Frances Fyfield is a criminal lawyer, a profession that has inspired and informed her novels, though not exclusively. She is widely translated, winner of the Crime Writers' Association Silver Dagger and the Prix de Littérature Policière in France. Several of her books have been televised. She lives in London and Deal.

Sarah Fortune Omnibus

SHADOWS ON THE MIRROR
PERFECTLY PURE AND GOOD
STARING AT THE LIGHT

FRANCES FYFIELD

sphere

SPHERE

This omnibus edition first published in Great Britain by Sphere in 2007

Sarah Fortune Collection Copyright © Frances Fyfield 2007

Previously published separately:
Shadows on the Mirror first published in Great Britain in 1989
by William Heinmann
Copyright © Frances Fyfield 1989

Perfectly Pure and Good first published in Great Britain in 1994 by
Bantam Press
Copyright © Frances Fyfield 1994

Staring at the Light first published in Great Britain in 1999 by
Bantam Press
Copyright © Frances Fyfield 1999

The moral right of the author has been asserted.

A CIP catalogue record for this book is
available from the British Library.

ISBN 978-0-7515-3881-6

Typeset in Plantin by M Rules
Printed and bound in Great Britain by
Mackays of Chatham plc

Sphere
An imprint of
Little, Brown Book Group
Brettenham House
Lancaster Place
London WC2E 7EN

A Member of the Hachette Livre Group of Companies

www.littlebrown.co.uk

SHADOWS ON THE MIRROR

To
Sylvia Norton,
Jenny Jones, Martyn Woodnutt,
Michael Kew and other colleagues
who make working life bearable

FOREWORD

He had loved her, she knew, in his vile, obsessive way, but she wished he had loved in a manner she understood. If he had ever loved her in some ordinary sense, he might have been here now, or she might not . . . But she could not cope with his kind of love or see herself as pet or instrument, could not live with being ugly.

The child laughing at her was the end. Politely she had ignored it, walked on and seen her face in the window, the same face she had tried to ignore in most mirrors, disgusted at itself, but smiling to make it worse. Then she saw her own reflection in the waters of the quay, hovering and hideous by the boats, lower than life, and told herself she had brought her arse to anchor here. Even without an audience, she had apologised automatically to Charles for the inelegant expression: he had never liked her crudity except in bed.

Then she went home for the pills.

Wherever she looked, she caught herself smiling at passersby, the way she always smiled in that other life. No good him saying they don't notice the stitches, only the smile, like a lighthouse beacon: he would not believe it, nor did she. Charles had married her for her beauty, which he had made all ways ugly, and she could not, would not live with it.

The final hope was revenge. Messages in cellophane in her purse and on her body bringing home to him, like ships in bottles, some sort of disgrace to damn him to hell. She could see

from her face now how much she had loved him and how much
she hated him now. Something the mirror and she could understand. She did not believe such a life could be redeemed as she
paddled across the low tide and walked towards the blue distance, unsteady but determined. The man, distracted by the boy
who had laughed in her face, thought she was drunk to walk like
that, lurching and slightly slow. The tide was well turned, forcing
her to wade through the water in the late evening sun. They
assumed she would come back, lie down with her hideous face
and sleep. She looked so tired.

Next day, Sunday morning, summery, and away they were,
down the creeks off the coast at Merton-on-Sea. He rowed out
down the creeks with the screaming child in the boat. Born here
and why not, can't complain, mad if he did, and he wasn't that.
No cloud in the sky, except this beloved stepson who couldn't
stand the sea. Silly little sod, about eight years old and cried like
a baby whenever he was taken out in the boat. The sky was full
of his wild sobbing, but they had Grandma's house on the quay,
he and the boy's mother. He could not afford a child who did
not like water. They slept each night with the sea, and the boy
would have to learn.

   But not this one, he wouldn't do nothing to order, not ever.
Put him in the boat, and he screamed fit to bust, so it had to be
done again and again, kill or cure, poor little bastard, hates it,
don't know why. The new wife said it was the flood, when the
tide put the boats right into the high street shops at midnight,
and the boy lost his dad after a night howling on the roof, waiting for the storm to die. The new father had loved this woman
too much and too long not to try. He'd have loved her with ten
children, let alone this funny little brute. There was another on
the way, light on the horizon, apart from the boy screaming and
breathless, frightened of everything, making him feel like a monster. 'C'mon, you little monkey,' he muttered. 'I love you better
than all the world, and if you think I'll like the new one better,
you're dafter than I thought. Stop crying now, good lad. This is

where you get out in the warm and paddle, and stop screeching. There now. Not so bad is it?'

He wanted the boy to love the creeks as he loved them. When the tide went out, water crept away through all these channels, leaving a trickle of rivers, with good shallow pools for swimming, safe as houses until the tide came roaring back and filled the gullies. When the tide was low, there was a playground of soft and sinking sand; when high, a riot of swift, deep water.

The boy recovered instantly as soon as he was out of the boat. He would run around a corner of the bank towards the nearest pool, forgetting the torture of the journey completely, singing and playing while the borrowed father dug for bait. Peaceful for the moment, basking in sun without wind in the snug seclusion of the channels. The man sighed with relief, pulled the boat further on to the bank, and sighed again with pleasure. Until he saw her.

If she hadn't been dead, lying with her gob full of sand, he could have killed her, simply for lying there waiting to give the child a heart attack. He'd always been worried they'd find a dead dog or something out there, something to frighten the wits out of the boy just as he was beginning to make some kind of progress. She looked like a bundle of rags, hands twisted in the heather, silly bitch. Sea must have come in over her and gone down again, leaving her covered with mud and sand. Once he knew it was a body, he'd chucked water at its face. Red hair she had, terrible scars, and Christ, he recognised her. She was the one the boy had laughed at only yesterday while his ma cuffed him. He'd go mad if he saw her now, sharp-eyed little bugger. Mad and frightened, he'd be, then there'd be the asthma, panic and rows. He looked up quickly for the child, heard him down by the pool, singing softly to himself, hardly out of sight. Noise was muffled in the channels.

Get rid of her. Nothing else for it. He could not let the child see. The banks were soft and easy, there was a shovel for bait in the boat and the muddy sand turned softly on the blade as he dug in the panic of haste, sweating himself like a pig to cover her in before the boy came back, soaking his clothes and gritting his teeth as he dragged the damp salty mass of her into a deep grave. He weighted her down before he slung the slodgy mud back on to her, closing his eyes and ears to the impact of its landing. What else to do? She had wanted to be found, that much was obvious, but not at his expense. It would take a tide or ten to shift her from there: next spring maybe. Maybe never. Sorry, lady. Silly bitch, you stay where you damn well are, stay down. I got my own to care for, he said, and this boy's done enough crying.

The woman called Elisabeth was buried without trace or ceremony. In the bedroom of his London home, a husband twitched and dozed full of the last nightmares. I loved you, my Porphyria, he told himself, but I shall find another.

Houses stirred into early evening. A fat lawyer and a young widow went out to dinner. Life went on as the hungry tide came back and covered the mound of earth, flattening it into innocence.

CHAPTER ONE

In the days before he had ever heard of Charles Tysall, and on the date when a certain scarred lady disappeared, Malcolm Cook was a very fat man indeed, but when he reared up in court with an energetic grace quite at odds with the huge size of him, the audience forgot to laugh. While they were expecting the idiot to overbalance his bulk, tickle himself, and tell jokes, his mellifluous voice was not only a surprise but the first premonition of trouble for those who knew him slightly enough to believe that the prosecution had fielded a buffoon. He was genial and twinkling, an old young man, so harmless when his fat laugh echoed round the foyer, a man with whom a defendant could feel safe, until, armed with his voice and his uncanny intelligence, he asked for his answers. They were kind, compelling eyes, betraying knowledge of exactly what it was like to be cast aside like the man in the dock, whatever he had done. The accused betrayed themselves to him by confident lies, tripping over details, looking at the fat man and forgetting where they were, keeping nothing but the dignity he would never steal from them. In the courtroom, Malcolm Cook, Senior Crown Prosecutor, was a man of charisma, compassion and great forensic skill, a gentle giant with powerful weapons. Everywhere else, he was regarded as a perfect clown.

It was beyond doubt that he was gross in size, but there was a finesse hidden in the bulk of it he was never encouraged to show, and certainly not in present company, as far as Sarah Fortune could tell. Bright brown glance, looking at women with eyes which knew they were not looking back, determined against embarrassment, blanked against longing. Malcolm's stories were famous, told in a dozen accents, and as for his antics, they made a party all on their own. A curiosity, with merely borrowed membership of the human race, freakish good value, everyone forgave the way he looked. Belinda Smythe would never seat as many as eight at her gatherings of lawyers, accountants, architects and assorted spouses without him being one of them, since his mere presence ensured success. Pound for pound, Malcolm Cook was worth the feeding since he provided a shoulder for weeping ladies, chest for pummelling children, mouth for laughing and merely sociable kisses, big clever teddy for the whole world. And he could drink. The legendary capacity was first joke of the evening: 'We've been down to the warehouse for you, Malcolm, here's your crate.' 'Thanks very much, see you're as mean as ever.' A benign exchange of seasoned insults, tokens of pleasure to meet him, all smiles and relief: he would see to the evening's entertainment. Sarah watched him closely, wondering if she was wrong to sense a kindred spirit, another outsider like herself, being used on a hostess ego-trip, someone who had arrived for dinner as an alternative to loneliness. Imagination had run riot in the six months of her altered status. She was sick of being invited out of duty and knew this was the last time she would accept. She tried and failed to dismiss her curiosity for the haunted man who laughed too much.

'Malckie?' shrieked Belinda, sensing from the kitchen the comparative lull which signified his absence from the room beyond when his presence was crucial. 'Where are you?'

'He's gone to see the children,' said Sarah, dutiful guest making salad-dressing.

'What's he want to do that for? Damn the man, we're ready to eat. Go and fetch him, Sarah, won't you?' Sing for your supper, Malcolm; Belinda was leaving nothing to chance. Sarah went, grateful her role in the guest hierarchy was less onerous than his.

It was far easier to look pretty, please the people and run errands, the last done most willingly for the excuse of brief escapes. She was sent to look for the warm-up man who had left his audience to wither without him; he must hurry back or they would miss him.

She found him upstairs, squatting at the bedside of a snuffling three-year-old, his stomach and chest meeting bulging thighs while the child giggled softly at the jowled faces he pulled. 'Noo, no, wait.' Conspiratorial whispers. 'Can you do this one?' 'Which one?' 'Like this.' Eyes pulled down by one thumb and fourth finger, nose pushed up and sideways by the other thumb . . . 'Ugghh!' 'Good, isn't it?' 'Triffic, show me how . . .' Sarah saw them both in the mirror, lit by the night-light left to comfort the child, a huge grown man lost in playing, the child transfixed with concentration. Each in his element, herself in the mirror, the silhouette of an interfering adult. She did not want to stop him; happiest in clowning to an audience who knew him with better instincts than those downstairs, but his dark eyes caught her brief movement, the barely perceptible warning gesture of hers which said, don't stop, you're doing fine, I did not mean to interrupt, and at once the face of him showed weary anger before a resigned smile. He turned to the child with a warmer smile, and tucked her arms below the sheet.

'Must go, honey, supper's ready.'

'Will you come back later, Malcolm, promise?'

'Promise, but you know how Mummy fusses about the food.' There was more giggling. 'Give me a kiss, Malcolm, please.'

'Ah.' Aware of his audience, he paused theatrically. 'I can't resist that, you know I can't.'

The child threw her arms round his neck and hugged for dear life. Malcolm's upper arm where the golden head was buried hid her completely in the breadth of it. Sarah thought of King Kong with his tiny princess, ridiculous, sad, but complete for the moment. The eyes meeting Sarah's over the blonde hair in his arms issued a brief challenge before the grown-up mask returned. 'See?' he joked for the adult not the child. 'Beautiful women find me irresistible.' She turned away from them and left, embarrassed by her presence at the scene of genuine affection and equally disturbed by the change her presence provoked. Next time she looked he would be one of the bosom buddies, a proper guest, one of the pack.

'He'll be back,' she told Belinda briefly. 'And by the way, what a gorgeous daughter you have.' The mother had her hands full, not thinking of children.

'Zoe? Yes, she's sweet. Adores Malckie of course, so does our son. There'll be ructions in the morning if he's spoken to one and not the other. He'll have to come round again. We all adore Malckie.'

But you don't, Sarah thought. You don't even begin to see him. You're giving houseroom to all that bulk simply because he entertains; you have no idea of what he is, what he does, or what he feels. He is here through loneliness and because he loves your children. If you were a true friend you'd put him on a diet rather than insist he eat even more than all the others, while you make him play to your gallery, damn your bloody silliness. And why do I come to your house when I don't even like you? Because you're my husband's friends, and because, like Malcolm, I'm useful. No, that isn't fair, I know it isn't fair, it was my choice I'm here, no one made me. Not your fault, but I've just seen something of big fat Malcolm you might not have seen, and I'll bet your daughter knows him a damn sight better than you. Sad man, but not pathetic. She could not move him from her mind.

Belinda and Martin Smythe were living happily ever after in the house he had converted from a mid-Hampstead ruin. Each visit there involved another guided tour, since some aspect of the house was bound to have changed. It moved and altered like a living thing, first a conservatory appeared, then another bedroom, then an attic created out of roof space, signs of admirable energy, but she could never quite understand why she didn't feel comfortable. The whole thing was violent and superficial self-advertisement and so were the owners. Sarah's husband had loved it; now it was time for dividing the ways. But she was here now; she should be grateful for the irritating insensitivity of their generosity.

And she wasn't bored, simply disturbed: no one was bored with Malcolm around, court jester, delighting them all with self-mockery.

'What do you do?' Someone asked him the inevitable party question.

'Obvious, isn't it?' he replied with the infectious grin, pirou-etting on the carpet, mincing his steps with one hand on huge hip. 'Male model for Aquascutum double-breasted. When I'm not doing swimwear.' Shrieks of laughter. He was a gifted mimic with his extravagant gestures, tossing imaginary locks out of his eyes, assuming the distant gimlet glare of the romantic hero, tripping over his own feet. 'But when I grow up . . .' – they waited with bated breath – 'I shall pose for Henry Moore. Why hide a perfect body like this?' Belinda was priming him for more. 'Where did you get that suit, Malc?' she said, pointing to his well-worn garment. 'That, my dear, was specially imported. It is the produce of wool from a thousand Falkland sheep who shrugged their fleece simultaneously as soon as they knew the size of the order . . .' And so it went on until Malcolm's antics had welded a group of relative strangers into an audience who could talk among themselves. 'Another drink, Malckie?' 'Oh, please, just give me the bottle and a straw . . .' Outrageous, he encouraged them all to their party pieces, stroking performers as he left them the stage, assuring all present that though they might feel foolish, he would be worse.

Sarah was nurturing a resentment she knew was unjustified, watching Malcolm Cook with a liking which grew in proportion to the loneliness of him, which glared towards anyone observant enough to see it. She saw the fat, asthmatic little boy he had been, standing on the sidelines as he did now, making up stories and pulling faces for attention, fighting his own demons. She liked him with a furious and defensive liking, intensely angry with him for clinging to acceptance where it was offered at the price of acting the fool. This much she had gathered by the time the sweet course was placed in front of Malckie in magnificent creamy entirety with a teasing flourish of stunning unkindness by Martin. 'All yours, old man. Thought you were wasting away . . .' 'So kind,' said Malcolm, 'but I always take cheese first . . .' The table rocked with well-fed mirth, and Sarah squirmed for the victim reacting to his cue, taking his poison. The man needed intravenous confidence, something to make him love himself. 'I know what you need,' Sarah told herself, '. . . and I should like to provide it, by way of experiment.' Not a whole cure, but a start perhaps.

Tutting for baby-sitters, looking at watches, everyone far later than meant, satisfying for smug hosts. Again, Malcolm had slipped away unnoticed to honour promises to sleeping children, returned for goodbyes lasting even later, reluctant farewells in the blast of wintry cold from the glass door. 'Ah well, cab for me,' Malcolm was saying between assuring Belinda how well he had fared. 'I'll give you a lift,' said Sarah. 'No need, really no need. Think I'll jog home and come back for breakfast.' 'I'll give you a lift,' she repeated. 'My pleasure.' He found a final joke irresistible. 'Send out a search party for us,' he said, 'after three days . . .'

In the draughty doorway of the house, the place for the last and best intimacies of the evening, Belinda fussily took Sarah aside in a sudden, guilty sympathy. Perhaps she should not have made it so clear that Sarah was a duty guest, invited on the coat-tails of a dead husband.

'Sarah. Haven't had the chance, you know how it is, but how are you really? I'm so sorry . . . we're still devastated, but you know where we are if ever we can help . . . Must be awful being on your own, how do you cope? What on earth do you find to do with yourself these days?' She was surprised by the sudden sparkle in the blue eyes, the amused appreciation in the ironic smile of all her obvious condescension.

'I manage, thank you,' said Sarah.

Hilly Hampstead spun with brittle ice. 'Tell me the way to

Kentish Town,' she asked, concentrating through misty windows
on the road ahead. 'I'm lost here.' 'What? Oh, left at the bottom,
then right. I'm lost anywhere.' Not joking, distracted, the first
sign of the evening's strain. Followed by silence. Malcolm looked
at her smooth profile as he had been looking all evening, the slim
elegance of her tucked into the seat, her round bosom parted
and emphasised by the seat-belt. Then looked away, sick with
longing to touch the thick red hair. Half hidden by coat, he could
picture the demure dress she had worn, skimming slim knees
descending to pretty ankles, soft-flowing stuff over firm, muscular hips. Fit, he supposed. Athletic, calmly authoritative,
competent and anathema, like all beautiful young women who
were the stuff of dreams erotic and otherwise, never pursued by
a man of his dimensions but very lovely all the same. Likeable,
attractive on sight, gentler than them all, but like every one of
her kind, could not be allowed to see this sickening twist of longing in the clown hunched into her small car. Would never return
such a look or volunteer to touch him. No one ever touched him,
and he never importuned. Malcolm Cook felt himself a leper
with women like this, but it did not stop him wanting.

'Here?' The car lurched to a halt and he fumbled with the
handle, suddenly clumsy.

'I'd like some coffee if I may.' He hadn't heard right, a humble
request in a calm, clear voice. 'Yes, of course, come on up.'
Hearing his own voice sulky with surprise, then firmer. 'Yes, of
course. I should have offered, but I thought . . .' An illuminating
smile on her face, full of forgiving mischief. '. . . You thought I
would want to offload you as soon as possible. But I don't. And
I need coffee.'

There were books by the thousand indoors, pictures by the
dozen, solid furniture which seemed to correspond with his own
weight and size. A man's womanly touch, clearly distinguishable
from a woman's touch, existed in the kind of austere comfort
produced. Small and tidy, the lair of an isolated creature who
exerted rigid control over his life, dared not encourage visitors
for the contrasts in their departures, and clung to his home for

the rock of peace it offered. Perhaps she was mad, perhaps she imagined it all, but from the moment she had watched him lumber into action like a well-trained and baited dancing bear manacled by mysterious grief, she had been drawn to this loneliness and knew she would not leave it untouched.

'Music?' he asked. She nodded, watched him fuss awkwardly with unaccustomed hospitality, unwind marginally and heavily on the sofa beside her. It was the only seating in the room, which left him without the alternative he would have half preferred, to sit outside touching distance.

'May I ask you something?'

'Of course.' Only slightly flustered, but flattered. The cold had brought a glow to her pale skin and the eyes were enormous.

'Why do you let them use you like that? You know exactly what I mean.'

He looked at the clear intelligence of the face, haloed by the red hair, began to bluster and decided not. His large head shook, puzzled and confused by the question he had often asked himself.

'I exist to be jester,' he said slowly. 'What else can I do?'

Abruptly he rose, poured a brandy from a decanter and handed her a glass without invitation. She took it and sipped, waiting. He was hesitant, wanting by now to explain it all, believing her sympathy, ashamed of himself for beginning to talk.

'. . . I suppose . . . I suppose . . . Why on earth do you want to know?'

'Just accept that I do want to know. Go on.'

'I'll have to simplify it then.'

'As simple as you like.'

'Not easy all the same. I'm fat, you see. Enormous. Ugly.'

'Not ugly. Who told you that?'

'The mirror tells me that. My mother told me that. Other women's eyes tell me that. I have always been gross: glandular baby, fatty child, ungainly student, fat man. So I immerse myself in criminal law, my work, which makes it worse. But being fat is my trademark, has its uses I suppose, and I don't know how to change it. I must make something semi-dignified from it. So, I make people laugh; relieves the monotony of existence, gives me a measure of acceptance. And if you say, lose the fat, I will say there will always be a fat man in me whatever I do. I daren't try in case it makes no difference.'

'Who comes close to you? Who do you tell?'

'Don't be silly. No one till now. The way I am? My world is far too competitive to confide in men, and I can't trouble women although I prefer their company . . .'

'Why not?'

He looked at her. 'Why not? Oh, come now, I'd always want more than friendship, although the women to date have never offered it. Since you're so keen on the pursuit of my humiliation, you may as well know why no woman would ever want me. She'd get lost in all this flesh, and I would have to watch her shrink away, with me dying of shame but still joking. I couldn't bear it, so bloody unfair to ask. Am I making this sound self-pitying enough?'

'No, but there is a hint of it. I never heard anything so silly. What do you do, shove the whole world to one side because of an extra bit of flesh? What would you do if you didn't have legs?'

'Beg, on my elbows, to be taken seriously sometimes. Or just to be taken.'

She laughed, close to him, innocently close as she stroked his wide eyebrows, tracing the arches with a finger. 'Fine eyes, good skin, thick head of hair. You've a lovely head, you know.'

'Don't.' Part embarrassment, some particle of gratitude made him hug her, conscious of the bulk of himself, if only to make her stop.

'I'm not being foolish, you are. Forever seeing yourself as you think other people see you, imperfect first, as if there was nothing there which couldn't be weighed in kilos. What an idiot, always asking yourself the same question, "Speaking as an outsider, boy, what do you think of the human race?" Not a lot.'

'Enough,' he said quietly. 'Don't confuse self-pity with honesty. Look at me. I'm disgusting. I'm the object of revulsion in half the human race, and I can't even blame them. I think that explains it all.'

'I'm looking,' she said. 'I've been looking all the time.' And I like outsiders like me, she added to herself. They make me feel at home.

Malcolm Cook, clown *extraordinaire*, stopped the tears inside his own eyes, swallowed the last of his brandy. Intent on the effort of self-control he failed to notice the swift movement which brought her closer. 'You idiot,' she said. 'You silly, silly idiot.' So softly said, he scarcely heard with her hand caressing the back of his neck, relaxing his whole spine, then touching his face, her fingers through his hair smoothing and soothing. He had begun his small protest before she began her kiss. 'Sshh, sshh, my lovely, stay still, don't send me away, not now.' Her mouth on his own with a sweet brandy smell, gentle, his tongue exploring the taste, his hand on her breast where she had placed it, moving, wondering, feeling the fluid flesh beneath the cloth and her nipple beneath his fingers. 'Please,' he whispered. 'No pity please.' Her thumb stroked the crease between his eyes, her lips brushed his forehead. 'No pity at all,' she replied. 'No judgement either. Stop thinking of yourself as a freak. You're nothing of the kind. I do this because it pleases me to do so.' Malcolm did not speak, looked at the calm grey eyes and believed. Slowly she unbuttoned the modest dress, kneeling beside him, touched with his tongue, he pulled her towards him as her hands pulled away his clothes. 'Sarah, Sarah, Sarah.' He had known her name but never said it, spoke it now like a litany, lifted her to the floor and himself alongside her. Miraculously naked, flesh upon flesh, tingling and weightless, aware and ashamed, stunned into agonising life, he wanted her to stop, but never to stop, helpless with wanting, conscious of warmth, enveloping affection, rhythmic movement of her hips against his own until the dim light of the room faded, everything faded in the mounting wave of sensation. Hold me, Sarah, hold me, please, I can't help it. Don't stop.

Calm. A quiet popping sound from the fire above the noise of his own breath, her head resting against his chest with one large hand still pressing her into himself, the other stroking her hair. Agony of relief, gratitude, apology, Sarah, Sarah. 'Sorry,' he mumbled. 'Not much fun for you.' The head raised above his own was flushed, tousled, alive with an impish grin. 'That,' she said, rubbing his nose with the tip of her own, kissing his eyes, 'was the beginning. Or are you going to send me home now?'

'No,' said Malcolm. 'I'm not.'

Talking towards dawn, he had never known how easy it was to talk when touching, how peaceful to speak of unmentionable things to one who listened by instinct, could even understand how he had arrived, by various routes, to stand on the outside of the world as a constant and lonely observer. In turn he absorbed the untold history of Sarah, the lost child, the emptiness. Two outsiders, finding truth in nakedness: absolute trust. He could scarcely believe how simple it was. Then, when they made love for the second time, he believed before he slept he had conquered the world, had heard her cry out in a kind of joy. He had done that, made her body leap and rear before she had cried out, convulsed around him. He had caused that pleasure, he and that great big body. Idiot, she had said again, the affection turning insult into compliment. Idiot to doubt yourself, now you know better, and he was proud, slept with his arm tucked beneath her. Hug me, she said, my lovely lover, and huge ungainly Malcolm Cook hugged after hours of talking, no longer afraid, and, no longer a freak, slept the sleep of a child. Then opened his eyes to find himself alone.

Bow Street on Monday morning, prosecutor Court One, Mr Cook. 'Thirty on the list, sir.' Street traders, hot-tog stalls, touts and drunks, easy. Three for soliciting prostitution, fighting the evidence. 'Them three's contesting, sir, but we can't find the papers. Better ask for an adjournment, sir.' Malcolm looked at the bold and tired faces of the three at the back, one of them bulky, pointing at him and laughing, one thin, one blank and black. He remembered the note left on his kitchen table in Sarah's clear hand. 'Being fat isn't the point. Being you is the point and, I'm telling you, nothing is lacking. You're a marvellous man, better than anyone else. You don't need me, you only need you. Please don't try and find me; you must change yourself, or it will not count for anything. Besides, you're on the way up, and I'm definitely on the way down. Just love yourself as much as I did. I shan't ever forget you.' Malcolm remembered the searing of grief, and the image of himself in the mirror, fat and stricken, half-naked. He made himself a promise: he would find her when he was a different man, a thinner, more dignified man, worth the loving of a woman of such peculiar and glorious qualities, but before then he would change simply because she had made him feel alive, was the first who had made him want to change. Clichéd thought, he made himself smile at it: this is only the first day of life.

In the meantime remember fairness, his hallmark along with his size.

'If we have no papers,' he said to the gaoler, 'put the ladies up first. I'll be offering no evidence. Then we can let them go. Who the hell are we to judge?'

There it was. Compassion always far more important than duty, living better than dying. Time to alter. Love did that, and he would always love her, for what she was and what she had done. He would find her when he had completed the revolution she had started; find her and love her although all he knew was her name. Then, looking up briefly at the ladies of the night, freed from the dock with squawks of relief, he wondered what Sarah had meant by saying she was on the way down, thought of the words with a flash of anxious intuition quickly dismissed as he lumbered to his feet for the next cue.

CHAPTER TWO

Within the next two years, Malcolm dreamed of many things, including his stepfather's office, but he never visited it, and knew better than to make inquiries about the progress of that empire, since any question sparked a row. Not many solicitors' premises, even bigger city types, were quite as sumptuous as these, and none bore a sign as ostentatiously discreet, 'Matthewson, Carman and Company, Solicitors', very small lettering on an enormous brass plaque. Nothing flashy, please, Matthewson had said, confronting the interior designer lady. Normally it was the sort of thing Ernest Matthewson left to his wife. His house was a mass of birds and flowers, curtains and chairs full of them. He could not see why the office décor mattered. Clients like Charles Tysall would not notice the colour of the walls, it would only make them suspicious about what was being done with their fees. Whenever Ernest, Malcolm's stepfather, thought of Charles Tysall, he felt sick and pointless, and nothing as banal as his surroundings was going to help.

Matthewson had built his practice on common sense, pats on shoulders, a large handkerchief, tea, sympathy and stiff drinks, and above all the ability to keep a secret, but success had exacted its peculiar punishment. Sofas like squashed elephants, forty-five solicitors and only one of them he liked. Whatever had happened to the place where he started three ulcers and one heart attack ago, God knew; he didn't. He was lonely and he missed his stepson more than ever, not daily, but hourly. There were only a few minutes a day, faced with the ghastly luxury of the reception, when he knew why Malcolm preferred his darker regions.

'It's not the same,' he would mutter to Penelope. 'Not the same at all.' Mrs Matthewson, known as Pen to her friends, would try to forestall the depression by planning an extra course on the evening's menu, food being the only panacea she knew. *Moules marinières*, perhaps. No, not in this mood. A sweetener the other end: *mousse au chocolat*, delivered to him without pointing out he had no real choice. For the firm, she meant, hadn't had any choice in a long time.

'That woman in Commercial is awful,' he would say. 'As bad as the bloody décor. How can anyone as frightful earn so much?' Pen would bring him a drink and suggest that cash was not always acquired by the same means as his own charm and common sense. 'Not like you,' she would say. 'Not your flair.' Fondling the back of his neck in the same way she fondled the space behind the ears of their cat, preferring Ernest's soft and bristly stubble, the creased warmth of it. 'Not like you. They can't all be so lucky. Her work needs brains. I mean, law does these days.' He did not take offence, knowing flattery was meant. 'At least they're all respectable,' Penelope added, by way of comfort. 'I wish they bloody well weren't,' he shouted. 'Stuffed shirts, every one. Thirty-going-on-ninety.' She soothed him. 'Not like Sarah Fortune,' he would say. 'No, dear, not like Sarah,' she would reply, stiffening her back, pretending to Ernest she resented such eulogies of praise which might follow for the widow Fortune. Then she would stride towards her kitchen in the direction of the good smells, walking across twenty-five feet of carpet with her plump tread, smiling to herself. Let him fantasise about Sarah Fortune. It did him good to think she might resent his praising Sarah Fortune. Penelope knew better and it did not do to let Ernest know he had been so thoroughly discussed. She also knew that the most romantic assignation Ernest ever had with this lady was to play cards with her in the basement of the office when no one but the caretaker was looking. Penelope and Sarah had found one another at the first Christmas party Sarah had attended in the new office. Between them, discreetly, they had got tiddly Ernest home. Penelope had squared up to Sarah. 'My husband is always talking about you,' she had begun.

'Is he really? I'm flattered. I'm very fond of him. And he's safe with me.' Then in a lowered voice, with a disarming smile of conspiracy, 'You see, Mrs Matthewson, he and I share something. We're the only lawyers here who don't know any law . . . we make it up as we go along . . . sometimes we have to confess, as well as hide. Then we have a drink.' Pen wished she had a daughter like Sarah Fortune, instead of the son. No, not instead of the son, as well as him. Penelope knew what Sarah did in Ernest's office, inspired guesswork and a few other things. They had discussed it, taking their turn with Ernest's whisky long after Ernest had fallen asleep that Christmas. Penelope knew when a girl could be trusted and when not. She had never told as much to anyone, or felt as safe.

Pen stirred the sauce. Ernest had turned on the music, a sure sign of recovery. At least this evening he was not going to dwell on the other two sources of grief: his stepson Malcolm, who so adamantly refused to join the firm or have anything to do with it, for reasons Ernest could not understand, and the client, Charles Tysall, who told poor Ernest the sort of secrets Ernest could never share, making him physically ill. Guilt, that was Ernest's problem. Couldn't bear to think he had failed, and when the guilt struck, thought Penelope, he ceases to judge them at all. Becomes immobile, like an animal hypnotised.

Eight-fifteen on the Rothbury Estate, finest statement of Victorian values for the poor, despised, these days, by most of them. Built around a well with a scrub of kicked-up lawn, ancient white brick, small windows, noise was echoing as the last of Joan's children clattered down the steps. 'Wait for me. Wait for meeee . . .' Jack's voice drifting back, forever plaintive.

She sighed and wished she had not shouted. Time to go to the office of Matthewson and become secretary to Miss Fortune, rather than mother to this bratpack. She tidied the room in a flurry of hate, pushing dirty clothes in a sack, food in the bin, dishes in the sink, leaving the beds and the washing. Mustn't grumble: just think if Ted were here, the mess would be worse. Ted Plumb, divorced husband, lived like a tornado, could reduce a room to a dump within minutes, and somewhere in the muddle, there would be a whisky bottle. Joan sat down on the sofa, suddenly winded by the thought. No, if Ted was still with them, they wouldn't be living here, would they? If not in a house, at least they'd have a police flat with one more room and a caretaker. The bloody Commissioner made his officers look after their families, even officers like Ted, and if they wouldn't, he did, in a manner of speaking.

But all of them were beyond such protection now. Ted had put it behind them. Disgraced, sacked, living in a grotty bedsit, God knows where, still with a bottle for company, and Lord alone knows what else.

'You really did it proper, didn't you, Ted?' Joan scowled into her mirror, adding a row of beads to the rest of the colours. 'You really blew the whole thing. Us, in a half-condemned council flat no one else wants, and you up shit creek. And now you want to kiss and make up. Well, sod you.'

She pushed the hat on her head, twisted the stocking sideways round her ankle so the holes would not show, picked up her bright red bag and slammed out of the door. Wait till she told Sarah what the bugger had done. Sarah would laugh and, despite herself, she would be made to feel better however much she might resent it. She might just turn up and offer to take Jack on Sunday, give her a break, the way she sometimes did. Odd woman doing that for nothing; why the hell should she? But she did. At least, Joan thought, I've got a job. I hate bloody typing, but at least I don't work for some bloke. At least I work for a woman, even if she is too bloody clever by half.

Teetering on high heels, adjusting the shoulder bag, Joan was thinking hard. Get to Tescos at lunchtime, beans, spuds, under-pants for John, socks for Jack, soap, and they all needed shoes. £19.99 a pair, kids' shoes . . . They needed everything, and what had he carried in under his arm as a peace-offering for the first visit in three months? A dog, a bloody dog, not even a puppy, probably stolen. A relic of a Christmas present. The kids had loved it. Joan had exploded.

'What the hell am I supposed to do with it?' Hissing, wresting it away from Jack, shoving it back into Ted's arms. 'Three floors up, no money for clothes, let alone dog food.'

'I thought the kids would like it,' he said, sullen the way he always was with every misjudged gift which had distinguished the marriage. She had pushed him and the dog into the kitchen away from the howling children. 'Get out,' she had said, con-trolling her voice with difficulty. 'You can't bloody provide for us, OK. But you don't have to make it worse. Just get out, and take that animal with you.'

Clattering up to the top deck of the bus, she remembered his slower steps, descending from the flat with an armful of smallish dog which had looked so large and hungry in their cramped living room. Remembered the hour spent placating the children in quiet fury. 'Why can't we keep it, Mum . . . why? Dad gave it us, not you . . . You're a pig, Mum . . . We'd look after it, Mum . . . we would really . . .' Would you hell, she muttered, promising treats in return, while it all rumbled down into quiet, solid resentment, each for the other. But even in the remem-bered anger, she could hear Ted's light steps going away mournfully. Always light-footed, Ted. Not known as the soft-shoed shuffler for nothing. To hell with him. But she wished she did not care what happened to him, wished she did not mind them being so ignorant of one another's lives. Didn't even know where he lived, or he where she worked. Better that way, probably. Tears threatened the bright eyeshadow and she blinked them back, staring ahead at the broad back on the seat beyond, clutching the bag on her thin knees, trying to think of food.

At ten-thirty in the morning, Sarah fled through the smoked-glass doors of the reception, noisiest person to enter and easily the latest. It was not for the golden receptionists to comment. Miss Fortune had been in a meeting since dawn, according to her secretary, and since Sarah's grin was catching and her wave towards them unrepentant as she took the stairs two at a time, the red coat rustling, her exuberance defied criticism. The other lady solicitors had been in since eight-fifteen of course, but there was something admirable in Sarah's defiant carelessness, so that, in mute conspiracy, they failed to notice the eccentricities or the appalling time-keeping, and smiled back.

The stairs led to a wide corridor, carpet still thick on the first floor, with well-tended greenery in tasteful alcoves cleverly lit against restful walls. No prints, almost spartan. On the second floor, decoration was more haphazard, the corridor narrow and the ceilings lower over rooms of smaller dimensions if no less immaculate. Solid reproduction furniture to compensate for lack of size: one chair for the desk, one for a visitor and the room was almost full, would have been elegantly cramped without the mess Sarah created. Her own pictures hung on the wall to pacify her spirit and hide the feeling of being a caged bird with ruffled feathers pining for a piece of sky. Apart from these, Sarah hated it, not as much as she hated being a lawyer at all, but certainly to the same degree. This might have been prestigious Mayfair, this ghastly, pretentious, stuffy office, but on four mornings out of five, she could not raise her head from the pillow without dropping back into that sickening claustrophobia provoked by the thought of this room. A sensation of dread compounded by the certain knowledge that any other employment which used the qualifications, which felt like her own sentence for life, would be better. What a wimp she had been, what a malleable weakling, to let herself in for a lifetime of legal wrangling. Time will come, she told herself, when I shall be no one else's creature. And when I don't wake up looking for yet another reason why I should not go to work today.

As Sarah sat, applying the everyday props, face crouched to

a cracked mirror in the drawer, wondering why her make-up bag always looked diseased and mascara was claggy only when she tried to apply it in a hurry, the door crashed open before Joan, a six-foot wraith bearing a large mug of coffee which was still complete with traces of yesterday's lipstick.

'Bloody hell, gel, where you been? You aren' half late.'

'Sorry. Thanks, who noticed?'

'No one much. Matthewson popped in, only for a chat, he said. Don't think he was checking up on you. Just lonely.' Matthewson was happier in these humbler regions. 'Come on then, tell me. Out late again last night, was you? Another of your deadbeats?'

'Another friend. Of the opposite sex. All right, another deadbeat, but very kind.'

'So you say. All your blokes sound useless to me.' Rich, though. Joan presupposed they were rich, Sarah's pleasant-sounding men with their secretive requests. They had rich voices! Sarah had rich clothes, richer even than all the other lady solicitors. 'You need a nice fella.' She sat down, coughed, lit another cigarette. 'Only don't marry a policeman. I'll tell you the latest when you've caught up. Ted's excelled himself.' She cackled, pushed the coffee towards Sarah, folded her arms, looked down critically. 'And do I detect just a trace of chemical poisoning?'

'Just a trace.' They had a common language. Joan considered that the chemicals in wine were solely responsible for the hangovers, and had coined a new phrase for an old condition. It looked better on a sick-note, and had confused personnel on several of hers.

'Well, gel, don't let it get to you. And in case you've gone deaf, that's your phone ringing. It's Watson and Watson. They're caving in.'

'Sarah Fortune, could you hold on a minute?' She covered the phone with one hand. 'What do you mean, caving in?'

'What do you think I bloody mean? You offered him ten thousand to settle the action last week. He was all bluff and "no, can't consider it", and this morning he's phoned three times, 'course he's caving in.' Joan strode out, thin as a stick, muttering mock despair. Panic in Sarah as she tried to remember which case, when, who were Messrs Watson and Watson, and what was the name of the client?

'Sorry to keep you. Who's speaking?'

'Mr Watson.'

'Mr Who?'

'Watson.' Roared.

'Which one? Oh yes, Mr Watson. Missed you earlier. At a meeting. Shame about that. What can I . . .'

'We accept.'

'Do you now?' Struggling with words and memory, fencing for time, with facts slipping away like eels from a net. 'Well, I'm not sure the offer stands. You refused last week. I thought again. I seem to remember my client was being generous.'

'We accept.'

'Nine thousand.'

'You said ten.'

'Then, not now. You refused then. Nine thousand, take it or leave it. I shan't ask for costs. Saves you some.'

'Wait a minute . . .'

'Haven't got a minute. Nine thousand. Just hang on a second . . .' Stuffing the squawking phone beneath a rubble of papers, the question of which case it was tugging at bruised brain cells, wondering why she argued on automatic pilot like a compulsive bargainer when she couldn't even remember who he was or what the hell it had been about, this offer, this acceptance. Then she couldn't find the phone, and when she did, the receiver was still warm with Watson's enraged acceptance. 'Tough lady,' he said, furious but admiring. 'Don't suppose you want a job?' 'Christ,' muttered Sarah. 'That's the last thing I need.' Must be an important client for Watson, whoever he was. At times like this, ignorance was bliss. Watson could not be expected to know the difference between a hardliner and a thirty-year-old woman with a slight hangover, defective memory and no line at all.

Miss Fortune knew she was a misfit in the firm, not obviously, but subtly so, simply slightly out of focus. The firm, that big amorphous animal with all the dull instincts of a modern dinosaur, knew it without analysing why, and compromised by relegating Sarah's menage to the nether regions of the second floor so that Joan's leopard-skin tights, strident laugh and aggressive face would not alarm the clients who padded to the doors in city suits and matching briefcases. 'Here's another clone for you, Mr P,' she had once said by way of announcement to a senior partner, and after that the second floor came to suit them best. Sarah accepted Joan without a qualm, knew every foible of Joan's health, history and energetic offspring, while Joan herself would cheerfully have killed for Sarah on a good day, murdered her on the next. She held a sort of defensive, utterly suspicious affection for her employer, allowing for giggling in both their rooms with defensive sulking in between such lassitude on Joan's behalf. She always regretted the giggles, the confidences she gave, but always gave them, grudgingly appreciative of a good boss in the full understanding that it was still a boss. With no accountant able to understand how it was that Miss Fortune made money for the firm more by luck than strictly legal judgement, no one entirely sure what she did all day, the mystification was shared by Sarah herself who did not understand it either. For half of the hours, she worked in an energetic muddle which, miraculously, generated acceptable income by inspired and soothing guesswork, bargaining and choice of barristers. For the other half she wondered how soon it would be before she was found out, planned her passage to freedom, and tried to think up new ways of shortening her day. A talent for guarding other people's money from litigious predators ensured survival, but nothing altered the fact that she loathed it. How could anyone in their right mind be interested in the Law? People counted, not the rules. The Law is an ass, but around Sarah, it brayed with enthusiasm.

There was a short interval of silence in Sarah's room while she looked at the mess of papers made worse by the scrabble for the phone. Then came a slight knock at the door, the diffident tap of someone who had evaded the eagle eye behind the outer desk.

'Come in, Fred.' It was a conspiratorial whisper. He hovered in the doorway, a down-at-heel caretaker, sloppy to the toe nails. Fred wore the same shirt most days. His braces were frayed and his eyes permanently bloodshot. The grin on his face showed pure affection and slight mental subnormality. Fred was permanently shunned, smelt of fish and the boiler room, even though there was no boiler room.

' 'Ere, Miss Fortune. Brought your bacon roll.'

'Thanks, Fred. I need it.' She fumbled in her purse, exchanging cash for the paper bag he held out like a precious gift, thankful and grateful for the very sight of his lopsided, sheepish grin. She grinned back, her face split in open welcome. They were friends, possibly the only allies under this competitive roof. The bacon roll lay there, comfortably greasy on her desk, cholesterol fix for the day. Fred, who had already eaten two, sat down and pulled out his cigarettes. Fred's fags were legendary. They smelt too. Sarah had simply never noticed, and ate the roll with the delicacy of a hungry red squirrel, talking between bites. 'Come on then, Fred,' she said. 'What's the news?'

He shuffled happily. 'Well, not much, see? But our Ernest has got the grumps. Going round like a bear with a sore head. Reckon the missus feeds him too much. Bad tempered as hell, couldn't cheer him up.'

'What, not even with a bacon roll from the corner?'

'Nope. Nothing doing. Go away, Fred, he said to me, bugger off. So I thought I'd give you today's tip instead. Couldn't get Ernest to listen. Usually does, though.'

'What tip's this then, Fred?'

He leant forward. 'Horse called Pink Jade in the two-thirty at Epsom. Bloke in the café really rates it. Says it'll go like a bomb, nothing to stop it. Knows a bookie. Got something on it himself. What do you reckon?'

'Two pounds each way?'

'Fiver to win? Be a devil.'

'Go on then. I'll have your guts for garters if it doesn't.'

The grin grew wider, dividing his face into two triangles as he shuffled to his feet.

'Sure as eggs is eggs. Tell you what, Miss F, how about putting something on for Mr Matthewson? Might change his mood if he wins.'

'OK. Two pounds each way for him. How's my account? Do I owe you any?'

'Naa. We're looking pretty good. You're always in credit, never let me down. See you then, better get to work.'

'Watch out for Joan. She's got the hump too.'

'What's different?' They shared the look of plotters and a mutual shrug without malice before the door closed behind him.

The morning was filled with little incentive schemes. Lunch was booked, and that could be stretched to two hours. Nevertheless, Sarah sat idly. Outside in the street, tyres squealed; there was a sound of impact. She shut her eyes, stung by the sudden memory, and did not move to look.

When Sarah Fortune's handsome husband had relinquished his uninsured life nearly three years before in a car crash of resounding stupidity, he had not been entirely sober, and was talking as fast as usual. Crossing a red light in fourth gear whilst engrossed in the business of discussing a better hotel room for the next assignation, resulted in the tidy compression of his chest, a bloodless crushing; no evidence on his face, so that his companion, protected by the seat-belt he had ignored, tried to shake him awake before the police arrived. It had complicated life for Sarah to discover that the companion in question was her own sister, who spilled the beans of this incestuous attachment at the same time as her stricken face imparted the news of death. Sarah's family had never been supportive – she knew them already for the tribe of treacherous bullies they were – but all the same she agreed to Jeannie's immediate request to keep this liaison with Sarah's husband secret from Jeannie's own. She remembered asking repeatedly, what about the people in the

other car? Were they hurt, tell me, were they hurt? No revenge
adding to the wreckage, but in retrospect, remembering herself
agreeing with Jeannie a story for public consumption, Sarah
wondered at herself. Extraordinary what one person will ask of
another, and what the other will agree to do.

No one had known, except a fat man called Malcolm (who
had a way with children and other bodies), met at a party two
years before. In the middle of the night she had told him and he
had seemed to know what she meant. All sorts of other things
she had told him too, even about the baby. Funny what she had
done then, in a passion of liking. Funnier what she had done
since. She had even told Malcolm about school, making him
laugh in the early hours. 'Brains,' said her teacher, 'bring res-
pons-ib-ility . . . do-you-understand?' Adding one more thwack
with each syllable for the rude message on the blackboard. 'And
the word cop-ul-ation spelt with one P, don't you know?' Sarah
knew, but it was someone else who had written. Her own childish behaviour was then as good as her childish spelling, but life
had the effect of shedding one moral principle a year and leaving a greater desire for fun than there had ever been for
obedience. She had never told anyone else, apart from the same
fat man, about the baby. Dead child of faithless spouse who had
impregnated a sister as well as a wife, and left his debts instead
of the result. Three months' life oozing away six weeks after his,
drenching another car seat, while somehow, in that red, embarrassing flow, there had slid from her the whole code by which
she had thought to have lived. I loved you once. You blocked my
view of the universe once, both of you, but I cannot lie down
and die. Nothing as insubstantial as fidelity, duty, honour or the
dignity of hard work seemed faintly significant after that, nor
had these old inhibitions recovered ever since. There was no
place for them. Kindness, yes. Honesty of her own peculiar
kind, but not the rest. Sarah stretched in her seat, one limb at a
time, smiled into the distance, then chuckled out loud. On the
whole, apart from the work and the grief, it had been a bloody
good two years.

She dictated letters, vaguely hoping that none of the stuffy partners downstairs would ever have cause to read them.

'Dear Mr Jones . . . Sorry about the size of this bill, but I did warn you Mr Justice Harvey is a mean old demon, and you were likely to lose . . . Better luck next time . . . Please pay us soon, we know you can afford it . . .'

The door thumped against the visitor's chair, adding another chip to the mahogany veneer. Behind was a vision in fake fur with the bright blonde wisps of dyed hair half-tucked into an orange toque. It was eleven-forty-five. 'Just off to lunch,' said Joan, defying her to look at the clock. Sarah did not look. 'That time already? Thank heaven. See you later.' No rebuke, not even a mild one. Both knew better than to specify how much later.

Freedom for at least an hour, secured by striding across the foyer as if *en route* to yet another meeting. Charles Tysall sat waiting for Ernest Matthewson, who was delaying upstairs, dreading the encounter. Charles was hidden behind one of the huge ferns Ernest so loathed, following Sarah's exit with puzzled eyes, half-rising from his seat in the desire to run after the mane of red hair, sitting back instead, with alarm and relief moving across his closed face. He would have Sarah Fortune. He was determined to let her refuse as much as she liked, but for now he needed to talk.

Plodding downstairs, Ernest felt his head begin to throb. Charles Tysall had him by the balls, and there was no one to tell. Although the firm did not handle more than half of Tysall's monetary affairs (luckily, they were spared the shadiest), they still needed him. As Ernest put it to himself, they needed the loss of Tysall as a client like they needed a hole in the head, and if they lost work generated by him, they would lose half the income of the practice.

Therefore, he had to be pleased, and he knew he had to be favoured, which meant long lunches with Charles, and even longer confessions. Halfway downstairs, Ernest looked at the pale walls, saw the same tasteful colours he had seen in Tysall's house, somehow spattered with blood. He had tried to make

Charles seek help, in the bumbling way Ernest did everything:
'Really, old man, it's a bit much, shouldn't you . . .' 'Shouldn't I
what?' Charles would say, looking at him over the rim of a glass,
smiling at his helplessness. 'Shouldn't I what? What do you
mean?' Ernest had failed, conspicuously; he had known the
man, and had never once liked him. Ernest had never before
found a client he could not like for something, even if it were
nothing more than the imagination of his dishonesty, but he had
never anticipated one quite so brutal. But he knew equally well,
from the oldest school of solicitors, from practices taught him
by his father and grandfather, that he should never reveal what
he was told, should be utterly bound by his client's confidence.
Whatever the value of the belief, he could not relinquish it now,
and Tysall was fully aware of that reliability. Ernest could only
hope the mere act of talking might curtail some of the excesses.

Damn him. Damn him. How long since, oh, more than a year
or two, when Ernest had asked that standard question, 'How's
the wife, Charles?' Receiving the cold reply, 'Dead, I think.'
Ernest had choked, and in the midst of the choking, listened.

'I tried to kill her. No, not really, but she was so very unfaithful, you see . . .'

Ernest did not see. He envisaged his wife, who had always
been unfaithful to her own son in her way, he could see that, but
never, ever to him. He listened to Charles proceeding, matter-
of-fact, unhurried, the calm, handsome face not even flustered.

'She was not in any kind of order. Unfaithful, according to
the evidence. So I had to cut her face, to teach her a lesson.'

'Had to?' murmured Ernest, remembering the wonderful
Titian beauty of the woman, a bit like Sarah Fortune when he
came to think of it.

'Had to? Surely not?'

'Yes, it was necessary. Women have to be punished.'

'I see,' said Ernest, and continued eating with his soul disturbed, each mouthful like cardboard. 'I see.' What a mistake, he
sometimes reflected, to even pretend you understand, especially
when you do not comprehend at all.

In the face of his silence, there had followed an account of the first attempt by Charles to strangle his wife, recited while delicate food expanded in Ernest's mouth, sticking in his throat. Then there had been more, the history of all the episodes since, the memory of all those cool anecdotes of horror. I cannot tell, Ernest told himself in a daily litany. I cannot ever tell. What is told to me in confidence, I cannot ever tell. So his father had said, God knows what he had heard: trust is a sacred privilege, as well as a curse. Beware of it. Ernest had armed himself, but he did not know what to do. Without a God to whom he should pray, he simply did nothing.

But he worried about the women. Whoever they were, escaping with their lives, they never complained. Charles Tysall was too powerful for that. Ernest knew it all, understood not a jot. Hoped against hope Tysall would never find a passion so grand it could merit the ultimate finale, some final, insane revenge from an insane mind. Even Ernest knew he was dealing with a madman of enormous civility. It made him fear him more.

Secrecy. All in the lawyers' code, a kind of vow, till death do us part. Ernest missed his son, for the jokes and the games and the telling of secrets, and, thinking of Malcolm as a kind of talisman, reached the foyer as Sarah Fortune left it, smiled at Charles, and gritted his teeth. To listen without forgiveness, to hear without an element of understanding, to endure his confidences in an endless, sickening silence, full of fear.

CHAPTER THREE

Malcolm did not understand his own persistence. Forgetting the occasional triumphs, at this single moment in time he shared Ernest's incomprehension as to why any man should take his considerable legal talents to the grubby back-streets of prosecuting crime. A life of litigation for the rich seemed infinitely preferable.

With one accord, he and Detective Sergeant Ryan had stopped by the railings and looked down. Neither wanted to move, both of them were utterly depressed. They might have parted at the door of Counsel's chambers, each to nurture, or drown, his own disappointment, but they had not parted, they stuck together in grim silence until they reached Temple Lawns, rounded the corner into a colourful sun. After nine years of it, Malcolm had tutored himself beyond the kind of impotent fury he used to feel when the guilty celebrated acquittal. Having resolved that these travesties would not be the result of poor prosecutions, shoddy paperwork and indifferent investigation, he tried to shrug his shoulders. Even so, trudging away from the chambers of Simeon Churcher QC, he had felt the weight of frustration like a sack on his shoulders, heavier than the papers in the bag. Not even an acquittal; more a question of horse falls at first gate due to sabotage. It was inevitable, he was accustomed to it, but never in a hundred years would Ryan relinquish the bitter disappointment, and Malcolm felt all the worse for that.

They had walked from King's Bench Walk, adapting their steps to one another as if handcuffed, Ryan had thought, but reluctant to part. Through Pump Court, silent still at four-thirty, early yet for the rush of after-court footsteps. Through the archway across Middle Temple Lane and into Fountain Court with pretty summer shadows and elegant fountain. Of all the facts of his professional life which Malcolm was able to absorb with such ease, the sheer prettiness of the Temple, its clubbish discretion, cobble stones and gracious buildings, filled him with wonder. Inside these well-proportioned windows, premium space was broken down into small rooms where disrobed barristers of various means and abilities sat with murderers, fraudsmen, uncomfortable policemen and defrocked bankers, distressed wives and violent husbands, giving unacceptable advice in calm tones. 'You must plead guilty, Mr X. Don't worry, you'll only get five years,' and yet no one ranted and screamed in this place, or even broke a window. Above, or below it all, the ladies and gentlemen of the Bar sailed out to play, leaving mayhem behind them.

Down on the brilliant green of Inner Temple Lawns, waitresses with black dresses and white pinafores were loading snowy tables. Glistening canapés appeared on plates, ice buckets stood to attention filled with unpopped bottles. Ryan licked his lips, and turned to Malcolm.

'What these buggers celebrating, then?'

'Being alive, I suppose. It's an annual event. One of several. Middle Temple Garden Party. Most of the Inns of Court have something like this. Then there's the Inner Temple May Ball, the Christmas cocktails, indoors, of course; Gray's Inn Ball, grandest of the lot. They like to enjoy themselves.'

'So I see.' The Detective Sergeant sighed, watching the activity, curious rather than envious. He preferred pubs, champagne made him sick. No, it wasn't champagne, it was weddings, the only time he encountered fizzy drinks, which made him sick.

'So that's why old Churcher made it a short conference. He

had to rush off and polish his tie. Dry old stick, isn't he?'
Malcolm sighed, hearing the sharp edge of Ryan's resentment.

'We wouldn't have liked him whether he was dry, wet or mid-
dling.' Ryan made a sound between a sigh and a snore. 'Bailey
told me this would happen.'

From behind them came puffing and rattling. A red-faced
boy stepped inside the gate to the gardens, deposited a crate of
champagne and a box of glasses with a dangerous thump, then
ran across the lawns for instructions. Ryan looked at the crate,
and Malcolm looked away. Ryan opened his huge briefcase, and
reaching deftly for one bottle of the champagne and two flute
glasses, placed them neatly inside the case with a wodge of
papers between them. Without a word, the two men moved
down the steps towards the Embankment.

'I reckon,' Ryan sighed again, 'since I hate barristers and this
little lot gets paid out of Legal Aid and such, while I just pay
my taxes, they owe me, not the other way round, and they
didn't ask us to their party. How about a seat by the river, Mr
Cook?'

In the end, they leant on the pigeon-stained wall, watching the
movement of the sluggish low-tide river. 'You do the honours,
Mr Cook. Makes you an aider and abettor to theft, you know,
and all you lot ought to try it once or twice. Besides, you'll be
more used to champagne corks than me. I don't go to many
garden parties if you see what I mean. Only weddings.'

The first glass had its reviving effect. Ryan noticed how
Malcolm preserved the posture of the fat man, distanced himself
even as he smiled, giving himself space even as he slumped.
Ryan took out a cigarette, passed the packet to Malcolm, lit his
own and inhaled with the deep satisfaction of an addict.

'Can't even bloody smoke in Churcher's chambers. What a
pillock. What the hell does he do down the cells with a client on
Monday morning?'

'He doesn't go down the cells with prisoners on Monday
mornings. He's not that kind of barrister, doesn't do much
crime, if any. Company and Commercial, all that stuff; that's

what he does. Real money. That's why I used him. We needed a
Silk with the know-how to sift through a mile of documents. To
tell the truth, I never thought we'd have much joy on the theft
side, but I hoped we might find something in Tysall's bloody
records which would give us a clue where to go next. Some
other way to get a crack at him.'

'Clever bastard.' The Detective Sergeant drained the glass,
looked round him with a grin, pulled the bottle from behind the
briefcase.

'Same again, sir?'

'Don't mind if I do . . .'

'This would be nicer with cheese and onion crisps,' said
Ryan.

Both sipped, temporarily content.

'Mind you,' Ryan continued, replacing the bottle, 'old
Churcher has a way with words. At least he'd read the papers.
Good of him.'

'And let us know he'd done his homework. Good customer
relations, only he won't want many customers like us. Not on
what the Crown Prosecution Service pays him. He'd rehearsed
it. This is the case, as I see it, Mr Cook. Mr Ryan . . . Pay attention, boys . . .' Malcolm mimicked Churcher's clipped tones. 'We
have Mr Tysall, our putative co-defendant, who owns several
companies. One of these is dealing in er . . . new technology.
Produces not very exciting er . . . packages, needs new ideas. He
spots a smaller company consisting of a little team of brilliant
graduates who've formulated a revolutionary new piece of software which, when harnessed, will put this struggling outfit on
the billion-dollar map. They've devoted three years and all their
capital to research. However, not all of them are otherworldly
boffins. By dint of seduction of one young graduate, female,
you'll be glad to know at least, and another young man in
Company A's team, our Tysall persuades them to come and
work for him, at exorbitant salaries. Provided of course they
bring the er . . . package with them.'

'Giftwrapped for preference.'

'Which it was. The defectors do not tell Company A, of course. Who do not know until market rumours tell them that Tysall's lot are launching a revolution sooner and better marketed than their own could ever be. Altered, of course, for cosmetic reasons, but still the same. Only we have to prove it's the same. Prove that the defectors have not created something out of their egg-shaped heads, but have actually stolen er . . . data, discs, whole programmes and ideas, solicited by our Mr Tysall. So, Mr Cook, Mr Ryan, you find a computer expert who says, for several hundred pounds a day, he will make a detailed comparison to show how this must be the case. There are few experts in this field, they are vastly expensive and all as incomprehensible as one another. The jury will not understand, Mr Cook, Mr Ryan. What is more, they will listen to three weeks' gobbledygook, and they will not care. It is not theft as they know it, it is employees squabbling, it is only money and computers. Even if a small firm faces bankruptcy and a rich one stands to gain revenue of ten million. Meantime, our expert and myself have bored them to death at vast public expense for a result we cannot guarantee. This is not, Mr Cook, Mr Ryan, a gamble I advise. Send Company A to the High Court to pursue his civil remedies . . .'

'. . . And you told him the complainant Company couldn't afford to do that, that's why he's come to the police. He don't want damages, he wants his programme, and is now on the brink of shooting himself. Remember what Churcher said?'

'Yes, I do. He took his glasses off, and said, "That is very sad, Mr Cook. I hope you advise him against it. Not a course I recommend." I mean, how would he know?'

Both men collapsed against the wall, snuffling with unexplained giggles. Again Ryan caught himself in surprise. Even in the midst of uncontrolled laughter, he expected Malcolm to be fat. It was odd to see the thinner man chuckle and explode as the fat one had done. Thank God some things don't change, thought Ryan, wiping his eyes, reaching for the bottle. 'He's not a bad old stick, Churcher,' he said, gasping. 'He just doesn't appreciate what it's going to be like telling this Young Turk we aren't going to prosecute and his company is going down the pan. But he did understand the difficulties, some of them. What was it he said? I know. "These days, Mr Ryan, we rarely have the means to prosecute fraud, or even complicated theft. You have my sympathy. Being in the Fraud Squad must be similar to riding a horse and cart in pursuit of a Porsche."'

'He's right, of course,' said Malcolm. 'He was right about everything. What sticks in my gullet is the fact that if it were a man on the factory floor, stealing bits from cars, or computers for that matter, only computer bits aren't useful, he'd be charged and put inside. Just because it's complicated ideas being pinched for a loss and profit worth millions, Tysall gets away scot-free. For the third bloody time, the third stolen company, on almost identical facts. All those ruined lives.'

'To them that hath it shall be given. The water always flows into the valley. Didn't know I went to church, did you, Mr Cook?'

'No,' said Malcolm. 'I didn't, and I wouldn't have guessed.' Both immediately dissolved again. Malcolm fell against the wall, stood upright, braced himself. 'Right. Shame. There's a good pub in Fleet Street; should be open by now. Time for a swift half? Between wives?'

'Not like you, Mr Cook, not these days.' Ryan shook his head. 'Can't get used to you being so careful, Mr Cook, I really can't. I'm pleased you still drink. I been worried about you. Still a big man, though. Room for a pint.'

'Sometimes. In good company I return to my old habits. Not often.'

They ambled past the Inner Temple Lawns. 'Shall I put back the glasses, do you think?' Ryan asked.

'I don't think so,' said Malcolm. 'Don't tempt fate.'

'But I'm an officer of the law.'

'And I, a solicitor of the Supreme Court. A serving member of the Crown Prosecution Service, aiding and abetting a police officer to steal champagne. The average judge would have a lot of sympathy, but what would you do if you were drummed out, Ryan?'

Ryan grinned. 'Become a pimp, or a private detective. Like Ted Plumb. Did you ever know him? Rochester Row?'

'No.'

'Lately of the Drugs Squad. Good copper once. Drummed out. Now all the things I've just mentioned, pimp, detective, bouncer. Works for Charles Tysall, I hear, but wouldn't talk to me. I did try.'

'Well, if you got the sack, Charles Tysall would give you a job.'

'Would he hell. Don't put me in the same bracket as Ted Plumb. I have my pride. I'd rather be a publican. That would suit me better.'

'Well, watch it, Ryan, will you?' said Malcolm lightly. 'Don't ever expect too much by way of results. It's disappointment makes policemen bent. When they cease to see the point of playing by the rules. If you see what I mean.'

'Yes,' said Ryan, just as lightly. 'I do see, as it happens.'

The lawns were filling. Black suits, wives with peacock hats, dark-suited ladies straight out of court, discreetly painted faces with just a hint of a frivolous frill at the neck, colourful against the green and the hats and the old young heads. Only Ryan paused to look back after they had passed the same steps, suddenly, vainly anxious for the boy who would have to account for the bottle.

'Hey! Mr Cook! I've just seen bloody Churcher talking to a lovely redhead, crafty old bugger. No wonder he wanted rid of us.'

'Good luck to him,' said Malcolm. 'I hear he's a widower. Whoever he talks to isn't even scandalous. Maybe she'll soften him up before we ever have to see him again.'

'Widower? Single man? All right for some. Not a bad old bloke really. Oh, come on, Mr Cook. If we're going to drink, let's drink. And not in bloody Fleet Street. I need a beer . . .'

Looking at his own haphazard reflection, Simeon Churcher was aware of something wrong but what it was escaped him. Like why it was the business of his day was so easy if complicated, while the business of his evenings was so awful. All his life he had been setting himself goals, achieving them more or less with the kind of precision useful to Queen's Counsel engrossed in commercial litigation, but these days nothing came naturally at all, while the mirror showed signs of the now familiar panic and Simeon was forced to recognise in his own lopsidedness not only how useless he was without a wife, but what a hash he was making of finding a replacement.

The incident of her death was remote now, like an old, but well remembered case. Mrs Churcher had usually been ill, but well enough to run her household with an iron hand, frequently discarding any velvet glove. The end result was Simeon in pressed socks and pristine appearance to compensate for years of virtual celibacy and incessant headaches, with his innocence preserved by twice-daily telephone calls to his clerk in order to plot his movements and nourishment as would a general for his army. Pleased to be the subject of such concern, he had never rebelled; but now when he strode down Fleet Street towards the High Court he kept his eyes fixed on the ground to avoid the distraction of what they might otherwise observe, bumping into short skirts with groans of dismay, Simeon was as hungry for an affectionate sexual encounter as he had been at sixteen, with a level of ignorance almost as complete. Two problems compounded by fifty-four years of total respectability. Simeon yearned for adventures with a kindly, instructive mate, and from the depths of his imagination, the new wife rose a phoenix from the ashes, while all the time there was something in his approach which sent all prospects scuttling for cover like hysterical ants in the path of his large feet. They did not walk away. They ran.

'Jesus.' Joan was speaking to Sarah. 'That was that Simeon Churcher. Again. Why didn't you see the danger signs with him, Sarah? He's rung for you three times today. It's like listening to a man fall over himself on the phone. You must've bowled him over at that posh garden party you was on about.'

'My heels were stuck in the grass. I was shrinking by inches, I couldn't move. Besides, he's a nice man. He's taking me out to dinner.'

'He's bloody what? You must be mad, and why do you go for such losers? You won't bloody go out with Charles Tysall, best-looking bloke who ever crossed this sodding doorstep, rich, handsome, gorgeous . . .'

'I did. Go out with him. Once or twice was enough, and anyway I thought we agreed we wouldn't discuss it.'

'Sorry, I'm sure. Won't mention it again. Was it because he was a client?' You poor cow, she thought.

'No. Besides, he isn't a client. Not one of mine. I only saw him because Ernest was out. Charles Tysall has problems beyond my slender skills.'

'Well, it ain't for me to comment, but you must have a screw loose. Bloody good-looking bloke. And rich. Wouldn't catch me missing a chance like that.'

Sarah stirred, fidgeted. She's all right, thought Joan. I like her really, and I bloody well owe her plenty, but it doesn't do any harm for her to worry from time to time. Nice to see it. Makes her human.

'I'm a bit frightened of him, to tell the truth.'

Joan snorted, and hoisted the files from the desk and under her arm. 'Never known you frightened of anything, Miss Fortune. Not you.'

Simeon considered he was looking rather pukka. As far as he was able to judge. He was a slight man, with grizzled, grey hair, bright eyes, a large mouth and hands which he used for copious gestures in court and could not otherwise keep still. The appearance in the mirror still worried him. Today he wore cavalry twills, and an ancient bluey tweed jacket devoid of shape and unpleasantly hairy, slightly at odds with his nylon shirt of brilliant yellowy-white and a half-purple, striped tie, saddened and twisted in the wash. His new shoes shone like plastic. The combined effect diminished and aged him into a retired colonel, without batman, and if he had wished to complete the general impression of dated ineptitude, Simeon could rely on his manner to do the rest. Excellent choice, the Travellers' Club. Pall Mall's faded splendour. It had been himself at fault, and he knew it, crestfallen when she said she had been there before, but how grand it was. Grinning like a pixie he had been when she had found him too early in the entrance, bestowing his smiles indiscriminately on all passers-by in case they were her, hopelessly surprised to find that this warm lady, met so opportunely on the Inner Temple Lawns, would actually arrive. Sarah Fortune had no sharp edges to distract from her neat and confident elegance and transparent intelligence. He did not understand women's clothes, but the combination of sexiness with complete respectability unhinged him completely. There was the ready laughter in her throat, so lacking in contempt, an understanding in the smile, and despite his twitching, he sank into a state bordering on calm.

Dinner had passed with relative ease, apart from his realisation that he had placed her facing the wall with the token vase of carnations between them, so that he gabbled and she questioned with both of them peering between the leaves. At one stage she had moved it to one side, and he had replaced it nervously without knowing he did so. The hands. He could never control the hands. New shoes were hurting as he tripped on the way down the staircase into the library, crushing her briefly against the banister, but she did not seem to mind. All going well, only three or four gaffes. If Miss Fortune had counted rather more than that, she did not say.

Too successful, of course. Simeon had relaxed too soon. As she lit a cigarette to accompany coffee, an automatic gesture on her part, his own reaction was spontaneous. Smoking had been anathema to Mrs Churcher, forbidden in her house: no smoke, no nicotine, all rooms immediately freshened, and Simeon had copied her set response. As the first curl of smoke trailed from Sarah's cigarette, he automatically produced a large red handkerchief from his bulging pockets and flicked it absently but loudly in front of him. Among the subdued murmurings of the library, the gesture was flamboyant, certainly clumsy. The edge of the cloth caught the cigarette in the ashtray, sent it flying on to the carpet before the second flick caught the coffee cup she had extended to him. Liquid and cup rose in the air for a brief and graceful moment, then crashed against the table as a huge brown stain appeared on Sarah's skirt.

'Sorry,' said Simeon, his voice manically loud and cheerful even in his own ears. 'My wife hated cigarette smoke.'

The girl's face was looking at him strangely, twisted slightly in a kind of grimace, reminding him, surely not, of someone attempting not to cry. 'Ah,' she said quietly. 'I suppose that explains it. Will you excuse me a minute?'

She was off like a shot, out of the long room almost at a run, leaving him to breathe heavily, rumple the handkerchief and wonder at his own offence. Down in the basement Ladies, Sarah Fortune relinquished stern control of her face, and collapsed in helpless laughter. He needed help. Carefully she wiped her eyes and repaired the damage.

But alone in the library, subjected to a few curious glances, Simeon was suddenly, blindingly aware of what he had done. People did not deserve to be abused, swatted like flies and covered in hot coffee for the simple antisocial crime of lighting a cigarette. They didn't deserve it; some people liked cigarettes, judging from those around him, many people. He might have been competent to advise on the devious shameful Mr Charles Tysalls of the world, but otherwise, his ignorance was profound. Being clever, he realised, was a hindrance.

Simeon prepared to leave, stiff with embarrassment. He did not blame her for not coming back, could see no reason why she should.

Two light hands were on his shoulders, and her face, curtained by sleek red hair, was bending towards his own, her eyes alight with amusement.

'Do you think I could have that coffee now, from the cup?'

For that deft touch of forgiveness, Simeon could have given

her the world. They had managed to speak as if nothing had happened, as if his pockets were not bulging with boy scout detritus and three handkerchieves, and parted, friendly and reserved. In that little absence she had somehow assumed charge, and given him hope.

Words were difficult. Two days later, Sarah reviewed the evening with Simeon and sighed. One task then, before forgetting all others. She had picked up the telephone with something akin to trepidation, telling herself it did not matter. These were the episodes she most disliked.

'Simeon?'

'Sarah? I'm delighted you rang. How are you?'

'Better for hearing you. Now, my dear, what do you think about another meeting?'

No foolish girlish promptings. No clues. No pretending that the circumstances of their meeting had been entirely ordinary or the evening perfect.

'I think about it all the time,' he stammered. 'You know I do, and how much . . . But it won't do, and I won't do for you, if you know what I mean . . . I want to, but can't.' That understanding teasing voice of hers, he could feel himself melting.

'Well.'

Strange how he knew what she was going to say before she said it, not the words, but simply the meaning wrapped in a great and sensitive generosity. And did not mind in the least.

'You aren't the answer to a maiden's prayer, any more than I'm a maiden, you know.' Gently said. 'You want a wife, and don't know how to court one. I don't want a husband, as it happens, but I like you well enough. Would you like it if we were to meet from time to time? Until the maiden answers the prayer? To make you fitter for her? You aren't at the moment, you know, but you don't need me to tell you that.'

'No I don't. And I agree. I'd love to see you.'

'Dinner next week, then. Or a play. Or an evening in.'

'All three,' he said earnestly. 'If you don't mind.'

She laughed, and his fists uncurled at the sound of it. A

happy laugh she had, as comforting as a hug and as full of promise.

'One problem,' he began.

'Which is?' From the first, he loved her mild, questioning voice.

'What if we don't get on?'

'What do you mean?' Not defensive, simply an insistence that he, rather than herself, should express any reservation.

'Supposing we don't accord, I mean, I'm not much used to . . .' He stopped in confusion.

'Oh, I wouldn't worry about that. We'll be fine.'

Such an airy confidence. He believed in her, felt the burden of inadequacy fall from his stooped shoulders like a pack.

'Are you sure?'

'Of course. I'll have to look after you if not.' Again that laughter, entirely free of scorn or condescension. 'Next week? Wait a minute, I'll get my diary . . .'

Sarah stretched very shapely limbs on a pretty sofa, sank into her glass of wine in a quick survey of a favourite comfortable room and the prospect of hours of silence. Oh, for a short life and a merry one, but look at the mess. It was not the larger, moral issues which ever troubled her conscience, not any more. They were shrunk into minor dilemmas the way she considered sensible, second to all the endless problems of how to keep the house clean, manage shopping for necessities, and hold all the thin threads which made life possible. She had run out of washing-up liquid again, there was always that irritating pile of cups on the draining-board, clothes to be mended or cleaned. She had avoided the corner shop on the way home, guiltily evading the sad gaze of the lady behind the counter and the thirtieth chapter of her life waiting to be told as the twenty-ninth had been told that morning. Sarah always listened, but sometimes it was harder than others. The fridge contained one egg, a piece of venerable cheese, two onions and a bottle of oil. Difficult to make a feast out of that. She had the depressing suspicion her bedroom was a mess, remembering the tights

flung on the floor that morning in the frantic search for a pair
with both legs, to say nothing of the earrings, tipped and spilt
in the usual hurried search for one to match another. Such
sophistication you have, Sarah. What a joke, what a glorious
muddle. Home. No food, nor ironed shirts for the morning,
place needing a dust. She looked at it from the safety of the
horizontal, squinted at the untidiness, saw the box containing
new shoes and a sideways view of a favourite painting alongside an open bottle of wine. What the hell. All right, there was
an hour or two of chores, then she would be able to sing in the
bath while washing away the day, before going out to look at
the world again. A night world, different and better balm for
restlessness.

Sarah moved with energy, crossing the hall by the mirror,
into her bedroom, waving at the glass dismissively. Don't ever
look in the mirror, she had warned herself, for signs of what life
does to you. You chose it, you can always opt out, but don't
damn well pity it. Don't look. You only ever grow old and ugly
by surrounding yourself with malice. And discontent. And that
office. You only stay sane by doing exactly as you please as
nearly as you can, with as much honesty as time allows. Which
is what I think I do. Too many years of doing the opposite,
being good for nothing else but being good, whilst being good
to no one.

The kitchen depressed her as usual. Maybe one day she
would have somewhere in a wilderness with all the total independence she craved, free from the dual tyrannies of mortgage
and employment. Maybe she would borrow some children,
paint pictures, live without a bloody answerphone. She played
back the messages on her own, absently dusting the table on
which it stood. All lawyers, all business. 'Hallo, Sarah. How
about lunch next week?' (She must remember to take the book
he had wanted.) Another. '. . . Just phoning to say thanks for
conference the other afternoon. When next? Soon, I hope.
Please phone.' Measured English tones: John's voice, Judge
Henry's voice, Albemarle *et al.* No, thought Sarah. I mean, yes.

Yes I will have another glass of wine. Cottage in the country, room in a lighthouse. Yes. But not yet, not for a while. I like this secrecy, I like this life.

And today my horse won. Pink Jade again, backed by Fred. Not bad for a girl.

CHAPTER FOUR

'How long have you been in the police, Mr Ryan?'

'Oh Christ. Since I was born.'

'No, I can't put that. Perhaps that's just what it feels like . . .'

'Thirteen years, then.'

'Lucky for some. Any substantiated complaints?'

'No, not yet. There've been some unsubstantiated.'

'Never mind. Those don't count. Any commendations, Commissioners' or judges'?'

'One.'

'Married? Children? Sorry to ask, but we have to know for the witness statement.'

'Yes to both.' And sod off if you want to ask anything else. He was sick of it. Two interviews in one week, one with CIB, MS14 or whatever the hell it was those maniacs investigating complaints against police officers called themselves these days. All because that bastard Tysall had (a) made a formal complaint about the seizing of documents from the offices of his computer company, even though they had all been returned, and (b) followed it up with a High Court writ against the Commissioner for damages. First, the interview by that faceless Scot with the obsessive gleam in his eye and the plain-clothes demeanour of a crafty thug, but at least a policeman, and then this friendlier chat with an equally faceless solicitor from the Commissioner's small fleet. All had been explained. 'The Commissioner is liable for the acts of his constables, by law. He is sued a few hundred times every year.' 'Oh yeah?' Ryan had joked. 'That's worse than the gas board. Now who would want to work for a man like that?'

Malicious, tight-fisted bastard. Tysall could spot money under a stone, and if he fell into his own cesspit, he'd come up smelling of roses. That's what Eton and Oxford does for you. Solicitors' department was airless, slotted into an ugly block along with Catering, Medical and Surveyors above a foyer smelling of onions from the traffic wardens' canteen in the basement. The complaints office was aptly placed in a building resembling Alcatraz on the south side of the river. Ryan almost missed his smaller, colder office in the Fraud Squad, and for a moment thought of it with affection.

'Listen, sir. Me and Fraud, we're incompatible, that's what.' So he had told Superintendent Bailey who had pinched him from District. 'I'm not too good at reading and writing, sir,' he had finished lamely. 'Too bad,' Bailey had said. 'You need the promotion and your wife needs the regular hours.' Stitched up good and proper, and to start with he could feel the thread cutting into his skin.

Paperwork forever, he thought. No street pounding, no pubs, no chases, no great gulps of outrage, only money. But that was before Tysall, before Ryan understood how he should have trusted Bailey after all. Fraud wasn't so bland, not once he cottoned on to how Bailey had got him on the squad to get his teeth into Tysall. There was a roomful of Tysall, and Ryan hated Tysall with a passion. Exactly as Bailey had intended.

Back in the chilly confines of his room in Holborn, Ryan rekindled the flames, forgot the humiliating interviews. On his desk, read briefly before he had left, was a slender report from District, slimline through lack of effort and a dearth of questions.

'Diana Steepel. D.o.b. 18.10.1960. 13a, Olympia Mansions, West Kensington. Suicide Report.

'On Tues, 15th August 1988, Ms Steepel was found by her neighbour who had forced the door of the flat to investigate a dripping tap. Subject had taken an overdose of sleeping tablets, plus large quantity of gin. One half-bottle remained. The flat-mate does not drink, and was away for a fortnight's holiday.

'It is apparent Ms Steepel intended suicide. The pathologist says that the attempt would not have been successful through a combination of alcohol and Mogadon if the victim had not woken, probably nauseous, but unable through weakness to vomit effectively, and without any help at hand. Cause of death: asphixiation. No note, but victim known to have been severely depressed. No signs of violence or disturbance . . .'

Perhaps a cry for help? Perhaps, but not likely. Ryan closed the file in disgust. Pleas for help were made with the clear prospect of rescue, and she'd deliberately chosen the time when her flatmate was away. She had not been seeking deliverance, Tysall's brilliant graduate, who had defected to his ranks with all her brain cells intact, but not the rest of her, apparently. Tysall lived less than a mile away, in a straight line. She'd probably moved to be nearer him, then been abandoned, poor cow. Probably wanted to sleep for ever. He'd had the body and used up the brain. At least Annie, pretty and plump, love of Ryan's own life, rebounding from him to be seduced by Tysall, was still alive. Back in her own home town, silent, only mentally scarred. Ready to marry the nearest worzel farmer if she hadn't done it already. Anything to remove the mortal sins of two seductions and one abortion.

At least I loved Annie. That bastard never loved anyone. Annie loved me too. Guilt surfaced in his mind, a kind of sudden heartburn distilled into fury and pain.

Ryan marshalled all his reports on Tysall, including the last in a varied and tragic line. Three or four bankrupt companies, and Steepel, bankrupt life, pretty kid. Just as well Bailey encouraged Ryan's empirical style of investigation and turned a blind eye to it. In the face of Bailey's Nelsonian telescope, Ryan worked by instinct, found himself a bad man rather than a good suspicion. Tysall had emerged into woozy focus from all the rumour-mongering, tales told by disassociated witnesses and informants, information leaking from other investigations. The Fraud teams worked like that, names falling off carousels or found in the brantub with irksome regularity. From all this dross, company frauds, bent mortgage applications, other men's double lives and sticky fingers, Tysall's name was always appearing as director of that outfit or this, never in a big way, but always there, owner of a hotel with a tax-evading accountant, major domo of a now thriving computer firm which stole software ideas. He was like a growing blob of mercury on the desk: if Ryan touched, he slid away, and if he hit, the droplet broke into a shower of smaller drops, easily reunited. But having sensed the rotten core, Ryan was not about to give up. A man could not be that bad without somehow breaking the law. Simply a question of finding how he had done it and how to prove it, and all he had got so far was the thumbs down from Simeon Churcher and a writ for the Commissioner. And the tortured memory of Annie's face trans-fixed with misery, the innocence which he himself had smirched finally turned into total disillusion. She might, just might, have got better without that. Might have written him off like any other girl, dusted herself down, got on with it. No chance now. Absently, Ryan bit his lip, and punched one calloused fist into his palm.

It would have been better if his conscience had been clearer in other, more professional respects, or if he had been warned less often of the dangers of keeping secrets, instead of pretending to investigate fraud while investigating something else. There had been this wife, see? Mrs Tysall, who used Harrods like a corner shop – well, she would, wouldn't she, nothing nearer. A brilliant looking redhead, weeping in the nick, stinking of frightened sweat and Chanel perfume, battered, bruised and bleeding. Twice, was it? Or more than twice, he couldn't remember. Statement taken, not usual from such quality, 'My husband tried to kill me,' touch. 'Why, madam?' 'I tried to go out . . .' But as usual, be it the rich or the council house wife, allegation with-drawn within days. No proceedings, please. I daren't. Besides, we've made it up. Me complain? Never. Silly me. And then the

Tysall wife had disappeared, simply disappeared off the face of the earth, or at least the pretty complexion of Knightsbridge. Nothing to investigate: no one reported her missing, no power to ask questions and interfere with the civil liberties of the husband.

'Seen the wife recently, have you?' Ryan had asked with his irritating wolfish grin, determined to needle that imperturbable face while pillaging Tysall's office under warrant for documents to show to Malcolm Cook. Charles smiled back, replied with bored dignity. 'She lives elsewhere, Mr Ryan. No business of yours. Have you finished?'

Ryan paused, smoked and slumped. He hadn't told Malcolm Cook about the Tysall wife saga, or about the other evidence of dismembered female lives, didn't trust him enough. Cook might have guessed, not entirely, and it was important he did not yet know that Ryan was not really pursuing a fraudsman thief, while Ryan knew he was chasing the tail of something worse. A psychopath possibly, a murderer almost certainly. Whatever Tysall was, it was dangerous. They didn't know the half of it.

Ryan piled and bound the reports, flicking back the last for a quick squint at Steepel's picture, taken from the flat, must be returned to relatives, but not if they failed to ask. Odd time for her to die. He'd spoken to her by phone the day before, thought again how strange it was with the educated ones, how it was they couldn't bring themselves to put down the phone on you even when they didn't want to speak. Too polite. His mind jumped over the photograph. Redhead, lovely curly redhead. Mrs Tysall, dead according to his instincts, redhead. With a great gulping need for life, gasping for the stuff, even as he had seen her, grasping at life, bruised but not beaten. Women like that don't disappear, not until they die.

Pity for them. Put out a general alert for all red-haired women of suitable age to steer clear of this bastard. Stay away, or number your days, he thought, while I think what the fuck to do next. Fraud, he supposed. A waste of time, he thought, with Tysall at large.

*

Charles Spencer Tysall was home early. No longer was he forced to work all hours, although the days when he had done so were still fresh in his mind as an exercise in stamina he never wanted to repeat. Speculation, clever investment in desperate companies forced to sell for less than their capital assets, sold at monumental profit or kept for more, all of that had ensured a measure of security, and he was nothing if not flexible in talents of management and acquisition. He liked to dabble, and the businesses he retained as director were varied enough for all his tastes. And they worked. Everything worked if you were creative about the means. There was his menage: Ted Plumb, the ex-detective, one or two tame lawyers, what more did he need? Somewhere in twenty years' achievement he had also laid hands on the Porsche, the Knightsbridge flat, the Paris house in the same sweep, and had mislaid one wife, or that was how he explained it.

Poor Porphyria. She was called Elisabeth, but he had always called her Porphyria, the only thing he had never really owned in forty-five years, never known or entirely subdued. Since Elisabeth's departure he had seen her in the streets, pursued her auburn image across counters and roads wherever sunlight had fallen on hair, and finally he had found her. Not her, perhaps, but certainly her graven image. She would live in this house with him, stay still without rebellion. This new Porphyria would learn from the old, would surely know better than risk Charles's style of combat. Wherever she was now, Madame Tysall the first must bear the scars, and Charles shook with the memory of his own anger.

Unhappy reflections shuddered away. Charles changed from his immaculate suit into cords and rough silk shirt, then sat in his leather armchair with the cold bottle of Sancerre at his side. Knightsbridge rush-hour hummed softly below the second-floor windows of the mansion flat, sounds dimmed to pleasant indifference by the double-glazed windows. The room was lined with books and marbled paper. The carpet was rose red, Charles's choice, not that of the dear departed who enjoyed neither that colour nor the olive Chesterfield which complemented it. Not a visible hair of woman or dog, nor a single speck of dust on the floor. All trace of her was expunged. He had even told Ted to destroy the wretched puppy she had loved so much it had become her inseparable companion. Now there was simply the red carpet, at home with the black speakers which relayed the spindly Mozart sounds softly into his ears. Above the marble fireplace a gilded Georgian mirror showed Charles's dark-skinned face, green eyes below thick-arched brows as black as the raven-coloured hair, a mouth chiselled rather than sensual, the chin cleft. Truly a very beautiful man, with the broad shoulders and long legs of a dancing prince. Such a beautiful man, reminiscent of every dark hero in paperback romances. Slim-hipped, strong brown fingers, arresting face, full of hidden authority, with that luminous power of masculine saints depicted in sacred portraits, mesmeric eyes and the charm of the devil. Penetrating gaze, sensitive, perfect manners, superbly cast and presented for the diplomatic role of a Pontius Pilate.

Charles sipped the Sancerre, not waiting for Maria, simply expecting her. When the entry-phone buzzed from the street he did not rise, but pressed the electric device by his chair, and sipped another mouthful. She would sense the nature of his mood from the fact that the door was not locked and he did not rise to greet her. She could sense his exact requirements by the fact that she found him seated, would know how limited her time. Maria knew his habits and never commented, would not have considered argument. She had the advantage of a regular call-girl. Now he had tied her up with Ted Plumb, bodyguard, bruiser and private law-breaker, they were both his creatures, suitably afraid of him.

Into the room she slipped almost soundless, darker, smaller, slighter than he, a radiant Filipino, more smiles than words.

' 'Lo, Charlie boy. Happy today?'

'Not particularly. Pleased to see you. I needed you.'

'Oh good, Charlie boy.'

He stood then and took off her coat. Maria giggled and

squirmed a little as he ran his hands over the smooth-sided
dress, shuffled off her high-heeled shoes, raised her arms to the
fastening behind her dress, revealing the absence of undercloth-
ing around her small breasts. Charles turned to his bedroom,
undressed more slowly, watching her stretch like a dancer on the
silk cover, her black hair around her. The image of a skinned
rabbit briefly crossed his mind, swiftly dismissed as he lay beside
her.

She moved to his side, ran her fingers across his flat belly, listening to his even breathing as she lay with her face against his
chest. Then she bit gently, tickled his nipples with her fingers.
He did not kiss her. Instead he fondled her neck, and pushed her
head downwards. Without further prompting, she obeyed, one
hand kneading the inside of one thigh while her mouth found
her target, crouched above it, held in small fingers as she began
a delicate circular motion with her tongue, slowly, then quicker,
waiting for the imperceptible signs which would show his pleasure. Charles lay still, already removed to the evening ahead,
admiring the cornice on the high ceiling, his thoughts absent
from the work of her mouth apart from the automatic arching of
his back and the moist sounds. As the sensation grew, he arched
further, felt her pull back, pulled her head down savagely by the
hair. And held it there, silently, throughout his own climax, and
her choking, panicking struggle.

There were times when Maria might have spat back, although
she did not contemplate it now. What did it matter, beautiful
clean boy. Better this fear, this coughing and mouthful of
molten, waxy filth than all those sudden spurts of hate for the fat
dirty uglies who actually tried to please. Sometimes, on a good
day, Charlie boy was normal. Other days he would practise on
her like a man tuning a violin, testing her body for sensation and
himself for skill until she had arched three times and lay gasping
like a fish filleted alive. Other times he wanted almost nothing, or
made her crawl between his fine legs, like a harem-slave. So
what? He always paid, always tipped and had never struck her –
well, not hard. Not yet. She thought of Ted, Charles's regular

henchman, and her inept lover, so undemanding by compari-son. She thought of Ted, and smiled at their mutual master.

'On the hall table,' Charles said drowsily, hands crossed behind his head, lazily watching her dress.

'Thank you, Charlie boy. Next Thursday, yes?'

'I'll telephone if not.'

'OK, Charlie boy.' Consistent clients were hard to find. She scooped the notes from the inlaid table by the front door and left, high heels clicking down the stone corridor into a grateful silence. Once out of earshot, she ran. Maria never knew why she ran from Charlie boy's flat, but she always did.

In the silence, Charles showered, then returned to his chair, the cool Sancerre, the music and the unfashionable volume of Browning. Poetry was his unwinding. Reading Browning he would think of nothing else. Not even the new lover would come to know all he had ever learned and enjoyed from the Marias of his world. There would be her image in his mirror, one day soon, owned, as he owned the mirrors in every room, where she would stand before him even now. In the meantime, he would make do with a passion for poetry, turn his eyes to verse for the appropriate images for a lighthearted mood. Browning, under-rated in twentieth-century terms apart from his affair with that suitably dutiful daughter, Elizabeth Barrett. Effortless poet, renowned for romance, cynical to the core, or so it seemed for all that. Charles read the poetic plays for early-evening soothing, the stray poems with his aperitif, and turned to 'Porphyria's Lover', the oddest of them all, for light amusement.

> . . . at last I knew
> Porphyria worshipp'd me; surprise
>   Made my heart swell, and still it grew
>   While I debated what to do.
> That moment she was mine, mine, fair,
>   Perfectly pure and good: I found
> A thing to do, and all her hair
>   In one long yellow string I wound

Three times her little throat around,
And strangled her. No pain felt she;
I am quite sure she felt no pain.
As a shut bud that holds a bee.

Good Porphyria, happy child who died so sweetly in the arms of a master, without pain. There was one imperfection in the mention of a golden head – he could not admire such flaxen hair – but even flawed, the poem always made him shake with quiet laughter, a familiar joke, but never stale. Soft, artistic hands against skin, his own curled around the neck of his wife, the disgusting vision of her bulging eyes and silent, resistant scream. One day, he was confident, the new and improved fac-simile of the old would seat herself upon his lap, Porphyria-like, with graceful back towards him, her trust a feature of a perfect, faithful wife. Unlike the old, Miss Fortune would change her name. Her own, cheap title was not fit for an auburn swan. Soon she would see sense and stop avoiding him. Each has its fate, and he, of course, was hers.

Charles looked at his watch. Ted Plumb had begun his obser-vation today; no doubt he would finish at six. Unless she began to co-operate soon, he would have to get Ted to look at her house. Ted was a faithful hound, and did as he was told.

Arriving home light-headed with exhaustion, Sarah found her-self waiting for the dawn, the effect of tiredness so acute it made her wakeful, active, loathing the idea of sleep and all the exhaus-tion of waking into another day. Better stay awake at five in the morning, a perfect and precious peace, which reminded her she could cope with everything except fatigue. Even that was pos-sible when grit-filled eyes watched the beginnings of light invading the windows, and the whole place clean and washed in that pale morning glow from the milky mist outside. Sarah shed her clothes, wandered naked as a baby in her own rooms. Alive. She wanted to postpone sleep for the hour of idle happiness and the regret which was bound to follow the lack of it. In these hours, uninhibited by clothes, she had been known to clean floors, polish silver, scour cupboards in a happy awareness of timelessness and order.

The wide crescent outside, full of early Victorian mansions, was an avenue of silent doors and swaying trees, her own for one silent hour. No hint of engine noise, one far-off trumbling train, yak yak, sleepily over the North London line, somnolent carrying of goods, too soon for human stock. Not even a motorcycle messenger or paperboy. Drawn to her large front windows, still naked, she watered the geraniums fading for water while she spoke encouragement. In the pinkening glow of five-thirty, she heard footsteps, ducked, and craned over the balcony, resting her chin on the cold iron curves of the rail, watching and curious. Down the park came the jogger, padding softly, breathing easily in sweat-stained black tracksuit, looking like a burglar returning home. Rhythmic pad-padding up the middle of the road without competition from machine or beast, a long, lithe body, moving with a smooth, slow sprint as effortless and elegant as a horse trotting back to the paddock having won the race without waiting for the cheers, owned by no one. His private time as well as hers: she ducked further below the ironwork in case he should see himself observed. There was a mild familiarity in those fine features which puzzled her in his quick upward glance. He had shimmied to a slow-breathing halt beneath her window, felt for the keys strung around his neck, passed a large hand through thick sweat-damp hair before jogging up the steps to the front door, impervious or indifferent to observation. Sarah could not recall where she had seen him before. New flat dweller, perhaps, using the side door to this largish block, while she always used the door in the centre. She was sometimes ashamed of how little she knew of her neighbours, pleased they knew so little of her. Jogger in black had the look of some woman's lover. May they go safely back to bed, where she, pursuing the freedom of restlessness, had been wakeful for half the night.

CHAPTER FIVE

'Don't know why you do this, Sarah, I really don't.'

Joan was truculent, grateful in an embarrassed, furious fashion which did not allow her to sound grateful at all. 'You don't bloody have to, you know.'

'I know I don't.' Sarah spoke with mild nonchalance as if she did not care either way. 'Can't have you dying for lack of sleep though, can I? Besides, I like him. Wouldn't have you for the day if I didn't, would I, Jack?'

'No,' said Jack, beaming at her.

'That's all right then,' said Joan, cuffing him lightly, speaking grumpily. 'Mind you behave. Bring him back if you're fed up. See you.'

The door had closed behind them with a hollow crash which echoed down the stone stairs, Joan both angry and relieved. So long as you don't think you're doing me any favours. Don't think I'm grateful, but God, I needed the peace. Why does she know when I'm at my wits' end, knows to arrive out of the blue and take one of them off me? How does she know? I don't bloody tell her. I could kill her for knowing, I really could, letting her do it . . . Little sod'll have a better day than he would cooped up with me, shame on me. Just don't let her think I can't cope . . .

The wind was blowing, stiff and hot. Sunday, Sarah's favourite day, improved by Jack, aged seven years and three precious months, relinquished into her care for a whole day through an offer of hers made with deliberate diffidence, accepted in the same vein. Free of the mother's watching eye, they were almost happy.

'Come on, Jacko! Race you!'

'Not yet. Sarah, what's Mummy doing?'

'She's at home, Jack. You know she is, you big softy.'

'Yes, but what will she be doing?'

'Sitting down, I think, with her feet up. Where we left her, probably asleep by now.'

'Will she be there when we get back?'

'When is she ever not? What's the matter, Jack?'

'If she goes to sleep she won't go in and tidy up my bedroom, will she? Then she can't find her birthday present, can she?'

'Is that all? Look at me, Jack.'

He paused, scuffed the new shoes she had bought him on the path, sighed and quivered. Jack suffered terribly for his sins, then he burst.

'Oh, Sarah, I ate the sweets you bought me last time to go with the present. Only some of them, then they were all gone. She'll find the paper.' Tears were gathering in his big pale eyes. No wonder he wouldn't eat. Sarah bent to his seven-year-old level and put her arms round him. He was a prickly little boy, but he put his arms behind her neck and wept into her collar. Spindly boy, over-anxious, protective of his single parent, and as far as sweets were concerned, the same as any child who saw them rarely and wanted them all the time. Sarah was angry with herself. Her own kindness was both brusque and cunning towards this household, but it should not have been insensitive enough to cause any distress. She should have known better. The devastation of tears was rare in Jack's life; normally he was far too well controlled.

'Jack, listen to me, you dope. It's not so bad. Sweeties are meant to be eaten, and I shouldn't have left them with you. Mummy won't know and I bet she wouldn't mind if she did. Anyway, you've still got the talcum powder and stuff to give her. You haven't eaten them as well, have you?'

A watery smile emerged with some reluctance. 'That's silly.'

'Well then, we'll soon make it better.' She wiped his eyes, handed him the handkerchief to blow his nose. 'Tell you what we do. We go to the lake, then the other lake, and on the way back, we buy some more sweets. The ones she likes. We'll get them wrapped up, just the same as the others. Only lots of Sellotape.'

'I'm not supposed to take other people's money. Mummy told me.'

Sarah sighed. Mummy would. 'Look, when you're as big as me, you can pay it back.'

'Can I?'

'Sure can. I'll bop you on the head if you don't.'

'I will, I will, I will.' Drat the child, brought up with so much pride. She would like to make him naughty, rebellious and proud of himself.

She watched the thin legs kicking in front of her as she raced him up the hill to the Heath, relieved that the small distress was so easily cured. Not all Jack's problems had such easy remedies: there was little she could do about his father's defection, his mother's uphill struggle to survive. Joan was stiff-necked with pride, would take nothing smelling of charity, and ruled her off-spring with a rod of iron. Unpaid bills and a rotten council estate were not going to turn them into delinquents, not as far as Joan was concerned. They would get an education if it killed her. Sarah knew them all, knew they deserved better, and did what surreptitious little she was allowed to do. The odd pair of shoes, the odd day out, anything she could sidle past the barrier of Joan's suspicion. She had endless patience; small children enchanted her. Charity did not, and unbeknown to Joan, she knew all about it.

They had climbed Parliament Hill to see the kites, run and rolled down towards the lakes, both of them breathless. This was a regular pilgrimage to see the fancy boats, chugging round the edges of the shallow pond, controlled by their owners from the shore. Serious recreation, power boats, remotely controlled, charged by Hampstead fathers and healthy-looking children.

Looking like tramps by comparison, and without a boat of their own, both stood and watched, Jack with his usual innocent curiosity, untinged by envy, full of wonder.

'Look at that one,' he whispered.

Sarah looked, and saw a man and a boy, tall, well-dressed father ordering a sturdy blond son to behave. Yards from the edge, their battery boat was idling and they could not get it back. Like a pretty, disobedient animal, it floated in splendour, refusing all instructions. Papa's irritation was all too clear. The child was sulky. The boat inched further away. Jack looked at Sarah and Sarah looked at Jack, and they both began to giggle. There was nothing funnier than impotent fury.

Then, as the man turned to gesture, Sarah recognised the face of Belinda Smythe's husband, one-time host of more than two years since, a souvenir of lately married days and married friends. The recognition was mutual: both paused until Martin Smythe's face cleared, lost its irritation and took on the glow of remembered manners. The widow Fortune, always fancied her. Didn't remember them having a son. Confusion needing enlightenment, must tell Belinda.

'Sarah, isn't it? Not seen you for ages. This one yours?'

'Hallo, Martin. No, not mine. Wish he was.' There never had been much to say.

'Trouble with the boat then? This is Jack . . .'

'And this is Benjamin. He's cocked it up.'

The two seven-year-olds looked at one another with mutual suspicion. Jack grinned: if in doubt he always grinned. Benjamin grinned with less certainty: he was more at home with adults.

'I didn't cock it up,' he protested to Sarah. 'We need Uncle Malcolm.'

'If you say that one more time, Ben, I'll scream,' his father warned through gritted teeth. 'He means Malcolm Cook,' he added to Sarah in explanation. 'Remember Malckie? You both came to dinner once, I seem to remember. Fat Malckie. He always used to relieve us of our children on Sunday afternoons. Perhaps we took him too much for granted, but he seems to

have disappeared. Bloody nuisance really. Malckie was a natural
with kids.'

Benjamin was restless, growing truculent. 'The boat. Daddy,
it's going further . . .' Sarah felt Jack's hand creep into her own,
gently pulling her on. They were all suddenly uncomfortable.
Martin gazed distractedly at the expensive toy, moving further
and further out of reach.

'You must come and see us again, Sarah. Soon.'

They moved away, turned to wave, and saw father and son
devoted to argument, the chortle of laughter from Jack hiding
Sarah's lightning blush. Of course she remembered Malcolm
Cook, never quite forgot him. Malcolm with the big gentle
hands, his clear, understanding mind, his instinctive way with
children. She would not think of Malcolm Cook, mere memory
of other days, one last sharing begun with a kind of compassionate experiment of her own, ending in the last real
conversation before she had slipped away wilfully into her own
self-sufficient world, unfit to help him then. She had run before
he could touch her or make her vulnerable, determined he
should not. She could not afford it. She had not wanted to know
ever again what that was like. Or even what it was like to be with
a man who seemed to understand so much, despite the earlier
clowning. Another outsider, surprised by nothing. Don't think
of it now. Both of them licking wounds, and he too gone into
hiding from the conventional world. A couple of freaks, giving
freakish comfort.

'I'm glad,' said Jack, relinquishing her hand to brandish his
own in the air, 'that I haven't got things like that boat. Costing
plenty, and then getting lost. I'd be very worried, all the time. Do
you know what I mean?'

'Yes I do, pet. Very well. Is it time to find a sweet shop?'

He grinned again and began to run, whooping and jumping.
She followed faster, the red hair streaming out behind her,
shouting with him, circling round him, letting him win.

Far behind, a large shambly figure stubbed out his cigarette,
coughed, swore and followed. Ted Plumb could not understand

it. In the distant but far from dim days of Drugs Squad observations, Ted had learned to control surprise. There he would be, stamping his feet on a cold afternoon, wondering if he could slope off for a drink and cover it carefully in his notes, when suddenly the least likely suspect, supposed to be miles away, would pop out of a back door like a genie, and force him to move. Surprise would have been confined to a curse on the breath, his body immobile against shock, as it was now.

He had left the bloody dog at home, and now he was grateful. Jack might have recognised it, just as Ted so clearly recognised Jack, his own son, romping over the grass with the pretty woman he had been ordered to follow. Well, well. The same woman who had such a preference for adult company, dressed for her men, smiled at them, playing here with a penniless boy. She certainly was versatile. He shrugged. No point being curious about it. He'd find the connection in time, but the sight of his own child was hardly a comfort, even to a man as bereft of paternal instinct. He had better not mention any personal interest in his report to Charles Tysall; besides, he was sure he was not supposed to report activities of such studied innocence as these. What the girl did with males of Jack's age was of no interest to Charles. Perhaps this woman lived near his own wife, perhaps that explained it, but he felt acute annoyance. He had supposed she was simply another of Tysall's targets, but what the hell was she doing with a child not her own, making Ted so impatient an observer, and even making him begin to like her?

He watched the boy, sighed and turned away. Let them be, but he wanted them back, some of the time. Not all of the time; not when he was in bed with Maria, but when he was out in the streets with that damn dog, going home to the bare room in Hackney, then he did. At least he had Maria. This woman, richer, peculiarly beset by gentlemen friends, had no one to call her own. Go home now. Nearly closing time. With surprising speed and neat steps, soft-shoed Ted ducked away, turned his feet towards the houses and the first drink of the day.

Sarah watched the flying figure of skinny Jack. Look at him compared with the elegance of little Benjamin Smythe. Fatherless, not quite rudderless Jack, just like me. Well, you little monster, don't grow up obeying all the rules, will you? Not worth it. Be yourself. Whatever else you do. Hope someone, maybe me if I get the chance, makes sure you shout when it hurts rather than lie down and cry so easy. See yourself in a mirror and punch the rest in the eye if they don't like it. She shrugged, and ran after him. 'Wait for me, Jack . . . Wait for me . . .' Sunday children, better by far than none.

When Malcolm Cook had next been invited to dine with Belinda and Martin three weeks after the time he had with Sarah Fortune, he had demurred. He had almost been rude, and deliberately obtuse.

'Have you invited that girl, you know who I mean, Sarah?'

'Sarah who? Oh, widow Sarah. No. Should we?'

'You invite whoever you like. Only, she gave me a lift home.'

'Nice girl, Sarah, but we do try to vary the list. Apart from you, of course. She's very quiet, Sarah.'

Malcolm paused. Not as he remembered, with his whole size quivering slightly at the memory. He must not ask after her, he must not pursue her. She had been quite clear.

'Well, my dears.' The old heartiness took over. 'Afraid I can't oblige your kindness. On a diet. Besides, very busy. May be absent for a while.'

'For how long, Malckie?' She sounded annoyed. 'The children will be impossible.'

'I'm sorry,' he said formally. It sounded as if he was going away for a long time. Visions of Captain Oates, as he walked out of Scott of the Antarctic's tent, floated into his mind. 'I may be gone for some time . . .' With his present stones of weight, and smaller stores of bravery, Malcolm felt he would have lasted longer than Oates. Easier to be brave when you knew you had no choice. Oates had meant them to use his supplies. Malcolm wished his surplus fat could be distributed with so much fairness, and felt the old familiar longing for company, any kind.

He felt he might give at the seams of himself with the sheer grief of his own rage, and in this deficient life of his, something would have to go. The bloody bulk of it. He smiled the first smile of the day at his own pun. Inside the reflection of his own size, normality had beckoned like a mirage not dignified yet by any real belief in it.

Two years forward and tidying his new flat, a different man moved easily from room to room, drastically altered despite the fact that he still expected the sight of his own flesh to crowd his mirror. It was strange to recall how much he had hated his new determination when he first began. How he had crawled up the steps to the front door of the old place at the end of that first, short run with his stomach trembling, his thighs quivering, calves on fire, a throbbing in his head and a hazy dizziness blinding his eyes along with the sweat which ran down from his hair. The two flights which led to the old flat seemed the last, impossible obstacle, and he had imagined the whole world must be aware of the deafening sound of his own breathing. All that for a stumbling run of two hundred yards, and the sight of the neighbour behind the first-floor net curtain, giggling at the sight of his comical distress, wondering between times whether she ought to call an ambulance. Poor fat sod, what did he think he was trying to do? Being fat was like being old, he had discovered whilst soaking in the bath, a dying whale, and waiting for the sickness to pass. All attempts to change it are regarded as inherently stupid and undignified. They were both of those, but no more than the condition.

'You must be mad, Mr Cook,' said the doctor, faced across the surgery table next evening as Malcolm eased himself off the chair like an invalid, paralysed by stiffness. 'Man of your age and weight suddenly trying to sprint. You'll give yourself a heart attack. Try diet first. A little gentle movement, perhaps.'

'I'm not a geriatric,' Malcolm had said mildly. 'No,' snapped the small thin medical man. 'Nor a child. Most people begin by touching their toes.'

But he could not start so slowly. Malcolm could not do the thing in stages. He would have to charge at it painfully, stocky bull at five-bar gate, ignoring slow and sensible progress. Whatever he did must hurt, show results, require courage. Gradual progression would be like watching the clock for the second-hand of failure. Malcolm ran again, then again, forcing himself further by one more street, hating the process as he had never hated anything, loathing the disabling stiffness which followed. He ran in the dark, spending the hours of light inventing excuses for not persisting, until he moved himself to the mirror to taunt his own fat cowardice, and, suitably disgusted, fled the house in running-shoes, into rain, sleet, warmth or thunder, not noticing or caring which.

Cruel laughter in the office. 'Have you heard? Cook's dieting . . . Lost an ounce so far.' He heard, and tried to smile.

The second reaction, after the sheer horror at the pain of it, was a wonder in the discovery of the ability to move on the day when he woke without groaning, suddenly able to put one foot on the ground out of his bed without the rest following in a slow and clumsy roll. Wonder, mixed with curiosity about the next stage. Could he move better, stand taller, stride out with more economy? How fast would he be able to go, and how far? In retrospect, he realised it was this burning curiosity which made him persist far more than the simple desire to be thin. Then there was another stage, one of intoxication after he had shuffled, run, jogged one whole mile. The stage when he knew with absolute conviction he would crack it even if it took forever, and one day he would be free of all this bulk. That marked the beginning of an obsession, a voyage of exploration across boundaries of pain, stiffness and teasing, through mindless mornings, hungry afternoons and breathless evenings, to see how far he could take himself and what lay on the other side. No time for dinner party clowning. But when Malcolm Cook emerged after several months looking an approximation of a normal plump human being there was no time for him either. He found the lightness of his frame had allowed him to move from half-way up the pinnacle of loneliness, occupied in bearable isolation, to a point at the summit where the air was very thin indeed, and no one pretended to know him at all.

Belinda and Martin were the first casualties. He knew too much, had been told too much, fat father confessor, and who could now confide in a thinner man, or weep on his shoulder? 'It isn't the same bloke,' said Belinda. 'Not the same at all.' Such an ordinary man could not tell jokes with the same wonderful pomposity as a fat man. Their parties could not cope with a clown *passé*. Other friends thought long and hard. They decided to avoid him, and finally decreed: Falstaff, be thou not thin. Your role was made for a fat man, you are a disappointment to us all. He was the same generous man, but they did not like him. He made them uncomfortable, and he found he did not like them much either, although there was nothing else to replace them. So Malcolm simply retreated into himself. Not comfortable, but not despised. Shrouded in work, saturated with all the antisocial knowledge of the criminal world, he lived alone.

The dramatic weight-loss, and the emergence of a startlingly good-looking son, worried Mrs Penelope Matthewson, who was having a difficult day, made infinitely worse by the fact that her only son, product of a brief and difficult marriage, had been missing for months and had installed an answerphone. She had not known what to say when faced with its pleasant message, spoken clearly in his familiar friendly voice, and she had only suppressed the instinct to chatter after the whining noise when she had realised that the message was the sum-total of the response, leaving her shouting into a vacuum and feeling silly, still full of irritated affection.

Penelope wanted forgiveness from her son for her neglect of his childhood, and knew she had it. She was grateful for Ernest's great love for his stepson, and irritated by that too. Swallowing pride, she dialled again, listened this time, and left a message after the bleep. 'Malcolm, I know you're there.' (Although she had no idea why she knew.) 'Phone me when you can. I need to see you. I'm very worried about Dad.'

He did not telephone. He arrived instead, adding to the guilt and still shocking her with his new appearance, even as her own, equally unerring instinct guided her not to comment, forced her to smile as if she did not find him changed. Malcolm, fat from the overfed age of eight, shoved from pillar to post among the debris of a marriage, and away to school at the age of eleven where he grew fatter and learned to survive on his wits, was the thinnest she could ever remember, slender, fit and athletic.

'Dear God,' she said, swaying in the doorway, smile frozen, 'you're even thinner. Would you like to eat now or later?' When he did not smile, she began to laugh at his handsome face, so like the mulish small-boy look he had worn when pushed too far, relieved to find him so familiar. 'Oh, Malcolm darling. You look wonderful. You make me understand why I fell in love with your father. Come in.'

He grinned at last. 'One condition.'

'What's that?'

'No food. You got me into this, don't hinder me getting out.'

She hugged him, melted her sweet-smelling arms around his neck, and led him in. Plump feet in plump shoes dinting the velvet carpet. Mrs Matthewson had never liked modern things or sharp angles, nothing harsh to the touch, even in the days when she had been Mrs Cook with a husband as liberal and progressive as her own Ernest was not. She sat opposite her son on a sofa which almost enveloped her in high colours of hummingbirds. The curtains matched, the walls reflected the soothing and vibrant colours, like the woman herself.

Penelope never admitted Malcolm was a mistake, but in a life now devoted to comfort and order, she wished she had produced a child of more predictable qualities, or one her second husband loved less. But in those dimmer days, Pen had always reserved the greatest devotion of life for the two husbands. Now she loved this son and this husband equally, and wished they would damn well do the same. She looked quizzically at Malcolm. Something was all wrong with the boy, and she knew by that smile of his, a wonderful smile, enlivened by enormous affection, curtailed by equally huge reserve, that she had better not ask what it was, for fear of an answer. In turn, he had sunk into a large, exquisitely comfortable chair, and was thinking with only the slightest regret how odd and spartan his own life had become in comparison to this, and to all his dear mama would want for him.

'How's Father?' Noticing her fidgeting with the desire to present him with the large measure of Scotch which greeted all visitors, and which she knew he would refuse.

'Not well. I'm worried. Will you come and talk to him?'

'Mother, you know I can't. He won't take advice from me. Not since I've refused to take it from him, insulted him by refusing to join the practice. He's never forgiven me, dabbling in crime, humble prosecutor paid by the state, and he won't confide in me now.'

'But, Malcolm . . . you could try at least . . .'

'Yes, I could. But only if he asks. Not otherwise. Come on, Ma, you know him. If he came in now, crippled with an ulcer, he'd start the same old argument within minutes. He can't help it. He'd ask how I was, slap me on the back, and say, "When are you coming into the firm, then?" Again. And I'd say, "You know me, Dad. I'm a loner, always was. Can't work for anyone. Better off with crooks and coppers, drunks and thieves," and so we'd go on until he sank into silence and me into mindless jokes. If I could get him to talk naturally, we might have a chance of being able to talk about himself, but then again, only if he would. And could.'

'He loves you, Malcolm. You know he does. I don't know why, you aren't even his, but he does.'

'You make it sound like an accusation.'

'Well, no. Yes. I mean . . . No, I don't mean anything. I mean I simply wish pleasing him wasn't so difficult for you. I try to understand; part of me does, part of me doesn't. I just want you both happy.'

Heavy tears gathered and slid solidly down her round pink cheeks before she brushed them away in frustration. Penelope was not a regular weeper. She would stoop to blackmail of most sorts, but not weeping.

'Mother, don't. It isn't me making him unhappy. It's the firm that makes him miserable. He made it, but he doesn't belong anymore in a big commercial partnership full of whizz-kid lawyers when he really belongs in the library, dispensing common sense over half-moon specs, giving out inspired pats on hand and "don't be so silly" kind of advice which never needs a law book. He always said he couldn't be bothered with law books because they were all print and no pictures, a bit like me really, but his kind of lawyer isn't in fashion. He's all at sea with the technical age. They haven't even got time for lunch. He might think he'd feel more comfortable with me in the room next door, but he wouldn't. Get him out more, encourage all his other interests.'

A smile broke through Pen's creased concern, and she was cheered by the prospect of positive action. 'Get married, Malcolm,' she said, unable to leave him with the last word. 'Provide us with a couple of grandchildren. We're both broody.'

He rose, dropped a kiss on her brow. 'Chance would be a fine thing,' he answered lightly.

Penelope continued, speaking to herself as much as to him. 'There's a gorgeous girl in the office, one of the young ones. Ernest has a crush on her. I pretend it annoys me for the sake of form, but I know it's not that kind of crush. She's a daughter-substitute. She stops him feeling lonely by being the only one there who can begin to think like him, or understand it. Besides, she helps me look after him. She keeps me informed,' she added darkly.

'Spies in the camp?' queried Malcolm. 'Not sure I like the sound of that.'

'No, no, no . . . she's no sneak. Not the school-prefect type at all. She simply understands him. When he gets upset, you know the way he does, she calms him down, and when the ulcer is on the march, she tells him jokes and stops him going on the rampage. Whenever his secretary threatens to resign, the others call her in and she makes them see the storm will pass, and makes them laugh. They talk about anything and everything, and when he's really on the warpath to the tune of risking another heart attack, she phones me up and warns me.'

'No secrets?'

'If he tells her any, she would never tell me, and if Ernest tells her anything about the firm, she wouldn't tell anyone else. She only tells me when he's really over-excited. I trust her. Lovely voice. Penelope, she says to me, this is an early gale-warning, and I'll know to give him a big hug when he gets back, to show he's still king in his own house. And a good supper. And not argue.'

'He's a lucky man. Surrounded by adoring women.'

'But not adoring stepsons.'

Silence fell into the sunlight passing through the curtains across Penelope's fresh flowers and her bonny, anxious face. Malcolm wished he could please her more, please them both, herself and the irascible stepfather he loved so much. Wished he had the means to restore that volatile old man to contentment. 'He has good friends,' Malcolm said firmly, watching the sunbeams dance on the polished wood. Pen looked at them too, pleased by the effect, secretly gratified to see her son discomfited. 'I must clean the windows,' she remarked, one of her *non sequiturs* which closed the conversation on family topics. It was always closed before she admitted too much. Malcolm was resigned to it. He knew she could not say there was more than that in Ernest's current high anxiety. Some client, some breach of his old-fashioned honour, some arrow lodged in his keen conscience, festering, which Malcolm could have discovered and she could not.

She sighed and rose slowly. She could not say more today, and this was not, as she had hoped, the best time to suggest to her only son the delightful prospect of a dinner at home, graced by a mellow stepfather and the lovely but suitable young woman. What this family needed was a decent daughter-in-law, a bit of romance, and Malcolm was thirty-three. He needed a wife.

Painting by numbers on the life of M. Cook was adroitly, respectfully resisted. He had fended off the far more serious questions concerning work and career by waxing lyrical to Mother on the subject of the new flat, although she sniffed at the very idea of living in one storey so far from the ground, couldn't fathom the appeal at all. 'Why not a house, Malckie, at your age?' She could not tell him all her fears any more than this son of hers could explain how he had emerged from the chrysalis of sixteen stone a strange, shy shadow of himself with no known place in the world, but full of silent fury, and acquiring some very eccentric habits indeed.

They always left their conversations incomplete, at the point where they should have started. It had become a habit.

'See you soon, darling.'

'Give my love to Father.'

'Of course.'

She moved to the kitchen for the therapy of cooking. Malcolm hurried to court for the therapy of crime. He would feel more at home there in the mess of files and accusations. And after court he would go on looking through the directories, make ten more phone calls. Malcolm was looking for Sarah Fortune. The process was slow, but absorbing enough to dismiss all thoughts of his family from his mind. This much he knew: she was a solicitor and a widow, but the Law Society could not help. No trace of Fortune, they said. She may practise, they explained, under her married name, but the registration will be under her maiden name, you see. If you don't know the maiden name, and she calls herself something else now, we cannot help. So, each day, time allowing, he rang another of the hundreds of legal firms in the Solicitor's Diary, to make his discreet inquiries. The response was often puzzled, the task embarrassing but necessary. Sighing, half in hope, half in frustration, he reached for the phone.

A long day, so filled with different preoccupations. Criminals, families, and the quest to find Sarah which had so far taken months, from the two years since he had seen her. And after this, his nightlife began, running the streets in darkness, looking for the man and the dog, regarding all he might see with his mild, forgiving eyes.

CHAPTER SIX

'You look like the nicest kind of sleepy cat. And I wish you didn't have to go.'

She smiled a wide smile, pulled a face in the middle of a graceful yawn.

'So do I, but there's just this little question of work in the morning.'

'It's only eleven. I'll get you a taxi. Stay on a minute. Talk to me.' He pulled her hand. She sat down next to him on the bed, half-dressed, nicely rumpled, obliging. Simeon's moves were all ponderous, not as heavy-handed as before, but she could still see him thinking ahead, like a child.

'Sarah?'

'Yes?'

'You know we agreed I wouldn't pry into your life. I've known you for three months now, and I feel a new man . . .' He smiled at her fondly. 'I can hold a knife and fork, I don't stop people smoking by waving things in their faces . . .' She stroked his head, and he grinned sheepishly. 'And I've honoured the agreement, haven't I?' She nodded. 'Well, I thought it gave me licence to ask. You don't have to answer. But why, why be so secretive with your life? Even though you seem content. You don't have to answer, but what made you?'

'Made me? Nothing made me.'

'I know that . . . But why, then? Why be . . .'

'Your mistress?' She dimpled.

'Your description. I rather like it. Every man should have a mistress at one point in his life, perhaps. It honours me, your description, but you aren't mine. And you are a lady, never anything less.' Even in his dressing-gown, with his eyebrows and hair pointing on end, like an endearing goblin, Simeon had relearned the gallantry of his youth, and he meant it.

'Why do you want to know?' She was buttoning the sleeves of a white blouse, the one she had worn into his house after her official life, and now he watched as she reassumed that other shape in front of his eyes, hiding herself in the good black skirt, silk scarf and all the everyday uniform.

'I want to know because I like you,' he said simply. 'And whatever our arrangement, I'd like to be counted as a friend. Difficult thing to be if one's as ignorant as this. I know some of the motivations, of course, but not all of them. Tell me why.'

She sat again. One flick of the hairbrush through that red mane and it would be too late, she would have become the Sarah known to the Law Society, not the luminous-eyed creature who, among other things, sang him songs and insisted he learn how to cook. (When you're indoors, eat properly. Enjoy it.) And redecorate his flat: make yourself comfortable and you'll make others comfortable. No, don't undo what your wife did, just adapt it to your own taste. A motto to alter his life. Sarah's service was comprehensive. He often forgot the bedtime bit when faced with her subtle capacity for mending lives, often regretted the restrictive nature of the association, but he never once counted the expense which followed in the wake of it. His flat and himself glowed with new health and his face was alive with questions.

'All right. I'll tell you why. Briefly. An exercise in making a long story short.'

'Not too short.'

'Very short. Call it the reaction of a disillusioned widow with a career which bores her to death, a kind of prison. In order not to see the bars, needs uncomplicated relationships on equal terms, with everyone knowing where they are. Will that do?'

'Far from satisfactory.'

'It isn't really very much more complicated than that. I like doing what I'm good at. I like you. You're good company.'

'Sarah . . . What do you do on all the other evenings in the week when you don't see me?'

'Ah. Clean the windows, wash my socks, see friends and twiddle my thumbs. In other words, with all respect to your curiosity, nothing harmful and none of your business.' It was said inoffensively with the smile he could not resist.

'Tell me about your family.'

'Genteel, poorish, brutally religious. Wanted the best for me. Threw me out with the onset of the first boyfriend. Forgave me for qualifying and marrying, a brief period of acceptance, but not for being widowed. Indecent, you see, bound to be my fault and very embarrassing for them. They always preferred my sister. Better I stayed away.'

In the calm tones, and although he lacked sensitivity, Simeon could sense undertones of terrible rejections, fights, abandonment. He hesitated.

'And your husband? What was he like? Did you love him?'

'Oh yes, I loved him, but he is a different story for another time. Not today.'

Nothing more detailed would follow. Simeon believed that widowhood was about as dignified as a poke in the eye, but did not see why it led to Sarah's solution of such a floating life. On the other hand, he could not see why not.

'You could always marry me, and give up the single status.'

'Don't be silly, Simeon my love. You know we'd never work on a daily basis, and anyway, you'll need a respectable wife. Someone really wifely, you know, someone intelligently normal. If you go for an appointment on the Bench, as well you might, you'll need a spouse beyond reproach, fit for all those Benchers' dinners and the occasional scrutiny of the press. Not a reprobate like me. Someone who would think like you and support everything you did.'

He sighed, thought of the outrage of the top table in the Inner

Temple Hall, shook his head sadly. Too glamorous she was, and far too funny for that august company.

'There's nothing I dislike about you, Sarah, except your dreadful realism.'

'Kiss me goodbye, then.'

'Until next time,' he added quickly. 'I still need you. Don't forget the Ball. You haven't forgotten Gray's Inn Ball? Big occasion for me, the final test of my greatly improved manners. You said you'd think about it. You will come, won't you? Please?'

'Oh, I don't know, Simeon. I can't, really.'

He was openly distressed. 'Please, Sarah. I've been out of circulation for so long I won't manage without you. Just once. Please. Why not? Is the thought of an evening with me in public so terrible?'

Pretty terrible, thought Sarah, but only because of potential embarrassments which have nothing to do with your company.

'Why not?' he repeated, taking advantage of her sudden and surprising nervousness.

'Well, half my legal acquaintance and some of my clients go to this thrash. I shall feel exposed,' she added lamely.

'Exposed to what?'

He regarded her with innocence, his concern touching her as he took her hand. 'Exposed to what?' he said again. 'I'm sure you haven't done anything wrong.'

'No,' said Sarah. 'No, of course not. I haven't done anything wrong at all.'

'Well then, you'll come with me,' he said triumphantly. 'I'll look after you.'

No one, thought Sarah, has ever done that. And I shall go with him. He's a kind man, so unused to having an ally – I must help him swim in those crowds. There was a glimmer of resignation as well as mischief which Simeon found puzzling, but dismissed in his pleasure at her acceptance.

'I knew I would win in the end,' he said triumphantly. 'You'll enjoy it, and of course, it won't cost you anything.'

'It might,' she replied.

On her way home, Sarah forgot the prospect of the Ball,
remembered Simeon's questions and regretted the luxury of
words. What little she had said had been entirely true, but however bland, any form of confession weakened the self-sufficiency
she carried before her like a talisman, and all the explanations
had been contrived. She did not know why she was as she was or
how she had so simply arrived at living as she did, alone but
accompanied by the balm of constant activity. There were precious few clues in either past or present. Perhaps she was just a
little wild. In any event, she hated introspection which nailed her
down on the crucifix of the past for nothing. A good girl, such
a good girl in childhood and marriage. Studious, anxious and
abused for her earthy beauty in the early stages, utterly devoted
in the second, pinioned by the constant desire to please. Sarah
thought of her blond and muscular husband, the friends of his
whose sophistication had puzzled and defeated her once. Maybe
she had not been much fun then. Well, I am now, she thought.
Now there is no one to disapprove, no one to look. As for
Simeon, again, why not? Don't ask, do. There was nothing to it
apart from all her lack of inhibition in contrast to all those dry
and dreadful rooms of the law, where loneliness and frustration
existed behind frozen smiles on faces refined by conventional
success, masking personal agonies. She would have no such agonies, would prefer to kiss and stroke such faces rather than
accept their severity, preferred to touch rather than stand outside gracious windows looking in. No, there was no explanation
to placate the logical mind of Simeon or anyone else who could
not understand the simpler pursuits of pure pleasure, the freedom of choice granted by money, both seen as an end in
themselves, a freedom. She was becoming eccentric, knew it and
did not care. Without showing the symptoms of freakishness,
she had always been the outsider who was never accepted.
Nothing had altered except for the fact that she had given up
trying. If in doubt, which was rare, Sarah followed base instinct,
and felt the better for it without realising how. It was the sheer,
determined joy in her which made her so attractive.

Sarah's taxi juddered to a halt outside her door, while the driver delivered the last of his homily on the troubles of married life. She had heard him sympathetically, listening from the outside in, standing on the edge, the way she always had, wondering why there was anyone left who kept to the rules. Envying them very little, there being no shred of envy in her, paying a large tip for the pleasure of being home.

Turning the corner of the street, jogging away from the basement entrance, Malcolm heard the taxi, turned back, padded on. Neighbours were neighbours. In the weeks of living above and alongside these, in his new flat, he had done his best to ignore their existence and they had reciprocated the indifference. As he skimmed over a patch of dirt, avoided the arms of a last drunken straggler from the pub on the corner, he did not care if his neighbours noticed him any more than he cared about the fact that he had become extremely odd, and if they were odd too, always coming home at midnight or three in the morning, so much the better.

The habit of running by night, generally only ever functioning by night at all, coasting by day on a few hours' sleep, working on auto-pilot, had become entrenched. He was sure now it was his chosen work, as much as his bulk, which had pushed him to the edge of the world. Sympathetic criminal lawyers, like policemen, know too much, and he knew himself to be uncomfortable company in the civilised world. Very little human society intruded on his isolation, and those who did were filtered by the answerphone. When all those slept, along with his neighbours, Malcolm came to life. Like Dracula, he thought. Once fat Dracula.

In the terms of his own description, defined by the friendly policeman who stopped him twice and with whom he was now on waving terms, Sir had become addicted to neon-lighting, finding sunlight pale by comparison. The constable did not say it like that; he had merely remarked on how Malcolm obviously preferred the night-shift as he did himself, and warned him against muggers similarly fleet of foot. Malcolm agreed. He loved the scenery of the night, that great divide of city darkness between two disparate ways of life, two whole societies. Sometimes he would run twelve miles, around Hackney Marshes and the Lea Reservoir, then back, or up to Hampstead Heath, avoiding nocturnal lovers, but mostly he preferred the streets. He had been running now for almost two years, and he was as lithe and as self-possessed as a cat.

So far, this preference was no more eccentric than that of a policeman or night-security guard. But the darkness inspired Malcolm with mischief; he could understand, if not copy, the vandal's secret glee of midnight desecration, Kilroy with spray. I was here, I tell you, but now I'm not. Since he was not yet free of a law-abiding nature, although his sympathies had come to lie with those who had the opposite, most of the mischief was faintly philanthropic. The Rolls-Royce in the square, the one parked nightly by an arrogant owner to the maximum incon-venience of everything around it: letting down those expensive tyres three nights in succession before the guinea dropped, might have been juvenile, but hardly wicked. Sprinting down the back alley of the same rich square to find a burglar half-way into a window, warning him of the imminence of discovery without doing more, was an act of debatable charity, but Malcolm could only empathise with the wild-eyed creatures of the night.

For years, he had met them all by day; he knew them better than they knew themselves and had somehow lost the knack of condemning. Malcolm's job was to prosecute the lawbreakers, read of them, question them, only nobody had ever told him there might come a time when he would cease to see them as outsiders, feel more at home with them, even if he did not emu-late them. Some of them, the regular car thieves, prowlers, dustbin-bag watchers, scavengers, saw him as a kind of harmless vigilante. Others, including the stray constable, knew different, and wondered how far he would regress. Those on the outside come to see nothing other than the outside.

Malcolm, reborn, became one of those completely at home in the midnight desert, blinking at dawn and the intrusion of light, and might well have forgotten even his sense of pity as his actions became more careless and his intervention more direct, if it had not been for the one regular sighting which niggled his bizarre contentment. Unlike the misplaced statues, the silly, changed direction signs, the other frivolous, absent-minded jokes he had played, there was no chance of humour with this pair. The man and his dog were a sight he had grown to dread in the last few weeks: both filled him with grief, the anger focusing on the man, leaving nothing but pity for the dog.

Always in the early hours, as if their respective needs could only be met long after midnight and without witnesses. A bulky man and scrawny animal, walking the mean Hackney streets, the only sight which, in Malcolm's growing indifference to humankind, almost provoked tears. A stocky man of indeterminate age, good clothes, but scruffy and careless, peculiarly light-footed, always more than slightly drunk or drugged, difficult to tell without smelling, as if this state, along with the hour, were a prerequisite to taking the dog for an impatient exercise which was far from a labour of love. On these swaying perambulations, the man muttered, grumbled and pulled with the dog's lead clenched inside his pocket, so that the animal danced, front paws scrabbling, strangled neck extended through every tortured step, whimpering for relief. 'Turn on him, bite him, and run away with me.' These were the instructions Malcolm formed in his mind, but he had never gone far enough to act. He saw them most nights, though not every night, and dreaded it, swaying, yelping, cursing in mutual suffering, man hating dog, but bound to each other. Burglars, sad prostitutes on Seven Sisters Road, some of whom waved and jeered at his useless custom whenever he passed, watching him waving and grinning back, all of them, theoretically at least, made some sort of choice. But poor bloody dog, he thought, did not enter the world with an owner's grudge, did not deserve it. Or a neck red-raw from the pulling, or the lead. Or slow abuse and slower starvation, poor bitch.

You must not interfere unduly in the lives of others, even to save them, and thou shalt not steal. Authorities exist to prevent man's inhumanity to man or beast. Wasn't that the rule behind all his prosecutions, the criminal law bible, as well as the commandments of his own English schooling? Malcolm stood in front of his mirror, not a deliberate move, but the mirror was there in his bedroom. In it stood a vision of mangled dog, by the side of a slender, cowardly man. Himself. Mirrors always carried into his life accusations, premonitions and waves of disgust. Malcolm picked up a chair and hit the glass, watching it smash into smithereens, shattered picture of a hypocrite who could act daily to imprison lawbreakers, but could not even rescue a suffering dog. Tomorrow, then, he would deal with theft. The day after, or whenever he saw them next, he would commit it. And after that, God knew what he might become. He did not particularly care, but old morals, old images, died hard. He was happier without the mirror.

CHAPTER SEVEN

'Just like old times, sir.' Ryan knew he sounded over-jovial.

Chief Superintendent Bailey grunted and eyed the walls. After the conference with counsel on the infinitely tedious subject of mortgage fraud, they had been aiming for the usual pub in Fleet Street opposite the High Court, the same gloomy place to which Ryan, Bailey and others had resorted with speed and several years of practice. Like camels, with the hump and the thirst, Ryan had said. Bailey, ex-Flying Squad, murder squads, and half the worst divisions in the Met, now basked in the relative predictability of Fraud, tinged with the quiet excitement of a late love affair, and these days rarely stayed out drinking. Not that Ryan imagined there was much temptation in a place like this. Bailey had shunned the regular haunt for its overpowering crowds, and they sat instead in the relative calm of the wine bar. Within minutes, the calm had been shattered by baby barristers baying for dry white wine. Ryan looked at his ice-cold continental lager. Not bad, for an arm and a leg. Man'd spend a fortune getting pissed in here, and he'd needed something stronger to duck and dive beneath the serene questioning of his lord and master which he knew was just about to follow. Bailey was wearing his gentle, inquisitorial air, and it was he who had suggested the drink. But drink made no difference. Whatever Bailey consumed never seemed to touch the sides, one of many reasons to admire him. And Ryan liked Bailey, respected him above all others, which was not saying much but was still considerable, although the liking was tinged with the reserve he would always have for indecently naked intellect and a copper who actually lived with a brief. Such a union was, as Bailey's Helen had put it, rather like a Montague actually joining a Capulet, placing Bailey even further outside the ranks of his own than he had been before, and her further still. Neither seemed concerned and Ryan envied them.

Cheshire's Wine Bar was all plants and bentwood chairs, subtly uncomfortable. The young barristers went there to see their friends, and to be seen; the older ones hovered round the edges. Police officers were a rare phenomenon against the painted woodwork. and all the tables wobbled. Get on with it, Ryan asked his companion silently. For once, he wanted to go home. Whatever Bailey was going to ask, he knew he wasn't going to like it.

'I was wondering how you were getting on with Tysall.'

Oh, oh . . . No beating about the bush then, no how's your father and the kids: straight for the jugular. Feign honesty.

'Bloody awful. I told you what Simeon Churcher QC said, didn't I? Can't find any more angles for now. I mean, except for the fact that he steals ideas and makes people bankrupt, appears to manage a brothel in that hotel of his, may have left the Stock Exchange before they caught him for insider-dealing, certainly steals from the taxman and trades in stolen antiques, and probably murdered his wife, the man's as clean as a whistle.'

'I see. You've joined his fan club? Look, Ryan, I know I've given you free rein, but we are supposed to be investigating fraud. That's why this is a Fraud Squad, if you see what I mean. There's supposed to be some connection with fraud in our daily lives, if you understand me. So if Tysall's a hopeless case for a fraud charge, forgery, deception, anything you like, you're supposed to report any other suspicions you have to his local Division, and let them run with it. Fraud is what we do.'

Ryan fingered the glass, brushing the moisture from round the side in straight lines.

'Are you telling me to do that? Sir?'

'You would insist on being so bloody direct.' Bailey's smile always transformed his heavily lined face, and Ryan remembered on sight of it how much he liked the man.

'. . . And no, I'm not telling you to do, or not do, anything. I'm just telling you not to get caught with your toes on the corns of some DCI on Division. Do what you like, with that in mind, and remember I don't need to know about it provided you're turning in a respectable amount of legwork on all the other cases. But it's limited to three months. That's all the time you have to find something. Is that clear?'

Ryan nodded. Bailey relaxed.

'Now you can tell me why you go into overdrive whenever Tysall's mentioned. I've never known you so keen. Come on, Ryan. Tell me something about the man I don't know.'

'You know most of it . . . Oh shit. Look who's here . . . Mr Cook, sir, coming over . . . He's seen us.'

'Yes,' said Bailey. 'I thought he might be here.' Rather than pull himself into the shadow, Ryan's instinct, Bailey was waving at Malcolm Cook, who forged a path to their corner. Ryan sighed. Sly old bastard. No accident avoiding the crowded pub, was it? Smoothly oiling us both in here, knowing bloody well he'd get old Malcolm into this conversation. Probably thinks I need educating, and need the restraining hand of the Crown Prosecution Service. Amid the prickle of resentment for Bailey's effortless manoeuvres and Cook's inevitable legal authority, Ryan nevertheless felt the stirrings of relief. He had been ploughing a lonely furrow after all, and the relief persisted even as the deliberate blankness of both his interrogators showed the prearrangement of the whole trap.

'Ryan was just telling me,' Bailey remarked, pouring wine for Malcolm and lager for the Sergeant with remarkable economy of movement on the small, wonky table which had come to rest, painfully, on Cook's muscular thigh, 'everything he knows about Charles Tysall.'

The 'everything' was stressed lightly. Ryan was in the middle, another subtle trick: he was the stockiest but smallest of the three, and it seemed best to admit defeat. It took a secretive man like Bailey to recognise another, and Ryan supposed Bailey had understood his own hesitation in talking to lawyers, even lawyers like Cook, and even lawyers on the same side, especially lawyers on the same side who had the power to stop you, but he'd thought Bailey might have forgotten all that, what with marrying one of them. Montague and Capulet indeed, posh stuff. Beauty and the Beast, more like.

'Everything I know about blue-eyed Tysall? Well, you can have it in one sentence. He's a bastard.'

'No, no,' protested Malcolm, laughing. 'He's innocent, like all those people in prison. But apart from making his own companies super-rich at the expense of making others go under to the tune of a dozen suicides? That's all you ever told me.'

'That's all you ever asked.' Ryan was still truculent.

'Ryan,' said Bailey delicately, 'thinks that Tysall has a lethal attraction for redheads. Not they to him necessarily, although that does seem to happen, but more the other way round. Ryan is very worried about Mrs Tysall, whoever, and wherever, she may be. Also other redheads. My Sergeant has a vested interest in redheads.' Annie, lovely Annie, had been a kind of ginger. Ryan shot Bailey a glance, half plea, half venom. Bailey shook his head. No, he agreed tacitly, they need not mention Annie. Not if Ryan behaved.

'Come on, Ryan. Drink up, and cough up.'

'I didn't know Tysall had a wife,' said Malcolm, thinking in a shocking moment of his own pipedream and shrugging it away.

'We don't think he has either,' said Ryan, finally admitting familiarity in the sudden desire to tell. 'Not any more.' Each took a strong pull of drink, and waited. Bailey knew how well Ryan could tell a story.

'Half of this is gossip, you know, but I used to work out of Kensington, three years ago, before Mr Bailey saved me from ruin.' He shot Bailey his best glance of wolfish friendliness, the look which had enraged so many prisoners and frightened not a few. Never touched them, sir, only smiled. '. . . And once upon a time, filthy rich Charles Tysall, getting better-looking all the time, the women said, moved into a mansion block opposite Harrods. Seen after that, when we raided a couple of clubs on a big gaming round-up, but not a gambler. Always with a redhead, who sat so close you'd think she was tied to him. Mrs Tysall, that was; very nice looking woman, real charmer. Same woman seen by me, as it happens, when I was . . . out with this woman . . .' No, don't say it was Annie, or talk about Tysall's personal revenge on his clumsy pursuer, seen as clearly as his own observation. 'Well, never mind what I was doing, but I saw her in this club, with a man who was not Mr Tysall, her lawfully-wedded husband. I got the lads to keep a look-out: seems Mrs T might have been over the side, once or twice. Anyway, she paid for it. Came into Kensington nick looking as if she'd been hit by a bus, three times over a year. Once she told us he'd tried to rip out her fingernails, but she wouldn't show her hands to the divisional surgeon. Don't know what she wanted us to do about it, apart from give her shelter until he'd calmed down, because she'd never make a statement, and she'd never charge him.'

Ryan sat back, brow puckered with puzzlement. No woman in his own life had been so slow to accuse, but he never aimed to find out what they'd have done if he'd hit them. He still couldn't understand anyone wanting to try. It was the one piece of male unfairness he could not understand.

'Anyway, one day I took her back home, bleeding all over my new car. She had a lovely voice, Mrs T, and I asked her why she stayed with him. Because he loves me, she said. Funny way of showing it, I told her. He can't help it, she said. It's the way he is. If I try to go out, or look at anyone else, he goes wild, and it doesn't even take that. He doesn't like me thinking, even. Stop thinking out loud then, I told her, or he'll kill you, and as long as you won't bloody sign the sheet, we can't help. Oh no, she said. I'm sorry to trouble you, but it isn't so bad. He never scars me. The day he does that, I'll know he hates me. Then this tomcat will really have marked his territory, and I'll have to go. That was the time he'd broken her ribs. Why wait, I thought. Suit yourself, I thought. I wouldn't wait, not even for a pedigree tomcat. Which he is of course. Eton, Oxford, cultivated bastard.'

'He's not the only one around who thumps his wife,' Bailey said mildly, although his fists were clenched on the table. Ryan remembered the night when Helen West, Bailey's woman, had suffered at the hands of an intruder, and understood more of why his boss was giving him a freer rein than normal.

'Or she the only wife who refuses to take any action whenever she's roughed up,' Cook added. 'The wives withdraw the allegations. Good God,' he added with a grin, 'how do some men get away with it? If we tried any such thing, they'd be queueing up to murder us.'

'There's a difference here, sir. This wasn't a lout coming home from the pub and knocking his punch bag round the kitchen. This is a bloke who quite likes refinement with it. Mrs T had been tied up and beaten. Obviously he'd threatened to cut her face or she wouldn't have mentioned it. She was terrified, only she wasn't going to make it easy for him by letting him go and hopping out of it herself.'

'A masochist maybe? Parlour games with a difference?'

'No, I didn't think that either. Wrong type.'

Bailey wondered. Ryan might have been a dogged detective, but he was an easy champion, not quick to spot perversion in a pretty face. The Superintendent knew how his Helen had been in the face of attack, brave, but with all the normal instincts to do anything rather than repeat it. Even, thank God, living with him. She would have gone to the ends of the earth to avoid the humiliation of physical assault, and so, were she entirely normal and as far from helpless as Ryan described, would Mrs Tysall. Mink coats were rarely that important to people who wanted to stay alive.

'Anyway,' Ryan continued, 'she disappeared, Mrs T. Clean went. Saw the light, you might say, and buggered off. But not before he'd had a good go at her, really chewed her up. She'd not been seen for three weeks. One of the uniformed lads checked every day with the caretaker and kept an eye on the comings and goings for me. No sign, no visits to the nick either, but a woman of her description, and there aren't many, had been in the Brompton Hospital casualty having twenty-five stitches put in her face. Even then she wasn't reasonable. Brought a bloody puppy inside with her. It sat and howled outside the ward. No one could shift it. I got that from a nurse I know.'

Ryan paused, looked at Bailey.

'And guess who took her to the clinic? Not Tysall of course, never does his own tidying up, but good old Ted Plumb. Never thought Ted was a good bloke, but he was once a good copper. What a way to go. No way but down. Getting your own car bloodstained by the boss's wife, being left with a howling dog.'

'Ted Plumb was a bad case,' said Bailey. 'In case you didn't know,' he explained patiently to Malcolm, 'Ted Plumb was a DC in the Central Drugs Squad. Peddled drugs, used them once I think, but not now. He did a very good job bargaining with the Commissioner to get out of criminal charges. Threatened to take a few with him. Anyway, you can't judge Tysall through his employees, or them through him. Yes you can, now I think of it. Sorry, that's only a sideline. Go on, Ryan.'

'All right. As I was saying, the lady stayed to get embroidered, then took herself to a private clinic in Mayfair. Couldn't get more than that. Then pfft! Gone like a cloud of red smoke.'

'Why couldn't it be investigated? Or am I being naïve?' Malcolm asked.

'With respect, Malcolm, you are,' said Bailey. 'Ryan only got hold of the medical stuff by accident. No way of getting hold of the records officially. No doctor was going to reveal them without the patient's permission, and no patient to be found.'

'You could have got an order under the Police and Criminal Evidence Act for privileged material if you could show reasonable suspicion of a serious crime,' Cook pointed out.

'Oh could we indeed? And then what? One set of medical records showing multiple facial injuries, one reluctant witness who'll say she fell downstairs if ever we found her, and one

Charles Tysall, who'd have a very expensive lawyer, and not say anything? We could get the records, for what? We hadn't a victim, we hadn't a complainant, and no one even reported her missing. I think he killed her. Not then, later.'

There was silence at this. And had Annie in between, thought Ryan savagely. He looked at Bailey, grateful for the silence, then took up the tale, tired of the sound of his own voice and bored with his own anger.

'They had a place in Norfolk – you know, pukka country cottage by the sea, complete with dishwasher, very rural – and she was seen there three months later. We're talking about two years ago now, but only seen for a couple of days. Walking round the village like a zombie, grinning at people, with a face like a battlefield and one squint eye. Then gave the keys to neighbours, said Ta-ta, she was moving on. No car with her, all tidy. Then no trace.'

'Has the yearning husband expressed an interest?'

'No, and no one else either. American she was, no parents alive, no friends, and no one expressing anxiety. So I can't, or rather Division couldn't, investigate, could they? What power have we got? You have to have a complaint before you can do anything, and all we had was him complaining of harrassment from me. I was told to lay off, and then Mr Bailey asked for me in Fraud. Come any closer to Tysall and what do you find? A man bristling with writs, who says his wife has simply deserted him, and what business is it of ours?'

'I see your point,' said Malcolm. 'Not even reasonable suspicion of foul play, and you'd have to explain your information from the nurse. Not much fuel in that even, if she's seen alive three months later. But that doesn't entirely explain your passionate interest in Mr Tysall, Ryan. There's more, isn't there?'

Here Ryan hesitated. Bailey knew why, albeit vaguely, Malcolm not. But only Bailey knew the signs of his Sergeant struggling with empirical conclusions, and struggling even harder not to look silly. Ryan drained the lager, shook his large head, appealed to the ceiling for help, and waved his hands in frustration.

'I dunno. Redheads is what there is. Not just a disappeared, hacked-about wife, but redheads. All over the shop. Looking at Tysall's files, raiding Tysall's office, the companies he's made bankrupt, having a look at his hotel accounts, there's always a redhead jumping out of a corner at me like those pop-up cards you give to kids. He seems to surround himself with them, and then they up and go.'

'Or are you just seeing redheads because you've got them on the brain?' asked Cook. 'My mother told me whenever she was pregnant, or even thinking of it, the streets used to be full of pregnant women . . .'

'Well, I'm not bloody pregnant. Or red-haired. Or female. And not quite daft either.' Malcolm could see he had not chosen the best parallel. He smiled an apology, and Ryan went on grudgingly.

'There must be plenty of redheads around, but our friend Tysall finds a high proportion of them. And some of them don't come to any good, and none of them have families. All those without families come to no good at Tysall's hands, let alone the world at large.'

'Like who, for instance?'

Bailey answered. 'The receptionist in his hotel. Seen on Tysall's arm, next seen looking the worse for wear. Leaves job abruptly. No complaint. No family, of course. The private secretary in his office. Starry-eyed, goes downhill slower. Heroin overdose but rescued with funny compression marks on the neck. Catatonic, that's the word, isn't it? Won't say anything. Then the bright girl from the computer company, very obviously seduced, bowled over by our Charles. Ditched when her usefulness was over. Committed suicide a few weeks ago, just as Ryan thought we might get something out of her. I don't know what they do for him, or what they have for him, but he seems to haunt redheads.'

'Or be haunted by them?'

'As if he was looking for someone. Or something. Then he throws them away, or deliberately hurts them. Sorry, when we say all this it sounds daft. Let's have another drink, what else can I say that makes sense?'

'No,' said Ryan. 'My shout, I'll go . . .'

Bailey placed a hand on Cook's arm, a gesture to prevent him from insisting otherwise. If Ryan was embarrassed by his tale of woe, let him buy the round, make himself feel better and sink the dying vision of Annie.

'Hardly enough for a search warrant, is it, Malcolm? Or even enough to approach the Crown Prosecution Service with the idea of an official investigation?'

'Official, no, but continued unofficial investigation with a modicum of surveillance . . .'

'Yes, I'd say that, but you never heard me say it. The Met Police solicitors are the ones you should ask, but I know what they'll say, and if it's a second opinion you wanted, there it is. I'm only a senior principal. You know I can't give you any kind of real authority, and no one else would give it either. But I'll keep an eye on Ryan if you like. We've several other cases together already.'

'Good. That's all I wanted. He'll hate it, he hates being watched.'

'Well, I won't be watching closely. Simply the odd question here and there, and I'll take him out for a drink. It always makes him expansive. He likes me as well as anyone, I think.'

'Kind of you. Leave it there.'

Ryan was relieved to return to the table and find them discussing no more than mutual acquaintances, Bailey issuing invitations to his home. Since the past but still clearly remembered days of fatness, Malcolm's confidence had been so altered, he could not bring himself to court invitation, preferred his own company. Bailey was simply reminding him of an open door. Malcolm grinned at Ryan as Bailey left them both for home. He too had realised how many strands, how many benign purposes there had been in Bailey's skilful arrangement of the evening.

'Crafty blighter. Great bloke,' was Malcolm's grudging contribution. They both laughed. As usual, Ryan's glass was empty.

'Don't know about you, Mr Cook, but it's like the other night. I've got the taste now, if you see what I mean. For talking and drinking, not sure which order. But not here. Can't go home early, terrible waste of a free evening. The wife's out.'

'Well, I'm going home. You come too, it's only a mile. See how the other half live.'

Ryan looked up in surprise. Friendliness from a lawyer was one thing, appreciated and mistrusted in equal proportions, even if you got drunk with them sometimes; but being invited across the portals of their precious houses was quite another, a rare occurrence, except perhaps between bent copper and dodgy brief. And yes, he would like to see how an honest one lived, and yes he did see there was something in the gesture which should make him wary. No one in Ryan's book, not even Mr Cook, gave something for nothing, but he would suspend judgement on that, for the moment.

Two hours later, Ryan left and returned to Cook's attic-flat laden with the Chinese food they had ordered. Conversation was flowing, freely. Ryan was finding a liking for wine. Cook could make him like the stuff, none of this poncing about with sniffing corks and that, and Ryan was even enjoying the prospect of being able to tell his wife. Most interesting evenings in Ryan's life could not afford that kind of follow-up, but he could tell her all about the visit, if not the conversation, thinking as he shambled up the street with the hot bag how odd it was that people like Malcolm Cook should celebrate their modest and educated success by going to live in draughty old houses. Nothing so strange as folk. Thinking hard on that phenomenon and others, when he stopped, and almost released his hold on the carrier.

There she bloody was. Mrs Charles Tysall to the life, tripping down the steps from the big front door into Malcolm's house, collar turned up against the evening chill, exquisitely, formally dressed, as if for work, with a flow of red curls catching the light from the taxi-meter as she bent towards the window. Mrs Tysall had caught his fancy more than he had told, and Ryan's heart stopped, until he saw the clean lines of that smiling profile, so close he could almost have touched, and heard the voice giving pleasant directions. 'Gray's Inn, please.' Sarah Fortune, off to meet yet another lawyer. No, not Mrs Tysall, he saw with enormous relief and some regret. Just her double, without her gravelly voice or cut face. Not quite her height, but near as dammit, and his heart lurched into movement again, along with his feet, as the taxi pulled away, cheerful island of light in a dark street, diesel engine thumping. What a cracker, though. Thank God she wasn't Mrs T, he'd have looked a real fool saying hallo. And why did such silly objections occur to him? He would have preferred her to be found. And thank God, whoever she was, she lived the other end of London from good old Charles: she was just his type. And he'd have to ask Cook if he kept a fancy woman downstairs. No sign of anything like that in residence with the prosecutor. He'd looked.

'You've gone pale,' said Cook indoors. 'Was it the wine, or the effort of getting to the corner?' Remarks had been made earlier on the subject of Ryan's small paunch.

'Do you know the neighbours, Malcolm?' First names were suddenly permissible here; when next met in court or office, Malcolm knew he would become Mr Cook, but for now he saw an easing. 'Only there's a right smasher just come out downstairs. Redhead. Thought you might be keeping something from me.'

'Don't know any of the neighbours. I haven't lived here long. Keep my head down, so do they. Perhaps I shouldn't.'

'Come on, Malc, you're kidding me. You couldn't have missed that one unless you're blind.'

'Well, I am, a bit. We all keep different hours, and when I go out, I go out to run.'

'Where does the girlfriend live, then?' Ryan asked, super-casual, ripping the foil-top from egg fried rice, sniffing appreciation.

'What girlfriend?' said Malcolm mildly, fetching plates to his fine polished dining-table, regarding his vegetable dish and Ryan's spring-rolls with something like resignation.

'Oh, come on, you don't look like a hermit. Not now you're so bloody slim. Where do you hide her?'

'Nowhere. There isn't one.'

'Well, stone me, you poor sod. I'm no advert for marriage, but I like to go home to someone, nice warm lapful.' He coughed, not wanting to repeat too much of the chequered Ryan history which at least gave him licence to lecture on the subject of women, but not to advise. 'And I couldn't be without the kids.'

'How many?'

'Two. Bloody babies, but the fact I've had two means Bailey at long last asks for my expert opinion on how to produce them, and that's a turn up for the books, I can tell you. No girlfriend, Malc? What's wrong with you?'

'Nothing. I just don't try. Well, I do, but not very hard. They're all so normal, the ones I meet. I'll take one out, sit down with her, then I think of this girl I met once, and I lose interest. Stupid, really. Can't ever get her out of my mind.'

Ryan wondered. He'd been that kind of dreamer once, not so very long ago, still dreamt of Annie before he'd had the sense to go home and Tysall had finished it all. Broken his heart. Only it hadn't quite put him off his stroke somehow. You might be with one of them wishing she was the other, but you still managed to do what a man has to do.

'Bit special, was she?' he asked with the sudden sympathy of fellow feeling.

'Yes, I suppose she was.'

'How long ago?'

'Don't know. About two years.'

'But look here, Malc, it won't bloody do, you know. How old are you, thirty-twoish? Two bloody years. That's a cop-out. You can't wait for everything to come right, you've got to get on with it. She'll be married to some other bloke by now. If she wasn't then.' So Ryan told himself firmly about the love of his life, every day. 'What you holding the torch for? Stupidity, don't want to get involved, some kind of loyalty, or what?'

'Not loyalty. Just hope I might find her again, though I never did know where she lived, and she didn't want me to ask. More a question of making comparisons, and no one else compares. She was . . . very kind.'

'Well, stuff it. Find another one. The best ones never come back. I'm not saying they're all the same, but there's plenty as nice as one another. You can have my wife for four days a week. The other two she's mine, and on Sundays she goes to her mother's.'

Malcolm laughed, ate. 'Perhaps I've just lost my touch. If I ever had one.'

'Well, you can come out on the town with me. I'll show you where to find them.' It was an empty invitation: both knew they would do nothing of the kind, any more than Ryan would ever choose to live in a flat rather than a house, but the gesture counted for something. Ryan ate companionably, wondering why Cook liked so many paintings and plants. Perhaps the walls were bad, something to do with damp, but he had to admit it was restful.

'You know PC Smith at Clerkenwell nick?' Cook nodded. 'He told me this good story. Roughly about women. About a man from Yorkshire, the only one who could ride the famous donkey on the beach . . . You know the one?'

'Which famous donkey?'

'The one no one else could ride, vicious brute. Bucked and reared, and reared and bucked, and no one could stay on its back. Thousands of blokes on the sands tried every year, all failed, knocked off, ground into the sand, trampled by the dozen. Until this Yorkshire bloke, he stayed there, gripped on like glue, nothing could shift him. So they all stopped and cheered and said, How do you do it, how do you do it, you've got to tell us . . . And he said, It's nothing lads, nothing, and they ask again. Where did you get the knack, tell us? And he says, It's nothing lads, really. I've allus been the same since the wife had whooping cough.'

Malcolm spluttered into his black beans while Ryan roared at his own story. Healthy attitude to sex is what Malcolm needed; apart from that he was pretty normal really, for a solicitor. He'd have to be to rise to that story. The wife hadn't liked it much. Nor had that social worker he'd told yesterday. Ryan's little test of humour showed he was happy.

One hour after, chirpy and dutiful, he went home for the train. Plenty to tell with a clear conscience, glad it was only midnight and also that, in comparison to Mr Cook's funny flat and empty bed, his own life seemed rosier. As he left, Ryan glanced at the front door of the huge old house, and the lit windows of the second floor, wondering which were hers. Nice to spot that redhead again. He may have been well-behaved these days, but there was never any harm in looking.

CHAPTER EIGHT

It was raining and dark after Ryan had gone, and Malcolm had the overwhelming desire to speak to his father. In case that wise old bird would extend into the vacuum some hint of affection, or even suggest he might know what to do with a financier like Charles Tysall. But no. To speak to his father was to try and speak a new language, and only ever served to renew the old quarrel. Perhaps at the Gray's Inn Ball, that grand annual occasion which both of them were bound to attend, out of long habit and his mother's insistence. Perhaps then, when they were both bound to be jolly, but not now. All Father would do now was scold, like an otherwise fair school prefect on a bad day, raise his voice out of the stiff collar of his outraged pride. Lowly public servant, he would yell, as he had yelled before. Struggling in the gutter for your trade, hardly like a proper solicitor, and probably damaged in the process. You fool. Yes, yes, Malcolm had said, all that and more. Exploited, bemused, saddened and maddened, usually on the losing side. You never change anything by prosecuting people, Father had shouted. No you don't, Malcolm had agreed, but then nothing changes people except luck, and at least this way I have the chance to protect the victims, that's the point. Besides, I get to laugh sometimes, which is more than you seem to do. But only sometimes. Not a dignified way of earning money, but my own, you see.

No, he would not speak to his father, however much he loved

him. Tomorrow he would make ten more telephone calls in the search for Sarah Fortune; maybe he would succeed. She might have been a stranger, but he never lost the urge to talk to her again, or the belief that she would understand him. He had tried to will it away as he would have tried to deny the existence of a toothache, with the same lack of success for an ache which grew. The thoughts were jumbled: Sarah, Charles Tysall and his own father, all somehow ill-fated.

He could not bring hope of a prodigal return to his father, nor could he defend himself. If neither Ryan, Bailey nor himself could even draw the barge of the judicial system alongside Charles Tysall's yacht, then Stepfather would be proved right. Even if he were interested in criminal affairs, which Malcolm doubted, he never had, as far as Malcolm knew, encountered violence. Instead of speaking, Malcolm resorted to his old friend, the night. He went out like a burglar at midnight, ignoring the summer rain. Padding his dark route on shiny warm streets, looking for the man and the dog, wanting something to rescue.

There they were, on cue for inspection, the dog thinner than before, ratlike with damp fur, dragged each inch of the way, not even whimpering protest, while the man shrugged on, fighting his private battle with the world. Malcolm passed them once, then twice, sizing the frame of both, looking for witnesses. Then circled the block and ran from behind, silent, full of trepidation. Stealing was far from easy. He had begun to think like a thief, but was not a thief whatever his sympathies. May have watched it, read of it, but never embarked at dead of night with real theft in mind. Whether the kidnap was of handbag, child or animal, there was still a violence in it he could feel as he gathered speed, accelerating for the task, rushed softly to the man, snapped the lead from his hand, lifted the dog into his arms and ran on, panting in a spasm of relief before he reached the end of the street. There he stopped and turned briefly. The man was watching, passive but confused, arms by his sides in resignation, gesturing nothing at all, swaying slightly. Without the whimpering dog in his arms, almost weightless through long deprivation, Malcolm might have returned. He knew this one sad man would not change, not ever or not soon enough, neither for RSPCA inspectors nor anyone else. Malcolm's role in life left him no belief whatever in authorities: nothing was ever altered except by individual will. It was one of the reasons why he respected thieves. 'Got you,' he murmured to the dog. 'Why did I take so long? You might have died.'

They jogged home, two miles before the weight began to tell. No protest from the animal, plenty from Malcolm's limbs as he carried his damp bundle upstairs, and closed his door behind them. Once released, the dog, who appeared on closer inspection to be half spaniel, half nondescript, placed her matted rump on the kitchen floor, and regarded him with caution, her neck rubbed raw of hair and her eyes still bleary. Malcolm found eggs and milk, remembering gentle puppy diets. She wolfed food, eyeing him nervously as she ate, in case he should regret such generosity. Then the two of them, both thin animals used to greater quantities of flesh, examined one another with some hesitation and mutual admiration, like a couple of lovers still uncertain of the affair on which they were due to embark. In the end, they removed to the bathroom, where he washed the dog gently and towelled her dry, a treatment she disliked but did not resent. He had thought of a hairdryer to complete the process, abandoned the idea for fear the noise would alarm her. Still perplexed, he led her into the living room and sat in his armchair, admiring his handiwork. She sat on the carpet, looking at him again expectantly, and, after the briefest of pauses, crawled weakly into the capacious seat beside him. Acquired in his larger days, it held them both easily. She padded and snuffled damply, until they were comfortable.

Later he took her into the garden behind the house, found she did not try to escape but followed him back. He was adopting the same principle with the dog as he would these days with a kept-witness: if you wish to ignore safety and go home to violence, I cannot make you stay, though I wish I could. They resumed the chair by common consent. Together, they were seen by a dawn trickling through neglected curtains over the bodies of both which twitched and dozed in profound content- ment. If it was a love affair, it was committed to continuance by the morning. In the course of the night, Malcolm's dizzy world returned to its own axis.

Ted Plumb's highly disturbed world was even worse than it had been. No matter if he forgot to feed it, or if the wretched crea- ture was a nuisance he disliked, it had still been his dog. His by default, and the property of no one else. As he sat outside Sarah Fortune's house, not suspecting the presence of the sickly animal indoors on the top floor, Ted's loss rankled. He pulled the half- bottle from his top pocket. Two hours since the last drink, may as well be at work if you can't sleep at two a.m., and looking at this building was work of a kind. The liquid was fiery in his throat, nothing like the initial gulp, the sheer warmth of it, wish it didn't mean he would have to finish whatever was left in the bottle. That was the problem, never a single sip, never stopping at the stage when it was merely comforting.

He must not think of the dog, hadn't wanted it, and did not really want it now. Elisabeth Tysall's puppy. God, she had loved that thing, cuddled it like a baby, then, daft bitch, it had been left to Ted to kill it. He could not do so, but could not love it either. The dog had not wanted to stay with him, cried for its mistress night after night, always searched for her whenever they went out month after month. Same penchant for red-haired women as its master. He had tried to give the dog to the kids, they had not wanted it either, and now some bugger had stolen it. However mean the relationship, Ted had not wanted the dog stolen from him. There were enough humiliations without that. Made him weak, standing there like a pansy for some tall, thin bloke to snatch it out of his hands and run away. A reminder of the fact that he himself was incapable of running, incapable of protecting his own. His own hadn't wanted the dog either.

Tears of self-pity gathered in Ted's eyes. He took another

mouthful, shook his head. Bugger the dog and let it rot, as well as the thief who took her. Look at the house first, where Sarah Whatshername lived, whoever she was. Then go home, sleep and think, Good riddance. But first, concentrate.

Buildings had once been an interest of his, in the days when he had interests. A very large house, semi-detached, late-Victorian he guessed, flanking a small park, nice and quiet. One huge front door in the middle, two side doors either end; must be like a warren inside. Old houses like that would have had two staircases each side, one for family, one for the servants. Ted supposed they'd kept both. The flats on the top floor could use one side staircase each, or the main one if they chose; same for the second floor, but the grander flats on the first would prob-ably ignore the narrower access. A sympathetic conversion, needing a coat of paint, but otherwise fine.

Ted was pleased, even for the damp summer warmth. Not unpleasant really, sitting on the bench in the small park opposite, quite pretty and peaceful, not the way it used to be, all teeming tenements at the back and faded splendour facing out bravely, neither poor nor quite rich. Respectable, he would call it, almost, but not quite grand.

Find out which flat she has, those were his instructions, or what he suspected were only the first part of those instructions. How long was he supposed to watch, he'd wondered, but had not asked. As long as it takes, of course, is what Charles Tysall would have answered. She'd been out till after midnight, came back through the big front door, then the lights had come on in a second-floor flat, left of the door. He'd watched two others go in, side entrance right, wondering who else was in residence here, not that it was worth reporting. He had stayed as he was until all the lights were out, then gone to see if he could check names on the door. No chance, entryphone systems on all doors, occupants identified by number only, a trick to make them feel safer, though the doors themselves were as vulnerable as any other. Never mind. There were eight flats: someone was bound to lose a key sometime. Ted knew what estate agents were, he'd worked for one once before someone had spotted him. Down one end of the building was a For Sale sign, 'Luxury garden flat. Two Bdrms', the obvious way to get a key, but if a key was what Mr Tysall wanted, he could get it himself. Since Tysall had the looks to con himself into anything, getting a key from an estate agent was hardly an unsuitable task.

'*Pas de problème*, old son, but you've got to find yourself an informant. Someone who knows her. Someone who can give me an inside clue what she does with her life. Need a starting point. Can't do this all on my own,' Ted murmured to himself, hands in pockets, looking for the last cigarette. That was the trouble with observations, you smoked too much, as well as drank. Shambling away from the scene, he was vaguely bothered by questions, like what did Tysall want? But the curiosity was soon dismissed: all that was not his business. Ted's police career, abruptly and disgracefully ended, had accustomed him to obedience and a 'do now, think later' routine perfected into fine art. He was as grateful to Tysall as he could be to any man for the regular employment. Pity about Miss Steepel, pity about Maria and the others, pity about Mrs Tysall, but none of it was his business and nothing bore his fingerprints. And when Tysall crashed, as Tysall would one day, there might be pickings in plenty for himself, Maria and Joan, who might welcome him back with a fistful of cash. Ted would wait. There were always fortunes to be found in ruins, rings on broken fingers.

Watch what she does, he'd been told. I want a picture of her life. He was used to that too, the painting of verbal portraits. A few weeks should do it, allowing for some invention. Nothing difficult for a Drugs Squad man. Even one who could not keep a dog.

Soft-shoed Ted left no footprints. In the morning light, everything was normal. She could tell herself, speaking to the slightly dusty mirror in the hall, that everything was straight, and everything in place. The hall mirror, very old, fine and slightly crooked, gave a focus to her flat, revealing to her a simultaneous glimpse of the two rooms flanking it as soon as she came through her door. Squinting into it now, she could see that order reigned, or as much order as ever was in her own home. Sitting in the sunny kitchen, Sarah entertained herself to a mental review, uncomfortable, but necessary, before she could face the office and everyone in it. Joan nagging more than ever, Ernest with his worried ulcer face, and all those life-histories from the corner shop to the reception desk of where she worked. Damn. Why did it all have to be so complicated when she had tried to make it so simple? She had run out of coffee, sugar and milk, wondered if it was sinful to eat chocolate for breakfast in the absence of anything else, thinking at the same time that she had a very strange notion of sin to consider it at all.

Everything was in its place in her complicated life, difficult but not impossible. No malice anywhere, generosity given from all her huge reserves, and received wherever she trod her diplomatic way, so why this unease? Charles Tysall was why. She was thinking of all her clients on the way to work, simply to remind herself of the comparisons of what had become standard in her life, and what was not, wondering if close knowledge of too many of the breed had weakened her imagination. Charles had ridden into her office like a god all those months ago, and no one but Sarah had been immune to his charm, and not even herself, at first. Stuffed in the perspiring crowds of the morning tube, she could only recall him with a shiver of frost.

'He's something special, Sarah. No kidding, promise.' Joan's breathless recommendation had been startling. Usually she was so scrupulous, so unimpressed by any client, however rich, who happened to cross the portals of the practice. Straggly Joan, so completely contemptuous of male charm, had been bowled over by Charles Tysall. Asked by Matthewson's secretary to take the man to Miss Fortune, she had embarked with ill-grace and mutterings. Stupid client insisting on seeing someone, having called in without appointment to see Ernest on a day off with the ulcer – his bad luck, wasn't it? Tell him to . . . Ernest had been the Tysall solicitor over many years, but since the firm must

appear to pull together, and Miss Fortune was so good at placating people, she could take instructions, surely, whatever they
were. She might not know any law, but she did seem to know
how to please people.

'Why me?' Sarah had protested. 'Don't know him, don't want
to know him, give him to one of the Commercial boys.' 'OK.'
Joan raised her thin hands. 'I'll try and head him off.' Instead she
had whistled back. 'You'll bloody well see him, gal,' she hissed.
'And if you think I'm taking someone who looks like a cross
between Michael York and Omar Sharif to see one of those faceless little buggers in Commercial, you've got another think
coming. Shut up, and comb your hair.'

So, Sarah had seen him. No, nothing urgent, he said. If ever
there was, he'd forgotten. It could wait for the next day, but since
he had been informed that she was more generalist than specialist, he had taken the opportunity of seeing her for a little
advice on Industrial law. Could she help? She wondered wryly if
he meant the same thing by 'generalist' as she did, and smiled at
the thought since she could not see this man willingly consulting
such a bodger of all legal trades, expert in none but vivid invention. Industrial tribunals were part of Sarah's mixed-bag of legal
tricks, along with divorces and domestic upset, the 'also rans' of
litigation. She had somehow found a role in the firm which was
the provision of the sort of advice which no self-respecting
Commercial solicitor could touch with a long spoon, and hers
was the loophole in the practice designed to prevent their clients
going elsewhere, forming other loyalties in humbler streets. In
any event, it did not matter how she came to be sitting in her
untidy office with immaculate Charles Tysall on a January
morning, while Joan fluttered in with coffee in borrowed china
cups, lipstick-free. Sarah shot her a glance of amused suspicion,
and Joan, scowling in response, almost patted the well-groomed
head of Charles on her way past.

Powerful certainly, leonine and handsome: he was all of those.
Also urbane, amusing and apparently modest, twinkling like a
star with the pleasure and success of his life, and bristling with

animal attraction. No one, thought Sarah, should have so much of it. They had achieved little in the meeting, except to agree what should be done with the dishonest employee, who Sarah suspected was no more than a polite device to hide the fact he was wasting her time, since he could not, or would not, speak of the real purpose of his visit, reserved for Matthewson's ears only. Then Charles Tysall had suggested dinner the same evening, and under the spell of very brilliant eyes, she had agreed and wished she had not. Attracted, but profoundly disturbed, dreading and looking forward without knowing why, feeling like a silly girl.

Meeting a strange man by arrangement in a strange place, a wine bar, was always an intimidation which none of Sarah's sophistication could quite dispel, but by the time she had arrived, she had given her mental defences a complete overhaul. Certainly Charles Tysall was a devastating man (she could only think of him, as Joan did, by resorting to teenage epithets), but with all the advanced instincts of her being, she knew he was an abnormal one, without pausing to define why. He was certainly not a potential client, nor a lover, nor a friend; friend least of all. She was early, willed herself into insouciance, ordered her wine, and, in the light and calm of the early-evening trade, read a book. Charles was late. She had known he would be late: men like Charles did not sit and wait.

She forgot the man, forgot to look for him, concentrated on the book, used her talent for losing the sense of time and place. It was the first contrast he could see between this and other meetings, the first insult and the first fascination. There she was, sublimely unconscious of his existence, lost to him, sitting in a corner and smoking without the smallest concern for the image she made, half-way down a bottle of excellent wine, carelessly turning a page, profoundly content to exist, with or without his presence. She was not allowed such nonchalance, nor could he know how difficult it had been to achieve, but it was unnerving all the same, greeting a woman who looked as if it would not bother her in the least if he had simply failed to arrive.

So why did he try? He who hated wine bars, assignations, anything unpredictable and women in particular. Hated the way they shrank from him, or opened up like sea-anemones looking for prey, every orifice gaping greedily in a panoply of slack mouths, glistening for himself, or for any other. Docile animals on heat. Equally, he loathed the others of sly reserve, with their tongue-tied giggles, looking and preening, wobbly and silly in response to the worst flattery, voluble after the most bland curiosity, as tactile as waxy flowers. He despised as much the brittle wit which proved itself with funny faces, wisecracks, street wisdom and worldly knowledge displayed to show how wise, how sharp the speaker. Charles had met only one woman inside the last fifteen years of his own life who did not fall into one of these three categories, did not respond towards one of these extremes, adulation, stupidity, or competition. While he, chameleon that he was, would enter into the spirit of all roles, changing colour or changing skin, shivering beneath it all with sheer dislike of playing games with those less skilled. For what? The horror of the prospect of failure, not of going home alone (although he would often circle the block rather than enter his own abode after midnight: not dread, simply disappointment not to find anyone there). Whatever he had hoped to find for her replacement proved as elusive as ever. For more than two years he had been in pursuit, been offered, looked beneath stones, while sexual gratification was always provided by some willing Maria, some commercial body paid for humiliation. Desire, naked or otherwise, repelled him. Indifference or refusal, any controlled or hidden reaction, had an effect dramatically opposite. Charles liked to hunt, but if he lost, was crossed, ignored, or worse, humiliated, the fury and the violence were terrible in manifestations cold, sharp and calculating.

And there in the bar was the graven image of his wife, before she was disfigured, the woman he had sought for two years. Sarah Fortune could have been the double in feature, superior in wit, but the nose, the mouth, the shape, the walk, all the same.

Apart from that quality of innocence, there was a shining kindness in her intelligent face, which Charles mistook for his ideal of purity.

He remembered the last Porphyria. I love you, she had said. 'How much?' he had asked, wanting to know at first, later shouting at her. 'Surely you can do better than that; you do not love me enough to serve me . . . Tell me something I can believe . . .'

'Why should I, Charles? I'm only your prisoner, so I'll say, I love you, Charles, and you can believe it or not, as you wish. I'll say whatever you want me to say . . .'

And then he had hit her, hated her for all that endurance in her refusal to bend to his will. She had clawed back at him, screaming. He could not remember any pain, nor, as she had told him later behind her mask, had she.

> No pain felt she;
> I am quite sure she felt no pain.
> Like a shut bud which holds a bee,

So said Browning.

Here was the new Porphyria, his wife before he had marred her. She was not dead, had never left him after all.

'You are very beautiful,' he had told Sarah Fortune.

'For the compliment, thank you. I shall treasure it. Although it isn't true. I don't think I have that quality. Perhaps I'm lucky; well constructed, built to last. But not, I think, beautiful.'

'Are you always so pedantic?'

'No. A response to awkwardness, a lawyer's trick. A desire to be exact, and seen to be honest. Even in candlelight.'

'Why awkward? Do I embarrass you?'

'Yes, since you ask.'

'Why?'

'You are a man of singular attraction, and I am slightly afraid of you. I tend to be pedantic when wary, or weary. At the moment I'm suffering from both. You must forgive me.' She sipped her wine, and smiled.

Bizarre conversation, so easily slipping from pleasantry and into this disquieting intimacy so soon. And the scarred faces he saw in his dreams faded away into this cool unscarred mouth which told neither truth nor lies, showed humour but no deference, both open and closed. Only after he had circled the block, pressed open his own door, entered his cold house, did he notice how skilful she had been. He knew no more of her life, her history, her tastes, and more importantly, where she lived than he had known in the beginning. Unwilling perhaps, but this time he was better equipped for pursuit and all the rest would follow. A pursuit he would not confess to Ernest Matthewson, but still a pursuit of his pure ideal, the chase to be surreptitious and delicate in tune with the goal. He had dreamed of her daily. O my Porphyria. Perfectly pure and good.

Put him out of mind, Sarah thought, pounding up the steps from the tube. No one watches you, knows you, no one ever has. Don't ruin it all by being a fool. Nothing is getting worse. He may have kissed you once, but he has not rung that bloody phone in days. (She remembered the kiss, an expert pressing of himself into herself, knowing she was too polite to escape or show the squirming revulsion of her mouth.) He had taken the refusal as a sign of innocence – dear God, what an irony. But he did not, could not possibly know where she lived. No one knew that, unless she had asked for them to know. Safe, so she was. Safe as daylight. And late again. Joan took the telephone calls for Miss Fortune, worried and resentful. Some of the many men left names, some did not. Fred could not wait to see her. Pink Jade had lost in the four-thirty at Leicester but, as always, he had another, better horse, which would make their fortunes brighter.

CHAPTER NINE

In the darkness of north Norfolk, horribly still after the noise of his familiar suburb, Ryan heard a dog bark, snuggled back into his bed, and dozed, wondering how he should be so content. All this was his wife's idea, but just because he was so anxious to please her these days did not mean that Ryan was putty in her hands. The resistance to her wishes and whims might have been token, but it wouldn't have done to let her know how anxious he was, so he did his clever best to hide it. In turn, she was well aware of the anxiety and took a smug satisfaction in it. Serve him right: infidelity was a dangerous game and it was he who had taught her how to play. Ryan's telling himself that she was only taking her revenge, a preliminary, perhaps, to their still tenuous marriage settling into equal terms, did not make his life easier. Cold comfort was his own counsel, recognised for what it was as clearly as he could see that the new hairstyle, prettier clothes and trimmer figure were not for him, but for someone else. A man met in the afternoons and early evenings of life. Ryan, receiving payment in kind, was humbled by the knowledge. Anything she liked, as long as she did not abandon him into that homeless wasteland he had inhabited when he had temporarily abandoned her. So now, while she preened a little, ruled her roost with a firm hand, and positively encouraged him to stay out late in the evenings, Ryan held his tongue, took the small mercies of her scrupulous care of him, and agreed with all her plans.

No foreign holidays this year, she had said. What's wrong with England? Too much money gone on clothes and her new car, Ryan thought, and made a big show of nagging which was met with the iron will he had expected. Ryan did not give a damn where they went. Family holidays were his idea of hell and a fisherman's cottage on the Norfolk coast struck him as a singularly unpleasant alternative, but after he had looked at a map and read a book of words, she had seen him become suspiciously resigned. He had learned that the place where they were bound boasted a pub which sold the best bitter in the world, and five miles away was Merton-on-Sea, the village and tiny port where Elisabeth Tysall was last seen. Busman's holiday, maybe a little scouting over the dunes, the thought of it obscurely cheering. Ryan laughed at the thought of himself as country detective; he had never spent more than a day or two out of the city, but especially in the context of his uneasy family life, the sniff of Tysall was enough to resign him to the packing, although it might not be enough to ensure a week of harmony. His was not that kind of family.

Ryan's boys were nine and six, and through all the hours when they drove him to distraction he loved them more than the world, and willingly accepted the wisdom of his wife's holiday decision when he saw them rushing in and out of the small, square cottage she had found. The dreadful details of the place dismayed him: the lack of light, the tired-looking beds, thin curtains and cold thick walls, but he could see it was all the details which so captured his children. They were howling with excitement. 'Dad! The garden's full of nettles, and there's a shed, Dad, with a door hanging off and all spiders inside . . .' 'Dad! There's a ditch at the front with frogs and newts, and my blanket's got holes, Dad, look . . .'

Wonderful, thought Ryan. Fucking marvellous.

But something was there which charmed him by the end of the third day, when the silence of the place had ceased to alarm

him and the strange creeks creeping inwards from the sea no
longer preyed on his nerves. They had actually, in the absence of
any other entertainment, swum in sharp frozen bursts, with the
wife neat and blue-skinned in a new bikini, which Ryan noticed
even between chattering teeth, liking the idea that for the first
time in six months he knew where she was for every minute of
the day. She seemed to like it too; their double bed was soft and
sagging, so they rolled into the middle, gratefully sleepy with
fresher air, but not that sleepy. Comfortable love and talking,
surprising chatter for a man of so few words in his own house.
By instinct, Ryan knew better than to force the pace of this intimacy by asking questions in those quiet and sympathetic hours.
Nothing would have wrecked the harmony more effectively than
him saying, 'All right, who is he, this other bloke?' So he stroked
her reddish hair instead, told her all about Tysall, with some
notable omissions which they could never discuss, and persuaded her to spend a day in Merton-on-Sea. With a couple of
hours off for him to amble into the local nick and see if anyone
had heard of a certain missing lady whom no one else believed
was dead. The wife was as full of new wisdom as Ryan. This
domestic peace, this actual confiding in her of something to do
with his work, was well worth the sacrifice. She and the kids
would find a boat. Ryan could wander at will, and would miss
them immediately.

He found the local bobby on the quay, gossiping and laughing with housewives, difficult to sound at first, calmly
suspicious next. But prejudice against a confessed member of
the Metropolitan Police, renowned to rural forces as being over-
paid, over-corrupted, arrogant and flash, had not fully
permeated into the mind of PC Curl, who simply liked people
and had a position in his own community tantamount to the
local vicar, only more important. He was easily persuaded by
Ryan's open face which was flushed out of city pallor by three
days of gusty sun.

'Not official, you say? Mr Ryan, you say? Elisabeth Tysall?
Oh yes, went off to America, didn't she? They had a house, up

there . . .' He waved uphill, away from the quay. 'Had an accident, she did. So she said, 'bout two year ago. Used to come here three or four times a year. Very nice lady, very polite.'

'Did they know many people here?'

'Not so's you'd notice. Not him anyway, but she'd talk to anyone. But it's a crying shame that house being empty. Plenty of young folk around here could use that house.'

Ryan listened, trotting beside the long length of PC Curl, laughing and praising, comparing lives. Finally, still talking of anything else but Mrs Tysall, they turned into the tiny police station on top of the rise.

'Open every day we are, in summer that is,' said PC Curl, proudly. 'No call for us much in winter. They have to go to Fakenham and report their missing dogs.'

The man's placidity was wearing, and Ryan envied the kids out on a fishing trip. They'd be full of it, he longed for them, while over a steaming mug of tea he was almost trusted.

'Now see here.' Even his voice was changing, developing the local speed. 'There's no inquiry going on about this Mrs T. Just me happening to think that her disappearing is a bit funny. No one ever saw her again after she was down here early part of last summer. No trace. Never came back.'

Curl shook his head dumbly.

'Why should there be anything? She don't live here. She's living in London, with her husband or without him, let him worry. She had a little puppy second last time, but didn't bring it back. Probably got tired of it, wanted a string of babies, that one. Strange creatures, women. And she said in the shop she was going abroad, see.'

They both watched vapour rising from the tea.

'But,' here PC Curl chortled with remembered worry, 'my nephew in spring, after the high tides, he found her bank cards.'

Ryan gripped the mug, and let it go hurriedly. Too hot, and the rest of him flushed with sudden heat from the fingertips down, sipping slowly to save it becoming obvious.

'Bank cards?'

'Yup. Them things, Access and Barclay. Can't like them myself. They get people into all sorts of trouble. But they don't perish in the sea. Most things do.'

'Did you report the finding?'

'Nope. Why should I? Checked with the bank places, all computers, Access and Barclay. Discontinued, they said, not lost or stolen, nothing else for me to do. She should have handed them back, they said, if she didn't want them anymore, but she probably just chucked them off the quay. People are always chucking things off the quay. They don't realise how they come back, eventually. Might take a year or two, but they usually come back.'

'Where did the boy find them?'

'Out in the channels, stuck in the sand-banks down a hole, he said. Little bugger used to be frightened of the water, now he can't get enough of it. Loves them creeks, ever since his dad got him a dog. Walks up there at low tide. Always bringing me things. Tell you what, he's not at school today. I'll call him in. He'd like to meet a copper from London. Make his day for him, but you'd better look fierce. Only lives on the quay. He'll be home now. Tide's high. Nowhere for him to go.'

When Ryan faced the boy in the bright daylight of the front office where no one seemed to consult the police except for a chat, he saw a golden child of spectacular thinness and more freckles than he had ever noticed on a ten-year-old. They had merged into a dark shadow over the bridge of his nose, making him look smeared, a permanently worried sand-boy. Quiet child, Ryan thought. Fit as a monkey, and, given the task of prizing secrets out of this little head, he would have felt more optimistic with a team of professional blaggers, each armed with a lawyer. Another half-hour, delicate questions unravelling from the child. Do all coppers in London carry guns? Has anyone ever had a go at the Crown Jewels, and if they did, how would they do it? And had the Queen ever come to where he worked? And where, at last, had he, over-polite boy, so different from Ryan's own, found the plastic cards belonging to Elisabeth Tysall?

'In the creeks, right out by the sea. You can walk all the way out there.' Well, fancy that. Did that mean they were actually dropped there? The child burst out laughing, pleased with superior knowledge. Oh no, it didn't mean that at all. They could have come from the quay, from a boat, or all the way from Brancaster, miles either side. The water, you see, takes things everywhere. No clue at all in where they were found, how silly of him.

'Anything else with the cards, was there?'

'No.' They had a pause of infinite length. 'But they had a piece of elastic keeping them together.' The mouth was firmly closed. 'I'd best go. Mum'll have tea . . .'

'And so must I,' said Ryan. 'Or my wife'll kill me. Thanks for the afternoon. Come and see me in London.'

All suspicion lost in their final easy burst of goodbyes, uncle and nephew united in secrets and opinion. 'Oh no,' they said. 'Don't mean to be rude, but you wouldn't see me dead in a place like that.' Ryan might as well have suggested a day in Valhalla, and he left them as he found them, courteous, closed strangers.

The boy had found the whole handbag trapped in the heather at the top of a bank. Or rather, his dog had found it, crazy puppy, new Dad's idea to reconcile him to life and his terror of the sea. A leather bag full of sand and wonder, half-chewed and stiff by the time he had rescued it by running half-way to the sea in pursuit. They might have taken away the puppy, or punished her, and the handbag was still in his own room, what was left of it. Good, salt-ridden leather. The dog was still chewing it. The coins in the purse had been tempting, but the sodden letters, tied up in cellophane like the parking-tickets his uncle gave to tourists, bits and pieces, rings, the purse itself, had all gone on Dad's bonfire. Only the niggling conscience, and the fear that they would not burn, had trans-ferred the plastic things to his favourite uncle, with half story, half truth. Uncle had understood. They didn't want trouble, either of them.

Best friend to man and boy, Malcolm's dog wanted nothing but his existence. He had decided to call her Dog, a name of dignity he thought, because he would never be able to think of her as anything else, and she was, after all, the only dog in the world. She loved the windows of his flat, loved the park with the children and the grass made brown by football players and walking populace, thick with dirt and rich in smells. She had a remarkable penchant for following women and fawning on them, but most of all she adored Malcolm with a devotion bordering on the manic, and the sound of his step on the stairs provoked such an exhibition of frenzied affection they were left exhausted.

'Down, girl, down, you silly mutt. Get down . . .' Vain requests against her panting enthusiasm and vapid attempts to reach his face. She was a kissing dog; she feinted and growled like a cat purring, great daft paws on his chest in ecstasy, only ready afterwards for a brief, unconvincing show of obedience.

Impossible to conduct a life of privacy with Dog, out of the question to resist her affection, or remember the frustrations of work in her company, and Malcolm felt a strange belief that this was the point from which he should begin his life afresh, and grow again. Any form of growth but size, he reflected wryly. Dog would bring him luck as he brought her health, but he wondered what he would do with her when he and his parents issued forth in the next week to go to the Ball. He hated the thought of excluding Dog from anything: the only time she suffered distress was from being left alone.

It was late afternoon when Malcolm looked beyond the dust of his office window, felt Dog hidden by his feet, and thought fleetingly of Detective Constable Ryan by the sea. Then he pulled towards himself, for the hundredth time, the Solicitor's Diary. Eight more calls to go in the daily hunt for Sarah Fortune. He had reached the Ms in the directory, and found, startling in its familiarity, the name of his father's firm. It was a laughable thought that Sarah Fortune could be working so close to home. He almost abandoned the thought of making the call but, led by a sense of thoroughness, persisted. His voice, if not his mind, suddenly official.

'Hallo. I wonder if you could help me? My name is Malcolm Cook, solicitor. I was in the High Court last week and a lady in the case after me lent me a good pen, which I'm afraid I failed to return. I believe she was from your firm, but I'm not sure . . . Do you have a solicitor, thirtyish, red-haired . . .? I believe the first name was Sarah, but I didn't catch the rest. You'll inquire? Then I could return her pen. Thank you.'

Tapping his fingers while the faceless receptionist was busy with questions. 'Here, Sylvie, I've got this bloke asking for some-one like Sarah, what do I say?' 'I dunno, put him through to Joan.'

Suspicious, but trained to be helpful. Usually, if a redhead existed within the walls of the office Malcolm was calling, he would be put on to herself or her secretary, and would know within seconds, by a mere detail of the voice or the description, that the trail was cold. This time it was a secretary with a voice breathing the fumes of a hundred cigarettes, and a manner as brusque as a sergeant.

'Sarah?' said the voice loudly. 'Sarah Fortune?'

There was a pause, whilst Malcolm held his breath, main-tained the indifference of his tone, and listened with rising hope to the sharp intake of breath.

'There ain't no Sarah Fortune here,' said the voice abruptly. 'Our Miss Winfield has red hair, but she isn't called Fortune, and she's retiring soon. Never goes to the High Court anyway. Must be a different woman.'

'Thank you,' said Malcolm, spirits sinking. 'I'm sorry to have troubled you.'

Joan's hand trembled as she replaced the receiver. She had not acted in response to orders, only to instinct, an automatic reflex of protection and fear. If Sarah had noticed how subdued her secretary was these days, she had not commented. Knew better from past experience than to try to force Joan out of one of her depressive moods, finding it wiser to grin and wait for the storm to pass into healthier rage before deciding how to help by whatever back door she could find. But there was no help for Joan to seek from Sarah's generous source, not now. Before her eyes, on the other side of the desk, there lingered the vision of that small, broad man who had found her two weeks before in the office, and whose presence had reduced her to this. Deception and misery, cutting Joan off from all support, Ted's favourite and most effective practice.

She had shopped late one Thursday night, returned to the office reluctantly to finish some work, a rare enough occurrence and one she would never repeat again. Tapping up the corridor, suddenly awed by the hollowness of the quiet, she had heard him, sensed someone in Sarah's room. Sudden fear had melted into angry curiosity, and her thin shoulder had pushed the door open wide before she had given herself time to wonder who was this shuffler of paper, or even to consider that he might be sinister. There had been this squat man, with his hands in a drawer and his small feet below the desk, scruffier than when she had seen him last, but still dapper, if thinner and slightly dirty, looking up from his task with something like resignation, well-established in Sarah's chair.

' 'Ere, what the fuck do you think you're doing?' Joan's shrill cry rang futile in her own ears before the other instinct made her aware of danger. She stood still, unable to move from the circle of his untroubled gaze, shocked by recognition.

Ted Plumb recognised foe and friend, his mind calculating with speed as he moved towards Joan's paralysis, holding her eyes until he reached her, then pinning her arms and forcing her down into a chair. He had been in the office for over an hour, slipping in as the stragglers moved out, had seen the children's photos on Joan's desk, recognised Jack, knew for the first time where Joan worked, and had also surmised exactly how she stood in relation to Miss Fortune, whose desk had yielded a surprising set of secrets. There were angles in plenty here, levers and weaknesses for blackmail. Feeling Joan's arms begin to tremble, he knew he could afford to be almost honest, and was suddenly ashamed by the hunted look in her eyes. There she was, his informant.

' 'Allo, doll.'

His own shock had struck and passed when he had seen the photographs and recognised the detritus of his wife's familiar presence. A new bag on the floor, identical to the old, Joan's hat, Joan's bits and pieces in her desk, the lipstick which would always have that chewed appearance, the cheap cosmetics, the colourful scarf over the chair which he had touched in passing, smelt for sentiment, stopped in his tracks by half-regret. Yes, he missed her, more than he had known, wanted to be in those photos, a man with his kids and a careworn, but still striking wife. Better than a bedsit, a pile of dirty clothes and the occasional company of a foreign tart.

Joan struck at the arms holding her still, calmer but still rigid with shock.

'No need for that, Ted. Get your bleeding hands off me. And fuck off, I'm getting the caretaker.'

He sighed. Work was work, and this was far too important for other loyalties. Act first, make up the ground later. One slap to stop this effort to escape. A loud slap in the silence of the empty corridor, a reminder of her real isolation compared to his physical strength. One blow was enough, the rest was words.

'Come on, Joan love. Don't be silly.'

A red patch glowed crudely on one cheek. She did not respond. He pulled the chair from behind Sarah's desk and placed it next to hers.

'All right. Don't speak to me, but listen, will you? I'm not here to spy on you, didn't even know you were working here, how could I? You never tell me nothing, Joan, do you?'

Silence.

'Now listen, love. I've got this job. Charles Tysall, you know him?'

She did not reply, but he saw the flicker of awareness in her eyes.

'Poor bloke's in love, see? Like you and me once.' Not a good comparison, so he hurried on. 'Only she won't have nothing to do with him, your Miss Fortune, I mean. Nice woman, is she? Helps with the kids quite a lot, doesn't she? Thought she did. I seen her with Jack. Am I right?'

He held Joan's chin and shook it playfully. She nodded her reply.

'Now,' he continued, confident of her full attention. 'Now. All we want is what's best for Miss Fortune, what's best for you and the kids. Quite easy really. You just do as I say, simply speak nicely to Mr Tysall whenever he rings up, tell him what your lady boss is doing, and try to get her to speak to him if you can. Give him a chance, keep telling her what a good bloke he is. Don't let any other blokes she doesn't know speak to her either. That's all, and then no one gets hurt. Nothing to worry about. Nothing at all.'

Nothing. An empty building, the light above the desk illuminating dusk in early summer, washing out the workday sanity of the place. Not a sound, apart from his voice, even the street quiet outside. Joan had thought of her own rowdy estate, shrieks, howls and yells, sandwiches thrown to kids through the window, all that lovely, irritating noise. She had looked at the flat eyes in front of her own and known, without needing to reason, how captive he was. In those eyes, in her own street, in this room, prisoner day by day to all the loyalties and necessities. Ted and Sarah: threats to Sarah would threaten the whole of Joan's life. He knew it, and so did she. Children galloped through her mind; pictures of broken legs, burns, scars, and the emptiness of the place rendered her hopeless before Ted, as hopeless as she had always been when faced with a plea in his eyes. She had loved him, missed him, worthless bastard that he was.

She bent her long spine into the chair, a small gesture of defeat. Trembling, she reached for her bag, looking for the inevitable cigarette which might help her pretend defiance.

'Steady on, girl,' he said quietly and gently. 'I'll do that for you. Day's been long enough. Don't want to upset you, honest I don't.'

He had lit her one of his cigarettes, and the sudden kindness unhinged her frayed defences. Ted knew when to vary the strokes. She took the cigarette first, then the hand, then tolerated the arm round the back of the chair. It was a male arm, unlike Sarah's slender one, convincingly broad. Ted Plumb came from the same frightened place; they had shared too much of it together. It was all so much easier, so much more regrettable than he could have imagined, simply a question of finding by accident another loyal servant, full of weakness.

'It's very simple, see? But your Sarah, lovely woman, won't see sense. Don't know why. Sorry to rough you up, but you know what I mean. I've no business here. I'll come back in the morning if you like. But I need this job, Joan, really I do. He'll put me back on my feet. Good money, and then perhaps . . .'

She did not like. Even withdrawing from him, there was a spell, a mystical charm, Ted Plumb's fatter face transposed on the thinner, handsome face of his master. Whatever she thought in her mix of love and bitterness for Ted, she could not believe wrong of Charles, and she had simply agreed. Guard Miss Fortune, tell me, and tell Mr Tysall whatever she does. Save your husband from the scrap heap in the process, without doing any harm, simply doing Miss Fortune a big favour. Ted always had a way of dignifying a task, rendering betrayal a thing of worthwhile purpose. It was only afterwards Joan began to wonder, but even then she did as she had been told, telling herself it was all for the best, and such was the mixture of hope and reluctant loyalty, she believed it most of the time. Money, he had promised. Money and security after this, soon.

But today was a bad, fitful, trembling day when she knew it could not be so harmless. A strange man asking for Sarah,

Sarah's very existence denied on an impulse. Joan lit another
cigarette. Not only that. Bloody Charles Tysall's now familiar
voice. What news for me, Joan my dear – a voice which caressed.
Well, she's going out to lunch, on Saturday she's going to a ball.
Where? Gray's Inn, something like that. She was talking about a
dress. He had found something significant in that. She had tried
to keep it brief since she could not see it was useful information
at all. Felt all her resentments of Sarah and the world, all the
reluctant respect, then put her head in her hands and wept.

CHAPTER TEN

Gray's Inn Ball, last word in effort on the Bar's social calendar of which Ryan and Malcolm had spied the first on Temple Lawns, the grandest ball for Cinderellas and Prince Charmings of all ages. Joan envied Sarah the Ball, Sarah dreaded it. There were too many memories, too many complications among all that glitter, and none of it was gold.

Reasons festered in several separate minds for hesitating. Matthewson, invited by Queen's Counsel as a gesture of thanks for all the expensive litigation brought to the fashionable door of chambers, hated the thought as much as Penelope loved it, and the loathing had driven the ulcer into a frenzy. Penelope wept with frustration at the defeat of her plans to reconcile father and son over the champagne. She and Malcolm would go to the Ball and make the best of it, she with her friends to meet him there. Malcolm placed Dog in his car, fingered his tie, and hoped it would rain.

Charles Tysall, non-practising barrister, had found it easy to organise an invitation through the old school contacts who would prostrate themselves to please so successful a contemporary. He would find Sarah Fortune, trapped by politeness, unable to refuse to speak to him, or even be touched. So far he knew her instincts well, and dressed for the Ball with easy determination. Porphyria would suit an evening gown.

Sarah Fortune, poised in front of her mirror, ready for flight, wished for peace and the end of all perplexity, stuck out her tongue at her own image and wished it was a night for a long bath with frivolous book to consume during an evening of wilful inelegance. Wondered too what it was like not to be playing a part. Wished she could recapture excitement, and wished for more than a moment that someone loved her, even that hopeless love in a vacuum once held for a husband, never reciprocated, always denied, finally betrayed. And in the mirror, she still saw a dumpy child, permanently unloved, surprised by the verdict of the world's attention, begging not to go to the Ball. There in the glass was the reflection of an anxious face, the drawn look irritating her own observation. She hunched her shoulders, scowled at the result. Nothing was going to make her any the less recognisable, the blessing and curse of her own appearance ever since childhood. She could not have left her house with unwashed hair but the clean version shone like a bonfire however she pulled, scraped and twisted it into pins. Nothing could make her unnoticeable, however soberly dressed in this shroud of shapeless black, anonymous below the subdued hair. Maybe a pair of spectacles and a paper bag for the rest of the face would complete the disguise, she thought savagely, but even Simeon would notice that. God, this is going to be awful. Impatience rose in her throat in the form of a few gentle obscenities addressed to the mirror. Damn and blast. I never cared for opinion, good or bad, I will not pretend, I will not. Then the mirror reflected the same ironic smile, same lack of dutiful gratitude which had made Belinda Smythe recoil in surprise two years before. Sarah unbuttoned the high neck fastening with one hand, began to release the hairpins with the other. Hair undone, dress at feet, she pulled from the wardrobe a very different garment of cardinal purple, soft and shimmering, pinched at the waist, flounced at the bare shoulder, still demure, but a dress of curves and vivid subtlety of colour. She left it on one side, went to the kitchen, poured a large gin, then shook her hair and threw away the hairbrush she had used to torture it, stepped into the dress and downed the drink in one. After that she stuffed keys, cigarettes, lipstick and cash into a bag, blew a kiss at the mirror and walked out of the flat into the last of the late evening sun. Striding over the grass towards the road, she resembled a hiker in her long-legged and determined stride, unimpeded by the dress which she held to the knees. Cigarette in hand, she waved down a taxi, failing to notice that three of them, together with one bus and a private car, all stopped in unison. Thank you. Gray's Inn, please. If I'm going to the Ball I'm going to the bloody Ball. Not creeping there.

Ten o'clock. Gray's Inn, in splendour for the evening, covering its elegant façades and squares in lights so much more entertaining than its daylight preoccupations allowed. Gray's Inn Fields, once a meadow, the past only betrayed by the present names, Jockey's Fields, Field Court, flanking Gray's Inn Square and South Square, both bordered with Georgian stone and gracious windows. Beyond these were the walks, one and a half acres of pristine lawns with bowed trees, the envy of top-deck bus passengers in the road beyond, who saw from their own captivity a sanctuary of peace railed and protected from the ordinary world. And now, with trees festooned with lights, the grass half-covered by huge marquees and a small fairground, all disguised with the final transformation completed by the entrance of hundreds of revellers in evening clothes. Pipe bands in the walks, orchestra on the marquee dance floor, alternative band in hall, casino in the library, jazz or films in the Arbitration room, dinner out of doors, breakfast in the refectory, and all survivors to assemble for photographs at four-thirty in the morning. High Court judges, Sarah, Mrs Matthewson and others hoped to be home before then.

Tables in one marquee, cramped and cheerful, a crowd as large as New Year in Trafalgar Square, Simeon in earnest conversation with the lady he hoped to impress, Sarah entertaining his guests, and all relatively well. Mrs Penelope Matthewson, instructing her son to replenish the wine supplies before the rigours of dancing, looked as happy as a child at Christmas, and Malcolm ran errands with good grace, pleased to please her for once. Until he stopped in his wide-angled glance across the vista of tables, shocked by the sight of Sarah Fortune, held out of touch by a sea of faces, delightfully familiar all the same. Forgot the wine, and forged towards her as the tables' parties began to break up and move on to other entertainments, obstructing his path by some ghastly common consent, so that by the time his 'Excuse me, excuse me' progress was complete, she was gone and the table empty even of crumbs.

Then he spent the next restless hour looking, seeing her everywhere in the shape of a dozen others, spying her in a distant crowd, whirling past him on the waltzer, moving across the lawns with a group of women, never once seeing him. The crowds moved like sparrows, debating and screaming at each novelty, fluttering on and off dance floors, around the incessant barbecues, the indoor cabaret, the disco, leaving tables empty until exhaustion struck, and whenever he saw her, she was not remotely approachable. He knew it was chance. A kind of weary fatalism overtook him, but still he looked.

Her movements had become frenetic. She had not bargained for being hunted. First there had been the initial embarrassment, probably worse for them she hoped, of encountering so many of the men from her past and present. Men whom she met alone, now firmly attached to other women, the men who had paid for the dress she wore. There they all were, in various combinations, glimpsed or met with partners on arms and Sarah introduced as a new acquaintance. There was Judge Albemarle, eyebrows in sky with a look of discomfited, amused surprise. 'How do you do, Miss Fortune? Have we met before?' 'No, I don't think I have the privilege of Your Honour's acquaintance . . .' Sarah's reply. 'And how do you do, Mrs Albemarle?' facing a grim smile from that lady who was eyeing the drink in her husband's hand with weary and puritan distaste. Then there was Michael the Mole, only recently persuaded towards better things, but still sporting not a wife, but a mother, strange man in his choice of persecutions. Then James, grinning from ear to ear, winking uncontrollably, nervous with laughter but masking it, just. How nice to see you all, how very nice. Yes, the lights and the band,

and everything are, is wonderful. I'm very well, thank you. See you next week. We have a conference, I think, said Henry.

Surprising how accurate each description was. She could always picture the partners and there they were. Maybe it was the facility of lawyers to talk so well. By the time she had found herself shaking hands with Leo the Lemon after Hugo Hyperactive, serenity was becoming difficult in the face of the constant threat of a serious fit of giggles, and her only gratitude was for the size of the crowd and the anonymity of it all. Sarah Fortune's entire legal cabal on parade, all in their Sunday best, the one funny aspect which appealed beneath the respectable glitter, the badges of honour, the judges' sashes and the general celebration of sublimely respectable status quo, none of it quite as it seemed, like a picture without focus. And then when she had absorbed the cynicism of this into a sense of its own joke and straightened out her face, ready for the next onslaught on self-control, she had felt, rather than seen, the presence of Charles Tysall, like unseemly fungus on a pair of shoes.

Difficult to fly through a press of people. She was not running as such, not in an evening dress, although that was the instinct, but merely sliding away gracefully round the edge of the lawns, out through the side gate used by the gardener, into a narrow lane of parked cars, all of them silent and cold even in the close sound of music and crowds. Thumping through the trees, the band began to play a persistent Latin American beat, overtones of flamenco, a kind of tango for those of an age to reminisce, catchy and carefree. Sarah hummed in the darkness, 'Da da da Da' (kick) 'da da da da' (turn) 'da da Da, da da Did . . . and then he hid . . .' cantered a few exaggerated steps, twirled and turned by herself. Nothing to lose, but I dare not go on that dance floor, Simeon will be worried, and all this is very silly indeed, but I am frightened, and I have always despised my cowardice. The presence of it, the heat of it among the cool shadows of this avenue, made her want to suppress a laughter which was half fear, half scorn.

She walked the length of the cars, calming her mind with

observation. Old cars, new cars, small, large, shiny or dirty, looking abandoned. Passing them slowly she wondered which belonged to whom, equating the grandest with the least likely, the worst with the prudent rich, until she saw the battered Volkswagen. Not a memorable car, except for the fact of there being a dog half-way out of the back window, a puppy of a dog with a lolling tongue, announcing delight at the sight of a human face with one quick bark of welcome. The dog had become stuck in the window in a frantic effort to reach her, beginning the effort as soon as she strolled into sight. Sarah laughed in delight, the hunt momentarily forgotten.

'Fine watchdog you are,' she said, stroking the head which pushed itself into her hand. 'Even if you weren't stuck with trying to get out, you'd let anyone steal anything, wouldn't you? There now, what's the matter? No, you can't come out. You wouldn't like it, I promise you, they're all as mad as hatters. Are you thirsty?'

She had noticed an empty enamel dish on the back seat. Dog had been supplied with water, and had finished it in a spate of anxiety. Sarah leaned through the window, opened the door, retrieved the dish, walked back a few steps to the tap at the gardener's gate, replenished the water and returned. She held the dish at chest height while the dog lapped with careless enthusiasm, eyeing her throughout, splashing the purple dress. 'Clumsy,' said Sarah. 'Never mind.' Then she put the empty dish back on the seat, noticing how careful the owner had been to provide comfort in the form of rug and bowl, his only fault being the failure to notice how easily the back window could be pushed by a creature of such agility. 'Can't stay long,' she said cheerfully. 'Only two more hours of hell to go. Now go to sleep. No more trying to get out. You'll be lost. All right?'

She wound the window up further to leave room for air but not for exit, shut the door and left reluctantly. Dog remained silent, remarkably responsive to reassurance, turned on the seat and settled. Sarah braced herself for a return to the fray, wishing that men were more like animals.

Charles had waited and watched, and like cat with mouse, caught her as soon as she emerged into the throng. It was only to be endured with calm. Wherever she turned in whatever company, there he was within yards, smiling his urbane smile, ignoring whatever partner or party, forcing an introduction into Simeon's group which, flushed with its own success, welcomed him with open arms. She could not refuse his choice to avoid the separate twitching of the disco for the closeness of the waltz. 'There, Sarah my dear, was that so painful?' His lazy question into her ear, holding her close with the ease of expertise while she responded to his fluid steps automatically, putting into her feet the irritation, the fear and the beating heart, all stopped in an effort of politeness which overcame distaste. Guiding her away from the floor with a light grip on her arm as effective as a vice, he had led her into the wide gravel of the walks, strolling by force towards the garish lights of the miniature fairground. A pair of romantic walkers, two of many careless, enraptured souls.

'Fancy! There's our Sarah Fortune,' remarked Penelope to her son, as they ambled themselves in the same direction, with Mother unaware of his distraction. Malcolm was silent, his eyes fixed on one graceful, retreating back, struggling with the impulse to run the few steps forward. 'Ernest will be disappointed to have missed her finery,' continued Mama artlessly, 'But just wait till I tell him . . .'

'Tell him what?' asked Malcolm, striving for control. 'Oh no, dear.' She patted his arm. 'Of course you don't know. Well, that girl up there, the one with the red hair? That's Ernest's Sarah, the girl in his office I told you about. And, would you believe it, she's with one of Ernest's oldest clients. Not old himself of course, but he's rich enough to have been a client of Ernest's since he was a boy. Charming man, came to dinner once. Charles Tysall.'

She stopped herself in sudden concern, reminded by the name of Ernest's strange preoccupation. Penelope usually saved words, but now was as good a time as any, and after today, her

son would go back to avoiding her bullying again. She pulled
him to face her, forcing him to tear his gaze from the scene
beyond.

'Malcolm . . . I wouldn't want to spoil the evening for you by
saying this, but you must come and see your father. He isn't just
worried by the things you said, it's more than that. Seeing
Charles Tysall reminded me. It's something to do with Charles,
but I don't know what. You know him and his conscience with
clients. He keeps their secrets, but wants to burst sometimes.
Will you come? Say you will, or I shan't move a step further.'

'Yes,' said Malcolm. 'Of course I shall.' He kept his eyes on
Penelope's earnest face, lit yellow from the trees, until her nod
allowed him to look back for Sarah. Looking between others, he
thought he saw her pull her arm from Charles Tysall's, make a
mock curtsey and hurry into the middle of a crowd flanking the
paths, darting away in relief. Without the strong arm of a needy
mother in his own he could have pursued, but his thoughts,
more than his obligations, rooted him to the spot. Charles
Tysall, Sarah Fortune, Ernest: all enmeshed somehow, an explosive formula for his ill-prepared mind. He watched the tall man,
wondered why Ryan had failed to stress his extraordinary good
looks, saw him moving now, unhurriedly but purposefully, in the
direction of Sarah's flight, and could not listen to his mother's
words, or any words. In his own eyes the glittering, ever-moving
crowds of Gray's Inn, the richest and fairest of London's legal
society, resembled clown-like children amidst the glowing lights
and fairground noises which gave them all the horror of painted
and poisoned creatures. Beneath the gaiety, the dignity, the high
spirits and the now flushed faces, the lawyers entertained in style
such strange corruptions of themselves. He hated them for their
stupidity as much as he suddenly despised Sarah Fortune for the
nature of the company she deigned to keep. He would never find
her in time. On the way down, she had said. More than halfway
down to be the glittering consort of a wealthy, dignified thief.
Malcolm placed his mama in the gentle care of her friends and
made his polite excuses.

At home, the image of her softened. Damn them all for fools, but not Sarah, please not Sarah. Let him find her now he knew how, but he was no longer sure if he should look. He had so small a right to intrude upon a life, whatever he had seen of it, simply because it had intruded so dramatically upon his own. Perhaps he had only needed the search. Malcolm felt entirely powerless.

Dog had greeted him with the usual affection, calmer than he expected, but in his car was a strange, sweetly familiar smell, like a distant memory. There was no pretence in Dog's contentment: to her, the scent was no new experience, not the height and colours of what she had seen. From the windows of Malcolm's flat, Dog had seen what he had failed to see, the red-haired vision of a former mistress, and had poised herself for adoration. Dog had found her after two long years of distracted searching, and was happy in the discovery.

In the hall of Gray's Inn, amid the Elizabethan splendour festooned with the judges' portraits, the crowd swayed to the alternative band of defiant reggae music. Points Dextrous and his troupe held them in thrall, even the older crowd on the minstrels' gallery, jigging surreptitiously in the dark, while below their faces cigarette smoke caught the floodlights in a haze of brilliant blue like a magician's flare. 'D'ya love me, honey?' yelled the band, 'd'ya love me?' while Charles skirted the crowd in mounting anger, stood on the gallery, the only immobile figure in that vast room, looking for a familiar swathe of colour and a familiar red head. Elisabeth, Porphyria, I shall find you.

Outside, at the back of the hall, servants' entrance for the use of, Sarah sat in the van which had brought Points Dextrous, his crew and all their electronics this evening. She sat on an upturned box, playing cards with Winston the driver, a bottle of wine between them. She had seen the open door, and found the only place to hide.

'Give us a break. Let me sit in here for a bit. Please.'

'What for? What you want, lady? Leave me alone. I'm sleeping.'

'Big man after me.'

'Very big man?'

'Well, very tall.'

Winston had chuckled. 'No surprise, lady. Come in. What you got there?'

'Bottle of wine.'

'Welcome, lady. You play brag?'

'Surely. Not as well as you.'

'We'll see. Close that door. No, not all the way. We needs the light.'

In the same uncertain vehicle, wedged between amplifiers and noisy conversation, Sarah had arrived home without question.

'I owe you a fiver, Winston. As well as a taxi fare.'

'You'll find me, honey. You'll find me. My pleasure. But you're needing more practice when it comes to cards . . .'

Dawn again. Another dawn with the same characteristic effect on flagged spirits. There was damp dew on cool grass, that peculiar and complete silence of the inner city. Pausing on the grass in the joy of being home, she thought what a nice man was Winston, how nice were they all, how lucky to find them. It had always been her only criterion, whatever the rest: they had to be nice, with the description 'nice' used in its least insulting sense. Decent, intelligent, kindly men, otherwise it would never have worked, she would never have got herself on the boil for the whole enterprise. And that brought about the whole vexed problem and the only source of guilt: how to cope when she actually, genuinely liked them all, wanted them to pay, but all the same could never give a bad deal, always wanting the best for each and every one of them. Neither a borrower nor a lender be, and no, she had been neither. Good value Sarah, with high value fellows and plenty of laughter. No reason why not, she had never seen why not. Respectable wives charged higher for services far more basic, not even dignified by the business arrangement it was. Not that she ever justified herself by this, or any other comparison.

Her mind turned to the clients, oddly comforted by them. All found by accident and design, in the very respectable corners of her own profession, discovered in barristers' chambers, court room foyers, meetings, even on the phone, by Temple Lawns and High Court annexes, her daily places and theirs. The more distinguished the face, the more the features could show the pressure, the greater was the need focused there, and sympathy was no less mutual whether or not it carried her own particular price tag. They found her without asking; she was simply there. For a lawyer, a lawyer mistress was a godsend, so discreet. A peculiar bonus if she made you laugh, so genuinely good at listening to worries. As far as she knew, she trampled on no one else's territory. This was not theft, it was simply an abundance of need and a dearth of companionship, paid for in familiar coin, dignified by affection.

Kicking the grass, smelling the air, she wondered if they all knew their nicknames. Probably. She had never hidden them, never hidden anything, except for all the things they quite deliberately failed to ask, such as, are there others apart from me? Better not to know, although they must silently have guessed. None of them were stupid; she could never have stood a stupid man. Even Hurried Hugo, workaholic with the ever-absent wife. Simeon, of course, known as Smoke, anxious widower. Georgie Albemarle, known as the dawn-raider for calling at six a.m., completing the inevitable within minutes, talking for an hour and a half (What sentence would you give this one, Sarah? Oh, as little as possible, I think. Be kind today. Good, I'm glad you agree . . .), all before departing with the wig and gown left by the door. It was the talking which seemed to matter most with all of them, the listening rather, and she never knew for what comfort they paid, had certainly never thought of sex and law as any kind of erotic combination. Which it was, even to James, Tax barrister, known fondly as Ticker because of a bad heart and the habit of counting in his sleep, and Henry Hypochondria, who knew hugging was good for his health. So far, she was committed to two mornings, two lunchtimes and three evenings a week. Her bank balance was healthy, there was the beginning of an escape route from the hatred of work, and even if her sense of humour and her energy was under strain, life was still tenable. As long as they were what they were, kindly, normal, needy men, quite rightly greeted with affection, lost with calm regret, and frequently as the result of her own advice. Go, young old man, don't bother paying me, I enjoyed you. You have better things to conquer, now you know how. She was not good at collecting fees, tended to forget them. Fun and money, never mind law, sex and secrecy, all made for different, attractive combinations, suitable for an outsider who had ceased to care.

'I'm a tart,' she told the moon. 'Tart with heart. And that means I have to get Winston to drive me home. I'm so rich with uncollected fees I come home by van. Think I can take it?'

What the hell. She threw the evening bag in the air, caught it and ran indoors.

CHAPTER ELEVEN

The summer was glorious, but it had been a long hard year, almost beyond curing. Ryan felt the lassitude of the heat, dogged by the slower pace of life he had come to adopt so easily on his country holiday, felt his brain was dulled, leaving only enthusiasm without energy, questions without answers. Besides, he had fallen in love with his own wife, embarrassing to say the least, dulling all memories, all other instincts. On his return he did not seek out Malcolm Cook with his slender store of fresh knowledge which all looked so insignificant against the grime of London, only spoke on the phone, sat in his stuffy office, his back to the small view of the sky, thinking of the sun and his wife in her blue bikini. Bailey had found him there.

'You look well. How was it?'

'Bloody marvellous. Great to be back. What's the news?'

The irony of the tone, accompanied by the rueful grin, made Bailey pleased to see him.

'I see a man with contentment oozing out of every pore, and what do you mean, news? It's all in your in-tray, the alarming size of which I have come to discuss. Any developments on Tysall? Either before you left, or since? You'll notice I was patient enough not to ask sooner.'

'Nope. Nothing doing, then or now. I found out that the Tysall wife threw away her credit cards in Norfolk. I think she's probably dead up there.'

'And that's all?'

'Yes.'

'Nothing else, in three months?'

'No. Nothing. Gone to ground. He plays at home and keeps his nose clean. No rumours, no reports, nothing.'

Bailey sat down, heavy with disappointment. 'Nothing. Only a civil action against the Commissioner listed for hearing in the autumn. Expensive claims for loss of profit and harassment. Perhaps that's why he's quiet. Certainly a reason, so I'm warned, why we should be the same. Anyway, enough's enough. Until we can say someone's in danger, we have to call it a day. Even unofficially.'

Ryan thought of his garden with sudden longing, irritated to miss the tranquillity of knowing where his wife was and what she was doing.

'Yes, I suppose we do. Stop, I mean. Funny, I don't really mind. Maybe I'll mind when the weather's cooler. For now, and for once, I want a quiet life.'

A depressed mood, Bailey sensed, the somnolence of enforced leisure. Then Bailey remembered Ryan had kept an eye on Tysall for two years, a long time for a man with a preference for quick results.

'Have you spoken to Malcolm Cook? I know he was interested.'

'Well, yes, a phone call. Nice bloke, Malcolm. We were going to have a drink, but he couldn't this week. I get the impression he's fed up hearing me bellyaching about Tysall. No one wanted to know apart from me.' There was a note of mournful self-pity, provoking Bailey to brisk reply.

'Best leave it then. For now.'

'All right, sir.' There was the familiar wolfish grin. 'For now.'

'He'll come back, Ryan. They always do.'

'I know, sir, I know.'

Ryan might be growing up at last. 'Never flog a dead horse, or you'll never make old bones yourself. Let sleeping dogs lie. My new philosophy, or should be. If you see what I mean.'

'I do,' said Bailey, mouth twitching at the mixture of metaphors. 'But I thought you'd mind.'

'So did I,' answered Ryan. 'But just at the moment, I don't. Much.'

Malcolm's indifference to Ryan's cheerful voice so soon after the discoveries of Gray's Inn Lawns was not entirely calculated, nor had he meant it to sound as clear as it had. It was simply the fact that he did not know what to do, and had no wish to discuss Charles Tysall until he was able to discover the role of the man in the life of one Sarah Fortune. He had no doubt that his father could assist with his knowledge of one or the other, but it was all a question of how to ask. Now he actually knew where she was, he was reluctant to act on the knowledge without acquiring more, afraid of treading on toes. So he waited. With all his lawyer's caution, Malcolm had never really believed in Ryan's ogre, and the belief was lessened by the awareness of the innate respectability of his stepfather's clientele. He did not consider that their respectability was anything more than surface, but could not envisage his father allowing thief and psychopath through the portals. Such characters, a source of fascination to himself, would bring nothing but revulsion for Ernest. Now, having seen Charles in company with Sarah, he hoped that his own assumptions were true, and willed them to be so. He was neither wilfully optimistic nor careless, but on the day when he would have pursued his father, healed the rift and found his answers, Ernest Matthewson was proving elusive. Until he could find his father, Malcolm did not wish to speak to Ryan, but the more he tried to make contact, the more he met with frustration. Ernest had chosen this day to disappear.

When Malcolm telephoned, Ernest was first of all sitting in a dim West End pub, then, on the second occasion, sitting in another, both chosen deliberately for their down-at-heel anonymity. Ernest was on a bender. An anniversary, that is what it was. A remembrance of the same day two years before, when Mrs Elisabeth Tysall had telephoned from a Norfolk call-box and asked him to help. 'Please, Ernest, please . . . I know you belong to Charles, but please . . .' He remembered how the word 'belong' had stung him, as if he needed a reminder even then. It had made him stiff with resentment, so that he had said, in his most pompous tones, 'I don't actually belong to either of you, but if I did, it would have to be to your husband, Elisabeth. He pays for exclusive service, so I don't know if I could help you.' As the phone had been gently and hopelessly replaced, he had regretted the words, and in the light of all he had learned since, regretted them more.

Hiding from the office, hiding from home, with an ache in his side and a bad conscience, all compounded by the nagging anxiety inspired by Pen's careless account of the Ball, and who she had seen with whom. Time for Ernest to break the habits of a lifetime, swallow his pride and enlist the advice of his stepson. Plodding further and further away from his office he could feel the pain which heralded sickness, worried by the prospect of a familiar pattern of stress and the prospect of seeing the son he had failed to meet for so long.

Deal with the stress first, his doctor had said. Do nothing else today, except hide, and make a resolution for tomorrow. Today was an ill-starred day. Leave it until tomorrow. Today he would think it out; tomorrow he would speak. And after that, he might salve his conscience if possible, take Pen down to the coastline which had been the scene of that haunting phone call from the woman he hoped still lived, who had been the source of his misery since. He was comforted by the thought of a journey of retribution. Wherever it was, this place from which she had spoken, he had always imagined it calm, blue and somehow sublimely peaceful.

The wind had blown, loud and chill, up the channels the week before, driving the tide to a new fury, so that even the boy was afraid, turning back to look for drier land before the water moved. Before this, he had stayed out until the last minute, pitting himself against the tide's speed, playing games with it, calculating close odds on which of them would win his self-appointed challenge, risking all the time. Now he did not dare: the weather was dangerous, the water unpredictable, making him turn and run before it, quickened with fear. The fishermen laughed at his anxiety: now you'll learn, boy, nothing stays the same, didn't you realise? You think you know these channels like the back of your hand, but they break in these freak tides, split and crumble in the floods, never quite the same again. Find a new place for your boat. Last time this happened the sea came closer and killed your father. Don't be surprised.

In the summer storms none feared the results more than the new stepfather, but inevitably, it was the boy himself who found her in the same spot where those exhausting attempts had been made to spare his eyes. Sand-woman, stained brown, clothed, but not recognisably so, imperfectly preserved in sand, mud and salt, scarcely human. She was betrayed by the existence of limbs and hair, the bones of five toes and fingers, but difficult to imagine she had ever breathed, or put the clothes on that decayed body, let alone spoken words through the sand-filled orifice which had once been a mouth. Slack tide when he found her, as indifferent as that mouth; part of the bank crumbled away, split itself into a fissure six feet deep, with fragments of mud left for the next tide's shifting, and there she was, a brown, lumpish thing lying in the gap, only the head of her washed into something vaguely recognisable, a shiny forehead, free of flesh. The boy had looked closely, then he was sick, and half ran, half waded to the safety of the quay.

No time to reach the pathologist before the tide swept back. Dear God, what was the point, she was very dead already. He could wait, so that after the boy had found his uncle and a posse of men he could lead them back. They believed him and followed willingly, but having looked and retched, all they could do was carry her back in the boat before the water caught her again. Her skull was covered, her mud-heavy skirt pulled down decently.

Ah, poor creature. A death not like a violent city death, made worse by this involuntary and undignified disinterment. Poor, poor creature, the doctor said. He was never a stranger to tears.

Take this down, I cannot write and examine at the same time. Colour of hair, red. (They had washed a morsel of it; even below the sand it had grown into a wild mane.) Human type: Caucasian. Eyeless, sand-stained, no colour left on the hefty brown remnants of flesh even after hosing down, but cleft to the cheekbones, skin might have shown scars. Hands: long, clever, some broken fingers, either cut or crushed, the skin receded from them. A slim-built, proportional woman of thirty summers, possibly more. Most likely cause of death under the sea, water in the lungs, in common parlance, drowning. Extracts from the bone marrow revealing the presence of the same diatoms found in the surrounding sea, proof she had died in these waters and not in any others. Impossible to say what had been in that bloodstream apart from salt, and equally hard to be certain about the times. No telltale organisms beneath the sand, the pathologist explained, not like a body in a field where he could have collected the squirming life still breeding on the carrion and sent them away for someone else to judge the time of death by the dreadful cycle of the predators. A dipocere, a waxy lard, present in abundance, preserving shape. She had been buried deep, most likely within a few hours of death to remain as recognisable as this. Before she began to hum, someone joked grimly. Clothes, synthetic material, virtually intact. Some damage by marine life. The eyes long since gone, the toes no more than bone. Another decomposition expert said again, poor creature, reckoned at least a year, never more than eighteen months since she had first lain there. All discussed in the pub on the quay, with the stepfather breathing a sigh of relief, thinking how well it was for experts to be so certain. Police Constable Curl looked at his brother and his nephew, shrewdly remained silent, as did they, the boy as taciturn as usual. Having each other, the mother and the sea, they needed neither trouble nor questions. They did not even form a conspiracy. As a silence, it was simply complete.

But Constable Curl remembered Ryan, and remembered what little else he knew on the science of dead bodies. Someone would find out who she was because of the teeth, even less destructible than those plastic cards. Dentists, strange beings, would be sent a diagram of those less than perfect, if only slightly mended, teeth and one of them would recognise that picture as easily as others would recognise a face. Experts in death found people by teeth even if there was nothing else left, and it only took days. Hardly the concern of PC Curl, but after many hours, with the London copper in his slow mind, the Norfolk constable telephoned Detective Sergeant Ryan. No point him saying it then, but he had known as soon as he lifted the decomposed legs of her into the boat, exactly who she was. What he could not fathom was who it was who had buried her.

Maria was submerged beneath blankets in her own tiny room when Ted had found her. Thin thing, lithe as a lizard, dark honey-coloured hooker, kind-hearted kid. As he looked at her swollen eyes and reddened cheeks, he could see in the pulsing finger marks on her shoulders the souvenirs of larger hands grasping smaller bones. In the distant memory of a luckier youth before he discovered the experience of constant abuse, Ted pitied Maria, weeping not for a lost life, but with all the confusion of a wounded animal.

'What's up?' He knelt by the side of her unmade bed, and smelt Tysall. 'Here, you silly girl, show me what he did.'

Slapped, that was all, held by one hand, slapped by the other, with fingers on that tiny throat. He could feel them, almost see them. Two bloodshot eyes, no white spots of suffocation, not so bad, although her ears must still be ringing. 'Bastard,' he muttered, 'bastard.' She winced slightly at the touch of his hands.

'He pull my hair, Ted. Says nothing, suddenly goes bang, Teddie. What did I do? Don't know why. He pull my hair very hard.'

'Who pulled your hair?' As if he did not know. She sighed.

'Who you think, Teddie? Mr Charles, who else? Bad man.'

'First time?'

'First time, yes, but before I was very careful. I leave too quick for him to do what he wants, then go, whoosh! In, out, run away. But I knew he would, one day; I always knew he would. That kind, Charlie boy. Not so bad, Ted, I promise; not so bad. I stop crying now. You buy me drink.'

'You can have a bucketful, sweetheart. Go and bathe those eyes.' Her thin arms clung around his neck, then she dried her eyes carefully. Ted could only stand so much of that; he would go if she kept on crying. He held her briefly, suddenly bereft, wondering if the state of her face were some kind of revenge.

It had been a Machiavellian touch in Charles to link the two of them in his service, worse to have seen them both in the same afternoon. They had been in Tysall's flat within hours of each other, separate times and entirely separate purposes; he at noon, Maria at four. Perhaps Maria had paid for the understated insolence which Ted had been unable to control; the thought made him clench his fists in impotent rage, relax at the thought of his own helplessness. He should not have taken a drink before arriving to make the report of the last two months' work, resenting his captivity in those graceful rooms as soon as he walked through the door, knowing that every word he repeated of his illegal activities put him further into Tysall's hands, further beyond pale normality, and deeper into the realms of blackmail. Being so thoroughly in Tysall's power had made him enjoy the man's discomfiture, but it seemed now as if Maria had paid. Ted did not count who else.

The profile on the life and times of one Sarah Fortune had been episodic, compiled over twelve weeks as far as Tysall's expense account was concerned, although Ted had discovered all he needed to know in less time than that, with a little help. Yes, he answered diffidently, he had been to the home today, and here were the keys Mr Tysall had obtained himself and Ted had used, safe on the table, while in his head was a history of her daily rituals. All of them, nothing excluded, from the early morning visitors to the destinations of her taxi rides, and the occasional, oddly misspent lunch hour. Ted knew whom she saw and the purpose of the meetings, and did not omit his own firm conclusions as to what this beautiful woman did in all her respectability, with any time about her slender person which could be called spare. However, he did not say why she did it, since even he could not account for that. Nor why this peculiar lack of vulgarity or greed in her, as well as a dearth of any conspicuous riches in her clothes, her choice of shops, her acquaintances.

'Do you really expect me to believe this?'

'I'm not paid to lie. Sir. Nor would I bother recording it if it wasn't what I'd seen. And concluded. Sir.'

Soberly said. Ted felt he could afford this hint of sneering in the face of the white shock on Charles Tysall's face. That shade of insolence in Ted's voice was registered, but provoked no instant retribution. Charles walked to the window, spoke softly.

'The woman's a whore.'

Ted shrugged, waiting in the silence. What was the point in telling Tysall, yes she was, but she was so much more than that; someone he had actually grown to like through simply observing her? A woman who took out stray kids on Sundays and had them screeching with joy; whose paying men regarded her with genuine affection? Not for him to describe how she was patient and popular, loved or liked by all who dealt with her. And what the hell was wrong with being a tart in the first place, keeping other men's desires as well as their secrets, and in this case, as far as he could see, preserving their sanity as well. It was not inconsistent in Ted's mind that a female of these proclivities should be also a funny and generous woman. Considerate, kindly Sarah Fortune proved it was possible, but the word 'whore' had been pronounced like a whispered curse.

'I didn't say that, with respect.' Ted's vocabulary still borrowed from the judicial. 'I was simply suggesting that, discreetly as may be, she sees plenty of men.'

'And keeps accounts of them, no doubt.'

'Possibly. Probably. Well, yes.'

Charles stood by his wide window, his back to Ted, while Ted stood uncomfortably in the middle of the floor, hands crossed behind back, shifting his weight occasionally and imperceptibly as he had learned through hours of waiting. He preferred to stand. Sitting rendered the relationship even more unequal, and standing he allowed himself a fleeting smile in the mirror.

'Damn Porphyria,' said Charles loudly, but absently. 'She was supposed to be perfectly pure and good.'

'What did you say, sir?'

The insolence was becoming more pronounced. Ted clenched his teeth to restrain it.

'Did you know,' said Charles, spinning on his heel and striding towards Ted so swiftly that he had brought them face to face before the words were fully formed, 'that my wife was a whore? And I have been combing the ranks of women to find her equal, as perfect in all respects, but without that fatal flaw. Did you know that?'

The words emerged with such venom that Ted stepped back, drew in his chest to increase the distance between them.

'But she wasn't . . .' No, she had not been anything of the kind as Ted recalled, a little flighty maybe, but not his concern until the end.

'It's not my business to know anything of the kind, sir.'

'Good.'

Charles wandered back to the window. Ted was shaken, wondered if he was dismissed.

'Won't have me, the bitch? She'll learn,' said Charles so quietly the words were no more than an outward breath.

'How, sir?'

Ted had finally spoken out of turn; he closed his mouth abruptly.

'That's all. Get out. Leave me the keys and get out. Forget all this, will you? My regards to young Maria.' The last words were affably accompanied by a smile. Ted had wanted to slap him. Instead, he left without gesture or word.

Looking now at Maria's face, Ted was glad his report had

been incomplete; more pleased still that he had not mentioned to Tysall the nuisance factors and all the coincidences which had made his task so bizarre. First, the connection with Joan which had helped so much; then, that bloody dog loping across the park last night, following the jogger into the nether regions of Sarah Fortune's house. Elisabeth Tysall's dog, then Ted's own dog; the impotence of seeing that animal was the last factor which made him try to warn her. A light warning, only by moving the chair a fraction, putting his fingers on the mirror which dominated the hall. He would have liked her less had her rooms been pristine, without the postcards showing normality, the dust on the mirror, the creased clothes. But in all of her belongings, there had been this strange and total absence of any vanity, and under its spell, against all his instincts, he had left some trace of himself and touched the mirror, moved the chair in one room, and hoped for her observation.

A woman so different from Maria. No powers of observation here beyond the minimum necessary for a creature of instinct, not a calculating mind like his own, currently moving with speed. Maybe Tysall would do nothing more; far more predictable that he should simply watch, but even if he merely abandoned his pursuit for less direct retribution, it was time for Ted to move on. With this skinny little outsider, perhaps; not ever with Joan and his children. Somehow the sight of the dog he had brought to them, so carelessly stolen from himself, underlined for him how far he had gone from ever being forgiven for what he was, or from making decisions at all. He had better try to save something from this. He put an arm round Maria's shoulder, and with the other hand reached for the whisky she had left for him on the table.

CHAPTER TWELVE

Propped up against the desk was the bouquet. Two dozen roses, twelve carnations in a savage harmony of red, offset with a cloud of fern and a crimson ribbon, like a funeral tribute. One tasteful card. 'CT.'

'Joan!'

'Yes?' No longer hovering for Sarah's arrival, Joan's startling look of guilt was almost as disturbing as the relentless colour of the flowers themselves. She had waited for Sarah's presence, nerving herself: today I shall say something. I shall tell her about Ted and all the rest, see what she thinks. I must tell her. About love's not-so-young dreamer. No harm in it, of course, but I must tell her. She's never been bad to me, I have to admit that. I should say something; she's never done me wrong, not in years. After she's seen the flowers; she'll surely like the flowers. Then I'll say something, but I'm not sure what.

'Who brought these?'

'Oh, a messenger, I suppose. All right for some.'

'I would like to know,' said Sarah quietly, 'how a messenger would know that I would be here to receive them. No one sends flowers into a vacuum.'

'I told him.'

'Told who?'

'Charles Tysall. Does it matter?'

The hurt and bewilderment in Sarah's flushed face, the

sudden understanding of some kind of subtle betrayal, made Joan wince.

'Does it matter, Sarah? Don't be so silly. They're only bloody flowers.'

'Joan, I asked you weeks ago, don't answer Charles Tysall, and if he rings, tell him I'm out. Why didn't you do as I asked?'

Joan was silent, struggling for words, mulish in her confusion. Then shrugged her shoulders, the worst and least attractive in her repertoire of self-defensive gestures, angry for feeling bad. Sarah's sense of isolation grew. She looked at the flowers, smelt the suffocating scent of blooms in warm cellophane, felt the tears of disappointment at the back of her eyes, and straightened her spine.

'All right. If you say so, Joan, of course it doesn't matter, but I thought you might know I wouldn't avoid anyone without good reason. Never mind. Not important. I'd better do some work.'

She softened the dismissal with a bright smile, but in Joan's condition it was the dismissal alone which registered. With the high colour and step of a puppet soldier she left the room of flowers and shut the door on her own sanctum with a crash. No telling secrets now which would have burst forth a few minutes ago. She might have wanted to confess, but forced herself into a kind of irritation instead, made conspicuous noises of industry, banging cabinet-drawers, typing with loud and furious inaccuracy. Let . . . it . . . bloody wait. She was there to work, shop, go home. Let . . . it . . . wait until Madam was more receptive. Joan made anger the companion to conscience.

Home early on the train, swaying with the flowers pressed against the back of the crowd, thinking fast and slow. I feel what I am, odd, outcast and cast out. Living in a way removed from anyone else, with no feelings much. Except fear, for the first time, fear. Waiting for the ghost of the following footsteps which had seemed to trail her days. Carnations and roses. Reminiscent of the last funeral, one husband buried at his own request on a hill, with all those wreaths, dead or dying, what was the difference? I loved you. There was nothing left for me but my own

kind of promiscuous sympathy after that. Anything for fun, freedom, admiration and the promise of self-sufficiency. Until now.
I am alive again now because I am afraid. You were worth it, you
know, whatever you did, and I know it now for the first time. I
might even do the same again, love someone like that.

She flung the bouquet into the skip at the edge of the small
park near the flat, watched the weight of the monster thing drag
itself from the top, turned and saw the last flash of crimson as
she ran up the steps to the front door, sorry for the blooms.
Then inside. Someone had been there. Almost imperceptible
traces, all reflected in the large mirror at the end of the hall. Only
a chair moved, a smear on the carpet and on the dust, nothing at
all. Gremlins, walking around in the emptiness, nothing.
Something to make her back away, promise herself to return
later, when the gremlins had gone to join the flowers.

'We are looking for Mr Charles Tysall, sir. Wondered if you
might have his current address on your files.'

'Of course,' said Ernest stupidly, caught in the emptiness of
his office at seven in the evening, more than slightly drunk,
bereft of secretary, clueless. 'Who are you?'

'North Norfolk Constabulary, sir.'

'But why,' asked Ernest, looking with slow despair at the bank
of slung files in the girl's room, 'do you want to find my client?
And why don't you know where he lives? Sorry, too many questions. But I should ask, you know. Protocol. Must protect my
client's interests.' He hiccoughed.

'Of course, sir. We do know, actually. But we found your
address in his office, and no one seems to know where he is. Or
won't say. Same difference isn't it?' The disembodied voice
managed a polite laugh, and Ernest tittered in response.

'Hope the bastard's in trouble.'

'What did you say, sir?' The voice had sharpened. Ernest
dragged himself upright in his large office chair, remembered his
duties to his customer. Father would be ashamed of him now,
drunk during office hours for the first time in years, with a

gnawing pain in his guts. No pleasure without pain – he should have known better.

'Nothing at all . . . officer. But I have to know why you need to know. If you see what I mean.'

There was a pause. 'Well, sir, we think we've found his wife, and we need to contact him. As a matter of urgency.'

'Oh.' Ernest squinted at the ceiling, remembered her voice with a sudden surge of pleasure. 'Oh. I'm glad. Is she asking for him?'

'No, sir, as it happens.' The voice could not resist its own sense of irony. 'If we're right, she's been dead for some considerable time. Eighteen months, we're told. I'd say about two years. Can you hear me, sir?'

Ernest slumped to the floor, holding the receiver away from the strange buzzing in his ears. The voice went on, more urgent, fainter all the time. Sliding into unconsciousness, slipping to the floor, Ernest hoped that the place of this death had been the same as the blue and tranquil scene he had imagined.

By midnight, Malcolm ceased the effort to find either parent and let himself out of the flat for the comfort of darkness. After a slow, sluggish, long run, returning fit enough for sleep but not inclined to it, troubled still, restless for the light which would excuse wakefulness. Only Dog was tired, recovering in sight of home.

He felt a pang of conscience. Dog was not so strong that he should encourage her to run so far. Rest, girl, where are you? Snuffling in the rubbish by the side of the skip at the entrance to their small piece of grass. Wrong again, he told himself. She still has plenty of energy, more than you, in those spindly legs of hers, half her body weight recovered in these few weeks of companionship. 'Dog? Where are you?' Standing in the middle of the green, he shouted for her rather than whistled in front of the big silent houses which stood around them in a large, solid crescent, dim windows, scarce street lamps. Shouting never disturbed such heavy doors, and Malcolm hated to whistle for a dog. A dog was like a child; you did not whistle for a child. Back she rolled, obedient by instinct, bearing her gift.

With all her impulses for kissing, Dog also had the tendencies of a kleptomaniac, and now she was holding in her muzzle her favourite substance, the cellophane rustling and crinkling after her, a red ribbon trailing from her teeth and several battered flowers held in her mouth with difficulty. Malcolm bent to see, curious about her treasures. She shied away, hoping for a game, mock-snarling, scampering off. Play with me, please, play with me, pretty please. Look what I've found. Slowly he followed her back across the kicked-up grass, noticing more of the flowers, carnations scattered in the dog's path, and by the skip, the remnants of the large bouquet, dispersed by nose and paws as she had parted the elaborate wrappings, wanting nothing but the sound of the cellophane.

'Give it to me, girl. Time to go home . . .' She barked, quick protest and sudden urgency. Downwind with the flowers, she had caught the new scent, familiar and friendly. Shying away again, she scampered to the big front door, snapping, inviting him to follow. 'Silly girl, why? You know we go in the side, like we always do . . . Come back.' But Dog pushed at the door with a wet nose, dropped the cellophane, waited. Puzzled and amused, Malcolm went up the steps in turn, used the unfamiliar key on his key-ring to humour her, opened the door. Even as the handle turned inwards, Dog sped before him, leaving him whispering empty commands. Here, girl, here, highly conscious of being a trespasser in the unfamiliar regions of his own house, following her in sheer exasperation. He paused mid-step, arrested by muffled sounds above his head.

London was huge and endless, full, she had once been told, of golden opportunity, and in the middle of it Sarah had walked, careless of the danger zones. Watched lights from hills and buildings, hopes reflected in the river from Blackfriars Bridge. Place of glorious chance and exciting dwellings, all of them barred to the homeless. She walked endlessly, to court danger and destroy the fear which had driven her out of her own abode; walked to find amusement in whatever she saw and calm the imagination which made her so restless, anything to restore the humorous equilibrium by which she lived. But there was a limit to walking. Her steps formed a circumference around known places and familiar sights, leading her away from strange territory, while all the time she knew she was moving because staying still would show her how much she wanted to talk, and there was no one to listen. She concluded this without self-pity; a fact of life was all it was. No family who would respond, no man whose home territory was sanctuary, her own way. Outsiders live on the outside, without any avenues inwards; she must live with that as she had always done. Slowly but surely, the combination of darkness and light soothed her, and by one o'clock, she had reached the big front door of her own building, solidly silent, with the park beyond bathed in moonlight. Walking for miles had been a meaningless gesture: she had known in the end there was nowhere else to go.

Unlocking the door, Sarah regretted her own anonymity, her total ignorance of all who lived alongside her. The block was almost empty; two occupants on the top floor she guessed, strangers both, one either end, with a tranquillised couple dead to the world on the side ground floor, and herself on the second-floor centre, no more than a fleeting glimpse, a polite curiosity seen at the end of a busy day. All the rest of the small family, successful couples who lived in this semi-elegance, had sloped away earlier on the same day, last Friday of school holidays, leaving behind no trace of childish weeping and wailing to mix with the hum of the city silence. Slower still, she climbed the stairs. Don't be silly, your imagination has stolen your sanity. You are not important enough for anyone to watch you. Get indoors, have a glass of wine and go to sleep. Besides you have no choice. What else do you do, knock on the door of some stranger neighbour and say, come inside my own flat with me please? Provocative thought which made her smile. She could always wait outside for the jogger, who latterly had shown no sign of life, equally out of the question, and besides, it was only a question of opening the door. She unlocked it with quiet confidence and a sigh of relief. Cured of anxiety all by herself, proud of it.

Half-subdued instinct warned her immediately of some other presence, and she dispelled the thought, pausing on the threshold and waiting for the sound of breath, hearing none. Then flinging down her bag, feeling foolish for a wasted evening, walking boldly up the short passage to run a bath, without closing the door behind her, whistling as she went, happy to be back. Stopped suddenly as she saw the mirror at the end, catching the reflections of the rooms on either side, silent tribute to good taste, giving an immediate view of all her possessions, but always dusty.

There was no movement, no sound from him, only a profile of his face behind the mirror. A composed face, immobile like his stance, as if he had ceased to breathe. He was not hiding, simply waiting in one room, their eyes caught in the glass obliquely before she could turn back towards the door. The statue of him sprang into life as soon as the whistling died on her tongue. Charles's reaction was instantaneous, peculiar facility for a man so languid and controlled. He was behind her, grabbing the thick hair in the same moment she had turned to run.

'Don't scream,' he said. 'There's no point screaming and I detest women screaming.'

Sarah stood still and did not scream. She clenched her hands by her side to stop the trembling, mastered it slowly while he waited, holding her so close she could feel the buckle of his belt pressed into the small of her back, close as any lover, but holding in his hands two fistfuls of hair.

'Sarah,' he said. 'Porphyria. Perfectly pure and good, I thought. Now I know better.'

She did not speak. There was the impediment of terror as well as the knowledge of futility. A stranger in possession of a key to her home, where he had waited, how long she could not guess, was not, she sensed, amenable to even tones, nor would he respond to either questions or orders. So she remained as she was, felt him lift the mane of her hair, and kiss the side of her neck with deliberate coldness. She flinched. The trembling, scarcely controlled, began again.

'Ah, Miss Fortune, afraid? Of me? How could you be? I was ready to give you the world, but you have humiliated me in return. You do not, I hear, flinch in the arms of other men. You sleep in their beds, and they in yours.'

'If I do, that is no concern of yours,' she answered, her voice surprisingly calm.

'Ah, but it is, Porphyria, it is. I wanted you, and all you can do is throw away my flowers, and open your legs for other men.'

She was silenced by the crudeness, thoughts in racing panic. All those footsteps in her mind, the presence of the follower she had never seen, or told herself she had never seen. There emerged some form to the fears she had tried, successfully, to dismiss; they had substance now, but no sense except for the logic of obsession. She tried to apply her mind to that logic and attempted to speak.

'Charles, this is the height of stupidity. Whatever you may need, you have no right to break into my house. Get out, please, before you're discovered. You may be powerful, but you aren't immune.'

He pulled the hair, her neck stretched back in one agonising movement. With her throat pulled taut, she was forced to stare up into the face bent over hers while he laughed briefly at the expression of pain and fear.

'Leave? Before discovery? One of your legal terms, is it not? Who fears discovery? Like a title for a play. You are the one who should have feared that. Besides, why should I have less licence with your house and your body than you give to anyone, every-one else, comparative stranger though I am? I hoped it would be otherwise. And if I leave go of your hair, darling Sarah, what will you do?'

'Call the police,' she hissed, her neck stretched further.

'And have them arrive? Surely not. Granted the benefit of a

few details of your life, I doubt they'll see fit to assist you much. They are busier with other battles.'

He paused, allowed the words to sink in, then slowly released her.

They stood facing each other in the hall, the mirror at the end reflecting a picture of part of her own white face in the single light, half-hidden by the lithe, black-clad figure of Charles Tysall. Odd thoughts filtered by panic and puzzlement, such as what a handsome man he was, even now, what a graceful head, what power there was in his slenderness. Should she shudder at the repellent attraction of him, smile, submit, joke, scream, stay silent? The world was asleep in a sleepy building. A policy in these respectable houses to ignore screams. A similar policy for the police, should she be allowed to call them, to do their utmost to protect the innocent, and Sarah knew she would never be one of those. Not guilty, but not innocent either. The knowledge weakened her, made her weary, beyond questions, reproach or anything other than temporary submission. For anyone weaker or anything requiring protection, for a child, for a friend, a lover, even a dumb animal, she might have fought like a savage, taken him by surprise. For herself, since it had been so long since she had cared for herself at all, even for the protection of her own body, she could not.

'Do what you want, Charles. Whatever you want. Just get it over with.'

'Like any other lover?'

He held her shoulders, turned her, stood back and regarded her face with a quizzical smile.

'Like any other lover,' she said gently, 'if that is what you need.'

Charles sighed exaggerated sadness. 'Ah, Porphyria. You will not even fight. But I forgot. You have no virtue left to protect, have you?'

'More than you think. I do not torment or abuse. I leave when I am not welcome. I am there when I am needed. I do not trespass or take anything from anyone. There is no malice in me. I like to live, that is all. I call that a kind of virtue. More than yours.'

'There are different virtues, then. I do not count those.'

He was stroking her now, his hands cupping her breasts, soft and firm beneath the cotton blouse. In the silence of the house, nothing stirred. She was aware of the open door behind her, equally aware that he had seen it and knew he could afford to ignore whatever remote help may have lain beyond.

'Take off your clothes, Miss Fortune. I have seen other whores. Let us see how you resemble one another.'

She could not see what it was he wanted; rape, or seduction at the knife-point of his presence, or more simply humiliation. Without direction, she hesitated.

'Go on, Miss Fortune. A familiar enough ritual, surely.'

The defensive power, poor though it had been, was gone. So was the power to form any words at all. How to say, yes, undressing was a familiar enough ritual, but not for this, not like this. Whatever I have done, with whoever it was, for money or for love, for simple pleasure or for a gamble, was done to please with at least an element of affection. Not like this. I am an entirely honest animal in my way; I have never cheated. Please do not make me do this. I am ashamed of everything beneath the shell of clothes – who could be otherwise in the presence of one whose sole purpose was to steal everything, perhaps even life, but certainly dignity first? I have always kept that, she thought wildly. I have always kept a little dignity and made sure others did the same. They could always have mine in return for their own. I am not as bad as he suspects, but he would not understand. I had better do as he says, and he may, just may, leave me alone. She undid the buttons on her blouse.

He sat in the chair pulled from the living room, next to the mirror, fingering the stone head on the table next to it, smiling, tapping his fingers.

'Go on,' he said.

She snapped in fury. 'What do you want me to do? Would

you prefer I did this to music, like a cabaret act? There are far better ones in the West End.'

Insolent bravado. She watched the jaw tighten and the grimace of a smile faded.

'No, just undress. As I told you. And,' he added, 'watch yourself, here, as you undress.' He moved sideways slightly, so that she could see herself in the mirror. For the first time, she turned her eyes to him in a plea.

'Please . . . I can't do that.'

'You can. You shall. Watch yourself in the glass. And I shall watch you watching.'

She began to cry, a motionless sobbing. Sarah loathed the mirror, hated for years the reflection of that unproductive flesh, whatever the pleasures it had given and received. Conventional clothes, a conventional house, a daytime conventional life, dropping to the floor. First the blouse, revealing tanned shoulders, then the skirt, then the slip. Left in bra and knickers, she hesitated again, saw his face and went on. Unhooked the flimsy piece of cotton last, felt her bosom fall free. Stood upright, resisting an impulse to fold her arms across her chest in memory of that last remnant of pride. She had not always hated this almost-perfect body, but despised it now. Impossible to look into the mirror. She turned her head aside, and waited, the slow trickle of enormous tears on her face the only movement of soundless desperation.

Charles stood up and approached her, twisted her face roughly towards his own, and kissed her mouth. Then moved to stand beside her, so that she was forced to face the mirror while, slowly, he ran his hands down the sides of her body, across the flat stomach, brushed his palms against her nipples. He stroked the cleft of her buttocks, and, bending, touched the bush of her pubic hair. She was shivering uncontrollably.

'I was right,' he said. 'I knew you would be like this, perfect, but perfectly flawed. Look at yourself, what do you see?' He continued to stroke the captive body, and she did not answer. Nakedness made her completely vulnerable, but her silence angered him. When she finally spoke, the repetitious weariness of her answer angered him more.

'Whatever you want, Charles. Just finish whatever you came to do. Whatever you want.'

The body behind her own stiffened, the hands ceased their rhythmic stroke, and placed themselves, disembodied, in the mirror, around her neck.

'Do you think it is as simple as that? I wanted you to want me, but how could any man want you now? Put myself inside you, diseased as you are . . . I am so tired of women like you. No, I want you to look at yourself, see, for once, how putrid, how ugly . . .'

She felt all that for different reasons, wanted to scream denial at the words, twisted out of his arms and ran for the door, escaping the nearly gentle touch for a brief second. He caught her hair, pulled her back, ignoring the futile scream, and with effortless ease dragged her to the mirror, then with the same ease slammed her head against the glass. Her forehead struck the cold surface with a resounding crack. In the dizziness and pain which followed, she heard the deafening sound of the glass breaking as the mirror shattered in a crunching, groaning impact. Pulled upright, she saw through scarcely focused eyes no image of herself or him, but a web of cracks. Still keeping hold of her with one hand, Charles tore the mirror from the wall and threw it on the floor of the hall. It bounced, the shards of glass split in twinkling, sharp confusion while the oval frame rolled sideways to rest crooked against the wall. Charles pushed Sarah up against the frame of the door, again twisting her face into his.

'Rape, little Fortune? Do you think I wanted only that, something simple, a mere favour? Did want, do want, but only if you were to be another wife, like my own, but not like my own, perfectly pure and good. As I have always wanted, never found.'

He pulled her to the floor, suddenly tender. She, naked; he, fully-clothed and stroking the huge swelling on her forehead, his fingers lingering on the blood oozing from the contusion at her hairline. 'Ah, poor Sarah, sit with me . . .'

Mad, hopelessly mad. In a fog of pain, slumped against the wall, her eyes catching the strewn glass glimmering in the light, she knew he was mad. Hysterical laughter rose in her throat. Madder than his impulses surely, this desire to laugh and stuff her fist in her mouth.

'You know what I did to my wife? No, that's not right, what she did to me, betrayed me, laughed at me. Made me hurt her. I cut her face with my best glass, and then her hands. I didn't mean to cut her hands; hands are blameless, but she tried to cover her face, so cut them away.'

The voice of him was almost a whine, Sarah's emerged as a rasp.

'Did you kill her?'

'What? No, of course not.' There was a mild, aggrieved surprise at the question. 'I only marked her. To stop her doing that again. I wouldn't ever have killed her; I only punished her. She did the rest.'

'She was your wife. I am no such thing. I owe you nothing.'

'But you are my wife, and you owed me better. You must be punished too, like all the others: you have made men mad.'

He knelt beside her. Then pulled her crouching form away from the door and pushed her to the floor. Sarah cried out briefly as the pieces of glass pierced the skin of her back and shoulders. Impervious, Charles knelt astride, pinning her arms wide for maximum contact with the glass, stopping the mewing sounds of her mouth with his own. Despite the piercing pain, she struggled, feeling the splinters cutting feathery stabs the more she moved, until it was unbearable and the struggles negligible.

'The passion of pain,' murmured Charles, unhurried, unhurt. 'Whenever I punished my wife, I made love to her. But not to you, Porphyria, not to you.'

Her arms had grown numb and she was aware of the floor sticky with blood. When he released his hold, she neither cried nor moved, watched him pick up the largest shard of the old pock-marked glass she had once loved, and draw it down her arm in a thin red trace. Across her belly, scratching rather than cutting, cat tormenting mouse. One long line up her torso, between her breasts, moving to her throat. Then she screamed and screamed, struck back, twisting and turning, feeling the broken glass cracking beneath her. Charles slipped; the triangular shard dug deep into her shoulder with the weight of his hand, and she kicked, struggled, clawed bloody hands into his eyes as he slumped towards her.

If I can push him on to the glass, let him feel this, let him risk his own perfection, stop him being sheltered by my pain, surely it will hurt him through cotton clothes. He will not risk scars . . . Charles was grunting with effort, off-balance, nearly falling, holding her wrists to drag them from his face, slowly winning, his expression contorted with fury. One hand was cut from the shard he held. There was a blinding curtain of pain, like glare through a windscreen multiplied by dirt, blood in her eyes and hair running freely from a dozen cuts. She was sinking, drowning in weakness, clawing at him with her back arched away from the vicious glass, losing second by second, warm, slippery, but growing colder and colder. He released one hand; she felt it turning her face to the ground, pressing her cheek towards the splintered glass, playing with her resistance.

I shall die here, she thought. I am going to die. Melodramatic to acknowledge it, unreal to have to imagine at the same time that she who had not wanted to live, did not want to die cut to ribbons without even a blow struck, not even a minor triumph on her own behalf, a death from someone she had never injured, no real ending . . . I did not live for this. Her tensed muscles bleeding slower, while the desire to fight suddenly intensified in inverse proportion to the means for trying, a kind of passive indignation mounting slowly.

Then the sudden power of sheer fury, a launching of faded strength as she struck back, kicked, clawed, tried to scream, and felt the impact of his surprise. At the same time, into the midst of them both, there erupted a howling snarling animal, a flurry of red hair, teeth, claws. A mess of three rolling bodies instead of two, and abruptly what had felt like silence was full of sound. The tearing of Charles's cotton sweatshirt, a roar of pain from him, her mouth full of red hair, the dog's and her own, as she rolled away across the glass. Dog was a moving target; Charles could not grasp the writhing shape, but shrieked like a child as he struggled, shifting forward on his knees towards the glass, beating the jaws away with his fist until the teeth took hold for a second time and sank into his wrist. Sarah rolled free, tried to stand, and watched in horror as Charles raised one large hand holding the same shard and chopped repeatedly at the dog's neck. The animal dropped away whimpering, then leapt towards him again, ignoring the glass in the fist, pathetic in wilful ignorance. Sarah could not bear to watch, flung herself at Charles, hanging on to the raised arm with the full force of her weight, knocking him sideways. He slipped, thumped against the wall, twisted out of her grasp and stumbled towards the door, pushing her away in a last violent shove which sent her reeling. She fell and lay still against the supine form of the dog, both of them panting. Below the stairs, she heard a confusion of noise, waited in hope for the sound of the front door slamming, and slid into numbness.

Not my kind of bravery, but I must do as driven by this devil, I who have no trace of violence in me. Through the open door of the flat, from the darkness into the light, Malcolm saw the glitter of glass, smelt blood, heard Dog howl in pain, before the man in black cannoned through him and down the stairs. Malcolm hesitated for a second, looked forward and back, shouted after the flying figure, and by instinct followed. By the time he reached the front door, he could see the figure beginning to move across the park in a slow trot. In a last practical gesture, Malcolm felt for the keys around his neck, thought fleetingly of the carnage behind him, and ran after the man, better-trained feet tearing at the grass, running as swift as an arrow towards the dark figure which turned and saw him, ran on with lithe speed. Malcolm leapt into the air, caught at the retreating back and crashed the two of them to the ground, rolling in the damp green, with the man's hands beating against his face. One of them was stronger: the blood on the exposed skin was like drying soap, tacky and slimy, difficult to hold or pin to the ground, while the muscles beneath were as hard as steel. In the struggling, panting darkness, Malcolm heard his own voice, furious and low: What have you done, what have you done? Questioning with his own repeated blows which struck that other body into slow submission. He knelt astride, only ceasing his own savage punching long after the end of resistance, aware then of the silence outside their own tortured breathing. In the distance, he heard a police siren, knew it was not for them. Without questioning why, he had realised this to be a private battle, no concern of any other. Sirens were second nature, part of his daily business, they carried his living to his door, but he knew he was beyond their authority, and so was the man who groaned beneath his weight.

In his stirring, and in the sharp movement of the head on the ground, Malcolm dimly recognised his adversary, but before the knowledge of that, was ashamed of his own force, regretted the blows struck beyond those which had been necessary, and in the midst of the dying anger felt guilt and shame. I am no better than any other thug who strikes again and again in mindless fury. Remembered the greater needs inside the building a hundred yards away, still silent, saw there was little he could do with this prisoner bar continue to strike him, stood away, and looked down. Charles turned on his stomach, pulled himself on to his knees, and stood upright slowly himself.

'I know you,' said Malcolm. 'You can wait for your arrest, or leave. I'll find you. I know you.'

The face near his own was smeared and swollen, but even in this transformed state twisted itself into a kind of smile before broken words emerged with breathless deliberation.

'She wouldn't like it, I promise you. Your Porphyria wouldn't like it. Too much to hide . . .' The voice trailed, but as the figure limped away, Malcolm thought he heard the sound of strange laughter. A childish giggle, sad and gleeful, only ashamed of defeat.

Silence. Moist silence. Spittle running down her chin, and a slow, ponderous drip, drip, drip from the shoulder now leaning against the door. Sarah looked at her feet. Red. Her own blood, Dog's blood, falling to the carpet like a weeping tap. A warm snout pushing against her thigh, urgent whimpering sounds like her own, a tongue making a half-hearted licking against her skin. She put out a sticky hand to the silken head in an automatic stroking, feeling comfort flow into her from the softness of the touch. She moved to stroke the dog's neck, felt the matted fur, sensed the blood, the serious wound. Her mind cleared into urgency: there was someone to rescue, the least she owed, and she tried to stand, like a shameless drunk, looking fixedly at the animal with red streaming down one flank, resisted the temptation to stay still, moving as fast as her limbs would allow.

Skirting the glass clumsily, she stumbled into the bathroom and wrenched two towels from the rail. One she wrapped around herself, dabbed Dog's wound with the other, then tied it round the animal's neck to staunch the flow. Then fell heavily against the door, holding the makeshift collar, waiting for the return of strength.

Into the circle of light, there swam a face of dim familiarity. Who was that? Difficult to tell. The fat man, the thin jogger, some woman's lover. Memory dimmed by blood, but the face was calm and competent, eyes she trusted. 'Please,' she said, 'please . . .' The recognition was slow but mutual. There was something in the way she lay curved and naked like a vulnerable foetus which reminded him of another, bolder Sarah Fortune. 'Help us, please . . .'

'Shh. Of course I'll help, don't worry . . .'

'Is he coming back?'

'Of course not, keep still . . .'

'No policemen, please. Don't do that whatever you do, please.'

'Shh,' he said again. 'Anything you say. Doctor though, and a vet . . .'

'Yes,' she said wearily. 'Look after that stupid, brave dog.' There was a grim attempt to smile. 'And a vet will do for me too.'

He lifted her into his arms, carried her into the bedroom, noticing the network of cuts, the great gash in the shoulder, the contusion swollen beyond recognition on her forehead. Pain stung her awake as he laid her gently on one side to avoid the fragments of glass which clung to the towelling and the skin. Dear God, how would he explain what had happened, how she and a dog had launched themselves out of a window, some incredible story like that would have to do. The slim body shuddered with relief. 'I'm sorry,' she was muttering. 'Sorry . . . Look after the dog. I never meant any of this.' Shaking slightly, a sign of life, even shocked life. Malcolm pulled the duvet round her, then looked at the cut on Dog's neck, a slice to the bone, frighteningly deep, but bleeding less, laid her on her side too, binding the towel tighter. He went to the telephone, listening in the silence to the slight noises of the two wounded. As he dialled, he could hear the muted sounds of Sarah's crying, and even when speaking his appeal for official help, could not resist the single wish, recognised as bizarre as it sprang into his mind through a haze of anxiety, that she would not ask him to leave if ever this was over, not ever, not at all.

CHAPTER THIRTEEN

'Fuck you, Malcolm. Surely you can get her to talk? What kind of bloody lawyer are you? You're a retarded idiot. Born with a brain, can't effing use it. You tell me she's told you she was carved up by Charles Tysall, and his bloody wife's just been washed up with the tide. All this, and then that, currently marked "No Crime", it makes me sick. If she could talk, we'd at least have a bloody angle to weaken him on the death of his wife, but all we've got is a bloody ancient corpse that can't talk, and one healing body who won't talk, won't put on paper what she's said to you. Bloody women. Most of them I know talk all the time. Do something for God's sake. At least get her to promise she'll sign the sheet when she's better.'

A week after the event, Malcolm regretted repeating to Ryan the greater part of what she had told him. She had said as much as she could, and there was more, of a different kind, to come. She had talked when she sat in a hospital bed, receiving a pint of blood through one tube, saline through another, but she had only talked to Malcolm on condition that he repeated to the doctors, who were far from convinced, the story of falling through a window. Now she would not talk anymore, except to him, and would not make any kind of statement identifying her attacker.

In the scepticism born of years of criminal practice, Malcolm could see why. Even five years before, in the days when he had still believed in the ultimate power of law, he would have been the gentle inquisitor, looking for the conviction of an evil man, probing, persuading, warning that truth will out, you may as well comply. In those days he would have said to the reluctant witness, Miss Fortune, you must take an oath and speak, for the sake of catching a breaker of the law who may well hurt another. You must write first, and then speak. Here, take my pen. When Malcolm thought of those he had met in the bowels of the court, refusing to give evidence, until his large and gentle insistence had made them, he blanched. He knew in his heart of hearts that he had persuaded people to believe they would not be hurt in consequence of words said on oath, and that he had never had to see or follow up the beating which would ensue from the friends of the pimp subsequently convicted, or the bruising of the girl-friend of the thief betrayed by her words. This was different, but more or less the same. These days he could see how many were outside the law by sheer influence, could see there were times when it was not worth ruining the life and the trust of one disturbed victim to bring an offender to book. Not even if the offender was Charles Tysall, and not even if other lives hung in the balance. It would make the rickety game of justice one of a life for a life. Especially now.

Malcolm's grasp of the criminal code was so complete he could envisage the trial and all which would follow. Sarah Fortune, pilloried as a greedy whore tormenting a man and suitably punished by falling over a mirror. And, to support the persecution of the witness, no doubt the names and lives of all the lovers, so carefully purloined by the defendant, would be revealed. Malcolm did not know this for sure, but his instincts, and the faithful repetition of Charles's words to Sarah, made him understand the possible extent of his research into her life. Sarah had expected Malcolm to be shocked, but saw no point in hiding anything. He was, after all, both rescuer and criminal lawyer. Malcolm had not been shocked. A life was a life; you did as you could. He did not care what Sarah had done with her body and did not regard it as dishonest. His tolerance was dangerous: a prosecutor was supposed to feel some moral outrage and show at least some sort of belief in his own society's rules, while Malcolm's attitudes, to say nothing of his affections, were going to get him the sack. He had reached that dangerous age when law and punishment mattered less than individuals. In the face of Ryan's fury, he was silent.

'It's all down to you,' Ryan said. 'You and your bloody father, and that woman. And too many secrets. All the secrets you lawyers keep. You aren't normal.'

'Not quite,' Malcolm murmured apologetically. 'And there are other things to consider.'

'Like what?' Ryan shouted. 'Your precious confidentiality rules, OK? And fuck the rest of us? The fact that you tell me that it would kill your father to step into the witness box and tell on oath what bloody Tysall told him about disfiguring his wife? Or the fact of the reputations of a few other lawyers in the club who've had the privilege with our Sarah? Sorry, guv, your Sarah. What the hell does all of that matter when we've got the chance of nailing a psychopath and a thief?'

'It matters plenty. We're supposed to protect, as well as prosecute, you and I.'

'Leave it out. You might. Protect? At whose expense? Shit. I'm sorry, Mr Cook, I don't get it, and I've had it up to here.' Ryan sketched a line across his own forehead. Malcolm thought of the stitches in Sarah's brow and shuddered slightly, silent against the other's indignation. Ryan tried another tack, the last resort of anger.

'I thought we were friends, Mr Cook, I really did.'

'I'm sorry,' said Malcolm formally.

There was nothing more to say. Ryan left.

Malcolm wished he did not understand it all too well, the anger and the frustration. Wished he had not, unwittingly, confirmed the policeman's view that all lawyers were either charlatans or fools. You're committed to failure, his father had said. Get out of this game, Malcolm; it's bad for the soul. Another hospital bedside, another revealing interview, made brief for Ryan's benefit. And what has your legal game done for you, Father? Sold you a client who has used you as he would a psychoanalyst, abusing you by seeing if he could rely upon you to keep untenable secrets, blackmailing you? Ernest had had the grace to laugh, a short, despairing sound. Well, Son, we who dabble in human lives must take the consequences.

And then there was Sarah, sitting as still as a plant, hiding her wounds in Malcolm's flat, less elegant than her own, more austere, but warm and complete nevertheless. She had not asked to stay, the ambulance had returned her there at his request, and she had not argued, simply demurred. At Malcolm's feet sat Dog, recovering from a fretwork of stitches, stable by his side, although in the time of Sarah's constant presence, the loyalties had become divided. Not divided as such, said Sarah, simply multiplied. After all, she saved me; she can't be stand-offish now, although she should bite me if she had any sense, since I got her those stitches. But for all the ease, Sarah was watchful like a cat, residing in the home of another because of a need, a weakness in herself she resented all the time. He wished she would simply accept the need, possibly with the same calmness with which she had accepted the serious injury, the permanently scarred forehead, still clear headed, obstinate to the end.

'Why won't you talk to the police?' he had asked, to establish an answer he knew full well after her clear account to him of the evening of her attack and all the two years which had preceded it.

'Because it would do more harm than good in the long run. And because I know the limitations of evidence. I don't object to the ruining of my unimportant reputation, or falling from respectability, but I won't risk the same for anyone else. I might not be an innocent, but the lovers were, in their own way. So is your father. Charles Tysall knows very well I wouldn't risk exposing them. I don't believe anything as clumsy as the due process of law could catch him anyway.'

He accepted that as he accepted all she had done with her life in the meantime between that single encounter of two years before which had been etched on his mind ever since. It no longer occurred to him to judge, condemn, or even wonder whether a thing was illegal or immoral: he could only see whether it was well-intended, harmful or not, quite different distinctions. Malcolm believed in nothing, but he knew that he loved her. He knew and wanted the heart of what he loved. Whatever had been done with the body did not matter. Pasts did not matter, only futures. There would be a long wait, but he had time. It crossed his mind what they would do for money once he had survived his forthcoming interview with the Chief Crown Prosecutor, to explain his harbouring of a refugee, as well as explaining his own refusal to contribute to the evidence, but that too was irrelevant.

Charles Tysall had sat for many hours in a dim interview room with a faceless Superintendent, a note-taking Sergeant, and his own, newly recruited solicitor, a man with a face like a weasel. Horses for courses: one solicitor to whom one confesses; another, eminently corruptible, in whose presence one says nothing of any importance at all. Whilst voluble Ryan had acquainted the interrogators with the reasons for the bandages on the hands of the suspect, the marks to his face and the slight stiffness to the walk, it was not their mandate to question him on the basis of hearsay evidence, or any evidence at all of events so recent. They had been removed from the confines of Norfolk to ask their suspect about older history than that. There was a sharp demarcation zone in their inquiries: what the man had done in London was London's concern, while the discoveries of Norfolk, confirmed by a Knightsbridge dentist, were theirs. As a concession to other inquiries, Ryan was allowed as inside observer, and as the greatest concession of all, Superintendent Bailey was allowed to ask some of the questions.

'When did you last see your wife, Mr Tysall?'

'Two and a half years ago. We quarrelled, and she left me. She had had an accident.'

'What kind of accident?'

'Domestic.'

'I see. Were you involved in that accident?'

'My client does not have to answer that question,' interrupted the weasel.

'The choice is his,' said Bailey, well used to the interference of legal representatives, while the Norfolk officers shuffled with indignation. In their own county, lawyers were more co-operative. 'I'll ask again. Were you involved, sir?' It was an automatic reflex to call Charles sir. In Norfolk, anyone not actually on a charge was not called otherwise. They were not fools, but they were invariably courteous. Charles was immobile, urbane and alert. Wearing that look the Superintendent recognised, and which told him a man would tell him nothing.

'If you don't mind, I shall take my solicitor's advice and not answer that question. Except to say I was aware of her accident, and how much it distressed her, as did our relationship, which was not happy. She sought treatment for her injuries; no doubt you will find evidence of that, but she made no complaint. It was not a criminal matter. Then she left. She told me she was going back to America. From whence she came. I did not pursue her.'

'What about money? What was she going to do about that? I presume she was financially dependent on you?'

'You presume correctly. Who knows what she planned?' He spread his hands, still expressive, even in bandages. 'If she had wanted money she would have asked, but she had the deeds of our house in Norfolk, in her name, a valuable property. I regarded that as her settlement.'

'Minor, for a man of your means.'

'Surely. But had she asked more, I would have complied.'

No you would not, Bailey had concluded, you would have fought tooth and nail to deny her a penny, because she had abandoned you. But he allowed the polite flow to continue.

'In any event, she had credit cards. I closed and paid off the accounts six months after she left.'

'And you made no effort to find her?'

'No. I find it preferable to sustain defection in silence, Superintendent. What would I have achieved by looking?'

'Peace of mind, perhaps?'

'My mind was not troubled. Besides, it is constantly engaged. I am a very busy man.'

No trace of her in the man's flat ('Will you look at this place, look at all this stuff? He must be loaded . . .'), scene of crime specialists beginning their task in hope, ending in frustration. Not an inch of carpet older than a year, nothing more than sanitised cleanliness everywhere, some long, dark hairs beneath the bed, that was all. Charles's address book and all his confidential correspondence locked in a safe in the weasel's office. The letter from his dead wife, informing him of her intentions and announcing the incriminating letters she would leave on her person explaining quite clearly the reasons for a self-inflicted death, had long since perished on a Norfolk bonfire.

There was nothing then, apart from a drowned body discovered in a sand-bank. And a placid man, with an alibi for all possible days eighteen months before, when he could show he had not left London for a single day, who knew he would not be charged with murder or anything like.

Disposal by hired help, the interrogator thought. Contracted death, hopeless, but not as cruel as the total absence of grief which stung the questioner most.

'Did you love your wife, Mr Tysall?' An announcement of a question, designed to shock, if only a little.

'What do you mean?'

'What I said. Love her, the way normal human beings do. Did you?' The colour drained from a pale face, leaving the bruises livid. There was a twitching of the limbs, a brief contortion of the features into a peculiar mask of anger and grief. The weasel stirred to restrain his client.

'Love her?' said the face loudly. 'Love her? Of course I loved her. Better than anything else in the world.'

Silence had fallen. Only the slight scratch of the pen on lined paper as the note-taker, unperturbed, wrote, 'better than anything in the world', finished with a slight flourish before the pen dropped.

'I think,' said the weasel, 'my client has had enough for now. Anything else I regard as oppressive.'

'Oppressive?' said Sarah. 'Is that what Superintendent Bailey told you?'

'Yes,' said Malcolm. 'He's the only one left who'll speak to me.'

'Oh, Malcolm.' She pulled Dog towards her in a gesture of affectionate despair. 'It's me who's oppressive. I seem to have isolated you. Nothing good has come to you ever since we met. Your job is at risk. You don't see friends. I've been a sort of curse on your life.'

Over the weeks, their conversation had assumed an easy, joking banter, hiding nothing.

'What do you mean, no good has come from you? Look at my slender figure.' He pirouetted in the room, grinning, a touch of the old Malcolm, ready to joke as a more dignified buffoon. 'That was you, though you may not know it. Then there's Dog, an indirect credit to you. What more could man owe woman? Friends I don't miss, except for the few I hope either to acquire or keep: Bailey, Helen West. And you.'

'Friends? Friends have to be equal, and whatever you say the balance between us is all in your favour. I owe you everything, including wanting to stay alive. And I'm hardly suitable material for a friend. Not even an acquaintance or relative to give me ballast. And, as an extra credential, two years behind the mask of respectable prostitution.'

'Do you regret that?'

She hesitated. 'No. I was always on the outside; being what I was didn't seem different. I would only regret if I had hurt anyone, so no, I don't regret it.'

'Good, I should respect you less if you did. Is there anything you do regret?'

'Of course. Like not having the comfort of moral beliefs. Making such an obsession of love, and such a cynical matter of its absence. Not knowing you a long time ago. Not having a baby. Or a dog.'

He was standing by the window watching the park settling for the evening. Dying sunlight played on his features, turning the thick hair blue-black, making his eyes deeper set and his profile sharper. Malcolm was long and lean, strangely authoritative and utterly relaxed in his own home with this company. Sarah regarded him with covert affection and respect, tinged with a vague longing she was frightened to show. The man deserved far better than this.

'It's time I left you in peace, Malcolm. Summer's turned autumn. I've been here six weeks. Too long.'

He continued to look into the park, examined the view, shrugged his shoulders.

'You must do exactly as you wish. Leave me in peace? If you must. But if you leave, I should not be in peace.'

'No,' she said softly. 'Nor would I.'

He spoke as much to himself as to her. 'Outsiders, both of us. We arrived at the outside by different routes, as unlikely a pair of lawyers as you could hope to find. Quite indifferent to the status quo we are paid to preserve. We may as well be on a different planet from the rest.'

'We are.'

'Well,' he said diffidently, 'it might not be a bad idea to circulate earth in company. I've always wanted a garden.'

'And I the dog.'

'Ah, if you had had either dog or child, you might not have had the lovers.' He was laughing now, and he turned back towards her, squatted by her chair and took her hand. 'So you may stay a little longer?'

'Please. Although I don't see why you ask.'

'Let's see how we go.'

She stroked the blue-black hair, feeling strength, new blood in her veins after a ritual bloodletting, she thought. A strange sensation after three years of caring for nothing, like the bends in the blood of a diver coming up from the very deep in search of air.

He sat beside her and kissed her lightly, a first time kiss.

'What shall we do?' she asked, smiling.

'Well, by degrees, we could shorten the distance between your room and mine. After that, travel hopefully. Far better than arriving.'

She leant into him, conscious of the warmth of him, the care he took with her, wondering why he should, but grateful.

'And if Tysall should come back, not here but elsewhere? Charles is on my conscience. Not him, but the harm he can do and I have not prevented.'

'We shall have to see,' said Malcolm. 'He may be beyond the law, but not beyond his own demons. He may destroy himself.'

'In rage, do you think?'

'Oh no. In cold blood or arrogance. What he may do cannot be helped. We have to fight our own battles.'

'Is that what outsiders do?'

'It is.'

'I do not want him to suffer. I don't want anyone to suffer, I want to believe people can change the course of their lives.'

'We shall prove that they can.'

Silence fell. Dog moved, and slept again.

'Malcolm, I have never trusted anyone before. Or not for so long that I can't remember what it is like.'

'Nor I. But we shall learn, you and I.'

'Shall we? Am I, at least, not beyond hope?'

'I don't know. I don't believe, now, that anyone is.' He smiled suddenly. 'But we have to try. We have our responsibilities, you know. There's a dog to bring up . . .'

She looked back at him, echoing the old mischief.

'Oh yes, of course. I forgot. That settles it then.'

Never trust a lawyer, or a copper, and trust the court least of all. Ryan was pushing his maverick trail out for battle rather than solutions, back on the course of unfinished business. Dead Mrs Tysall and the vision of Annie freshened by his own impotence and a fair degree of new guilt. I hate you, you bastard. If I do not have you, I do not sleep and cannot get on with my life. And I am angry in my bones for turning away, when I, more than anyone, should have kept on watching.

'It's Mr Tysall, isn't it?'

Charles looked up. The bruises had disappeared, the face was cold and distant, and although the level of sublime self-assurance was less, the responses were as controlled as they had always been.

'You don't need to ask, Mr Ryan. You know perfectly well.'

'May I sit down for a minute?'

'I'd rather you didn't, but I can't stop you.'

Ryan sat, pretending a nonchalance he did not feel in this airy coffee shop where he had followed Charles and watched him eat a frugal breakfast. One small croissant, three dark coffees.

'I was looking for Ted Plumb, Mr Tysall.'

'I don't believe you, but you look in vain. Mr Plumb has disappeared.'

'People connected with you have that habit, sir, don't they?' Ryan remarked conversationally.

'Yes. I have to concede that. Especially wives. But Edward's disappearance is not of that kind. He will reappear, like the proverbial bad penny.'

'I see. Not like the wife, then.'

'As I said. But she reappeared too.'

Ryan sipped the coffee he had brought from his own table. In the weeks intervening since the discovery of Elisabeth Tysall, his anger had faded into a dull curiosity, blunted by a sense of futility. He required some kind of reaction from this calm face more than he needed explanations. Ryan was learning that there need not be any explanations, but it irked him, the powerful frustration flowing from a man who was beyond hurting, whose physical wounds healed with the same even speed as the rest, and he wanted above all to needle a response. He wanted to prickle and hurt like those little pieces of glass he had seen in Sarah Fortune's flat before the doors were closed against him. Not your case, DS Ryan, not anyone's case, thank you. Oh, Mr Tysall, you are beyond the law, but not beyond suffering, surely, nor quite outside all those little devils which trouble me. Besides, I'm curious. I saw you react, just the once, when you announced you had loved your wife. Perhaps you did, like I love mine. Like I loved Annie. You were hurting then; I want to see it again, you bastard. Then I shan't feel so useless. I hate you, Charles Tysall, you stinking mixed-up coward. Hate you for failing to understand you at all, and because you didn't even have the guts to kill anyone. You just made them want to do it themselves and sent me on a goosechase. You've made a monkey of me, Charles old boy, so I shall try to needle you with the unanswered question you do not seem to have considered.

'Do you have to sit here, Mr Ryan? Surely you have other duties? I don't have to speak to you.'

'Shan't keep you, sir. You don't have to answer, but I hoped you might, and if you do, it isn't for the record . . . One question in my head, the rest I can live with . . . I have to, don't I?' Charles nodded grimly. '. . . But your wife, Mr Tysall sir, Elisabeth. One thing defeats me. It seems she may have killed herself, but who,' here he paused for effect, 'buried her? Dug her in, I mean,' he added to emphasise the point.

Charles stirred and clasped long fingers together, faced luminous eyes on the broad features next to his, then turned his attention to the half-finished cup of coffee, the hand holding it trembling slightly, Ryan noticed with satisfaction.

'Buried, Mr Ryan? The sand buried her, or so I understand. A natural process: the force of water moving sand to cover an intrusion. Maybe she died in a natural hollow and was covered. No one mentioned burial, not in the terms I understand.'

'No?' said Ryan. 'Fancy that. But then you were being questioned about her disappearance, not her burial. I promise you she was buried, sir, in a bank which split open later. Buried deep, sir, or there would have been nothing left to see. There was nothing natural about the burial, sir, human hand, not nature's. You could always go and look, sir, ask the locals if you don't believe me. Someone definitely dug a hole and put her in it . . .'

'No,' said Charles, cup crashing against saucer, his voice unnaturally loud.

'Yes, they did,' said Ryan, grinning his wolfish grin, teeth on the jugular, pleased to have found the weak spot with his usually faulty instinct. 'Yes they bloody did. Sir.'

Charles's right hand clenched the edge of the table, a white scar on his dark skin glowing against the wood.

'So,' Ryan went on relentlessly, pursuing his advantage, 'she didn't just fade away, did she? Someone had their hands all over that lily-white body right at the end, and not yours either, I suppose. Poor Elisabeth, always partial to a bit of the other, wasn't she? I hope he was a good strong man, well-endowed, if you see what I mean. Gentle, passionate and sensitive with it; you know, all the things a woman could ever have wanted . . . Hope he made her scream before he buried her . . . I can see it all, one last night together on the sands: Elisabeth darling, I'll show you what a man can do . . .'

Charles choked, the pale skin blotched. He pushed at the table and half ran for the door. A waiter stepped into his path and stepped aside, seeing the rapt expression of a man on the verge of nausea. Ryan turned to watch the departure, then resumed his cold coffee, suddenly unperturbed. He sat back, smiling. All right then, no answers at all, but at least he'd kicked where it hurt, clever enough to have found the spot. More than one way to skin a cat. The bastard. He signalled the waiter.

'More coffee please. And don't worry,' he jerked his head in the direction of the door, 'I'll pay for his breakfast.' Then I'll go home and sort out the wife, he added to himself, catching his healthy reflection in a mirror on the wall.

Who had buried Porphyria, stoked her into the mud in her final, obscene abandonment? Charles arrived at the quayside during the Saturday business of mid-afternoon. The sense of holiday was gone, winter in the air, stragglers peering at boats, leaning over the sea-wall to feed the birds in the channels; then disappearing into the warmth of the cafés and amusement arcades. Fish and chip front down to the east end of the harbour reserved for fishermen, where the wind blew colder and the water was relatively empty, the tide low, leaving acres of mud and sand exposed between the swift channels of water running in between the banks. He had witnessed this scene before, never with the same fascination. Elisabeth it was who loved the sea, the peculiar mystery of this double-edged landscape, at once a bleak view of colourful earth and muddy rivulets, filling with tide, until it seemed as if the ocean had come to land leaving only the slightest trace of tufty ground. The surfaces above the channels were covered with sea-lavender, a faded but vivid carpet as far as his eye could see. Cardinal's purple, Charles thought, a pall for a coffin, but I never saw her buried.

He began to walk down the old stone steps of the quay wall and across the mud where boats lay like beached whales waiting for water. Absently, he removed his shoes before wading across the nearest channel to the opposite bank, surprised at the coldness of the water and the strength of the current pulling around his calves, flowing inland. It was all innocuous, peaceful and calm in the stiff breeze. He walked on, skirting the glittering water, feeling sand beneath his feet.

'Mister!'

There was a small boy crossing his path, walking back purposefully towards the quay, stopping Charles's progress towards the skyline of the distance.

'Mister, don't go far up the creeks, Mister. The tide's turned, see?'

He looked at the child with the contempt he had always reserved for children, angry to be disturbed by a human voice.

'What do you mean, boy? Get out of my way. There's other people further out.'

'Coming back, though, not going out. They're coming back in, don't you see?'

Charles did not understand. Nor did he wish to know the child's nonsense, but the boy stood firm, ready to elaborate his explanation. Irritably, he pushed the slight figure out of his path and walked on.

He had in his mind the picture they had shown him of where she had been found. It was imperative to discover the place now, not later or another day but now. In the slow churning thoughts which had governed his actions since the morning, there had been one burning question demanding immediate answer. Who had buried her, intervened like a lover in that last chapter of her life. He needed to discover the place. To ensure Ryan was wrong. Once he had seen the place he would surely find what he needed to know. That there had been no lecherous undertaker willed to Elisabeth's side in final infidelity or in death. There would be no peace, no sleep until he discovered that patch of sandy earth, and found it innocent. The wind was growing colder. He moved quickly.

The boy was faster, ran after him, caught up, pulled his arm. 'Don't go, Mister,' he was shouting. 'Tide'll be high today. Too much east wind. And there's nothing to see.'

Charles looked down at the anxious face, seeing nothing but obstruction, interference and sheer insolence. He raised his arm and struck the child a casual blow to the head as he would have thrashed at a branch obstructing his path. Unprepared, the boy sprawled sideways into the sand with a grunt of surprise, scrambling up within seconds, ready to fight back. But he saw that the man had moved on without a backward glance, and his own eyes narrowed as he rubbed his jaw, felt the beginnings of a dull pain and involuntary tears in his eyes. By his side, slow to protect, a small dog barked anxiously and licked his hand.

Pain turned to anger. The small guardian of the creeks saw the long figure striding into the distance, walking along the banks, following the path where he himself would have taken the boat, disappearing from view as the very last of the walkers returned back to the harbour-wall. The sky was turning ugly grey in the last of the daylight. Let him, then. Don't interfere or tell him his business.

Don't tell anyone else either.

'Come on, boy,' he said. 'Time to go home.'

'Where would we go,' said Sarah to Malcolm, 'if we did not have to live here?'

'To the sea I think. I find it soothing.'

'And dangerous.'

He put his arm round her with the familiarity of a brother. 'We can and we will change our lives. The privilege of being human. Nothing is safe, but nothing is hopeless either. Look in the mirror.' He hugged, less brotherly, turned her to face the new mirror on the wall. 'What do you see?'

'You and I against the world?'

'Yes.'

'We can do anything then,' said Sarah.

PERFECTLY PURE AND GOOD

To the esteemed
Charles William Fyfield OBE
– otherwise known as the uncle
who enriches life.
From a niece, with love.

PROLOGUE

It was an ordinary place. People lived and died in it. On Sunday mornings in summer, some of the men who lived nearest gathered on the quay to gossip. News of death was underplayed; views of life, casual. For most of them, like Stonewall's new father, who did not frequent the pubs unless driven by a louder-than-usual row indoors, the occasion was a mixed relief. All of them made it look as if they had met by accident. When they dispersed, they did not arrange to meet again, same place, same time. That would have been some kind of admission, as if they needed one another. Which they did, but could not say.

The overgrown village of Merton-on-Sea boasted a population of eight thousand, doubling in summer. The high street formed the undulating backbone of the village, flanked by alleys and uneven cottages spreading out like crooked limbs. The main thoroughfare, too narrow for the dustbin van, wound uphill away from the quay into an almost elegant square surrounding a green. Here, where the merchants in wool and grain had lived a century before, the houses were large and ponderous, governed by the Crown, Merton's only hotel. The town-cum-village, large enough to form a metropolis on this underpopulated length of the flat East Coast, fizzled out further inland beyond the council estate and the church, the last cottages giving way to rich farmland with never a hill in sight.

Merton was a conurbation which had grown on trade and

fishing, been eclipsed and grown again without the benefit of planners or preservers, so that the visitor's abiding memory was one of obstinacy rather than beauty, haphazard charm rather than style. If Merton had aspirations, they were humble, a desire for consistency rather than change, an understated pride which could never see the point in the newfangled, a sense of order which would always defy chaos and a self-sufficiency made necessary by isolation. The inhabitants were ruled by good sense, kept promises to one another, did not mind their own business and only fleeced the holiday-makers enough to make a modest living. They neither noticed nor cared how the blatant vulgarity of the quay's front marred the Victorian splendour of the rear enough to deter any serious follower of taste. The people who lived in Merton liked it the way it was.

So did the holiday-makers and holiday-home owners. Those of lesser luck or affluence, unable to face the forest of bed-and-breakfast signs, where the landladies made no concession to foreign habits, rented a caravan on the camp site a mile from town, reached on foot by the raised causeway along the sea defences. This path, hiding the road on the landward side, ran alongside the wide inlet which led to the busy public beach, the lifeboat station, the pine-woods and the miles of unadulterated sand which stretched west. Sometimes, where sea joined inlet, seals would play. There were beach huts, mostly old and crooked, flanking the woods.

At high tide, Merton became part of the sea. The inlet filled with water deep enough for the passage of small steamers which occasionally anchored, along with fishing vessels and an increasing number of pleasure craft of the less expensive variety, hobby boats rather than yachts, in keeping with Merton's obdurate lack of style. At low tide, the view altered dramatically. Gazing seaward from outside the amusement arcade, there was nothing beyond the car park but boats listing sideways and sand-banks topped with reluctant vegetation in a vista of browny-green land, full of hidden detail invisible to the eye. People parked on the quayside car park, peered down at the moored boats, saw the same flat view to the east, and ate hamburgers with onions from the arcade or fish and chips from one of three sources. In July it was something to do. Merton's entertainments were not otherwise sophisticated.

The men on the quay on Sunday mornings gathered thus only in summer: in winter you could scarcely stand out there. Male gossip was more restrained than the female kind, and only the youngest men ever dared venture a remark on the girls passing by, reserving any unkindness for strangers only. Stonewall's stepfather never felt quite comfortable standing there on the edge of the water, particularly if the tide was down and all that stretched into view was the peculiarly inviting, earth-and-sand-smelling channels leading out to the sea. He never stood there without thinking of himself as a kind of pretender, a man who kept secrets. When one of the lads gave a low wolf-whistle, he could only quiver with embarrassment, think of the woman he had watched, two years before, drunk and scarred, staggering along on her unsteady way out for a morning walk down the creeks. Or rather, he had not watched; the boy with him, little Stonewall, had watched, pointed, sniggered and been cuffed gently round the ear for his rudeness. They had watched her go down the high street, bypassing the medical centre although she looked as though she could use a doctor, then seen her grinning at her own hideous reflection, first in the shop windows, then in the water. The man still shuffled when he thought of that, shuddered when he thought of what happened next after they'd gone out in the boat. Poor Stonewall had hated the water; he had to be forced to learn because no one who lived as close to it as they did could afford to shy away.

'Nice day for it,' one of the men would always remark, never specifying further and never being asked, while Stonewall's stepfather wished that the sea would come back and obscure the vision of his mind's eye. First that woman with her cloud of red hair, Mrs Tysall he had later learned, looking so drunk and so tired, teetering out over the muddy sand in her unsuitable shoes, a real townie; and then the same woman, without shoes and without life, lying with her hands twisted in the sea heather up at the far end of the creeks, her mouth full of sand, her red hair damp and matted, a smell beginning to rise from her, still mainly the smell of the sea, which reminded him of sex. Saw her living one day, found her dead the next when out on another outing with that miserable kid, Stonewall, that parcel of skinny, asthmatic baggage which came alongside his beautiful widowed mum, and had to be taught to understand the tide.

Stonewall would scream whenever he was put in a boat and rowed up the creeks to find a place where the water formed safe and shallow pools, but once there, the child changed tack completely and became calm, ready to play and sing to himself for hours, leaving the man he would not yet call Dad free to dig for the lugworms he needed for bait. The relief when Stonewall stopped crying was always tremendous. The crying, a breathless keening, always made his stepfather sick. If he did not get this boy right, the whole edifice of his marriage would crumble, he knew it like he knew the time of day and he knew these creeks. Silence down here, a sense of contentment and the brink of a breakthrough with the boy; peace.

Until he had turned to one side, seen that red-haired lump with her long brown legs spread and her heavy skirt plastered with mud. Two years of Sundays had passed and he could still feel the panic now, like a mouthful of salt water. Remembered himself thinking, The silly bitch, how could she do this to a boy? Lying there, obscene in death, her head half embedded in the bank, her hands raised above, twisted into the heather as if to anchor herself there. Waiting for a child to find her and begin the screaming nightmares all over again.

No Merton-born man travelled ill-equipped and, besides, he had come prepared to dig for bait. Inside fifteen furious minutes, using his spade and closing his ears to the sound of sloppy sand on dead flesh, he had buried her, right there in the depths of the bank, just before the boy came back from the pool. He had meant no harm, he had meant for the best. Let someone else find her; someone unburdened by an hysterical child and a heavily pregnant wife. Let the tide hide this red-haired bitch here until tomorrow when he was at work and the boy was safe. Let it hide her, preferably for ever.

From that day on, though, Stonewall had stopped his screaming, took to the creeks like a duck. It seemed that some god somewhere approved.

'Found another body, they did, so I heard, off Stookey,' one of the men said, covering a gap in conversation, while a thin thread of smoke from his cigarette drifted upwards. Stonewall's dad jangled the coins in his pockets to hide his own discomfiture. The friendly coast yielded three or four bodies a year, swept from God knows where. Mostly men, overboard from a tramp steamer, big men, rarely identified, the homeless of the sea. A corpse was always a matter of remark, but hardly news any more and never in front of the children. Sometimes it was difficult to tell how long a man had been in the water or rotting in the sand where he was found. Mrs Charles Tysall had taken a whole year to surface, as far as anyone knew. Unlike the indigent sailors, she had been identified, her death the subject of speculation, her strange reappearance the stuff of long, public-house and hairdressing-shop debate. Stonewall's stepfather had never said a thing: he had been either too wise or too shocked. A body was only a body. He had his own kin to look after.

The guilt only lingered on the Sabbath, when he thought of that woman's husband coming back to look at her after she was found. Stricken by grief, walking out over the sands to see where she had lain, never coming back. She would have been a beautiful woman once, before she had acquired that dreadful, lacerated face. Someone must have loved her, ached for her, yearned for her in the year she had lain buried before the freak storm broke the bank and sicked her up.

That Charles Tysall had indeed loved her in his vile obsessive way, was something his wife Elisabeth had never doubted, but the nature of the love had been as cruel as the tide, requiring the same complete possession of everything it touched, punishing insubordination with violence. She had played for attention, misunderstood the nature of the madness, flaunted her red hair and her own perfection. Therefore, in complete accordance with his own logic, it had been entirely justifiable to beat her into submission, beginning with the face.

The men on the quay knew nothing of this, then or now. Nor what Elisabeth had thought while lying there with her hands self-imprisoned among the heather, waiting for the pills and the gin to work and hoping this would be revenge on him, and then thinking, too late, of what she might have left. Thinking of how she should not be doing this, dying without a whimper or a warning. It was so unfair to whoever followed. She, who had never been a friend to women, felt suddenly and sharply for her own kind, knew with terrible certainty what she had begun. Without her, Charles would simply find another obsession, some other red-haired pet to torment. Elisabeth murmured a prayer for her successor, let the thought of her slide away, closed her eyes, waited for the sea, slipped at last into the oblivion she had craved for days. Waited for the tide and never felt it.

A body was only a body, the man on the quay thought again. Since that woman had died, and then punished him by coming back, he had acquired twins and his wife was pregnant again. It was only because he so loved his own woman that he felt guilt for that other husband. The guilt was wasted, had he known. As the sea had swept over the slumbering form of Elisabeth Tysall, her husband Charles lay on a couch in their extravagant London home, reading his favourite poet, Browning, remembering his wife in the days when she was perfectly pure, obedient and good.

> . . . Happy and proud; at last I knew
> Porphyria worshipped me: surprise
> Made my heart swell, and still it grew . . .

I love you, my Porphyria, he had told himself. Did you not know? Come back, before I find another.

One death alters nothing and everything. As Elisabeth Tysall's hair floated out beneath the water, the erstwhile landlord of her holiday cottage felt the first intimations of mortality. In a large house half a mile beyond the end of the quay in the opposite direction from the public beach, Mr Henry Pardoe, entrepreneur, self-made man of frugal habits and large pretensions, played Scrabble with his timid little wife and found, to his amazement, he enjoyed it. She let him win, of course, something he half realized but blocked the full knowledge. He rubbed his chest where the faint, but nagging pain was a constant reminder to him to make a will sooner rather than later, although he did not seriously believe in death as a concept and was damned if he'd pay that old rogue Ernest Matthewson his London rates the way he had always done in the past. Daylight robbery. Mouse would help him draft a will. He looked at her faded prettiness with affection.

Life went on as the hungry tide came back through the channels and covered the earth. The coastline shifted with the seasons, flooded at high tide, drained by the low. Which meant that everything was the same, no matter who lived and died.

The men on the quay broke ranks. They made laconic farewells, drifted indoors for the innocent pleasure of the Sunday meal.

CHAPTER ONE

Malcolm Cook, advocate for the Crown, legal if cynical vigilante against injustice, was dark, lean, thirty-five. The only weight he carried was a surfeit of knowledge. He knew more about man's inhumanity to man, and rather less about domestic harmony, than he liked. While his work was merely the reflection of human perfidy, his own reflection was something he tried to avoid. An aversion to mirrors often sent him out of doors wearing odd socks.

This morning he could not ignore his own image as he shaved, and as usual, felt himself flinching. A mirror was a cruel object. The contrast between himself as he had been before, a grossly fat clown of a man, and the thing he was now, streamlined by his own efforts into the shape of a marathon runner, was a sight which occasionally amused him. He would shake his head, smiling, expecting the old self to return, knowing the new one was merely a figment which did not fit the description of handsome, however often it was applied. These days, the contrast he saw in his own expression was more immediate. He looked old and worried, like his adoptive father in the throes of illness. The comparison between this and the person who sang through his morning ablutions was one which wounded him. He was losing something, and with it, all his fragile self-esteem. It felt like losing his teeth.

'Get down, you silly girl,' he muttered without taking his eyes

away from the mirror. At least the dog, with her constant need
to be close, never wavered in her affections, followed him from
bedroom to bathroom like a silky, red shadow, so grateful for the
sight of him she could not stay away. It did not do to make comparisons between this affectionate creature and Sarah, or to
hope the gratitude of the one would inspire the same devotion in
the other, but he made the comparison all the same with rueful
humour and a slap to his own wrist. After all, he had saved them
both. A pair of red-haired beauties, both in need of a champion.

Who looks after me? Malcolm thought with a sudden wave of
self-pity, which he suppressed only when he saw to his horror
how his eyes filled with tears in the privacy of the bathroom.
Quite right to avoid mirrors: he had always been too emotional
for a man, even a fat man. His father, Ernest Matthewson, had
said so. Ernest had exercised the right to speak his mind since
the day he had married Malcolm's mother and become the
benign but tyrannical influence he was. Strange how roles
altered themselves when no one was looking. Who looked after
whom these days was a moot point. Ernest Matthewson, senior
partner, a man of old-fashioned principles and terrifying,
irrational loyalty to clients of the firm, no matter how frightful
they were, was also the indulgent employer of Malcolm's Sarah,
but his powers had waned into frail irascibility in the last twelve
months. Anyone serving a client like Charles Tysall deserved to
be ill.

Malcolm snorted, waving his hand at the mirror. There was
nothing to envy about his father's career. Ernest had the sumptuous office and the salary to match, but Malcolm felt he had a
certain moral advantage. It was not one which could ever make
him oblivious to Ernest's good opinion. Malcolm loved Ernest,
Ernest loved Malcolm; they were stuck with it, even if they rowed
like enemies to hide an attachment they simply could not avoid.

He might despise my relative poverty, Malcolm thought, but
at least I am licensed to tell the truth. And at least I can sneak my
dog into my office without anyone worrying about the furnish-
ings.

Nor did he have to care today about the fact that it was too late and getting later, and he did not give a damn. The dog's lead evaded detection. Must be in Sarah's flat, that's where it was; she had been the last to walk the beast. Malcolm stroked the spaniel's silky head, felt the warmth behind the ears, the thump of her tail. At least there was some consistency in his life.

They walked downstairs from his spacious attic in the huge Victorian terrace on the side of the park, round to the front door, inside with the key and up one floor to another door where a small brass plate announced 'Sarah Fortune'. Somehow in the intervening year, they had lived between the two places, tending more towards his, especially in the early days. That was during the time when her flat was being cleared up, to put it mildly. The contrast between then and now hit him again as he opened the door. There was a new mirror, winking at the end of the hall, new carpet on the floor, a mushroom colour in a hall lined with pictures, all slightly dusty. He could never forget what had happened here, even on a fine morning like this when the sunlight sanitized the memory.

The trust of the dog was infinite. She never growled on crossing the threshold: it was Malcolm who did that. She should have murmured at least, he thought resentfully; she was badly hurt in here, but then she has nothing of which to be ashamed. She does not suppress memory; she simply forgets everything but the next meal. It was a knack Sarah should learn too.

There were a few new marks on the clean paint by the kitchen door. Spilt coffee, tribute to Sarah's domestic carelessness, at odds with her flair for making things beautiful, translating junk into elegance. Coffee stains, or wine, not blood. Malcolm was beginning to understand that he might be stuck with the memory of the blood, however much he encouraged it to fade. Each time he came here he felt as if he was retracing his own fleeting steps, following the dog up to this apartment where she had led him twelve months ago, inspired by her mischievous curiosity. Disobedient dog, running amok at the end of a late-night run, cannoning into the insecure front door, up the stairs, leaving him no choice but to follow, cursing her.

No, don't remember it. Memories were for old men. Past accidents, old horrors, should be recognised, of course, put into the scheme of things so that life could continue as soon as possible. Too much analysis only increased the weight of the baggage and both he and Sarah carried plenty of that already. Malcolm sighed, resigned to a mental ritual. OK, run through the facts on record, including those which embarrassed him personally, as if explaining them briefly to a stranger, then put them back on the shelf where they belonged. It was his way of dealing with it. So. Charles Tysall, Dad's super-rich handsome bastard of a client, got involved with Sarah, whom he met through Dad's firm. No, correction, not involved, obsessed. Had this fixation, see, with red hair. Sarah gives him the cold-shoulder, so he breaks in here one night, waits for her. There is a fight in which a large mirror is broken. Sarah falls on the glass, has lots of nasty little injuries all over, though not on her face, God knows how. Led by his daft dog, he, Malcolm, had intervened and pursued the attacker out into the park, and this was the bit he most loathed to recall. Bringing the man down like a Rottweiler after cattle, hitting him far too hard and too long for the purpose, and, oddly, enjoying it. Malcolm hated violence, had never known he was so capable of it.

It had been a cruel way to bring Sarah into his life, he would concede for the record, but since he loved her with every ounce of his sinewy frame, the means of this savage introduction were less important than the ends.

The dog's lead was in the kitchen. Malcolm found it and then took a quick tour of the rooms, guilty again, looking for the negative, for some signs that she was not packing up and leaving. She could not do that now, not with all the exclusive knowledge which bound them together. Knowledge of Charles Tysall, not only as that rich and privileged businessman-thief, whom Malcolm had pursued with all the futility of the law long before it was made apparent to Sarah what else he was. Bugger the past. It was the future Malcolm wanted.

The dog froze at Malcolm's flank, leaning against him. Red hairs from her long coat already decorated the trousers of his suit. Footsteps, upstairs in the flat above, harmless, unhurried. They both relaxed. The dog shook herself; he felt inclined to copy. Dog lived in the present; so should they all. Charles Tysall was dead. He might have mutilated his own wife and driven her to suicide, then turned his attentions to Sarah, but now he was dead. Dead as an old potato chip.

That was all right then. Perhaps all himself and Sarah needed was a holiday. Brisk sea air, that sort of thing.

I am only an ordinary man, Malcolm told himself. An ordinary man who tries to be decent and honourable. I should not have memories like this, complications like this. I only want to love and be loved.

Back outside in the sunshine of summer, crossing the park to the road, he made himself think of sea air, but his thoughts only shifted back. That was the problem with reliving memory, even in the tidy way he did: it infected everything, like rancid oil in cooking. He could not think of sun, sea and sand without thinking back to Charles. How the man who was the closest thing to evil he had ever encountered went on being so, even in death. Only Charles Tysall, moving unit of harm, could choose to despoil some innocent seaside resort by committing suicide in it, just as his wife had done. Had the man never heard of preservation?

Life, Malcolm thought to himself, is a bitch. If he could ever have thought of Sarah as a bitch, it would be easier.

Watching the dog lolloping away, he began to laugh. The laughter was the result of suddenly seeing himself introducing Sarah to others. This is my wife Sarah. We met in the hall, beneath the mirror, through an extraordinary set of coincidences you would find impossible to believe and so do I.

The word 'wife' stuck in his throat. He wanted to be a husband; take this wonderful creature and make an honest woman of her. Laughter ceased. Oh yes, he told himself, you can lead a dream to water, but you cannot make it drink.

Sarah Fortune had been taught by her mother never to complain. She had also been warned that there was an element of indecency in her nature; that her energy was a nuisance and that a woman's lot was not happy. Parental ambition had amounted to a kind of Calvinism, a constant push in the direction of career over frivolity which dictated that Sarah keep her nose to the grindstone and her red hair in ugly plaits until she was qualified to earn a living. With the double standard of a mother, Sarah's had still wanted her daughters wed, the sooner the better; wanted them free but still suppressed, clever but stupid, independent but biddable. By damning with faint praise, she nurtured in Sarah a profound sense of worthlessness which secured obedience to all expectations. The girl passed examinations, became a lawyer, acquired another as a husband and everything seemed well, until the point when he died behind the wheel of his car, distracted by recent sex, not with Ms Fortune but her sister. He was a lazy opportunist who went for the nearest. In one fell swoop, red-haired Sarah lost trust, a spouse, a sibling and all her mother's values, as well as the foetus she carried at the time.

After a period of recovery in which she remained, as always, a reluctant but efficient professional, she set about shedding the work ethic as easily as she shed her clothes, an exercise she could complete with incredible speed and efficiency. Ms Fortune recognised no moral principles other than thou shalt be kind, few instincts which were not positive and no incontrovertible fact other than that men always leave in the end.

She retained that bitter sense of worthlessness, saw all the accidents of her life as a reflection of it. Sarah could no more believe that someone truly loved her than she could have flown over the moon. She saw sex as an enjoyable necessity, love as a variety of claustrophobia, a fine deceit, a trap. She was warm as fire, generous to a fault, occasionally as cold as ice. She took nothing for granted.

Miss Fortune, at thirty-three, was contemplating the dreaded moment of saying goodbye to Malcolm Cook for a number of reasons which made eminent sense in the middle of the night, rather less in the bright sunlight of a July morning. He had loved her from afar for two years, at closer quarters for one, saved her life and continued to offer the kind of single-minded devotion he himself received from his dog. He was fuller of natural goodness than a bowl of cornflakes and it drove Sarah beyond distraction. For one, she knew she wasn't worthy of that; for two, she did not want to receive what she knew she could not give; for three, he would be better off without her; fourthly, she was already too far involved with his family; fifth, she felt like a prisoner and was not the stuff of a good wife.

These were the reasons she counted on her fingers as she reversed her car into the wall and heard the back wing crunch against concrete. Each reason had an element of truth. Malcolm would demolish them like a row of ninepins, argue with the full force of his finer feelings and his enlightened compassion. Finally, he might threaten her with ownership of the dog. Sarah was feeling sufficiently liberated by the satisfying sound of mashed metal to recover her sense of humour. Perhaps that was all she wanted in the first place, not a lover who lived in the same building, whose father was her employer, but a dog.

The car was easily the flashiest of Sarah's possessions, a misguided bonus from the firm to keep her happy. The engine leapt into willing life at the merest touch, rather like Malcolm. From the outside it looked as if things had fallen into her lap. Which they had in the last year, with such crushing weight she reminded herself of a shopping trolley and it made the same sense as giving the world tour to a small, red squirrel.

Ernest Matthewson, close to retirement, inhabited a huge office decorated by his wife, which was why he could not get rid of all the humming birds climbing up the blinds and fluttering amongst the fabric of the chairs which were intended to make him feel thoroughly comfortable, a reminder of how he lived at home. Cushioned, catered for, resplendent, like a pasha on a throne, with a loving woman who bashed the heart and the ulcer by alternate feeding and starving of same. He considered the dreams of slender youth, currently advanced to closeted luxury, weight control, client accounts, computers, goodwill, diplomacy and language. Sarah Fortune had been his choice: he had interviewed her years since, when she was freshly widowed, but he couldn't pretend she was partnership material, not in today's grey world. She was also the girl his wife favoured as daughter-in-law.

'I disagree,' he said aloud, banging the desk, wincing. 'All right, ALL RIGHT! I still disagree!'

So: Sarah might well have turned his fat and isolated stepson into some semblance of a human being and brought him back into the fold, but one look at the child was enough to show the liaison would be a disaster. Women envied, youths simpered, clients salivated at the sight of Sarah, and although Ernest, out of respect to his age and his fragile health, did not follow suit, he considered his protégée as a jewel beyond price who belonged, for safety's sake, locked inside a watch. He also loved her dearly in a manner which made him feel only slightly treacherous for hoping she would go away, even though a morning when her feet went by his office without pausing was a bleak day indeed. Having made his announcements to an empty room, Ernest listened.

She usually fell at the bottom step opposite his door, where the bad carpet curled against the good leading away from where important clients trod in quality shoes. The worn patch caught the headlong rush of her steps whenever she was blinded by the armful of flowers for her room and the minuscule briefcase containing some pretence of overnight work. As she tripped, she swore loudly. The sound of absent-minded obscenities made Ernest curl with laughter. He did not like to think what they did for his errant son.

'Oh shit a fucking brick. Not again.' She spoke it in her low, musical voice, like a person reciting poetry. Ernest flung open his door, pretending to be angry, terrified in case she should be gone.

'What's wrong with you, woman? You do that every time and you always swear. I don't know. What's the matter with your vocabulary?'

'What's wrong with your carpet, more to the point? Does this too, every time. I've just put a dent in the company car, nobody else's motor involved, you understand. Just some fucking concrete pillar.' She was standing there, grinning like a recently fed cat with half-clean paws, every inch of her unsuitable for the office of a solicitor of the supreme court, more like a bouncer at the Hippodrome if only she wasn't so tiny and so highly coloured. The colour came from the freckled skin and the brilliant red hair. No one could say she dressed like a siren, in a perfect camel brown dress, but there was something about that great, wide belt of soft, tan leather which made her look as edible as the bacon sandwich she proffered in his direction, shrouded in greasy paper, the whole gift presented with a grin.

'Yours,' she said. 'Oh, yes, and the racing pages. How's things?'

Ernest relaxed. His large stomach growled and sagged like a parachute landing. Sarah always made a man mindful of his girth, first to suck it in, then to let it out in glorious relaxation.

'Terrible,' he said. 'Awful, really. Come in. I've got a case for you. Should take you out of London for the summer. Come in.' The words came out of his mouth before he could stop them and he turned away abruptly, winded by the devilish inspiration which had been incubating for many days and only now came into words. It was like delivering a baby with a knife. He was saddened too, at this instinctive combination of wanting her out of the way while knowing he would miss her. There was something about the effect she had had on their late client, Charles Tysall, to say nothing of his stepson, her ability to make strong men putty, along with something else which smacked of love and a profound suspicion.

'Only if you want,' he added hurriedly, sitting to hide his confusion, lunging towards the bacon sandwich. Monday was always one of Mrs Matthewson's sensible days, Fridays were better.

'I'm only suggesting you leave for a while to save me from this,' Ernest mumbled with his mouth full, feeling the decadent bacon grease creep down his chin. 'You're not good for my insides.'

'The bread's wholemeal,' said Sarah, tranquilly, as if that made all the difference. 'Full of fibre.' She never had believed in diet, ate anything which was not moving. Looked at him with that complete acceptance she granted the human race. What she thought behind those great big eyes he never questioned for fear of being told. Looking at his fidgeting, she thought how it was just as well that she and Malcolm and Malcolm's lovely mother had conspired to subvert Ernest's post bag and save him from the worst demands, as well as the hateful revelations, of his clients. Also, how she and Malcolm had managed to excuse her absence last year by saying she had suffered an accident. She was a gifted liar. Making him ooh! and aghh! about the effects of a broken windscreen had been far better for his explosive ulcer and fragile heart than telling him the truth about a client. Charles Tysall had done enough damage, most of it still unmended. Some people needed the truth. Others needed saving from their own beliefs that all clients were good chaps. Ernest was one of the latter. He might not have been once, but now his health made him so.

'Tell me about this case, then. I need amusement.'

'Very important client,' Ernest mumbled again.

'It can't be, or you wouldn't be sending me.'

Ernest sighed. 'Important by my standards, not by those of the partnership. Clients I've had for a long time.' He meant clients not eligible for the seduction of his junior partners, who rubbed grey-suited shoulders with bankers and accountants, captains of industry and Government officials, drinking mineral water at lunch-time, for God's sake, not a human being among them. Ernest was well aware of being slightly redundant in the new generation, retained for the weight of his age and the number of nasty facts he knew about others, but Sarah had no chance. She was tolerated in the attics of the low-earning litigation department because someone had to do the odds and ends. The someone was preferably a woman without ambition. No partner would miss her for the summer. None of them guessed how valuable she was.

'Well, if these clients are important to you, I'll make them important to me. Why out of town? When do I go? And what nasty thing do you want me to do?'

Ernest nearly fell out of his chair. For an idea with such a difficult, if spontaneous conception, this was all growing suspiciously fast. Not that she was usually unamenable to suggestion; the passivity hid the obstinacy of a mule, just like her smile hid depths of despair and a strange knowledge beyond her years, touching the parts other women did not reach. Too late, Ernest remembered Charles Tysall and where he had died.

'A family estate', he began, 'needs sorting out. By the sea. You're always saying you like the sea.'

'I know nothing about probate. Or the sea.'

'What's that got to do with anything? Look, we're only talking about a family who need their heads knocking together. Just stick around, work out what they want, get a draft agreement on who should have what ... the boffins and the Court of Protection can do the rest.'

Sarah dusted crumbs off her skirt. Ernest so admired the way she ate, like a delicate wolf.

'I haven't got the faintest idea what you're talking about. You'd better explain,' she said. He took a deep breath, prepared to mix fact with fiction in order to make the prospect more appealing.

'Large house in the country, right? No, not an ancestral mansion, but plenty of land, and ... no, I'm not going to tell you why the estate is as big as it is. You can let that titillate the imagination and find out for yourself. It needs an entirely fresh mind, so the less you know the better. Family consists of two sons, one daughter, eighteen to thirty-four, I think, all of them at war. Why? Dad died two years ago, left the whole caboodle to his wife for life, and then,' he rummaged on the desk, flicked the pages of a grease-stained photocopy, '. . . I quote, "to all my children in whatever shares my wife should decide". Perfectly poisonous will; he should have asked me to draft it, ungrateful sod. I did everything else. He must have been out of his mind.'

'And was he?'

'Probably, but not provably. The point is, his wife is. Off her rocker, barmy, barking, out of her tree.' He liked to mix metaphors. 'She's never going to be in a position to make a valid will. If she dies intestate, disaster. Terrible tax implications. The children aren't exactly carving each other up, I think they have straws between their teeth, or would it be sand? Needs an outside mind to construct an acceptable arrangement, working out who'll get what and when. Then they can run their lives peacefully until the old lady pops her clogs and even then, the transition will be easy.'

Sarah rose gracefully. 'You need an estate planner, not me,' she said.

'I need a litigation expert who knows how to make people avoid litigation. I think you've got to be on the spot, hopeless otherwise. They'll put you up, always a spare cottage, they rent them out, saves expenses.' He was full of admiration for himself: everything dovetailed so neatly without him thinking at all. In fact, he rarely indulged deep thought.

She was standing over his desk, reached forward and pinched his cheek.

'Wake up, Ernest, will you? This is me, Sarah. You must detest these clients, or you wouldn't consider foisting me on them simply because you would like me to be a hundred miles away from Malcolm.'

'Sarah, nothing was further . . .' He was blushing like a schoolboy caught smoking in the lavatory, and she was smiling like an indulgent teacher who was going to forgive him.

'Nothing was closer to your mind, Ernest dear. Don't worry about it, please, but don't treat me like a fool. I may not deserve much, but I deserve better than that. Of course you're right to think I'm all wrong for Malcolm in the long run. I know that; he doesn't. Yet. It may take him some time. Now, do we understand one another?'

He could have wept. She sat down again.

'Don't fret, Uncle Ernest, please don't. Worry's infinitely worse for the ulcer than a bacon sandwich.' She looked at the grease-stained photocopy of a badly typed will. 'But is sending me to this particular part of East Anglia a clause in the master plan? Same village, I see, where Charles Tysall walked off and drowned, mimicking the actions of his wife the year before. You want to punish me or something?'

'No, no, I promise you . . . Sarah, I swear!'

'You've just told me not to do that. I believe you, but if you'll excuse the pun, I thought you might have wanted me to lay the odd ghost.'

Malcolm Cook did not have his stepfather's shrewd business acumen, nor did he think his life was ruined by the omission. He considered that less pay for more enlightenment was a good bargain. As for the rest of his limitless kindness, he had learned his compassion as well as his tolerance on the sharp learning curve of his own loneliness. The metamorphosis from laughable clown to thin athlete also made him an incurable optimist, most of the time, although not on this particular evening. 'You don't know anything about women,' Ernest had warned him, a truism liberally applied to the whole male sex, but one which was, in his case, less accurate than usual. Malcolm's former fatness had only preserved a habit of celibacy, not innocence, making him a confidant rather than a practitioner, without rendering him naïve. So had childhood illness. Even a once-fat man, helplessly in love and struggling to disguise it, knows when he is being abandoned.

There was no point in going back over old ground trying to

work out where one or the other had failed, no point arguing; no purpose in analysing performance and saying 'if only'. He knew you cannot make a person stay if they want to go any more than you can make a tiger a truly tame beast, and with Sarah the analogy was sound since she had that sleekness, with none of the ability to maul or scratch. Nothing had been said, neither in her flat (where she hid her shopping from him), nor in his, where he had nursed her more than a little following the ministrations of obsessive Charles Tysall. They had survived a hot summer of healing wounds, a companionable winter of hot toddies, laughter and warm blankets and he had thought she was his for ever.

He should have known how no man is allowed to assume anything. In the spring, he could feel her straining the leash, like the dog guided away from the daffodils. He could feel the numbness of loss from the moment of realisation when he began vainly arming himself. He must not carp, he must not complain, he must not. He could never go back to what he was before and if he loved her, he must let her go with grace, make himself run into the distance without complaint.

'Where the hell have you been?' he said peevishly as she let herself in at eight o'clock. So much for grace. Grace is a virtue, virtue is a grace, Grace is a dirty girl who will not wash her face.

'Your father sent us some wine,' she said, humbly. 'He and I went out for a drink.'

There was a pause when both of them turned to the task in hand, she to taking off her jacket and making a fuss of the dog whose greetings took precedence over all other formalities, he to watching rice boil, while both privately, desperately, considered whether they could get away with another evening of pretending nothing was happening. Ready to eat and fill the air with smells and brittle conversation, drink to cure emotional indigestion, pray that neither would say anything real. She came into the kitchen, followed by dog.

'Your father has a job for me. Norfolk, somewhere.' She was ultra casual, foraging for food. 'So I'll be away.' She shrugged her shoulders as if she had no choice. 'Don't know how long.'

Malcolm stirred the rice unnecessarily, hiding his face in the steam.

'That'll suit you fine, won't it? You must have persuaded him. No one litigates in Norfolk. What does he want you to do, go and dig up Charles Tysall? Pay your last respects?'

'Charles was buried in London. Your father gave me the client's address. You know how vague he is on that subject. I honestly don't think he even registered it was anywhere near . . . Old client, he says.' He turned on her, his face hot, his throat choking and his eyes full of salt and water.

'My own father, who professes to love me, enters the conspiracy! Well, well, well. As if you needed help to escape. You've been detaching yourself from me for three months, only you don't know how to say. Am I right?' He tried to keep his voice light.

'Right.'

'Don't say sorry, will you?' He poured a glass of wine with a shaking hand, then stuck a piece of kitchen roll near his eyes as if it was the heat which troubled him. The day had been long and hot; he was hungry.

'I would say sorry since I mean it, but not if you'd prefer I didn't. Listen, Malcolm, it's nothing you've done or haven't done: I love you and I owe you, but I can't breathe.'

He was an articulate man, a large, kind man who liked to cook, a patron of defenceless animals, a natural lover, and all he wanted to do was hit her. He caught that look of mute terror in her eyes and heard the warning growl of the dog before he knew that one arm was bunching the front of her dress in his fist, while the other arm was raised, ready to inflict the futile blow which would never connect.

Malcolm slumped, let his arms drop to his sides.

'I love you, Sarah,' he said. 'I love you to pieces. I'd never hurt you.'

'I'd better go,' she said, the terror still in her eyes.

'Yes, you'd better. Just go.'

She went with door closing softly behind her, the dog pawing against a panel already ruined with her claws. Malcolm's appetite for anything went with her. The dog slunk back and pressed her wet nose into his groin, waiting for him to be pleased. Instead he pushed her away with his hand so tightly around her muzzle she began to protest and he stroked her instead. Couldn't hit a dog, could have hit a woman, and the mere temptation to violence was a kind of death of anything in which he believed.

It was finished. She had left him ashamed.

Mrs Ernest Matthewson dumped a tray on the table in front of her husband and watched fondly as he struggled from the depths of the plump sofa to stare at it.

'What's this?' he barked.

'Poached cod. With samphire.'

'Samphire? Seaweed?'

'Full of iron, dear. Better than spinach.'

'It looks disgusting. Do I get potato?'

She wagged a finger, roguishly.

'Not today. You've been drinking. Eat it up and I'll get you pudding.'

'And what might that be?'

'Low-fat yoghurt.' He groaned, shot her a murderous look which turned into a smile.

'You remember the Pardoes?' he asked, looking at the sea-weed.

'Oh yes. Awful great house on the coast somewhere. A long drive from here. We used to go and see them quite a lot, didn't we? In the days when we had to do that kind of thing.' Mrs Matthewson shuddered. She left home as rarely as possible, did not rue the days when loyalty dictated dreadful social visits to clients.

'Didn't he make his fortune out of socks, or something? Tried to become a country gentleman, didn't know how? All sorts of fads and all sorts of mistresses? Bought half the village he lived in? Vulgar taste?'

Ernest nodded, holding her eyes and taking a long slug of her wine. He did not underestimate his ever-loving wife, but there were times when she was easier to distract than divert. Reminiscence was the cue.

'I saw that, Ernest. Don't think I didn't. You know, I can't work out why Jennifer Pardoe put up with all her husband's playing around.' She glared at him, as if infidelity was infectious. 'Such tolerance that woman had, such marvellous, I don't know what, qualities. Serene, somehow. She was called Mouse, wasn't she, because she was like one, small and brownish, pretty, ineffectual little thing, you had to like her. Sympathize, I mean. No one took any notice of her.'

Ernest shuffled and coughed. His wife's memory always amazed him.

'One son came out good, daughter a bit of a dope, nice girl, other son, well he was a nasty little thing, always playing nasty practical jokes. Luck of the draw. You told me it all came all right in the end, with Mouse and her husband, didn't you? He had that gold hair I'm so fond of. He seemed to fall for her all over again. Then he died. By God, you lot take it out on us. We damn well earn our pound of flesh.' She patted her stomach, comfortably.

Ernest cleared his throat, waved his hand and grasped her glass like a man in need. She did not protest. He tried to swig with nonchalance, couldn't quite manage it.

'I'm sending Sarah there. Mouse – was Jennifer her real name? – well, she's gone mad. Got to get the estate sorted before she dies too. Sarah's the right woman to do it.'

Mrs Matthewson lowered the second glass she had poured while this information was passed with a vague hesitation, incapable of fooling her for a minute.

'What are you planning, Ernest? Why on earth send Sarah away from our Malcolm? Someone else could have gone. You could have sorted it all out from here. Who'll cook his meals?'

'Good God, woman, you don't think Sarah cooks his meals, do you?' he roared, putting into his voice all his own guilt and his dislike of the fish.

'She does other things, then,' said Mrs Matthewson defensively. Ernest sniggered.

'I'll bet she does.'

'That's enough, Ernest.' His bark was worse than hers, but not as bad as her bite. She threw back her wine as if it was water, allowing the silence of her disapproval to sink in. After a pause, she went on.

'You don't know anything about Sarah and Malcolm. You know much less than me. Mind you, he always tells me everything's fine. Such a liar, that boy. I suppose he takes after you. Send her away? You must be out of your mind—'

'Sarah will sort out the Pardoes,' Ernest interrupted more firmly, recognising a mutual capacity to lie. 'She's a catalyst, she analyses dreams. And,' Ernest continued as if his wife had never spoken, 'she'll never marry our boy, you know. Never in a million years. No grandchildren there.' This was a cunning move.

'How do you know?' she wailed. 'She led him out of the wilderness and she loves him too, in her own way. You just can't bear the fact she knows too much about you. And the wretched clients. Oh Ernest, what have you done? What have you done?'

'I've done nothing!' he shouted. 'She wanted to go! She wants the sea!'

She hesitated for a full minute.

'Charles Tysall's dead, isn't he?'

He lost his rag and his skin went red.

'Of course he is! Dead for a year! Wife dead for two, though it took them a year to find her. What more do you want, woman? Sarah Fortune's as strong as an ox.'

She held her peace.

Sarah had long since bought the new mirror for the hall of her flat. Like the old, it caught the reflection of herself as she entered, greeted her at the end of the corridor on to which the door opened, revealed her with the cunning of an old enemy. The replacement of the mirror was supposed to be therapy, a positive step towards putting things back the way they were before the former mirror was broken. A gesture to prove it was not all her own fault, as everything else was. Sarah Fortune knew she was beyond redemption. Leaning out of the window with her arms on the wrought-iron balcony, staring into the night, imagining the sound of the sea and the wind in the trees, waiting for thunder, tears and some sensation of liberation, she was feeling nothing, apart from a desire to run back up to his flat, demand entry and say, I didn't mean that, can we just go on as before? An impulse so overpowering she had found herself halfway there, twice. Then crept back, regretting as much as anything the failure to explain, the sheer cowardice. But if she had said, It isn't as if I don't love you, as well as revere everything about you, he would have laughed and said, How can you love and leave at the same time? And she would say, Because I cannot be what you want me to be and in the end you would hate me for that.

He did not imprison; he was too kind. At least not with stone walls or shackles, only with constancy; the terrible patience of waiting for her to arrive and the unspoken denial of what she had been and what she was. She saw him come out of the big front door at midnight, dressed in a track suit, the dog alongside. Jogging away across the park, running for company, his nightly ritual. One lover, the best and most honest of them all, padding across the brown grass, back into his world. And she to hers.

Only if she put her hands very firmly over her own ears, could she conjure up the remembrance of dreams, the instincts of courage, and the sound of the sea.

CHAPTER TWO

There was no fence to separate the small figure of Stonewall Jones from the scrubby garden into which he stared, or from the greenish, mud-coloured land which stretched from behind his thin back into the distant strip of gold which meant the sea. From his small height, he could see everything he wanted. When he was as still as now, he merged with any landscape, a colourless little boy, whose pale orange hair corresponded with the freckles all over his skin and the eyes which seemed merely to reflect, without any shade of their own. Stonewall suited his nickname. Others were called Jack or John and came to fit a more aggressive mould even at eleven years old, but Stonewall blended effortlessly into ageless scenery as a born observer. No one noticed him at home any more either. He had once been the apple of his mother's eye, but that was when he was a baby. She had new babies now and there was no room. He was good for nothing but hanging round in school holidays, coming up here with the bait he dug twice weekly for Edward Pardoe and which he had just delivered to the kitchen at the back.

'Baah,' he breathed. 'Kchoo, coo, coo.'

Stonewall desperately wanted to be loved, even though his own habits of silence discouraged affection. There was no way to express his own love for the sheep in the garden except by making a sound like a pigeon. Birds he could magic from the skies, lugworms from the sea, but none of it helped a boy who was looking for a dog. Sal had never behaved; she had been a russet-coloured flirt, skittish as a sandpiper, which was why she could have been spirited away so easily by a thief. Stonewall was quietly craving possession of this placid sheep for something which would love him unreservedly and mutually. He also liked the house, simply because it was more than half a mile from all other houses and looked as if the inside was big enough to swing several cats.

Not that he would have dreamt of such barbaric methods of measuring space since animals of all kinds, not only dogs, had the effect of melting his bones. His own dog had been given to him to act as a constant companion, keep him safe in his wanderings and make him more forthcoming. The failure of the latter purpose, and the presence of baby twins gave some explanation as to why he had not been encouraged to weep for her loss in that small, cramped and shrill-voiced cottage where a dog had been a luxury and everyone encouraged him to get lost. It was not as though they did not care, he simply felt he took up too much space. He supposed they would let him have another, but he couldn't think of that, yet. A sheep with twisted horns would be less of an obvious substitute for a walk through town. Stonewall smiled widely at the very idea. It could graze on the ever-present washing in the back yard. He could get it a lead.

'You're a silly thing,' he murmured, then shook himself and sighed. Sheep always seemed so content. The breeze made his hair stand on end. He was not bored on an idle day like this, since that was a condition he could not understand when left to himself, but he was a trifle restless. Rick would not play this morning: no one wanted to go looking for ghosts. They all talked about a white-haired ghost who stole bits and pieces from the dustbins, but no one, not even Rick, was going to believe his sightings. It was a mistake, Stonewall reflected gravely, to be known for both silence indoors and exaggeration elsewhere.

He turned for one last look at the house. From an upstairs window, an indistinct figure in bright clothes was waving at him. For a moment he was startled, then waved back, putting energy into his arm, twirling and dancing for her benefit, watching her double over in laughter.

That was no ghost. It was mad Mrs Pardoe, always ready for a game. Funny the way she noticed everything, even himself. He thought of cantering across the lawn, telling her he'd left the sodding bait wrapped in newspaper by the back door, and would Edward please pay him some time? Or shouting, Have you seen my dog? He did neither.

On the way home for the sort of dinner he despised (shepherds pie and peas), Stonewall formed the conviction, on slender circumstantial evidence, that the ghost had got his dog, only because it was better than believing she was dead.

He slouched the half mile back into what he thought of as a town.

A fly buzzed at the window. The room was full of half-read books, usually less than half. Edward Pardoe pretended he had read them all, so that he could quote the odd bit of poetry or drama and dazzle the hayseeds with whom his superior artistic tendencies were forced to slum. At his feet was a painting of Joanna. Edward read from his pocket book of Browning.

> That's my last Duchess painted on the wall,
> Looking as if she were alive . . .

She didn't. His sister's face looked flat and dead, a bad piece of chocolate-box art. Edward threw the book away, kicked the painting under the bed and turned to the doll's house.

'Enter the dreamers,' he murmured, and they obeyed. Inside the stage set on which they performed, each tiny wooden figure could only bend and gesture in strict response to his own fingers. They could sit on chairs with legs crossed, lounge on beds, raise their arms, look as if they were running for their lives. He often played with the doll's house he had made. Other grown-up boys of twenty-two played with steam trains or computer games, depending upon the early taste of their fathers, but Edward was different. He was like the God of Eden who could never quite leave his creatures alone.

'Oh Mummee, Mummee,' he whined, as a little figure held in his hand sat in a sulk with her ballerina skirt sticking straight to expose a wooden crotch and miniature sexless limbs. 'Oh Mummee, I've got a headache and my dress is RUINED!'

'Shut up,' Edward replied. The little figure lay down on her back, knees apart. 'You be careful, Jo,' Edward murmured again.

Crouched over the doll's house, he concentrated on the mummy puppet on a sofa, decked out with ribbons and looking like a dead tin general ready for a funeral. At the dining-table sat the tiny figure of Julian, coated in a little tweed suit. Joanna had made that in the days when she humoured him more. Real men don't sew, she had told him. They may create houses, but they don't sew. Edward had always wondered why not.

'Oh God!' The genuine Joanna, too tall, too broad and shockingly blonde, exploded into the room. 'What are you doing, Ed? It's too hot to be in here.'

'Go away, Jo. Leave me alone.'

'You should have locked the door if you wanted peace.'

He stood with his back to the doll's house, his wiry frame too small to hide his preoccupation, his face unable to disguise his pleasure in seeing her.

'Playing!' Joanna said, contemptuous but nervous. 'Playing happy families, I suppose. You'd be better off painting. Why don't you grow up?'

That was Edward's problem. He refused to grow up. Wanted to be king of the castle without doing anything to earn the crown, his father had said scornfully. Joanna always felt slightly guilty about the disparity between their father's treatment of his second son and only daughter. Edward could never do anything right. She could do nothing wrong.

'What?' he jeered. 'Grow up like you? Progress to the amusement arcade? Very sophisticated. Completely mature.'

Joanna was not in the mood to take offence. Edward's teasing lacked any real force, unlike his elder brother Julian, who could make her weep with a mere glance. She flung herself on the bed, began chewing a length of her blonde hair, twitchy and insecure as ever.

'Oh big brother, I'm so miserable. Do you know, I could feel him trembling when he held my hand? Now he avoids me. Weeks, not a word. What did I do? Am I too fat? I want to die.'

'Of course it isn't anything to do with the way you look. I've told you why, how many times?'

They both knew the subject of Joanna's religious fervour. The conversation was stale, but it was the only one which would have tempted her into his room. Edward shook his head. The room was full of sighing. He moved to the window through which the sun streamed, leaned on the sill, looked at the view he had examined a million times before. The front garden led down to the narrow road; beyond that, flat land spread out in a brown plain until the sun caught a yellow spit of sand. To the left was the village and beyond that he could just see the ground sloping up into gentle, pine-clad dunes. On the stillest of nights, the sea was audible; by day, never more than a ribbon flecked with white. The view swam before his eyes in the shimmering heat. In his mind's eye, he planted exotic shrubs into the flatness, ripened the sea-lavender which would change the dun colours into purple during August, included a bit of yellow corn and a few dappled deer, added alien palm trees. An artistic eye could always create such an improvement.

It was so much easier to amend the landscape than it was to acquire the skill to portray it in paint. He had tried to learn, but like everything he did, the discipline defeated him. He blamed the teachers. Blaming others for his own laziness was Edward's first and last resort. Silly old farts.

'What gives?' said Joanna, peevishly, changing the subject in deference to his indifference, still chewing her hair like a little girl. He liked her like that.

'You're home early. Don't tell me you've got the sack again.'

Another sigh. Edward had turned back to his doll's house,

about to replace the dolls, but the gust of his impatient breathing knocked over the sofa on which Mother sat and sent her tumbling to the floor. She lay with her head in the fireplace.

'No, not yet. I didn't have much to do today, honestly.' He shuddered and Joanna shrugged in sympathy.

'All right, don't sound so defensive. You know what I think? I think the idea of you being an estate agent is ridiculous. There, I've said it and that's all I'll say. Anyway, since you're here, I could do with a bit of help.' She was lying on the bed with her arms folded behind her head, her bare feet leaving dirty marks on the coverlet. It was this last detail, along with her bitten nails, which reminded him that the languid attitude was not one of a willing courtesan in a painting, but the artless, unselfconscious sprawl of a teenager. 'I need help,' she continued, 'because of this awful solicitor woman coming to stay in the cottage. Do you think you could clear up some of your fishing tackle? It does get in the way in the kitchen. And the hall, and the dining room. I suppose supper ought to be better than usual.'

'It's always good,' Edward said gently. 'And often marvellous.'

She flushed, the pleasure quickly hidden by a flick of the hand across her pink face.

'Oh, pooh. Not what Julian says. He says if you really want to cook, go away and learn how. Why does he want us both to go away?'

'You know perfectly well,' Edward said gently. 'Neither of us can, can we? Julian wants to grab everything and shove Ma in some horrible home the day after we leave. How many times must I tell you?' He lightened the sombre tone which always caught her attention. 'Anyway the cooking does a lot for me. You could even make me fat.' Jo grinned at him, threw a cushion from the bed towards his head. He caught it, threw it back, growling; she seized it again and hurled it harder. Edward let it drop, then went into his King Kong mode, lurching towards her with legs splayed and arms raised with the elbows above his shoulders, fingers twitching. Jo behaved like a maiden waiting for a dragon, wringing her hands and shrieking, 'OH! Oh! oh!' until he came closer and there was a hint of real fear in her laughter. Edward dropped the pose.

'You don't take me seriously,' he said. 'No one does. Oh dearie, dearie me. I'll never get to eat a virgin.'

'Sturgeon, maybe,' said his sister, leaping off the bed noisily, shaking out her skirt. The waistband was loose round her small waist, the skirt itself extra voluminous, old-fashioned, flounced and girlish to hide the wide hips she detested. If only, Edward thought, I were larger all over . . .

Joanna also detested her white skin, her cheeks currently blooming into pink as they always did in response to the slightest emotion or exertion. Edward frightened her sometimes. He always took a joke too far.

'And of course I take you seriously,' she added carelessly, retreating. 'Though maybe not as a maiden-snatcher. Oh, I wish someone would snatch me. Listen, do you think Julian will lay on wine for dinner? In deference to the Law amongst us?' Julian, tyrant, despot, unfair critic and spoiler of everything.

'I expect so,' Edward murmured, suddenly depressed. 'Provided we undertake to keep it away from Ma.'

'Oh yes. Easier said than done.' Both lapsed into silence. Edward moved back to the doll's house, where he replaced the little figure he had blown off the sofa. He felt Jo bending beside him to look into the room with the same old fascination she found so easy to scorn and he so quick to rekindle. At moments like these, they could have been the same childish age instead of he four years her senior. He wanted to pull her closer. The effort to restrain himself was almost too much: he could feel her breath, the babyish talcum powder smell of her and it made him want to faint. His fingers itched to feel the warm patch at the back of her neck.

There was a sound from the road which separated the summer garden from the channels beyond. It was a tinkling parody of Big Ben chimes on the hour, Da dah, dah da, dah da, da dah, garish and eerie. The ice-cream van, calling to Joanna like the music of the spheres.

'Oh no!' she wailed. 'It's him! And I look so awful!'

Edward clenched his fists. The door slammed, the room shuddered and everything in the doll's house fell over. Edward peered inside and took the ballerina figure and the small doll dressed like an artist with a smock and placed them with their arms around each other on the master bed of the biggest room upstairs. Then he threw a cloth across the whole construction as if he was silencing a parrot in a cage and took up a station behind the window, out of sight.

The ice-cream van drove down the drive, where weeds had almost overtaken the remnants of gravel and the lawn, where a sheep grazed, somehow expanded into the grassy flower-beds. Mist was beginning to roll in from the sea, warm and wet, promising oblivion. He watched as the ice-cream van stopped below, still tinkling, shut his eyes, tried to imagine the sound of the distant waves, failed. Please don't run, Jo, please don't. He could not abide to witness her humiliation or watch her bitten nails pushing through the blonde hair; could not bear to see her preen the way she never had for him. He clenched his fist. 'Why is it I never get what I want?' he murmured petulantly. 'Things will change, Dad, just you wait and see.'

As the van drew to a halt, with its monstrous bells still ringing to the faithful, a figure emerged from the front door of the house with a joyful scream. Edward closed his eyes again in the instant he recognised that high-pitched shrieking and the jumble of excited words which followed so harsh on his ears. He looked, without amusement, as a plump figure banged on the side of the van, yelling, 'Hallo, hallo oh, goodbye, darling thing, are you being good today?' The van stopped, lurched forwards a few yards, part of an act. The bright little figure ran after it, whooping with laughter. Edward relaxed. At least this little fool wasn't Joanna. Only his own darling mother, sweetly dotty and harmlessly senile. He looked down at her with more indifference than contempt. As soon as he could manage it, she was going to live in a zoo. If not a zoo, at least behind bars, and a grave would be best of all.

Joanna, money, this house to pull down and this landscape to alter. If only. He wanted never to work, and to go on as he had so far, in the careful cultivation of an image of himself as a cunning player of games and a deeply interesting, deeply unpleasant young man. Oh, yes, and maybe a better fisherman than his father. Nothing else mattered.

Everyone mattered too much.

'Nice evening in store, Doctor?'

'No,' said Julian Pardoe, writing the prescription as he spoke. 'I very much doubt it.'

'Why's that, then? Lovely big house, yours. So I'm told. People says.'

'Ah, the word of authority. People says. Lovely house. You should try living in it. You should try coping with leaks and delinquents of all ages. You should try . . .' He stopped, not embarrassed, but ashamed for listening to his own voice rising into a petulant yell. Miss Gloomer, obdurate spinster, eighty years old, chronically and courageously ill, sat across the desk in his surgery, knowing her manners, while he forgot his. Her face was a map of pain, patience and fortitude. She managed to sit in her chair without trembling only because of the stick with the ornamental duck's head she clasped with both hands pressed into the top while the ferrule was digging a hole in his carpet, absorbing the constant trembling of her limbs. I'd be so much better, Julian thought, if I talked to them more, the way I used to, but I can't bear it. Women of virtue like this are the worst, so patient and kind they take a piece of you. I've nothing to give them, even when I like them as much as this, I can't be patient. He turned the bark into a laugh and finished the prescription. 'Mustn't complain, mustn't complain,' he said, testily.

'Why not?' she said surprisingly. 'It's allowed. We all got problems. Perhaps you should try living alone. You've been the same since your father passed away. There was a time when you had a kind word for everyone. I suppose they call it stress.'

Snatching the prescription quickly to avoid more than a split-second release of the stick, she was on her way to the door. Oh Lord, he thought, I should be helping her, instead of sitting here like an inconsiderate dummy. In his own confusion and her rumbling movements, he still recognised something horribly astute.

'I appreciate it's very hard living alone, Miss Gloomer . . .' he began to say, trying to make amends with a particle of conversation. She stopped dead and cackled.

'Don't you believe it. Only thing I ever got right. Even if it is frightening, sometimes.'

'I'll probably see you later.'

'No need. Only if it suits you.'

This time his smile was right from the eyes. He heard the stick guide her down the corridor and waited before pressing the bell. Living alone seemed like a vision of heaven and he would appreciate it now if the next patient was a hooligan tourist deserving of rudeness. 'Next!' he yelled, when the bell brought no response. Nurse popped into the room, smiling, her endless cheerfulness like sand in a graze.

'You've been through them all like a dose of salts today, Doctor. Reckon that's the lot and you can go home.'

'Oh. Dr Freeman finished too, has he? Or would he like me to take one of his?'

She shifted uncomfortably. 'Well no, I don't think so. He's got a couple waiting, but they're his regulars, if you see what I mean.'

Dr Freeman was far more popular than Dr Pardoe. Nor did nice-natured women freeze him in his tracks. Once upon a time it had been the other way round.

Julian did not know if fury or relief was uppermost in his mind as he strode to his car. Relief to be out of the ugly modern medical centre with its compassionate efficiency, or fury with himself for skimping time with the patients and shying away from the opposite sex as if they could sting him. If only he could emulate the charm of Dr Freeman; give each one his undivided attention, instead of champing at the bit, brooding, hating himself, moving from one captivity to the next, taking no comfort. The interior of his car was overpoweringly hot. It had been cleaned that morning in readiness for house calls to patients who would tell him about ghosts, as if he did not have enough of his own. Freeman's car was carelessly filthy and parked beneath a tree. Julian wondered what had happened to his comfortable dreams and the endless sympathy he had once commanded, felt faintly savage, ashamed of himself for his own, dogged misery.

There was a smart red car with a dent, parked next to his own in the space marked 'doctors only'. The sight of an inconsiderate outsider only increased his irritation.

Sarah Fortune felt a stranger, off territory and slightly confused. She was not due to reach the Pardoes until early evening and it was only early afternoon. She had several motives for reaching the village sooner than expected, but was unsure which to take first, so she dawdled in the high street, trying to orientate herself. In briefing her for this task, Ernest Matthewson had been deliberately economical with the background information he had given her, which consisted of an Ordnance Survey map, directions and little else. She was left to glean what she could of the family who were paying her fees and giving her a place to stay while she earned them. Which was why, on a whim, in a state of indecision and not relishing the next task, she found herself in the hairdresser's. Hairdressers knew things and it was a place to sit.

'On holiday, are you? You've been in here before, haven't you? I'm sure I know you from somewhere.'

'No,' said Sarah, smiling her disarming smile. 'No to both. I'm working. For the Pardoes. Do you know them?'

The woman towelling her wet head of hair did not pause for a moment, but chuckled.

'Course. Everyone does. I got no worries. I pay my rent. How do you find Mrs Pardoe? Comes in Monday mornings, all the clobber. Mad as a hatter, but still independent, you know. I suppose they'll have to get someone to look after her soon. Poor little Mouse.'

'I haven't met her yet. I'm not due up there until this evening. Thought I'd have a look around first.'

'And get your hair done? Good idea.' They eyed each other in the mirror. 'Blow dry, or set?' Sarah looked at the row of four ancient hairdryers, beneath which sat a selection of dozing women with hair tortured into rollers, their hands crossed on ample stomachs, a comfortable sight, along with the smells. In the ample bosom of Sylvie, conversation and coiffure would be more rewarding.

'What kind of work are you doing for the Pardoes?' The curiosity was mild, so innocuous it demanded an answer. Sarah never saw the virtue of being entirely honest when a vague evasion would serve the same purpose and, besides, she wasn't entirely sure. Ernest had been infuriatingly vague. You need an unsullied mind, he had said.

'Oh, something to do with their house.' The woman nodded, understandingly.

'Oh yes? I've heard they could do with a bit of decoration. Mr Pardoe was always adding bits on. He was a dreamer. Never finishing anything off.'

Perhaps Sarah's clothes, smart in comparison to what she had seen outside, suggested interior decorator rather than woman of letters. She smiled again as her hair was brushed with rough efficiency.

'That bad, is it?'

'Well, old Mrs Pardoe isn't up to doing much, poor soul, is she? Daughter does her best and all that, the doctor's too busy, I expect, and that Edward's no more use than a sick headache, spiteful, lazy little sod. If only his sister would see it, but she won't, worships the ground he walks on. Funny things, families. Mary!' she half turned to yell at her girl assistant. 'Turn Mrs Smith off, will you? Otherwise she'll melt.'

It was pleasant to be spoken to as if she knew them all.

'Poor Mr Pardoe,' she said solicitously. 'How long is it since he died?'

'Fell off his roof with his heart attack, you mean? About a year, I suppose. Mind,' she lowered her voice and switched off the dryer, 'there's other things he could have died of, only I think he'd given that up.'

'Such as?' Sarah ventured. The blow-drying started again.

'Falling off a big woman!' Sylvie yelled, breaking into raucous laughter, then subsiding into the confidentiality of a stage whisper audible from a hundred yards. 'He did a lot of that in his time. All right, Mrs Jones? You waiting for me? Please yourself.' She coughed impatiently.

'That Mrs Pardoe was wise, though,' she continued shouting. 'Never complained. She just pretended she didn't notice, waited for him to stop his nonsense. They all come back in the end, don't they?'

Sarah nodded, slightly unsure of what kind of worldly wisdom it was she was endorsing. It never seemed to her worthwhile to wait for anyone to come back. Her head was hot, her hair floating away from the brush.

'Lovely colour,' Sylvie yelled. 'Natural, I can tell. Used to have a customer with hair exactly like this. What was her name, now? Oh, hallo. Look what the cat's brought in.'

The door of the shop had opened, the bell clattering. On the threshold stood a large young man, twenty-one or so, Sarah guessed. For all his astounding good looks, he had an air of shy uncertainty. Next to him, standing proudly in his shadow, was a boy the colour of sand. Sarah, her back to the door, screened by Sylvie, watched them through the mirror.

'What do you want, Rick?' said Sylvie, snapping as if scolding, but patently pleased to see them both.

'Boy needs a hair cut. He got chewing-gum in it.'

'Get your arse out of here, the two of you, and send him back in half an hour, all right? Can't you see I'm busy? You want spray?' Sylvie bellowed to Sarah all in one breath.

*

Sarah Fortune, with her cloud of clean hair and her small sum of knowledge, walked out beyond the town, away from the people and away from the sea. *En route*, she bought provisions for the cottage the Pardoes would provide and left them in the car, except for the flowers, which she took with her. This last action made her define the real purpose of being early, not merely to explore – something else far more important. She had craved the sea for the last few days but once in view, found herself afflicted with a strange reluctance to look at the creeks, the channels and the quay which existed at the bottom of the street and ducked into the town instead. She was suddenly an alien, far from the metropolis which was home, and if not afraid, at least wary.

Tomorrow she would crave the sea again: the mere thought of it made her excited. So often she had dreamed her ignorant dream of living in an unpretentious place like this, inside a cottage with roses round the door. The dream had become a habit of familiar escape. Similar visions of privacy and non-accountability prevailed as her greatest ambition, the tawdry golden thread of her adult life. Somehow she had come to imagine Elisabeth Tysall might have felt the same.

On the edge of the village-cum-town stood the church. According to the Ordnance Survey map, the only church, bearing bravely the signs of neglect as evidence of the dwindling faithful who needed no more than the burgeoning graveyard and the occasional blessing of a half-remembered God. Elisabeth Tysall, twice-buried, once beneath a sand bank and, later, here, had needed both. It was her consecrated grave which was the purpose of Sarah's pilgrimage. The newer graves spilled into a field, less attractive than the mossy stones surrounding the church at crooked angles, like drunken friends on the way home, the names obscured, the grass growing between. The interments of the last two years were less cheerful for being still remembered, harassed in equal terms by grief and dead flowers. Some had already begun to sink into the unkempt; others bore vestiges of fresh planting. A temporary wooden marker bore the legend of Elisabeth's name. No one had requisitioned a stone, but then Charles had died, had he not, so soon after she was identified. The grass grew round it freely. On either side, the close-packed graves bore bright, white stones, the soil packed with pansies to the left, a bunch of tired flowers in a plastic container to the right.

Elisabeth, who had chosen the wrong one to love. Sarah wanted to weep for her.

'I'm sorry,' she was saying. 'I'm so sorry. I should have come sooner. Maybe you know how it is. I should have come to your funeral, but I didn't know the full story. Still don't. Did anyone come to your funeral?'

She found she was raising her voice to the level of one commonsensical woman talking to a friend on equal terms, a person who was businesslike, ashamed of sentiment, but always prone to it. Sarah parted the grass to lay down the flowers, wishing she had bought something grander; there was no impulse of which she was ashamed, except meanness. Buried beneath was a suicidal woman of youth and beauty, unmourned, unnoticed, and that was an abomination. Sarah began to tidy, until her fingers struck razor points and she withdrew sharply. Blood appeared on her knuckles; she sucked her fist, squatting back on her haunches to look again. Covered by grass, there were thistles lurking, dead, massed into a bunch beneath another bouquet of fat, desiccated roses, purple with indeterminate age, which crumbled at her touch. Sarah parted more grass and laid her own daisies, level with the feet, not the heart. The silence of the place was extraordinary.

There was a posse of black crows congregating at the bottom of the field. Two years before, Elisabeth Tysall, wife of Charles Tysall, had walked out at low tide across the creeks. She had been presumed the victim of an accident. Sarah could hear the cultivated voice of Charles telling her of the need for punishment and knew the version was not true. His Porphyria had lain down amongst the lavender and waited for the sea to take her. She may have covered her own elegant limbs with sand, the better to remain buried for a whole year before the tide broke the bank and released her.

'Why?' Sarah asked her. 'You let him win. I do wish I'd known you.' A redhead you were, like me. A beauty, since Charles would have wedded nothing less. You should have been mourned, whatever you were. Not only by Charles, who loved you in his own, perverted way, followed you into the sea to find your resting place, drowned in the same, aberrant flood.

Sarah looked again at the grave, the dead roses and the scornful thistles. Who loved you? Who cared for you then? Where did you go? You and I, we could have been friends. Instead, you were merely the catalyst in a story and another source of my endless guilt.

The silence struck again, like a blow to the ears, making her long for a voice in return. The intensity of it, the dearth of birdsong, made her look round, notice for the first time the mist of the now late afternoon, obscuring the sun, hiding the wicketgate to the church. She stood and looked down at the daisies.

A headstone for Elisabeth Tysall, something to mark her life, someone must. Something grand and beautiful for a woman who had wanted to live as much as the woman who stared at the flowers now.

Sarah walked back to the landward side of the village where she had left her car and took a wrong turn out of the town, looking for the coast road. The red car with the dented wing crawled through the lanes, following instructions, driving like the locals in second gear. To call this a town was a misnomer: it was a village. She imagined the populace from the hinterland trucking in on Saturday nights, like cowboys from the desert, in search of liquor 'n' entertainment. A fish-and-chip frontage and a Victorian behind, was how Ernest had described it; a sort of harbour flanked with an amusement arcade and signs saying don't park the car on the front, or the tide may take it. Drive along the quay, Ernest had said, ignore a bend. Go straight on, he had said, off the main road, keep the sea on your left until the track runs out. The house is there, half a mile at most. You can't miss it.

She did miss it, because she detoured round the town out of curiosity and found herself stuck in a narrow lane against a wall lined with hollyhocks and someone waiting patiently behind. She went back to the quay, found it swathed in mist and wondered what Ernest meant about keeping the ocean on the left when she could not see a glimmer of water. The receding tide moved in a dirty little channel out beyond brown banks towards the invisible sea. The garish lights of an amusement arcade hit her back and the din was raucous. People sat on a wall which separated quay from road, eating fish and chips; the air smelt of salt, vinegar, petrol. It was all so messy and so normal, shabby holiday life, nothing sinister in the pedestrian litter. The mist was puzzling rather than frightening; it spread round her like a warm blanket, bringing with it a premature darkness and making her realise at long last that she was very, very late for the Pardoes.

There was a cake on the kitchen table, a lopsided travesty of a confection which looked more like Plasticine. Two slabs of solid matter, wedged together with a gluey icing made with flour in mistake for sugar. One of Mother's better efforts at occupational therapy, Julian thought. The kitchen looked like a bomb site after her efforts. At the best of times it was a good enough kitchen, despite Edward's fishing mess; the oldest part of a patchwork house. There was a big pine table, large, heavy chairs which did not match and an old-fashioned Raeburn stove which Joanna loved for all the trouble of tending it and all the unreliability of the oven. A heavy kettle stood on top, simmering endlessly. The room was always warm. The pantry beyond the ancient fridge was cool by contrast, a large, walk-in store with stone-flagged floor, netted windows and pale shelves crammed with stores. On the floor in there, at all times, were two or three bundles of Edward's always superfluous fishing bait, worms, inelegantly wrapped in newspaper, an unlikely source of protein for the inmates of the house. The cake, Mother announced in one of her very rare comprehensible sentences, was for the guest. Joanna looked at it in horror. If only Mother wouldn't.

'She's late, this rotten old bitch of a lawyer, thank God she's late, the cow, nothing's ready.' Joanna's temper was running high; Julian's likewise.

'Don't flap. It doesn't suit you. What do you want me to do? Worry about impressing her? I doubt if she's a cow or a bitch, it's physically impossible to be both, she's only a sort of hired help.'

'We should have a lot in common then,' Joanna hissed. 'Only I'm not paid.'

'No, but it's patently obvious you're well fed,' said Julian. This marked the end of the shouting. The row had caused the delay and rendered a light cheese sauce inedible. Joanna had started again, which was why she was not going to cry now. The poached halibut required no extra salt.

Impatiently, Julian stacked two fishing rods against the wall. Edward's fishing tackle seemed to penetrate every room in the house except his own. Wherever he went, he seemed to fall over Edward's deliberate attempts to impress as well as dominate. Fishing and Edward did not really go together. He only did it to be manly, like his father.

'Did you check her room?' Joanna snapped. 'You know, the cottage? I suppose you managed that?' It was a poor attempt at sarcasm, her voice too shrill for impact.

'Yes, but I don't see why you didn't ask Ed first, he's far more time than me. It's fine. Could have done with some flowers, though.'

'She's only the hired help,' Joanna hissed, pleased with herself. The pleasure faded quickly. No one should have mentioned flowers, or even thought about them. Mother could sense a word from a mile away, also a row and the way to make it worse. She had the uncanny instinct of appearing on cue, in the wrong role and always the wrong costume like now as she stood in the kitchen doorway, holding an enormous bunch of dandelions in one hand, a clutch of nasturtiums in the other. She had a full bottle of wine poking out of the pocket of her coat. An evening gown swayed round her ankles beneath a mackintosh and there

were three ostrich feathers in her hair. Julian took away the wine
and placed it on the table in a swift manoeuvre, well practised if
devoid of humanity. Mother's eyes filled with tears. She had
always been so infuriatingly defenceless, he thought. Earned her
nickname of Mouse for always weeping like her daughter, neither able to stand their own ground.

'Why did you do that, darling? Oh, I'm hungry.' She moved
unsteadily towards a small pile of grated cheese on the chopping
board.

'No you don't,' Joanna said. 'Leave it alone, will you? What
do you want?'

'Something to eat, I think. Just a little something. Don't you
like my cake?' She stood centre stage, smiling at them both
through bright, watery eyes.

'Are you going to change for dinner?' Julian asked ironically.

'Should I? It's only a bitch or a cow, you were saying. I was
just going to put flowers in its room—'

'No!' Joanna shouted. 'No you won't. Not after I've swept,
hoovered, put out towels, no you don't.'

Mother's upper lip trembled. She looked at both her hands,
the one holding garden weeds, the other, *pissenlit*.

'Yes, I will,' she murmured. 'I'm sure the cow will like them.'

She scuttled sideways, swifter than a crab, towards the front
door, just as the bell rang. With the row and all, no one had
heard the sound of an engine, usually discernible from a hundred yards. Each knew the sound of their various old cars,
parked outside like a row of sentinels. Edward was feigning deaf-
ness in his watchtower, pretending to paint his rubbishy daubs
and reading poetry, defying the necessity to earn a living, while
his sister suspended life through cooking and pretending that
was enough. Julian surveyed them all with despair. Mother was
agile. She reached the door first, could not work out a way to
open it with her hands full, stood back, grinning like a cat.
Edward bounded downstairs, straightening a big floppy cravat;
Joanna stood back and Julian hesitated. They were not used to
guests.

Another knock. None of them could answer the door. She would have to open it herself.

A figure stepped into the gloom of the hall. Mother staggered forward, still grinning, dropping the flowers at Sarah Fortune's feet.

'Oh,' said the guest without a hint of discomposure. 'How lovely. You shouldn't.' She stopped to pick dandelions from the floor, carefully and swiftly, like a person used to gathering weeds with great respect. They watched, fascinated. She had straightened up with the flowers in a neat bunch by the time Julian switched on the cruel hall light. Dressed in khaki, she was, a princess in her brown freckled skin with her red hair kinking over her shoulders and a tan belt round her waist and small hips, clothed in nothing which was not utterly neutral while remaining a mass of colours all the same. A humorous face, a square jaw and a smile which embraced the giver of the dandelions. Not beautiful, but stunning.

Mother picked up the last, ceremoniously. Sarah bowed and stuck it down the front of her dress. Mother beamed.

'Would you mind coming straight on in? Supper's ready. No time for washing and all that stuff.' Joanna spoke roughly.

Sarah nodded. 'Of course. I'm really sorry I'm so late. I wouldn't have been but I'm such a silly cow, I got lost.'

'Cow!' Mother collapsed in giggles. Sarah took her extended hand.

'What fabulous feathers,' she said. 'I wish I was allowed to wear those.'

CHAPTER THREE

They all stared aghast. It was love at first sight. Before grace, before dinner. Before the second batch of burnt cheese sauce and before anyone heard the sound of the distant, ghostly tinkling of the ice-cream-van bell. There was a full second of silence until the sound died. Mother clapped her hands.

'What the hell's he doing here?' Edward snarled. Sarah turned her gaze on him. He wilted.

'I'm afraid that's my fault. I stopped at a, what do you call them, amusement arcade, to ask directions, and this man volunteered to lead me here. I thought it was charming. I've never had such an escort.' Joanna was brick red. She no longer cared if dinner was edible. Instant love turned to instant hate and then to love again as she fled to the kitchen. Edward looked amused. This was only a woman, not the gimlet-eyed professional he had slightly dreaded; she was too attractive to be a threat. Julian led her inside. His manner was barely less than brusque; he was shaking slightly and he did not seem able to take his eyes off her hair.

Outside, Hettie the sheep bleated. Mother had placed a bow round her neck. Only a youth called Rick noticed and remembered fondly as he drove back to work.

Stonewall hung about the amusement arcade as long as he could and as late as he dared, sick with anxiety and knowing that, sooner or later, he'd be shooed away. There had been twenty minutes of sheer bliss, when he'd been left in charge when Rick came in from a quick stroll on the quay, talking to someone, said he'd be off for five, would he, Stonewall, take charge? The arcade belonged to Rick's dad, who was a sort of uncle, like everyone round here, but not Stonewall's favourite by any manner of means. Especially not when he came in drunk and found Stonewall in charge of the till. There'd be trouble when Rick got back, which was why Stonewall hung around, because someone had to protect Rick from his dad.

It was no good. Even with his new, short haircut, to which his fingers flew all the time with nervous pride, Stonewall didn't have the power and it made him want to shout. Hit me instead, he wanted to say to Rick's dad, as if Rick would ever have let it happen. Instead, that surly man went out for another drink or two, came back and took Stonewall by his newly exposed ear and pushed him in the direction of home. Rick didn't prevent him.

'Go on with you,' he said gently. 'See you tomorrow.' Stonewall felt the urge to kick shins and scream. Rick's dad didn't like witnesses.

'Go away,' Julian muttered in his sleep. 'Physician, heal thyself.'

He was dreaming of a girl with red hair who had run on the beach. The background of the dream was the strident, fairground sound which emerged from the arcade, as if such sound could travel the half mile to where Julian Pardoe attempted to sleep and cursed himself for his own insomnia. There was no excuse, no cause for alarm. The meal had been easier than anticipated, the guest, whose expertise could lighten his own burdens, had been the soul of charm to disguise, rather than hide, those over-intelligent eyes and that blatant talent for perception he somehow knew she possessed. Julian felt she could read his soul and all the shame printed on it, dismissed his imaginings as the kind of nonsense induced by red wine and over-ambitious food. Besides, he had no soul to reveal. By day

he was an automaton about his business, by night a heap of restless limbs, made fanciful only because he had embarrassed
himself staring at her so much, read too much into those blue
eyes, felt again that sickening guilt and despair. Take your time,
he had told Miss Fortune, formal beyond the point of rudeness,
wondering even then how soon he could phone Ernest
Matthewson and get this paragon recalled to the safety of her
own city.

Instead he found himself saying, Come into the surgery
tomorrow and I'll tell you a bit about the estate, have the rest of
the weekend to think about it. Don't feel you have to take meals
with us. Don't feel you have to stay.

Edward was acting out the role of serious, unconventional
younger brother, quoting poetry and describing the land. He
made it sound as if he owned it all, puffed himself up to look like
a small man with a big career, like his father, instead of a boy
who failed at everything he tried. The guest listened intently.
Mother put half-eaten food on the stranger's plate while Julian's
own abruptness shocked his sister and nothing fazed the guest.
He had wanted everything settled, his father's family safe, but
not like this. Not with the aid of a woman with hair like that, and
those calm, amused eyes.

They had taken her over to the cottage, followed by the sheep
with the crumpled horn which lived in the garden and was fed
by Mother. Miss Fortune didn't seem to mind that either. There
was nothing to surprise her frightful composure.

Julian turned restlessly, hearing again the creaking on the
stair he had heard before and never wished to investigate.
Could be his mother prowling, Edward going out fishing, he
did not want to know, could not watch them all the time or even
half of it. As long as it was not Edward going into Joanna's
room, something as yet unprecedented, but hanging over his
household like the threat of thunder. How immoral to wish
away his sister's virginity on the first unrelated youth who tried
to take it, but that was what Julian wished. If only she would
leave before some accident of desire should upset her life . . .

better if Edward went out fishing, even if it was to foul the sea shore as he did, leaving lines and hooks for seals, just as he littered the house with equipment and the pantry floor with buckets of soft-shelled crabs and lugworms for whiting.

The silence of the night increased the rattling in his mind. Julian felt responsibility without strength or confidence. He had killed his own self-respect, found himself left with nothing but impotent knowledge.

From a great distance, he thought he heard a scream.

Worms beneath this mud: good for bait.

'You don't know nothing, boy. Nothing. You don't know your arse from your elbow, or where to put that big dick of yours, or even where you want to put it. Dirt all over the van. You want to put dirt up her fanny? That what you want? I bet you bloody do.'

The sound which followed was a soft grunt, the noise of the boot into the ribs almost inaudible in itself, except for the air dispelled in the effort and the boy's biting back of pain. Both of them were covered in mud. The boy curled away on the bank, his left shoulder embedded in mud. Black mud bubbled where his elbow sank below the surface. There was blood inside his mouth, tasting of iron, salt and slime. Rick thought of the ragworms below the surface, imagined something slithering down his throat, struggled to sit, spat, coughed.

'I could have killed you, Dad.'

He was spitting out weary words, fielding another blow to his ribs, thanking heaven for his father's boots being so heavy with mud he could scarcely lift them. It could have been worse, had often been much worse. No blow had connected with his groin; he had turned on his back, wishing he had learned the trick when younger, before the damage was done and before he had realised the whole ritual of violence was far quicker if he did not resist. Lie there, let the boot go in, never mind about the shame.

'Kill me, you little fucker? Kill me! You could scarce kill a fly. You let that little runt look after the till while you're out running after that tart? You need to be towing the line. With a hook. I'd stick it through your mouth. Or up your bum.'

The boy allowed himself to be lifted out of the mud, shaken like a rat, dropped back. He could have taken his father then, knocked the old man's teeth through the back of his head, but he lay like a puppet and listened to the breath in his chest. Out of the corner of his eye, lights from the outside of the closed arcade shimmered on the water, blurred by mist. He could hear the tide running swift and deep through his head and his skin, vibrating through each portion of his body. Dad raised his wet face and sniffed like a dog.

'Best move,' he muttered. 'Water's coming on.' He was suddenly cold, shivery, adrenalin gone, replaced by a sensation which was the nearest he could get to shame. No more punching, rolling and snarling at the east end of the quay. The boy was right. He was strong. He could take his old dad any time, better watch it.

'Come on home, boy,' said his father, almost humbly, the way he was when it was far too late. 'You'll catch your death.'

'Bugger you. I got my own place.'

'You could do with a wash. You and me both.'

'I could do with a new set of balls after what you've done to me over the years. That's enough, Dad, do you hear me?'

Weird, to be speaking like a pair of blokes who had gone for a drunken stroll to look at the stars. They struggled up the bank. Past midnight, everything as silent as the grave. The apologies, oblique and humble, were the feature of Dad's drunken violence which Rick found worst.

'I thought you were taking that bit of Pardoe stuff out. You mustn't touch her. You know what that poxy little bastard told you, leave his sister alone. Otherwise no job, no arcade, no nothing. We're doing all right, boy. Don't rock the boat.'

Rick adjusted his trousers, tried to manage a laugh.

'Dad, I do leave her alone, but for my own reasons. I might have gone to the boat by myself, when I could still walk straight.'

'Don't give me that. Leave her alone? You've been up that

house twice today, bashing the van over that track. I saw you, I heard. Kids might be robbing the till and off you go.'

Rick took a deep breath, which hurt to the degree where he knew he would live.

'Dad, I goes the first time because Mrs Pardoe likes ice-cream, poor old bat. I goes the second time because this bird came in the arcade and asks directions, doesn't she? Said she was working up there. Christ, what a looker. A bit old, but a looker.'

Dad grunted. Sometimes he knew the truth when he heard it, not always.

'What do you mean, old?'

'Thirty. Something like that. Said she was a lawyer. A cracker.'

His father gave a great shout of laughter, flung his great thick arm round the boy's shoulder. Rick flinched. He might act for now as if there were a reconciliation but he had done it once too often. All he wanted was a clean body and sleep. And a dream. Running the arcade all by himself. Swimming in the sea with Jo Pardoe. Lying with her in the hot sand . . .

'Old! Thirty! So you lead some lady lawyer up there in the bloody ice-cream van! Doesn't that beat all!'

Rick could see him, telling the story in the Globe, the Ark Royal or the Golden Fleece, any of them would have done. The wet and weighty arm descended back to his shoulder and Rick let it rest. He felt for his groin. No soreness this time. His clothes were soaking and stinking, the body beneath weary beyond relief.

What a life. Work hard to keep your body in one piece, let alone the dreams. Not many of those left. Not a body worth a prayer, either. Not a thing to take to Joanna Pardoe.

The sheep had surprised Sarah. It had wanted to come indoors to this strange little cottage, last in a row of three, standing in grand isolation, thirty yards to the left of the house. I suppose this was once a farm, Joanna had volunteered, chatty and shy, a nice, nervy child. Workers would have lived here, years ago. Dad wanted a farm once; he wanted to do everything once. I'm sorry you haven't got the best one, but we had a fire in it a few weeks ago, still don't know why. Might have been the village ghost, we've got a new one this summer. Good night, sleep tight, sweet dreams.

The cottage was a shoebox of a house, living room-cum-kitchen, stairs to a bedroom, bathroom and tiny room under the eaves, explored in half a minute. Any sounds were the mere echo of her own activity. In her bedroom she faced a storm-proof window, open for airing, with a breeze moving pretty chintz curtains. Someone had made sporadic efforts, leaving the place less spartan, with an ancient hot-water cistern, older lavatory, clattering pipes, the kind of thin cord carpet which chilled the feet; two hangers in the wardrobe with a loose door, an over-soft bed.

She was absurdly disappointed that she could not hear the sea, let the lawyer in her take over to quell the disappointment. What did she know about the Pardoes and whatever was she supposed to do for them? She had a glimmer of their personalities, none of their supposed riches. Julian, the doctor, sandy-haired blond, churlish, driven and tired; Edward, a young, cunning braggart, self-consciously keeping himself the rebel and the subject of his sister's devotion. The girl, bright with gilded innocence and the friendliness of a puppy, watching her mother as if someone was going to take her away, while Mother herself overplayed to the gallery the loud rituals of her madness, comic and irritating by turns. Find out the dreams, Ernest had said without giving her a single clue. Find out, then work out how to finance them fairly: that's what lawyers should be for. Instead, Sarah thought of Elisabeth Tysall's punctuated dreams, the colour she might choose for a headstone, and the right shrub to plant.

The air from the window was like a drug, closing her eyes although the bed was cold. Not damp cold, but lonely cold, intensified by the quiet. No distant music, shouting, footsteps, no humming city life where neither silence nor darkness was ever quite complete. There crept into the chilly vacuum of her bed the panic of separation and the muck sweat of fear.

Her fingers touched her face: there were lines forming round her eyes; she could take great clumps of skin and pull them off, could lift her scalp away from the bone, feel the scars on her shoulders and her arms, force herself to think of the healing sea which would cure it all. Perspiration trickled down her back before she slept. It was not the countryside of which she had dreamed.

The day bore no relation to the night: from burial in the terrible silence, she was suddenly elevated into the delightful cacophony of dawn. Birdsong first, little fatty thrushes squabbling for attention and clattering on the roof; then the soft cooing of a pigeon, stupidly repetitious, two high notes, one low, no variation but long pauses, and at last, a wholly man-made sound, cutting across the natural like a knife. The mournful wailing of a distant siren, swelling into a full-bellied moan, fading, rising again to a steady wail, diminishing, howling, three, four times. It sounded like a crowd in anguish, an animal in pain, a prayer for the dead, a muezzin calling from the turret of a mosque and she listened spellbound. Minutes later she was out of doors.

There was nothing but clear sky and a view without ending. The village, with a long bank of land curving away from it seaward like a question mark, lay on her left, half a mile away. In front of her, opposite the house which stood the width of its garden from the cottages, a vast expanse of land amounting to nothing. She watched idly as she walked, until the nothing began to move as the light caught the surface, showing random, glimmering channels full of chuckling water. Sarah in plimsolls jogged towards town. The channels became wider with each fifty yards, the deceptive flat land gave way to channels of water no longer lapping but guzzling louder and louder in the ten minutes it took her to reach the quay. From the evening gulley of mud and sand, it had become part of the ocean upon which it fed. The sea lapped high against the harbour wall; boats which had been invisible the night before now rode proud and level with her eyes, bobbing and straining with lazy ease. Remnants of tufty land which she had glimpsed standing high and dry in the mist, poked above the surface of the water, like the uncertain remains of hair on a smooth, bald head.

Early. Salty, fish-smelling. Two men throwing open boxes out of a boat, slamming them on to the stone. The boxes were full of wet, heaving fish. Another man sluiced the deck of the boat from which they unloaded. Blood, mixed with water, ran down the sides. Sarah tried to hide her nausea.

'Excuse me . . . What was the siren I heard?'

'Siren? Oh, that. Lifeboat.' They did not waste words, not unfriendly, but busy.

'Do you fish with hooks?' she asked stupidly, eyeing the watery blood.

'Hooks are for fun. You only catch one at a time with hooks. Nets, we use.'

The fish smell defeated her, she was ashamed to be asking the obvious, risking their mild contempt. The village lay glistening. There were swans in the harbour, carried along by the tide with comical, dignified speed. The amusement arcade was emphatically closed at an hour still too early for the postman. A youth was hosing down the pavement outside, oblivious to bold seagulls whooping over waste-paper bins in search of yesterday's chips. The same uncertain but gentle giant who had appeared in the hairdresser's with his charge, and, later, escorted her beyond the boundaries on her regal progress, recognizable even when the pale sunlight illuminated the fresh bruises on his face. He seemed too lethargic to resent interruption, leant on his broom and watched her cross over from sea to land side of the road, trying to smile in mutual recognition.

'Hallo,' she said. 'Look, thanks for showing me the way last night. I told them up there,' she nodded in the direction from which she had walked, 'that I felt like the Queen. It was very kind of you.' This time his grin managed to emerge, splitting the face into dimples and making her remember what a star he had looked, in his tight-fitting jeans and brilliant white shirt, among the lights of the arcade with bingo going on in the corner, how politely he had listened to her above the din. A contrast to his dull-haired misery of the morning, no longer a king but a servant.

'That's all right then,' he said. 'My name's Rick.'

'What did you do to your face?' The question would be asked two dozen times during the day and for others he would invent a story, make them laugh, but the hour was too early for con-coction.

'Nothing. Had a fight with my dad for taking the van out.' There didn't seem much she could say about that, except what she did say.

'I'm sorry. I'd rather have stayed lost than got you into trouble.'

'What makes you think you're that important?' he flashed back, jeering. 'Doesn't take a reason for Dad to hit me. Fact is, he thought it was funny, me taking you out there. Didn't like me leaving this place, though. Might have missed taking money or something.' Rick was suddenly uncomfortable, talking so much, but she didn't waste his time being shocked or anything. She looked fresh out of bed and besides he hurt all over and wanted someone to know.

'Do you look after all those machines?' she asked, pointing to the arcade.

'Yeah,' he muttered. 'All those crappy machines, all that row. And I do the ice-cream-van round. Smashing.'

'Do you? What a marvellous place to live.' She knew as she spoke that the question and the observation were fatuous. He spat into the gutter.

'You've got to be joking.' Then he spat in the road, to empha-sise the point again. She was mildly irritated, not much.

'OK, OK,' she said. 'But you're far too good-looking to let anyone cover it in bruises. Why don't you dump your dad on a boat and tell him to sail? You're big enough, unless he's bigger.'

He let out a great shout of laughter, then clutched his waist because laughter hurt.

'For Christ's sake,' she said. 'Give me the damn brush and sit down.'

'I can't. My dad—'

'Give it me.' He did, slowly crossed to the wall opposite and lit a cigarette, then sat there watching, waiting to be amused. Sarah swept the pavement in front of the arcade like a furious housewife with only moments to spare, picking up fish paper, hamburger remnants, shoving everything into the plastic sack with which he had come equipped. Then seized a wash leather out of his bucket and cleaned the windows with the deft movements of a person who hated housework, endeavoured to complete it in the shortest possible time with all the refinements of sheer impatience. She scoured door knobs and scuffed panels of paint, covered every inch in ten, hyperactive minutes. The emotions of the last few days had driven her to scour her flat from end to end with the same relentless energy in a practice made so perfect her swipe of the last window-pane called for a slow hand clap. Rick ambled back across the road.

'Are we quits?' she asked.

'How much do you charge an hour?' he asked, still trying to jeer, the smile less painful, strength coming back into his limbs. She was a looker all right, a lovely bum when she bent.

'Oh, I couldn't possibly tell you. It depends what for.'

'You really a lawyer, like you said? I knew the Pardoes were expecting one. Mrs P. told me. Said it would be some old cow.'

'That was a perfectly accurate expectation. Here I am.' They were both grinning broadly now.

'I don't know anything about them,' she added cunningly. 'Why would people say, for instance, that Edward was a shit? Someone said so, in the hairdresser's.'

'Because he is. Because when he goes fishing up yonder,' he gestured beyond the far distance, 'he won't even stop if he sees a seal. Leaves hooks and line for other things to swallow. He likes nasty practical jokes, Edward. And that ain't all.' Yes, she was a looker. Not old at all, with her jeans and the smut on her nose.

Then his mind went into overdrive, remembering Pardoes in general, discretion in particular, wounded pride and his dad.

'Come out for a drink tonight, I'll tell you.'

She'd laugh, of course, a woman like this, find an excuse. He picked up the bucket and hurled the dirty water into the road, swirling the last slops towards her feet, playfully, watching to see if she would scream or move, half hoping she wouldn't, a challenge.

'Yes,' she said, ignoring the water. 'Where?'

'Meet me here? My night off,' he said, thinking of Dad with inexplicable triumph.

'See you then.'

She began to walk back. The quay was suddenly busy. A small boy, the colour of sand, stopped at a corner and stared at her. The stare was similar to a public undressing, all the more intense for the childish lack of inhibition in the dropped wide mouth and the lack of preening which went with it. The stare followed her as she passed and remained lodged somewhere at the back of her neck. A clock on the wall of the harbour stated the time of high tide and low, and next to it was a record of the highest the water had ever risen. Sarah liked that, wondering what else it was could rule these lives.

Here it was Charles Tysall had died and his wife before him. Charles, who had chosen her as his next obsession. Punished her as he had punished his wife, and then walked out to seek the spot where the wife had died. Charles, whose love destroyed what it touched. She felt her arms, suddenly cold. There were the ghosts of spoiled dreams, shimmering above the water.

Mrs Jennifer Pardoe, always known as Mouse, had a fondness for things which glittered. She took her wardrobe seriously and the morning selection occupied an hour. For this hot summer, evening dress was *de rigueur*. Ball gowns, and her several euphemistically called cocktail frocks, were ideal for late July. When worn for their proper functions in wedding marquees, stuffy dinners in draughty old houses, charity dos in barns, openings of horrid little galleries in picturesque villages, any frocks which were chiffony, *décolleté*, short-sleeved, were always too cold for comfort. No wonder a girl needed a fur coat: a girl was usually well advised never to take the damn thing off. Mrs Pardoe had once described the sailing club dance as an acre of gooseflesh sprayed with starch, not a remark, even whispered as it was, designed to win either friends or the plaudits of her spouse, who was, in those days of his social climbing, ashamed of her.

Today, she thought she might wear the silver lamé shift, *circa* 1973. Her stylistic roots were with Marilyn Monroe, while her figure, small and plump like a trim-waisted frigate, dictated a preference for the loose fold rather than the tight twist. Joanna inherited the same curves and one day the child would learn it did not matter.

Mouse uttered a brief, emphatic, 'Huh!' when her wavering concentration lit upon a vision of her deceased husband scolding her for filling cupboards with frocks for occasions she had never wanted to attend in the first place, but did anyway because she simply did not know how to disagree. Then the whole concentration went into the moment. Which one? The mid-calf, gold fabric shift without sleeves or back would do fine for the simple reason it was going to be hot. Big, glittering ear-rings, a golden bangle shaped like a snake with little green eyes and a pink stone in the tail; perfect. Nights of agony in crippling high heels came to mind wistfully as she selected what she had always secretly yearned to wear then, a pair of pink training shoes. Thus attired, she went down for breakfast with her coat on top.

Champagne cocktail for preference. Brandy in the bottom and sugar round the top, cornflakes on the side.

It was a big, ugly house, Sarah observed as she approached on her way back, seeing it clearly for the first time and realising with something of a shock how the Pardoe mansion was no jewel in a simple setting. Had it been reached via a long curving drive, it would have been a huge disappointment and even as it was the monument grew straight out of the sky with every step nearer revealing another, discordant detail. East Wind House was a marriage of additions. The tiles were a new and vicious orange, ill-suited to the mellower brick of the walls and making the whole edifice resemble a person wearing the wrong hat for the occasion. The bright blue of the eaves and the guttering added extra disharmony along with the extension at the back in the wrong stone at the wrong height; windows had been replaced with modern replicas of originals. All in all the house looked like a woman dressed in a fit of indecision with more money than taste, a vision of half-executed dreams, absent-mindedly amended and finally worn for a careless fit like an old cardigan.

The massive front door, made of oak and curved to a point at the top, belonged to a church and only added to the impression of a folly. Sarah ignored this entrance and strolled round the back, her feet wet in grass which swayed to the knees. There were remnants here of a vast kitchen garden dominated by rampant rhubarb and a smell of unculled vegetables. A row of ornamental cabbages thrilled the eye with purple splendour. The sheep with the twisted horn hanging drunkenly over its wall eyes munched and burped next to a pot of uncontrolled nasturtiums flanking the back door.

What the hell game was Ernest playing? There might be an element of expensive eccentricity, the sense of money spent unwisely, but there was nothing in this establishment which had the perfume of riches, a scent Sarah Fortune found easy to detect in a client and often easier to despise. Charles Tysall had the odour of an arrogant minority, but there was nothing yet discernible here to attract the hourly rates of Ernest's London partnership. Not even the row going on in the kitchen, to which she listened without shame.

'Where's Mrs Tysall? Doesn't she eat breakfast? She looked very thin.'

'Shut up, Mother. Just shut up . . . And will you go and change out of that horrible dress? She's not Mrs Tysall, she's a lawyer from London and she's going to think you're even madder than you are, dressed like that.'

'Mrs Tysall and I would like champagne.'

'Oh, for Christ's sake. Julian, get her some lemonade, will you?'

'I don't want—'

'Yes you do. You just said you did. Drink your tea, you look like a—'

'Don't hit me,' Mummy was whining until Julian's voice rose, deceptively calm, with a hint of weariness.

'Don't be so silly. No one's going to hit you, never have, never will. Why did you let her wear that dress, Jo?'

'Oh, here we go again. Let her! Have you ever tried stopping her? She does what she wants. How do you suppose I stop her? I've got enough to do—'

'Sitting on your bottom all day? Playing house? Leaving dirt everywhere and the garden a mess? Pretending to cook? I don't know where you get the energy.'

Sarah remembered the elaborate meal of the night before, the polish on the furniture, the semi-tidiness, her own clean sheets, and reflected that Julian was being less than fair. Joanna's voice now had a hint of tears.

'Oh what's the point? I do nothing while you play God with the sick. Bet they're all queuing up now, praying for the chance to see another doctor. You look like those dead cod off one of the boats.'

'At least I work. One of us has to.' His voice was dangerous. There was a pause, a clatter of cutlery, then a crash.

'Oh, what a pity!' Mother's voice rose to a giggle. 'No champagne for Mrs Tysall!' Julian ignored the interruption.

'I'd have more to offer the sick if I wasn't surrounded by idiots at home. A brother who can't work and can't get a job unless I get it for him, a sister who thinks she deserves to be kept.'

'OK,' she howled, 'give us some money and we'll go. Isn't this what the lawyer's for?'

'Mrs Tysall, please,' Mother chanted.

'Money?' Julian taunted. 'Other people start their lives without.'

'I'll go,' Joanna shouted, 'and you can keep Mother. But you wouldn't, would you? Would you?' Her fist was pounding the table, her voice rising in hysteria, then sinking. Mouse began humming tunelessly; there was the sound of a chair scraping back on a stone floor. Julian's voice again, dismissive and distant.

'Tell Miss Fortune, when she deigns to appear, that I'll be in the surgery at twelve, and do remember what else I told you. Don't forget to give her directions. Don't offer to feed her either, not tonight, not any night. She supports herself as long as she's here and I don't think it will be long.'

Sarah waited. There was the remote sound of a door banging somewhere inside the house, silence but movement inside the kitchen, a sensation of relief. Sarah knocked on the open door and stepped inside.

Joanna leapt to her feet and turned back to look busy at the vast Raeburn with its large simmering kettle, rubbing her eyes with a tea towel, while Mrs Pardoe's mouth formed into a startled OOOh of something like pleasure. She looked as welcoming as a placid baby with exactly the same span of concentration. There was a stale-looking edifice of chocolate cake in the centre of the table.

'Good morning, Mrs Pardoe,' said Sarah. 'It's a lovely day.' The sleeveless gold lamé dress was only as shocking as the enormous ear-rings which hung down to bare shoulders, tinkling as Mrs Pardoe finished chewing her toast and dabbed at her mouth with the corner of the tablecloth, leaving small traces of marmalade.

'Good morning to you, Mrs Tysall. How nice to see you.'

Sarah felt cold as Joanna, flushed and uncertain, came back to the table with a pot of coffee.

'I do so hope you enjoy your stay, I made you a cake. I'm always making cakes and things, but no one eats them.' Mother was continuing in the same, fluting tone of a hotel receptionist fresh from a training course.

'Oh Mother,' said Joanna uneasily, embarrassed, but all fight gone.

'And I do wish,' said Mother, rising from the table and affording Sarah a glimpse of her pink trainers, 'that you young things would wear frocks. Trousers, my dear, are made for men.' With this she swept from the room in a cloud of perfume, a bright smile and fluttering of fingers to indicate her blessing. Joanna looked at Sarah across the table and tried to smile. Tears still lurked, not as well controlled after a quick appraisal of Sarah's appearance in the light of Mother's remarks. Joanna did not notice the dirt on the jeans, only their immaculate fit and the vibrant silk shirt ending across slim hips, and the fact that Miss Fortune's appearance in trousers bore no resemblance to her own.

'Did you hear us having a row?' she asked abruptly.

'Think I caught the tail-end. Sorry.'

'That's all right then. You must have missed the worst bit, when Edward was in on it too. He stormed out a while ago. A morning ritual. I should stay in the cottage if I were you, until after eight-thirty on weekdays. After that, it's only me and Mother. Have some coffee? Toast?'

'Please. Coffee.'

'By the way, you've to meet Julian at his surgery, about twelve, he said. I'll take you, but I'm under strict orders not to discuss business beforehand, not that I know much, not about the estate, whatever you call it, and all that.' The words were rushing out in a fit of apology.

'That's fine. I wouldn't expect you to disobey orders.' They smiled at each other conspiratorially, two women mourning the dominion of men. 'But can you answer me two things? First, why does this family need a lawyer to sort out who should inherit what? Why can't you do it for yourselves?'

Joanna waved vaguely round the mess of the kitchen, the tea spilt on the wooden table, rubbish stacked at one end, two fishing rods next to the Raeburn, the smashed glass on the floor. 'You can see why, can't you? We're not exactly good at the art of

communication. Bloody Julian gives the orders and buggers up
our lives, Ed looks after me. He and Julian never speak, that sort
of thing. What was the other question?'

'Why on earth', Sarah asked casually, 'does your mother call
me Mrs Tysall?'

'Search me . . . Oh, I remember, Edward said something
about it when she started this morning. There was a couple
called Tysall had a holiday cottage down here, a few years ago,
he said. Mrs Tysall had red hair, like yours, she sometimes came
here by herself. Then she had some kind of accident and
drowned. Ma used to talk to her in the hairdresser's. Well, everyone talked about her, I gather. It was a bit of a scandal at the
time, because the body got stuck somewhere, wasn't found for a
year, after a high tide. Must have been horrible. Lots of red hair.'

'What about her husband?'

Joanna thought hard. 'I dunno the details. More scandal, but
you'd have to ask Julian about that. He dealt with the bodies: it
suits him, he's better off with dead people.' She laughed at her
own wit. 'Oh, yes, once this Charles was told where his wife was
found, he thought she'd run away, or something, you see, he
must have walked out to see and got caught by the tide. He got
washed up in Holkham the next day. Must have been love.
Romantic, isn't it?'

Joanna was pouring more coffee, enjoying herself with ghoulish tales which did not touch her own life and mattered less than
her eighteen-year-old concerns with love and spots. Or so Sarah
guessed. The passions of the over thirties were obscene mysteries to teenagers.

'Charles Tysall was a client of ours,' she volunteered without
quite the right kind of indifference. 'I knew him.'

'Did you? I never did,' said Joanna, wondering how a person
managed to acquire a figure like Sarah's and the jeans to fit it. It
must be a combination of smoking instead of eating breakfast,
and living in the sinful paradise of London which she did not
crave.

'Well, knew him slightly.' She sipped her coffee, black. 'What an action-packed place this is,' Sarah added lightly. 'Family fights, suicides, sirens, death and all other adventures. Even a ghost, you were saying last night. Everything happens here.'

Joanna shot her a pitying glance of incredulous impatience.

'What on earth are you talking about?' she wailed. 'We own most of the village,' she added mournfully, 'and absolutely nothing happens here. Nothing at all.'

CHAPTER FOUR

The medical centre could have been anywhere. There was nothing rural about it and the clean, hygienic smell, still reminiscent of sickness, made it somehow a fitting place to discuss a will.

'. . . the residue of my estate, whatsoever and wheresoever, to my wife Jennifer absolutely. For her to dispose of between my children entirely in such shares as she sees fit.'

'Look,' Julian was saying from the opposite side of a depressing metal desk, oblivious to her curiosity, cutting short niceties and looking at any point in the bare room which did not include Sarah's presence, 'I can't pretend I like this because I don't. I don't like any of this business and I regret the necessity for your presence here. Ernest Matthewson was my father's lawyer for half a lifetime, but I don't always see the sense in his ideas.'

'I thought it was your idea,' she interrupted. Julian looked blank. A brief, forced smile touched his features like a magic wand, to reveal a glimpse of humanity on a face carved from stone, distressed by chronic pain which may or may not have been his own.

'My idea? Ernest simply told me you were coming. Never mind. You ARE here, for better or worse. You've looked at the will, but not the list of assets which form my mother's property as it is now.'

She waited for signs of smugness, saw none as he handed her three typed pages, headed with the name of a local estate agent.

A glance at the list showed a longish list of houses, business premises and shops. Sarah wondered fleetingly if there was anything freehold left in the village belonging to anyone else.

'About two thirds of it,' Julian said, guessing her thoughts. 'Took him twenty years. My father,' he continued, 'believed passionately in bricks and mortar, exchanged the proceeds of his manufacturing concerns for nothing else. Hence it was apposite for him to be on a roof when having a heart attack, because, at the age of seventy, he chose to clean leaves from the gulley. He always was an over achiever and a lousy delegator. Since his death, my mother has been as you see her; it appears to be a permanent malady. She can no longer read or cook, has no sense of property or propriety, no sense of time, no sense of fear, absolutely no insight into her own condition and no perception of ours. She's difficult, irritating, demanding, vulnerable and quite incapable of dealing with her own affairs since she doesn't even know what she owns. Neither do I, entirely. I believe Edward does. He works at the estate agent's who manage things.'

He sighed as if bored by the whole subject. 'Father was copping out, you see.' Julian went on with the same suppressed irritation. 'For such an astute and materialistic man, he was very indecisive. He left it all to Mother to sort it for him. Amazing. I thought he loved and trusted me. Obviously not.' Sarah watched him flinch.

'For the last couple of years, he and Mother seemed to rediscover each other. They behaved like lovers, told each other jokes instead of him simply issuing orders. Father even gave up social climbing, she hated it anyway. He perfected his skill at fishing. Talked about raising rare breeds of sheep. There's one left, in the garden.'

Sarah wanted everything. She wanted to know where Mrs Pardoe had worn her gold dress for the first time and what Mr Pardoe had been like. She wanted family portraits, anecdotes, signs of grief, instead of this unnerving formality. All she could see from here was that husband and wife between them had created a good-looking tribe, disparate in appearance, Edward, dark and slight, Joanna fair and rounded, and the eldest, sitting opposite, stocky and attractive with a jutting chin, red-gold curls, the blazing eyes of a fever and no inclination to wander from the point. Sarah supposed she had better act as she had always done with clients and pretend that she had more to offer than educated common sense. The pretence often became real.

'Look,' she began, 'it's a perfectly valid will.'

'Yes, I know that,' he said rudely. 'And it leaves me, as the eldest, to administer an estate over which I have no power. Mother can't make a power of attorney in my favour, because she'd have to understand what it was. I've tried and failed. I manage to collect rents, pay cheques and run things only because the bank manager's a patient, but I've got responsibility without authority. I also know, before you deign to tell me, that if she dies, Edward, Joanna and I would inherit in equal shares. Meantime, we're all stuck. We've got assets without a huge income. Enough, but not generous. Mother could last for thirty years.' He made the last statement fondly, a glimmer of admiration in his voice. Sarah caught him smiling, smiled back and watched his face harden, a man coarsened by bitterness and a loneliness beyond his own curing. Sarah was watching the fleeting betrayals of a condition which was second nature to herself, saw a man who had passed harsh judgements on himself.

'So,' she said briskly, 'this is what we do. Itemise the estate, then value it. Decide on how it should be managed, whether in or outside the family. Then go to the Court of Protection with our plans. They can write a will for your mother.'

'Simple,' said Julian ironically, the smile coming back.

'No. Not simple, but possible. It'll cost you the price of a house on a Monopoly board, but I don't suppose that matters, you seem to have plenty of houses. The object of this planning is to make sure your mother is safe, happy and well provided for. That's the primary aim. Then, to free up enough capital for you, Edward and Jo to spread your wings and fulfil your dreams sooner rather than later.'

Julian laughed, surprising himself. There was irony in the laugh, but at least it was laughter.

'What dreams? What dreams could a simple country doctor have?'

'Everyone has dreams,' Sarah protested. 'Your father must have had dreams to acquire as he did. Jo tells me that Edward has dreams of being an artist. She may dream of being a cook. Money's for refurbishing dreams. Why else work for it?'

'Some of us don't.'

Surely she could not believe Edward had honest dreams. So much for her wisdom. Edward dreaming of being an artist only meant the same Edward who blamed all his failures on being bored, growing from spiteful boy into lazy man, drifting through one job after another until his father had got him a sinecure in the local estate agent's office. His ability to concentrate was pathetic, his lack of convention a sham. Julian looked at Sarah and decided her neutral expression was a clever sham too. She might repeat what she was told, but only believe what she chose.

He sat back. This time the smile did not retreat into the gauntness of his face.

'Miss Fortune, I believe you may be a witch. I was waiting for you to accuse me of cupidity and you talk about dreams. I suppose you also exorcise demons?'

Sarah shook her head, smiling. 'I find it easier to pay them off. Gremlins, demons, goblins, regrets. They're the symptoms of life after thirty.'

Julian allowed himself another bark of laughter, which stopped abruptly to coincide with a knock on his door and the entry of a buxom nurse who bustled towards the pile of notes in a wire basket on the edge of the desk, smiling her professional smile. Then she stopped, face to face with Sarah, ceased smiling, grabbed the notes and scuttled away without apology. The door clicked shut angrily behind her. Sarah pretended to study the list of Pardoe assets Julian had given her. 'Amusement arcade, East Quay,' was a description which sprang from the page. The room was suddenly hot.

'Is that enough to keep you going?' Julian asked, back into the persona of a doctor asking if the medication would last the week. She wanted to slap him, but rose gracefully, tucking the papers under her arm.

'I wonder if your nurse thought I was a malingerer? Asking for a sick note to sit in the sun, or something of the kind? She seems . . . a little possessive.' She felt unreasonably angry, looked down at the pristine slacks which had replaced the dirtier jeans, too smart for a village surgery, noticed that Julian's skin resembled the colour of chalk.

'I'm sorry. You must have given her a shock. Actually, you gave me a shock when I first saw you. You happen to be the graven image of a patient of ours, oh, two years ago, but she was . . . well, difficult to forget.'

'Mrs Tysall,' said Sarah flatly. 'Your mother calls me Mrs Tysall. Someone in the hairdresser's said I was like an old client. It's extremely disconcerting, a person could get sick of comparisons, but I suppose you all mean Elisabeth Tysall who resides in the graveyard, without even a headstone on her grave. Wife of Charles.'

He had risen from his seat, still pale, twisting a pencil in his large hands.

'Your sister says you dealt with both bodies, Elisabeth and her husband,' Sarah went on artlessly, driven by the same flat anger. 'She was your patient, you say. I always wanted to meet someone who knew her. Was she very lovely?'

The pencil snapped.

'Get out of here. You're right. Comparisons are odious. You don't resemble Elisabeth at all. No one does.'

Sarah stopped, watched his rage crumble into a thinly disguised distress, the veneer of control exerting itself slowly.

'Demons and gremlins,' she murmured. 'I didn't mean to touch a nerve. Was she a friend of yours? She certainly needed one.'

He shook his head, reverting abruptly to the original state of officious rudeness.

'Please go, Miss Fortune. I doubt if you're at all suitable to help us. Spend the weekend in the cottage, as our guest. Then we'll reconsider.'

'As you please.'

Stonewall Jones ran from the amusement arcade, left down the quay, left again and then cut through a crooked alley leading to the main street. On the way, he could nod in several directions to houses where various relatives lived, first his mother, out at work at the moment, her carefully made sandwiches mashed in his pocket, his baby brothers three doors up with Aunty Mary, Uncle Jack round the corner in the police station. The place was a mine of people who were good for a fifty-pence touch, and those who would, in various scolding ways, let him in had he asked, but not one compared with Cousin Rick.

Rick had his drawbacks, but as a hero he was faultless, while as a spy, Stonewall was the soul of discretion, with the added talent of being able to lie convincingly, although truth was his natural inclination. He also had a memory as long as his fleeting stride and a fine eye for detail. Which was why he was now so excited. The redhead.

The memory was visual rather than verbal. Stonewall talked all the time to Rick, sometimes to his mates at school, while anyone else got short shrift. The redhead girl came back before his eyes from a time when he had been smaller, but not such a baby he'd fail to remember a woman with her face full of stitches, coming out of the medical centre, crying. That was two years and a whole lifetime ago; but he never quite forgot because he had not had the chance. First he had found her credit cards and stuff with her photo on it hidden in the creeks. Then he and his stepdad found the body, exactly one year after.

Dad had been terribly sick, which Stonewall had not considered a good example. Tutored by illicit, adult videos, seen in the house of a mate, he wasn't that shocked himself. The redhead looked like a real dead dog, not a person, the impression accentuated by the long hair like red spaniel ears covered in muddy sand, floppy, silken, gritty and wet. She was a thing, not to be confused with anything live.

The man they had found a month later, well he was different. This time it had been him and Rick, the rovers of the creeks in their idle hours last summer, looking for flotsam, only Stonewall secretly hoping they'd find another corpse, because of all the fuss people made of him last time. Being famous gave him a wonderful, fleeting insight into being noticed.

They'd been so brave, they could still make themselves shudder at the memory. The second body, a man, had only been in and out of the sea for two days and was so nearly alive they couldn't look at him. A man with his face in the rictus of a smile, another gob full of sand as he lay on a bank, sluiced with mud, his good trousers dragged off his ankles and his bottom a little white mountain. Turned him over and his goolies fell out. Hung like a donkey, Rick said. They had sniggered while trembling, called Uncle Jack who panicked and talked about sending for the lifeboat. More sniggering, hugging themselves, as if anything more than a rowboat could get near at low water, he'd have to go by land. Seen one, seen 'em all, said Rick. They had stood in the tideless channel and rocked with mirth until the doctor came and seemed to know who it was. Then it was harder to laugh. In the end, it was he who carried the corpse away with their help, brought his car as far as he could, using a piece of Rick's dripping sail to lug the thing over two creeks and into the boot; it was all anyone could do with the tide rising all the time.

Mostly, though, it was left to the doc. Everyone else turned away; so had Rick and he, but not before they had both seen what they had seen: the doctor, kicking the corpse as if it had been a football. Just a couple of kicks, but hard. Stonewall could still hear the sound of a shoe going into a waterlogged chest, could not quite recall the sight of it, since even he had turned his head, but he could always recall the sound. Schluck, schluck, schluck, the thudding of mad hatred. Funny at the time. Everything with Rick was funny, but they never, ever discussed that bit again. Stonewall had felt sorry for the drowned man, later. He reckoned that if he drowned, he would be taken away and buried somewhere like the man was. His mum and dad wouldn't come to the funeral either. They'd be too busy.

Stonewall pounded on the door of Swamp Cottage, then opened it. There was a lock which was never used, nothing to steal; burglary was not a problem in the village, except recently, when it could be called the work of tourists or the ghost. The door led straight into a tiny scullery where only two dishes lurked in the sink and a fly buzzed at the window, down a step into a living room where a TV blared. Rick sat in an old sofa, his finger easing stuffing out of a split in the arm as he gazed at the screen. The sight of the haversack on the floor and the bruises round the eyes threw Stonewall into a panic.

'You're not going, Rick? You're not going away, are you? Your dad'll kill you.' His voice was high with anxiety.

'He already tried,' Rick grunted. He got up, towering in the gloomy room, his head inches away from the ceiling as he ruffled the boy's hair. 'Don't fret, boy, it wasn't so bad. Only I might go on the boat tonight. Then again, I might not.'

'Can I come too?'

'Nope. Only in the mornings. Your mum'd miss you. God knows why.' Stonewall relaxed. If Rick was teasing, he must be all right. The boy took up occupation of the sofa and began to play with the stuffing, rolling flax between his fingers. He was utterly relieved to find Rick so normal, had news to impart which made him as full to bursting as three rounds of chips followed by chocolate.

'Tell you what, Rick, I just seen a ghost just now. I did, honest. A woman.'

'Oh yeah?'

'I saw this woman, see? Same one as I used to see, long time ago, when my dad started taking me out in the boat—'

'And you were scared to death of the water. Oh I remember that. You'd cry like some mating cat in heat, you would.' Rick taunted without malice. 'Wait a minute,' he added, still teasing, 'you mean you saw one whole woman ugly enough to be a ghost? Just the one? There's dozens out there!' His laugh hit the rafters.

'It's the same one,' said the boy stubbornly, 'that came up out of the sand. She went down the creeks, drunk, her face mashed up. I was with Dad, he ticked me off for laughing at her. Course, that was MY body, the one I found with Dad, not the one I found with you. I'd never have remembered her if it wasn't for her stuff, with her picture in. Anyway, this one I just seen got the same red hair. Lots. Got to be a ghost. Or a twin?' He wilted under Rick's glare.

Stonewall could not resist the importance of being present at the finding of two bodies, made reference to it whenever he could. He'd been a cosseted celebrity in school twice over. Rick, on the other hand, had only ever found the one. A few dogs and cats down the creeks, a couple of swans poisoned by lead weights, a seal killed by massive fishing hooks, but only one corpse. It was the only feature of Stonewall's little life which gave him any superiority. He milked it.

'Red hair? You saw a ghost with red hair this morning, did you?' Rick jeered. Stonewall was deflated.

'Saw her this morning, when I went out looking for you. Saw her again, walking into town, with your girlfriend,' he said cunningly, but Rick only shrugged.

'That weren't no ghost, baby. That's a lawyer, so she says. Belongs out with those Pardoes. They could do with a gardener, never mind a lawyer. And Jo isn't my girlfriend.'

'Oh no? Not what I heard,' said Stonewall, looking so much the little man. Rick wanted to laugh at him but hadn't the heart.

'Anyway, I follows them both. That's how I come to reckon the red one was a ghost. Your Joanna went in the grocer's; the ghost went in the doctor's. Just like that other one with the hair used to do, all the time. My Aunty Mary used to say it was shocking.'

Stonewall loved to be the purveyor of adult gossip, which lost none of its sparkle in his eleven-year-old eyes for the obscurity of its implications. He simply liked the tone of it, knew they were talking about sex when they lowered their voices and went into corners. In his own home with two babies, he was not a power-ful person, always last in line, listening. Brilliant, Rick would say, sometimes in genuine amazement at what this child, so silent indoors and so loquacious out, could collect as second-hand knowledge. Stonewall sensed attention was beginning to wander.

'Going to get your girlfriend on the boat?' he asked, to rekin-dle interest.

'She ain't my girlfriend, I tell you. You deaf?'

'She thinks she is,' Stonewall muttered.

Rick swaggered. 'Her and who else?' he said, then caught sight of his face in the cracked mirror propped over the mantel-piece, let his mouth drop in a leer. 'Her and Granny Pardoe, at this rate, any woman draws a short straw with me,' he muttered. 'Fancy an ice-cream down on the beach?'

The boy hid his enthusiasm by shrugging, nodded, followed with a little skip and a sigh of pleasure which somehow got out before he could stop it.

'And there's another thing,' he began as they went out into the alley.

'Oh yes, another ghost, I suppose. The one with white hair? Tall bloke? Come on, everyone says they've seen that.'

'Maybe ghosts come out at the same time.'

'Well, I don't know,' said Rick admiringly, cuffing him round the ear. 'I think you need glasses, boy. Dark ones, with wipers, stop you seeing so much.'

'That ghost got my dog,' said Stonewall stubbornly, horribly ashamed of the way his eyes filled with tears. 'He did. I saw him, and then Sal ran away.'

Rick was thinking of his evening date, half wishing he hadn't made it. Thought of Jo and tried to put her out of his mind.

When Sarah got back to the homestead, wondering whether it was better simply to pack up her bags and leave before she was sacked, two sights met her eyes as she went, like an old familiar, to the back door. The first was Mrs Pardoe, sunbathing in the cab-bage patch. She looked like a religious emblem, lying in the pose of a crucifixion with her legs discreetly crossed, the dress hoiked up and the arms spreadeagled. A little dirt didn't seem to matter. Sarah approached with caution until her shadow fell over the body. It was very hot; her own longing for the sea was intense.

'Hallo.'

'You're taking my sunlight,' said Mrs Pardoe, shifting in irritation. 'Give me back my rays.'

'Can I get you anything?' The body laid out on the earth still had very good legs, the face resembled a pixie, oddly ageless.

'Ice-cream,' said the lady, dreamily, then closed her eyes.

The second sight was Joanna crying in the kitchen, with none of her mother's aplomb, but again, there was a sense of absent beauty.

'Sorry,' said Joanna, beyond embarrassment. 'Sorry. I can't help it.'

'Is it your mother?'

'Oh no, I'm used to her. She's fine, honestly. Absolutely fine. You sort of adjust, you know?'

Sarah didn't know, but nodded.

'I mean, she's quite safe by herself and everything, and she doesn't ask for much, never did. I mean, I could go out this evening, even though Ed and Julian are always out on Fridays. I mean, I think Ma quite likes a bit of time to herself and anyway, she goes to bed ludicrously early, so that's fine, she doesn't need a babysitter; but I can't go anywhere, can I? I mean, not even round to Caroline's, can I? Even though she's asked me twice and I said I would . . .'

Sarah continued nodding.

'Because I'm different, and Caroline's very together, you see. And she knows I was going out with Rick who is, let's face it, the best looking boy around, but he won't talk to me now. Julian warned him off. And she'll have her friends there, and I've got to pretend I just don't care, you know, have a glass of wine and make a joke of it. Which I just about could, just about, even if it isn't true and it's only a small party, but not like this. Not when I've got nothing to wear . . .'

Sarah nodded. An obscure dilemma, one she remembered well. King Henry offered his kingdom for a horse. A love-sick teenager would offer hers for the right suit of clothes. Twice seen, Joanna was remarkably badly, almost childishly, dressed. Sarah settled into an uncomfortable wooden chair and kissed goodbye to her dreams of a distant beach for the afternoon, pulled out her cigarettes, lit one, did not offer the rest. The child was a smoke-free zone.

'What sort of clothes,' she asked gently, 'do you think you need?'

'Classics,' said Jo, fervently. 'I read it in a magazine . . . Caroline reads it too. Stuff that makes you look sophisticated. You know, older, thinner, all that stuff. Expensive stuff. Julian says I can get them if I want, but Edward says don't, it's bad to grow up too soon. I always laugh, tell him it doesn't matter, but it does.'

Sarah felt a recurrence of spontaneous dislike for Edward Pardoe.

'Classics. A bit of nice jewellery? Just a bit?' said Sarah thoughtfully.

'Exactly. Edward would murder me. I can't afford it anyway, I promised him a new fishing rod for his birthday, they cost a bomb—'

'Stand up.'

Joanna stood, much taller than Sarah.

'I've got some lovely shirts, fit anyone. Leggings for the bottom? Come with me.'

'Oh, I couldn't, Miss Fortune, honestly. I'm really sorry, blubbing all over you, scarcely know . . . Oh, it's so awful . . .'

'Sisters under the skin,' said Sarah lightly. Clothes could be the stuff of dreams or the staff of confidence. 'I wouldn't listen to Edward,' she added kindly. 'Men are no good on these things. A nice, bold colour, no patterns, is what you need.'

'Black,' said Jo fervently. 'Then I could cope.'

There was darkness and privacy in the pine woods which

covered the dunes and led to the beach, but when the man with snow-white hair came to the brow of the last ridge, the wind took away his breath into a vast, galloping sky, leaving him shocked. Memory played such tricks, even since yesterday. He had forced himself to walk this far with his military steps; the sea should have been closer, instead of that distant, mocking promise. The tide was a fickle woman who never obeyed orders. The man saw only the horizon, noticed no details, felt no pain and counted nothing but the minutes.

The sand was soft, his ill-fitting shoes suddenly struggling for a sinking foothold as he thrashed the air with his arms, overbalanced, fell with his jacket flapping, rolling over and over, sand in his hair and his mouth, landing on his back on the beach. There was an initial sense of fury, then exhilaration in letting go like a child, falling into a blissful, uninhibited waving of limbs without any sense of danger. He wanted to do it again. The sky was blinding blue when he opened his eyes and laughed. A face came into focus above his own.

'That wasn't very graceful,' said Edward Pardoe.

The man grunted, sat up, stroking his luxuriant white hair which curled into the back of his neck. His clothes were the ill-assorted garments of a tramp, too heavy for summer, but he folded his long, thin body about itself and clasped his hands to his knees with a kind of elegance. Strange, how wearing the clothes of a person of no importance could turn one into exactly that. He was beginning to perceive how disguise became habit. The transition had frightened him once, not now.

Edward considered that the face beneath the stubble of beard had been handsome once, possibly exceptional. They sat and said nothing for a while.

'I'd like to reorganise this shoreline,' Edward remarked, frowning. 'It's so . . . imperfect.'

'But it's here,' said the man.

'Yes, I know, but the sea should be lapping at my feet. The trees should be more exotic than these drab pines. A few extraordinary shrubs. Flowers in winter. I could do it. I shall do it.'

'After art, nature,' the man murmured. 'These kinds of dreams are expensive.'

They were silent again. The sea stayed the same distance, the man staring at it as if mesmerised.

'Have you been seen?' Edward asked as if it did not matter.

'What do you think? From sea or land? I suppose so. A beastly little boy and his dog. The dog ran after me. I loathe dogs. I move about, beach hut, boat, occasional empty cottage where people obligingly leave me their soap. The village is crowded with holiday-makers, ignorant pigs. They don't notice anyone who looks so venerable.' He touched his white locks. 'People don't notice me now.'

'They may have done once, when you were younger,' said Edward nastily.

'I am a person of no fixed abode,' said the man quietly. 'That is my choice, not my destiny. It does not mean I am a person of no consequence.' Even as he said it he wondered very briefly if it were true, looked down at his hands. Of course he could still remember how to pare his nails.

'What did you do about the dog?'

It was disturbing the way the man exerted superiority so easily with his patrician voice and his air of sheer indifference. He looked like an outcast and behaved as if he were a prince.

'The dog? Buried it. It was only a dog.'

Edward swallowed.

'You aren't invisible,' he said sharply. 'I've been hearing local rumours about a ghost with white hair committing minor burglaries. You're obviously perfecting this talent of yours.'

'Mrs Tysall was good at picking locks,' the man volunteered irrelevantly. 'She was never fond of keys, but she could always get in, or out.'

'I never knew Mrs Tysall,' said Edward, profoundly irritated. 'It was my wonderful brother who knew her, as I told you in some detail.' Both were staring seaward, their eyes never meeting.

'I have to be sure,' the man said.

'How to get into the surgery,' Edward continued, 'is something you must work out for yourself. As I said yesterday, you'll need the keys to his desk.'

He dropped a ring of keys on the sand in between them. The man never took his eyes off the horizon as he felt for them with long, lazy fingers.

'By the way, don't stay in any of the cottages nearest the house again, will you? We have a visitor in the end one. My mother calls her a cow, but she seems quite observant.'

'Aah, your lovely sister.'

'Leave her alone, she's mine,' said Edward sharply.

'Of course I shall. I didn't doubt it for a moment. Ah, the love of a sister. How could you be ashamed?

'"Say that we had one father, say one womb
Are we not therefore each to the other bound
So much the more by nature? by the links
Of blood and reason? One soul, one flesh,
One love, one heart, one all?"'

Silence again.

'Who wrote that?' Edward asked softly. 'I like it.'

' *'Tis Pity She's a Whore*.'

Edward clenched his fists.

'John Ford. A play. I'm not being personal.'

Edward relaxed.

'Here,' he said roughly. 'Be grateful for the love of a sister. She made these sandwiches for me. She does every day. Pity you can't fish for food. I could give you a rod.'

The man took the sandwiches without thanks, opened and ate them with the voracity of a dog before the daily bowl, swallowing rather than chewing. His teeth were brown. The silence was punctuated only by the sound of his jaws, the soft shushing of the trees behind them and the distant shouting of games. Edward could imagine the thin man eating carrion, crumbling bones and all, and shuddered slightly.

'Food', the man announced, 'is a matter of complete indifference. I detest the vulgar business of eating. I suppose it would be useful if I had learned to fish. Can you fish?'

'Not well. I go out at night to learn,' said Edward, miserably. 'When no one's watching. My father fished,' he added inconsequentially. 'He said it made a man of you.' The silence stretched again, unbearably.

'However did I come to meet someone like you?' Edward asked facetiously, simply to interrupt it. 'You've quite enlivened my summer.'

'Dreams,' the man said abruptly. 'We are all entangled in dreams.' From his mouth, the word sounded oddly obscene.

'Oh yes?'

'You met me,' the man said evenly, 'when you found me trespassing in that cottage of yours. It seemed to amuse you. You said you wouldn't turn me out immediately, would even show me another empty place to stay, provided I was good enough to set a little fire inside it, enough to stop it being used. It wasn't much to ask of a man on holiday.'

'We seem to have gone on from there,' Edward murmured.

'Into the dreams. You dream of changing the landscape. For which you need your brother destroyed and your mother dead.'

Edward would never have put it so baldly. He felt the prickling of his scalp, a terrible tingling in his limbs of dreadful excitement.

'And you?'

'On my master's behalf? I dream of the proof of wickedness and adultery. I dream of revenge and the satisfaction of honour. "Death, thou art a guest long looked for; I embrace thee and thy wounds."' Edward scrambled to his feet, lightheaded. Enough was enough.

'Don't tell me what my dreams are. I'll see you here, same time, tomorrow or Sunday.'

The man nodded, the breeze lifting his long white hair off the once spectacular face, his eyes still staring towards the sea.

Sarah Fortune had packed a case for all eventualities except the extremes of country life, being ignorant of what it was; black could be provided. A sueded silk overshirt with the elbow-length sleeves she always wore, slightly padded shoulders, cool and elegant over leggings, completed by a deep cerise belt and a discreet but heavy silver necklace and ear-rings. The child looked ten years older, transformed into a sleek, black cat with a whole decade of confidence.

'Shirt needs an iron. Where is it?'

'Oh, in that cupboard. Oh, Sarah! This shirt is positively divine!'

A lawyer dressing a client for a night on the town. If these were the worst eccentricities of country life, Sarah thought she could take to it. In the course of this long foraging through her suitcase, she had heard plenty of family history since Joanna talked non-stop. Such as, Father being a lovable tyrant, they'd all wept buckets; Julian a despicable one. Such as Mother never getting her own way about anything when Father was alive, poor thing. About Edward being marvellous, but constantly misjudged, and about how all Joanna Pardoe wanted to do with her life was to learn to cook properly, get married and have a lot of babies.

Sarah had agreed that feminism was overrated, no, a career was not always a route to happiness, and that yes, family life was a perfectly honest ambition, if you had the temperament for it. Then she heard all about Rick and how wonderful he was and how he didn't love Joanna any more. Julian had told him to fuck off.

'I suppose,' Joanna finished wistfully, putting on the freshly pressed shirt, which looked easily as expensive as its price, 'that's a better reason for being rejected than being too fat. Heavens, look at the time.'

'Fat? Who's fat?' said Sarah. She had dragged a mirror from the bedroom. Joanna pirouetted in front of it, giggling, half convinced, but better than that, being sure she could convince others of profound sophistication.

'What did you do to my hair?' It was twisted above her head: it would fall throughout the evening, gracefully. Blonde tendrils escaped round her ears. 'Look, are you sure I can wear this?'

'You can be sick on it if you like. I wouldn't have ironed it otherwise, would I? Eat your heart out, Caroline what'sit. You look a million dollars. I'd kill for hair like yours,' Sarah added fervently.

'But yours is so lovely.'

'No, not always,' said Sarah.

Mrs Pardoe had removed her station to the upstairs window where she often waited throughout the late afternoon, in case the ice-cream van came, not every day, but often enough to warrant her vigil.

She watched her daughter, crossing from the cottages where she had seen her go earlier with the old cow. When she saw Joanna striding back like a modern princess, head held high, face enlivened by a rosy glow of hope, she sat back and sighed with profound pleasure.

Ernest Matthewson was an old friend, one to be trusted. He had such good ideas.

Ernest made her think of food: ice-cream, chocolate cake, steak and champagne. And all those years of being called Mouse.

CHAPTER FIVE

Malcolm Cook sat with his stepfather and his mother over the evening meal they shared once a fortnight, sometimes under sufferance, although never when Sarah had been included. There were no apologies for absences; the food was elaborate since it never took long for plump Mrs Matthewson to recover from a period of dietetic austerity. Ernest was spared the low-fat yoghurt in the interests of feeding Malcolm, a son who was far too thin in his mother's estimation. She did her best by hiding cream in the soup, serving hot garlic bread ostensibly made with low-calorie spread. Her husband ate heartily while Malcolm failed to be fooled, played the game back, complimenting everything, eating only what he needed.

'Want some more, Malcolm dear? Another potato?'

Everything calm so far, just like a normal Friday dinner, as long as she was careful not to leave them alone for too long. So they all sat with their coffee, their spines sunk into the feathers and the humming birds of the chairs and behaved as if nothing had happened, until the phone rang in the hall and Mrs Matthewson thought it was safe to leave them.

'Father,' said Malcolm, 'why did you send Sarah away?'

'I didn't,' Ernest responded indignantly. 'It was her choice, she volunteered. Couldn't wait to go. She wanted the sea, didn't mind where it was. She's always talking about living in the country, by the sea. Good chance to experiment. Nothing to do with you.'

Malcolm felt in the cigar box on his left, set on an ornate table decorated with more birds. He withdrew one of his father's best, tucked it into the open pocket of his shirt, then lit one of his own cigarettes which Father despised. Ernest winced at the subtlety of these gestures of insolence.

'You must think my stupidity is entirely comprehensive,' Malcolm continued in the smooth, authoritative tones of the advocate he was. 'But sometimes it lapses into an aberration called intelligence. You may have been right about Sarah and me, I doubt it, but did you have to be so cruel to her?'

'Cruel?' Ernest blustered. 'Who said anything about cruel? All right, I thought it was time both of you did a bit of thinking and it seemed like a good opportunity. I must admit to not quite realising where it was I was sending her. She said it didn't matter. There was something she wanted to do in that part of the world. Someone to see.'

'Of course you knew. You were once friends with the Pardoe family. You sent her to sort out an estate which could be sorted out better by someone else in a matter of hours, to the place where Charles Tysall's wife committed suicide, and he followed suit.' He kept his voice calm. Ernest was at his least reliable when alarmed. All he could do at the moment was grunt.

'What happened to the Tysall business empire, Father?'

Ernest snorted in disgust. 'The estate will take years to resolve. What do you know or care about business? You like it down where you are, prosecuting grubby criminals—'

'And what else was Charles? The soul of probity? Eton educated he may have been, good family, yes, but he founded his companies on stolen ideas, drove people to ruin, brutalised his wife—'

'There's no proof about that,' Ernest muttered. 'He may have told me things, but he may have fantasised. Don't speak ill of the dead.'

The Persian cat sprang from its cushion as Malcolm leaned

over his father. There was a little hiss from Ernest of post-
prandial sleep, only possibly feigned. Malcolm, ever aware of the
shame of violence which was subsumed in himself by the habit
of running twenty miles a week, was far too humane to strike
someone already unconscious, although the temptation was certainly there. If only this old man were not so Machiavellian; if
only they had talked more, instead of just enough; if only they
had really exchanged information about what had happened to
Sarah immediately before Malcolm found her. If only the son
and the mother, in the interests of Ernest's health, had not
sought to protect him from information which could shock and
alarm, and if only it were not too late now.

'I'm thinking about Sarah, not your bloody clients,' Malcolm
muttered, more to himself. 'Because she taught me about loving,
Dad. That's what she did. That's what she does. I don't mean
just sex; I mean loving.'

Ernest jolted out of a dream, rubbing his belly.

'Tart. That's the problem. A bit of a tart,' he muttered.

'What did you say?' Malcolm asked. 'I was talking about
Sarah.'

'So was I, but what I meant was that I shouldn't have eaten
that pie. Too tart,' Ernest grumbled, still stroking his paunch. He
looked at his stepson pleadingly.

'Do you know your loyalty to your clients is ludicrous?' said
Malcolm. 'You take the code to extremes. I thought you'd have
been cured. Would you tell me, for instance, if Tysall was alive?'

'No,' said Ernest. 'He isn't, but I wouldn't. Not for you to do
what you were trying to do before. Prosecute him for fraud
when all he ever did was steal other people's ideas. Perfectly
good capitalistic practice. I couldn't let that happen to a client of
mine. Not even a dead one.'

Again, that terrible temptation twitched in Malcolm's fingers,
made him ball his hands into fists and keep them by his sides.
The ample figure of Malcolm's mother stood frozen in the
doorway, the whole of her suddenly forlorn. After all the work
she and Sarah had done, there they were, father and adopted

son, back at loggerheads, with love, that dangerous and volatile commodity, as elusive as ever.

'You see? I love it, see?' Rick yelled above the din. 'I mean I just do. Could be all I know and that's for why, but I love it. Can't help it.'

'Can I try?'

'Course you can. Pity Stonewall isn't here. He's the expert. Which one do you want? Try this one, this one's really good.'

Sarah wasn't confused by choice, only the row. There was a background and foreground of thunder, of bleep, bleep, bleep, explosions, machine-gun fire, electronic voices issuing commands, the muffled explosions of a dozen bombs, the sound of falling cash. In the corner of the large room, separated from the rest by age, the older generation sat to play bingo in a serious, dedicated row of grey heads with handbags on laps, listening with all the earnestness of a congregation in church to a voice echoing sonorously through a microphone. 'Number eleven, go to heaven, take a dive, number five . . . on its own, number one . . .' Above them hung the tawdry prizes for which they concentrated as though their lives would be altered by lime green furry bears, brilliant pink dolls, plastic skeletons, jigsaw puzzles and on the top tier only, dusty under the unforgiving lights, glass and brass table lamps with heavily frilled nylon shades, brilliant vases, sets of cheap tumblers, bigger teddy bears with bows, grinning pottery cats with glittery eyes, none of it worth the price of three tickets for a game or the yearning it inspired.

Sarah sat on a pedestal as comfortable as the seat of a bicycle, inserted fifty pence and watched a man with a mask run up the street on the screen in front of her. Windows opened each side of him; the enemy dropped bombs on his head, emerged from doors and windows with the sole purpose of assassination. Pressing a button and pulling a lever in an unnatural feat of co-ordination would shoot the killers into the sky and save the refugee from the gang of thousands. She failed dismally: he was dead within seconds, gone in a big boom, noisier than all the rest. Game over, said the screen.

'You know what you are,' Rick yelled in her ear. 'Useless! Another?'

To her left, a boy stood, his body braced, his hands moving so fast they were blurred, his eyes transfixed by green monsters which bathed his hair in the same colour, his screen emitting the rat-tat-tat of a rifle and the muted sounds of artificial, bloodless agony.

'No thanks. Where do you go to draw breath?'

'Why?' he shouted.

'Is this all there is?'

He grinned. 'Isn't it enough?'

He liked the noise, but heard the message, led her to the back of the arcade where a voice still had to be raised to make sense, although not as much. She was temporarily deaf and blind. The light was eerie here, the carpet ran out into a couple of ante-rooms, one containing a table, chair, sink, kettle, cardboard boxes and signs of disuse, the other, more machines, untidy, unlit, strangely lifeless, lurching towards one another. They reminded her of the graveyard.

'Dead ones,' said Rick. 'I don't like to see them really. Some broken. Mostly gone out of fashion. They change all the time. Nothing lasts long. The kids master them, want something else. Don't want to see the dead ones. I stay out front. There's nothing else out here, only a back yard.' He opened a door beyond the silent machines. The remnant of fast-fading, natural daylight on the cusp between late evening and summer night was faintly shocking after the dazzle of the screens. In that light, Rick looked exhausted. The bruises had merged into the lights of the arcade; out here, they formed extra shadows to his handsome face. An attractive boy, ten years her junior. His face should not have held the merest line. The world should be his for the asking: he should be full of dreams.

After an hour in a pub called the Globe, he had volunteered to show her the arcade, or was it because she had asked? He couldn't remember, forgot as well how he had worried about this rash offer of a drink in the pain of near dawn when she had done his housework, just liked being where he was, with her, half hoping everyone he knew, except Jo, of course, would see. Which they did, good bit of gossip tomorrow and a lot of explaining to do to poor old Stonewall. Then, looking up into the stars visible from the back yard of the arcade, he felt suddenly sad, bereft, lonely, wanting to spill his guts, tell her stuff he never told. Also sleepy, the bruised ribs and early rising taking a toll. Must be the beer, the unaccustomed silence, the perfume. He slid down the wall and stayed at the bottom. She squatted beside him.

'Sorry,' he said. 'Things catch up, you know?'

'You've gone all pale, Rick.'

Without thinking, he felt for her hand. Must be drunk.

'You're nice, you know? Why'd you say you'd come out for a drink? You said you fancied a walk by the sea, but I'm a wreck, look at me.'

'A nice wreck. Place is full of your friends.'

He struggled to his feet. 'Think that's good enough reason to go out the back way. Cup of coffee's what I need. I live round the corner. Goo'night. Sorry.'

'I like coffee too.'

There was a shame in it, sneaking through the alley from the back yard of the arcade on his night off, back up the road to Swamp Cottage, letting her in with him to see the place where he lived. Tidy, scruffy, but clean; he was good at cleaning, good at nothing else. Strange the way she took over without being bossy, just as she had this morning. Made toasted cheese sandwiches without asking where anything was, terrific. You'd think she'd been here dozens of times, it was like being with Stonewall only not like that at all. It was food he needed, food he had forgotten all day. A whole day with nostrils full of hamburger onions or ice-cream with a chocolate flake stuck on top; a man forgot to eat, he explained. The room came back into focus, leaking sofa and all, he was still proud of it. He loved the way she ate, long fingers, nibbling mouth, and he still wanted to spill his guts. Wasn't much good for a bargain, was he? She'd wanted to have a look at the sea, talk about the Pardoes and he'd never mentioned anyone but himself. And Jo. Oddly, it hadn't felt like a betrayal, talking about Jo. It felt nice when she'd told him about Jo dressing up earlier to go out with the girls. Not with some other bloke. That was the point when the room refocused with shocking clarity. He'd been talking about Jo for twenty minutes.

'Why did Edward warn me off?' he asked out loud.

'Edward? It was Julian. You told her.'

That was what it was like, being with a woman who listened. You didn't have to explain anything, all your disjointed, drunken, exhausted thoughts were assembled for you.

'No. I met her once. Told her how her brother told me to fuck off. I meant Edward, of course. Julian's all right. He wouldn't do that. He wouldn't threaten you if you were behind with the rent, no more than his dad would have done. Edward told me to fuck off or get evicted. Not that there was any need. I love Jo, you know? We've played together since kids. I fancy her rotten, but what's the use? I'm not much use to a gorgeous bird like that, am I? Even if I love her. Even if I want her so much I think about her all the time.'

'Why?'

It was the only piece of his evening's rambling conversation which she did not seem to follow, she who seemed to piece together what he said even while he said it, she should have known this last bit, but how? Christ, she'd had half the story of his life, the arcade, his dreams, all but the greatest. She'd been more than perfect, she'd raised his stock with the multitudes, including his dad, sitting in the corner of the bar with his mouth open, serve him right, and she still didn't know nothing. About him being a virgin, at his age, the only one never quite able, out of fear of failure, and even after fumbling efforts, to do anything but grope.

'Why aren't you any good for Jo?' the woman was reminding him gently.

'I got too many kickings from dad!' he yelled, loud enough to be heard over a thousand screens filled with computerized deaths and loud heroes. 'He did for me, Dad did. I think.' He was holding her hand again, didn't know why, there didn't seem too many minutes since he first had, sliding down the wall of the yard, and then here, a moment or two before the focus on his own room came back, still holding. He could smell her, wanted to smell her. Cheese, toast, perfume. Long sleeves of stuff he liked to touch, felt like suede. Here was this fancy bird, watching him crying like a kid. Just like Stonewall had on the beach this afternoon, when he'd found his dog's collar come in with the tide, as if he'd needed any confirmation that the bitch was dead.

Still holding hands, him and this older bird, sitting on his couch, in tune with all that old corrosive despair and shame. Her doing something else, touching something else, saying not much, putting her chin on his chin, tiny as she was, no doubt so she could look into his eyes and laugh herself sick. Only she wasn't. Smiling but not laughing, she was doing something else. She seemed to have lost her shirt. There were pretty little marks on her arms, like a series of meaningless tattoos.

'Kicking,' she was saying from a distance, 'doesn't do an ounce of harm, never did. Big man like you.'

He thought of the big man he and Stonewall had found, hung like a donkey, skin so white, dead like his attributes. It had mattered more to him than any imprint from Dad's boot, and he also knew he'd seen the last of those. The last, the last, the very last, of both sensations of disgust.

He would wonder later how it was he lost either his fear or his virginity on his sinking, third-hand couch with the stuffing hanging out. He would have liked to remember the details, recall them for inspection.

Rick woke, admiring himself for what he knew he had done for the first time in his twenty-one years. Fucked someone, slowly, beautifully. Someone who left him with a blanket up to his chin, his feet out of shoes, his head steady, a waft of perfume and a sense of pride which owed nobody.

Edward lay after dark and slept. He could have gone fishing, but he didn't. Fishing to prove he could do something, or to please a dead father, or simply to gain power over the fish, he didn't know which. It was an addiction. The old silk coverlet was twisted, the space next to his own body empty and cold. Ever since little Joanna had crept into his bed to tickle him awake in an orgy of innocence each morning, a practice she had suspended long since of her own accord, Edward woke with the expectation of finding her there. She had crept into bed at a dangerous age for a boy teased at school, tormented by his hormones and scolded at home for laziness. He had simply let her remain etched on his mind and imprinted on his skin as the only desirable girl in the world, rehearsed in wet day-dreams his own part in her deflowering, envisaged her whimpering joy and the slavish passion to follow. He saw them both, she blonde and round, he dark and slight, copulating in the sand of the dunes, riding each other, and then racing naked into their own private stretch of sea. The result was simply himself, getting up fastidiously, to change the sheet.

The light was gone. The doll's house in the room was covered. Edward now stood with his easel facing the window. A piece of watered paper was stretched on a frame, showing under the light a portion of Ordnance Survey map copied on a larger scale. Instead of the marked paths and the symbols, he had drawn depictions of the things themselves. The pine woods along the coast formed a forest of tiny, dark green trees. The footpaths were bordered by bramble bushes, hung with miniature fruit. There were untruthful innovations on his version of the map, such as the village church being Mediterranean white, the fields corn-coloured, the gardens full of palms. He had moved the graveyard nearer the coast, depicted highly coloured half-human figures like his mother, dancing and digging their own graves; made the high street houses Georgian dwellings of immaculate proportions to replace the crooked, uncontrolled and irregular cottages. All this gave Edward a sense of power. The village and the coast became an elegant habitation under his rule. All of it slipping away, like his rod when he cast, like the fish he always failed to land, however savagely he tried with whatever expensive equipment. Like Jo.

Perhaps it was a vision he was simply too lazy to shift. Such devotion. Sandwiches every day, whether he needed them or not, a hot bottle in his bed at night, his shirts ironed, his paint brushes clean, even his fishing bait kept under her eye, a child seeking his approval in everything. But that was the other Joanna. Not the one flaunting herself this evening, not the girl who once let him choose her childish clothes but was now immune to his criticism and who looked as if she could stop a party by simply standing in the door. In whose clothes? With whose expertise? Sarah Fortune's. The hired help Joanna had previously referred to as the cow, suddenly friend, confidante and creator of glamour, all in one destructive day.

Edward had abandoned all thought of fishing. He had glared at his giggling mother with murderous eyes as she waved Jo goodbye. Knowing how capable he was of striking her, Mother giggled more, withdrew to the kitchen, then to bed, while he went to his own room to brood until after dark, which was now, when hunger struck.

The normal Joanna would not have left the house without leaving him something for supper. For him and him alone. Not his brother.

They collided in the kitchen doorway, both of them looking for the light switch, each recoiling from the other.

'Sorry, Julian. Didn't know you were in.'

'Sorry, Ed.'

Each wanted food, but rarely the company of each other which they avoided as often as possible, except breakfast, dinner and the more than occasional late-night snack which could be necessary after one of Jo's more experimental meals. Their habits made her claim she could never keep stocks, never quite knew what there was.

Julian was looking at the newspaper on the floor of the pantry. Edward's bait for fishing, given pride of place because they were Edward's; fish hooks in the drawers of the kitchen table, reels and bits all over the place. Julian could not look at the bait without imagining the lugworms lying so docile on the inside. Lugworm, harbour ragworm, white ragworm: they could live for a few days in newspaper, but Edward was always over supplied as if it increased his own chances to acquire them and let them die. Julian could never pass the supplies on the cool pantry floor without wondering why it was so many of the civilised men he knew could bear to pick up a worm and spear it so bloodily on to a hook, simply in order to fish for the dabs they could easily buy.

'I wish you wouldn't keep these in here, Ed,' he said, keeping the irritation out of his voice.

'They can't get out, you know. I'll put them somewhere else, if you like.'

Edward was being conciliatory, even jovial.

'Want a drink. boss?'

'Yes,' said Julian, surprised into acceptance simply because he wanted what Edward offered, a single slug of indifferent-quality whisky which made his mouth pucker. Julian did not keep the stuff near him: it had been dangerous in the past, cured no ills, turned insomnia into nightmare.

'Where's Jo? And Ma?' he asked, not because he needed to know, simply for something to say.

'Ma's in the land of nod. Jo went out earlier. I saw her as I was coming in, wanted to have a word with you about Jo. And about our learned lady solicitor.' Edward practically spat the last words.

'Oh.' Julian was wary, always in the habit of mistrusting everything Edward said, especially if he was serious. He could always give Edward his seventy-seventh chance, but since childhood the boy had never departed from being liar and cheat, features Jo simply refused to see, while he saw them all the time, that and the idleness. Be fair, he told himself. Mother had always spoiled the boy, while Father had seemed to dislike him from the moment he could walk. He could resist the opportunity to be fooled yet again, but not the chance of discussing Miss Fortune, however obliquely. The very same unsettling creature he had seen, minutes before, as he passed the arcade, sitting on a pedestal seat like one of the kids, playing a game with enthusiasm while under the wing of some unidentifiable lad. The sight had given him the same terrible jolt of recognition as last night when she stood in the doorway. So much for his original estimation: the woman was a lightweight, a silly cow ... The violence of his own unspoken descriptions appalled him in their patent unfairness. He was simply looking for excuses.

'Look, Julian,' Edward was saying, 'I just don't like that woman. She's far too charming to be anything other than a bad influence.'

'What? On you?' Julian joked.

'No. On Jo.' Julian waited for explanations, warmed to his brother's seriously concerned face, thinking, Perhaps I misjudge him, I must not be so hard.

'Listen, when I came back home this evening, I met our sis going out, highly pleased with herself, showing off to Mother. Dressed in that solicitor's clothes, I ask you. Done up in black, like some high-class call-girl. That isn't Jo. That's somebody else. She's still a child at heart.'

Which is what you want to keep her, Julian thought wryly, somehow pleased. How often had he urged Jo to dress like a young woman instead of a juvenile? He dismissed the thoughts easily, knowing they would return, willing to suspend criticism of Edward's suspicious resentment in his own wilful search for an excuse to get rid of their visitor, simply because he found her disturbing. Edward's eyes shone with the sheen of sincere dishonesty, the guile of his own, strange corruption; Julian chose to ignore it all. He rubbed his hand over his forehead.

'Sorry, been a long, long day. I just went to Miss Gloomer's.

She's been burgled, poor soul. Some bastard holiday-maker. A
loaf of bread and her stick, pathetic. She said it was a ghost, but
I think she's just picked up on gossip. A man with white hair: she
saw him going away, couldn't move. Wouldn't have a sedative,
so I prescribed sherry, it made me hungry. Anyway, you were
saying, Sarah Fortune?'

Edward was blushing slightly, swallowing fast, never hesitant
for long.

'I think, since we need a lawyer, we should get someone else.
This one's too ... subversive. Impertinent, over familiar. She
makes Mother hysterical with excitement and Jo bolshie.'

They looked at each other in a moment of rare complicity.
Julian nodded.

'I agree. We'll tell her tomorrow.'

'Fine.' Edward moved to leave.

'Ed? Talk to me more, will you? For what it's worth, I know
you think you've had a rough deal, and I'm sorry. It's not been
an easy year.'

'No,' said Edward, horribly surprised and touched. 'No, it
hasn't.'

The ghost with the white hair and the all too human face moved
no further away than the garden immediately beyond Miss
Gloomer's tiny patch. This allowed him to watch the doctor
come and go, wait for the fuss to die down, sit on the still warm
ground and eat the bread in great gulps, three slices at a time,
rolling it into a doughy ball, swallowing it whole. He would have
killed for the services of a dentist on his back teeth. He supposed
it was vaguely dangerous to stay where he was; there were other
things to do, the beach hut he had chosen for the night's lodging
was a long walk. In a year, he had not driven a car, eaten a
decent meal, entered a shop or looked any living person in the
eye. His own worm ate him, kept him alive in the process of consumption.

A year which had sped, or rather eclipsed, since the day he
had been caught by the tide. Made himself float on the cold

water under the warming sun which saved him, surprised that it was time to die until he became indignant. Acted cunning with the tide, moving minimally to save his strength to make a burst for the shore five miles from where he had begun. The naked-ness of his state, the liberation of it, had made him run for cover, hide in a half-derelict church while putting up two fingers at God, revelling in the sheer pride of outwitting even the ocean. He felt omnipotent and free, intensely alive, at one with the flat wilderness of the coast, wandering through it like a king survey-ing his country.

The newspaper, bought with stolen money, since stealing was always easy, told him he was dead. It amused him that some stranger had apparently died in his place; increased the feeling of power to do whatever he liked. It was as if he. had been able to commandeer that other man's death. Any investigations into his own life would presumably die with the same speed. It had sud-denly seemed an excellent idea to remain dead. He could do what he had to do undisturbed, then reveal himself and resume his place, like a phoenix from the ashes, horrify them all. The man had told Edward he was on holiday, but time slipped and slithered in this limbo world, while he tried to get a fix on time, circling round the coast and hinterland, slipping from village to town, sleeping through the better part of a winter. Each day seemed like a minute. In the spring, Merton called. He had been idle: there was work to do. Memories had altered focus too, all except one.

Who buried her? Who touched, who buried her? And there, in the light coming out of Miss Gloomer's door, was the enemy. A fond enemy, speaking softly with evident affection for the occupant inside, but still the enemy; while in his own pockets, out of the surgery desk, was the proof.

After an hour, he removed himself with the casualness of an invited guest who has suddenly remembered the time, slipped out into the high street, back down an alley and into the yard behind the arcade. The back door yielded easily: there was no attraction in a patch of mossy stone, warm rooms containing

silent machines which stood like sentinels. He felt sick, burped in
the darkness. He dreamed of himself, being hunted across the
dunes and out into the sea; the sea closing over his head and no
boat coming. He dreamed of the pack being led out to hunt him
by the boy with the dog which had followed him, stayed with
him, eaten some of his precious food with the surreptitious
speed with which he ate himself. A red dog; the outrage had
sprung into his fingertips, round the animal's neck, holding her
whimpering and trying to kiss while he slit the throat with a
piece of broken bottle off the beach, untying the collar first
because it stopped him getting a hold. How foolish to exercise
his own strength in this way, but he had needed the reminder for
himself, in case the strength should slip away. Like a woman
with red hair, slithering out of his grasp and onto the ground,
still breathing. He thought of gravestones, coloured red, chest-
nut trees spreading tentacles beneath a buried body, wished all
these colours would emigrate from his mind, but he never once
doubted his reason.

'. . . all and each
   Would draw from her the same approving speech,
   Or blush at least. She thanked men – good! but thanked
   Somehow . . . I know not how . . . as if she ranked
   My gift of a nine hundred years old name
   With anybody's gift.'
   His Porphyria, Browning's last duchess, they all became con-
fused.

The air was fresh and warm; Sarah was beginning to learn the
sound when the tide was changing, the musical clanging of the
halyards of boats in distant channels, the night-time mewing of
gulls, the fact that there was no such thing as total silence, only
the subdued noises of intense life. She was growing used to
walking, choosing not to use her car, but in what seemed a year
rather than a day, she had still not seen the uncontained sea.
Only these mysterious inroads, lying quiet but running deep in
the quay, gurgling in secret, incoming streams across the land,

intriguing, pretty, mysterious yet inadequate to suffice the craving for some vast blue sky, a wilderness edged with powerful water.

The Norfolk coast was full of such according to her map. Tomorrow, the Pardoes could wait, if they had not already told her to go; for tonight, she was faintly exhilarated. The tide was out but coming back; she could feel it. She could breathe, she was fully herself. Behind her, a boy was thoroughly asleep; sweet dreams, young man, and more to follow.

Here it was safe in the dead of night. Outside her cottage, where the roses trailed round the door a trifle sadly, bitten by the wind from the sea which she had not yet felt in the heatwave, Sarah looked at the isolated terrace as she might a home. That crazy sheep stood ready to greet her, making her laugh, butting her in the side as she opened the door and felt for the switch. Another thing she knew by now: there was no such thing as total darkness.

The electric light was brutal. On the floor of the kitchenette there were a dozen large worms, oozing flesh, lying inert on a double sheet of newspaper. They were lazily twined with one another, like the head of a Medusa. One moved, very slightly; the rest were patently alive, confused into inertia or dying.

They were meant to make her scream, but they brought into her throat the bile which prevented her scream, made her choke instead, and then the sheep saved her. Hettie blundered through the narrow entrance behind her, blocked her retreat, sniffed at the wet mass of corrugated, underground flesh with every sign of complete indifference and belched loudly. Sarah's heartbeat, remaining abnormally loud in her own ears, became slower and slower. Her skin was hot; life flowed back, and with it, the remembrance of the wellbeing which had walked home with her and a faint sense of the ludicrous. She had not come so far or lived so long to be frightened by worms. She had wanted country life and now she had it.

Eyes averted, teeth clenched to prevent the nausea, she found a plastic bucket, picked up the corners of the damp paper, put the whole collection inside. Holding the pail in one hand she stepped out and over the road, flung the whole container as far as she could. There was a bouncing thump and splash; she was absurdly pleased. Then she doused the kitchen floor with bleach. Only then did she find room for anger.

There was a light on over at the house, across the other side of the lawn. One light at the front door, directly opposite hers, another glowing from the back. There were two cars: Jo was home then, so she should have been at two in the morning. The anger drove Sarah over the wet grass; the sensation against her bare legs, dragging at her skirt, oddly inhibiting, slowing her steps. By the time she reached the back kitchen window, she was hesitant and stealthy.

They were a household which went to bed and stayed inside with their cars parked like guardians. Not all of them. Through the kitchen window, Sarah saw Mouse Pardoe sitting at the table. Without ballgown, *pissenlit*, jewellery or anything else but a dressing-gown and a pair of glasses, looking like the Queen Mother without hat and the same soul of concentrated sanity. She was eating a delicate sandwich which she had clearly made herself, reading the *Guardian* with easy concentration. There was none of the theatricality, the divine display, the endless smiling.

Mrs Pardoe turned a page and refolded the paper with effortless co-ordination and long practice, sipped a glass of wine with decorum. She turned to put the big heavy kettle on the Raeburn, rubbed her hands, went on reading.

As a woman, Sarah did not understand caution. As Ms Fortune the lawyer, she did. She went back to her cottage.

CHAPTER SIX

Joanna was as jumpy as a cricket. She swooped by Edward's seat at the kitchen table without pecking his cheek, moved on.

'You were late last night,' he said with surly accusation.

'Was I? Not particularly. Oh isn't it nice it's Saturday?'

'What's good about Saturday?'

'The clouds lift, Caroline says, but that's because she's got a job. Maybe I should get a job. Caroline says she could get me a job. Takes your mind off things, she says. Anyway, I've left your sandwiches in case you were going to go fishing or something. Only I'm going shopping, all day . . .' She turned away, breath running out.

'I thought you might come with me. Look, I'm sorry if I laughed at your grand clothes yesterday.'

'S'all right. Perfectly all right. Got to go, I'm busy.'

Something of this new, unprecedented independence, its blustering bravery, words spoken with bold resolution, break-neck speed and underlying nervousness in case he should mind, touched him like the breath of an icy wind.

'Ed,' she was saying, 'what were you eating in here last night? There's nothing left.'

'Worms,' he said grimly. He hated being called Ed.

'Grilled or fried?'

The worms were bothering him, bothered him more as he sat in the kitchen and watched the sun stream through the door.

Taking the bait from the pantry floor on a malicious impulse was something he slightly regretted like one drink too many. Everything, including sleep, conspired against him and the only thing which was right was Stonewall Jones delivering more lugworms first thing this morning. Edward wanted to grumble out loud. He had detested his mother and Julian for as long as he remembered, was accustomed to receiving dislike ever since he had played his first childish trick, not dissimilar to the one played on the guest, but he did not feel easy. The man with the white hair should not have taken Miss Gloomer's stick; Jo should not put herself first; Julian should not have laid a hand on his arm and said he was sorry. Any minute now, Mother would float downstairs and blow him a kiss and the whole fabric of comfortable hatred would begin to fray.

'Here,' said Jo, thrusting a bag on to his lap. 'Do us a favour, will you? Take these back to Sarah, I mean Miss Fortune, don't look so vacant. Tell her thanks a million, and let me know if she wants to eat with us tonight, will you?'

'Julian made it quite clear not,' he said sternly.

'I like Sarah and I live here too.'

It was something, if a slightly uncomfortable thing, to do. Crossing the lawn, Edward hoped Miss Fortune had already packed her bags and gone, since if that was the result of his handiwork, he wouldn't feel again this strange compulsion to apologise.

Halfway across the lawn, he could see her car was missing. He persisted, looked through the windows of the cottage which someone seemed to have cleaned. The room inside looked different. There was a bunch of flowers in the sink; beyond the kitchen areas, he could see a shawl thrown over the nasty settee. Hettie the sheep was guarding the door, bleating loudly. Edward kicked her, felt his foot sink in the woolly fleece as she sprang away, adept at such manoeuvres and used to his casual attempts at brutality. He left the parcel of clothes balanced against the door and hoped the daft brute would eat it.

He could go fishing all day with the sandwiches he so often

left in bins. Should he go and see the man on the beach this morning, progress the plan to rid himself of all his family restrictions? Make him a present? No, too late already. Let him wait. By tomorrow or the day after, the bitch from the cottage would be gone and everything would be clearer.

Sarah was looking at a display of cakes. There were buns and flapjacks, scones, enormous sponge slabs stiff with butter and all with the lopsided look of the honestly homemade. The cakes were under glass in the high street café where a plump girl struggled with solid wedges of white bread sandwiches for a dozen customers and their equally lumpy dogs. Over the road was a shop window full of knitting wool, a wry reminder of what an honest woman might expect to do with her long, winter evenings.

Sarah was not an honest woman by any but her own standards, had rarely baked a cake and knew she was a freak. Baking had never been part of her obligations with any of the men she had ever known and the thought filled her with wry amusement.

'Have some more,' a woman was urging a man. 'It's good for you.' Sarah ducked her head, light-framed and light-hearted. Would Julian sack her for lack of tact, and did she mind? Yes, she did. She had been examining with care the exhaustive list of the Pardoes' assets. They owned this café, a boat or two, the freehold of a pub, the hairdresser's, the amusement arcade, half the shops, over a dozen houses. They owned, in fact, the lifeblood of the town. They could strangle this mini seaside empire, set like a semi-precious stone among the dun-coloured, waterlogged land.

Sarah sat and considered dreams, thought in the same loop about Ernest eating cake laced with worms and hoped it choked him. Thought of Malcolm refusing to eat cake and missed him with a poignancy she had so far managed to avoid; pictured him here with his lack of prejudice, the dog sniffing in gutters with selective enthusiasm, a thoroughly streamlined beast, that dog, compared to these. Last night, in the conversation which had preceded his second pint, Rick had told her about Stonewall and his dog. And about how Stonewall earned pocket money, digging up lugworms for other men's bait. She had been glad of that knowledge, later – it had defused the effect of the worms on the floor.

The coffee arrived, weak and insipid, served with triumph, not the stuff of dreams, but Sarah's sense of taste was blunted by indifference and she had no dreams left, save the lingering vision of innocent and self-sufficient country life. With her eyes still on the impressive list, she felt a hot, non-apologetic stab of envy when she considered the dilemma of the Pardoe family and their unquiet expectation of riches. No one should be allowed to inherit so much and then spend their lives sulking. Once upon a time, Sarah had regarded wealth as an end in itself, the means to change things and forge a link with freedom. She sat back in her uncomfortable bentwood chair, watching the eating of sandwiches and wishing she was hungry. Dreams were food, like riches, to be vicariously consumed by simply looking at the other consumers. If she herself could no longer define her own ambitions, let alone fulfil them, had neither the stamina to earn millions nor the compulsion to steal, she could still advise others on the subject of wealth. How to use it, enjoy it, or, if that was the best thing to do, give it away.

A man in the corner roared with laughter. He wore cheap clothes, fed his red face on ice-cream in a state of uproarious contentment. He was not rich. The Pardoe children should be happier than him, looking at the world as a cake for nibbling, not moping about with their private disorders, listless, lovelorn, bitter. Their money was a privilege, their behaviour an abuse and some time during the day, the brothers would foregather and tell her to leave.

A shadow fell over her table, the girl with the coffee, twittering. Rick stood towering, bruises fading, grinning widely.

'Not stopping,' he said. 'Only I wanted to show Stonewall here that you weren't a ghost.'

'I have no illusions about that,' she said primly, the dimples of a big smile forming in her face.

'No,' he said. 'Neither do I,' and his laugh hit the roof. 'Is it a ghost, Stoney?'

'Nope,' said the boy. 'And nor's that other one, either.'

'Oh,' she breathed. 'Two ghosts?'

Stonewall squirmed, torn between silence, a sense of loss and a desire to do whatever Rick suggested. He could feel an undercurrent here, adding to his normal anxiety and the constant challenge to make Rick believe him and never send him away again.

'What would you like?' she asked. Rick shouted with laughter again.

'Don't ask a lady that, she might tell you.'

'Ice-cream?' Stonewall said mournfully.

'Two,' she said cheerfully.

Rick got up to order, none of this sitting around politely when he knew he could jump the queue as long as he grinned. He swaggered a little.

Stonewall looked at Sarah and Sarah looked at Stonewall. She was all right, he thought desperately, must be all right, Rick likes her and she isn't no woman I ever saw before. She, on the other hand, simply considered him beautiful.

'It's a ghost,' said Stonewall, when his ice-cream arrived in a big glass dish stuck with wafers like a ship in full sail. 'Went into Miss Gloomer's.'

'I'd told you to go home and stay there,' said Rick sternly. The boy ignored the interruption. What else was a window for, but to afford an escape?

'I seen him go in. I seen him last night and I seen him down the beach when I was getting bait. Ed Pardoe knows him, this ghost.'

Rick looked worried.

'Tell me about me,' Sarah teased, not quite lightly. 'Me, before I was the ordinary mortal I am now. Whose ghost was I? What did I do?' Cold ice-cream in too large a mouthful made

Stonewall swallow with a gasp. Everyone listening: he could make them wait.

'You used to go in the doctor's a lot. You were married. To that other ghost, I think. The one who sits and talks with Edward Pardoe. You got run over by a bus. You went off walking into the sea, didn't come back. I saw you, but it wasn't you, it was someone else.'

Stonewall could guess what Rick was going to say. He'd say, You shouldn't eat all that ice-cream so fast, makes your brain go soft; but the woman with the hair listened intently, her skin suddenly paler, so that the red hair looked redder than ever. All Rick could do was grumble, even though he was outrageously happy.

'Why didn't you do something when you saw the ghost go in Miss Gloomer's, you twerp?'

Stonewall ducked his head. 'Cos my mum would know I was halfway out the window, wouldn't she? Don't be daft.' He looked hopefully at the empty plate, the last icy morsel trailing down his throat.

Anything else would require a bigger fee from a stranger. Despair filled his eyes. Everyone was more important than him.

After they had gone, Sarah rubbed her arms beyond the confines of the full, elbow-length sleeves of her shirt, her fingers feeling instinctively for the tiny scars which adorned the fleshy part of her upper arms. They'll grow smaller in time, the surgeon had told her with manic cheerfulness; no one will notice.

Enough. Saturday afternoon, holiday time: families, ghosts, moral obligations and bleaker memories had no place. She wanted to shrug off the whole human race, their unhappiness, their miseries, above all, their presence, sink them into the sea with her own inadequacies. Wanted, as she walked back to the top of the crowded street, to cleanse herself and all her fears in the vastness of the ocean she had been craving. Once inside her car, the sun beating down on the roof to make the sense of confinement worse, she looked briefly at the Ordnance Survey map, propped it against the wheel, drove back through the town and miles beyond. Such a flat, deserted coast. She wanted what she knew she could find: a place where others did not go. A desert with water, the emptiness she had been searching for to heal her own sickness.

She drove fast, then swung away into narrow lanes where the meadowsweet lurched from the banks and touched the roof. She kept the coastline ahead of her as she bumped down tracks designed for smugglers and bird-watchers, until finally, land ran out. The map had led her to a place where no one needed coke or ice-cream.

Two more cars were parked on the same spit of terra firma. Four people, muffled despite the heat, sat on shooting sticks, binoculars aimed towards the hinterland, each looking as if breakfast and lunch had passed while they waited so long for the sight of the rare bird which had drawn them, that they seemed to have become permanent features of the landscape themselves. Sarah ignored them as they ignored her, left her car unlocked, handbag and keys under the front seat, jogged towards the sea. A year's rigorous punishment of her own body left it lean, shapely, hard. She stopped a hundred yards from the indifferent spectators, peeled off every stitch of clothing and left it with her shoes balanced on top as a marker, the bright purple of the silk shirt iridescent in the sun to guide her route back, then jogged on towards the flat horizontal of blue. The sand looked as smooth as baize, dipping into valleys which were velvet on the feet. She ran on and on, but the ribbon of waves seemed to recede. Then, when she stumbled into a narrow stretch of shallow water as warm as a bath, she gave up the pursuit. The water was soft as silk and the breeze a silent fan. Lying with her naked limbs tickled by salt felt utterly natural but at the same time blissfully decadent. The sand bank acted as a couch, moulded to the shape her body had designed for itself, while soft water crept up her neck into her hair. Some sybaritic millionaire would pay a fortune for this. As she lazily splashed water on to her flat belly and her thighs, she felt again, with a little frisson of disgust, the tiny white scars on her abdomen which mirrored those on her arms and her back and reminded her of maggots. She wanted to scrub at them with sand until they disappeared, but somehow, in the water, they were less offensive and she could no longer imagine them shifting and moving like the vermin on a carcase, eating away at sanity, and the will to live. The sun was hypnotic; she could not be sombre under the merciful glare, sprawled like a cat before the fire, dozing to the sound of soft breeze and silence.

Ten, fifteen minutes; she could not guess how long she had lain in her feline pose. Neither did she know what woke her, whether it was the sound of distant shouting or the sudden sensation of a deep chill curling round her. When she opened her eyes, she saw the greater expanse of water all around her, lapping greedily at her bare breasts, colder water mounting above her knees, pulling slightly as if inviting her to float away. For a moment she was tempted to let go, simply drift like a rogue vessel, but sat up, watched her pool expanding before her eyes, the surface corrugated by breeze as she scrambled to her feet, alarmed, disorientated, still in a muddle of a dream. From the rim of the rise on which she stood, the ribbon of sea seemed ominously closer and clearer, the wind on her face sterner. She looked back to the shore for her clothes and could not see them; two pin figures stood by their toy-like car, waving and shouting as if cheering some invisible team, dancing in a fury of agitation. They seemed a long way off and the rim of the sea even closer.

Sarah began to run. The route back bore no comparison with the careless route out, when she had imagined the golden surface flat beneath her feet. Now the sand dipped and rose before her into gulleys where water collected into swift rivers, pulling at her knees like an hysterical child. The first channel was easy; the second brought the breath to her chest and fire into her veins; the third rose against her like an engine fuelled by hatred. She did not pause to look again for her clothes, pushed through the skin-ripping flood with her hands above her head, bending into it, the tide tearing at her waist until it receded like a tease at the moment when she thought she could no longer fight the relentless, inland pull. The steps became firmer; she splashed through a dying current, shrinking to a gentle tugging at her calves, and walked unsteadily up the incline to her car. The prickling of thistle and sand grass marking the point where the tide did not reach and land began, felt like a blessing. A woman stood with a brace of binoculars round her neck, stout shoes on her feet and tears of consternation on her red face.

'How could you be so stupid?' she yelled. 'He wanted to go for you,' pointing to the man on her left who stood shivering, leaning on a stick. 'Wouldn't let him! We've been shouting for hours, you'll give him a heart attack, you wouldn't listen, I could kill you!' Then her face crumpled into lines of relief. 'Oh, you silly, silly girl. Don't you know about tides? You must have been so frightened.'

Sarah stood before her dripping and shaking, humbled and ashamed.

'I should have thought. I'm sorry I gave you such a scare. Thank you. You woke me. The shouting wasn't wasted. Thank you both.' The shivering grew worse.

'Your clothes,' the woman said, softening more. 'Your pretty coloured shirt.' So much for assuming they would not notice.

'You'll probably get them back,' said the man, helpfully, needing to say something to control his own shock. 'They'll probably wash up in the harbour down the coast. Or somewhere.'

She felt a terrible desire to giggle, put her hand over her mouth.

'I think I'll get in my car where it's warm.'

'Do you want a blanket or something?'

'No, thank you, thank you.'

She had to get inside, start the engine and move because until she did, they would watch, without prurience but with an honest concern which made her feel far more exposed. The heat from the driver's seat spread through her buttocks, she dripped into the fabric, the steering wheel was warm on her white knuckles and through the windscreen she saw the advancing sea, marching inland like an enormous army with white halberds and a silent war cry, unstoppable, irresistible, the oldest enemy. She watched until the chill subsided and she could flex her fingers. From their own vehicle, the couple watched her.

The back wheels of the car spun in the sandy gravel, a satisfying sound. The bumping, jolting progress back to the main road made her want to sing. For the joy of survival and for the revelations it entailed.

First, if Elisabeth Tysall had lain in such a pool, warm, drunk, drugged, to make her own death simultaneous with blissful and uninterrupted sleep, she had chosen a tempting method, full of dignity, and that was an obscure comfort. The nature of Elisabeth's death had always tormented her. Secondly, Sarah could now see how she had never possessed such a well-matured desire for death even though the number of temptations were beyond counting on the fingers of both hands. She had so often wanted to die. She found a cigarette, lit it awkwardly, and felt a moment of euphoria which was warm and wild.

Late Saturday afternoon, people trailing back from their beaches passed Sarah's car, not looking, but seeing enough to notice a naked bosom level with the wheel. And that was another thing. Death and risk made clothes seem irrelevant. A man stalled and whistled as their cars paused alongside, each waiting to turn right. His children in the back giggled and squirmed. Sarah waved at them demurely, laughed at the minor traffic jam outside the amusement arcade as holiday-makers looked for places to park, and pulled into the side, still grinning. A small bullet of a head with hair on end appeared at the nearside window. The face of Rick appeared on the right. While the boy averted his eyes, he did not.

'Lost again, are you?' She had time to notice how the bruises round one eye had darkened into purply striations, well on the way to recovery.

'What's this then?' Rick said grinning. 'Legal services?'

'Doubt it. They'll fire me. I just went swimming.'

'You go indoors like that,' Rick said. 'They'll keep you for ever.'

★

The early evening was warm, but the sky had grown troubled. Edward loved that phrase, a troubled sky. When he owned his birthright, he would paint a troubled sky, with angels interrupting the clouds and coming down to bless him. He shut his eyes and thought of it, until Julian called everyone downstairs into the horrid gloom of their Edwardian dining room, where the chairs cracked shins, and dead flies fell from the plum velvet of the curtains as soon as they were drawn. Edward stayed silent while Julian conducted the meeting like a headmaster in front of the assembly hall, telling them all, Mother included for all that she would either notice or care, how the solicitor sent by Father's executor was not suitable for their purposes, did they not agree? Mother laughing herself sick, saying nothing except, No, no, no, you've got it all wrong. Joanna upset, wondering if it was her earlier referrals to their guest as the cow, or the arguments at breakfast yesterday which had made Julian so obdurate. Edward merely nodded his agreement, thought of the easel waiting upstairs and the man waiting on the beach tomorrow. They did not need a disruptive lawyer who made his sister cry as she cried now.

When he watched Joanna weeping, he felt on his own skin a flush of irritation which was the very opposite of desire. If only he could, for a minute, imagine wanting someone else: boy, girl, woman, whatever the body was, as long as it was not this plump, snivelling, beautiful child.

'We're decided then,' Julian said without turning it into a question.

Edward now sat facing the long windows where the paint blistered off the frame and the glass was cloudy with salt from the shoreline which they owned, travelling across the drab marshes, which they owned, to the house, which they owned, while he owned nothing. Bitterness rose like a painful cough. It was warm and airless: the windows were stuck in the dining room. Mother, giggling in her evening dress, plucking at the hem, finally picking it up so the fabric hung around her knees while she chewed at a thread, suddenly springing into life as a car drew level with the front door and she rushed to the window. They all followed.

'Oh,' said Mother in tones of wonder. 'Oh my dears!'

Joanna and Julian moved to the window where Edward stood, languid but transfixed.

'Whoever it is she needs a drink and so do I,' Mother said. She stood very still, none of her normal twitching and constant adjusting, a wistful note in her voice, a hidden chuckle. You wicked old crone, Julian thought with more than a hint of fondness.

Sarah Fortune stepped from her car, presenting a perfect half moon of buttock with a well-defined swimsuit mark as she reached inside for her handbag, then stood up with the strap parting her bobbing bosom as she slung it across herself and stepped back, naked as the day, to slam the door with a careless foot. Her hair was a frenzied cloud, her shoulders tanned and she was perfectly controlled. Joanna felt she should not look, stared and held her breath instead. Sarah walked away across the lawn towards the cottages, resting one hand on the handbag as if she were wearing a suit and strolling to a business appointment, no hurry or anxiety in the stride, careless or oblivious of the scrutiny. Julian bit his lip in a rare moment of sympathy, Oh Lord, how terrible for her, not to know they were all there, judging her finest details with the scrutiny of a jury; she would be mortified. But then as he watched, Sarah stopped, looked at the ridiculous appendage of her handbag, flicked it off her shoulder into the long grass and raised her arms in the air. The grass was warm and moist; she seemed to enjoy the sensation of it round her feet. Expensive tan leather bounced on the lawn: still they watched. The sky was pink in an early sunset; she seemed to glow as with an unbearably slow and graceful precision the perfect figure turned a series of perfect cartwheels, hand over hand, twirling in front of their eyes with only the damp red hair marking where she was. Then she picked up her handbag, placed it on her head, walked towards the cottage where they had put her, strolling with her arms outstretched to keep her balance, her naked feet swishing through the grass. Hettie the sheep followed, keeping pace, bahhing piteously. There was a shred of bright orange nasturtium hanging from her jaw as she trotted after. The sun sank like a big, red stone into water.

They were spellbound, until Edward let forth a bellow of delighted laughter. Joanna expelled the breath she had held for a full minute, joined him in a frothing of mirth which made her eyes water.

'Well,' said Julian, shaking himself. 'Proves my point. About her not being suitable.' Edward caught on his brother's face a terrible, naked look of despair.

Mother turned on him, dropping the hem she had chewed. Her voice was cooing and fluting, talking as she would talk to a baby.

'Will my little boy sack a lady from her job for taking her clothes off? Would he? Would he be so silly? Should know better. No man got sacked for taking his off, not even a doctor.' Her voice sank by a whole octave, emerged as a grim rattle, whining but perfectly articulate.

'If Julian gets rid of this lady, his mummy will break everything in sight. Is that understood?'

He turned sharply, met for a moment a pair of eyes hard with purpose, moved towards her. She sprang back and began again her chewing of the hem, saying nothing, looking away. Then he looked towards Edward for moral support, found Edward also looking away, gaze fixed on the footsteps through the long grass of the lawn. Joanna evaded his glance, arms crossed resentfully, her ever-ready tears still in her eyes, but her body obdurate. He felt the meeting had passed without a definitive vote, but if asked, he would not favour the initial resolution. Oddly, he did not mind.

'Look,' said Joanna, desperate to break the ice, 'I'd better go and ask if she's all right. I'll take her something to eat. I mean,' she added, flustered, 'she must have had an accident.'

'I doubt it,' said Edward drily.

'Fuck off,' Joanna replied with far more calm than she felt.

Edward was always on the outside, never feeling anything, always analysing: he didn't care if a person felt cold, and stared at her in the way she had found disconcerting for as long as she could recall. He moved nonchalantly to put an arm round her shoulder.

'What would you give for a body like that, eh, Jo?'

She turned on him, furious and pink, picking the arm from round her neck and throwing it back as if it were inanimate.

From the kitchen came the sound of breaking glass. The Mouse was making her point.

CHAPTER SEVEN

'Left you, has she?'

'You could say so.'

'Thought she would.' Squinting across the table top towards Malcolm Cook, Detective Sergeant Ryan, his erstwhile colleague in many a case, neither looked nor sounded sympathetic, not through lack of affection for his friend, but simply a well-tried patience with the whole breed of men who called themselves lawyers, a breed deficient in common sense, particularly regarding women. Ryan knew his own record was far from perfect, his attitude to the fair sex ranging from possessive passion, through the straightforward lust which could not remember names, right down to daily fondness and the acceptance that there was nothing you could do to keep them, since life and women were in one great conspiracy. His own contribution to Malcolm Cook's loss was going to be the provision of as much alcohol as he could get the man to take.

'I have to say, Malc, you were more fun before you two got together. Was a time when you were a great big lad, liked a pint and never moved your bum off a chair. Then you took up running, fell in love with a redhead, lost all the fat and got serious. You never sit, you bloody well sprint. She's worn you out, old son.'

'Get me a drink.'

'Surely. Doubles. Few packets of crisps?'

'No.'

Ryan didn't like the way Malcolm stared into the middle distance like that, ordering a refill every five minutes and showing not a sign of Saturday-night fever, not a tremor as he raised his hand. All the makings of an expensive night even in the sort of downmarket pub they both preferred. Malc was a mate, as far as any lawyer could be, but that wasn't the same as wanting him crying on your shoulder. It got your jacket all wet.

The drink went down quickly, not quite as quick as the last. Malcolm smiled. When he did that, he was a different man.

'Look, I'm not here to weep, I'm here to drink, understand? And I want to raise an old, dead subject, OK? Charles Tysall, your friend and mine. My father's been nagging at me again. No, I don't mean directly, just getting under my skin as usual. The man's not well, supposed to keep calm, but as soon as I mention Charles, he has an apoplexy. He's re-creating that man as a plaster saint, all because he's dead and was a client. All clients are heroes, the hypocrisy makes me sick. I want to tell him what Charles did to Sarah – I told you we kept all the details from him at the time – and spell out to my honourable old dad what his client did to other red-haired women. I want him to know. People should know the truth, even sick old men.'

'You really aren't happy with him, are you?' asked Ryan, mockingly.

'He sent Sarah away. To Merton, of all places. He . . . precipitated things.'

'Oh, I see. Revenge, is it? One good turn deserves another. You lose the girl and give the poor old git a heart attack. Come off it, Malc, it wouldn't help anything, would it?'

'No.'

'Anyway, what that Charles did to your bird never came to court, did it? She refused to give evidence of the attack. With your support. I wanted you shot.'

Malcolm raised a hand in protest, let it drop.

'She had her reasons. I didn't want anyone looking into her motives, still don't. Besides, Tysall saved everyone the trouble.

When his wife's body was found, off he goes and follows her into the water. What I want to know is how did he come to do that? I never really understood. He never struck me as the suicidal type. All those times we tried to nail him for fraud, and you for the women he plundered . . . He always wanted to live.'

Ryan looked smug.

'Nothing to do with me. I just happened to meet the sly bastard in a coffee shop. Made the suggestion he'd like to go and see where his lady wife was buried. It might not have been the tide covered her up, see? It could have been, course, probably was, but I made him think she'd been buried. Last rites delivered on her lily-white body by another man's big, chunky hands. I knew it would drive him mad. He might have beaten his own wife to a pulp, cut her face to ribbons, but he couldn't stand the thought of anyone else touching her. Listen, I couldn't have prayed he'd walk into the sea like he did: I just wanted him suffering.'

Ryan took a sip and it was gone. Time to go on to pints. Whisky was fine in spots; he'd go back to it later. Something nagged him, something he didn't like and knew Malcolm wouldn't either.

'So Sarah's gone off to the seaside, has she? Not her kind of place, I wouldn't have thought. Not very classy. Fish and chips, big amusement place, caravans down the beach. I can't see your Sarah in a place full of yobs.'

Malcolm smiled again. Ryan decided the smile was sadder than the scowl.

'You don't know Sarah. She has . . . simple tastes.' He seemed to hesitate, draw back from saying more, plunged on. 'What I want to know is anything which may affect and upset her. The sort of things people might still gossip about, take her unawares when she ought to forget. You got to know the local cop in Merton when you were investigating. You know what people said, I never did; lawyers never do. How long did it take them to find Charles Tysall and what did he look like?'

Ryan was wearing that shifty look, the one Malcolm knew all too well as sending shivers of alarm up his spine. The expression

worn by a police officer choosing economy with fact, sitting
where he was, assessing the odds on the consequences of truth,
a hesitation complete in the second it took to weigh up the fact
there was nothing to lose.

'They phoned me up when they found a body,' Ryan said
carefully. 'I gave them a description, and it tallied. Tysall was
seen walking out of town with the tide coming in anyway, so it's
pretty clear already. Then this doctor turns up on site, used to
know Tysall a bit, and, oh, yes, by the way, according to local
rumour, knew the wife quite a lot better.' He let that sink in. Any
deceased, in Ryan's eyes, had few virtues and high nuisance
value, especially women.

'Anyway, the doc is told in advance the body is probably
Tysall, and he agrees, so Tysall it is. Mind,' he added, shifting
with ever greater discomfort, 'they also say they get three or four
bodies per summer off that coast. Unidentified. Tramp steamers, suicidal fishermen. Christ, I'd hate to live in a place like that.
Three pubs, one church, nothing else to do. The wife loved it.'

He knew he should not have spoken. His own reservations
about that flimsy identification should have remained exactly
what they were, his own. If he talked long enough round the
subject, maybe Malc would forget where he was. No chance,
Ryan thought, looking at the calm face only slightly flushed with
alcohol while his own was glowing; should have known better.
Malcolm was staring at him. Once you've let some cat out of a
bag, Ryan thought, you can't shove it back in.

'I wouldn't regard identification by a slight acquaintance of a
drowned man sufficient beyond reasonable doubt,' said
Malcolm, refusing to register anything but polite curiosity. A
policeman under attack, even a friend, could become as wooden
as the table. 'Do you know that close relatives misidentify their
dead with monotonous regularity? If you believe a person is
dead and you see a dead person, it seems to close the circle. I
think we need another drink.' He walked to the bar with the
bouncy step of a runner, one hand feeling for his wallet. I should
never fool with lawyers, Ryan thought, especially when they can

drink. He patted the silky red head of Malcolm's dog which grinned in response. Now there was a good female, constantly obedient, loving, asking no questions, telling no lies.

'Just one thing more,' Malcolm was saying as he sat. 'You gave the locals a description of Charles which tallied with the corpse. What description?'

Ryan wrinkled his face, genuinely struggling for memory. He knew Charles Tysall, oh yes, knew him from the files and the cheats and the women. Knew he was a murderer perforce, a man with a passion to destroy, looking all the time for perfection in ideas and the opposite sex, knocking it into pieces when he did find it, but for all Ryan knew, he'd only been face to face with the bastard twice. The dead wife, whom he'd taken to hospital in his car, he'd seen more than twice, each time less recognizable than the last, sometimes talking, sometimes not. His brow cleared.

'I gave them the description Elisabeth Tysall gave me. I sat with her, waiting in casualty. She told me what he was like.'

'How?'

'She said he was hung like a donkey.'

The man in the beach hut made tea. He had a small gas stove stolen from an empty caravan, water which he collected from the lake near the small caravan site, a camping gaz cylinder stolen from another beach hut. These wooden edifices he liked above all; they reminded him of doll's houses. They stood along Merton's public beach, stringing away down the coast with all the grace of wet washing on a line in a downpour, irregular, highly coloured, lumpish and graceless, decorated to individual taste as if they could ever be permanent. They were a series of garden sheds with stable doors on stilts, hired for the season, subject to wind and flood, raised far above the sand to cope with the high tides they were so unlikely to withstand. Some did, more by luck than judgement, remaining upright with peeling paint and all their romance gone long after some family moved on to where the children had alternatives other than an amusement arcade in the rain, and the parents were not sick of a caravan, the cold, the moaning and the spartan splendour of the beach. Merton's claim to holiday-making fame was for those with old-fashioned stamina, a taste for chips, sticky sweets, pints of ale and mugs of tea The leftovers were abundant. The man with the white hair was grateful for that.

My name is Charles and I have no name, he chanted, rocking back and forth in the small space of the hut, watching the dawn rise on a Sunday morning. I rose from the sea like Christ from the dead. Sunday is a day of grace for sinners and I am not one of those. My name is Charles. There were occasions when he almost forgot. Just as he forgot what it was he had been when he had the name, until he remembered again. The beach hut, last of the line, was slightly askew; the stool on which he sat also slightly crooked, so that he leaned constantly to one side. The stick with the carved duck's head assisted him to redress the balance. It was against the local by-laws to stay in a beach hut at night, in case the wind got up and encouraged the endless hunger of the tide. People obeyed the rules. Charles held such people in contempt. Also those who treasured the small possessions he stole, but left them out for him to steal all the same.

People without names cavorted on the beach in front of the hut by day, looking to their own pursuits, their games, their dogs, their delicious children, never to left or right and never towards anyone old. He could walk amongst them as if he were invisible. When there was a crowd, faintly excited, they sounded like the geese which had travelled over his head the autumn before, when he decided his new existence became him so much it was better than the one before. Who needed prestige, when they could reach out and reclaim it whenever they wanted? Who needed a fine apartment when an empty holiday cottage would do? Places like the one where Edward found him. Looking for Elisabeth and who had buried her, giving himself a reason to live. When he had done that, meted out his own version of justice, then he could go home.

It was necessary for a man without a name to have a reason. From his casual and contemptuous observation of humankind, no one else needed such a thing. They just existed, like lumbering animals.

A child was attempting to clamber up the rickety steps of his beach hut. A plump little thing with a nappy rump and curly hair, grunting with the effort. Charles peered over the top half of the stable door, hissed, bared his teeth, watched as the child met his eyes, waddled away, crying. Good. Oh, it was a clean little thing. He could have cooked it. The thought made him dizzy.

The tide was out again this morning, fickle bitch, leaving a huge expanse of mud and sand for the fools to play on. If only they knew how difficult it was to keep clean. It was the desire for fresh water which drove him the half mile into town, made him careless.

Between the daily business of eating and cleaning, cleaning was the worst. He slithered down the steps of the hut with his stick, dived behind and up the bank into the dunes, to find the place where he met Edward, if the young man deigned to arrive. Sandwiches would be nice: he could live on sandwiches and save himself foraging time. It was only when he was hungry that the urge to destroy became so paramount. A hypoglycaemic rage, he would have said, when he had a name. Which he didn't, now. Nor half the command of words. Snippets of poetry was all. The haunting and cynical voice of Browning, all he remembered from a thousand books.

'The moment she was mine, mine, fair,
perfectly pure and good: I found
A thing to do, and all her hair
In one long yellow string I wound
Three times her little throat around
And strangled her . . .'
He sang the words to the tune of a hymn.

From inside the worn pockets of the track suit rescued from behind the church hall, he pulled out the crumpled letters, the medical record card and the envelopes he had taken with such fastidious care from Dr Pardoe's desk in the surgery.

'Darling Julian,' he mimicked, reading in a high and breathy voice. 'How wonderful to know that I shall see you soon . . . Your loving Elisabeth.'

Oh yes, he loved you, darling Elisabeth; the good doctor loved you to death; look at what he did for you, in case you should cause him a scandal. Look at the record of what he did. The last billet-doux, a prescription on the record card for enough diazepam to stun a crowd of women, let alone one.

Charles without a name looked out to the sea. 'Escape me?' he murmured. 'Never.'

Flames danced in front of his eyes, the morning sun blazing over shallow stretches of water left by the tide, moving and dazzling. He could burn down the Pardoe house, that was what he could do, a house he had entered and left a dozen times, all of them so mad or so preoccupied they never noticed. Charles could hear the crackling sound of fire, imagine the sight in the dark, as they rushed out screaming, for him to pick them off with a knife or a stick, one by careless one, until finally, he would stamp on the hands which had touched his wife, buried her without permission.

The images were soothing; Sunday was a day of grace. Charles without a name listened for the church bells, hearing nothing but the wind in the pine trees at his back and the desolate mewing of the gulls on the beach before. One day soon he would go home. He wondered how he would ever get clean enough to go home – and where home was.

Edward despised the mere notion of going to church, quoted religion as the opiate of the masses. Joanna went to accompany her mother, also to put flowers on her father's grave. There had been no ordinary plot for Mr Pardoe, of course: he could not have been buried in the serried ranks of the others who now stretched out into the field behind, not he, but in a plot in the old graveyard, bought from the vicar long before as the price of charity. Joanna thought of it now as she sat in the congregation with her mother, saw for the first time how people might resent Pa's privileged resting place. She was thinking too, of how much better her own life would be if the family did not own so much, how pleasant if she could ever present herself as an ordinary contender for friendship instead of a race apart, unable to enter a shop without putting someone in mind of owing rent. Perhaps if she had nothing, Rick would love her, but on this footing, she could never be equal, never belong, even here with her elders, singing the same hymn in a great, slow groan of tuneless sound.

Mother sang lustily, Da, da, da da da daah, her voice loud and cracked, humming without words, the feathers from her hat curling over her face, another evening gown of purple trailing round her pink-shod feet beneath the mackintosh, her face flushed from yesterday's sun. Nobody minds, Joanna thought defensively, so why should I? Mother was popular, always had been; men flocked to say hallo after church. Men had always flocked in that direction, Joanna realised, surprised at her own observation. Poor little Mouse, to be so pitied.

On the other side of the feathers, Julian gently took his mother's hymn book and turned it the right way up so that she could at least pretend she was reading the words. She ignored the gesture. On the last hymn of the service, he sensed rather than saw Sarah Fortune slipping out of the pew behind, late arriver, first to go, with her hair concealed under a straw hat. He shut his eyes for the final blessing, seeing nothing inside his own skull but the vision of her body in those circus cartwheels, hand over graceful hand across the lawn.

The sun struck with cruel brilliance as they emerged blinking from church, the sound of the organ receding behind them, the bells taking over. Groups formed on the paths between the graves, women with women, men with men, a division as old as time. Julian counted a small congregation of largely advanced years, hinged together by habit and the continuity of their lives rather than belief or commitment to virtue. That was certainly true of Rick's dad, from the amusement arcade, sedulous as ever towards the doctor even though he must have known the evidence Julian had seen on his own son, signs of drunken violence which were always explained away as the boy falling downstairs. Rick's dad, his cousin, PC Curl the village copper, others who may have needed God's forgiveness as much as Julian felt he did himself, but never prayed for it, believing, perhaps, as he did not, that a visit to church wiped the whole slate clean. There was a murmur at his elbow.

'Can we have a word, Doc, before you have to rush away?'

He liked the presumption that he was always busy, always in demand, disliked the deference. If it had been towards him for his qualifications and his value, he would have been pleased, but they bowed to a Pardoe for the supposition of money and influence. It was that which put him beyond companionship, nothing more, not even his own brusqueness, which they tolerated.

'What do you think, Doc? Time we began to take this ghost business seriously, don't you think? I mean, after Miss Gloomer, not fair, is it? Could have been this white-haired bastard did the fishing shop, other places too. I mean, he's real all right. He ain't a ghost at all.'

'He hasn't hurt anyone, has he?' Julian said sharply. He couldn't make himself care, except about Miss Gloomer. If there was a poor, summer vagrant wandering about at night stealing the surplus, it wouldn't be the first or last to go of his own accord. The idea of hunting him was vaguely repellent, although not to Rick's dad, nor to PC Curl who always dramatised problems of law and order.

'My nephew seen him plenty,' Curl murmured. Julian laughed. Stonewall Jones was his favourite child, stubborn, discreet, incredibly brave in the face of a cut arm, chickenpox and anything which had ever ailed him, but not, surely, a reliable source of information.

'S'not funny, Doc. Something's got to be done.'

'Such as?' he suggested lightly, refusing to take the lead. They were silent. No one else wanted to do anything other than talk.

'Such as locking doors, keeping your eyes open and letting him be?'

They nodded, each following the other. Pass the word, that was it, the full extent of civic duty on another day so warm it should be treasured, Sunday lunch beckoning as a prelude to an afternoon's doze. The heat made them lazy, turned their minds to other things. Rick's dad fingered his tie, tight at the throat, uncomfortable. The mood of vague purpose fragmented into nothing; Joanna called for her brother. The vicar stood next to her, the verger on the other side, planting a kiss on Mother's powdered cheek while she embraced him, the powder falling on to his dark jacket without him seeming to mind.

We could set off through the streets, Julian thought with sudden, savage amusement, in my car, with Mama waving to the locals like the Queen. She's the only one of us they can love, because she requires so little. They passed through the church-yard gate. There was no sign of Sarah Fortune's car with the dented wing.

'Just a minute,' Julian said. He walked back to the gate, sprinted through the old graveyard, into the newer environs of the field where Elisabeth Tysall was buried.

The same temporary headstone, disgracing him; the rest tidy. His old dead roses spirited away and at her feet and her heart, fresh flowers in new vases.

The chimes of the ice-cream van rang out to the faithful long after the church bells ceased. Down by the beach, they rang to a greater effect and the formation of a sporadic queue by mid-afternoon. They were parked on the edge of the caravan site, by the main track over the dunes on to the beach, ready to catch the comers and goers, who came forward as if the van, next to the refresh-ment hut, but somehow more enticing, was a mirage in the desert.

'What's the matter with you, Stoney? You suffering heat sick-ness, or what?' Rick was doling out a double 99 cone with Cadbury's Flake on top, watching it melt even as he presented it out of the window to a lad who'd have to be quick to get it all down in time. All down his vest, more likely. Talking over his back to where Stonewall lounged, ready to dive into the freezer for a Mivvi or a raspberry split or those iced lollies built like space ships which were so popular this year, but so phallic in appearance he and Rick sniggered over every sale, especially to girls. Nothing was funny this afternoon.

'Nothing's the matter,' Stonewall said sulkily.

'Whenever you say that, I know you're lying.'

Oh, Rick was on the ball today, jokes to customers, the bruises round his eyes making him look like a pirate, hands over the ices quick and deft, shirt shining clean and his hair falling over his forehead so he could flick it back and wink. There was a pause in the line. Give it half an hour, when they all started trailing home, business would be brisk. Rick checked stocks and whistled.

'Come on, Stoney, talk to me.' There was a shuffling. Stonewall looked out the window.

'Are you going out with that redhead, Rick? Are you?'

So that's what it was, a little *frisson* of jealousy, a little bit of the old insecurity creeping back, as if it had ever gone since the boy lost his own father and screamed in his sleep.

'Course not. I like her, that's all. You be nice to her if you see her, Stonewall. She did me a good turn on Friday night.' Rick laughed uproariously. He'd been laughing like a hyena all week-end, imploding with silent jokes Stonewall didn't understand.

'What about Jo, then?' Rick stopped what he was doing, and the laughter.

'That's something else,' he said sharply. Stonewall kicked his frayed training shoe against the door. He was miserable without knowing why.

'Cheer up. We got things to do after. My dad says we got to go looking for that ghost. Your white-haired ghost. Typical, doesn't want to bother himself, lets us do it.' He whistled again.

'Did you really believe me, then?' Stonewall asked, his voice quivering. 'No you didn't. You just pretended you did in the caf, to please her. You never believed me until other people did. You never believed that ghost got my dog.'

He had carried the stiff, twisted collar in his pocket for the two days since he had found it. Rick could see it now, protruding from the side of his shorts above the thin, pale brown legs with their covering of freckles. Stonewall was such a thin, sandy boy: even his legs weren't significant.

'And,' he was saying, his voice high with anxiety, 'when you go looking for the ghost, you'll send me away. When you get a girl, you'll send me away. That's what you'll do. Everyone does.'

There were tears now, coursing down his slightly dirty face, leaving rivulets made worse by the smutty hand which attempted to push them back. The face of a customer appeared at the window. Rick produced three of the phallic lollies, took the money, slammed the window shut and sat on the floor among the refrigeration hum, pulled Stonewall down beside him. He grabbed a sheet of kitchen towel and applied it roughly to the boy's face, absorbing phlegm and tears, put his arm round the skinny, shaking shoulders.

'Now listen here, you snotty bastard, and listen properly. You're my mate, my very best mate, you hear? And if I can't have you round me all the time, that doesn't make any difference. You're still my best one. I used to go about with Jo Pardoe when I was your age, bit like you and me now, loved her the same way, only it changed, and it all had to wait. My fault, I suppose.'

Stonewall grabbed the kitchen towel, blew his nose, failed to stem the tears.

'You love her more'n you love me,' he whispered. It choked him with shame to mention the word. Saying 'fuck' or 'cunt' was easier.

'Well, well, well,' said Rick, wonderingly, running his spare hand through Stonewall's stick-up hair, a gesture the boy would always pretend to dislike, but loved as much as Sal had loved a stroking. 'That's a damn fine haircut you got there, boy. And as for love, well, I'll love you for ever and nothing in between, you hear? And if I love someone else, they'll have to love you too. Jo would, she does already, even if her brother never pays you for digging up bait, like you did again this morning. He never catches anything, you know, don't do it again, you hear?' He paused. Another face pressed itself against the window of the van. Rick stuck up two fingers. He had to get to the end of what he was saying, since whatever it was, was important.

'There'll be times I'm busy and you're busy, but there you'll be, first and last, bad moods, good moods. Any fucker comes near you, meaning harm, I'll tear his fucking head off. Course I love you, Stoney, better than anyone. It'll always be the same until you tell ME to fuck off. See? I'll love you to death, boy, just you try and stop me.'

There was a knocking at the window. Rick got up, turned on his chimes and began to whistle again. The sky overhead had darkened; for once they came off the beach early. A week of heat, a season of drought; even for business and his dad's pleasure, he could not be sorry about the rain. One day, he and Stonewall might have an empire. Then they would only be nice to people they liked.

'Three Mivvis,' he yelled over his shoulder. 'On the double!'

Stonewall kicked him in the shins to show he was alive, sauntered to the freezer like a millionaire bar lizard in a small, select space, obliged the order with flourish. Four Mivvis, then they ran out, two double Ds, five phallic symbols, four caramel torpedos, nearly as bad in shape, six straight vanilla tubs and a bombe, Stonewall grinning throughout. Felt a hand on his shoulder, Rick's of course, there was no room for anyone else and no need either.

'Stay down there, boy, just sit down. I think I seen your ghost.' Preternaturally tall, striding down under the darkening sky which made his white hair look as if it shone, was the man with no name. Had he shuffled with an armful of family burdens, whingeing kids, bags of windshield, Thermos flasks, towels, damp clothes and plastic bottles, he would not have stood out. The others were purposeful. He looked confused.

'Tall,' Rick said tersely to the figure at his feet, clutching his ankles. 'I mean, really tall.' He didn't say handsome instead of long, tall, lean, regular featured, a face and frame tending towards the cadaverous: neither of them reckoned anyone over fifty could ever be called attractive; they just didn't count at that age. 'Big thatch, white hair, can't see his ears, bit of a beard, not much, trousers don't fit. Track-suit bottoms, too short?'

Stonewall nodded in the sheer ecstasy of being believed, not caring. The white-haired man paused in front of the window, sunken cheekbones presenting themselves first, the patrician voice echoing next.

'I'd love what you have for sale,' he intoned, 'but I haven't any change.' Rick leant forward confidentially, so that he was half out of the van and still looking as if he was telling a secret, putting his hand over one side of his mouth as he spoke in a hiss.

'Tell you the truth, mate,' he leered, 'we've had a good day and it's melting. Have one free. On the house. Only don't tell,' he added, tapping the side of his nose in a cockney parody, unconvincing to his own ears, not to Stonewall, still clutching his ankles in a paroxysm of terrible giggles.

The ice-cream fridge was on the right. Rick dived in, scooped out from on top a double cone, filled both, delivered it. The man did not pause to offer thanks or smile. Rick knew it was a giveaway to stare, so he pretended to prepare for the next on parade, noticing at the same time how the creamy floss had gone down the man's throat like a mouse down a Hoover, all in one, in a great big gulp, terrible, Adam's apple going in then out and a whole cone gone in a swallow. The man could have eaten a dog, the thought made Rick swallow too. Something wrong with his teeth. Another queue had formed behind him, discretion overcame the ghost's obvious desire to ask for more and he left without a wave.

'Think he's hungry,' Rick muttered.

'So he isn't a ghost,' said Stonewall, finally, lazily, leaving hold of the ankle, standing up.

'Four double cornets left,' said Rick. 'He could have ate the lot.'

'Perhaps he ate Sal.'

'Give us the mirror, Stoney. He made my hair stand on end.'

*

Her hair stood on end like a series of wire fences, and nothing a
soul could do. Mrs Pardoe wore it squashed under a hat or
turban, depending upon occasion or season. She maintained her
feathery boa and frightful hat as she tripped across the grass to
the small terrace of three cottages on the right of her overgrown
lawn, her feet landing neatly without the high-heeled shoes
which might have dug in so far as to root her to the spot.

The roses round the door looked glad of the rain which fell
out of the sky in droplets as big as petals, weighing down her hat
and waterlogging the feathers. Mrs Jennifer Pardoe knocked on
her own with a terrible urgency. The door was open. In
she went, all of a flutter, which stopped like a toy with a run-out
battery as soon as the door closed behind her.

Sarah Fortune stood up from behind a pile of papers in the
lounge area. She looked tired as if the heat had struck and she
was glad of the rain. So was Mrs Mouse Pardoe. She shed her
toque and her mac and sat down comfortably.

'Oh, lord, what a relief,' she said. 'Do you think you could
make some tea? I can't stand this any longer.'

The movements were deft and forceful. None of the totter-
ing, none of the giggles; a normal old lady of sixty-five years,
oddly dressed, nothing more than eccentric. She sat herself
comfortably among Sarah's papers, picked them up casually,
glanced at a copy of Mr Pardoe's will, put it down with a smile.

'Working, dear? It's so bad for your eyes. Don't you like this
simple will? It was all my idea.'

'Shall I draw the curtains?' Sarah said thoughtfully. 'In case
we have visitors?'

'They're all out, dear. Don't worry, I have ears longer than
stalks, and why do you think I insist on keeping a sheep? I'll
know as soon as I hear a car and if anyone comes to this door,
Hettie will bleat for me, then I'll just go back to being senile and
you humour me, all right?'

'Of course,' Sarah murmured. 'I quite understand.'

Mouse Pardoe beamed. 'I knew you would. Ernest said so.'

CHAPTER EIGHT

'The late Mr Pardoe,' said Jennifer Pardoe, 'was a bit of a bully. Full of charm and also full of shit.' She belched slightly after the use of a rude word whose sound she obviously felt was agreeable. 'He was very lovable and very forceful and I was always known as the Mouse. I loved him greatly, hopelessly, but also realistically. I didn't have much option, even if I thoroughly disapproved and considered then, as I do now, that most property is theft. My opinion was never heard, my wishes never considered, until, when he grew older and beyond temptation, he started to listen and I suppose I got the upper hand. He had a passion for respectability, although he wasn't in the least respectable. It's a shame so many things come too late.' She sipped tea out of a mug with all the grace of a thirsty labourer, looked at Sarah over the rim.

'No,' she said, answering a question which hung in the air. 'I myself am not in the least respectable. Neither are you. I have always regarded the mere notion of respectability as such a waste of time.' Sarah nodded a mild assent.

'Anyway,' Mrs Pardoe continued, 'we made certain confessions to each other, my husband and I, long before he died, which somehow put us on an equal footing. I won't elaborate now. He ceased to care about property and such, and made the will you've read because he trusted me. He trusted Julian too, but Julian was on a bender at the time, not booze, you understand, the other kind of addiction, misguided love. Then my husband died in a typically stupid fashion. People surrounded me, immediately, telling me what I should do. They hemmed me in, and even if I'd finally got my better half into the habit of listening to me, no one else did. The children, never. I knew they were going to push and pull me in all sorts of directions, and I knew exactly what I wanted to do with all this property we own, so did he really, getting it in the first place was only a sort of game to him. But I wasn't going to be allowed to have my own way.'

'Who,' Sarah asked, 'was going to stop you?'

'I merely made a suggestion about what we should do with all this property and Edward hit me. I ruined Edward as a child, let him get away with everything. He was such a pretty baby,' Jennifer Pardoe said simply, as if that was explanation enough. 'No one was going to listen, as I said. The tradition of not listening to me was far too well established and I really can't stand confrontation and conflict. So I decided to go mad. Remove myself into the realms of the harmless and also make sure I got attention. You get a lot of attention when you're mad. I've rather enjoyed it, even though it is a bit of a strain, sometimes. When mad, you can be a total exhibitionist, something I was never allowed to be, wear what you like, say what you like, marvellous, you ought to try it.'

'Lying in the cabbage patch?' Sarah asked.

'Yes. Wonderful. But if I did it without being mad, some fool would call an ambulance. I've realised I'm probably quite a bit mad to begin with. It must help, don't you think? I like walking about with the sheep too, and talking to the birds, why not? Only I couldn't if I were supposed to be sane, could I?'

'I don't see why not.'

'My dear,' said Mrs Pardoe, patting her knee, 'I know that you have the uncanny knack of understanding almost everything, but one thing you can't know at your age is how much power you lose in the world when you grow old. You have to create another power base as your own crumbles. Basic politics. Mine, by the way, have always been slightly left of centre.

Ernest Matthewson never used to approve.' She peered at a Mickey Mouse watch. 'I'd better go. We'll have to continue this another time. I wonder, will that boy Rick come up with ice-cream and my newspaper today? Probably not, what with the rain and all.'

She gurgled her tea again and proffered the mug. All confessions, Sarah noticed, needed some kind of liquid accompaniment. They could not emerge from a dry mouth.

'That boy Rick is in love with your daughter,' Sarah said. 'The feeling is reciprocated.' Mrs Pardoe nodded.

'Calf-love, I hope.'

'Calf-love can be real.'

'Well, there couldn't be a better candidate. A nice working-class boy, just like Mr Pardoe once was. Given the right chances, he'll go far. I must go.' Sarah wanted to stop her but there was nothing she could do against such steely determination.

'I suppose,' Mouse was saying, 'I should get a stick if I'm going to keep up this doddery charade. By the way, girl, have you any idea what should happen to this estate?'

'Yes. You've just endorsed it. It was you gave the instructions to Ernest, wasn't it? Not Julian?'

'Of course. Only it was supposed to look as if it was Ernest's idea, I mean anybody's but mine. I told him I wanted the children to realise that they had everything they needed already. I want them to realise of their own accord, without anyone telling them. I wanted them to know how you work out your own destiny and money only makes it harder, sets you apart.'

'And why did he suggest me?'

Mrs Pardoe looked away, put on her hat and let the feathers hang down to her chin.

'They're supposed to go at the back, these feathers, more fun this way, aren't they?' Sarah's gaze did not waver; Mouse met it.

'My old friend Ernest never does anything without a dozen motives, you know?'

'I never knew he was quite so clever.'

'He isn't, he's simply cunning. What he really said about you was . . .' she paused, her first hesitation, as if the symptoms of insanity were resumed with the hat.

'Yes?'

'You were a catalyst. Does that mean a very sleek cat? Can a catalyst do something about Hettie the sheep? She's been driving me mad.'

Mrs Pardoe lurched across the wet lawn, singing in the rain.

Catalyst is not what Ernest said, Sarah thought. He would never have used such a word. Nor would he have understood that someone who acts out another role, like Mrs Pardoe's madness, becomes the part they play.

Miss Gloomer was dying. When Julian came back from his ten o'clock call, he drew level with the house he could never quite love as home since his father had died there, although he had loved its classless eccentricity once. He pulled into the drive, sat where he was with his hands on the steering wheel, watching the windows through the rain. Mother woke and slept early; no light shone from Edward's room with its sweeping view of the coast. I should not think of him as a spy as well as a failure, Julian thought. I should not delight that he and Joanna are likely out of the house in separate directions for fear of what they might do to comfort one another on a wet night like this; I have an evil mind.

He watched the lawn, noticed with weary guilt the way it resembled a hay field. The night was cooling fast; drizzle made the grass glisten. Tomorrow, time allowing, he could scythe it, tonight all he could see was the ghostly vision of Sarah Fortune, naked against the green. Then he was out of the car, walking automatically towards the cottages, his feet soft on the surface, hissing in the grass. He could say he thought he had heard an intruder; he could say he had come to enquire after her health after Joanna had told him the story of the rogue tide; he could say there was no time to come sooner, which was a lie. He could mention Elisabeth Tysall's headstone and ask Sarah's opinion, but he was still afraid; it was ridiculous and he turned to go back, saw the lamp outside the cottage they had given her, illuminating the scrubby roses and against the block of light from the open door, her figure, bent double. He heard the pitiful bleating of the sheep, heard Sarah's voice, soothing in return. Julian quickened his step. She did not seem remotely surprised to see him.

'Oh, it's you. Look, we've got to do something about this sheep.'

'Why?' His own voice sounded like a bleat of protest.

'She's been making a noise all evening, that's why, all afternoon too, butting her head against the door. Took me a while to realise it wasn't a simple desire for my company. One of her horns is growing into her eye.'

Julian squatted on his haunches. The sheep flinched; Sarah pressed the fleece against the frame of the door. He noticed that the left horn was partly swathed in a steaming rag, then saw with horror how the tip had grown at a crooked angle, so that instead of being level with the forehead, it grazed the ball of one bloodshot and weeping eye. There was a hideous sore patch beneath.

'She's in pain. She'll be covered with flies in the morning,' Sarah was saying, matter of factly. 'I've tried to yank the horn back, she's been very good, but the horn's too hard. So I wrapped a hot dishcloth round it. Thought it might soften it. Is that the right thing to do? She doesn't like it.'

Julian swore under his breath, trying to remember any jewels of animal husbandry his father had learned in that last of his many enthusiasms. What was it Father had wanted to do at the time, or was it Mother's idea, collecting rare breeds of sheep? Put something back into the land, Mother had said.

'I can't see properly,' he muttered, feeling the animal tremble beneath his hand. 'Do you mind if we take her inside?'

It was bizarre, standing in the cruel light of the kitchenette where a kettle bubbled on the cooker, with the sheep trying to back away from where he held her between braced legs.

'The heat does seem to soften it. Here, hold on to her muzzle.' Sarah obeyed with both hands. The terror in the wall

eyes of the animal seemed to fill the room. Slowly, with considerable strength, Julian lifted the horn with a wringing motion of
both his arms, twisting it up and back, well clear of the eye.
Quickly Sarah wiped the moisture which had gathered round
the wound below. Hettie bucked and reared. Enough was
enough. They let her bolt for the door in shambling haste,
dishrag unwinding as she went.

'She looks like a woman coming out of the hairdresser's, half
done, I never knew sheep needed similar attention.' She had
turned to wash her hands in the sink, up to the elbow. Julian did
the same.

'I wouldn't have seen you in the nurse's role,' he said lightly.

'Oh, I wouldn't know about that,' Sarah said with equal lightness. 'Would you like a drink? Plentiful supplies.'

Any animosity between them was gone. He felt himself
shiver, remembering the crumpled horn, boring into an animal's
head like the memories penetrating his own skull. The cottage
was cool indoors, designed to repel heat in summer, preserve it
in winter. Sarah was dressed in a cotton sweater, short-sleeved
with a deep V, buttercup yellow, her hair springy clean, the smell
of soap, shampoo and perfume easily overpowering the farm-
yard traces of sheep and the lingering medicine smell of Miss
Gloomer's bedside. They sat in the small living room. A large
shawl of many colours was flung over the sofa; an ugly table
lamp had been removed to the floor to diffuse the light, trans-
forming the place so much that even the single bar of the electric
fire seemed cheerful. On the first sip, he noticed that her whisky
was excellent and she sipped her own with the evident pleasure
of a connoisseur.

'Did you detour this way to tell me I was fired?' she asked
without rancour, as if the answer did not much matter.

'No. You're retained for having a certain expertise with a
sheep. How did you learn that?'

She shrugged. The sweater fell away a little at the neck; he
noticed two small, raised scars, as if a mole had recently been
removed.

'I really don't know. I don't have any skills, animals are easier than people. Would you like some more?'

The whisky had gone in the twinkling of an eye. He nodded. She rose gracefully, her arm catching the light, and he noticed three more of the little scars above one elbow, white against the golden brown of her skin. There was nothing disfiguring in any of the scars, but the sight of them filled him with a peculiar anguish.

'We spoke on Friday,' he said abruptly. 'About the late Elisabeth Tysall. What do you know about her?' Sarah followed the direction of his gaze to the marks on her neck, pulled the neck of the sweater closer to her ears with both hands.

'Nothing while she was alive, but I came to know of her. I know that her husband considered I was her double. I know that he abused her badly and she killed herself off the coast down here. Let herself drown. Yesterday, I almost found out how. Do you know, if it had been warm, like yesterday, if she was drunk enough, drugged enough to lie down and sleep, it would have been a peaceful death, a simple letting go. No pain.'

'Do you think so?'

'Provided she had no terror. Provided she had consumed enough to want to drift away.'

Julian looked at her closely for signs of flippancy. Now he could see they were not the same, Elisabeth Tysall and this woman at his feet. They had little resemblance apart from the hair and the membership of the same league of female beauty.

'I should like to know about Elisabeth Tysall,' said Sarah wistfully, 'because no one ever asked.'

Julian took a large swallow of the whisky and put it down. The prospect of shifting the burden of guilt by speaking of it made him react like the sheep at the end of the unexplained pain, silly and slightly skittish.

'The Tysalls had a cottage here,' he began. 'At least, she made it very much theirs with improvements, but it was rented from us. They appeared to be enormously rich. I suspect the kind of rich who actually owned very little. Not our kind of rich. This isn't a glamorous place, but Elisabeth Tysall liked it. Charles, her husband, let her come here alone, although he was extremely possessive. I supposed he reckoned there was no temptation in a little seaside town. We aren't exactly endowed with adult attractions. No casinos, no places to be seen. You don't get in the county calendar if you sit in the amusement arcade.' He looked at her meaningfully, met an innocent stare.

'She used to walk a lot. So did I, in those days when this landscape held magic for me.'

He remembered to sip slowly, feeling slightly intoxicated already, speaking faster.

'So I walked with her. I'd met Charles twice, when Father had had them up to the house for a drink. Charles saw me as a boring country bumpkin, the plain man I am. I met Elisabeth for longer in the surgery when she came in for a prescription. I don't know how it happened. I couldn't keep my eyes away. Life became a vacuum between meetings. A week when I didn't see her, and there were plenty of those, was a week in hell. She wrote letters in between, teased me, made me stand back. She was a wise flirt, warned me about Charles's savage jealousy. I told her, leave him: I'll take on the whole world for you; but she said no, you don't know me and no one ever wins with Charles. Then all of a sudden one weekend, she succumbed. I can't describe it,' he said simply. 'I'd sound like a boy if I tried to describe it.' Julian sat back, exhausted by the memory.

'I remember telling her, you are so beautiful, you'll immobilise me completely with any other woman. What am I to do if you don't stay with me for ever? Leave him, marry me. I shall never react like this to any other woman, you're so perfect. Don't say that, she kept saying. Please don't say that.' He began to tremble, reached for his glass, let the good whisky slop on the floor.

'A fortnight later, she came back. You know how it is when you miss someone so much it hurts. I'd got myself into a pitch of anger because she hadn't been in touch in any way, no letter, phone call, nothing, and of course I couldn't get in touch with her because of Charles, but I was still mad to see her. My perfect Elisabeth, the fulfilment of all dreams. She wasn't perfect, though, not even remotely beautiful any more. In fact, when she barged into my surgery, she was hardly recognisable apart from the hair. Her face had been cut to ribbons. It might have been glassed: it was difficult to tell with all the stitches and the swelling. I couldn't look at her.'

Julian put his head in his hands, briefly, toyed with his glass, his palms sticky with sweat.

'I asked her how and why, of course. I think part of my reaction of revulsion, no more or less, was guilt, in case our affair had triggered what had been done to her. It was difficult for her to speak clearly; her mouth had been slit in one corner. She said it was nothing to do with me, Charles had done it on a whim. I didn't believe her. I was stunned and revolted and frightened, so I behaved like an impatient irresponsible doctor. I prescribed for her massive doses of tranquillisers, sleeping aids, told her she'd do best by the healing process if she slept for twenty-four hours. I rang the pharmacy, didn't even volunteer to stay with her. Instead, I went out and got drunk. Paralytic.'

He emptied the tumbler.

'May I have some more of this please, with the reassurance that I'm not going to repeat the exercise now? I've never been drunk since, though God knows I've tried.'

He closed his eyes and listened to the sound of the liquid gurgling into his glass. A generous measure, enough to make him shrug to attention. The hand touching his as he took the glass, was warm, encouraging.

'I suppose it was the next day she disappeared, when I couldn't raise my head off the pillow, cancelled Saturday surgery where, I gathered later, she called to see me. She might not have received a friendly reception, despite her state. They thought she was bad for me and they'd never exactly liked her manner, which was imperious, to say the least. I suppose a woman as beautiful has the right to be rude and defensive, so many people must want to touch.'

He was nursing the whisky rather than drinking it. Sarah sensed a man of iron self-control, who drank not for pleasure, only for oblivion.

'I assumed she had gone back to her husband. I got a letter from him, some time later, terminating the tenancy on the cottage. I felt, as I should have done, extremely guilty, also relieved. The guilt then was nothing to the guilt a year later, when she was found in the sand-banks, half a mile from the quay. The buried body, come back into the land of the living.'

'How did she come to be buried?'

'No one knows, or if they do, they won't be telling now, but the creeks change shape all the time. A section of bank could have fallen on her, buried her, then split apart again after months. There was a storm tide the day before she was found. It was the growth of hair, mainly, which indicated how long she'd been there. Then the police investigation, her husband saying she'd never gone back to London at all, he thought she'd gone home to America, which is where she came from originally. Elisabeth was under the sand from almost the day I spoke to her last. I wish there was some doubt: there isn't. I shall always know it was I who put her there. She came to me for help. The one who was her lover gave her the means for suicide. The last straw. I may as well have ordered her to go and die.'

The whisky was untouched and the room was silent. Julian coughed, painfully.

'Charles came to look at the body of course. He phoned me and I told him he could stay in his old cottage if he wanted, but all he kept asking was how his wife came to be buried in the sand, as if I should know. I was angry with him, short, said I didn't want to know, shouted at him, he should have loved her. It was the same week Father died, my behaviour before that might explain why he didn't trust me. Charles simply wouldn't accept any of the explanations of how Elisabeth had been interred there so long, he wanted me to take him to see the place. I couldn't, wouldn't. Then I was called to remove his body from where it was washed up. I knew it must be him. Do you know what I did? I kicked that sodden bundle in the ribs, put the last nail in the coffin of my self-esteem. Then I came home to bury my father. I knew then what I've known ever since.' He began to count on his fingers. 'Namely, I'm not fit to be a human being among all these decent people here, let alone a doctor. I killed her, you see. I may as well have killed myself.'

Sarah got up and moved into the kitchen area where he could see her putting the kettle on the stove, lighting the gas. A moth came in through the window, fluttered in front of the mirror Joanna had used to dress, reflecting the light from the floor. Julian wanted to stop the sound of the flapping wings round the light.

'Coffee?' Sarah was asking.

'Yes.' He waited, leaned forward and caught the moth in both hands, got up and released it through the open window. Sarah came back, put the coffee on the floor beside the lamp, sat where she had been at his feet. There was nothing submissive in the pose, only a command for attention.

'Now you listen,' she said. 'There's something you should know. Don't ask for the sources of information, just believe, Elisabeth Tysall did not kill herself on your account. She planned it before she came here that last time and nothing was going to stop her. She had written a letter to Ernest Matthewson, deposited with her bank, to be forwarded to him only in the event of her death being confirmed. The bank followed her instructions to the letter. Ernest was ill, his wife intercepted the letter and finally, gave it to me. I showed it to a friend – no one else. Elisabeth stated on page one exactly what she was going to do, how and where. She said she'd had several affairs in the past, all as revenge against Charles for not loving her any more, but the suicide was pure revenge for her disfigurement. She couldn't tell tales about him while he was alive, but she planned for her body to be found, her injuries examined and him exposed. She didn't know much about the workings of the law, it wouldn't have stood up in court. Also, she didn't have the remotest will to live, something she had lost a long time before. She didn't need your tranquillisers either since she already had an arsenal of pills. There was supposed to be another sealed letter on her when she was found, but that was lost.'

Sarah twisted to sit on the other hip, gracefully. Julian could feel a wild heat course through his veins. Anger, relief, remembered, unexercised desire, until now, dormant along with the dead. Fury, guilt.

'That doesn't mean,' Sarah went on softly, 'that your reaction to her face was not horribly cruel, something to be ashamed of. But it does mean that it didn't influence events. You didn't kill her. Charles killed her. As for kicking his corpse, a corpse has no feelings, leaves those with the living. Your father had just died. Grief makes us all knock on the doors of insanity. When my husband died, I wanted to kill, maim, torture. You hardly did that.'

Julian was leaning forward, hungry for hope, staring into her flecked eyes, finding them fathomless, generous, lonely without sadness. He did not move when she took his face between her hands and kissed him. The kiss went on: he recoiled slightly, then responded with a groan, drawn into the embrace with a long, shuddering sigh.

'Sarah, Sarah . . .'

'Don't think,' she murmured. 'Just don't think. Except of killing demons.'

He thought he also heard her say that Charles Tysall could not be allowed to claim so many lives, but he was not sure of anything she said. He heard only the rustle of clothing, himself climbing the stairs in her wake, entering the dark bedroom where the moonlight shone, pulling his shirt over his head, falling with her into a warm tangle of silky limbs, joined again by the kiss which seemed never to have stopped. Remembering her slenderness, feeling her strength, trying not to claw or to grasp. Shivering until she calmed him, guided him into one cataclysmic moment when he knew he shouted. When he swam back into the planet, he wanted to cry. Instead, he slept like a child.

The wheels of Edward's car spun on the gravel; not the swishing sound of a well-raked, richly coated drive, only the spinning of worn rubber on worn pebbles sunk into mud after warm rain. Fishing: why ever would a man want to fish? Especially the way he fished, a sort of clandestine activity, often at night, for the romance of moonlight on the waves, but mostly for shame, because fishing was something he did to acquire a skill other men might envy, because a man of his vision should have been able to pull fish out of the sea as easily as far lesser men and he had to make his attempts at night because, so far, they were conspicuous failures. The fish would not bite, even after the hours he had spent over two years, they stayed beneath the water and laughed at him. The rods were state of the art, the bait was right according to the books, and that boy Stonewall swore it was, managing just a touch of scorn in his silent servility. Edward admitted he needed a teacher, if he were humble enough to learn. He could cast, but he could not catch. It was like everything else – his failure was in proportion to the effort. If only Dad had taught him.

The house felt empty. 'Joanna!' he shouted up the stairs, careless of whom he might wake; how dare they sleep when he needed company and food in that order? Silence. Her car was gone, out with one of her bitchy friends, as long as that was all. He slammed down his fishing tackle on the kitchen table, emptied his jacket pockets of boxes of hooks, floats, casting weights, the detritus of failure, along with sandwiches in greaseproof paper, silly cow. The lightweight plastic of the box of hooks cracked, spilling them on the table, small things these ones, no bigger than a thumbnail. Edward scooped some of them into the kitchen drawer. There were signs of his impatience, signs of his desire, all over the house. New rods, new reels, hooks in every drawer. Mother, Julian, even Father before had let him spread this litter. They all thought fishing might make a man of him. If he had heard that once, he had heard it ten dozen times.

'Joanna!'

Nothing. Edward went up to his room, hungry and bored,

and looked out of the window. The rain had eased to a soft drizzle; the sky was clear for another day's fresher heat tomorrow.
He was suddenly forlorn, still angry. The doll's house stood covered. He brought his fist down into the plywood roof, heard it
crack and crumble, the contents inside skitter as the edifice tot-
tered, groaned and stood still. Unable to bear examination of the
carnage, he turned to the window; unable to look towards the
sea, he looked towards the cottages.

A light in a window over there. Hettie the sheep grazing in
front of the one door out of the three which had roses. An
upstairs light and a downstairs light. Julian's car parked by the
front door of their house, as usual. Edward suddenly knew
where he was. The knowledge made him feel sick.

He clattered downstairs in case he was wrong, passed via a
wide detour to the back of the house where Julian's room
stood next to Jo's, both doors ajar, both rooms empty. Back to
his own room, looking out again. The light above the front
door shone out to welcome everyone home, illuminating the
grass. He could see Sarah Fortune in the nude, walking away
from him like a contemptuous ghost, a model for a painting
with her handbag balanced on her head and her arms outstretched for balance in perfect poise. Save me from desire, he
told himself with all the fervour of the prayer he despised.
Save me.

Back down in the kitchen, he tripped over his rod, swore,
tripped over the newspaper on the pantry floor, swore again. He
seized a fistful of bread, felt a tickle on the back of his neck,
turned. Mother was behind him, still in the feather hat she had
worn that morning, a tweedy coat over the same dress. She was
clearly startled. More satisfyingly, she was also frightened.
Retreating before him like a slave, back into the kitchen, putting
her hand on the hooks on the table, screaming short little shrieks
like a parrot, raising her palms as if about to pray, before he hit
her. A punch was all, to the side of that ridiculous hat, but hard,
making her fold, clutch the back of a chair with a hook or two
still in her palm. She gasped but would not fall, straightened up,

clasped the table for support with the other hand and stood straight, swaying slightly. The hat was knocked even further sideways, the feathers curling and brushing the left ear lobe, from which a drop of blood began to form and slowly fall. She opened the palm in which two fish hooks were embedded and sighed theatrically.

'What did I do, Ed dear? What did I do?'

There was a draught of cold air from the back door. Joanna stood, hair damp, frizzed by rain, looking at the tableau of mother and son. Mother sat with great precision and began to tease the two hooks out of her palm, wincing only slightly, tut-tutting under her breath. It was the barbs, pointing backwards, that got under the skin and went into the bone of a fish without causing pain; Joanna had listened to a thousand expositions and explanations from Edward. The hooks did not look painless inside a hand.

'There!' Mother said, triumphantly, easing out the first, holding it to the light and going to work on the second. 'You just have to do this and then you go this way, see? Easy peasy.' Joanna was comforted. Accidents will happen, fishing was silly sport. Then the drop of blood oozing from behind Mother's hat, a single drop, plopping on the table before Mother caught it in her injured palm, sucked greedily. All gone, that bright red speck, all gone. Then she saw Joanna for the first time. Her voice became defensive. She looked at Edward, fearfully.

'All gone!' she said, gaily, retrieving the second hook. 'Time for bed! Time for bed long ago! Should not have got up!'

Edward was filling the kettle at the sink. Joanna looked long and hard at the hunch of his back as she guided her mother out of the room.

'Want a sandwich, Ma?' she asked as they went slowly upstairs. 'Are you hungry?'

'No, thank you, thank you no.' Then as an afterthought, 'Mustn't wear ear-rings, darling, they hurt if you fall over.'

Joanna was glad Mother wanted nothing like a sandwich. She did not want to go back to the kitchen, with all its lingering body heat, the claustrophobic warmth, the accusations, the denting of faith in the brother she had trusted. Not yet.

The tide receded. Hooked against a rope in the quay, looking jaunty in the moonlight, hung a purple shirt like a church gown left out to dry at the end of the Sabbath. A pair of sandals danced and sank, moving on elsewhere with the fish.

Julian Pardoe stirred in Sarah's arms, bereft of guilt or pain.

'Sarah?'

'Yes?' Moving closer.

'When grief makes you insane, what do you do? What did you do the first time?'

'This,' she murmured sleepily. 'Only this.' Then later, another murmur. 'I never was much good at the law, you see, never much good at anything, but I am good at this. The law is so slow. It's no fun at all. It should be more than arithmetic . . . There are so many better ways to cure an ill.' He did not understand: it did not matter, he pulled her closer, back into the kiss, felt those strange scars on her arms, too late for questions, let himself drown in the oldest medicine of all.

CHAPTER NINE

They could go fishing for the ghost and earn themselves glory. Stonewall and Rick were down in the boat, a battered old rower with a put-put engine, half a horsepower, Rick said, but good enough for the creeks and if you let it go with the tide, it could win the Olympics. They were waiting for the water in the kind of milky sweet dawn which made Stonewall shiver. The boat lay snug against the harbour wall. He leant over the side with his line, looking for the crabs he could sell for bait or more likely throw back if he caught them, found instead a purple shirt drying on the mooring rope, wrapped it round his skinny middle and felt absurdly happy with his prize. Rick lay supine and looked at the sky.

He stood to stretch his legs and yawn, his head below the level of the quayside wall when he heard Edward Pardoe pass in his unseasonally heavy shoes. Rick balanced himself on the central bench of the boat, clutched the wall and sprang over. Intent on his own progress, looking briefly at the swans which dithered with the tide, Edward noticed nothing else. Rick put a finger over his mouth as Stonewall sprang to attention beside him. Both silent by common consent, they leaned with their elbows propped on the bonnet of a car, looking through the windscreen and out the back to watch Edward walk towards the road which led out to the beach, the caravan park and the woods.

Rick snapped his fingers and jerked his head in Edward's

direction in a parody of military command, instantly appreciated. Stonewall made a mocking salute, trotted away in his filthy
training shoes after the disappearing figure. Rick shaded his eyes
with his hand, still acting the role. The sun was brighter by the
minute; Stonewall's mum would blame him if the lad was not
home by breakfast, time enough for that. Now what was that
bastard Edward doing? He wouldn't rise early in the morning
for nothing, wouldn't rise at all if he could help it. Rick turned
and spat on the ground, always did him good to spit, even if it
was a habit recently learned and one which shamed him.

He'd acquired it first a few weeks since, when Edward came
down the arcade and warned him off Joanna. What's it to you
who she goes out with? Rick had said. I'm not going to do her
any harm. Just lay off, that's all, she doesn't even like you, just
pretends, laughs at you behind your back, Edward had drawled,
so leave her alone, or we'll see about your amusement arcade,
your job and your dad's living, plus all those other souls who
work in there from time to time. That's when Rick spat, more in
response to the first half of the message than the second, powerless, the way he often felt, story of his life.

Pardoes and fathers have the last word. Not any more. He
looked across the road at the kingdom of his arcade. Even with
a dad like his, he was good enough for anyone. He'd been thinking about it all. Today was the day to find Jo.

Rick folded back the doors to the arcade, went inside, moving
from switch to switch. The place was suddenly full of flashing
light and wonderful, raucous sound which gave him strength.

Stonewall thought he had got the drift of Edward's purposeful
direction, since on this road there was very little choice. Maybe
the lazy sod was going to dig up his own bait for a change, but
he carried nothing. The road could only lead to caravan site,
beach or woods; Stonewall couldn't see a Pardoe having much
to do with caravans. Edward walked on the bank parallel with
the silent road, with Stonewall shadowing, shielded from view
even with the piece of purple flotsam round his waist, as he

trailed behind, slightly excited, more irritated than thrilled, for once, slightly insulted by being so inconspicuous. He was hungry, he was following Ed who owed him money, committed to the pursuit, even if he was cross enough to risk a short cut. Stonewall launched across the caravan park, flitted like a shadow between the sleepy, slug-like vehicles where morning life was just beginning, into the woods where the wind moaned softly. Ed must have gone to the beach; he would head him off. He followed a series of tracks which led through the scented pine woods, dipping through sandy valleys, up and down to the final ridge of trees on the edge of the sand. There was a path across the ridge, again dipping into gaps where entries and exits had been forged or grown. Stonewall scanned the beach, moved slowly left. He had first seen the ghost talking to Edward, right out there. They had met in the middle of the wilderness, like two people about to fight a duel.

That was weeks ago. This time he heard the voices first and almost stumbled across them, sitting halfway up part of the steep slope which led from woods to beach, out of the breeze. Two of them, Edward and the white-haired man sitting in his old clothes with the palms of both hands on the pommel of a stick which Stonewall also recognised. Miss Gloomer's stick. Stonewall fell flat to earth as if he had been shot, lay with his hands propping up his head. He could scarcely hear them, what with the wind in the trees behind him and the mewing of the gulls on the beach below, struggled to listen for the sake of having something to report. His stomach grumbled, he farted and almost apologised aloud. People did not do that on videos and the prospect of doing it again stopped him crawling closer.

Rick loves me: he said so.

The sun was beginning to filter through the branches above him and warm the back of his head, not the sand beneath. The light was intermittent, like being in the disco above the Ark Royal with strobe lighting. Stonewall shivered with an uncomfortable sensation of fear, watched the sand flies leaping in front of his nose. What did you do with my Sal, you, you with the white hair like the headmaster? Sal's collar still dug into his groin; fear was displaced by anger, then by his own importance in seeing the ghost in which others now believed. They'd catch him all in good time, Rick and he.

Rick loves me. We can do anything.

A spider was creeping along a dew-defined tightrope of web, suspended in front of Stonewall's freckled nose. Edward and the old man beneath were certainly not talking with the ease of old pals. The conversation was clipped, infrequent, with much staring out to sea and long pauses, not men at ease, not like him and Rick.

'That's a new stick you have,' Edward was saying. 'Where did you get it? I thought you hadn't any money.'

'Oh, I stopped by to visit some old dear, for tea and chat, of course. Somehow acquired the stick on the way out.' Edward made a tut-tutting sound of warning, played with a blade of grass.

'You shouldn't do things like that,' he said petulantly.

'A man must eat. I shouldn't break into your brother's surgery either, but you didn't have qualms about that.'

Silence, the wind moaning, blurring sound.

'. . . did you find?'

'The medical records of one Elisabeth Tysall. Details of a complicated prescription for soporific poisons. Particulars of an adulterous murder, to my mind.'

'Oh no, not quite that,' Edward protested. 'Not as such.'

'Yes, as such. Letters from her which he received. Bitter letters to her he never sent. Why did he keep them out of his own house?'

'Because my mother is so inquisitive, I suppose.'

'I could kill him,' said the man calmly. 'That's the idea, is it not?'

'You mean Charles Tysall could kill him?'

'With his bare hands,' said the man laconically. 'Although I daresay he'd endeavour for a little more subtlety.' Edward wriggled uncomfortably. The man shifted in sympathy and moved further away. His piercing blue eyes abandoned their constant survey of the shore and bored into Edward's own. They seemed slightly out of focus, the man himself more of a vagrant than he had ever been before. Only his speech was perfectly controlled.

'Which would suit your purposes, I presume, as we discussed, however obliquely. It would suit you even better if your mother perished in the same accident. You and your beloved sister, lord and lady of all you survey, now that would be a lovely landscape to play with.'

'I suppose so,' Edward muttered, still uncomfortable, but his body tingling with excitement. He would still have preferred his ambitions to be guessed, remain beyond definition, carried out without his knowledge. In the light of morning, his dreams became violent and vulgar; he wanted first to cherish and then, postpone them. Plans were so much more pleasant before they became real.

'We've still got this woman staying,' he said hurriedly. 'Makes it a bit awkward.'

'The one your sister called the cow.'

'She doesn't do that any more. Look, we ought to think about this.'

'Of course. I think all the time.'

'I mean, lie low, for a while—'

'Are you changing your mind?'

'No, no.'

'You would prefer, perhaps, not to know?'

'Can we just arrange another meeting, say two days' time? I've brought you a key to a caravan, all mod cons, fourth row down on the left, on the end . . . What's the matter?'

The long, thin man was heaving with mirthless laughter, an unpleasant wheezing sound which shook his whole frame and made the stick vibrate.

'Nothing. It's too late to change your mind. Do you really think I'll stay in a place of your choosing, where you can find me?'

'I can turn you over to the police,' Edward blustered.

'For what? And have me repeat our conversations? Really!'

Again, there was that revelation of the balance of power between them, which Edward tried to pretend did not exist, but had been there all the time, since the very first, denying his control of the man, giving the lie to the little illusion that he was a grand benefactor and this was the grateful servant.

'Just don't do anything until I tell you.'

The man raised his eyebrows, spread his hands. 'Would I? Did your sweet sister make you sandwiches today?'

'Yes, sorry I forgot them.'

Edward left without a backward glance, breaking into a jog along the beach, running awkwardly, disturbed, anxious to be away. The man rose too, moved to the left, out of sight.

Stonewall had missed most of the talk, apart from the odd bit about caravans. Something froze him, belly down, the inertia of hunger which stopped him getting up and following the ghost, the sun on his head, his long squinting at the spider, the light falling in lumps through the trees. Thinking of his mother's wrath, wondering if it was better to wait here longer until her anger would be tempered by anxiety, thought after ten minutes' indecision how that might well make things worse. Thought, too, of which lies to tell to explain sneaking out of doors so early on a Monday morning, drawn by the allure of Rick's boat, not able to mention where he had been in case that meant a total ban, and somehow, in between all these anxious machinations, something more than the memory of Sal nagging at him, like being halfway to school on games days and realising he had forgotten his shoes. Stonewall hated Monday mornings like that: they were the days for guilt.

Rick loves me.

Reluctantly, he scrambled to his feet and turned to run downhill back into the woods. Stopped, took a step back, heart in mouth, tripped, fell heavily on his bottom, winded. The white-haired man was standing there, towering above him from nowhere, looking at him, leaning on his stick like a man who had no need to lean.

'I know you,' said the man. 'Don't I? And you know me.'

Stonewall shook his head in frantic denial, tried to scramble up, but the sand slipped from beneath his feet. Oh yes, he knew the man now. Almost a year to the day, that man striding out over the channels, Stonewall trying to stop him and tell him about the tide coming in faster than anyone could run, getting pushed over for his pains. A man who seemed to have grown taller and thinner and acquired this halo of bright white hair. He must have lived like an animal to change from that to this. His arms were like sticks, he was dirty.

'You're a spy for the good doctor,' said the man softly. 'You're just a spy. You even look like the doctor. Did you help to bury her? Did you put your grubby little fingers all over her, you and the doctor? Is that her shirt I see on you? Did you touch her tits? Did you?'

The boy was opening his mouth to protest, I never did nothing. I don't know what you're talking about, lay off, leave me alone, what did you do with my dog? There were no words, only a single sharp scream.

Stonewall's hands had flown to his head: the pommel from Miss Gloomer's stick broke three of his fingers. The second blow thudded into his skull; he could feel the crunching without pain, like a tooth coming out at the dentist, hardly felt the third blow at all. His body, halfway upright, curled into itself, fell forward, rolled down the slope through the pine needles and spiky grass, the thistles and the brambles tugging at his shorts, nothing hurting or feeling, his eyes awake to the light sparking through the pines, the moaning of the wind turning into a roar and then into a great big silence. He ceased to notice the sun, felt a mild surprise as his body jerked again and then lay still, foetally curled with his hands to his head the way Rick had taught him to land if he fell. The final sensation was of resting against a brown tree trunk where the bark scraped his cheek and at last, that graze caused pain, humiliation, a vague sense that he was in the wrong place at the wrong time, foolish, just a baby who wanted to cry and not be teased like this. He could not close his eyes but there was nothing he could see.

Rick loves me.

The man looked down dispassionately. If he followed to finish what he had started, he would probably tear his clothes and he did not have clothes to spare. Nor enough clothes to go home. Wherever that was.

It was a mild breakfast, big brother in mild humour, Joanna noticed. Mother took hers out into the sun; there was no sign of Edward and no ill will from anyone. Mother had dressed in Monday best, wore a turban with a brooch. With a reluctant sense of fairness, which had always distorted itself to champion the younger of her brothers, Joanna was admitting to herself how it was that Julian was best with Mother, adapted to her childish level, played her games except sometimes when she went near the stove. There was a bruise she had noticed to the side of Mother's cheek, the imprint of yesterday's ear-ring neatly reproduced, a lower level of attention-seeking in her lunacy today, uncharacteristic, a deviation from the way she never sought to hide her battiness, always thrust it under their noses. The dress beneath the turban was turquoise and shimmery with leg-of-mutton sleeves, the pink plimsolls the same as yesterday. Joanna could see her now, beyond the kitchen door, feeding the birds by scattering crumbs in large, unnecessary flings. Joanna sensed her restlessness. She was restless herself, wanted to tell Julian about the scene she thought she had seen last night, Edward and Mouse, something terrible. Loyalty forbade revelation, even to herself. Edward would never do such a thing; her imagination was playing tricks. It was all part of some spirit of energy which seemed to have afflicted them all since Sarah Fortune had arrived, a long few days before.

'Jo, don't bother cooking today,' Julian was suggesting pleasantly. 'Mother doesn't much care, seems a waste of the heat. Look, I meant to ask you ages ago, what happened to that boy you were seeing? Rick, from the arcade? Nice lad. I stitched his knee last year, he was extremely brave, I know we don't talk about these things, but I mean, I never even told you I liked him—'

'First I heard!' Surprise and the restless energy made her hiss. 'What on earth do you mean?'

Mother came back indoors. The full turquoise skirt was tucked into her knickers on one side. She did a waltzing turn, then beckoned to Hettie the sheep to follow from the doorway.

'Can Hettie come in?' she enquired with smooth politeness. The sheep seemed to snigger; they were only as silly as one another. 'Only she's so much better today, I've asked her for coffee.'

'Not on weekdays, Mother, you know that,' Julian admonished calmly. 'Joanna, what do you mean? What happened to Rick? You two fall out or something? I hoped, well—'

Joanna exploded in fury. How could he be so calm and concerned when all he wanted to do was put Mother in a home where they would never let her wear her own clothes? When it was he who wrecked her chances with Rick in the first place, drove him away with threats?

'I mean,' she hissed, 'that no, we didn't fall out. But it's a bit difficult for a man to go on taking a girl out when her big brother tells him not to bother because if he doesn't, he might lose his living. See what I mean? And don't lie about it. Rick was shy enough already. You just made it worse.'

She was shoving breakfast dishes into soapsuds with shaking hands. Julian's calm only fuelled her fury.

'Jo,' he began.

'Don't call me Jo!' she screamed. Mother erupted into laughter and then went back outside, humming in some strange sort of satisfaction. Julian let it all ride for a full minute until Joanna's frenetic movements became slower, then joined her at the sink, drying as she washed, sorry all of a sudden for not doing more often as he did now. Unbidden, Sarah Fortune came to mind. Life is too short to bake cakes, she'd said, sometime early this morning; made him laugh, made him smile now. I love my sister, he thought, only I never say so. I love this place, if not this house, I'm not the worst doctor they ever had. I can live if I let myself live.

'There's the door,' he said. 'Go down to the quay, I should, and ask your Rick which brother it was gave him a warning. All I can say is it wasn't this one. Oh, and do bear in mind the fact it could be simple nervousness makes a man give up on a gorgeous girl like you. You beautiful women never seem to know how terrifying you are. You scare us to death.'

She was still defiant, horribly doubtful. So much easier to blame rather than act, so much simpler to wallow.

'Gorgeous!' she spat.

'Oh, ever so, ever so gorgeous,' said Mother, nodding like the sheep in the doorway.

'Extremely good-looking, if you want to be pedantic,' said Julian gravely. 'If only you saw yourself as other people do.'

'Such as?' she flung back, still defiant, tossing her hair out of her eyes. He pretended to consider, think of an opinion she might value. Not the vicar, the genteel verger who kissed Mother after church, not any male in their small circle he could quote.

'Sarah Fortune says so. She told me, I didn't ask. Takes one good-looking woman to know another.'

The front door slammed. Edward's distinctive cough echoed in the distance. Joanna couldn't face Edward. She stuck two fingers in the air, roughly towards Hettie, aimed towards all present, speechless, mollified, flattered, unable to say anything with grace, still trying to suppress all those warning chords in her head which had been humming with the strength of the church organ, about anything Edward had ever said.

'Come in and have some more coffee, Mother,' Julian was saying. He was trying to distract her from her obvious efforts to introduce Hettie into the kitchen, as if she needed a watchdog, but also to turn attention away from Jo's dilemma since the girl could never make a decision with the spotlight on her. Look at them both, Jo thought with fleeting concern, would he ever put

Ma in a home, like Edward said? In the end, she didn't want to think about either of them at all, she simply wanted to run.

The dramatic stripes of her light cotton skirt flowed round as she walked briskly down the road, the effect of it reassuring. Sarah Fortune's influence had made her root through her wardrobe and the local shops for things which actually pleased her. If she were Sarah, how would she tackle Rick? Calmly, directly, without going pink or beating about the bush, saying, Can I talk to you, please? That's what Sarah had said when they talked about it. She said, Find out the truth and then, if you have to, find someone else. A long talk it had been, with the clothes.

The amusement arcade was an empty hall of sound, not yet fit for the crowd who would filter through later, clog the quay-side with cars and sit like dummies munching chips. Joanna did not smooth her skirt or preen her hair, but went into the relative darkness, temporarily blinded. Rick was polishing. Thunderbirds V, she read; Street Fighters, Space Wars X, Kung Fu, a veritable graveyard of fun. He stopped and looked at her.

His face broke into a slow smile. From the darkness behind, his father's large, florid countenance appeared. A gnarled hand laid a warning grasp on his son's arm, while the opposite hand tipped his cap to Joanna. Hypocrite, she thought, bully and hypocrite. Rick's bruises were still faintly shocking. She looked from him to the old man and back again, challenging. He seemed to shrink in front of her eyes.

'We'll take the van,' Rick said.

Driving out to the woods by the beach, Rick rang the chimes, ignoring the early posses of children who waved. Joanna sat upright. Beyond the caravan site, where a pitted road marked 'unsuitable for vehicles' led into the woods, Rick turned left, stopped after two hundred yards. The human compulsion to congregate had always amazed him in its sheer perversity. Once off the beaten track, even so short a distance from two thousand other souls, there was rarely anyone at all. You'd think, he'd told

Stonewall, that human beings really loved one another the way they went on.

'I've been wanting to talk to you,' said Rick to Joanna, resting over the wheel of the van. 'But you called me out, so you go first.' Her hands were in her lap; he could see she had been biting her nails and now she was taking an extra deep breath.

'Rick, do you like me, even a little bit? Oh, that's a silly question, you can't really say no, can you?'

'Yes I could, but it wouldn't be true. Course I like you.' He was furious about the tremor in his voice. 'You and Stonewall, you're all there is for me.' Then he copied her deep breath, entirely without affectation. 'Only your brother Edward said you were only playing games with me and I couldn't take that, could I?'

'Edward?' she said slowly, in tones of despair.

'Who else? He also said he could take away the arcade. I shouldn't have listened Jo, should I? I shouldn't, should I?'

She had begun to cry, whether from a sense of relief or one of betrayal, she did not quite know.

'No, you shouldn't. We wouldn't do any such thing. Dad wouldn't, Julian wouldn't, Edward . . . You know what we should do with all this stuff we own? We should just give it all back, all that stuff we have, get rid of it, let other people have it.' The tears embarrassed her.

Out in the woods, it was cool. They walked for a while in silence, moving by instinct towards the sea. You could live here ever so long and never fail to be drawn to the sea: all steps led in that direction, winter or summer. Rick wanted to make love to her there and then, on the pine needles, the way he had wanted to for months, too nervous to try because it mattered too much and he was so terrified it wouldn't work, slid his arm round her waist instead. The crying ceased, slowly.

'I've been so miserable, Rick,' she said with a great tremulous sigh. 'I've tried to stop being miserable, but I can't.'

'You and me both.' He tightened his hold. 'You're fading away. Don't you go getting any thinner.'

She wanted to laugh, still wanted to cry, turning to him as he turned to her, burying herself in his chest, her hair floating over his face, him stroking it into smoothness, looking down at the top of her head in wonder. Then moving on, arm in arm, looking for an even quieter place to sit down, somewhere where the sun would reach them but not intrude.

'I could kill your brother Edward,' Rick murmured. 'He was out and about early today, though. I got Stonewall to follow him, for a game.' Joanna did not like mention of Edward. She wanted to believe that the conjunction of Edward and mean little lies was a kind of mistake, all to be made clear, some other time.

'Stonewall didn't do so well then. Edward came home as I left.'

Rick stopped, faintly perturbed, not enough to distract him from the beating of his own heart. Much further and he would die; as long as he could sit with her, hold on to her, the rest could wait.

His feet felt the smoothness of sand in a couch-shaped hollow to the left of the track, shielded by a crooked tree halfway up the last slope before the top ridge and the alien openness of the beach where two seekers of kinder light knew they did not want to go. They sat together, peaceful but awkward, he suddenly with all the patience in the world, wanting to do everything right with time as his ally.

'You do want me, Jo? Are you sure?'

From out of his mouth, the shortened name was fine, she loved it, gazed at him, and then, the expression on her face changed slowly. From one of dazed and mesmerised beauty, her huge pupils narrowed, defied the love in her eyes, became a mask of puzzlement, almost pain.

'There's a person, watching us,' she murmured. 'Over there.'

Rick twisted away from her, shouted loudly, 'Who's that?' focusing in the alternate light and dark made by the waving branches, listened, heard nothing but the sighing of the wind. Looked round in deep suspicion, fists clenched, ready to fight, saw a flash of purple.

A sleeve and a hand extended from the other side of a tree, a thin stream of blood forming into a bright red drop at the end of the fingers, suddenly caught, looking as if it would never fall. Rick would not have recognised a mere hand, but he knew the colour of that piece of silken flotsam. Stonewall, the stupid spy, always playing games, the silly little runt.

'Come out, you daft bugger!' Rick bellowed.

Slowly the hand slipped. Both watched, hypnotised, ready to be amused. Stonewall's face, contused, streaked with dirty red, his eyes staring wide, emerged first. The hand moved in the semblance of a royal wave, making a big, slow, theatrical gesture until gently, violently, a slight trace of foam around his mouth, Stonewall slumped towards them.

Shortly after Julian had left, before eight o'clock, she supposed, without checking her watch, Sarah felt that great stab of pain which made her sit on the side of the ancient bath, holding her head in her hands. The clanking of the plumbing which produced steamy hot water by chance rather than science, pipes reverberating inside walls like the tuning of an organ, stunned recollection, forbade thinking, encouraged screaming. The same with the pain itself, intense, dying slowly, inducing panic because she knew it was not hers and there was nothing she could do, could not divine the source or the cure, only feel and pray it would go.

It was the same old affliction, an excess of vicarious knowledge. She was always able to sense loneliness across a road or a room, similar to an Exocet missile finding heat, but now all pain, physical and mental, seemed to find her, echoed from another body into her own and settled in her limbs, to be treated only by her own equivalent of prayer to no known god, the prayer as often a curse for the empathy she had somehow acquired.

A sort of telepathy, Malcolm said dismissively. Grist to her mill, in the days before Charles Tysall and Malcolm when she had augmented her income by discriminate prostitution, less concerned about profit than fun and freedom, merely a woman in pursuit of a talent. She had never considered herself a therapist, simply a person without conventional morals of the kind which seemed both irrelevant and obstructive. Besides, she loved sleeping with men provided she liked them. Affection or respect was the key; either would do. Some of them preferred to chat: not many. Being a tart with a heart meant listening first or after, it did not matter what they wanted, provided she gave value and as often as not, received her own reward.

Sarah washed with thoroughness, killing the smell of sexual contact with some regret. Losing the habits of genteel promiscuity because of being with Malcolm, did not mean losing either the empathy or the instincts. Malcolm's kind lived by one set of rules, she lived by another, was all; she could not even see anything odd about hers, could not even see it as a strange way of going on.

Or even a strange way of being, until she looked in the glass, as she did now, with the steam melting on the bathroom mirror and all the smell of sex gone, the pain receding into a dull ache, somewhere around the head, the ribs, the hand. She wanted not to stare at herself and could not close her eyes, they seemed to be stuck, staring wide. She turned on the basin tap to make more steam, scratching at those little grubs on the back of her arms where Charles Tysall had been, knowing he was alive, leaving his scars on her skin, like Elisabeth, now on someone else. The pain increased. She stared into the steam. There was a brief wish that someone, anyone, would stare back, that a hand could appear over her naked shoulder and brush away the worms, as no one had ever done, not Malcolm with his best efforts, no one, since no one ever did.

Sarah did nothing, stared towards the blurred reflection of her face, concentrated to keep her eyes open, in case other, more innocent eyes should close.

CHAPTER TEN

'All gone! Everybody gone!'

Left to her own devices, Mrs Jennifer Pardoe tended to potter and talk to herself, a mild eccentricity, she thought, a measure to preserve sanity in the face of the constant charade. The trouble was, it was becoming difficult to tell which persona was which. She kept finding herself acting oddly, even in privacy. Daily domestic help was long since vetoed: acting mad in front of the family was exhausting enough, though less of a strain recently. Mouse Pardoe was more than happy to justify her own existence in the meantime. By a gentle, none too efficient polishing of the furniture, a little playful baking, the occasional stroll with the vacuum cleaner, since it was not as though she had ever intended Joanna to be a slave, although it had often crossed her fertile mind that excessive domestic burdens could provoke the child to rebel enough to get the men to do it. This ploy had not worked: Joanna as housekeeper had a dedication well beyond her years.

Mouse sighed. A pretty girl of eighteen should find better things to do than think about the kitchen, or allow her brother to impose his presence everywhere by the clumsy means of all his fishing mess. Look at it, always taking up one end of the long table, reels, weights, ugly things, all there to exert male power. Mr Pardoe had done the same. In Mrs Pardoe's languid tidying of the kitchen and pantry, there were vague, but varied purposes. It allowed her to hide the tracks of predatory forays into the larder in the early hours of the morning; made it easier to blame her own, quixotic, greedy tastes on the men of the house. She could succumb to the desire to make another truly ugly cake which no one could eat and that gave her magnificent licence to irritate. No one had eaten the one she made to greet Sarah Fortune.

'They're all in their own worlds, dear,' she said to Hettie who stood sentry at the back door, a cunning watchdog who would warn if anyone approached by the simple means of a subdued bleating, which reminded Mrs Pardoe of someone coughing in church, a polite little rattle behind a handkerchief. Thinking of which, the verger who had greeted her so affectionately on Sunday was coming for tea this afternoon, which would be very nice indeed, the way it had been for years of Mondays. Mrs Pardoe laughed, a snuffling, giggling, finally trumpet-like sound which she smothered with a tea towel, her chin resting on the table. I'll be coming for tea, oh yes. There were certain phrases did this to her, such as the vicar saying, I'll give you a tinkle, meaning he would phone; Joanna asking, Where is the crevice tool for the Hoover? Such rude descriptions, shouted aloud with such innocence. Mouse sat at the end of the table with her head on her knuckles and chuckled until the onset of the sobriety which usually followed private laughter except on special occasions demanding silence, when the giggles would go on and on until she wanted to be sick in a sort of secret drunkenness. Share this with another and they become a friend, a bit like a joke with sex, and that, she told herself firmly, was enough of that.

There was something she had meant to tell Sarah Fortune. Something important. Oh dear, oh dear, oh dear. Memory gone. Perhaps she was really going round the twist after all.

Her tidying at table level had disturbed a collection of hooks in packets. Similar, but larger than the feathery, coarse-fishing kind she had collected in her palm the night before. She looked at them with caution and a dull hatred. Edward's little toys; Edward, fishing to compete with his father, using fishing as an alibi, like his father. Then the same suppressed levity came welling up within her again, a desire to play with things. A mischievous impulse. She would hide all the reels, throw away the weights, tie knots in the lines, sweep up the hooks. Then say, I was playing, dear. I was only playing; like you were when you hit me.

There was a dish of soft butter on the table, along with the milk, a bowl of soft liver pâté in the larder, cheese, soft sliced bread in the bread bin. She would make the men a sandwich. Then she would make, not a cake, but scones to greet them home. They would never eat them, and the waste of what they would not eat would really rile them.

Julian thought he would be haunted for ever by the sound of the ice-cream bells. They met him on the road on the way back from the graveyard where he had gone to make his peace with Elisabeth Tysall, measure with his eye the small length and breadth of her grave, pray mutual forgiveness, consider the headstone. The Big Ben chimes, distorted by speed, met him as he strolled back to the surgery. When he clambered inside, shocked by the sheer amount of blood on his sister's clothes, impressed by her quiet lack of hysteria and the way they had arranged the boy and kept him warm, it seemed best to continue as they were. The country ambulance could take some time to arrive; the hospital was several miles distant, the van a stable machine and he himself a pragmatist.

A doctor was always presumed to know what to do and he did not; everything was obscured by blood and anxiety, while for the sake of everyone else it was imperative to pretend. The lanes through which they rode were full of meadowsweet; the vehicle proceeded like a hearse. Joanna drove with cautious competence. Rick kept a loose hold of Stonewall's hand while the doc kept a dressing pressed to his head and a commentary of competent clichés between the boy's ramblings, disjointed words, slurred through a thick tongue.

'Talk to him,' Julian said to Rick. 'Tell him things. Make him blink.'

The eyes of the child were wide and rolling. Rick told him things.

'What do you think, eh, Stoney? I reckon that Omen III game is a load of shit. I thought we'd get that one with tigers in. Street Fighters VIII? Bit easy, you reckon? Such a smart arse, you are, just 'cos you can do 'em all. Tell you what, you can order one all of your own. I'll get you a special cushion for the seat. Like the Queen. No? I'll get you a pin-up then, Madonna. Who done it, Stoney?'

'Ghost,' the boy said loud and clear. 'That one. Drowning.'

'You were right about Omen, I'm telling you,' Rick was saying in a conversational murmur. 'Crappy game, that was. Could do with a game about drowning. Ghost, you said? Didn't know about that one.'

'Ghost,' the boy said. He raised a hand in protest and closed his eyes. Rick turned his head away, fierce with fury.

'Is this any good?' he muttered. 'That bastard. Is anything any good?'

'Perfect,' said Julian. 'Perfect. Keep talking. Everything's fine. Keep talking. Ask him things.'

'About ghosts?'

'Anything to make him blink.'

The day had been long. The people were fractious, holiday-makers fussy, demanding the spice of the Mediterranean to go with the weather, rebelling against chips. There was a near riot down by the caravan site when the shop ran out of ice-cream and the van did not appear. Inside the hairdresser's, the heat was stifling, the gossip stifling too, old repetitions of everlasting tales without topical edge, no one wanting, yet everyone needing a storm, not a mild belt of rain like the day before, but a storm with noise.

When the news filtered through, about Stonewall Jones some-how running into a tree, going off to hospital in Rick's ice-cream van because Dr Pardoe reckoned it was quicker than waiting for an ambulance, it was no more serious than the accident that

morning on the Norwich road, or someone failing to return a
rent-a-bike from Mr Walsingham, getting drunk and throwing it
into the quay. Someone went to see Stonewall's mother, but she
was out, gone to pick up the pieces, the way a woman did. Inside
the hairdresser's, where sweat trickled out behind cotton wool
under the three dryers (40 per cent discount for senior citizens),
they could have done with Mrs Pardoe, simply for the colour
and the smell, turquoise or gold or silver, and the wafting scent
of Yardley's lavender.

They waited for her at noon, again at one; then they looked at
the sky and waited for rain.

Charles, coming off the beach, noticed before the others the
signs of preternatural darkness, waited his turn for obscurity. He
watched the other fools from the stable door of his beach hut, all
of them, English holiday-makers who should have known that
rain and cold were never more than a breath away on a coast
which did not have a climate, only weather; watched them bal-
ancing the act until beyond the last minute, gazing, commenting
on the lowering sky as it sank so low it merged with the land,
continued watching, saying, Will it rain? Scrambling for cover
only when the big spitting fell and it was far too late to avoid a
soaking. Like other Anglo-Saxons further afield in fêtes and
garden parties, the result the same as with these bewildered
troops trailing away from the beach, along with Charles, wondering if he could beg another ice-cream on the way as long as
his white hair was plastered to his head, his shirt sleeves rolled,
trousers turned, his jacket over his arm, his eyes pink and full of
sand.

No van, no food, simply the burning which spread from gut
to brain and back again, an infection which began to consume,
while he began to march, like a prisoner, along with the others
who shuffled away into caravans, the bedraggled few who could
still laugh, aiming for the town down the causeway.

He was beyond food; the paper in his back pocket, dry as his
bones, crackled when he touched; hatred replacing hunger.

Other visions, fables of revenge and failure. Lying, rolling, groaning in the dark while a man went on kicking. Sticking glass in the neck of a red-haired bitch. The dog on the beach, his hands round a neck, what was her name? Sarah. What had he done to Sarah? There were benches along the causeway. Towards the end Charles sat. The sky was black, each feature of every building clearly defined. The short and vigorous shower stopped, temporarily out of mischief, leaving the light of thunder, the fantastic, promising light before a storm.

Sarah, that was her name. One of the other redheads, the whore. She who had so captured his fancy when he had seen her flying through the foyer of Ernest Matthewson's office, the soul of innocent perfection, grinning like a little girl who found life nothing more than a glorious joke. Wearing a red coat which clashed with her hair in a deliberate anarchy amounting to a kind of brilliance when combined with that untouched sophistication which seemed to be her hallmark. So Ernest had said, through several layers of suspicion, when asked. Ernest always answered questions from valuable clients like Charles Tysall, not always truthfully. Our dear Sarah, he had said; such a celibate young woman, devoted to her career. Charles had pursued. Asked her out to dinner and made her wait; discovered in her an unnerving indifference, followed her, had her followed. Felt himself hounded by her, the facsimile of the old wife, the ideal model for the new, touched, as yet, by nothing but loyalty. Perfectly pure and good, fine, fair ... Other women jumped through hoops like circus dogs, responding to the click of his fingers. Not this one. Not this whore who slept with old men and young, judges, silks and boys, sullied herself with life's lonelier inadequates, ignored his superior gifts for a careless, dirty life like that, and so disgraced him. Imperfectly pure, imperfectly good.

The thought gnawed at him, like a rat on leather. Nothing could meet his hunger then, or the different kinds of hunger now. Charles examined his hands, noticed the veins, the knuckles made more prominent by receding flesh, then saw with a shock that his intertwined fingers were resting on the pommel of Miss Gloomer's distinctively stolen stick, clutching it like an old man. Foolish, stupid, beyond bravado, sitting on the edge of town nursing a prop dishonestly obtained by local standards, if certainly not by his own. He had taken it because he wanted it, therefore, logically, it became his. Like a wife, or a lover, or money. Until one of them refused and made a man descend into this darkness. A man had beaten him. He had lost all his power until he had floated out of the sea.

Scornfully, Charles donned his damp jacket, buttoned it over his thin chest with the stick concealed, the pommel forming a lump inside the shoulder and the end of the stick protruding like a shortened third leg. He began to walk, across the quay, by now deserted save for those sitting inside cars in a state of martyred enjoyment, obscured from view by the rain outside and the condensation within. The amusement arcade heaved with people, music, electronic sound, the smell of candyfloss and onions making Charles faint. He swallowed, turned up the collar of his coat, went on walking down east quay and beyond, as innocent as anyone hurrying home. His home was the beach hut, the barn, the church porch. He knew no other.

Remembering his purpose, to make the hunger work, he turned towards East Wind House.

'More tea, sweetheart? I'll go.'

Mouse Pardoe lay on her bed alongside the verger, each with a cup of tea in one hand and a cigarette in the other, the coverlet over their knees. Everyone applauded the verger's good.works in visiting the sick and the elderly (of which breed he was one of the more able-bodied), while only himself and his friend Mouse knew that these weekday visits were not exactly philanthropic. They simply knew one another, in the biblical sense. They had known one another for a very long time, a knowledge of herself which Mrs Pardoe had shared with several men of the village who had the right qualifications. Namely, that they must treat her with an entirely non-possessive affection during Mr Pardoe's long business trips, and that their discretion should be bigger than their body weight. She liked them small and neat, in direct contrast to the bulky physique of Mr P. Such teeny-weeny infidelities of hers began as a game of tit for tat, then they became quite a delightful habit. One had to get on with life.

These days, she and the verger were usually content with a cuddle and the delicious comfort of secret trust. In both their eyes, a proper Christian attitude only meant refraining from judgement, hurting no one, and taking God's gifts wherever they could grab them.

The verger was about to agree to a little more tea and perhaps a soupçon of alcohol to go with the splutter of the rain on the windows, when Mouse, as much by instinct as by fine tuning, heard the watchdog bleating of the sheep at the front of the house below her window. She did not spoil Hettie for nothing. She put a finger to her lips; the verger replaced cup in saucer with elaborate care, grinned without alarm since this was not the first time they had been interrupted. All he had to do was to move to the chair by the bed, adopt the less comfortable position of a Church of England comforter while Mouse adjusted her dress and put her hat back on straight. Then she would start talking loudly and that was all there was to it. This time she shook her head.

'Wait,' she said. 'No car. I'll go and see.'

The pain in Sarah's head somehow lifted when the heavens opened to release the rain and the sky began to rumble like a giant's indigestion. She had spent the morning working on the estate, tabulating lists of properties, how long the lease, how easy to sell, value per area, inspired guesswork dogged by the stabbing behind the eyes. Frequent trips to the kitchen window showed the absence of cars outside the big house, all except her own. Another was parked well short of the grounds, probably a walker. Perhaps Mrs Pardoe, all alone, did not like the rumblings of thunder; Sarah did not fool herself that she crossed the wet lawn for charity but as much for company, the continuance of yesterday's conversation, which had begged more questions than those it had answered, left her curious for more. There was something about Mouse which made her feel kindred: something she liked and a degree of unscrupulousness she could only admire.

The sheep cantered towards her and then wandered away, appreciating friend rather than stranger. Sarah went through the open back door into the kitchen, where all was quiet with mid-afternoon languor. A pile of crazy-looking sandwiches lay on the pine table, bread cut to the size of slabs, the fillings of yellow cheese and pâté uninvitingly solid and nasty against the white dough, the whole edifice like some comic, plastic joke, a sandwich made by a child in its first stumbling lesson in home economics. Next to it, a row of sunken, sultana scones which made those in the tea shop a study in refinement.

There was another motive in her visiting, apart from the desire, part personal, part professional, to intrude upon Mrs Pardoe while she was alone. Sarah needed milk. It seemed impolite to call through the house as though summoning a dog, so she crept instead out into the hall which led to the front door, into the dining room and living rooms, sensing the warmth of recent presence, the smell of erratic polishing, noticing the dead flowers left on a table from last Thursday's dinner, the half-drawn curtains and on the first rung of the stairs leading up, a feather from a hat. Knowing she was an intruder, Sarah went on upstairs, stood on the landing at the top. From one of the front bedrooms, she heard the murmur of voices, backed away, then paused. Another door was ajar. Sarah went towards it, peered inside.

Edward's room, she could tell at a guess. There was an easel by the window which commanded the best view in the house. It was the view which drew her first, then the easel, depicting its strange, over-precise, hate-inspired version of the view. She turned away from it, disturbed. Then she looked inside a doll's house, the roof of which had collapsed, the rooms inside intact. Little figures, grotesque, clutching one another. Books on the floor, the room of a dreamer. Embarrassment flooded over her:

her behaviour was that of a spy. She could not call out for Mouse now, not when she was already upstairs. Quietly, she crept out, back down to the kitchen.

She could just collect the milk then, for the fourteenth coffee of the day. A large and venerable refrigerator rumbled in the corner of the kitchen, *circa* 1955 with a rounded shape and a crusted handle. Inside, a medley of food and leftovers, but no milk, and she could not somehow take the milk from the table. Then Sarah remembered Joanna getting pints from the larder and went in that direction.

She stood inside the door, amazed. The place was armed for a siege with durable products, jam jars by the dozen, full and empty, honey and lemon curd, sugar bags in rows, enough tea for a year, six pints of milk, two open and rancid, as well as four half-eaten pies, some weary lettuce, two cabbages from the garden with a faint smell of age, four loaves of bread, a side of ham, a dish of pâté, a half-eaten trifle, a dozen tins each of peaches, pineapple, tuna, sardines, sweetcorn and beans. It looked like the style of provisioning suitable for a bunker. The crooked chocolate cake she had seen before, untouched and not improved by the keeping, although the air in here was as moist as a cellar. On the flagstone floor was newspaper, damp and messy, incongruous among the food.

The door swung to behind her, the pantry suddenly dark with some light from the storm-laden sky penetrating from a single, small window, covered in wire mesh to deter the flies which had penetrated in small numbers and circled round the light bulb lazily, ignoring all else, especially the cake. Sarah felt the perverse desire to lift that paper on the floor, a test of strength and curiosity, a way of manufacturing bravery, since she knew what dwelt in a state of inertia beneath. Their brothers had been on her kitchen floor.

'Oh, bugger . . .' someone swore beyond the door.

The someone was in the kitchen. A hacking cough. Sarah froze, suddenly conscious of her squatting, interfering pose, doubled up further at the prospect of embarrassment. She was a licensed visitor, sir, so the law would say, allowed across these portals by common consent, but not to grub around on the flagged tiles in a pantry while no one else was looking. There was something else, an ear for sound, which told her the cough, the shuffling out there, was neither Edward, Julian, Joanna nor the Mouse. Each voice had a pitch, an intonation as unique as a favourite singing star who could not be copied, and this, while still a faintly familiar, patrician voice, was not one recently heard. Outside the wired pantry window, Hettie the sheep was bleating with a pathetic aggression, the sound first in the distance, hidden by rain, moving closer as if she had turned a corner and yelled in surprise.

'Oh Lord.' It was not the tone of prayer, only a curse, but mixed with wonder as whoever it was bumped against the kitchen table. There was a scrabbling sound: paper, a chair scraped back, a sudden silence, a gulping noise, a burp of satisfaction, all seconds apart. Sarah knelt and moved towards the pantry door. It was not a door which could ever quite shut, warped by decades and no one ever noticing it should be able to shut, a door which banged but never quite closed. Through the aperture, at the wrong angle to see more than half, she tried to look, in desperation moved the door a fraction to see the man at the table. A long tall hobo. Whitish hair scraped back into a small rat's tail, not the friendly rat of a cartoon character, seizing the last of the monumental sandwich, gulping at the open pint of milk, eyeing the scones, not for taste or shape, merely for size . . .

Mouse Pardoe clattered downstairs, cramming her hat to her head. She seemed to have lost a feather, picked it up on the bottom step, stuck it into her bosom, made her walk the one of dignified senility and entered the kitchen. There was a man sitting at the kitchen table with his finger making imprints on a single scone, digging at it once and then putting his fist in his mouth. He was wearing a jacket, something she had seen before; something which might have been collected out of a wardrobe upstairs where all things worn by the late Mr Pardoe still remained, unlooked at and forgotten, she recalled, later. For the moment, she remembered only her lines. Adjusted her hat to a daft angle, twirled the feather picked up on the stairs between her fingers, flipped the skirt of her evening dress over her knee and stepped lightly into the room.

'Hallo . . . oo,' she cooed. 'Hallo, haloo . . . ooo!' It was a salutation fit for a pigeon, soft and dulcet, but commanding.

'Are you making tea?' she demanded, moving in the direction of the sink. 'Oh, do be a darling. I want some too, but I don't know how. Nothing like a man to help.'

Dumbly he rose, lifted the kettle from the edge of the Raeburn, shook it. She took it from him with a manic beam, and banged it down again, her ample hips swinging to some unheard beat, humming throughout, the humming emerging into operatic singing, accompanied by operatic gestures.

'Say, gentle ladies,' she trilled, 'eef love you know . . .

Is love this fever, troubling me so . . .

Ees love this fe . . . ever, troubling meahh, so?'

Then she beamed at him again, leant forward as the kettle, still warm, began to simmer, pulled the lobe of his left ear playfully and whispered into the right.

'Got a friend upstairs, if you see what I mean,' she said with a lascivious wink. The act was going well, Sarah could see from her vantage point, good to the point of ludicrous. Mouse Pardoe deserved an Oscar, but the man did not like a flirt.

'Do you come here often?' she trilled. 'Oh yes, of course you do. I've seen you before. You're a friend of my son Edward and I think you're wearing my husband's coat. Oh dear, oh dear, you've eaten those sandwiches. Silly boy!'

She was on the other side of the table from him now, leaning across, scooping the scones towards her with frantic movements, her back to the Raeburn.

That was too much for the intruder. He had winced when she pinched his ear; the touch was overdone, broke the trance in which her performance had held him, as if Mrs Pardoe had suddenly stepped out of the spotlight, become human, threatening.

Her scooping up available food before his hunger was sated confirmed his irritation. He moved swiftly and clumsily, the stick beneath the coat knocking against the chairs as he lurched round the table towards her. He picked her up roughly by the straps of her dress, hoisted her upright so that she stood with her body pressed close against his. Then he whisked her round and in one swift movement, grabbed hold of both her hands, clamped the palms firmly to the sides of the kettle and held them there. There was a delayed reaction, both of them breathing deeply.

From her viewpoint, Sarah did not immediately comprehend. Actions of sheer malice were difficult to fathom, created paralysis rather than instant response. A high-pitched shriek of fear and pain burst forth from Mouse Pardoe's lips; she began to struggle, but Charles braced her sagging frame upright, his knees pressed into the back of her thighs, held her hands in the vice of his own, pressed them firmly as the kettle began to boil, and then Sarah understood.

There was no thought in her reaction. As the shriek descended to a whimper, she crashed through the pantry door holding the newspaper, flung the contents at the same moment as the scream descended into a pleading moan. Something brown, damp and inert suddenly moved on the neck of the white head; squirming animal life landed on the Raeburn with a hiss. Lugworms met the heat of the kettle and the stove, more landed on the man's arms and round his feet. He sprang back, slipped on the flesh, steadied himself, staring at the floor, seeing a serpent.

He raised his eyes slowly until he met those of Sarah, standing three feet away with the newspaper still in her hand. Their gaze locked in confused recognition. She should have known, she thought later, should have known from the first glimpse who he was, the style of his embrace, the clutching to himself of the thing he was about to torture. She should have known, from what she remembered.

Mouse Pardoe's whimpering rose again to a crescendo, descending into a sobbing. Then there was the sound of heavy footsteps overhead. The man backed away from the two women and the worms writhing on the stove and floor, without taking his eyes away from Sarah's face, his hands reaching for the scones and the milk on the table, grasping them blindly but accurately, as if he had rehearsed and memorised their position, shoving them in his pockets. The stick, banging again on the legs of a chair, made a loud sound. Against her own judgement, Sarah found herself advancing towards him, possessed by an anger which knew no fear, acknowledged no risk, desired nothing but violent retribution, a growl in her throat. Her hands had formed into claws; her voice emerged like a spitting cat.

'Charles . . . you shit.'

The door from the hall crashed inwards, the verger cannoning through and into Sarah with her hands poised to strike and her face white with fury. He grabbed her, holding her wrists shouting, 'Here! what's this?', blustering with breathless energy while she twisted. Charles melted away through the door, into the rain. Sarah felt the rotund, miniature shape holding her own, shrieked in turn, 'Let go, you stupid shit, fucking let go!'

'No,' Mouse Pardoe shouted, shaking but suddenly firm. 'No, don't, not yet. That's the last thing you should do.'

Sarah came back to earth and knew the Mouse was right. No one should pursue a ghost.

The thunder rolled away, but the rain persisted, tumbling out of the sky in sheer impatience. Miss Gloomer liked it. After a particularly satisfactory tea, she had risen from her chair to look for her stick, an automatic reaction for which she chided herself, reaching instead for the substitute, a lesser favourite, then decided not to move at all and drew a rug round her knees instead. The nice doctor, who did not know he was a good man, would call at six. There was no need for him to do that and he might not stay long because he never intruded, he was brisk and respected her privacy. The burglary had shaken her, left her weaker, but not so weak she could not think. What one needs in life, she was telling an imaginary audience, as she would tell the doctor when he called, is an infinite capacity for forgiveness. People are only little, busy things, babies and animals, you see, they do what they can; they are thoughtless and selfish, they love nothing better than their own flesh and blood and that is the way they are. If you want to be on the inside track, Doctor, get yourself a family.

On that thought, of what she would say when he came in for a small glass of sherry, Miss Gloomer's small and obdurate frame gave up the task of living. She died in her upright chair, wearing her winter and summer shoes, thinking of children and how little in life she really regretted including her inability to make a cake, why bother when you could buy better from the baker? This was one of life's greater mysteries. Julian found her. He sat and held her cooling hand, called for the ambulance, which would take some time. Composed her eyes and her mouth, watched the instant, facelifting effect of death.

Rick took Joanna home, with the kind of absent kiss she understood without trying, then took the van back and parked it outside the arcade. Course he'd live, daft little sod, he had to live, made of metal, the doctor said, hit that head one more time and a stick would bounce. A weary sickness made him slow getting out, drawn to the row and the smell and the noise and the temporary end of thinking. He did not walk straight inside; he saw sense and went further down the quay where he bought fish and chips and ate them without tasting anything, standing in the wet without noticing that either. Getting food down and keeping it there was vital. He belched but did not spit and went in to work.

'You're late, boy, we've been taking serious money here, where the fuck you been?' his father said. Rick seized him by the lapels of his jacket, shook him until he rattled and then sat him on the floor. There were no words with this brief exchange of views, only the breathy sounds of a precedent being established. It was enough.

'Listen, Dad,' said Rick, picking him up with absent-minded strength, 'you got to do something useful tomorrow.'

'Oh yes, what's that, son?' his father asked, almost respectfully.

Rick paused. 'We've got to have this place for our own so we don't owe anyone. But first we got to get our act together and find this ghost. He might have done for Stonewall. We got to find him.'

Malcolm Cook looked round Sarah Fortune's London flat, standing disconsolately and a little defiantly, facing the elegant mirror which dominated the narrow hall, giving a view of anyone who entered and also the rooms either side. He never expected it to be quite the same as the last time he had seen it, since Sarah, who loved and acquired beautiful things, also gave them away with the same ease and moved them round, restlessly. Malcolm was the opposite, preferred the spartan and the durable objects he would preserve for ever.

Next to his flank and keeping close, the red-haired dog, ever immune to the reverberations of the place, could not resist the introspective mood.

Start again. Open this door and think about it. Look at it from her point of view. Would the new paint on the walls have changed anything in her mind? Would she miss the place at all in view of its history? If he was ever going to understand her, he would have to make himself go over every step of her ordeal. At first, he could only see himself in here, using his enormous energy to clean up all the stains, so much blood he could only marvel, forced himself not to remember, but to feel, shivered.

So this was what he had done for her first, swept through the flat while she recovered, covering all traces with gloss and emulsion, three coats each. Maybe that had been wrong, just as encouraging her to forget the finer points, put the whole episode to one side like a useless gift, had also been mistaken. Perhaps she should have been forced to relive it again and again, exorcise the helpless pain of it, come to terms. Instead of which he had been saying, Look at me. Look at me, please, take me instead of looking back; I'm here for you, all yours.

The apartment had the stuffy heat of a place enclosed in summer. He wanted to fling open the windows but desisted, imagining instead the place in darkness. Forced himself to think. What would have been the worst thing about that one night last July, the importance of which, as far as he was concerned, was to thrust Sarah, bloody and bowed and needing, into his arms?

He walked back to the front door, turned, as if coming inside for the first time, as she had done in the near dark, careless, lovely, amoral Sarah. Entering her own domain with a slight feeling of trepidation. Seeing, through the mirror in the hall, Charles Tysall lurking in the room to the right, waiting. Turning to flee, too late. Charles behind her then, embracing her, making her watch herself in a mirror like this mirror, making her strip in front of her own reflection, teasing, taunting, announcing his litany of hate and disappointment, calling her filth. Then flinging down the mirror which had rolled and broken into a thousand shapes, large shards, sharp-edged pieces and smaller slivers, twinkling. Charles, pressing Sarah's naked body into that bed of bloody pain, holding her there, while she writhed against the glass and he waited to end it, to cut her face, her throat, whatever he would reach as she twisted away and he slashed, not caring if he cut his own, long fingers.

Malcolm shuddered again, his mouth hanging open, his eyes seeing again what he had discovered then. Led by the dog and her merciful passion for open doors, strange places, raw meat smells, they had come upstairs. Charles had penetrated the dog's russet-coated neck with the biggest piece of glass, almost killed her. Canine blood, mixed with the human; the same smell.

So much blood, so much glass, he had not known how to move her. There was all the gore of an abattoir, none of the convenience. He had wrapped her in the white towels she had soaked, all contact with her skin giving rise to small, breathless screams, which she bit back so hard her mouth bled too. She could not stand, sit, faint or recline, a creature flayed by the glass, the place reverberating with her whimpering.

What would Sarah remember most, when she touched those

little scars which marked where the myriad shards of glass had pierced so deep, leaving her arms, part of her abdomen, her back, her shoulders, littered with souvenirs? She touched them often: they itched, she said, excusing herself as someone would with the hiccoughs. He tried to analyse the pain, in a way he had never quite tried before, because he had been busy offering (instead of imagination) comfort, warmth, forgetfulness and the panacea of love.

Humiliation, that was what Sarah would remember. She would be most crippled by the inability to fight back, by her cowardice, by loss of control, by the obscene pleas she would have spoken to make the taunting stop. There would be the shame at crying in his presence, begging for life and a scintilla of dignity. It would be the poison of the shame, for doing nothing to prevent him, for letting it happen without seeing it was coming, for never fighting back until too late, misjudging, becoming helpless. That would kill the soul and leave the vacuum full of hatred.

Facing the mirror, he could feel it with her. Malcolm had been ashamed of his own furious ineptitude, but it was nothing like her shame. He should have made her talk. No one earns a future by repressing the past, and pain like that, he saw clearly now, never goes away. He had merely done the equivalent, he supposed, of treating a wound with a bandage when only surgery would do.

The dullness of logic prevailed. Tomorrow was a full day's work. Also the day after. He could rearrange his life to go and find her, a quest fit for a man who professed to love, rather than merely possess.

When he was calmer. When he could think of her not as what he wished she would be, but as what she actually was. Imperfectly pure: good by her own standards only, indelibly scarred.

CHAPTER ELEVEN

Edward came home shivering. The almost tropical dampness made him long for foreign territory and a bath, but he could not bring himself to go indoors. All morning he had sat in the estate agent's office where he worked, unable to get the white-haired man out of his head. If he looked out into the street, all he could see was white-haired men. Even his white-haired boss seemed threatening instead of contemptuous.

Edward hated working in the estate agent's, hated working full stop. This latest of jobs, a sinecure, was one he liked least, reminding him all the time of what his family owned in property and making him incubate the worst of his dreams. The Pardoes did not own a single beautiful building, he explained; nor was there one he could see in the village. Otherwise he might have cared about his work. The place needed pulling down, how could a man of taste love it?

Today, both his aggression and his defensiveness seemed to have disappeared. He felt naked, vulnerable and mean. It made no difference, working in an office which the Pardoes virtually owned. Conscience could always undermine money.

Edward knew he should have been able to identify the white-haired ghost by at least a name, but it had never been important when all they were doing was playing games. He should have been in control of the trespasser he had found, but he was not. With his estate agency knowledge, Edward had housed, sometimes fed, the malevolent spirit for three months. All in the interests of fun and the somewhat malicious, somewhat romantic dreaming which fed his own daily existence and made it worthwhile. It had made him walk taller but now made him want to hide. He had meant mischief, but the reality, the look of hatred on the man's face, somehow extended it further than his own cowardice allowed. Edward might have hit his own silly mother from time to time, he might have detested his brother, but wanting them to disappear was not quite the same any longer as wanting them dead.

The discomfort, which had begun when he heard about Miss Gloomer's burglary, increased somehow because of the mere presence of Sarah Fortune and solidified into an indigestible lump after this morning's conversation, like much of Jo's cooking and all of Mother's playful cakes. Increased threefold when his two colleagues came back from a makeshift lunch at the pub which the Pardoes also owned, talking about the ghost. Above the cheese-and-onion which Edward could smell as they spoke, the pungency overcoming the waft of a pint of lager between them, he learned all about how Stonewall Jones had met the ghost in the dunes and had his head caved in with a stick. The lady behind the bar worked in the surgery up until noon, then moved sideways into a less sterile atmosphere. Best gossip around, she was, with her dual sources.

Edward's blood ran hot, the slow digestion of the news creating a sweat under his cotton shirt, once perfectly ironed by Joanna and now a mass of wrinkles. The news made him itch all over, as if bitten by insects and carrying poison. Edward had never been anywhere where he might catch malaria: he had never dared, no money, no courage and no stamina, preferring the sneering discontent of home. Sitting outside his own house, he longed to go as far away as any aeroplane would take him. To any other kind of jungle where no one knew him.

There were cars lined up outside the front door as usual, Jo's, Julian's, the visitor's, plus another, the house apparently the

scene of a conference. The rain was easing. Edward felt allergic
to them all, especially Joanna. On the wet grass of the lawn,
another ghost, that of naked Sarah Fortune, still travelled, pale
and tantalizing, in smooth circles across the green, the only thing
of objective beauty he had seen in weeks. Oh, come on, he told
himself, as the rain drizzled mildly against the windscreen of his
car, come on. Be manly or something. A man should be able to
fish, like his father, a man was not ashamed to be whatever he
was, even if that made him idle, artistic, self-seeking, incestuous.
A man should be large, not small, indecisive and afraid. Edward
looked at his own neat hands in a hot flush of realisations he
wanted to avoid. The hands shook, more than they had shaken
when he lost his temper and hit his mother last evening. A man
should achieve control of his actions. He should also have someone to tell.

Wavering lights, out there, as he sat looking over the marshes
towards the sea which he wished would come closer, even
though its proximity made him afraid, as well as the house itself,
lit like some ugly Christmas tree. One thing he knew now, above
all others: he had loathed this place for as long as he remembered. Squinting through the glass, he could see two things.
First, the strange car belonged to PC Curl, their only full-time
member of Constabulary; second, from the near distance, the
light outside Sarah's cottage beckoned like a flickering star.

Nine-thirty, he read on his watch; the mere beginning of a
summer night. Closer, the light shone more like a keep-out sign
than a welcome, a warning, a weapon against this early dark created by the long, mocking storm. It was ironic, he thought,
beneath the lingering anxiety, that he should follow his brother's
footsteps so meekly, treading the same route with similar humil-
ity. He knocked loudly on the door, making a tune out of it,
rat-a-tat, rat-a-tat, instead of just banging once, something to
prove he was a nonchalant son of a bitch who would go away
whistling if there was no response, waiting all the same.

She answered after a long delay, less winsome than before,
still beautiful. A woman with a fierce look on her face as she

looked out of the window first, then said, 'Come in,' with a purely neutral friendliness.

'To what do I owe the pleasure?' Sarah said coldly. 'I've been visited here by all members of your family. You give me the impression you're more comfortable out of your own home than in it. Sit down.' The charm and the warmth were back, the teasing note uppermost, some of the edginess gone.

'Have you been home yet?' she asked in that steady, reassuring, conversational way. Edward, in common with his colleagues after lunch, smelled slightly of the pub where he had gone and sat for an hour or more after an abortive and hesitant search of the caravan site and the dunes had revealed nothing of the white-haired man. Emptiness and sunset had ended the search: Edward was secretly afraid of the dark. He shook his head.

'I went to look for someone,' he muttered. 'Why?'

'Ah, you might not know then. The village ghost took human form this afternoon. He came up here and attacked your mother. She's all right,' she added, watching him closely, standing away from him, arms crossed. Edward sat heavily, rubbed his eyes with a pathetic gesture which made him look like an overgrown baby.

'Not the first time he's been here, though, is it?'

Edward did not answer, his silence an affirmation.

'I was present, you see,' she went on, 'when this non-ghost arrived. Your mother said to him, and I quote, "You're a friend of my son Edward, I've seen you before." She sees a lot, your mother. I suppose I imagined from that that it was you who acts as his liaison officer. Difficult to see how any man, even one as resourceful as Charles Tysall, could stay alive in secret when he's supposed to be dead. Not without assistance. Not much, perhaps: he likes to move alone.'

'What do you mean?' Edward was suddenly angry. 'Charles Tysall? He was drowned, last year. My . . . acquaintance said he was sent by the family, the wife's family, that is. Maybe the wife's brother. He was having a long holiday, he said, experimenting with living rough. He said he wanted to know—'

'Who had buried Elisabeth Tysall in the sand,' Sarah finished
for him.

'Yes,' Edward said, dumbfounded. 'How did you know?'

'Edward,' Sarah said, 'I'm beginning to think you're an idiot.
Not the genuine article maybe, but a very good pretence.' She
unfolded her arms. He looked up at her like an animal waiting to
be whipped. She smiled slightly. It scarcely lessened her intimidation.

'I offered your brother a drink, so I suppose I'd better do the
same for you.' It was grudging. Watching her move about,
Edward was paralysed with the sense of his own weakness and
an awful physical desire which he knew, even then, was going to
loosen his thick tongue.

'I knew Charles Tysall,' she was saying. 'I also know he was
obsessed with the fate of his wife. There's no doubt about identity, so where do you come in?'

'He hit Stonewall Jones this morning,' Edward burst out,
ignoring the question. 'I can't believe he did that. I can't think
why. He's not a ghost, he's a monster. The boy's badly injured.
Oh God, I never meant this. Honestly, I never meant this.'

Sarah's hand flew to her head with a brief cry. She felt along
the side of her face where the pain had been, tears welling in her
eyes.

'Oh, poor boy, poor child. Oh, I wish I knew how to pray.'

Edward sipped his drink, wondering if he should respond to
that since he felt nothing for Stonewall Jones, could only see in
his mind's eye the relative sizes of tall man against small, helpless
boy. Julian would have liked sitting here, sipping excellent
Glenfiddich, he thought by way of distraction. The thought
came upon him without a trace of bitterness. Jealousy merely lingered.

'I shouldn't play games, should I?' Edward asked. 'I found
him squatting in the cottage next door to this.' He jerked his
head to the right, winced. 'It seemed amusing not to report him.
I didn't want tenants in the place this summer, hate them, kids,
buckets and spades, cars, spoiling the view. So Charles, if we

must call him that, started a small fire for me. Nothing too drastic. Nothing which would spread.'

She inclined her head, as if understanding completely.

'There were also a few of my paintings in there. Joanna in the nude. Didn't want her to see them if she spring-cleaned, didn't know how else to get rid. They were a bit . . . suggestive. Watercolours, easy to burn. Painted from imagination, of course. Wishful thinking.'

'Are you in love with her?' A gentle question, without criticism or condemnation. He was grateful for that.

'Am I? I don't know any more.'

'Jealous of other men, though?'

'Yes.'

'Jealous of Julian?'

'Yes! Yes! Yes!' he shouted. 'He's so dependable, so bloody adult, so sodding disciplined and my father loved him. He doesn't even need to learn to fish!'

He subsided as suddenly as his voice had risen, flung himself back against the plaid-covered sofa, petulantly. His own native defences of self-justification surfaced. He looked at her unforgiving eyes, looked away.

'Anyway,' he mumbled, 'owning a ghost was good sport for a while. I'm so bored, most of the time. Then he began to ask about Julian, how well he'd known Elisabeth Tysall. Well, I knew all about that. Julian just about lost his mind over that bitch, I watched him. The ghost wanted proof that Julian had something to do with her death. I pretended it existed but I knew it didn't. Julian's too soft to hurt anyone.'

'Elisabeth Tysall was a victim,' Sarah said sharply. 'Don't dare call her a bitch. You don't know what she was.'

'No,' Edward conceded. Guilt was corrosive, it caught in the throat like a fishbone.

'So,' Sarah said, 'you played make-believe with Charles as your creature. Thought you had the upper hand. Where is he, Ed?'

'I don't know,' Edward whispered. 'I just don't know. I gave him the key to an empty caravan. He isn't there. Maybe a beach hut, somewhere on the beach, he likes the beach.'

She was so powerful, she seemed to draw the words from him, like a fish on the line with no power to escape. Still standing in front of him Sarah pulled her shirt over her head. A pretty colour, russet silk, Edward noticed, thinking at the same time, Christ, she's mad; she's going to strangle me with it. She pulled the shirt as far as her shoulders, left it bunched round her neck and turned her back on him. The gesture was shocking and bizarre; made him recoil with a small, half scream.

'Please look at my back,' she commanded. 'Go on, look. With your artistic eye. Look closely, report what you see.'

He wanted to avert his eyes, escape from this threatening action, but he stood awkwardly and looked. A graceful spine, curving into a tiny waist, the silky flesh criss-crossed with scars, three or four larger gashes, the majority small pit marks, white against the brown of her skin, ugly. She pulled the shirt back over her naked torso abruptly, leaving him relieved, shivery, revolted but aroused.

'I just wanted to make a point,' she said wryly. 'Cuts like that are what you get for playing games with Charles Tysall. He makes you roll in broken glass. He holds you down among the fragments of a broken mirror. And when you've finished bleeding, although you never really do, he'll leave you thinking it was all your own fault.'

Edward had stared. With his eye for colour, he could imagine the vibrant blood welling from those wounds, flesh and skin mashed in ritualistic flogging. He could see the cool smile of the man this morning, the precision of his movements, the air of efficiency.

'He did that?'

'Oh yes. Slowly.'

Edward stumbled into the kitchen and retched into the sink. Bile was all he could produce, the residue of a day without food, no sisterly sandwiches to fill the gap, nothing but two pints, three sips of whisky and a diet of anxiety. He drank some water, looked out into the dark, recovered himself, came back with a mumbled apology.

'That's all right,' said Sarah, equably, but dry. 'I confess I don't usually receive quite such a flattering reaction when I take off my clothes.'

Edward blushed, relaxed more than slightly. Even like this, so serious and frightening, she was able to make a man think there was nothing incurable about his own condition.

'What shall I do, Sarah? What on earth shall I do?' he asked humbly.

She noted that he asked nothing about her own history, nothing about the scars, nothing which expressed concern about anyone other than himself. Men *in extremis* were always thus; she was used to it in the adult version, and this was a mere, play-acting boy. She sized him up, considered her own code for dealing with misery by the simple if temporary means of bodily comfort. The men in question needed to command affection and respect, this one commanded neither. All he deserved was a chance of redemption.

'I don't know. Stop dreaming of wealth and changing the landscape into something you might like. You hate this place, leave it. You're the younger son, the underachiever, your sister says. You'll always be powerless here. Make a break for somewhere else, before your last friend rumbles you.'

'Leave? With nothing?' he asked incredulously, glancing at the table, full of papers, brief notes in neat handwriting, valuations, lists.

'Yes. Enough to sustain you for a while, perhaps. There won't be much of an inheritance anyway. Not after your mother's finished with it.'

He looked at her, the pink spots on his cheeks an alien version of his sister's. Sarah spoke patiently.

'She wants to give it back, Edward dear. She wants to give back all this property to the local people who need it. That's what she wants.'

He started to laugh. A whinnying chuckle which went on and on until his eyes streamed.

'You need food and an injection of sense, Edward Pardoe. You never felt this way before working up at the estate agent's and discovering how much you might have, did you? You can get away with dreaming and painting and doll's houses, Ed; you might even make a living at it, but you can't get away with murder.'

Food. The thought was no longer beguiling. Charles lurched in the narrow alleyway which skirted the back of Miss Gloomer's cottage, leading by a route as twisted as her frame into the high street. The village was criss-crossed with similar environs, ancient rights of way, coal- and fish-delivery routes before the days when anyone would even dream of pulling a horse and cart in front of their own small doors, when families lay cheek by jowl in houses Rick found adequate for one.

Food was not the problem for Charles: enough for the day was all he could contemplate after the sandwiches which had scarcely touched his rotting teeth. Something in the solidity of the scones, like hairs tickling his throat, made him cough, stand where he was and gag, left him thirsty even after the milk which had washed them down.

There were fresh-water taps on the caravan site, easily found by dark when no one looked. Too soon to go back to the beach, too far to go without water.

'Give me water,' he whispered, 'and there is nowhere I cannot go, nothing I cannot do, even if I am beaten by women; rendered impotent by the weaker sex, when I could have snapped their necks like killing chickens, just like that.'

He had no plans, there was no point in planning, but a dim feeling that he was running out of time for revenge. The image of Sarah Fortune, snarling at him, superimposed itself on the image of his Elisabeth's face, but then these two images had always been blurred. Red hair, red bitches; a feeling of weakness. Was I always like this? Was I never strong? Who loved me?

There was a tap in the graveyard. Perhaps if he went to the second grave of his wife, where he had left the thistles, she might let him in to sleep. Come back to him, chastened, beautiful, the way she was before. Porphyria. Perfectly pure and good. He would tell her he forgave her, raise her from the dead, the way he had raised himself from the sea.

His footsteps were quiet in the dark; an old man padding through a village, unable to force himself to the brisk military walk, tardy, irritated by his own lack of strength, spitting on the ground in contempt of his own sloth, failing to see the blood in the phlegm on the road by the wicket-gate. By the side of her grave, he could almost believe she would rise and greet him; knelt, suddenly humble, felt for her shape in the dark.

His hands felt the petals. Someone had prepared her. The ground was covered with fresh flowers, damp from the rain, smelling of heaven. Gifts for a lovely lady.

Someone. Some man, some thief in the night had borne these tributes. Charles scattered the flowers in a fury of moving hands and kicking feet, ignoring the onset of pain as he bent and tore at roses and daisies, breaking the stems, flinging them as far as he could, kicking the containers, not caring about the sound, stamping on petals as if putting out a fire in a ritual dance of fury, finally lying down on the naked earth which covered her. An innocent piece of earth. Even beyond death, even now, just as he forgave her, someone else had laid their claims first, just as they had before. It had all been for nothing.

No one has claim to my image, Mouse Pardoe thought, not liking the indecision, not one little bit. She was being allowed only one ally at a time, most of them leaving her for diplomatic reasons, the verger first, Sarah later. They had talked a little about the ghost and who he was, and all this time, Mouse kept her hands in icy water. The verger, fisherman born, had dealt with the worms; there was now a ghastly smell of roasted flesh about the place, centred round the Raeburn, drifting through windows but determined to linger.

The sky remained the colour of gun metal. Mouse thought she would always remember the colours of the room; the verger's black against the pinkness of his skin, Sarah's pallor, her freckles, the hair, the russet colour of her shirt, then the colours of the best Pardoe hat with old feathers on the table, the surface of which seemed to glow a dirty yellow. She only noticed then the total absence of the yellower scones with their little bullets of burnt sultanas. She must have been mad. How could she? She talked to Sarah, a little irrationally and over-expansively, about her life, burbling, she said in apology, and all the time she looked at the space where her baking had been. There had been no one looking when she had made those scones and still she had made them.

Mouse was chill beneath her evening frock and woolly dressing-gown, a combination of garments she would otherwise enjoy. A little lonely, too, but not enough to shout down the earlier suggestions of getting a doctor. 'I've got one of those,' she said to Sarah, 'and a daughter, although I hate the thought of relying on either.' Mouse noticed, quietly, that dear Miss Fortune had been uneasy as well as practical about calling the police. They met each other's eyes over the dialling in a mutual suspicion of authority. The police might question, Mouse thought, the quality of her baking. And the motives, which she could not now remember.

Then Joanna came home. After thirty minutes of PC Curl's questioning, a process as slow as Sarah's delivery was quick, she took the Biro from his hand and wrote it all down for him. Then Sarah left too, just before Julian arrived and there they all were, the whole business protracted by news which put it in perspective. *En famille*, with all the complications of being so. Oh dear.

The trouble was, Mouse Pardoe did not know whether she should go on being sweetly mad or loudly sane. It had been so pleasant, even with blistering hands, to talk to the only two people in the world who knew she could think. She missed it sorely, could not decide whether to keep up her act with her daughter and son, could not even quite remember when it had started or why, could not imagine, above all, how she would explain herself for all these months of calculated pretence. Julian was looking at her closely. The stuff he had put on her throbbing hands had been applied, she noticed, with peculiar gentleness. No. Good Lord, no; she could not keep up her twittering bird-song, not after hearing what the same ghost had done to Stonewall Jones, the boy who had waved and danced for her in the garden whenever he brought up bait for Edward. Her own hands, her own fortune, were not important enough by comparison, and besides, her children were listening to her, really listening, not even pretending.

'I think the shock seems to have cleared your mind a bit, Mother,' Julian was saying, without talking as if she was deaf all the time. She glanced at him slyly. He did not seem to be playing games; like Joanna, he was honestly and simply concerned, listening with both ears. Jo flitted round the kitchen, bringing back bits and pieces of bland food, the panacea for all ills; Julian offered the wine. Each time Jo passed, she hugged her mother. Mouse had missed the hugging which was something a mad woman denied herself, if not with the verger, certainly with her children.

'Yes, dear,' she said demurely to Julian. 'I do believe my mind is feeling better. Now, what is PC Curl going to do?'

'Send out a patrol car regularly overnight to us, then organise a search party in the morning. That policeman can't do anything too quickly. He isn't the type.'

His father was not slow, Mouse thought, with a secret, reminiscent smile. Now there had been a neat and nimble figure of a man with a twinkle in the eye to match, oh yes. Tuesday afternoons, for a long time, he was.

'A ghost hunt,' she murmured, forgetting to add a manic giggle. Should she say who she knew the ghost was, or say she had seen him with Edward? She could keep her powder dry until she found out what other people knew. Her conscience was variable in its hints, but he was always on it, whatever he did.

'I don't think the search party should include Rick,' Jo said. 'There's no telling what he would do. Julian, what's the hope for Stonewall? Rick loves him.'

They sat at table, comfortably elbow to elbow.

'Well, I can only say that will help.'

She rested her head against his shoulder, briefly, the first time they had touched in as long as she could remember. He ruffled her blonde hair fondly; she did not resist.

Mouse looked at them. Children, love one another; and where is my little changeling, Edward? Love me, love one another, but listen to me sometimes. That was all I wanted. I think. She chuckled.

'When that Stonewall comes home in the ice-cream van, I shall dance like Tallulah Bankhead.'

The kitchen shuddered with giggles and delicious, hysterical comfort. Julian poured more wine. They did not think of Sarah Fortune, united in the forgetfulness of all outsiders, although each of them, with separable and secretive degrees of worry, thought about Edward.

'I expect he's gone fishing,' said Joanna, apropos of nothing, in a gap between laughter.

Mouse looked at the space on the table where the scones had been, and knew how easily laughter sat with grief, how the madness was not always feigned.

The silence had grown longer. Sarah remembered the smell of worms.

'Will they know?' Edward was asking. 'I mean Jo, Julian, anyone else for that matter, about me knowing this man Charles? The ghost?'

'Yes, if your mother tells them so. She could tell them you've let Charles into the house before, and into the cottage next door. If the boy Stonewall recovers and remembers, he'll say if he saw you elsewhere.'

'Christ.'

'Not that they'll know what you discussed,' she said distantly. 'You could have been sorry for him. You could have been passing the time of day with a fascinating stranger.' She spoke with a touch of bitterness.

'And what will you tell them?'

'Nothing to contradict what you say yourself. I'm a lawyer: we only repeat what we should. I'm well-schooled in that.' Ernest Matthewson came to mind, like a malevolent spectre.

'There's a price. Help find Charles. Help save your family, and yourself.'

'Is that all?'

'Enough, not even much. You encouraged Charles. You conspired to rid the world of your mother and brother, even if it was a malicious day-dream. Didn't you?'

'Yes.' The voice was dry.

'Well,' she said with a finality not quite approaching either threat or promise, 'I think it would be best all round if no one ever knew about that.'

'I think I'd like to go away,' said Edward shrewdly. 'Try living somewhere else.'

'What a good idea,' she said with a quiet approval of such intensity he could almost believe he had thought up the idea himself. 'And I suppose for now, you'd better go home.'

'Do you want to come over with me? I mean, should you stay here by yourself? For your own safety?' The onset of genuine concern upset him with a sensation as pleasant as a warm swallow of tea. She seemed to consider for a moment.

'No. Thank you. Taking refuge isn't the best way to deal with fear. In case it becomes a habit.'

'Perhaps I should stay with you, then? For the same reason?'

She seemed to consider it, shook her head.

'No.'

'As a guarantee of good behaviour in the future?'

'To stiffen the sinews?' she suggested ironically.

'Something like that.'

*

The wind had risen with the tide, pushing the water, encouraging the movement. Not the howling gales of winter whipping the waves on the open sea, a nudging wind, swollen with rain, eclipsing the shore line as the sea rode gently forward, filling the quay, lapping over the edge, covering the car park, wavering at the edge of the road, creeping towards the front doors of the amusement arcade and the gift shops, shifting the litter of the evening and finally dragging it back, prudence dictating a pragmatic retreat on the eve of destruction. Stuck behind the hull of a forgotten boat, the bloated corpse of a dead animal was dislodged and floated away to another part of the coast. Two Dutch boys from a tramp vessel borrowed the dinghy and rowed for shore in search of bright lights.

On the beach, the sea nibbled at land, obeying the wind without enthusiasm. Those in the adjacent caravans stirred in the night, the ground beneath them somehow softer, the weight of their shelters settling more solidly after the rain. The sea crept right to the edge of the dunes, way beyond the high-tide level of the afternoon outlined by the sluggish boundary of variegated weed which led the unwary to presume it could invade no further. As the faintest of punishments for man's arrogance, the creeping water brushed the legs of the two furthest beach huts, eroded by similar attacks. The one requisitioned by the ghost collapsed to one side with a sighing groan, settled to sleep like a drunk on crutches as the retreating water sucked from the upended floor Charles Tysall's stolen blanket and other souvenirs.

A yacht suffered for the pride of its owners who ignored guidance and sailed into a sand bank where they stuck and keeled sideways. In the early hours of the morning, the lifeboat siren made its own unearthly call, wailing and weeping in anger for the nuisance.

Julian heard it from the depths of a sleep in which he dreamed of murder most foul, his family, the inadequacies of medicine in the area and the body of Sarah Fortune. Heard it like a requiem for the dead, put his hands over his ears, shutting out any message which did not sing of hope.

CHAPTER TWELVE

Rick was running. Running with clumsy grace towards the lifeboat station, the village glistening behind him. The inlet was half full, the banks of the sea defences exposed in muddy splendour. Waddling, wheeling birds he had never bothered to identify, caught his vacant eye, birds which sprang, trotted, screeched in some kind of defiance, part of his landscape and he never even noticed them. Stonewall got down on his knees to talk to birds in the days when he was learning to love the creeks and Rick had laughed at him then; a boy, talking to birds, there's practice for you. How long did it really take to get to know someone?

He ran, one step after another, beginning to pant, wanting the excuse to stop, kept running.

One mile to the lifeboat station, where the inlet met the broader beach, so much further on foot than by transport. Stoney knew all that at half Rick's size, knew all about the birds if not the bees. Rick ran, seeing it all anew, the curlews, the footprints in the mud of the banks, the things which Stonewall saw.

He ran for oblivion, so that the screaming of muscle accustomed to different use would clear his mind from recent conversations of ghosts and retribution, talks with his uncle police officer, the lack of good news, and the tearful insistence of Jo, Don't go with them, Rick, please. If love was a question of conflicting demands, he could only obey the strongest which was not yet hers. So he ran the full mile to the beach, avoiding the woods, passing the lifeboat station, leaping straight down the bank onto the sand. There he jogged slower, the sand soft, his feet wet from patches of shallow mud, the breeze noisy in his ears, a brisk day with a fitful sun, the promise of wind and only the few real diehards out to play. A good day for hunting.

He jogged past the beach huts on his left, saw how two had collapsed but did not know if it was recent, noted it in his mind as just another fact, broke into a proper run on a smooth patch of sand and then began to tire. Perspiration trickled into his eyes; he rubbed them absently and uselessly with the back of his hand, blinked, stumbled, blinked again.

There was a dog running towards him, for a moment he thought it was Stonewall's Sal, the sight so shocking and the expectation of seeing Stoney himself so acute, it made him stop, stagger and choke.

The dog skidded to a halt and then ran round him, barking, ready for a game. Despite his pounding heart and the hairball in his throat, Rick felt the slow beginnings of a smile. Of course this was not Stoney's russet-coloured mutt, but a floppy red spaniel, with nothing in common but the kind of silly, fussy, excitable temperament Stoney would like. It gave Rick an idea, the first positive thought in all the confusing negatives. Buy the boy a new dog: that would make him better.

A man was following the dog, running in the same direction with the sun behind him, moving with the experienced grace which Rick had never mastered, admired for being so different from his own awkward arms and legs swinging everywhere, wasting energy and breath. The man's style of movement was an economical, effortless sprinting, so that when he shimmied to a halt, it was almost a relief to see that he shone with sweat.

'Morning.' A pleasant voice. 'Don't let her bother you. She just likes everyone.'

The hairball in Rick's throat would not go away. He had never quite understood the boy's passion for his dog; now he did as he stroked this one's soft ears and felt against his bare, damp legs those delighted vibrations of infinite trust.

'So did Stonewall's dog,' he blurted. 'Like people. Too much.'

The dog leant against his trembling knees. Having started, Rick had to go on, otherwise this odd piece of information, delivered so randomly to a stranger, would seem even odder. He made his voice harsh, as if his first words had some retrospective purpose instead of weakness.

'You want to be more careful of your dog,' he admonished. 'There's a maniac on the loose round here. Eats dogs for breakfast and tries to kill boys.'

'You're joking.' The man called his dog, which trotted to heel. Rick was stung.

'No, I'm not. The police are organising a search party along this stretch. We called him the ghost, but he isn't a ghost. So you just watch yourself, running along here alone. Even running as fast as you do.'

He was envious and gabbling. He needed to gabble, talking to a stranger was easier than trying to make sense to himself. The man suddenly stuck out a hand. Rick looked at it as if it was a turd.

'Malcolm,' the man said, with a smile which brooked no refusal.

It was such an incongruously formal thing to do, shake hands and announce names in the middle of a beach, that Rick did it, although it made him want to laugh, relaxed him more than a little. Maybe it was the running did that. They fell into step, walking back the way Rick had come. To where the search party formed on the spit by the lifeboat, a motley, serious crew, anxious to do duty.

'Perhaps I can help,' Malcolm said.

'Reckon you can. Just look at 'em. What a geriatric crew. Anyone's welcome. Even with a daft dog like yours.'

There was no one young in the group. Rick looked at them sourly. This bloke Malcolm was the youngest apart from himself, better take him on. The rest looked like a congregation from church.

They were old enough, though, to work without complaint, with the thoroughness otherwise devoted to their gardens; perhaps Uncle Curl knew what he did when he chose, but even with effort, they did not find the white-haired man by the end of a long day. Not Rick, the London stranger who proved such an asset, three dozen others walking through the woods. In and out of the caravans, taking apart the beach huts, one by empty one, wading across the flats, looking inside boats. Moving into the village, ignoring the populous quay where no one could possibly hide, sweeping forward from the coast to look inside empty holiday homes, further inland through the council estate, the church, into the barns of the hinterland. The two of them who walked through the graveyard tut-tutted at a mess of scattered flowers until they saw the stonemason erecting a headstone of fine white marble, stopped briefly to admire. Looking for a man with a stick and white hair, a form without needs or substance, otherwise held few rewards and less glory. They began to consider he was indeed a ghost, who had fled or gone back from where he came, into the embrace of the sea.

Rick and his ally Malcolm sat in the bar of the Crown on the Green, Merton's only hotel and a place where Rick had set foot twice, ever. It was Malcolm's invitation, said he was staying there. Posh. Let Dad cope with the arcade.

Stonewall Jones dreamt of the sea, the amusement arcade, his dog, and remembered someone loved him, best.

Night fell over land, without a whimper. Sarah Fortune was packing her bags, sensing her own impending redundancy without bitterness, preoccupied. She knew, from walking the town, sitting again in front of that unedifying display of cakes, what went on around her and did not want to know more. They would find him, she supposed; that desperation of his would make him careless. But she did not want him found. Except perhaps by herself, as the fulfilment of a whole year's dreaming nightmares, in which she discovered him bound and helpless and made him feel what he had done to her, what it was like to be so diminished. Finding him thus would pacify that burning which ate her from within, that yearning to watch him crawl, to scratch his face with long, polished nails and watch him beg. Naked, as she had been, screaming and whimpering as she had been in an empty house, suffering as she wanted him to suffer, with the knowledge of that helpless loss of pride.

There was a pain in her stomach; she diagnosed it as the result of all her self-restraint, the application of charm and manners to her daily life instead of howling for the carefree person she had been. A pain which came with the incipient grief for Elisabeth Tysall and for herself which would not go away. An ache which was the effort of her own agnostic prayer and the residue of all her violent and foul thoughts towards him. If home was where the heart resided, there was no such thing as home. She packed listlessly, half of her waiting, all of her ignored.

Mouse Pardoe crept away from the bosom of her family, ostensibly upstairs to bed and then out of the front door, bandaged hands lighting her way in the darkness. The deference of the children over a day, their affection, their overwhelming concern brought forth an unnatural sensation of guilt, a kind of emotional indigestion which alarmed her. Guilt of any kind was not second nature to Mouse: it made her tiptoe across the lawn, already resentful of the necessity of Sarah Fortune, who knew too much about them all and was now, for the lack of anyone else to tell, about to know more. Hettie the sheep followed after, but Mouse was not afraid and it was only the reasons why she was not afraid, not of the ghost at least, which made her faintly ashamed.

'What are you doing?' she cried, facing the cottage living room as the door opened without hesitation. 'I came to see if you were all right,' she added with less conviction. Both of them knew it was not the truth. Sarah had fulfilled her purpose. Mouse had plenty of reason to be grateful to Sarah, and that was enough to stop anyone caring. The shawl which had covered the ugly sofa was gone, the table lamp back in place, the room bereft of the flowers which had made it homely, the whole thing back to the anonymity of just another place to rent.

'Packing up my travelling bordello,' said Sarah with a smile. She made it so easy, Mouse thought bitterly, to like her. This was no woman who would kiss and tell, she was as tight as a drum, but somehow, horribly relaxing, all sorts of ideas in her eyes and her mind, but none of them including the slightest critical judgement.

'Packing? Whatever for? We need you, dear.'

'No you don't. I've finished.' She waved a hand towards a neat pile of papers on the floor. 'Valuations. Edward helped last night, that's why I kept him here so long.' Their glances met and slid away in recognition of a lie mutually accepted. Mouse seized a bottle by the kitchen sink, two glasses from the draining board, poured without invitation. She assumed the claret was for her: she was slightly drunk already, aimed to get worse. Such was conscience. Why should she care? If a trespasser ate the food and burned her hands he deserved to deal with his own digestion.

'You Pardoes', said Sarah without any hint of complaint as they sat, 'tend to be heavy on the rations. Anyway, if you can read the hand-written notes . . . I have very clear handwriting, nothing ambiguous about it, what I've done is suggest the properties you can get rid of soonest. Selling them, at absolutely knock-down prices on ludicrously easy terms, to the people who currently own them. Those are the businesses, beginning with the pub and the amusement arcade, then the shops. Give back the lifeblood of the town. Right?'

Mouse nodded, gargling the wine, lovely stuff.

'You don't want to be destitute,' Sarah continued. 'The business end of all this, as well as further education for Edward and Jo, a modest nest egg for all three and fine wines and parties for yourself, will be financed out of the holiday cottages you have. Selling them at very low prices, to be bought by local people to raise families, still leaves plenty, properly invested, for your own old age. Whenever that occurs.'

Mouse liked that touch. She proffered her glass for refilling. 'We won't need Ernest Matthewson to sort it all?'

'You don't need him, no. He won't like it, but you don't. A local accountant, an honest estate agent . . . yours isn't, by the way.'

'Awful in bed, Ernest,' said Mouse reflectively. 'Such a hurry.'

Sarah sipped without comment. Mouse sighed with satisfaction.

'Such a relief,' she said brightly. 'I mean really. We've all talked about it today, and they all want the same thing. They live here, they want to belong. Such well-brought-up children. All the right attitudes. They all agree that none of them wants more than strictly enough. Enough is always enough, don't you think?'

'Absolutely,' said Sarah with the right amount of fervour to make Mouse continue. The pain in her own abdomen was becoming intense, beyond the reach of wine, a hunting pain, which sought other places to attack.

'After all,' Mouse went on, accepting more alcohol as if she were a favoured guest, 'wouldn't it be awful if I'd had to tell them in order to get them to agree? Frightful!'

She was back in her hotel receptionist mould which Sarah realized had not been entirely mad.

'Awful,' she agreed warmly.

'I mean, if they hadn't listened? I didn't think they'd ever listen when I got Mr Pardoe to make that will. When he had those little heart flutters, you know? We were getting on so well, I knew he didn't notice how the thing was phrased. All my children . . .'

Oh, yes he did, Sarah thought. He might have seen Stonewall Jones in the drive, delivering bait and known. That boy was going to grow big and tall, like his real dad, with eyes like Julian Pardoe, all his colours and all his stockiness to become in the future the mirror image of his much older brother. When you lay with a man, you knew the colour of his eyes, knew when you had seen them before in another face, along with particular gestures and a way of eating and drinking. You knew.

'I would have told them,' said Mouse. 'I would certainly have done, if they hadn't agreed we should give it all back, all this property stuff, as soon as we could.' She sighed. 'I mean I played the scene a thousand times in my head before I decided to act mad. There we would be, none of them listening, sitting round a table with Ernest Matthewson sitting at the top. Reading out that bit from the will. How does it go? I should know, I constructed it. "To my wife, and then to all MY children . . ." Meaning, his children. Not his and mine, HIS. Those wearing his jeans, sorry genes.' She spelt it out as if Sarah could not see the pun, hiccoughed, recovered her poise, continued.

'HIS children? Well, I suppose Julian is his child. I've every reason to think so. The others? Joanna, probably. Edward, no. It seemed obvious to me. Perhaps that's why he and Mr Pardoe never got on. It's so difficult to tell. Now I don't have to tell.'

'Don't you?' Sarah's question was sad.

'No,' said Mouse. 'Not any more than you have to tell the person before who you slept with last. It's all right for you young things taking the pill. Nature helped me: I could have had lots more babies, but I didn't. Which is just as well, I'd never have known whose they were.'

'I've drafted a separate bequest for your new will,' Sarah murmured. 'Half the residue of your estate, to include a decent house and a piece of his own coast, to go to Stonewall Jones, after your death.'

Mouse nodded, did not even question.

'I entirely agree,' she said. 'I'd already thought of that. I may be selfish, but I'm not dishonest.'

'Well, all's well that ends well,' said Sarah, pouring the dregs into Mouse Pardoe's glass.

'Not entirely,' said Mouse. 'I didn't mean to bang on about my family, now we're all sorted, after a fashion. They aren't really on my conscience, nothing lingers there long. Except these.'

She fumbled in the pocket of the dressing-gown, worn over a frilly nightie up to the chin, and ear-rings which dangled about the pie-crust collar. Produced a small packet, split at the top. *Size 2/0,*

Sarah read. *Super-sharp fine wire: designed and perfected for shore fishing.* She turned the packet over, read more . . . *Top-quality hooks made from high-carbon steel.* She shook one of them into her palm. The point was needle sharp, with a neat, inverted barb. The hook was black; she felt it against her own skin, harmless until the barb took hold. The black hooks, each with a small eye at the top of the stem, curled sweetly in their innocent, polythene envelope.

'Only one thing bothers me,' Mouse Pardoe was saying, carelessly, 'I put lots of these in the sandwiches. And the scones.'

She tipped the glass over her nose.

'I only did it as a joke. Edward, leaving them all over the place, drove me mad. Hettie could have eaten one. No one ever eats anything I make: I only do it to annoy. All those years I *had* to cook; now I can do it for play, like making sandwiches. I would have told them about the hooks before they went near. To make the point to Ed, because then he would never have left anything in the kitchen again, like his father did before. Or hit me. What exactly did you DO to Edward, dear? He's being so nice.'

Sarah saw Charles Tysall, backing out of the kitchen, stuffing yellow scones in his pocket.

'Only that man, that Charles,' Mouse was saying airily, 'he ate all the sandwiches. I don't know how he did it, but he did,' she added with a trace of self-satisfaction. 'Ate the lot.'

Sarah looked at the hook curled in her palm, remembered the sound of the gulping of food and milk. The hook was such a fine wire, one inch long, small enough, only just, for a starving, hungry man to swallow. She pressed the small, inverted barb, between thumb and forefinger, felt it pierce her skin.

'Sharp, aren't they, dear?' Mouse remarked.

The pain in Sarah's abdomen became intense.

'Sleep on it, I would,' said Mouse, abdicating every decision with a smile. 'He deserved what he got.'

* * *

Rick never could take drink: a little went a long way, so he had been careful, was not drunk now, merely loquacious. How awful, in the village where he lived, to need the company of a stranger on a night like this. No news of Stonewall: he had checked with Jo and the doctor. He might as well stay where he was with this easy man, both of them dirty, other customers in the smart bar giving them space. Two pints simply brought emotion nearer the surface. Rick wanted Jo to hug, but he stayed, giving Malcolm all the information distilled from Uncle Curl and everyone else. Malcolm's gentler cross-examination techniques worked as well in a bar as they did in a courtroom, especially when the victim was emotional, malleable and confused. Malcolm knew the name, the identity, the local history and the persona of the man they hunted. Like Sarah Fortune, he was all too real.

'Your Cousin Stonewall thought that this Sarah Fortune woman was Mrs Tysall, did he?' Malcolm was asking.

'Only at first. My second cousin in the hairdresser's did too. What do you think the ghost wanted up at the Pardoes'? Apart from it being a lonely place where he might get food? A place with nothing to guard it but a sheep?' Rick's eyes widened, alcohol in flight in the face of realisation. The mention of Sarah Fortune made him blush; he thought of her with guilty fondness and a slight tightening of the groin, felt himself pulling his flat stomach flatter.

'You think he might have gone up there for Sarah? Aw, come on, it doesn't make sense. He wouldn't even have known she was there.'

'Listen,' said Malcolm. 'In his other life, Charles Tysall had an obsession with Sarah Fortune.'

'Did he now?' Rick mumbled, foggy again, but leering. 'I can see his point.'

They drank reflectively. Not this lad, Malcolm thought. Surely not, not even Sarah.

'So maybe he'll go back there, then. S'all right. They got someone watching the place, Jo said when I phoned. And there's two men up there anyway, well one and a half, if you count Edward. I reckon he's long gone. He managed months without people, why should he need anyone now?'

Rick drank the last of his pint, did not want to say anything more. Malcolm spoke slowly.

'Oh, I don't think it's a question of Charles going back to find Sarah. Not a question of Charles leading the way to where Sarah is. More the other way round.'

'What do you mean?'

'I mean Sarah leading us to Charles. Sarah will find him.'

Rick did not understand.

'Tell you what,' he said. 'Meet you outside the arcade. Seven o'clock if it's sunny. Eight if it rains. Right?'

Malcolm was silent, the taste of his good whisky, sour.

The room in which he sat had become terrifying. He repeated like a mantra phrase, 'My name is Charles and I have no name.' When at last he moved, towards the cracked, disused mirror against the wall in the opposite room, level with the high stone sink, all he could see was his face glowing yellow, his brown teeth, eyes which were pink and dry. So long without a mirror, the sight unhinged him. If he had even used a mirror in the last year, he would have seen the damage of the changes; seen how impossible it was to go home. He was beginning to smell. Blood and dirt and cold, hot sweat and putrefaction. Something inside him mortally wounded. Step to one side and watch me, darling. Dying. He had opened his mouth and raised his hand many times, let the hand fall back to wipe the froth which congealed round his perfect mouth, the lips stretched with pain, the forehead puckered with the knowledge of helplessness, his long thin body bent. There were portraits on the wall where he grew up. Red-haired women with the threatening white complexions of his forebears, himself the saturnine changeling.

Finally, he had bellowed with rage and frustration, shrieked like a child in the grip of hysteria and heard his shrieks descend into weeping. Shuffled closer to the opening when he knew the time was well beyond daylight. The lights fell across his face and his dirty white hair; he was ten feet from help, but no one saw, no one heard, the place was full of sound.

The rat-a-tat of machine-gun fire, eerie music, echoing gongs, popular songs at colossal volume, the sound of a fairground, the clack of coins and children screaming from afar, sounding triumphant. In the interludes, a droning voice, 'On the line, fifty-nine, legs eleven, number eleven, sink and dive, fifty-five . . .' The sounds bleep, bleep, bleep, wailing songs, heavy beat, and the mystical calling of the machines selling their wares to the possessed.

The effort of screaming drove him into a paroxysm of silent laughter, something to excuse the tears. The irony of a cultured man, enduring this orchestra of vulgar, electronic sound, with the purple lights playing upon the yellow skin he felt he could pull away, while his long hands clutched at his abdomen.

Someone on a misguided expedition to find a lavatory which did not exist kicked the legs sticking beyond the entrance of the ante-room, swore, went back. Later, another, ignoring him even while his mouth opened to scream again, left him for drunk instead of dying. The thought of a drink made his throat contract; he was thirsty, had only come in here for water which he could not reach, never left in twenty hours.

Charles dozed; when he opened his eyes all sound had ceased and he gazed into the peace of total darkness, the opportunity for rescue ending while he slept. Panic now, blood in the pee which soaked the track-suit trousers, the smell of himself disgusted him. He crawled.

Away from the dead machines, which stood like coffins in the back room, across the eerie moonlit floor, illuminated from the windows of the fold-back doors leading on to the road and the pay-and-display sign for the quayside car park. Clutching at the inside handle, feeling it rattle and the whole edifice of the door shake as he raised himself to his knees and looked out into the night in an attitude of supplication, looking for the moon and redemption.

Saw a figure turn, stamp feet, turn back, light a cigarette to illuminate its uniform, stub out the cigarette as someone passed by and said, Good-evening, officer. A woman, treating a police officer with polite deference as her dog bit his heels. Better die like a dog than live like one.

He began to crawl back, slowly, leaning against Omen III and Street Fighters IV. Thirsty, thirsty, thirsty.

'Room after room,' he whispered,

'I hunt the house through . . .

Next time herself! Not the trouble behind her.'

Browning in the mouth. The stanzas a litany for a shuffling old man who could remember nothing else but obscenities. Not a self-created vagrant, a real one. Once back in the room of the dead machines, he shat himself. The shame was so insupportable, the act of it so painful, he wept.

Stonewall Jones woke, with an urgent desire for the lavatory and a sense of shame in that. He was confused, but very clear about his needs. Coke, not milk; the embrace of his mother, not the nurse.

Sarah had never managed the art of travelling light, nor of counting back into her baggage what she had put in. In the dim light of dawn, she still noticed that there was less, one purple shirt, with the trousers and shoes donated to the greedy sea, one black shirt, with leggings, which she hoped Joanna would enjoy. The child had not been near, which she did not find strange in one normally so considerate; Sarah knew she bore her own kind of contagion, a kind of hidden, moral embarrassment which afflicted those of normal tendencies with a kind of unease.

She bent into the pain. Charles had occupied her dreams, the sense of his presence overpowering. The knowledge of the poisonous hooks in his body consumed her. She woke to the sound of gossiping birds, shrill and cheerful. Perhaps it was the signal they had found him.

The sea mist had descended, the air soft, damp, light struggling through.

Was it cowardly to leave after this fashion, skulking away at dawn in this chilling mist, to a home which was not a home, never had been since Charles had invaded the casual, clandestine, delightfully promiscuous progress of her life and called her a whore? Cowardly to leave, before anyone should find him first and ask her to identify their prize? To go with the same fear, the same lack of a conclusion, the same shame, back to the same hopelessly damaged life?

She closed the door of the car with the crumpled wing, leaving her things inside it. Hettie the sheep bleated with satisfaction. There was no hurry after all.

She walked to the village-cum-town, listening to the gurgling of hidden water. Walked beyond the quay and out on to the causeway. The red roof of the lifeboat station was scarcely visible, the siren, having issued its warning against the fog, remained silent. Sarah paused, turned, scanned the quayside. It was small and manageable, harmless. She could see the folding doors to the arcade slightly open and a man cleaning the windows without enthusiasm before he walked away from the task. Then a shaft of struggling sunlight pierced through the thin mist, illuminated the glass of the windows, disappeared as suddenly as it had struck, like a signal. Sarah knew with a complete and illogical certainty where Charles Tysall was. She began to walk back, watching her feet, feeling the quickening pain in her guts and listening to the vengeful messages of her own heart.

CHAPTER THIRTEEN

She was screened for a minute by the cars which seemed permanent fixtures of the car park, the shellfish van and a slow rumbling lorry full of animal feed, the sound of the growling engine ominous in the silence. When Malcolm reached the quay, to meet his appointment with Rick in the expectation that Rick might be late, Sarah had gone. There was an oldish man, with a figure stiff with resentment, coming round the corner, chewing on something, cap over one eye.

'Excuse me, have you seen a chap called Rick? Works here?'

It sounded like an accusation: Rick's father blenched.

'Nope.'

'Only I was supposed to meet him here,' Malcolm said, feeling useless.

The older man laughed, nervously. 'He don't like the early morning, our Rick. Told me I'd have to clean the windows, not him. Thought he'd got some woman in to clean 'em. Saw her. A looker.'

'Where did she go?'

'After Rick, I expect. They usually do.' Rick's dad laughed, taking pride in his announcement. Maybe he'd get some fun out of Rick's conquests.

'Where did she go?' Malcolm repeated patiently.

Rick's dad was thinking of nothing much; comprehension dawned slowly, remnants of another conversation coming back to cloud his early-morning brain, reminding him of the current primary purpose, which was to find a male ghost, not a woman. He supposed the question was related, didn't think why, but guessed wildly in order to please and get this bloke off him.

'Think I just saw someone going up the high street.'

They both turned, uncertainly, uphill.

Sarah could smell him first, an animal in a lair, surrounded by the stench of faeces and fear. He was lying with his back propped against one of the dead machines, levered against it for support. The pathetic outline of him emerged first from the half light in there, then the details. The track-suit bottoms had slid down from scraping along the ground, his thin hands were clasped over his stomach above his genitals which flopped in pathetic splendour. Hung like a donkey. His face wore the rictus of a smile, a dirty face, furrowed with tears.

She tried to make her voice harsh, summon up the hatred.

'Something you ate?' she said, standing over him, willing him to look at her with the unblinking eyes which looked towards the light instead. 'Shame on you, Charles Tysall, you made me offer to rut like a pig, and now, you look like a pig.'

How pathetic an insult, and then, suddenly she was weeping. He had been a handsome man once, lithe as a tiger, long limbed, broad shouldered, a prowler with infinite grace, a predator, but such a beautiful man, proud in his body and his obsessions, fastidious, wicked and still beautiful. Never a man to crawl: it became him as ill as a wounded tiger, a rogue elephant with no notion of human distress. She thought of the hooks which might not have damaged a younger, stronger man, but tore at the weaker fabric of this gaunt and starving fugitive with the terrible glitter still in his piercing blue eyes. The rictus turned into a recognisable smile; he held out his hand, the long, elegant fingers flexing, then trembling, trying to summon into a small gesture some remnants of the old arrogance.

'Imperfectly pure and good,' he whispered. 'Look at me, Elisabeth. Are you satisfied?'

She remembered the hands, slender, manicured, soft, caressing her body, spanning her neck, the buckle of his belt biting into her spine, the softness of his balls a cushion against her buttocks before the glass splintered and with it, all limitations on his calculating savagery. Felt the last, great spate of anger against him, remembering that torture, and then even with her own screams in her own ears, the anger died. She tried to retrieve it, hold the need for revenge, felt it slip away as she watched, disgust mixed with compassion, with the treacherous, wasteful pity for him winning in the end. The body was merely a man, a thing, twisting and grimacing, trying now to pull up its trousers in some pathetic attempt at half-remembered modesty. She stooped, indifferent to the smells of sweet, sour and rancid, helped him. He was warm and clammy, screamed when she touched him and there was no satisfaction, even in that.

Water for the saliva crusted round the mouth: she did not want him to be seen this way, sharing for a brief moment the pride which made him want to cover himself, but when she rose from her haunches to find the sink, he uttered a groan of despair. The tap in the other room yielded water onto a rag; when she knelt again and applied it to his face, he moaned again with pleasure, sucked at the cloth with the greediness of a baby on a nipple.

They stayed thus, wordless, she holding him round the shoulders, feeling the bones, keeping the cloth to his face, murmuring nothings, wondering what next to do, with the tears still coursing down her face, dropping onto his skin.

'Do you forgive me, Porphyria?' the voice rattled, bubbling from the chest.

She could not say so, could not utter a clear word. She did not forgive him, either in her own right or on behalf of her friend Elisabeth, but she could not bear to see him suffering either.

The door to the back yard opened with a scraping sound; there were soft footsteps, a pair of training shoes, an increase in the light and then a tall shadow towering above them. Charles had hold of her hand, her arm wrapped across his chest; she

tightened her hold, felt the papery skin of his palm, while she listened to a gasp of anger, felt the alien tension of bone and
muscle, the intake of breath before effort, the scent of violent
rage which would never emanate from Charles now. She held
him closer, looked up like a fierce little animal. Malcolm stood
above her, fists clenched, legs braced, a fighter ready to pounce.
He spoke through gritted teeth.

'Sarah? Is that Charles? What's the matter with him? Christ,
he's aged ten years. Is he hurt? The bastard. What are you
doing? Let go, for God's sake.'

She looked at him absently, his appearance a secondary consideration, spoke quietly.

'If you hit him, I'll kill you.'

Her own voice came from a great distance, followed by the
cough which was Malcolm's effort to control his voice before it
became a murmur, strangled by his own, bitter emotion. He had
slept with this woman. She had touched him. Now look at what
she held, with the same intimacy.

'So, Sarah my sweet. How could you? Is there anything you
can't touch? Anyone you don't despise? How could you?'

She could not summon scorn. Could not say, Look, this is no
more than a hunted man who is dying in pain and that is all I
can acknowledge. Could not in her contempt of Malcolm's futile
clenched fists, even attempt to phrase a denial.

The pain drifted away and she still held him, protectively,
knowing only that it was once handsome and proud Charles
Tysall who held her hand as a talisman. Knowing too that there
was nothing else she could do but hold on and lend warmth.
No one should die alone.

After the room became safely crowded and the rattle in his
throat had ceased, she relinquished him calmly, watching the
face turn from flushed to waxy pale, the lines of age and pain
easing away in the immediacy of death. She walked out of the
arcade past a silent phalanx of the men of the town and the
hunting party, each staring more accusingly than the last. She

walked the gauntlet with her head high, the mist teasing curls into her wild hair, blood on her hands and dirt on her clean clothes. Walked beyond the murmuring crowd, past the rising tide in the channels and the graceful swimming swans, until, beyond their sight, she broke into a run. The mist was wet on her face, the sea birds were silent, the earth was still, her stride punctuated only by the fierceness of her sobbing.

Hettie the sheep was still at the door, sporting her unequal horns and endless good nature. Oh to be sheeplike, docile and untroubled, satisfied, until the pointed horn of your life grew into your eye. Sarah picked the roses round the door, they owed her that, and put them in the back of her car. She rummaged in her case on the back seat for clean clothes, stripping and changing where she stood, obscured by the mist, wiping her hands on the garments she dropped, buttoning a clean blouse with shaking but efficient hands. She kicked what she had worn to one side, ever careless with her apparel, whatever it had cost. Clothes did not matter, they never had and they never would. Hettie began to eat her second outfit that week.

Late breakfast in the Pardoe household in a kitchen free of fishing utensils. Edward was giving up fishing, he was going away. Somewhere, he said. Joanna had long since told herself that in doing whatever he had done, he thought he was doing the best, although his notion of the best was no longer hers. It was more difficult to relinquish adoration than it was to relinquish love, everything would be all right in the end.

Julian and Edward were arguing, nothing altered except the tone, the tenor, the result, Edward still with that endless, hard-done-by element in his voice which he would have for ever, and if he ever found out why, he would only be worse.

I shall have to say goodbye, Sarah told herself at the door, look Edward in the eye to make my promise of blackmail stick. Julian was arguing in measured tones. Joanna cooked at the Raeburn, flushed and serene, with that hint of high anxiety which would always be hers. Mouse sat at one end of the

mess-free table, eating nuts for breakfast, wearing a swim-
ming-costume under her dressing-gown. She had things to do
later; she would never make concessions to clothes, or ever
buy new ones. She might, reluctantly, abandon the hats.

The appearance of Sarah, fresh and pale, sunny and clean,
riveted attention and brought to the surface of every face a slight
blush of shame. Joanna blushed least, for being nothing but in-
attentive to the guest in the face of greater dramas, but then it
took little to activate her guilt towards what was only the hired
help and ever so briefly, confidential friend and exemplar. All
the same, her skin grew the colour of ripe strawberry.

Julian's blush was more moderate, reaching up towards his
sandy hair with the same sting of hospitable conscience as Jo,
but also for his confessions and his cure, for what he had said
and done so joyfully in the middle of the night. The mild col-
oration of Edward's sallow skin was merely the result of a
temporary worry about whether the guest had come to tell on
him, a momentary sense of panic soon dismissed. Sarah's smile,
the conscious cheerfulness reminiscent of the ideal girl next door
rather than the airs and graces of a high-powered lawyer paid by
the day, made all of them feel better. She sat as if she could never
take offence in a million years, looking like someone on the way
out to play netball with the team. Joanna pushed a mug of coffee
towards her which she took with exaggerated thanks. They all
began to relax. Except Mother, who kept her nose buried in a
newspaper.

'All's well with the world,' Sarah said lightly, looking towards
no one in particular, ignoring the little lump in her throat. 'They've
found the ghost. Poor man, dead at the back of the amusement
arcade. Something he ate.'

From all sides of the table came a palpable sigh of relief.
Julian caught her eye and smiled with full magnetic glare. Sarah
wished she could afford dislike for mere weakness, but that,
along with hatred and judgement, was a luxury.

And I'm going home now, she was going to say, before the
Big Ben chimes of the ice-cream van impinged, first distant then

strident, dah da, dah da! Louder and louder, scorching not to
the front door of the ugly old pile, but the back, by the cabbage
patch, the van itself assuming a new intimacy with this terrain.
They would not be the landowning Pardoes for long. Everyone
would be welcome.

'Ernest will send in the bill,' Sarah yelled at Julian above the
din of scraped-back chairs and the headlong rush to the door,
led by Mother, all of them wanting a distraction.

'Of course. Thank you for everything,' was all he said.

When the red car with the dented wing drove slowly past the
front of the house, the ice-cream chimes still rang, like church
bells at a wedding, the harbinger of good news, so demanding
no one noticed the sound of an engine going away. Rick's news
would be repeated a thousand times, like the tune of the chimes.
Stonewall, back on the road of living and loving, demanding a
video, and could he borrow the sheep for a visit and what kind
of dog should they get? And Rick knowing exactly the right
kind. And that other fucker, that ghost, well he's really dead.
This time.

In a half-hour wake of the van, another car, small, blue,
undented, well looked after, pulled hesitantly to the front of the
house. Malcolm Cook decanted his long limbs, walked in the
direction of celebratory sound. No one had turned off the ice-
cream bell; it grated in his ears. Rick was high on coffee and
wine, slow on the introductions. For the moment, the tall, dark
man who could hunt so assiduously and run like a dream was
just another stranger.

'Come to collect Miss Fortune,' he said with the half-apologetic,
half-aggressive tones of a taxi driver.

'She's gone,' someone said, he was not sure who. 'You're too
late.' Rick looked at him sideways, wondering, for the first time,
exactly who he was.

'Too late,' he chanted, sounding just like Stonewall.

Well beyond the town, out on the coast road, travelling fast, until

she found the turning and bumped down the track she had
found before. She moved the car to the very edge where shingle
met sand on this flat coast. The mist was peculiarly local: ten
miles away from Merton's quay it did not exist. She looked at
the retreating sea, the stretch of warm sand, stayed inside the
confines of her car, with the bordello in the back, the shawl to
decorate a room, the virtue to decorate a life, the odd crate of
booze, the remnants of fear packed along with the clothes, and
felt no longer drawn to the water. Thought of Elisabeth Tysall's
headstone with remote satisfaction. Who loves you, beautiful? I
do.

Thought of pleading with Charles Tysall a year ago, standing
in front of the mirror in her flat while he accused her. You have
no virtue to protect, do you? he had said, despising the offer she
had made of her body in return for her life. You are nothing: a
woman is nothing without virtue. Looking at the sea, Sarah
remembered what she had replied, and what she would say now.
She had said then, Of course I have virtue. I do not torment or
abuse. I leave when I am not welcome. I do not trespass or take
anything from anyone, except my own payment which need not
be money. I keep every secret which is entrusted in me. I do not
really know the meaning of malice. I like to live without rules,
that is all, and that is a kind of virtue no one values.

Virtue all the same. She left the bleakness of the warm sand
with all its temptations, turned away from the coast. Found a
deserted lane, full of meadowsweet so prolific, so untouched by
human hand, it hid the car from sight. She took a bottle of warm
champagne from the supplies in the back and a beaker from the
glove compartment in the front. After she had disposed her legs
comfortably through the window, she lit a cigarette and wondered, Now where shall I go next? What shall I be next, now I
am free?

There did not seem anything wrong with going on exactly as
before.

STARING AT THE LIGHT

To Gill Coleridge and Esther Newberg,
with love and thanks.

ACKNOWLEDGEMENTS

I could not have written this novel without assistance in the research. All those mentioned below had the grace to hide their incredulity at my ignorance and they combined to dispel the lingering myth in my own mind that those with a scientific bent might be *dull*. Particular thanks to Leslie Payne, BDS LDC DMCC, and to Janet Payne for allowing me to glimpse the sharp end of dental practice, and also for access to Leslie's unique library and network. If either of you should ever read this book, you will recognise some of the scenery. Thanks also to the memorably kind Elisabeth Allen, who set me on the right track, and to Dr Norman Mills, who got to the root canal of the matter, gave me good ideas and provoked me to write this in the first place. Otherwise I could never have paid the fees. Thanks also to Howard Hersch and to Greg Woolgar, and finally to Peter Gurney, MBE, ex-Chief of the Metropolitan Bomb Disposal Squad, for the clarity of his explanations and the infectious quality of his laughter. Between you all, you manage to prove that there is more courage in so-called ordinary life than fiction would ever allow.

PROLOGUE

Guy Fawkes favoured gunpowder because that was what he knew. An artist, after his fashion.

It had been an exceptionally mild autumn after a wet summer. Winter was not quite real yet, although Sarah Fortune never did think it became quite real in the metropolis. They were all cocooned here, benefiting from body heat and the borrowed warmth of buildings. London was made for winter, became a garment all by itself.

Here and now, in one corner of it, comfort clothing was the order of the evening. Bonfire Night was hardly an occasion for style, especially since the entrances to the park were marked with notices exhorting crowds to beware of pickpockets who would take advantage of the dark and the distraction of lights. There were anoraks and wool jackets, and shoes dirty from muddy grass. A kindly mist had covered the day's preparations. The witnesses from the gracious crescent of late-Victorian houses had been unable to spy from the windows exactly what had been done out there to make the monster bonfire from dry, eco-friendly rubbish and set up the fireworks in the cold, all of it surrounded by sufficient mystery to cause anxiety. The mist, not quite a fog, had been enough to obscure it by daylight, and if it had continued, no one would have seen with quite the full splendour the extent of the council's generosity in the form of the annual firework display. This would have been a cheat.

The locals to the park scorned the event, complained and campaigned about it, and yet felt unable to resist. The crowds gathered. Gradually, the inhabitants of the crescent began to emerge. Their children insisted. Watching a bonfire from the front windows was not the same: you had to watch it with the crowd; feel it, fear it slightly; observe with watering eyes. The annual protests against the use of the park, the crowds, the racket, the drunken bums, the mini fairground and the thieves had given way first to grudging acceptance, then to excitement.

In the interests of the liberalism that persisted among the local worthies, there would be no ritualistic burning of an effigy of Guy Fawkes. The man had flair, but he had been found out. He had only tried to blow up Parliament, no more, no less – a perfectly respectable ambition after all: an almost unbroken succession of persons had been trying to do it by one means or another ever since, although none of them had been publicly eviscerated. Sissy Mallison, from number fifteen, told her daughter to stop moaning about the absence of a Guy Fawkes to throw on the fire. It was an emblem of hate, she said, perfectly barbaric; you would loathe it if you saw it. It is obscene to burn the effigy of a once live man and watch his limbs curl in the blaze; even dogs go mad and bark at such a thing.

I want one, said the child. We had one last year at Mary's house; it was great.

Mary was a little swine. Mary's family are a bunch of heathens, was all Sissy could say. Roman Catholics never burn Guy Fawkes: he was one of us. Out of spite, there had been a local movement, which Sissy declined to discuss, that perhaps there *should* be some sort of dummy to burn. Any unpopular figure would do. There seemed to be a strange sort of yearning for that sort of sacrifice. The child submitted to hat and scarf, whingeing.

There was an urge to feel the fire; it was imperative to stand near, or at the very least in sight of flushed faces. There was a general settling down after the first, paraffin-induced roar from the edifice of planks and branches. A *whoosh* fit to satisfy the soul of an arsonist, into which category Sarah Fortune put most children and many others of the population. A cheer, a few screams of delight and a few squawks of alarm, until it died down to a steady crackle. Then the fireworks began.

They sounded to William like a series of bizarre bodily functions but, then, William had always supposed he had little imagination, which, such as it was, extended over fifty-two years and tended towards the basic. He had been a mere youth when he had wanted to be a painter. If you closed your eyes, which was, of course, *not* the object of the exercise, all you could hear, he told an imaginary companion, was a series of dramatic burps and farts. *A pimph, a pamph, a tiddly pamph, a cushion creeper and a tear-arse*. A cracking groan of sound with the major rockets (rumoured to cost a hundred each: he was glad he did not live in this borough); a sigh of desperation, like a dyspeptic hiccup, when the multicoloured stars burst forth towards the end, falling to earth in a whine of relief. The colours blinded him, the fumes sickened him, so he concentrated on the sound. He had missed the person he had come to meet: he was always losing things.

Superficial observation revealed that some of the crowd were drunk, in contrast to the quiet and respectful parents, clutching children and instructing them in science. Then there were the semi-adult kids, and the self-grouping gangs of men and youths who formed their own momentum, chanting, *We WANT a guy, WE want a GUY*, or was it *WE WANT A GUY*? William wasn't sure, and was equally unsure that it made any difference what the hell they wanted, apart from the sensation of power from making a noise.

The display ended with a setpiece of gigantic proportions. I wonder what *that* cost? he heard someone murmur, wondering to himself, mourning his own prosaic tendency even to think of what kind of a noise it would make, or if it would reveal a message in the sky. And, if so, what it would say. *Phoomphh, phoomph, woof, woof, wooof!* It filled the firmament with rebellious sound. *Pshaw, shaw,* screamed the lesser starbursts, which went on and on and on, *crick, crack, crick,* another and yet another, louder than the OOHS! and AAHS! below, before the last of it fell to earth. There was another sigh, almost of anger, as the light went out of the sky. While the sparks fell, he could see the crowd as a picture, all those faces, upward-turned and vulnerable with hope, still wanting more. Anticlimax; dull with wonder.

They seemed at first oblivious to the greatest sound of all. A huge *WHOOMPH*. An air-sucking, ground-sucking *WHOOMPH*, which made him tremble. No one seemed to notice it. It was part of the spectacular effect, and it was only he who had been listening for sounds alone, keeping his eyes shut half the time.

And then, gradually, the crowd began to turn. Not the group who resumed the chant, *GUY, GUY, WE WANT GUY, WANNA GUY, WANNA GUY,* oblivious of anything but their own momentum, but the others, children first, readier to abandon one sensation for the next, little feet better able to feel the trembling of the earth. His section of the crowd, the one safely away from the heat of the fire, those who had most carefully chosen an avenue of escape, began to flutter and mutter and turn their collective head. He thought of a hydra, a single creature of many heads, turning simultaneously, uncertain of the direction to follow. Finally, there was selective comprehension.

The last house in the crescent, the biggest and the best, was collapsing in front of their eyes. The windows spat at them, pane by pane, a small distraction of smashing glass. As if by some magic trick, part of the roof crumbled out of sight. Like mother and child, locked in some ghastly embrace, the walls disappeared inside themselves with a shudder. There were no flames shouting for attention, simply an ominous, gut-churning rumble as debris fell. After the fireworks, it was curiously discreet. They were mesmerised, puzzled, as William was, but, all the same, he felt an obscure desire to cheer.

Some of those around him wanted to break ranks and run, but they waited, still unsure whether this was merely an extra spectacle. Others simply did not notice. Many people were transfixed in the act of chewing – bonfire toffee, hot dogs and beefburgers – while their pockets were picked. The crowd near the fire, kept back with increasing desperation by the guardians of the blaze *(We believe in safety first! Please stand back!)*, still chanted, WE WANT GUY! The fire gave a ritual groan, settling itself with a sigh.

One section of the audience watched the house come down. There was a tendency to laugh, as if the whole thing were a pantomime, while a few began to move uneasily. William was with them, until he stopped. Turned back towards the fire without the slightest knowledge why.

WE WANNA GUY! William closed his eyes, registered the pull in the opposite direction, shuffling movement on the periphery nearest the collapsing house; while, close to the fire, the chant went on. A central group of young men, disparate sizes and shapes, was hauling a carcass towards the blaze. A low-slung, dead-asleep body, peculiarly weightless, held between six sets of hands, swinging. William started towards it, yelling, *Noo,* no, no, screaming at the top volume of his lungs, listening to his steps and still screaming as he pushed through a crowd hell bent on the opposite direction. He was as heavy as the oldest, as inept as the suddenly screaming children; he was aware of the barking of dogs and he was too late. The band swung their figure, in a strangely disciplined fashion, on to the fire. *ONE, TWO, THREE! Yeah! Burn, you bugger, BURN!*

He shrieked. He pushed his way through, found himself yelling again without hearing an echo. And then standing there, a complete and helpless fool, as the thing landed on the embers of the fire. It curled into a phantom of itself. A corpse of packing material, foam and chips, dying painlessly in an instant of grotesque, twisted disfigurement. Those who had thrown it paused, the laughter and the chant quiet now. Someone tried to whip up fervour by a cheer, but that, too, died.

Then, across his line of vision, hurtling from the direction of the crescent, came a small, round figure, moving with a strange progress. A man, running with his hands above his head, holding a piece of paper, which he tore in half. The hands were gloved. The man ran all the way round the circumference of the

fire. 'Have it, Johnny!' he was shrieking. 'Have it all!' His voice
was high and feminine, muffled by the scarf round his face. The
dummy curled and melted, intensifying the heat. Then the man
stopped moving, his hands empty, still raised above his head.
Turned and faced the fire. Ran towards it, howling.

William knew what the man was going to do; felt as if he had
known as soon as he saw him. He was, obviously, going to throw
himself onto the fire. It was a conclusion that followed a shameful thought, which had crossed his mind far earlier in the
evening, an idle thought: what would he do if he was ever called
upon to rescue someone who was burning? What would he do?
Something or nothing? Would he take the ignoble course and
stand back, because his own soft and flexible hands were far too
precious to risk?

He watched with horror. There was nothing to be seen but
the strange little man, vaguely familiar and silhouetted against
the fire, as if everyone else had disappeared. The man was
already exhausted by his own screaming: he shuffled towards the
fire rather than sprinted. He was measuring the distance for a
final leap into the flames, and all William could do was watch,
paralysed. Until another figure entered, stage left, cannoning
head-first into the running figure, butting him in the hip, bringing him down, clasping him round the middle, just as his
extended hands reached the flames. Then there were two figures, locked in an unholy embrace, rolling together on the hot,
ashy ground and snarling like fighting dogs.

Then others closed in on them. William heard only a shrill cry
above the rest. He could not distinguish if it was anger or pain.

He felt sick in the knowledge that his hands were safe.

He walked two or three steps backwards, repelled, yet drawn.
Turned away, finally. There was the ominous sound of sirens.
The house at the end of the crescent was no longer a house.

Breeze blew the litter over the park among stampeding feet.
When William looked for the very last time, the fire stood alone
and deserted. The raised arm of the carcass waved a last vale-
diction.

No harm done. A joke. But he thought he knew who they were, that grappling pair. Two people who had touched his life and threatened to engulf it, like the flames. He must be wrong: he was often slow to recognise faces, even those he knew best. A piece of torn paper teased at his feet. He picked it up idly, because he was tidy, read a line of clumsy writing.

OK, lover, I'll make you a deal. You've hidden her for three months, clever boy. Now how did you manage that? She'll change, you know; they all do. And your friends will change, because we have no real friends; we never did . . . Let's play the game for one more month . . . I can't go on for ever . . .

He felt like an eavesdropper, even more than he had just felt like a voyeur. He dropped the torn sheet into a bin and went home.

PART ONE

CHAPTER ONE

There was never enough light in late November, not even in the morning. She lay, brownly naked, sprawled in a huge armchair upholstered three decades since in cherry cotton, now a dull colour of rust, rumpled and torn in places. She looked as if she had been flung into it by an almighty force, then shoved down and left, stunned and broken. Her buttocks were sunk into the cushion, one arm behind her head supporting a mass of red hair, which was pulled half over her face. A hand extended itself beyond the hair to clutch the back of the upholstery, the fingers plucking at the frayed fabric. It played on his conscience, this endless, distressful movement of her long fingers, as if she was copying him. He had been so busy with his fingers. Delving, stroking, stirring. They were fat, broad fingers, he had, poking out of swollen, ugly fists.

The breasts were smaller than he liked, rather languid things resting against her ribcage as she lay in the hair with her torso twisted, the legs splayed over the arm of the crooked chair, ankles close, feet arched An auburn bush exposed. Her left hand lay above her cleft, as if to protect it. Too late: his eyes had seen, his fingers explored, greedy, greedy, greedy, and his hands were still steady. Not like hers. She was touching herself, almost absentmindedly, one finger twisting a small clump of that abundant pubic hair into a tight curl. He imagined the bush decked with ribbons. Apart from these minute movements of the hands, she was perfectly still. A woman satiated by every kind of abuse it was within his talent to inflict. Her mouth was slightly open. Breathing deeply, blowing away a wisp of her thick red hair.

He almost regretted what he had done to her. She looked so exquisitely helpless. So pliant, so biddable, so deliciously responsive to commands. Nothing about her was beyond imagination, and still her fingers kept moving piteously. She was *willing*, he told himself angrily; she asked for it. Look at the way she lay now. Wide open. Trusting. He was the mere beast to her beauty. She had *asked* for it.

It was a room that cried out for devotion and expertise to make it into something of habitable beauty, although that was a matter of indifference to him. The air was damply warm, condensation streaming down the ceiling windows, dripping now and then, somewhere. He wore gloves and a scarf. When the heat rose from him, the scarf began to smell like an old bandage, with overtones of turpentine, antiseptic and sweat. His nose was red, adding to the melancholy of his features. There was misty, diffused light; still the brightest light of the day. It was his torture chamber, decorated with his triumphs and disappointments.

He smiled now. His face rearranged itself from one set of folds into another, reminiscent of someone pulling up a set of ruched curtains to let in the sunlight. When he was serious he looked like an idiot, with a chin that seemed to reach his chest, but as soon as he grinned there was a massive rearrangement of everything: his furrowed forehead seemed to disappear into his hairline, his dark eyes were almost lost, and he seemed like a rumpled boy. The volume of hair made his head look overlarge for his thin shoulders. When he smiled, he looked perfectly, malevolently mad. Which, in his sober moments, in this room, with his bed in the corner, he knew he was. One had to be mad to inflict this abuse. He felt wretchedly older than his thirty-three years. Such cruelty pained him. At the least, the very least, he should have tried his hard-earned domesticity and offered her coffee. Dreadful coffee, but still a gesture towards hospitality.

'Are you cold?' he asked. 'I mustn't let you get cold. Must I?'

'No. But I have to move. Dammit, I can't move.'

But she did move, cautiously. Leaning forward, the torso twisting in a way that made him wince, she reached for a packet of cigarettes that lay in the ashtray on the footstool beside the chair. Lit one, inhaled and put it back in the ashtray. Then she stretched out one leg and clasped the toes, extended it fully, grasped the calf with both hands and stretched the whole limb, still in the chair, until her foot was level with her ear.

'What do you mean, you can't move? What do you call *that*?'

'I mean I can't stand up. Until I've done this.' She grasped the other leg, held it with both hands behind the knee, straightened it. There was a small *crick*. Then she swung her feet onto the floor, raised herself on tiptoe and stretched. Thinner than he liked. As unselfconscious as a cat.

The shifting of the tableau and the moving of the image saddened him. Sarah Fortune was the perfect model. No vanity. She was a perfect piece of design, and his fingers were tired with the painting of her.

'Let me see,' she asked, moving towards him with the cigarette in hand.

'No!' He was shrill. 'And don't come near me with that thing. It makes me want one, and I shouldn't.'

'Pooh. I don't know why you think of it. You could do with a few more antiseptic cigarettes. Every single bloody thing you do is bad for your health. But I won't look if you don't want.'

'Not yet, please. I'm ashamed of it.'

He shielded the canvas with his body, not trusting her, quite, although in his way he trusted her absolutely. She had that effect: she was natural and warm and generous to a fault, but the habits of mistrust were so deeply ingrained in him that they had become the natural response. Just like his shuffling walk, like a man avoiding the middle of the pavement and clinging to doorways, always looking for shadow. She had long since supposed that he had always been a little like that. It was not merely a response to his current circumstances. He would always have looked far older than he was, even as a boy; over-matured and slightly shifty, even in his innocence. He was still innocent now or, more aptly, a man who had never mastered the social code that governed the rules, constantly, almost childishly, uncertain.

'Do you know', he said, with more than usual animation, 'that you have one leg longer than the other? At least, you do in my version of you. I shall call it *Miss Sarah Fortune with unequal legs.*'

'No,' Sarah said. 'I never knew I had one leg longer than the other. But thank you for telling me. I shall have to amend the way I walk. Do you know what time it is? We're going to be late.'

'Late? Does it matter?' Cannon had a limited view of what mattered.

She was pulling on her clothes, retrieving them from the three-legged chair over which they were draped, neatly, as if they were important, which, as she smoothed on the dark tights, fastened a bra of white lace, buttoned the tiny pearl-coloured buttons of her blouse, he had to suppose they were: they turned her into something else entirely. No suit of clothes had ever done that for him. He sat down, weak with fascination. *I used to be a tart*, she had told him, long since. *Still am, but more of a hobby.* Naked, he could imagine that; when she was clothed, he could not. A tart with a heart. Sarah Fortune seemed to know about love: she gave it briskly and unstintingly. But, judging from the state of her body, she was also familiar with brutality.

'I don't suppose it matters in the long run', she was saying, 'about being late. But it does create a poor impression. And it's bad manners. Have you got any other clothes? Something cleaner?'

The question surprised him. It was totally irrelevant to anything in his mind. He was watching the slow transformation of naked girl into woman. She brushed her hair and tied it back, shrugged on the jacket of the suit, reached for her fawn raincoat and the tidy leather briefcase. A set of innocent-looking pearls gleamed round her neck. The small nuggets of gold in her ears had never come off. He plucked the single daisy from the milk bottle in which it resided and handed it to her, hoping to make amends for the lack of hospitality, which shamed him even here.

'Thank you. How kind. On second thoughts,' she said, 'you're best off to show yourself exactly as you are. Only you'd better wear the coat that smells of smoke. Then no one will want to come near you.'

He smiled. Then the face fell back into its bloodhound folds. 'Not many people *do* want to come near me,' he said matter-of-factly.

She patted his shoulder, ruffled his hair and planted a kiss on his cheek. 'Hardly surprising, is it?' she said. 'You snarling the way you do. Come on, now.' She paused. 'I'm forgetting the most important thing of all. Have you still got his letter? The bits you have left?'

He nodded, plundered the pocket of the coat to pull out a charred half-sheet of paper, badly crumpled.

'You were crazy to tear it up,' she said. 'I'll keep it, shall I?'

'I'm crazy full stop.'

'Does he mean what he says?'

'Yes. Even Johnny has rules. Even Johnny has to set limits.'

The day outside was cold and raw. He pulled the odoriferous scarf round his face and shoved his hands inside his pockets. They throbbed and hurt, but the pain, the glorious pain of them, was a comfort. It meant that they were functioning. He followed her meekly as she clattered downstairs from the attic, swept into the road and hailed a taxi. The driver slowed and listened to her crisp instructions to take them to the Strand, wondering, as he pulled away, what such a woman was doing with such a man. Maybe even a man down on his luck could afford a hooker these days. The cab seemed to smell of smoke. Woodsmoke and paraffin, overlaid with soap, and the high-class tart threading a daisy through the top buttonhole of her coat as if the faded thing was made of gold.

'Hurry, Cannon, please hurry,' she was saying, pushing him out first, proffering towards the cab driver a note that was far too much and a radiant smile that made him, sour though he was, smile back. 'Stop *sulking*, Cannon. I tell you what,' she continued, '*smile* at the buggers. Mesmerise them . . .'

Obediently Cannon sustained his smile as they sidled past
Security, where Miss Sarah Fortune's evident familiarity shortened the process of bag searching, to which she still submitted
with a brief exchange of banter. She towed him through behind
her, although their gaze followed him with jealous suspicion.
Briefly. The High Courts of Justice were well accustomed to
eccentrics and at least this one was wearing clothes. An unnecessary number of clothes.

It was important to be on time for Master Ralph, but also
pointless because the appointment schedule never ran to order,
usually erring on the side of lateness but very occasionally, the
opposite. Sarah Fortune, solicitor of the Supreme Court in what
her employers, Matthewson and Co., described as her spare
time, knew these corridors well but, in common with half a million habitués, never quite conquered the unmasterable
procedure. It was a place where unhelpfulness was an art form
perfected into a refinement of itself. The Masters dealt with the
dull preliminary business of civil litigation. Cannon was before
the court to be reminded of his obligations and Sarah, who
hated this establishment with as much hatred as she could
muster, was determined to enjoy it for once. She was good at
enjoyment.

Another surreptitious cigarette. The woman from the Crown
Prosecution Service, who arrived to demand the immediate exe-
cution of the confiscation order against Walter James Smith,
better known as Cannon, criminal manqué of this and larger
parishes, was highly amenable; in other words, nice. A lame
enough word, for a civil servant with a civic duty often executed,
as Sarah knew, with a rigour bearing on the ruthless. *Nice*, in
Sarah's courtroom vernacular, meant approachable, reasonable,
articulate, lacking in messianic zeal as well as egotism, and
having the perfectly reasonable attitude of wanting to get out of
these Gothic halls as soon as possible. Sarah knew that half the
art of all this ritualistic confrontation was common sense and the
achievement of a dialogue with the opposition. Get it down to
basics. The Crown wanted immediate possession of Cannon's

house, and that was for starters. They wanted it on the basis that it was an asset accumulated from the proceeds of crime and that although Cannon had served his sentence for the crimes it was not the same thing as paying his debts.

Cannon took a seat on the uncomfortable bench. He did not look like a criminal as much as like an outmoded anarchist of a vaguely Middle European school. He was still smiling, content to sit with his arms crossed, hands still in gloves, surveying the scene. 'Do you think', Helen West said to Sarah Fortune, each of them greeting the other with the kind of mutual recognition and liking it was natural to disguise from their clients, in case amity was seen as complicity, 'that you could get him to stop doing that? I'm so afraid his face might get frozen, like a salesman.'

'He does something with his jaw,' Sarah muttered. 'And he's very proud of his teeth. He can keep up that smile for hours. I can't control it.'

'Oh, yes, you can. His coat smells. Did you arrange that, too?'

They were in a line for Master Ralph. Some litigants could spend a while in there, while others were spat out with all the ceremony of phlegm. Sarah did not want a conflict with Helen West, not when she held all the cards and a client who was unpunishable by law because he was, for the law's purposes only, as mad as a snake. Helen West was wincing, not paying attention to any kind of portentous news, feeling her jaw, pinching it with the spread fingers of her capable-looking right hand, as if pressure alone would stop it hurting. 'Bloody tooth. Hurts like hell. Sorry.'

'Nurofen?'

'I want my head cut off. I've had every damn thing done to this damn tooth. Still hurts. Look, give me a break. Just get him to sign over his house as part payment of his bloody debts. Then we'll all be happy. I don't understand why he delays.'

'He wasn't living in it and it was never really his,' Sarah murmured, rooting in her handbag for pills.

'Never *his*? Like he never made any money? Oh, yes? They all say that.'

'He grew up in Belfast, you see. Making bombs was play-time . . . His brother—'

'Nobody's saying he's a terrorist. Simply a destructive exploiter of knowledge. What kind of excuse is that for selling the stuff? What does your client *want* out of life?'

'Babies. He's crazy for a baby. Got a good dentist, have you?'

'Not if you judge by this.'

'Look; about the house . . .'

The queue before them seemed to dissolve. An angry posse marched out, arguing and blaming. Then they were in, Cannon hanging back like a tail and Helen West hissing, Why did you have to bring *him*? Does he ever stop smiling? and Sarah felt a moment of sincere regret.

Master Ralph was a disappointed man, who found the incessant struggle to administer decisions to the ignorant inside a room that resembled a dungeon with a high ceiling too much of a challenge, even before the realisation that every person who came before him was less informed than he and always would be. Every legal *ingénue* went this route until they were old enough to send someone else, leaving him to witness an endless parade of inexperience, all wanting something they could not have. It was not the iron that had entered his soul, but rust.

'I appear for the Crown,' said Helen West in her quiet and authoritative voice. 'The Master is familiar with this case.' Out of the corner of her eye, she had the vague impression that Sarah Fortune and plain Master Ralph had actually *winked* at one another. Master Ralph was suddenly uncharacteristically cheerful.

'Mr Cannon has been concerned in the illegal manufacture of explosives. He has been convicted of unlicensed supply to the building trade and others, served a sentence, and all that is history. Since he profited from this, the Crown wants his money. You have all these facts, sir, from previous appearances. Mr Cannon, otherwise known as Smith, was in business with his twin brother but, alas, they are not alike. Under the cover of his brother's respectable property development and building industry, *this* Mr Smith diversified into the manufacture of explosives. He was an expert for hire to the worst end of the trade, because he *liked* it. He would have been an asset to the Army. He also used the legitimate business to capitalise himself with a property and, we suspect, valuable paintings, by effectively stealing from his brother's business. Mr Smith, Cannon, considers himself an *artist*.'

'He *is* an artist,' Sarah mumbled. 'A *framed* artist.'

'Did my learned friend say something?'

'I heard nothing,' Master Ralph said. 'Go on, Miss West.'

She went on, 'The only asset we have been able to trace is his house in Langdale Crescent. We want that house. This hearing is purely about that house. The other money we must pursue as best we can. But Mr Smith – Cannon – has agreed he owes us the house. *When* he finds the deeds and chooses to leave it.' Here, Helen West gave a look of disapproval to Sarah Fortune. 'Mr Cannon has asked for an adjournment of the order. He is, of course, quite consistent in such a request. As he would be.' She grimaced, a brief illumination of currently pale, beautiful features.

Sarah rose to her feet. Hers was an infectious grin. 'On the contrary, sir, my client has seen the sweet light of reason. My client no longer wishes to adjourn the issue. The only reason he's delayed with the handing over of the deeds is because he could not find them. They were not in his hands. He did not *live* in the house. The Crown is welcome to the house. What's left of it.' She sat.

The Master raised his hand for silence and began to examine the documents in front of him, the better, it seemed, to delay the disappearance of anyone who could formulate a sentence. He glanced up from time to time, enjoying the view.

'What do you mean,' Helen muttered, 'what's left of it?'

Silently, Sarah handed her a Polaroid photograph. Helen fumbled for her glasses. 'That's *his* house?'

The photo showed a ruin, one quarter of a house clinging precariously to the end of a crescent. The most prominent feature was the stairwell, with a bath balanced on the top step. There was something so entirely ludicrous about it, like a surreal painting, that Helen began to laugh. Mirth inside the Master's room was as dangerous as laughter at a funeral. It became infectious, subversive, travelled round the body like a missile, rapidly out of control, ready to emerge as a noise more animal than human. Then both women were half double, making small weepy sounds, like puppies, and for some unfathomable reason, without even knowing the joke, Master Ralph joined in.

'Look,' said Sarah Fortune, on the steps to the high court. 'You can't go back to work like this. I know a fantastic dentist. If I phone him, he'll see you straight away, I'm sure he will.'

'No, thank you. It's gone. Well, it's gone for now. I need a dentist who copes with hysteria. I'm terrified. As soon as pain goes, I find an excuse . . . And it's gone. Well, it's gone for now. Where is he, this dentist?'

Sarah jerked her head in Cannon's direction. 'A dentist who can cope with Cannon can cope with anyone. Wimpole Street.'

'Can't afford it.'

'Oh, it's not too ruinous. Although it has to be said,' Sarah added in confidential tones, 'it *is* far cheaper if you sleep with him.'

Helen was not entirely sure she had heard correctly: she was dizzy with the end of the pain. She took the offered card, watched Sarah Fortune summon her client with an imperious wave, received the last blessing of that wide, outrageous smile and realised, once they were out of sight, how she had failed to record details of W. J. Cannon's current address. Yes, he was an artist; she remembered that. An almost incredible combination, but at his trial he had sketched them all, capturing their likenesses with uncanny flair. A man transfixed between opposing urges to create and destroy; a thief who probably made explosives for other thieves, stole from a twin brother, and even the gaolers liked him. Married to a wife who was going to reform him, common enough mitigation, speciously received. They all said that. She remembered more. He had looked different then.

There'd been a suicide attempt in prison, so why did he look so much better three months out from two years inside? She gazed after them. That was the difference. That smile. His teeth. She did not want to think about teeth and she did not want to go to the dentist. She would wait, like a fool, until the next time.

Cold outside. Warm within. A morning of contrasts. A garret; a courtroom; an office.

I am lord of all I survey, Ernest Matthewson told himself each morning when he passed the plaque bearing his name on the office wall, knowing each time he said it that it was a lie. He was merely an ageing senior partner in the monolith that had grown from the microcosm of his once modest legal practice and he did not really control anything. He could not control the staff or their relationships; he could no longer control the character of the clients, and he often reflected how the firm provided unique opportunities for the wrong people to meet each other in some-times advantageous, sometimes poisonous ways. One tried to *choose* the clients, but he no longer knew who they were and could only remember the nastier ones between the many. Charles Tysall, who had stalked and hurt Sarah; Ernest would always feel guilty about that. John Smith, the builder without manners he had passed on to ambitious Andrew Mitchum; clients with nameless needs, not always legal. Useless clients, ungrateful clients and barking-mad clients, who seemed to suit Sarah.

'Are you back? Oh, there you are. Do sit down.'

These days, Ernest Matthewson adopted an elaborate for-mality with Sarah Fortune. It had come upon him like a cloud, this awkwardness, and he could not shake it off, a mixture of artificial reserve replacing the easy friendship and slightly naughty camaraderie of old, which he missed but could not resume – as if someone had told him she was subject to fits and he was waiting all the time for one to happen. Or as if he knew how she knew his weaknesses and his vanities and he could not forgive either her tolerance or her affection which, once faced

FRANCES FYFIELD

with his coldness, simply incorporated it and behaved with the same good nature. Sarah's a good woman, his wife said, again and again, a *good* woman with a big heart, and she only makes you feel guilty. Ernest was neither analytical nor introspective. Questioning his own motives was anathema. Ah, yes, the firm was a network all right, like an unruly family drawing to its bosom, via the children, a number of unsuitable friends. Sarah had once been more like a daughter during her year-long affair with his own son, Malcolm. Such hopes Mrs Matthewson had had then, but Sarah was like a fish refusing to be caught and he was aware that he had been punishing her ever since.

Now, he simply told himself, this was the promiscuous gal who had thrown over his boy, thereby catapulting *his* wife into an orgy of recriminatory disappointment. As an excuse for a retreat into behaviour that would have suited someone inter-viewing an upstart applicant for the wrong job, it was adequate.

There was more to it than that, as they both knew. She was totally unfit for her purpose, for a start. She never had cared a toss about the practice of the law, although after her fashion she was genuinely good at it. Totally irresponsible in the commercial sense. Couldn't give a fuck, he growled (aware, even as he for-mulated the word, of Mrs Matthewson's strictures about bad language). She was immune to lectures, annual reports, training courses on the equation of time spent per hour to cost, and all that invaluable kind of thing, and although he was not fond of modern management systems either, at least he had always had the knack of charging the client until the pips squeaked and making it look convincing. The endless committees that ruled the life of the firm never voted Miss Fortune into partnership, but whenever her severance was suggested there was always this strange reluctance to act on it. She filled a gap: she took on the duffers, the no-hope clients related to other clients; the ones who wanted a spot of divorce or litigation so that they could get on with the business of making money. Clients who had once been rich. The children of clients. Clients they were not supposed to turn away without taking the risk of losing other clients and appearing to have no soul. Nobody knew where she got her clients: she seemed to find them herself and they came by the back door. For absorbing the misfits, Sarah was allowed a generous enough salary, unless it was compared to the partnership Turks – and how Sarah Fortune, glamorous widow, justified her existence remained a mystery.

She had recovered completely from past traumas, he told himself. None of it was *his* fault. She was decorative – that much was universally conceded: small, slim, agile up those stairs, watchable, without being classically beautiful. All the men felt better for seeing her around. The women looked out to see what she was wearing today. Ernest's wife often asked him wistfully to report on it. He suspected they were still friends, talking about him behind his back, but he could not prove it, and it infuriated him. Women were the devil for secrets.

'Are you well?' he asked formally.

'Never better.'

Court gear with a bit of pizzazz, he'd tell Mrs Matthewson, the way he would tell her every single detail of his day, especially if she asked. He was observant about women's clothes. Not exactly a black suit, he would say, but a sort of soft charcoal, with a long loose jacket over a gored skirt, which swung round her ankles. Cream shirt . . . Why does she always have them buttoned so high up her neck? But an old thing, antique even, with tiny buttons matching the pearls. And a belt? Mrs Matthewson would ask eagerly, waiting for Ernest to shut his eyes and remember. Ah, yes, grey again, but darker, velvet, I think. Broad belt: her waist is tiny.

She stood in front of his desk with her hands thrust into the pockets of the unstructured jacket, oblivious of his attempts to record the design. He would see it again, of course: she was artful with clothes (she was artful anyway); it would appear in several guises over trousers, over a short, straight skirt with a nice length of leg and, yes, he looked forward to that.

'Do sit down,' he repeated, the sound of his parlourmaid voice making him cringe, but there was nothing he could do about it. He loved and missed her in a way that made anything else impossible; but, by God, for all sorts of reasons she would have made a terrible daughter-in-law: flouting the rules, both moral and social, was all very well, but not with one of his own.

She sat. Elegantly, of course, leaning back into the chair with her arm over the back, legs crossed under the fluid skirt, at ease, cigarette lit. Useless to remind her about the no-smoking zone. They had been that route before. Oh, Lord, he wished he was not fond of her. Sarah, for God's sake, help me out, was what he wanted to say. I'm a half-way redundant old man in a firm that has outgrown me and I need you to act as my protector, the way you do for everyone else.

'How did you get on with Cannon? Our artist?' he added sarcastically, suddenly remembering that obscure and disastrous client. Where *had* she got *him* from? God alone knew. *She* said *he* had seen the name of the firm on headed paper on a relative's desk and come along by chance because he knew no other lawyers, had been sent upstairs because he was scruffy. A feasible but unfortunate explanation. They did not normally deal with criminals, unless purely the white-collar kind.

'Oh, fine. Someone blew his house up.'

'Oh.' Sarah had this tendency to exaggerate; you couldn't believe a thing she said.

'And the opposition had toothache and the Master got the giggles,' she added.

He was lost, so stuck to his own agenda, changing the subject, not daring to say, You know what you should do with Cannon? *Dump him.* Dump him like you dumped my son, only I don't understand why we all still love you. Instead, 'Still househunting, are you?'

'Yes, of course.'

'We've a new project,' he announced briskly, after coughing and clearing his throat. 'Every other leading London legal firm is doing it, so we have to do it too. Get an art collection.'

As a change of topic, this took some beating. She shook her

head to clear her face of incredulity. 'This firm wants to collect *art*? For what?'

'Not wants, Sarah. Needs. Helps raise our profile in places where—'

'Rich corporations go in order to raise theirs,' she finished for him crisply, rallying faster than a Centre Court tennis player.

He nodded. 'Part of the image, you see. Doing our bit. We get a few dozen paintings, maybe the odd sculpture or two. Decorate the foyer. Place looks like an empty cricket pitch with walls, anyway. Then we put them on show, oh, wherever these things go on show. Our logo all over the place, of course. It was these Japanese chaps started, buying *Sunflowers*. Hopefully we make money on our investment at the end of the day. But we can't have things like that man with his dead sheep in tanks. None of the partners knows the first thing – and none of them has got time. So we thought . . . you.'

She laughed. Another reason why they could never bring themselves to get rid of her. This easy, non-contemptuous laughter that embraced them all, without ever accepting the ethic of any one of them. A potential blackmailer, too, of course.

'Is there a theme to this collection?' she asked. 'I am not, emphatically not, going out in search of stags at bay in Scottish Highlands. Or dogs on cushions.'

Personally, Ernest liked the idea of anything featuring food, especially if it was going to include dead game ready for the pot, but he shook his head, then changed it to a nod. The worst was over. She had not said no, or told him he was being ridiculous.

'Investment pictures. Modern art, but not too obscure, right? Why don't you just go to one of the reputable dealers?' she asked.

'Bunch of charlatans. Take huge commissions. Besides, *you're* artistic. Only another mug's game, isn't it? You just swot up on it and away you go. Why pay anyone else?' There was the implied suggestion that Sarah was already paid too much. A slight threat, *Do this, or else* . . . He nodded, agreeing with his own wisdom. Nodding had become habitual. He tried to make it look wise rather than foolish.

'What's the budget and the time-scale? Do I have complete freedom?' Now she was going too fast for him, as usual.

'Oh, a few weeks at least . . .'

'Yes. I'll do it. Three dozen. But I will, of course, need time out of the office. More than usual. I'll have to go to all the exhibitions, scout round dealers, that sort of thing. Time-consuming. Ernest darling, what ails you? Talk to me, please.'

'The budget's generous, Sarah. We've to prove we aren't a bunch of Philistines. Get out of here, will you? Just go.'

She went. Uncurled those slender limbs without a word, and went. It was only after the door began to close behind her that he remembered he had meant to enquire what else she had done with the morning. Without adding the question he never asked – namely, whose bed had she left before she began? Her own?

'Oh, Sarah, one more thing . . .'

'Yes?'

'You've got to get rid of that ridiculous Mr Cannon. Where did you get him from anyway? We simply cannot subsidise our clients. We *can't*.'

She paused delicately, hand on hip. 'Oh, I don't think so, do you? He's a very knowledgeable artist. He'll help with the collection. He'll be an unpaid consultant, and where do you ever find those?'

The door closed softly. Ernest remembered a stray piece of information. The child had grown up in a convent. She could be vigorously clumsy, noisy, ebullient, and yet oh-so-silent. Even when she had the last word. He put his head in his hands and groaned.

Miss Fortune climbed the stairs to her office, which was a very small place as befitted her almost itinerant status, and a pretty cluttered space in accordance with the way she was. The services of a secretary had been withdrawn. Yesterday's flowers still looked fresh, but the rug on the floor was crumpled, showing signs of intruders. People stole into Sarah's room, sometimes to weep, avoid the open-plan, or sleep off the hangover. Space was at a premium in Matthewson's firm, while privacy was even harder to find. Which, of course, made it all the more ridiculous that they should have such a large foyer as proof of prosperity. The shop-front, like a marble cave, long, narrow and high, a perfectly natural art gallery, the rest a custom-built warren. She sat, yawned and stretched. Got up, closed the window, prowled around the room, which took a matter of seconds. Felt, although she had only just come in, the same old claustrophobia and the desire to be anywhere else. Looked longingly at the envelope full of estate agents' particulars. Pulled a face at herself in the tiny mirror by the door. How the hell, she asked her reflection, did God and man between them ever make a lawyer out of you? Because if it wasn't by divine intervention, it was otherwise a miracle of misjudgement.

She smoothed out the charred fragment of letter given her by Cannon. He had told her what the rest of it contained; she had to take his word for it as she struggled to read the remainder.

> . . . *rotting away. I tell you what, if you can keep this up*
> *until Christmas, I promise I'll leave her alone. Promise. Let's*
> *see who finds who first, shall we? But you won't keep it up.*
> *You'll get careless. You'll realize what's* GOOD *for you . . .*

Cannon said he believed this promise, and she had to believe Cannon. Someone must. She yanked open the neck of the blouse. Fingered a small, white scar on her clavicle. There were others spread over her torso and arms and, just at that moment, she felt a strange pride. She *had* taken a look at Cannon's portrait, and he had not noticed the scars. No one did. She was proud of that. It was as though they had disappeared. Little white scars, pieces of history. The work of a *client*. One of Matthewson's *better* clients, which was why it was odd that he should be so fussy about the rest. It was not as if they were saints employed to deal with sinners.

Nothing mattered now, except loyalty.

The door opened and a young man sidled in. Sarah stifled a sigh. A reputation for a sympathetic ear and a room that doubled as a haven for frustrated smokers was not always an advantage, attracting as it did not only the gossipers, the jokers and the anxious, but also the others. There was no such thing as a legal firm consisting entirely of nice people; there were always the sedulous, the ambitious and the jealous. Andrew Mitchum entered the room as if he owned it, sat without invitation, lit his cigarette and looked round with lazy appreciation. He coveted this room.

'You'll never guess who I had dinner with at the weekend,' he drawled.

'Jamie Lee Curtis?'

'Ugh! Darling, how could you? Why waste my time on trash like that? Prince William, more like. No, he's too young for money either. I only dine with clients.'

'Who, then?' She was watching a grasping young man, verging on the theatrical in a less than attractive way, convinced he was God's gift to both sexes while clearly preferring his own. The stories of his conquests bored her, but she was not going to say so. Instead she smiled encouragingly.

'John Smith. Our mysterious Mr Smith. He with all the houses. My God, you should see *his*. Vulgar, my dear, beyond belief.'

She kept her face clear of all reaction but polite, impressed curiosity. 'Oh, and what did he want? Another acquisition?'

Andrew Mitchum wagged his finger. 'Secret,' he said teasingly. 'A little extracurricular activity is all. Wants me to do a bit of research for him.' His eyes took in the pictures on the walls, yesterday's flowers, the heavy blue ashtray, with indiscreet approval. 'I'm good at research,' he added modestly. 'I've found out quite a few things about *you*, for instance. Such an interesting life.' He sat back and scrutinised her with frank, asexual curiosity, watching the anxiety flicker over her face to be replaced with an even wider smile.

'Not a lot to know, Andrew.'

'No? I don't understand you. All you had to do was marry the boss's son and you would have been a partner. What stopped you? Ah, I know. A penchant for the wrong kind of man and entirely the wrong kind of client, I gather. You were the one Charles Tysall fell for, and when you wouldn't have him he beat you up, right? Tut, tut. No ambition. The man was as rich as Croesus.'

'A long time ago, Andrew. Another country. And he's dead.'

She was relieved that that was all he wanted to impart; equally relieved that he was so dismissive of her clients. She did not want him examining their identities and seeing any connection between her waifs and strays and his moneyed men; far better that he should be as contemptuous as he was. His ambition was not distracted by imagination. He fingered his immaculate tie, unembarrassed by the silence.

'So what *are* you doing for John Smith? Screwing him?'

'If only. The dinner was wonderful, but he doesn't seem interested in food.'

If there were more to tell, he would tell it. He would not be able to resist. Ernest had hired this boy but, then, Ernest's judgement was not always sound.

'I suppose having been attacked yourself is what gives you sympathy with all your dozy victims?' he said, without really expecting a serious answer.

'No,' she said, rising to open the window and wishing he would go. 'Not always. Look, Andrew, take a tip. Do *not* take money from John Smith for this *research*. Everything you do for John Smith has to go through the firm's accounts. You might think Ernest's a woolly old buzzard, but if there's any hint you're raking in a personal cash profit you'll be out on your ear. *Finito*. End of career.'

'Oh, ho, ho, occupying the moral high ground, are we? From what I hear, that's not like you, Sarah, really it isn't.'

'Oh, yes, it is. Sometimes,' she added demurely, smiling again to defuse the malice in his tone. 'Are you staying for coffee or are you going out to make money?' She fumbled in the top drawer of her desk and handed him a red apple, slightly dusty. 'Want one? They're good for you. The man on the corner . . .'

He looked at the mess of letters on her desk, mixed in with estate agents' particulars, the arm outstretched with the apple. 'Eve offered Adam an *apple*, Miss F. I suppose some poor version of Adam offered the same sort of thing to you. Pity about you, Sarah. You could have had it all. What do you want?'

'A house with lots of white walls,' she said, and sank her teeth in the fruit.

White. Should be the favourite colour of a dentist like me, William thought. But white, my boy, is a non-colour, a state of nothing, a mixer. White is never white: it is either white mixed with yellow or brown, or bloodstained pink; skin is never white, it is multicoloured; white is never pure, it is muddy or creamy or tinged with grey. Or, at least, it was when it came to teeth.

He paused, paintbrush in hand, about to advance on the last wall of the waiting room. What colour, then, if he was aspiring to match their teeth? Make them feel at home when they saw their own teeth in a monitor. For God's sake, paint the place white with a hint of apple green. He paused. Isabella, his ex-wife, would loathe this colour and the thought exhilarated him, although he still wanted her approval. Isabella, the stuff of dreams and nightmares, probably at this very minute examining some new abode with her new, second-hand lover. Isabella, met all those years before in the curtain-material department of John Lewis, he confused by choice, she revelling in it. Houseproud Isabella, to whom the pursuit of perfection indoors was a kind of holy grail. A frustrated designer, a design snob, but what a series of cocoons she had made for them. White shaded green? *Dated, yughh!*

There was one small alcove to go. He continued with the off-white apple green, humming . . . droning, since his voice could never hold a tune, any more than his hands could have played a fiddle, or done one of the many things he had once aspired to do. They were pretty hands, his mother had told him, the exact opposite to the way a surgeon's hands were supposed to be. Splayed, to be honest. Short-fingered with a broad span and no arthritis, every damn finger working with an individual dexterity, capable-looking hands. His were the elegant, long-fingered things of a woman whispering behind a fan. His hands, with a permanent tendency to irritation, fungus, fast-growing nails and a dislike of any chemical, were currently enclosed in gardening gloves with rubber gloves beneath, and it was quite insane for a Wimpole Street dentist, with a practice surely lucrative enough to get someone else to do it, to be painting his own public rooms. The private rooms, both above and below, were ignored; they were beyond aesthetic redemption anyway. Why, then, William, why? he droned. Because you're an ass; the prosperity is all on the surface and, let's face it, you have nothing active left to do when everyone has gone home. And you are fascinated by the technique of it . . . and, besides, everyone else makes such a devil of a mess.

The doors would have to remain wood-coloured doors. There were too many doors and too many locks. He liked the arrangement. Reception desk by outer door; short corridor to large waiting room; surgery off that, with another damn door opening to reveal not the immediacy of the surgical area and the chair but another little seating area for consultation to the left, out of sight of the door. A non-threatening view.

He tried to whistle. What emerged was a breathy, piping sound, unrecognisable as the tune that had been going round in his head all day. 'All things bright and beautiful, All creatures great and small . . .' Such a well-known hymn, coming out of the blue to irritate. As far as his patients were concerned, all things bright and beautiful meant nothing more than teeth.

He finished and took the paintpots and the brushes into the bathroom, which was beyond the reception room and flanking the surgery. *Yes*, he had made it nice, this public part of the whole damn thing. What always amazed him was the way the patients always asked permission to use the lavatory when it was clearly marked, not in a dozen languages, perhaps, but quite evident for what it was, and the notion that he would want any of them sitting on his chair with a full bladder was so extraordinary that it made him shake his head. The bathroom, too, was filled with paintings. Perhaps that put them off; in which case, too bad. Pictures stayed.

On his way out of the bathroom, he detoured into the surgery. White upon white. There was something perfectly appalling about a surgery with no one in it, like a car park without cars. It had all the impersonality of a laboratory. The chair at lowered level, the machinery on a swing, far out of reach, his chair, with back-rest, crouching beside it, the footpad ready for his feet. No one there, and yet it all looked alive. Blue and white in here. Nothing superfluous. All of it chemically scrubbed. Cupboards full of equipment, as little on show as possible; no labels. Everything in sterile packages hidden from view, as much for the sake of hygiene as for fear of causing alarm. The place had been made to look like a high-tech kitchen display in a shop window, not exactly inviting, but efficient, at least, with the implied promise that there would never be any mess, spillages, stains, the distinctive burning smell of dentine dust, or failures.

William sat in his patients' chair. It was an eccentric habit of his to do this when the place was empty, and made his assistant feel uneasy if she caught him at it first thing in the morning, but he did it often enough. It was important, he told Tina, to keep on reminding himself of what the patient could see from this chair, and whether the view could be improved. There had been a series of soothing pictures on the far wall, limpid watercolour scenes featuring very blue water, until Tina had tartly reminded him that what the patient in the chair watched, as often as not, was the arc-light, until the name of the manufacturer, Siemens, was emblazoned on their eyeballs. She suggested, in her youthful and heartless fashion, that he put goggles on the patients and be done with it. Then they would see nothing and he would not have to bother about the view. No, he told her. That would only have the effect of refining their concentration on what was going on inside their mouths: they needed to see so they would *hear* less.

Tina had nodded; she had the benefit of perfect teeth, a child of the fluoride age. But at least, she added, if you put them in goggles, they won't have to see what they see almost as often as they see the light. Your face, looming over them in a mask. Was it such a bad face? he wondered. Nooo, she had said doubtfully, examining it with those cornflower-blue eyes of hers, which held not a moment of doubt. It isn't your face would frighten anyone. It's the height of you. I'd stay sat down, if I were you.

No respect, that girl. Beanpole, she called him – a slight improvement on the school name, which was Telegraph. Six feet and three inches was not such an unusual height, was it? Inconvenient for canoeing, horse-riding, bicycling, certain team games he had never liked anyway, and quite an advantage among school contemporaries who would otherwise have bullied him, although it imposed the necessity of owning up to any crime because he was always so visible. It had forced him to develop a slouching stoop, which even now he found difficult to correct; nothing more than a slightly lopsided air but, he thought, at fifty plus, he was used to it. Ah, he thought, oh, please, never let me see myself the way other people do. Let us all be spared that.

He was tired, but not tired enough. He supposed a good night's sleep in a dentist's chair was possible, although it was difficult to imagine anyone wanting to try it. People lay in it under sedation happily enough. It was an awful thought, that the only time patients looked serene was when they were deep asleep. Not anaesthetised, but slumbering without memory. It was then that they sometimes made pathetic efforts to co-operate and even to join in any conversation. It was then, instruments allowing, they muttered about their deepest preoccupations.

William left the chair rapidly, and hit his head lightly on the overhead gantry, which reminded him of one of his first mistakes in the early days of practice. 'Right, you can get up now,' he would command gaily, only to have the poor sap stand and hit the equipment, or trip over something else on their grateful way to the door. All exit and entrance paths must remain clear, even if they were not in a straight line, as his were not. If only the patients knew how much trouble he took, maybe they would loathe him less. No, they wouldn't.

He had moved to the bathroom. Green paint dripped beneath the tap. 'All things bright and beautiful . . . all molars great and small.' He felt the same thing when *he* went to the dentist. A defensive fear, as if the man *meant* him harm and was positively relishing the mere prospect of causing pain, giving him that wary handshake he might have afforded a self-confessed sadist, telling him immediately how much he hated being there, just in case the man did not know – the way his patients did to him *ad nauseam*. When the causing of pain was unavoidable, it drained him; on those rare occasions, it was excruciating. He dreaded it as much as the patient. It made him sleepless and hyperactive, like now, as he painted the walls green in the hope that it would never happen again. But it would. He could not wish pain on any living thing. Except *her*, except Isabella, and then it was not so much pain he wished but something else, which made him profoundly ashamed.

The whiteness of the room, contrasting with the black panes of the night, made him dizzy. It was a bad habit of the time of year to make the light so short and the nights so long. Christmas was beginning to look like a blot on the horizon.

The flash of the orange silk flowers in the waiting room reminded him. The flash of fireworks and red hair. William picked up the phone, dialled and, when she answered, felt a grin creeping across his face. 'Sarah! Why aren't you here?'

'Because I'm here, silly. How are you?'

'A bit low. Nothing too bad. Half-way down the pit, or half-way up, whichever way you look at it.'

'Half-way up, I would. Light at the top. Has that bitch been in again?'

'Nope. She's due tomorrow.'

'Tell her to get lost.'

'I can't. I just can't. You know I can't. Look, are you busy?'

'Never. Can you come over?'

'I thought you'd never ask. With my toothbrush?'

'Behave like a good boy. Yes.'

'Fine. About half an hour? Look . . . It was you by that bonfire last week, wasn't it? You and Cannon?'

There was a long, unembarrassed pause. 'What *bonfire*?'

And that, he supposed, would enter into the file of things they did not talk about.

CHAPTER TWO

'Lady in red,' Sarah yelled along with the radio, turned high to give her the gist of the tune over the sound of the vacuum-cleaner while she improvised the words.

'You're so perfect *tonite* . . . forgive me please . . . you have no knees, but that's *all right* . . .' She gulped the first gulp of wine and grimaced as she put it down – there was something odd about the taste. Slowly, she took another glass and polished it with a paper towel. The music was nicely relentless. 'Love the one you're with, love the one you're with,' she hummed, then stared at the glass. Filthy.

If she were a good housekeeper, there would be no need for this occasional and frenetic activity. *If* she were the kind of person who could host a party without looking round in a panic for the exit . . . *if* she had enough sense of the future even to take the risk of keeping a cat, she would be calm and collected, as quiet a closer of doors as she was in public. She knew she would never be able to keep a cat: they would have too much in common. Malcolm Cook had told her that on the day they had parted. She remembered him with regret. But I would never be catty enough to use my flawed good looks as a passport to a new billet if I was fed up with the old, would I? she hummed. That's the difference. I'd just go, starve or not. And who would take me in, covered in scars, like a feline with fleas, unsuitable for human devotion even if I were fun enough to stroke for a while? I did love you, Malcolm, but you didn't *like* me and, besides, I'm congenitally incapable of living happily in a pair. Leaves no room for other loyalties. *Love the one you're with.*

Find the life that suits. Like whoever you want.

Enough wine, as always, even if the glasses were dusty. There was rarely enough food. '*Yesterday!*' she bellowed to the music. 'I don't believe . . .' She pounced. Yes! A result! Two pound coins under the overturned cushion even before she had thumped it. Life was rich. She was perfectly comfortable living alone with her inexplicable devotions and equally eccentric retinue of lovers. Liking was more important than loving. She seemed to have turned into a bit of a gipsy, encumbered with a small mortgage and very little else, her ambitions lessening with each succeeding year. She wanted the flat with the white walls, and the freedom to be untidy in her life as well as in her own home. How else would she ever find the surprising coins behind the cushions and revel in the enjoyment of strangers?

Looking upon herself as an outsider, she decided she lived not only in an unconventional moral zone but also in a cultural vacuum. That much was clear from her taste in music. She scarcely knew Beethoven from Bach, and the omission had never yet cost her a sleepless night. She knew Thackeray from Trollope, since reading was a passion, and as for fine arts, she could certainly tell Rembrandt from Renoir and Degas from Van Gogh. He was the one who cut off his ear.

Her apartment was full of pictures. She would say, glibly, that this was another result of the vacuum of the soul or possibly the avoidance of any other decision about interior design, and because things hung on walls were less likely to get broken. The mirror had been an exception, and she did not think about the mirror.

Except sometimes. The old mirror had been smashed by Charles Tysall, a man in pursuit of perfection, disgusted to find it did not exist in her. He had broken the mirror into tiny pieces and forced her to lie among the shards. Life had begun after

surviving that: she had never since experienced the luxury of
hatred – not even for him when she encountered him again,
pathetic creature he had been by then. Neither did she pursue
perfection, but delighted in its non-existence. She was in love
with flaws.

As it was, the two large rooms and the smaller bedroom had
enough pictures to furnish a gallery, provided the owner had
taste as varied as hers. Paintings were acquired with zest and
compulsion, sometimes in unusual places, some thrust upon her
in payment of a debt, some purchased out of pity; and on the
basis of this highly random selection, which spread into her
office, Ernest Matthewson had come to the conclusion that she
was artistic. He should have known also that, although her eye
was good, she never bought anything for investment and she was
hardly discriminating about anything. Not a fussy person.
Unlike the patient of William's who had brought them into contact in the first place. William, another back-door client,
introduced on the recommendation of a friend and all because
of a girl with porcelain veneers who was suing him because,
infuriatingly, the veneered teeth glowed a different shade of
white in certain nightclub lights. Sarah had settled that case
fairly rapidly by the simple expedient of finding the plaintiff and
getting her drunk enough to confess a life history of similar legal
pursuits featuring plastic surgeons and hairdressers. Ruthless,
perhaps, but vanity was not, in Sarah's view, a matter for litigation. It was a matter for you and your mirror. Meeting William
had been timely. She hadn't had her teeth checked for years
before that, and she *liked* William.

She crossed the living room to the open French windows,
and looked out across the green from the tiny balcony. This
was the best feature of the place she was seeking to leave – with
a degree of regret, even though movement and upheaval came
naturally. It was a nice flat, but it was not home; it never could
be home after that broken mirror; she felt like an alien in it and
the urge to find *home* had become a mission. You had to take a
robust view of interior decoration when you had seen your

walls spattered with your own blood; you covered the new paint with pictures to remind you of other vistas and other lives. Or you did if you were *frivolous*, she told herself, repeating one of Matthewson's favourite accusations, echoed by his son. *Deeply frivolous*, she told him. Dedicated to it; life is far too short to be taken seriously. All those pictures on the walls, though. When she took them down, the place would look as if someone had been round with a machine-gun.

The dark was soft and damp. Across the narrow stretch of grass, she could see and hear the noise of the road. A figure moved between the shrubs. She wanted to shout a warning. It was dangerous out there. So dangerous there was no longer any point in being afraid. Not for herself anyway. Not any more. She had become fearless ever since all her fears for herself had become transferable into fear for others. She owed Charles Tysall that liberation. He had thrown her a kind of death, but it was he who had died; she was alive.

'William,' she called. 'Don't just stand there. *Do* something. Come in from the cold.'

He knew what he would find. Warmth. Pictures and a fire, handsome objects frayed at the edges as if they had all been rescued or recycled rather than purchased new. Always something broken, as if she could never quite preserve anything fragile in its entirety; always something so old it would no longer function without brute force. A lamp that required dismantling to change the bulb; a door with a non-turning handle in pieces; a tap in need of a washer. William was not sure if she failed to notice these things or attempted to mend and repair with such haphazard abandon that the task could never be complete. It was a contrast to all of the many abodes he had ever shared with Isabella; he was not entirely sure he liked it and he knew, with slight satisfaction, that Isabella would *hate* it. Things should *function*. Always assemble your tools before you start, he scolded. Make sure you have what you need. Look: it's easy. Do as I do. Before the patient arrives, I have a tray of equipment

ready, sterilised and waiting. You don't have a single tool that
works.

A foolish little lecture, because he did not really want Sarah to
be proficient in that way. There was nothing he liked better than
fixing things and, in any event, his ability to do so was an essential part of their understated relationship. It was payment in kind
for what she offered; so much so that, if there was absolutely
nothing for him to do in her house, he felt profoundly disappointed. He owed her rather more than a discount on treatment
and the proper instruction on the maintenance of her near-
perfect teeth. He owed her stimulus, interest, sexual affection . . .
a number of irreplaceable things that had enriched the latest
months of his life. William disliked the sensation of being in
debt, and it was one of many reasons why he always had to put
his foot in it. Insist on redefining what they had, if not every
time, often enough. Especially if there really was absolutely *nothing* to do to ease him through his first moments of
awkwardness.

'You've got paint in your hair,' she said crisply, as soon as she
saw him at the door.

'I was painting the waiting room. I'm in excellent painting
form. I could do the kitchen in, oh, under an hour . . . I could—'

'No,' she said firmly. 'Absolutely not.'

'But it *needs* doing.'

'That', she said flatly, 'has nothing to do with anything. Sit
down and have a drink, will you please? And take off those
gloves.'

He looked down at his own long hands, saw them still encased
in surgical gloves, made a strangled sound of agonised embarrassment, which emerged as a brief yelp. He clawed at the gloves,
the wrong, cheaper kind which gave him an allergic reaction
even if they did afford protection. They tore at the palm as he
ripped them off and threw them away into the corner, where they
lay curled on the carpet, looking almost alive. She would pick them
up tomorrow, maybe.

'New dress code for travelling the underground, is it?' she teased him, pressing his hands round the bowl of a glass. There were faint bubbles in the wine. He stared at them, fascinated. 'You must have looked a little . . . odd. Over-fastidious, perhaps.'

The glass was emptied before he spoke. She had an amazing facility for silence: she seemed able to maintain either that or ceaseless chatter exactly as the mood demanded. Suddenly he felt a whole lot better, found himself smiling for no other reason than that image of himself, reading a newspaper on the train with those oh-so-obvious, not quite flesh-coloured rubber gloves, as if the print would contaminate him, and he could not bear the proximity of other kinds of dirt, humanity included, for that matter. He laughed because it might have been true.

'Must've thought I was the burglar. Ready to avoid fingerprints. Dressed to kill. Or one of those men who goes round poisoning rats. Something like that. Give me a hug, will you?'

She did. An almost all-encompassing hug, hands scratching the back of his neck the way he liked. They stayed like that for some time. He could feel the warmth of her enter his bones, struggled against it; failed. He tried to tell himself she was amoral, feckless, promiscuous, insincere on that account, untidy, dishonest, disloyal, insensitive, unkind, calculating, and knew, as he recited to himself this litany of adjectives, that he was really thinking of someone else entirely. Applying to Sarah those angry descriptions that best suited Isabella was hardly fair, although Sarah *was* amoral in a way he never cared to define and certainly untidy. She was also far more than a fair-weather friend, but still he had to ask.

'Are you *sure* there's nothing I can mend? Do you *like* me at all?'

'Oh dear,' she said, removing herself from his lap and fetching the wine. 'You *are* in a bad way.'

'No worse than usual. Better for seeing you,' he added, in an attempt at grace. She did not come to the surgery for treatment these days. She claimed to enjoy the ambience, which flattered him – although he doubted it was true – even though she had helped to create it. First, there were the additional pictures, which added something to the waiting areas; she inflamed his existing enthusiasms for collecting and made him bolder in his choices. Then there was the increased flow of patients. Sarah recommended him to everyone she knew, and Sarah knew a lot of people. Some of them were strange enough to have crawled out of very peculiar woodwork, but they were still people with teeth. And, one or two of them, people with whom he could empathise without quite understanding the process. Especially Cannon. Cannon was nicely mad; both he and Cannon had gremlins. How Sarah had organised an artist and convict into his surgery was another thing he could never quite fathom. Networking. One day his life had been normal; the next he found himself spirited into a prison to see a patient, then launched into bureaucratic obfuscation to get the patient treatment. A client in need, she had explained: Do this for me, William, *please*. You're the only dentist I know who's treated people like him before. He needs you. She wouldn't tell him much about Cannon, pleading professional confidence, but he never minded that. Cannon's treatment had been a triumph, and William was profoundly grateful for the pride it gave him. Oh, for another patient like Cannon. It might be enough to dispel the dreams of inadequacy.

'Still haunted, are we?' she asked gently, sitting away from him to light the cigarette, despite his disapproval. (They are *bad* for your teeth, Sarah darling. They inhibit the circulation and retard healing . . . accelerate periodontal disease . . . *bad* for you, wanting to say it, but admiring the precise way she smoked.)

'Yes,' he said, sighing. 'I couldn't bear another night of the same nightmares. But you told me *not* to mention her name.'

She settled onto the floor by his feet and shook her head. 'Nothing is absolutely forbidden, you know it isn't. Break me in gently. Tell me about the other nightmares first.'

Tell me again, she might have said. William's nightmares were constants, variations on a few themes with different pictures. They were the result of the pursuit of perfection and an underlying guilty conscience that would not shift, and although the recitation of the dreams had lessened considerably in the time she had known him, they saddened and irritated her because William did not deserve such afflictions. No man of such conscientious kindness deserved them, and that was why she listened. He did not deserve to remain half in love with his shallow bitch of an ex-wife either. That was a private opinion.

'Well, take last night. I woke up convinced that the hall was full of brilliant paintings, and I'd painted them all. Although, of course, I hadn't, when I came to look at them, never could have, never shall.'

She shrugged. 'You can't paint pictures when you're obsessed with *technique*.'

'Don't interrupt,' he said crossly. 'I don't *mind* about not being able to paint. I haven't minded for years. But there were three people in the hallway, looking at the paintings. They were sharpening their nails, ready to tear them to pieces and, after them, me.' He gulped the wine too fast and felt the bubbles go up his nose. 'There was that child, Adrian. You know the one I mean, the one I told you about?'

Yes, she knew.

'Pale and ill and coughing, like someone who's blocked off half a lung. That piece of amalgam I dropped down his throat locked inside his lung somewhere, and no one knowing why he was so ill. All skin and bone he was, but as for his sister, well . . .' He shuddered.

'She was the one where you *think* you took out the wrong teeth?'

'Yes.' He patted her shoulder, grateful for her recall, as if she had never heard these nightmare stories before. 'Overcrowded mouth. Had a lot of them at the time. Got the records muddled up. Didn't concentrate. Only realised what I'd done after she'd gone.'

'*Might* have done.'

'*Must* have done. Otherwise, why does she stand in the hallway in my dreams with two ugly incisors on either side of two huge gaps? Her smile was *obscene* and, really, she could have been so pretty. So beautiful. And, of course, you can guess who had brought them in to mash up the paintings and haunt me all over again? *I* couldn't trace those children, however hard I tried. But *her. She* could.'

'Your ex-wife. Who else? No doubt she was looking perfectly wonderful.'

'She was, actually. She always does.'

'William, how can you be so helpless? Why do you allow her to tease you? I never heard anything so insane. Both of you. She wrecks your confidence and betrays you and comes back for treatment, and you *let* her. Why can't you say, "*Go away*"?'

'I don't *know*. Habit, I suppose. Perhaps I really enjoy the temptation to put the drill through the roof of her mouth. Perhaps I like to think of her nicely sedated while I sew her lips together. Stitch her tongue to her back teeth to stop her talking. Wouldn't do a great deal of harm.'

Sarah rose with her usual grace. 'I think', she said, 'that even Isabella might notice something like that. I'm ordering pizza.'

The nightmares always faded into nonsense as soon as he talked about them – another thing that shamed him. It seemed to mean they might have no significance at all because they were soluble in wine, digestible with food and they never survived time with Sarah. But the night had its own inexorable, bullying pace, taking him straight back into a broken sleep, even after pizza and too little lust. Far too tired for that, hugging instead, grateful for her body smelling of clean cotton, curled against his in a neat fit. Grateful for being accepted without demands or criticism, nothing but affection, which always felt exclusive at the time. That was what saved him from the trouble of having to think about love and all its strictures.

Of course he did not *love* Sarah Fortune; lover and friend was all. For William, love meant a grand passion, a gnawing of fingernails, intensity, anxiety and being connected at the hip; it was not supposed to be tranquil like this. This was a matter of mere liking and glorious convenience. Not the same thing at all.

And she thought, as she often did, about how the longing to protect other people had become so habitual that it was far more important than love. A mental check: everyone she cared about relatively safe for the moment. Aunt Pauline, Julie, Cannon, William. Falling into sleep, she wondered, briefly, what Cannon might be doing.

There was a rustling in the dark, in the back there, over by the wall where the nettles were thickest. Wet and dank, they had covered the sound of his fall, and now they whispered with life. Cannon half sat against a wall, which felt strangely warm against his jacket, watched the nettles with mild curiosity, content to wait until they settled. He was not afraid of the dark: he liked it. It was something he had tried to explain in paint, about how the night was never completely silent and the darkness never entirely impenetrable. Look, he mouthed, wagging a finger at the moon. Look at you, you old bugger, shining on. It was mirrored in the back window of the chapel, which held its own light, visible as he had clambered over the high wall and snagged his trousers on thorns. He was willing to take a bet that the noise in the nettles was some rat. Rat or snake, ferret or tiger, he didn't care. As long as it was not human. See? You can even read your watch by the light of the moon, my love. Why worry about the dark?

The clouds were moving across his vision, racing to catch up with the moon and wrap it round, pull it down and rein it in to serve some God his supper; a nice half melon of moon. Not a new moon, or Cannon would have paused, taken off his hat, bowed his head in the cold and made a solemn wish. Now that he was older and wiser, he would not waste the wish by using it to wish for three more wishes. One would do. It was time. He knew it was time without squinting at the watch: it was the slight shivering of his limbs, thin under all his garments, which made him realise. A numbness to go with the shaking; a fever that owed something to anxious delight. He swept softly through more of the undergrowth, feeling a tin can bend beneath his feet while the other boot scrunched on broken glass before he reached the door. Even as he reached it, it opened slightly, revealing a chink of subdued light. The iron latch made a sound like a small animal in pain. Dear Lord, Cannon thought, even a piece of metal resents us.

'Is it you?' He had meant to speak perfectly normally, but it was impossible. What he produced was a sibilant whisper, a sign of the fear he hardly felt, but which still infected him. It was only the dreadful fear of finding nothing behind that door.

'Of *c-c-c-c-course* it is. Qu-quick, come in.' She copied the sibilance of his whisper: he felt it could have been heard a million miles away, as if she was shouting, but she never did shout. She looked too small to produce any great sound, apart from an uncertain stutter, and as he enveloped her in his great big woolly embrace, hugging the life out of her, he felt as if he could have wrapped her up and put her into one of the capacious pockets of his coat. She seemed to sense it, too, getting her small self inside the jacket so she could snuggle closer, struggling to put her arms round his middle, worm her way through all the layers into his heart. He touched her hair, level with his chest, amazed as ever by its softness; then he felt blindly with his stubby fingers for the sockets of her eyes; kissed them first, one by one, and only then her mouth. The skin around her eyes was dry, her mouth against his lips warm, and her hands, beneath the jumper, hotter than burning coal. He was twice her volume and he staggered beneath her impact. Only her nose was cold.

He knew this was the sacristy to the chapel, although he had never quite established where it was in relation to anything else, or whatever it was that lay beyond. This was the only entrance he knew, always approached at dark as if he was approaching a place of pilgrimage on his hands and knees. Cannon would not have minded the bare-footed progress of a pilgrim.

They moved from sacristy to chapel, through the rows of seats to the back where a small light illuminated a statue of monumental ugliness. A garishly coloured plaster saint with a chipped red robe, lovingly dusted along with the rubber plant on the table supporting both. Cannon was carrying her: he felt as if he was carrying every single thing that was precious in his own life inside his arms, but still he paused, his face puzzled as he looked at the statue that gave them light. There was a dragon curled at the feet of the saint, a harmless-looking thing in the act of being pierced by a spear through the mouth, wide open to welcome such intrusion. The dragon looked as if it were an invalid being offered soup, while the saint looked smug.

'Not his best side,' she whispered into his ear. 'And the dragon has lost its teeth.'

'I'm a dragon,' he growled, pulling her closer, listening to her gasp. 'Only I found my teeth. Why did I waste all that time?'

'I don't know, I don't know, how should I know?' He could feel her laughter, along with her whisper, vibrate down the length of his arms and jolt his spine.

Her hands were finding his and he was trying to hide them beneath her skirt. Thick tights and skinny shanks: she could feel him through every centimetre of her skin. She felt the bandage. 'Oh, Cannon, is it still sore?'

'Nothing, lovely, nothing. I don't know what came over me. Fireworks madden me. Won't happen again. Are you all right?'

She nodded against his chest. 'Why did you d-d-do that, Cannon, *why*? Clumsy man. You need your hands. You don't need d-d-dying, not yet. Not a long while yet. And if you go alone, I swear to God I'll kill you. Honest I shall.'

'It was a bad day,' he whispered lamely. 'And it was never *our* house. I wanted him to know what I thought of him. I wasn't living there. He left me a note. Telling me he'd get the house back for me if I'd come home. Don't let's talk about him.' Then he stood with her still in his arms, that little strong scrap of her bound to him like a limpet as he bowed towards the altar and then sat down again. There was a smell of polish, which he rather liked.

Oh, to make love in a big, light room to the sound of the sea through a window. He had never envied anyone, but he did now. Never believed in a God either, but he did here, temporarily, in the hope of the fulfilment of his single wish. Listen to me, God, please. I shall obey every letter of the law, and if you let us free, I shall sacrifice whatever else I hold dear. Paint, canvas, fine wine, notoriety, curiosity and my few friends. You can have them all. Vanity and ambition are long since gone, so you can see I've made a start. *Free me from my brother; free Johnnyboy from me. And free me from the urge to destroy things.*

'How do they pray in here?' he asked into her ear. 'Isn't it too cold to pray?'

She shook her head. Soft hair touched his face and made him want to moan with longing.

'They wear a lot of clothes. And it's only cold at night.'

Cold, but not lonely; not with the statues and the altar light and the moon through the windows.

'Are they still kind to you?' he whispered urgently.

'Of c-c-course. And I'm busy.'

That was a relief. Idleness had never suited her. She felt guilty if her hands were free of work. Born to it, took to it like a duck to water, proud of it. His wife, who should have been breeding babies by now – three already if she had not had to wait for him to grow up and free himself and watch him make a mess of it, a process begun as soon as he clapped eyes on her. Waited for his self-discovery, and then his discovery by the rest of the world, and now, still waiting for this long process of revenge to work its way out. Never, ever blaming him. There's no such thing as a future you haven't built with your own hands, she had told him with her sweet stutter, which was worse when she was cross. And I don't see how you can build one on destruction. You may have grown up with bombs and evil. You don't have to continue.

'We shouldn't have stolen from him, should we?'

It was kind of her to say 'we', when all the decisions had been his, wrong decisions of course, however justifiable at the time. Stealing from Johnny because Johnny had never paid him and had told him to get rid of her. Knowing that even if Johnny had put one of the houses in his name, it didn't mean it was his. Futile to try to take something from Johnnyboy. Oh, yes, he'd stolen quite a bit and let Johnny frame him for more. He thought of the explosives made at Johnny's behest; shuddered; never, ever again. Thought of the picture he had bought to launder the money, and the fact that it was now all that was left, with his dwindling reserves of cash. Thought of Johnny's revenge, played out in this game.

'What's happening out there?' she asked.

They were warming each other: she pressed his hands between her thick-clad thighs. Her own palms were calloused with work; he fancied he could feel them rubbing his back. Cannon coughed quietly, loud in the silence. 'Not so much yet. I got rid of the house. We just have to wait and see. Until Christmas. He promised. He keeps to the rules as long as it's him who makes them.'

'Why don't you just give him everything? Give him what he wants? Everything. Even the picture.' It was a sad question, not really expecting an answer.

'You know why. Because it leaves nothing. He'd burn the picture. I couldn't bear it. And because it would never be enough. It's *me* he wants. Me, coming home.'

'Yes, yes, I know. D-darling, I know.'

Just as she knew why she was here. She was both his strength and the weak link in his fence against the enemy. His hidden weapon, his vulnerability. Because she knew, as well as Johnny knew, that Cannon would lose his mind if Johnny ever attacked her again. She was small, brown-haired, otherwise insignificant, except to him. And she knew there was no worse enemy than one related by blood; no worse adversary than a lover betrayed; and Johnnyboy Smith was both.

The tingling of blood was impervious to the chill. The embrace on the hard bench becoming frantic, his hand now beneath the two layers of sweater, cradling her breast, full and soft, large for her miniature person, perfect. Ah, he could paint a naked woman, but never desire any other than this. She had taken his scarf and wound it playfully around both their necks, binding them. The kiss was an endless kiss. There was nothing to say, everything to do.

'Cannon, we c-can't. We *can't*.'

'Yes, we can . . . Oh, I do love you. And the babies we'll have . . .'

'Oh, you and your babies,' she said. 'That's all you want from me.'

'No. But we *must* have a baby,' he said. 'We *must*. I'd die for the chance and I'd die for you both.' He wanted to climb inside her for safety; he wanted the baby to prove what he was.

The light was suddenly blinding: he felt he heard it rather than saw it, coming at him like a monster and assaulting his eyes. A torch shining straight at his face, catching his white skin and making it glow red. Then the beam played over the length of his body, with hers curled inside his coat, and dropped, modestly, to play around his feet. Instinctively, he curled his feet beneath the bench, clutched his wife closer and, for a moment, forgot to breathe until he heard her whimper. He clutched too tight for comfort. The light snapped off. There was movement away from them before the light clicked on again, illuminating the linoleum floor and another pair of feet that were clearly not his own. They were half covered by black cloth.

'No,' said a voice, whispering like their own, but louder and far more precise. 'No, you can't. I'm awfully sorry, but you just can't.'

Cannon felt a jolt of sheer relief run through him like an electric shock. Julie shivered in embarrassment and a similar relief, struggling to sit upright, if not quite detach herself: she could not bear to do that.

'I'm sorry, Sister. We were c-c-c-c-carried away.' Her small voice was apologetic.

The torch illuminated a pale hand, waving a gesture of dismissal. There was a flurry of shushing sound as the woman sat down beside them, arranging the folds of her robe with one hand and adjusting the rosary beads that hung from her waist. She must have held them as she moved, put them in a pocket. Such silent creatures they were, these nuns; only the beads gave away their presence with the polite clatter they made in movement, like a version of a motor horn. So silent, he wondered how they knew the presence of each other.

Sister Pauline was sighing gustily. 'Oh, Lord. It wasn't apology I was wanting,' she said. 'It's I who feel I should do that. We aren't very hospitable at this hour of night, are we? But you can't take your clothes off in the house of God to make babies. Quite apart from anything else, you'll catch your death.'

They were silent.

'Mind you,' Sister Pauline continued, 'I doubt if He would mind. If you've created man in your image and liking, you can hardly be surprised if he behaves in the way you designed him. I'm not attempting to speak up for God, you understand, only for the sisters in this order who would not like it at all. And they'd know, of course.' She adjusted her robe. 'Imelda can detect a fingerprint in here at fifty paces, let alone anything else. Although I suppose if she were to put sins in categories it would be the discovery of a cigarette end would really give her the vapours. I had a hard time with that, I can tell you.'

Last week, a cigarette in here. Cannon shook his head. He had never been more ashamed of smoking in his life. If his presence in this place was going to be revealed by something so venal and stupid, he did not deserve the fulfilment of any wish.

'I imagine we all grade sin in accordance with our own understanding,' Sister Pauline mused. 'Imelda was probably tempted to smoke once. As for sex, I doubt it somehow. She grinds her teeth instead. And now, I suppose,' Sister Pauline went on, 'I'll have to pretend I made a bonfire in here. You must do something about that coat, Mr Cannon. Get a new one from Oxfam. I don't know how your wife puts up with it.' She sighed. 'I knew I was right to choose God. He never snores either.'

Julie giggled softly. 'Oh, Sister . . .' Her voice trailed off into uncertainty. There was a tiny rattle of the rosary beads. Light from the window caught Pauline's features. A large hooked nose and a wide, mobile mouth, slightly sunken eyes with bushy grey brows, and a bony forehead. The contours of her face predominated over the detail.

Cannon thought how much he would like to paint that face, but this was not quite the time to suggest it. An idea formed. He could present himself as travelling artist, offer to paint the whole order one by one . . . No. He could do nothing that in any open sense connected him to this place because Johnny would find out but, all the same, he liked the idea of painting a face like this, so bereft of vanity that its owner would not even have been able to define what the word really meant. How old was she? Seventy? Difficult to tell: they were ageless.

'And now will you tell me, Mr Cannon, how much longer is this charade going to go on? I think I know why you can't arrive by daylight like any other visitor. My niece told me, and I don't doubt her since she's not exactly subject to paranoia. I must say, a visit from you in the parlour would be nice. You could pose as Julie's long-lost suitor. The sisters would be totally delighted. They adore the very sniff of romance. But not, however, in the chapel.'

The silence was companionable. Cannon bowed his head deeper into his chest. It was difficult to meet the intensity of Pauline's gaze and he was grateful for the gloom. Seen in sunlight, he imagined her eyes would have the effect of lasers and her voice, ascended from its current whispering murmur, would probably stop a herd of elephants with a single order. She would not need to fire a shot. Her teeth were very white, whiter even than his own.

'Only I know it's all very well for God to be relied on to provide,' she said, 'but the devil flourishes on ignorance. I, on the other hand, do not.'

'It's better that way, Sister,' Cannon muttered, and Julie nodded agreement.

'Oh, is it, I wonder? Or do you and my niece persist in the sweet belief that a nun cannot comprehend the wicked ways of the world without fainting from shock? You really should know better. And so should she.'

Julie squeezed Cannon's arm, reminding him not to argue. '*I* don't think that, Sister.'

The nun laughed softly, and leaned across Cannon to pat Julie's hand. 'No, I shouldn't think you do.'

Julie shook at the touch, remembering, as she always would, that it had been Pauline who had first seen her naked state when Sarah brought her here, her back scored as if she had been flogged through her torn clothes, ribs cracked from a kicking, the lacerated arm dragged across concrete, not an inch of her unbruised. She had mended quickly with tender, loving care; the eyes had lost the emptiness of terror, but if ever this child were to be tortured in any such fashion again Pauline doubted that she would survive it. It had crossed her mind to wonder why the torturers had not used a more subtle approach, if it was mere information they had wanted. Tricked her, persuaded her, fooled her, perhaps. Julie was disposed to see goodness even where it did not exist, Pauline thought, wryly, but she was not cunning. She might prove harder to conquer than subvert; persuasion or deceit might have been more effective. The sight of that skinny body, like a plucked chicken, covered with bruises, haunted her still. There was no other rhyme or reason for taking the child in, except that appalling need and the persuasive powers, as well as the purse, of a niece. And a very tall story about a psychopathic brother-in-law and a husband still in prison. An insistence on a ludicrous degree of secrecy.

Sister Pauline raised her eyes to the dim outlines of the crucifix on the wall to her right. Forgive me, Lord. If she asked them both to get down on their knees and beg for the same thing, they would do it only to please her and because, for that minute, they were in her power. Such power was corrupting: she doubted the Lord would approve, so she contented herself with a question. 'Why, Mr Cannon, did your brother go after her and not after *you*? Why are *you* free to roam the world at dead of night and Julie isn't? Why does he hurt her if it's you he hates? *Why?*'

Put like that, he wasn't sure, or at least not sure of an entirely correct answer, which he knew the question

demanded, and he struggled with some approximation, unable
to explain: *He doesn't think he hates me, he loves me*.

Intelligent he certainly was, Pauline surmised, but that was
not the same thing as good with words. She stared ahead, composed, her hands in the long sleeves of her robe.

'Because my brother doesn't want to hurt me, on account of
him being blood, and all,' he said. 'Inhibits him, see? Besides,
he'd tried that before, tried it for years, and he knows what it
does. He's beaten me more times than either of us could count.
Makes me so dumb, like I've lost any command of my tongue
first and my bowels next, and he's squeamish, see? He's not as
squeamish with a woman, provided he doesn't have to look at
her. He thinks women are the very devil . . . Easier to hurt me by
hurting her, believe me. That's why we're both hiding, but not
for much longer, and—'

'*Shhhhh!*' Pauline whispered. 'Shuttit,' she hissed, for emphasis. '*Lord help us.*' They sat in wordless silence, hearing nothing.
But she had heard with those antennae that decoded convent
sounds, nodded to herself in confirmation. 'Quick, in here,' the
command reinforced with gestures that steered them back into
the sacristy with a speed neither thought possible. Not a mutter
from the beads.

Cannon thanked his trainers for the lack of sound over the
wood floor, Julie her slippers.

Pauline drew the door closed behind them with a soft click.
No doors were ever slammed. She glided back to the place where
they had all sat, spread her habit around her, knelt with her bony
thumbs pressing into the side of her nose, wishing to God there
was no lingering smell. Gradually, the sound became clearer.
Shuffle, shuffle, rattle, shuffle, shuffle, rattle, rhythmic but slow, so
slow, in fact, she was tired of waiting for the sound to take form,
Oh, hurry up and get it over with, for God's sake, forming at her lips
as she waited. Imelda moved like a snail, slowed by a sense of
duty. Imelda woke in the night as a result of grinding her teeth;
she wandered and she gossiped. Pauline saw her now as an elderly pig, hunting truffles. The thought was not charitable.

Why should a man want to destroy his brother? Pauline sighed, manufacturing out of it a massive yawn. *Or his brother's wife?* The corridor entrance to the chapel was by means of a swing door, supposed to be soundless in the interests of latecomers but it still made a wholesome creak.

Sister Imelda saw the empire and the sanctuary of *her* chapel arranged before her, with Pauline, sunk in an attitude of abject prayer, in the *wrong* bench, taking up plenty of space. Not that there wasn't space to spare, especially at midnight and beyond. Imelda hesitated for a moment, sniffed the air and moved forward, with her usual infuriating hesitations. Pauline was forbidding: although one could never fault her perfect manners, she was difficult to touch, even in the best interests of friendship. Pauline detested those she managed to intimidate; she had said so, and Imelda remembered that. She did not pause to consider her identification of the robed nun in the wrong pew. She knew who it was, and if ever interrogated about identification would be mystified by the questions. There were only three in the order who still wore the full robes, with the rosary; but, with or without them, they all knew one another by instinct.

'Sister? Are you all right?' Imelda sniffed again as she asked. Strange smell: foreign. Her sniff was loud.

I shall never understand, Pauline said to herself, why someone with such dreadful halitosis and a teeth-grinding habit can be so sensitive to smells. She sat upright with dramatic flurry, moaning and gripping the front of the pew with two surprisingly large fists, which glowed an unearthly yellow, like bleached bone. 'Is that you, Imelda?' she asked faintly.

'Yes, of course.' Imelda sniffed yet again.

'How nice. I came down to pray. Only I don't feel so well. Could you help me back to my room?'

'Oh, my dear, of course. Do you know, I thought I heard noise?'

Pauline accepted an arm, leant on it heavily and awkwardly, propelling Imelda towards the door.

'It is a sin, dear Lord, to take advantage of kindness,' she murmured. 'Really, it is. *I am so sick of kindness.*'

Back inside the sacristy, Cannon wanted to weep. 'She humbles
me,' he said. 'She protects you, exactly as she's been asked to do.
She accepts. She doesn't insist on knowing why. How can she be
like that?'

'Faith,' Julie said. 'It's called faith. Don't question it. But d-d-
d-don't ask it to do the impossible. And please don't leave me
with her much longer. I'm ch-ch-ch-ch-changing, Cannon, and
I d-d-don't want to change. I love you.'

Making love through all these clothes was a fine art, almost
perfected and still imperfect, full of longing for nakedness and
warmth and row, instead of mouths clamped shut against noise.
'I adore you,' he whispered. 'I adore you.' And then, as they
rearranged themselves, he said, 'I'm not a bad man, am I, Julie?
Am I? Not any more. Would their God forgive me?'

She whispered, 'You are not your brother, Cannon; you owe
him nothing.'

He kissed his wife's hand, passionately formal in his leave-
taking. The skin was rough with housework.

Oh, yes, I do owe him.

Perhaps, he prayed, they had made a baby.

CHAPTER THREE

Nobody knew John Smith. Andrew Mitchum made a guess that no one could. Smith was a man of brief appearances, strong aversions and no loyalties.

Seven in the morning: bleak and cold outside, overheated indoors, and they seemed to be discussing the brotherhood of man.

'I am not my brother's keeper, sir.'

It was disconcerting to be called 'sir' by someone older. Andrew, a twenty-five-year-old solicitor flirting with dishonesty in this extra-curricular work, had never been called 'sir' in his life and recognised this as more of a conversational tic than anything to do with respect for his opinion, but it was uncomfortable all the same, especially with someone not even a decade older bearing all the gravitas of middle age. 'No,' he said. 'Of course not. Sir.' It stuck in his throat to reply in kind and he realised, too late, that he might be mistaken for a mimic. There was no jauntiness or sense of irony in John Smith. This man had neither logic nor humour, which did not mean to say he lacked charisma; only that he looked as if he had never laughed, except as a private and derisive reaction to something horribly personal, which Andrew did not like to consider. Aside from that, he was attractive, if only as an acquired taste. A folded face was what he had, jowled and lined in a way that might make a sallow French film star attractive and a pale pink Anglo-Saxon

resemble a certain kind of pedigree dog with a long tongue and
plenty of spit. There was a faint scar leading from the left
corner of his lip. Imagining John Smith in the privacy of his
bedroom was not therapeutic; neither was it sufficient to stop
Andrew Mitchum from being afraid. Or to prevent him from
wondering how it was that a man as rich as this should have
such terrible teeth. The better to eat one with. One ceased to
notice after a while. One never ceased to be surprised.

'What I fail to understand', he found himself saying, with def-
erential but genuine curiosity, 'is why it matters.'

'Why what matters?'

'Finding your twin brother. If you aren't his keeper. Sir.'

'You miss the point entirely.'

'Perhaps I do.'

John Smith emerged from behind his desk and stood by the
window with his back to Andrew, looking out and jingling coins
in his pocket. The window overlooked a large garden, level at this
height, with the branches of a horse-chestnut tree festooned with
the tattered remnants of a few orange leaves. Andrew imagined
the ground below littered with conkers. No one would collect
them.

'If ever I leave this house,' John Smith was saying to himself,
'I'll leave it empty and let it *rot*.'

This announcement was entirely irrelevant to any that had
preceded it. Andrew allowed himself to be differently distracted.
The house already seemed wasted. Nobody, surely, needed so
much space or so much ornament. The curtains drawn away
from the vast windows were as opulent as something borrowed
from a theatre – the opening of them demanded an overture.
The carpet yielded to every step: he felt as if he was walking
across a sand dune inside a house unnaturally quiet. If the statue
of a preying eagle, carved in silver and standing guard on the
mantelpiece, were to fall from its prominent position to the floor,
it would make no sound – and it would take a very long time
indeed for this house to rot. As for the pictures on the walls . . .
Andrew shuddered.

The paintings were all reproductions, highly coloured to the point of being inflammatory. Above the fireplace, cornered by the eagle, there was a battle scene, *The Charge of the Light Brigade* or something of the kind; men with muskets and red uniforms, many contorted in dramatic attitudes of death while non-specific Hottentots appeared to be on the winning side. On the opposite wall, in similar, massive scale, two battleships of 1914 vintage were engaged in furious combat on the high seas, one sinking in scorching water. They were vivid enough to make Andrew imagine explosions and screams, without being subtle enough to stir his emotions. The canvases were extraordinarily shiny. In the hallways were Andy Warhol-style posters, huge heads and one-dimensional faces heavily framed as if they were Victorian, looking odd against flock wallpaper and Edwardian picture rails. The whole house was a riot of garish acquisition.

'It would be perfectly easy to find your brother, even though he is . . . a trifle elusive. I *did* manage to get access to his prison records.'

'Part of them,' John Smith barked. 'What did you do? Pose as his doctor? You found the fucking *dentist* they gave him. That's all.'

Andrew had to concede that it was not a lot, just as much as he could achieve with the chance phone call of an amateur, but it did not explain why John Smith should go into such spasms at the mere mention of the word *dentist*. 'The question is, why do you want him found?' he queried, opting for the holistic approach.

'He stole from me.' It was a flat statement, without undue emphasis.

You have plenty left. The obvious remark was on the tip of his tongue, but Andrew refrained from making it. From lawyer to client – albeit one in strictly unofficial consultation, moonlighting and currying favour without the knowledge of his employers – that would have been impertinence, and John Smith, man of mystery, was a perfect client. A cow for the milking, with an undefined business that seemed to consist of

acquiring and selling. Others collected newspapers, conglomer-
ates, manufacturing plants, shops; John Smith, on a lesser scale,
collected houses. Started life as a builder, Andrew recalled, not
the first to reach such a pinnacle of reclusive respectability,
which made it even odder that he should spend so many of his
waking hours now thinking of nothing but his twin brother. He,
Andrew, would never be like that. Once he was rich (a state of
life devoutly to be wished, by any means whatever, and soon), he
hoped he would abandon all resentments, relinquish all tedious
family ties and realise when enough was enough.

Smith gestured to the wall above the fireplace. 'All my life I
tried to get Cannon to paint something like *that*,' he said carefully. 'But would he ever? Like shit he would. He wanted to paint
tables and chairs and draw silly little patterns and *women*, for
God's sake. Mind, he was good with a bomb, I'll grant him that.'

'Good with a *what*?'

John Smith sat. 'You heard me. A bomb. If you're going to
build anything, you nearly always have to clear something away
first. Trees, earth, another building. Besides, a small blast late at
night can bring down the price of a house wonderfully. I've had
a few bargains that way. Lord, we had such fun. Raised in
Belfast, you see. Bombs are only toys, and boys are boys and
they play with them. My daddy taught us how so we could
wreck places and he could make money building them up again.
Taught us everything, the bastard. You could always find a use
for a bomb. Don't ask whose side we were on, I can't tell you. A
shame you couldn't find his lovely wife.'

John Smith was not a conversationalist. Andrew knew he was
privileged. He remained silent. For a moment he had relaxed,
but the creeping feeling of unease was back, like a breeze round
the nape of his neck, making him feel as if someone else was in
the room, the other persona of polite, respectable Mr Smith,
stalking behind him like a tiger. Andrew Mitchum told himself,
with the wisdom of his over-qualified years, that Smith was *not*
a gangster. But gay, for sure, in the current use of the word; not
at all the same sort of thing as being festive, in the other sense.

This was homosexual screaming for release, and then another
appalling thought crossed Andrew's mind. Perhaps that was why
John Smith wanted to find his brother. No, no, no. Incest had
gone out with the Middle Ages.

'He stole from me,' Smith repeated.

'Yes, he used the business to make things for other businesses.
He siphoned off some money,' Andrew said impatiently. This
was old ground.

'*No. Love*. He stole *love*. As if it were simply a commodity. He
stole *my love*.' The shrill, unnaturally high voice rose to a shout.

'What will you do if you find his wife, *sir*?'

'Hurt her so much that this time she'll run. Thought I'd done
the worst I could, but no. This time she'll really scream. He
won't want her back. He'll come home to me. But I've only got
a couple of weeks more. I promised him, fool that I am. We
always played games, but you have to have rules. Like a boxing
match. She *stole* him. The *bitch*.'

Suddenly Andrew craved to be beyond these doors in the
street, jogging for a bus, home to his lover or back to his office.
Out. Instead, politeness ruled hysteria, so instead of taking his
leave he laughed nervously. The sound was subdued by the
room. There was nobody else in this house, except the silent fat
man, the house servant and factotum who opened the door. The
one Andrew knew had been deputed to track down the dentist
and find out, casually, what the damn dentist did with his week-
ends. Smith had mentioned that over dinner. *I want to get a look
at him*, he kept on repeating, *measure him up, the cunt, see if he'll
do, but I don't want him seeing me*. What strange and pointless
preoccupations he had. This client was warped, but rich.
Exceedingly rich. Too rich to be needing love. 'Love? Oh dear,
if that was all, everybody would be suing,' Andrew spluttered.
'For *love*? I mean, suing like mad.'

Smith had opened one of the windows, which led on to a
small balcony. 'I bought him a house,' Smith said, with a hint of
sadness. There was never more than a hint of any emotion.
Spread across the desk was a double-page article about someone

who had won the lottery, and bought seven houses with the proceeds for members of his family. It was possible to imagine Smith doing that: there were houses enough, although only God could guess at his motives. It takes the average family man twenty-five years to pay for a house, Andrew thought, with contempt.

'I'm grateful,' Smith was saying over his shoulder, 'that you were able to get here so early in the morning. Even if there is so little to report.'

Andrew shrugged modestly. 'He's gone to ground. The wife entirely so. I, er, didn't tell a soul about my researches, like you said. Or this meeting,' he added.

There was an approving nod.

'Do come and look at the view.'

Mollified, Andrew approached. After all, they had *dined* together the week before. Hadn't that been some sort of overture? Smith, asking questions, eliciting hopes and fears, apparently confiding his own. Telling him about a deserting mammy and a builder daddy, who had sent him and his brother away to make good here when they were fifteen, and hadn't they just? Well, *he* had. Told him about the freakish brother who had somehow learned to paint, even when all they had been was a pair of urchins, abandoned by women, abandoned by everyone.

They stood together as the sun rose, slowly dispelling the mist. The view from here might be tremendous on a good summer day. It was an area of vast older houses: on his way down the long road, Andrew had passed a convent and two nursing homes, suitable uses, he thought, for houses of that size. He felt John Smith's massive hand, tracing with a gentle touch the cleft of his buttocks, under the flap of the jacket, one finger only along the smooth fabric of his new Marks & Spencer suit. Thrilled to the touch. Stared ahead, muscles tensed, not even suppressing the thought that this could be the way to *serious* money; a house, perhaps. The man had plenty of houses and he, Andrew, was a very handsome boy. Then John Smith put his right hand onto Andrew's left shoulder, turned him to face himself, the jowled face lit with a smile, the powerful body bent. 'Andrew? You've been a great help, a real comfort to a fool like me. Really.' The charm was sincere; felt like a breath of summer.

'Whatever you want, sir.'

They seemed to have arrived at an embrace. John Smith was touching him with both hands, grasping for hold; Andrew suddenly floppy, preparing himself for his own reaction to a kiss . . . And then, in a shade of second, he went over the balcony, hoisted by his groin and his shoulder as if he were a lightweight. Two floors down, crashing softly through the branches of the tree, bouncing from each to each, clutching at twigs, first suspended by his jacket, then snarled by his tie, at once upside down, then scrabbling for purchase until he clung by his hands, more by luck than by judgement, oblivious to the scratches and the grazes, looking at the ground. The branch dipped; the buttons on his shirt ripped. He swung like an ape in a cage, a child at play the way Mother said, '*don't*,' and finally plumped to earth on a damp, dark lawn, before he had time to scream. The seconds had felt like minutes. There was blood on his forehead, razor grazes on his hands, and nothing he saw fit to notice yet. The last drop had been a mere ten feet from the last, dipping branch. A game, that was all, with a tree especially designed to save him.

He told me too much. If I repeat it, he'll kill me.

The mist drifted back. He watched it in a peculiarly disinterested way, as he lay on his back, stunned by the sky and the omnipresence of the branches rustling angrily, as if scolding, shaking themselves in indignation.

He moved his limbs slowly, propped himself up on his elbows, had some dim, unpleasant memory of where he was. Including the realisation that if John Smith thought this was a game he did not care about the consequences.

He shuffled forward until he was in a kneeling position. Felt the first surge of relief that he was whole, if not entire. Then saw the man looming above him.

'Don't *wink* at me, boy. Don't you *dare*. What do you think I am? Some *pansy*? Such lovely *teeth* you have, my boy, you useless little *cunt*. All the better for smiling with. Now, go and tell your boss how you were moonlighting. See how long you keep your job and how long it takes to buy your house. Greedy little faggot.'

He saw the piece of wood in John Smith's hand, the size of a piece of fence, crashing into his face as he made to stand, his mouth open in a scream of protest. Felt three of his teeth crack, his jaw shudder. Rose to his feet with his hand clapped over his lips, backing away, choking the scream, hawking blood into the carpet of leaves and damp grass.

The fat man bowed and showed him to the gate of the garden, as if he had been an honoured guest.

No one was going to get close to John Smith.

Whistling on the walk to work; that was the way to do it. Planning as she went, but not a precise form of planning. Thinking with glee of the excuse Ernest had given her to bunk off work, wondering if he had realised it yet; contemplating the rest of the week and how to manage it. Go to see one of the lovers, the one she called Mole, pick up a tip or two on how to form an art collection: he would know, there was always someone who did. Look up where that exhibition was that showed them all; check on Cannon, and if he rang, as he often neglected to do, ask him to go with her. With all that, the done and the undone, the other clients with their divorces and problems, Sarah was glad to be alive.

She stopped by the fruit-and-flowers stall. Michaelmas daisies, shaggy and purple, or should it be three of the monstrous, drooping orange chrysanthemums, or no flowers at all but pounds of the cold russet apples for biting later? When in doubt buy both, and take a full five minutes in a talkative set-the-world-to-rights chat along with the purchase. Early yet. The reception hall was empty. She paused for a minute, picturing those barren walls alive with decoration and, as she envisaged some large canvas of huge colour and conspicuous obscenity fit to make the senior partner choke, she grinned to herself. Then she whistled up the endless stairs, proving she could whistle without breaking step or breath – it was the swimming that did it – kicked open the office door, which was scuffed from this daily attention because she always seemed to arrive with her arms full.

There was that peculiar smell, instantly recognisable only to those who knew it. Blood, unmasked by antiseptic. Andrew Mitchum sat in the chair facing the desk on which he was more accustomed to place his feet, stemming blood from his lips with a teacloth he had found, rocking back and forth, moaning incoherently, dabbing at the droplets on her desk, mixed blood and tears. There was a hideous sense of *déjà vu*. Her step arrested in horror, until the horror receded into a kind of weariness. He, too, had got up all these stairs; he wasn't dying, only bleeding. She should be used to this, seemed to attract it. Don't make a fuss. And don't run screaming for help without checking first. When she had been rescued after being attacked, it was the last thing she had wanted anyone to do, so she herself was not going to do it now. Touch him, tell him it's all right. Don't scream and dial 999 until she had found out what he needed. She should know by now that not every walking wounded wanted to go public. She dropped the burdens; the apples rolled across the floor while she pressed his shoulders lightly to quell the shaking. 'There, there,' she said. 'Tch, tch, what have you been doing? And you such a handsome man, too.'

He quivered. Gently, she prised the cloth from his fingers while his eyes remained fixed and wide, looking in terror for a verdict on the damage. Vanity mixed with fear, a sign of health. She remembered what she had done, looked for a mirror, wanting to know the worst.

'Seen worse,' she commented. 'You'll be as gorgeous as ever inside a week, I wouldn't wonder. Who did this, you daft bastard?'

Seen worse. Herself. Cannon's wife, Julie. She was trying to shake herself free of the purely personal remembrance of injury, the shame of it, the humiliation; trying to make him realise that it was temporary while already it must feel endless. Trying to refine her own memory of what it was she had needed then. Touch; reassurance; the apparition of despised common sense. A joke in bad taste.

'A man . . . I thought he fancied me . . . Didn't . . .'

'And what did he want? Sex? Something easy like that? You shouldn't be so desirable.'

The nod was painful but clearly negative.

'Yesh. But he didn' wanna. I didn', either. Hit on me . . . hit me . . .'

'Sure about that, are you?' she asked, chafing his hands, examining him. If she buttoned the blue serge of his jacket and wrapped him in her shawl, favoured today over the favourite coat, the blood on the shirt would not show sufficiently to shock. She could pass him off as a nosebleed; she suspected that that was what he would want.

'Inna club . . . Nithe place . . . Nithe client . . .'

You made a pass at him, you little tart, she thought without saying it. Andrew was always making passes at clients with money. Oddly, the thought of ambition frustrated made her more sympathetic. The boy had had injury *and* rejection, not nice at all and not any easier to bear just because he was a creep. There were sounds downstairs, Matthewson's voice shouting an order, his first-thing-in-the-morning attempt to exert control. Andrew's eyes closed in a different kind of terror.

'You were moonlighting, weren't you?'

He raised a hand in acknowledgement. The shaking was slightly less.

'And you wouldn't want anyone to know that, would you?'

The hand moved.

'So I think we'll go out the back way, don't you?'

When Isabella came to William's surgery, she was treated like royalty, red-carpet service except that the front-hall carpet was claret-coloured already. The thought of her filled William's day with a shadow of grief.

'Mummy's got a bib on!'

'Yes, she has, hasn't she? Are you on any medication, Mrs Oakley? Turn your head slightly to one side for me . . . Feeling OK, are we?'

William knew he should get out of the habit of asking more than one question at a time. Even during a check-up, which in this case was half designed as a pantomime exercise to teach the child to feel at ease. Mummy first, you next, the child a new patient, three years old, and William with no idea of what he would find – a mouthful of caries or nothing at all.

'I'm on the pill,' she whispered, as if the information was classified or somehow embarrassing in front of the child. 'Doth that coun'?' He was probing the gums, half of his mind elsewhere, with the muted sound of the radio, the joyful memory of the previous patient, the disturbed memory of the night before, while the other half registered what he did and heard. The surgery was blissfully quiet. He had taken in what she had said about the pill and shaken his head. Long may she remain on it: the previous pregnancy had wrought havoc with her teeth and he did not want his mending undone. Isabella and he . . . Would it have been different with children? No, she didn't want them; she wanted the perfect house; she would still be searching for it now.

'An X-ray this side, I think.' Nor should he ever say I *think*: he must sound definite. 'Bite down. Lovely. Thanks.' He moved to the door, beckoning the child with him, stepped back after the button was pressed to remove the saliva-coated square and hand it on behind her head. Never pass anything across the patient's face, least of all a syringe: let it find its way into the mouth before they knew it was there. William's mind went back to the last patient. Such a nice man. Impervious to the whine of the drill, the hiss of the aspirator and the final ignominy of the impression. Lying there dreamily peaceful, with his mouth full of bright red gum, so gentle and vague and comfortable that he had had to be persuaded to bite. William wondered if he would insist upon crowned teeth at that age – such a nice old man. Probably not, but everyone was allowed their priorities. The rules in this practice were dictated entirely by what came through the door. William strove to see himself merely as an engineer and a pragmatist. It wasn't the demands that fascinated him: it was the challenge of technique.

The child clambered into the chair without a qualm and happily revealed a set of even milk teeth. Mother's dental history made her careful; she would be strict on his diet and do her damnedest to make Baby brush, although no one would save him from accidents; no one could.

'Very *good*,' Mummy was crooning. William's mind wandered again. An unbusy morning, but he missed the hyperactivity of his former National Health practice, as well as the anonymity of sheer numbers. Conversation had been minimal in those days, the patients mainly stoic and silent. He did not miss the ignorant and terrified children who had to be anaesthetised to keep them still. That had been barbaric. What he resented now was the expectation from every one of his fee-payers that he should form some sort of personal relationship with each of them.

'Do you like sweeties?'

'Yeth.'

Such beauty would not last. Better to eat the sweeties and never bother brushing at all.

'Do you mind if I take a photograph? I'll give you a copy. The teeth are so perfect.'

'Course.' The mother was pleased, as if he had complimented the child's brain. He could see it now: a photo of the child's teeth alongside one of his face in school cap. A photograph for the family records, alongside those of innocent, babyish nudity, produced some time to embarrass a girlfriend, a reminder of fluoride, genetic good fortune or sucrose-free babyhood. The child obliged for the camera, then waved from the door. William felt the vaguest stirring of affection, and then remembered the children of his nightmares: the one with the suffocating chest and the one with the missing teeth, the others crowding crooked into the gap.

His receptionist, a young Australian female of whom he was secretly afraid, sat at the outside desk engrossed in conversation with Tina and an ancient rep flourishing a fistful of brochures, who had failed to notice in the waste-bin the similar stack of adverts for new hygiene aids deposited there every morning. William hurried by, baring his own teeth in a semblance of a smile, carrying with him the wax mould from the old man's teeth, making a brief wave with it. There was a humming from the autoclave, which was sterilising the implements.

Past the pictures in the corridor, the coffee machine in the immaculate waiting room, the silk flowers, the greenish carpet and the newly painted walls, through the door, past an old, decrepit dental chair he could not move, and down the stairs. Shabbier with each step, full of crap, the detritus of an old surgery, the residue of the last dentist and his father before him, neither of them, like William himself, ever quite able to throw away anything. There were oxygen supplies; there was the heart defibrillator he had never had to use. There was an outdated steriliser, kettle-sized for small implements and awaiting repair, an old Hoover, ditto. Three cupboards, one with sundry dried and diet foods and the girls' supply of tea, coffee, sugar, snack soups, which they made down here; another with stocks of crystallised mouthwash, throatwash, plaster for making moulds, an old chair or two awaiting rescue, a blanket, looking worn in the light from the window leading on to the dim well of the basement. One of these days he would spring-clean in here. William liked making moulds for crowns. He found it restful.

He picked up a plastic bowl already scored with the remnants of the last mix, half filled it with water from the single cold tap, which dripped into a sink spattered with white. By the sink was the telltale sign of Tina's unwashed ashtray, also covered in white dust. He shook the powdered plaster into the bowl, small amounts at a time, swirled the water until all the powder was absorbed, stirred it, picked up the brush and quickly painted the plaster mix inside the impression left by the teeth. Such cunning contours they had, teeny little ridges, grooves and dents: the liquid was refined, but not enough to reach them all. He painted again, added more, wandered round, waiting for it to dry, sighed with sheer pleasure.

There were rows of models on the table: imprints of jaws with three teeth left; distorted jaws; facsimiles of huge mouths and others of adult mouths so small he could barely insert an instrument. He had once felt a vague envy of a veterinary surgeon invited to treat the totally articulated jaw of a rhino. The conversational requirements would be nil and the teeth accessible with a pickaxe handle; the dentist as carpenter. He came here to fiddle and to dream, to quell the dread of the next hallo! and because it was archaic, the whole damn thing, far removed from the gleaming refinement upstairs. And also because it was quiet and draughty and full of souvenirs. He could shut the door on it. His own small flatlet was above the surgery. He liked the sense of occupying this extended fragment of a house but, best, he liked the self-contained peace down here.

Until he heard the feet on the stairs and Tina, yelling out of more than a need for attention, her shoes clattering on wood, her face flushed. 'Jeez,' she said. 'Disgusting. Get outta here.'

He didn't know if she meant the room or the situation downstairs. 'Got some bloke needs a hospital bleeding all over the furniture . . . and a friend.'

'Drunk?'

'Hurt.'

He was a privately paid dentist now, at the front of a big, protective house, only an entryphone to connect him to the street. He did not need to deal with the unruly, the occasional inebriate suddenly aware of pain in his mouth. His duty was to existing patients, not to the rest of the suffering public.

'Your other patient brought him. Sarah.'

'Oh. Bring him through to the back.'

'I can't stop them, can I?'

A strange procession came into view at the top of the stairs.

The man of the pair sat abruptly in the old dental chair, obviously under the impression that this was the end of the road. He held a folded, blood-soaked tea-towel over his mouth.

Sarah Fortune was patting his shoulder, beaming anxiously at William. 'Hallo,' she said calmly, as if she had not seen him in a while and this was an everyday occurrence. 'I found this in my office so I thought I'd better bring him here. He won't let go of me, anyhow.' The young man was holding the cloth in one hand and using the other to clutch at Sarah's coat. His face was runnelled with tears. William put his palm to the boy's forehead. This *was* still a boy: William regarded thirty as the threshold of the martyrdoms of adulthood and anything below that as boyhood. His hands were ice-cool from the plaster; the skin of the boy's forehead searingly hot.

'He'll only say that he collided with a tree,' Sarah said helpfully and incredulously. 'Maybe a lovers' tiff. And he won't go to hospital.'

Gently, William prised away the tea-cloth. It was decorated with yellow roses, now red. He murmured to the young man as if he were a child, 'There there, there there,' thinking, as he uncovered the teeth and curled back the blood-filled lower lip, to see the cut, that this was exactly the playground injury he might have expected to see in a child who had run hard and crashed into a wall; the sort of injury incurred when there was no time to flinch and exactly the kind his three-year-old patient might acquire soon.

'Accident and emergency,' he said firmly.

'Neuuuuugh!' The boy began to thrash in the chair, turning his head back and forth, pulling on the coat he still held in his hand. At least he hadn't broken his jaw: it was only teeth and shock. Only.

They moved him to the surgery proper. William noticed the filthy mark of a bloody palm on the fresh paint of the walls *en route*. He sighed. 'What's his name? What does he do?'

'Andrew. Not the most promising lawyer. Brawler, by the looks of things.' She smoothed the lank hair away from Andrew's forehead, smiled at him reassuringly, the smile negating the lack of compliment in the softly spoken words. *She doesn't even like him*, William thought. *Why doesn't she ever walk away?*

'Look in his wallet. Any prescriptions, notes about medication, stuff like that?'

'Nope. Mid-twenties, belongs to a squash club. Fit as a flea. Gay. If you do the wrong thing, I'll make sure he doesn't sue you.'

'Thanks a lot.'

Don't pass the needle over the face. This one needed restraint, he did not belong here – and when William tried to get inside that mouth the boy vomited. One of those. Make him comfortable; sedate him; calm him. That will be all for now. A lot of fresh blood on the shirt . . . How had she got him here without stopping the traffic? He felt a guilty relief that he was still wearing gloves. He also felt a brief surge of irritation against Sarah Fortune – her, outside, making arrangements on *his* phone, doing it *again*. Creating mayhem. Bringing the unpredictable off the streets and into his life. How did she do it? Why? What had he done to deserve it, with his quiet life? The boy's eyes were wide with fright. William touched him gently. *There, there, there*.

William Dalrymple was afraid of the dentist himself. It gave him a terrible empathy, and *There, there, there*, was all he could ever say.

It was eleven in the morning. Sarah should be elsewhere, profitably – or at least accountably – employed. She did not want to think about what frightened version of the truth she had been told. *Don't tell anyone, don't tell, I'll lose my job . . . please*. If he did not tell her more, she was not going to insist as a condition of helping him. Help was not a conditional thing. She did not need to know which frustrated loner had punched Andrew in the mouth. It did not matter.

Sarah walked with the speed of a racer, crossing Oxford Street and diving into Bond Street, tripping past shops in her low-heeled shoes, not pausing to stare. Reaching the far end of galleries, arcades of pictures, thinking of Andrew and her own alibi. Outwardly cool, almost languid. *She had to account for this time.* Staring into windows, Agnew Galleries, Bond Street galleries. There was something alien and arrogant about the galleries in Bond Street and St James's, which defied the casual visitor to enter. Even from the outside evidence of heavy glass doors, security systems refined into elegance, the absence of prices, the hushed, church-like atmosphere, they seemed designed to intimidate all but the initiated, while inside there would be the supercilious glance of some slender gallery girl, designed to repel the provincial plod who did not belong. She could see herself wiping her shoes on the doormat as a preliminary to flight: this was not where she could come to shop for art. On the way back, she paused in front of a sober display of old-master flower paintings, glowing with priceless splendour, and thought she would prefer the flowers themselves. *Why does it have to be art, Ernest? Why can't we collect plants? Or rare vegetables?*

There was nothing in these streets of excellence that she wanted, and nothing she wanted anyone else to want. She had once thought there were things she *needed* in environs such as these, in the days when she had *yearned* for the beautiful clothes and the intoxicating power of money, just as Andrew Mitchum did now, so she should empathise, and she did. But there are no short-cuts, Andrew, there never are; and it's never enough, don't you know yet? John Smith can buy what he wants, and what has it done for him? Will you please *look* at the clients, Andrew, before you want what you think they have?

By the time she was half-way back to William's surgery, the swift walk had accelerated and the mind had gone back into overdrive. *Poor little boy.* Juddering and weeping in her room that morning, spitting out words, exhorting her to secrecy about nothing. Well, she excelled at secrecy. He was safe in that regard, and so, she thought with guilty relief, was Cannon.

There was a dress in a window, on a single elegantly stately mannequin. High neck, closefitting sleeves, a moulded sheath of scarlet wool crêpe with a broad belt in the same colour. She stopped and stared. Gorgeous: dramatic, striking. Now *that* would perk up Master Ralph in the high-court gloom. She was almost in there, tearing it off the model to try it on, until she saw the reflection of her hair in the glass. Some women could get away with a mix of auburn and scarlet but she was probably not one of them. She moved on, thinking that she had left her yearning fingerprints and the slight blur from her nose on the window, and that it did indeed help to be frivolous. Better to be haunted by a dress than by blood.

When she returned, Andrew was in the back, dozing on the old dental chair, cleaner than he had been and supplied with one of William's shirts, she noticed, with a flush of gratitude. National Health practice had made William difficult to surprise. The door to the surgery was closed; she could hear the drill. With a vacant grin that merely suggested forbearance, the receptionist saw them off the premises to a taxi. *Not much I could do*, said William's note, *except stabilise his condition. When is someone going to do that for* you? *Explanations, please, in unmarked envelope to my address.*

When she had delivered Andrew into the arms of his flatmate with a sheaf of prescriptions and instructions, she went back to work, armed with a set of spurious excuses for his absence (road accident) just as he had requested, plus another set for her own. She took the stairs two at a time, feeling only vaguely guilty about all the lies, thinking that the note she had left for William was a shade inadequate. *Thank you, dear. That's your good deed for the day. Now you can be horrible to Isabella.*

Isabella did not simply enter the surgery, she floated in like a dream, a star demanding modest acknowledgement, flashing a smile that was supposed to make them faint, and had roughly the desired effect. They became like hotel staff with a celebrity, *Let me take your coat, madam, please*, the faithful greeting a guru of no known faith. Her entrance was, in all senses, ridiculous, but charming since she never could or would forget a name. 'Hallo, Tina, how nice you look. What a lovely day outside.' Her musical voice flowed on with a stream of social burble punctuated by sallies of laughter. There was a cry of indignation when she saw the colour of the walls, but remarks on any changes over the last two months were not criticism as such, simply an implication of sartorial superiority. William's estranged wife always told them where she had come from, where she was going next, enveloped the girls in an infective intimacy that seemed to subsist between visits, until William appeared. In that few minutes' interval, she would have asked about his welfare, shared a sweet little joke or two at his expense, united them against him, made them wonder how he could live without her shrewd beauty, shake their heads at the very idea of this failed marriage, which could never have been, by any stretch of the imagination, the fault of Isabella. Nothing was ever Isabella's fault, and yet he could not prevent that treacherous leap of heart when he saw her, or that racing-pulse guilt, which was related to nothing he could define. Not jealousy and no longer quite the same as desire, but a feeling of powerlessness all the same. She reduced him to a state of juvenile dependency; he became a person, suddenly, with no real will of his own. A look from her had always been able to dictate his mood. Isabella had made him what he was, driven him on with a whip, revealed him as inadequate and dull. She was the princess: he the lucky courtier.

These kinds of nerves, subtly different from any other kind, made him falsely jovial, shouting an avuncular hallo!, accompanying it with a swift peck on the cheek, just to show how amicable, natural, friendly and civilised a relationship with one's ex-wife could be, three years down the line; everything still hunky-dory and bitterness a dirty word. Never a mention of how she had rendered him so completely . . . impotent, then and now; the very smell of her enough to make him shrivel with the shame of failure. At least she knew he was a good dentist; everyone said so.

He led her round the corner to the chair; she settled herself with the ease of familiarity and laced her fingers together over her flat stomach, her legs crossed at the ankle, while she winked at Tina to her left. William adjusted his mask, reached the light to the right angle.

'Do you *have* to wear that thing, darling? I'm not infectious, you know.'

'Of course not, but I might be.' He laughed immoderately.

Tina looked at him strangely. 'Do you need me?'

'No.' She left the room, slightly miffed. William hummed as he began to examine Isabella's teeth. It was the one point in time when the balance of power was reversed and he could feel this perverse, guilty enjoyment. In this context alone, she trusted him: she had given herself no choice and, in this moment, all her vanity was revealed. Her eyes stared upwards vacantly, the interlaced fingers were more tightly interwoven and one foot moved slightly, as if remembering a long-forgotten dance. He could see the lines around the eyes and the mouth, wonder at which stage in her life she would try plastic surgery. She wouldn't, because it hurt and because Isabella's mirror would always be allowed to tell her lies. She would not accept age: she would simply fail to see it. And on the back of that stray thought came another vexed question to self: How on earth could he be, or ever have been, in the control of a woman so utterly self-obsessed that she would deny any inconvenient fact? She could eradicate knowledge like killing weeds. She was superb for the lack of any self-critical faculty. She was monstrously stupid and he was still in awe of her.

'All right?'

A crinkling of the eyes and a very slight nod, managing even now that shade of amused contempt.

I could really hurt you, William thought grimly. I could say there were caries in this back tooth, inject you not near the nerve but into it; make you scream. Go through a vein, give you a lovely haematoma; invent a treatment; take out a tooth, try to leave half behind, abscess, swelling, pain and more pain. He could not have done it any more than he could have hit her. What he was doing was probably worse.

'We did X-rays last time, didn't we?'

'Yes,' he said shortly.

'And everything's fine, I suppose?'

'Yes.'

'Good.'

'Do the gums ever bleed?'

'*My* gums? Bleed? Whatever for?'

They bled when he probed. Deep pockets round the upper palatal and lower lingual teeth, more than six millimetres, significant recession of the bone at the back. To admit to bleeding would be an admission of imperfection, another inconvenient fact: she would not believe the significance. *The whitest teeth are not necessarily the strongest.* She had teeth that gleamed white in her professionally bleached smile, her care going into what showed; the rest, to use a non-dental phrase, grimy, especially the distal and mesial surfaces. There was more time spent on the care of the face. He remembered the rigorous beauty routines before bed. Perfection was hard to achieve: there were priorities.

Just you wait, William told himself. Just you wait.

She could not be less than perfect and she would always be so stupid . . . and yet the profile, turned to him in a practised way, moved him unbearably. Vanity and ambition made her so vulnerable; criticism, however phrased, would make her shrill, and even the most conservative of constructive suggestions about any aspect of her appearance would make her flush with fury. *You must clean your teeth rigorously* would make her feel a slut. *You have subacute periodontal disease and, while plaque may be simply a feature of the mouth, to you it is fatal* would sound like yet another lecture. Why say it? She would not hear it. There was little joy in this dereliction of duty, although it also gave him a slight satisfaction.

'Issy, there's something . . .' He stopped, arrested by her expectant stare, her constant, amused waiting for the dreaded moment of some personal revelation, some statement of continued desire.

He realised, as his voice trailed away, that he was standing with his feet turned inward, hands clasped, body bent into an anxious and graceless stance, reminiscent of himself at five years old, the little boy again, making a desperate plea for the lavatory.

'Yes?'

He shook his head.

'Must go, darling. Lovely to see you.'

Her eyes began at his over-large feet, travelled the length of him, taking in the red hands, the mask, absentmindedly forgotten and pushed up off his face like a misplaced party hat, and she smiled her gentle forgiveness of all his ineptitude, using her eyes to hold him still for one long, pitying moment before she swept past on her way to the door in a trail of Givenchy. There was laughter from the other side of the door; a murmured instruction, *Keep him in order, won't you?* as if he was a prized, albeit delinquent, possession, loaned into the care of others until he was ready for collection at a later date.

William moved to the window so that he could see her cross the road, three flights down. A swirl of olive-green cashmere cape, a quick look at her watch, the hand raised for the taxi, the dull gleam of her dark blonde hair, and all of a sudden he was overtaken by a feeling of sheer malice so intense it shook him rigid. The *first* thing she would know would be loosening of the back teeth, due to perishing of the bone. Then one or two would fall out; then more. Her face would sink; her lips would turn inward; she would scream at her own reflection. Rant and rave. Remedial treatment would be slow, expensive, unguaranteed, with the alternative of dentures to clack while she ate her delicate food.

He wrote up her notes with a shaking hand. *Never make personal comments in patients' notes: all prejudice will turn upon you.* That did not exclude lies. 'Patient urged to have X-ray to monitor progress. Offered hygienist. REFUSED.' Revenge, if conscience allowed it and she continued to encourage it, might indeed be as sweet as the caramels she ate.

Tina sidled into the surgery and began the routine wipe-down clear-up routine between bums on the chair, her silence a mute expression of hostile curiosity. 'You must still *like* each other,' she ventured.

'I don't think that follows,' William said dismissively. 'I don't think it follows at all.' He was remembering the dream and the size of his feet. Seeing Isabella coming in the door with the two children who were not theirs, leading her little beauty parade of all his failures, the boy with the collapsed lung and the girl with the fangs.

He would write her a letter about her periodontal disease: he would; he should. *You are like the poorest patient I ever had, Isabella; it is only here such ignorance lurks, but ignorance in your case is wilful. You never wanted to know.* And when the pen went to the paper, he would remember all she could have learned and all the times she had so obdurately refused to listen to anything that concerned him, and then he could not get over his unholy glee at the thought of Isabella and the shrinkage of the skull beneath her skin. May God forgive him.

He tore off his gloves, scrubbed his hands vigorously, letting the pain bite. Perhaps if she married she would release him from the spell. William stared at her open notes, flicked from them an imaginary speck of dust.

Notes. It was a myth that he knew all his current patients: it was a knack of reassurance that he could pretend that he did. There were few enough of his patients he knew, only some he remembered. The notes were impersonal: they rekindled memories of the teeth, not always of the face or the personality. He liked it that way. It was four in the afternoon, and the day, in his current state of emotional exhaustion, felt endless, as if it had never once been light, only as dark as it grew now. Rain drizzled against the window. One more to go. William saw the name on the page and began to smile. He looked at his notes about Cannon and blushed at the way he himself continued to ignore his own best advice about keeping them impersonal. 'Nutty and delightful,' he informed himself from his own prose, wondering at the same time if it was not a better description for chocolate.

'Brave': not a description he often found occasion to use. 'Surly today; painting well', would hardly give a clue to the man's dental problems, but he had still included it. In the box on the first page, where he invariably wrote the name of the person who had referred the patient to him, it simply said, 'Gaol'. William rushed out to the waiting room to embrace him. Cannon was one of his triumphs, one of his rare affections.

Cannon sat, huddled into his evil coat, staring at a painting on the opposite wall, wagging a finger at it, measuring it with his eye, giving it the thumbs-up sign, lost in a dialogue that meant nothing to anyone else. It was one of many indefinable reasons why William liked him: their gestures and their nervous habits could have been those of cousins. The *non sequiturs* of their conversations made illogical sense. Cannon talked to paintings as if they were alive: he began each conversation with whatever it was on the top of his mind, scooping it into words like froth.

'He's got the fucking hands all wrong,' Cannon said, jabbing his finger at the portrait as though rebuking it to improve. It was a portrait of a benign old man. 'God bless the poor bastard. At least I'm not alone. Every bastard does it. You can paint the tits and the hips, but the hands and the mouth – total balls-up.'

He stood, level with William's chest, grasped his shoulders and gave him a big, smacking kiss on the chin. It was audible: Cannon could make a kiss echo from wall to wall and start a hundred rumours. The grin seemed to dislocate his jaw.

William found himself returning it. 'Why the hell have you made an appointment? No need.'

Cannon was pulling a parcel out of a rucksack that had seen better days. The parcel was wrapped in tissue, secured with inordinate amounts of string. 'Needed to talk, that's all. Listen, I got business for you.' His skin glowed clean; his coat smelled of earth and damp, a contrast to the pot-pourri, and William laughed for the first time in the day. After a time it felt like exercise, a relief for some hidden set of muscles, undetectable except through disuse. Cannon tore at the paper wrapping of his parcel. A painting.

'What business? I've got plenty. I don't need any more.'

Cannon sat on the floor with his legs crossed, eyes on the painting propped against the sofa, mind in focus. 'A tribe of nuns?' he asked. 'Gave up with the dentist years ago, costs too much, and one of the poor creatures grinds her teeth. So much for God, eh? I'm paying. Didn't I say I'd see you right? And, while we're at it, can you keep this for me? Only I haven't got room for it at the minute.'

A nude. William stared at it, transfixed. It brought light into the room. He stared at the painting and then at Cannon. There was a certain bond between one man and another if they had met behind prison walls, even if one was fresh from outside and the other a sulky, suspicious suicide-risk.

'You just look after this for me, will you? And you'll like the nuns, I promise. Oh, and when you phone up and offer your fantastic services, don't mention all that cosmetic stuff, will you? They won't want to know. And don't say I asked you. Say . . . say Sarah Fortune put you in touch. She knows them too. Not too soon for a drink, is it?'

William was never surprised about whom Sarah knew. After all, she had sent him to Cannon in prison and got Cannon round to him, just as she produced others of her peculiar clients to visit him in his more usual surroundings. By common consent, they went downstairs to the glory-hole. In his treatment Cannon had been allowed free range of the place, originally to keep him away from the staff and the respectable customers, then as a concession to a man who came with his own gaolers. Let him and his minders stretch their legs, fulfil their curiosity about how everything worked. Difficult to imagine Cannon being acquainted with nuns, but he looked like he needed charity. Faith and hope seemed in reasonable supply. William knew not to ask questions. The glory-hole suited them best. On the three occasions post-prison when he had come back, shyly, to chat, this was where they had sat.

A dentist, and an artist who had given up making bombs and buildings: the contrast delighted William. He had minimal knowledge of the man and how he lived now, and did not need to know. Cannon asked for nothing, even brought his own whisky.

'Christ, William,' he remarked, looking round, admiring the mess. 'This place is an arsenal, you know.'

'I should tidy it up, I suppose.'

'No, don't do that. I like it here.'

William admired the smile he had made.

CHAPTER FOUR

BOOM, BOOM . . . CRASH. I'll blow your house down . . .

I'm going to do it now, Little Red Riding Hood . . . You'll never get a penny from me . . .

She woke with a short scream of surprise from a mid-afternoon doze. Day-dreaming, slipping into torpor, and all the images converged, *crash*. A woman in an exquisite red dress was orchestrating the demolition of a house, chanting through buck teeth the complaint of the divorce client whose file was on the desk and whose bleated fury stared from the printed page. *He said he'd never give me a penny and he hasn't . . . Nothing's safe, not even houses . . .*

Sarah blinked and took a slug of cold tea, wishing it was gin, lit a cigarette, pushed away the deposition and retrieved the other papers, which had slid to the floor with the wakening *crash*. This was better. Given this kind of literature, she was anybody's. Art catalogues were the picture-book stuff of speculation, but the particulars offered by property agencies held another kind of magic. They were made for dreamers. They were read by Sarah Fortune with all the fervour of a person who believes that it is better to travel hopefully than to arrive.

I want to inspect unoccupied properties, she had told the agents. I need to view them empty, so that I can see the possibility of myself living inside them without having to speak to an existing occupant and I don't know what I want. Houses,

apartments, whatever makes a home. Price range, madam? She
shrugged her shoulders expansively. Depends on the house,
the apartment, the street. They looked at her clothes and her
air of confidence, sent her everything they had because she
looked like a well-kept lady. There was the same assumption
she had noticed before, namely that if a woman is well dressed
she is automatically assumed to be intelligent, her mouth
framed to speak perceptions beyond the normal range, as if a
flair for visual self-enhancement were anything more than a
knack. There were similar assumptions, she had thought, as
she moved insouciantly from one prestigious property agency
to the next, such as the idea that a painter with visual skills
would be articulate, an actress interesting and a tart also a
philosopher. Or that women were sisters under the skin.

She was on the second sheaf of particulars when the word
'sister' came to mind, a memory purloined from the sheaf of
glanced-at unanswered messages on her desk. Some were
already redundant; half were asking her to account for her time,
and Sarah rarely attempted the impossible. '. . . charming ter-
raced house with small garden, lovingly maintained in quiet
road . . .' No. '. . . small, second-floor apartment overlooking
green sward, near tube, small balconies . . .' These could be the
particulars of her own abode, reduced to a terse description and
thus acquiring a kind of glamour, appearing to her own eyes
exactly the kind of thing she was looking for. '. . . *living room, 12'
× 12'; two bdrms, 12' × 10' and 8' × 10'; bthrm,10' × 4'; ktchn, 6'
× 8'; use of lge gdn . . .*': what an odd shape it sounded, so impossible to visualise. She turned to the next. The text was compulsive
reading: '*Overlooks canal . . . huge recep! no mod cons! Ideal investment opportunity!*' And if it were, the market, with its best
gambling instinct, would have absorbed it many months ago.
Damp and empty, was what she read, and chewed her fingernails with a gentle, inquisitive motion as if they might provide
interesting food. She had to be *here*, dropping tiny fragments of
nail into the ashtray, rather than out there, on her way to the
ideal investment opportunity, which was so ideal that no one

wanted it, the very thought of the thing creating a surge of excitement. More than a dress; more than a coat; more than a painting. This was *real* shopping.

The phone rang. She could hear the background roar of traffic. Then a muted swearing; a muttering of formless, threatening syllables that sounded like obscenities – and might have been no more than the human sounds of a stranger struggling with a phone card in an unfamiliar place while besieged on the outside by aliens.

'For God's sake, is that you?'

'It is, it is. What's the matter?'

'You're always out, is the matter. I hate this phone card you gave us, is the matter. Can't hear myself speak either. Mother of God . . .'

'Where are you?'

'I'm stood with my head in a bubble in a place where a dog pees down the side of my habit and the world thinks I'm a freak. I need to see you. Soon.'

'Yes. I think so too. I've got to look at a flat. Can you come? About six?'

A chuckle; the sound of a kick. 'Tell me where. I'm a sucker for a house, as long as it's empty. I've got strips to tear off you. Things to ask. I'm out on errands.'

Sarah looked round the office. *Everything you ever wanted.* She looked at the elegant frontage of the place advertised in the particulars as she recited the address. *Everything you never had.*

'Why do you *need* it?'

They stood outside a grey terrace in the dark, Sister Pauline and her niece Sarah, waiting for the agent. Pauline had a box with her containing her errand, which was a duvet. 'For Imelda,' she explained, as if such a luxury required explanation. 'We have to spoil her to stop her grinding her teeth.' The girl from the agency had a cold: she was immune to Sarah's charm and jealous of her coat, and she was intimidated by the firm handshake of a nun with a face like a hatchet. She fumbled with keys and

opened two doors leading into a raised ground-floor flat. From
the windows at the front, the waters of Little Venice gleamed
dully. The inner door was stiff, requiring a shove, first indication
of the overpowering smell of damp. The girl shivered. 'Why
don't you go and sit in your nice warm car?' Pauline demanded.

'I shouldn't . . .'

'You should. We might be a while.'

She went, ungratefully. What did it matter? Twelve times
she'd shown this place; no one would buy before the spring.

'Why would you *need* it?' Pauline repeated. 'All this space.'

Sarah did not answer, drew her coat closer. The main room at
the front was huge and echoey; the room behind half as large
and darker. The walls were fifteen feet high with a cornice and
a crumbling central rose from which there hung a solitary bulb,
swaying in the draught from the door. Cold. There had been an
ornate fireplace, untidily removed to leave a cavern in the wall
and a black hearth. There were holes in the walls for the missing
light fittings. The floor-covering was garish in the electric light,
with big splodgy flowers. They moved through the wide hall into
the kitchen. Grubby yellow units with gaping doors, gaps where
the white goods might have stood. There were droppings in the
corner; an acrid smell.

'It was burgled,' Sarah told her aunt conversationally. 'The
agent told me. The owner can't be bothered to clean up or get it
done, doesn't seem to care. Puts a jinx on it for buyers.'

The air of neglect was almost palpable: they could taste it and
breathe it. Anything that might have given life to the rooms was
gone. The width of the house was narrow; it was deep from
front to back, with the kitchen and bedroom facing on to a back
garden area. The rear rooms were meanly proportioned for their
height: even in daylight, they would be dim.

'I'd want to knock these walls down,' Sarah said.

'You have a penchant for knocking down walls,' Pauline
replied equably. 'Now, will you tell me why you've dragged me
along to look at this dump? And tell me what's happening to Mr
Cannon. I don't care if that little girl out there perishes from

frostbite. I'm not leaving this filthy place until I know . . . well . . . a lot more than I know now. Julie Smith's been with us three months. I'm not sick of hiding her, but I need to know how long.'

Sarah found herself suddenly defensive about the flat, as if by having elected to view it at all she had acquired a stake in its reputation. 'It's a *glorious* dump,' she insisted. 'Look at that front room. Give it money and care, it could be *magnificent*. I *love* faded grandeur. The bathroom's OK, and as for the back, well, you could hide in it. No one would know you were there.'

'Ah,' said Pauline. 'I see. Distraction. Somewhere magnificent in which to hide. That's why you house-hunt. That's why you've been house-hunting for a year. You're a courtesan in pursuit of faded grandeur. Needing a new face some time soon. Or a new place to hold court. You can throw bread to ducks from the front. Or let them eat cake.'

She swung her arms wide for warmth and folded them across her chest, tapped her feet against the cold of the kitchen floor; her long habit rustled and the beads rattled. Sarah took out her cigarettes, extracted one and proffered the packet in Pauline's direction. Pauline took one greedily; they lit up in silence. Sarah heard a sigh of satisfaction. 'Go ahead and bribe me,' Pauline said. 'It's easy.'

'I believe,' Sarah said, in the tones of a tour guide explaining the finer points of the museum, 'that this flat, as part of this house, is owned by one John Smith, Julie's brother-in-law. It has all the hallmarks of a Smith property. He buys them, sometimes lives in them, then moves on. Lets them to destructive tenants sometimes. He can't quite bear to let them go. What is *his* can't possibly belong to anyone else, or not for a long time. He doesn't have the same sentimentality about office blocks, so he has plenty to indulge his little hobby. He won't knowingly sell to a woman buyer, which restricts it a bit . . . and the price will be too high, which restricts it further. Smith puts them on the market and makes it impossible to sell. He'd rather let them rot.'

Pauline was silent.

'He sells in the end. When he's besieged with offers and fed up with the game. When it's so decayed its own architect wouldn't know it.'

'Sarah,' Pauline said, 'you are wasting my precious time. My God, it's so cold, I should wear this thing.' She kicked the duvet box. 'Here we are, looking at a place you're never intending to buy even if you could, and you're telling me facts – interesting facts, I grant you – which do not really help me. At all.'

Sarah stubbed the box with her toe, pushed it to one side. There was a sale sticker; Pauline could scent a bargain from the other side of the street.

'They should,' Sarah said. 'Although I'd rather not be telling you. John Smith is Cannon's brother. Brother-in-law to Julie Cannon, who, I think, you have grown to like.'

'I don't just like her,' Pauline interrupted, 'I love her. I care for her profoundly. A girl who drops out of school, chucked by family, and brings herself round from drugs . . . clever . . . decent . . .'

'I thought it might be useful for you to see a John Smith property,' Sarah continued, 'because it might give you some idea of his attitude to possessions. He can't relinquish or respect either people or things. This includes his brother as well as his properties. He wants his brother back, body and soul. Dangerous men don't understand their own motives.'

They were surrounded in a grey cloud. The cold stuffiness made smoke linger in the air.

'So how comes it, niece, that *you* understand them? Are you so well versed in the mind of man you can decode it at a glance now you've slept with so many of them? Is that it?' She blew smoke into the air, the action somehow contemptuous, the words quiet. 'You used to seek attention as a child, you know,' Pauline continued. 'Not that you got it the few times I saw you, for all your trying. Such a fine little storyteller, with just that *grain* of truth.' She snapped her fingers to show how little. 'Don't know why I chose to believe you now but, then, I suppose I live by faith. One way and another.'

'You know what he can do. You didn't learn that from *me*.'

'I know what *someone* can do. *Did* do. To Julie. She has this quality of goodness which is appallingly addictive. She shines.' Pauline spun on her heel, gripping the beads of the rosary. The habits of silence were instinctive. It seemed wrong to make a noise here, even though she wanted to shout. 'He whipped her,' she said wonderingly. 'You told me and I believe you because I saw the result. He got to her, a fat man, just before Cannon was due out of prison. He and another man brought her to a place like this, had her whipped and tortured for the sheer impertinence of being alive. Covered her face so he wouldn't have to see it. He thought she would run. She didn't. You found her. She told me she knew it was *him* because of his *teeth*, I ask you.' She slapped her palm against the wall, which felt wet to the touch, withdrew it hurriedly. 'I want to know *why* . . . and how *you* know *why*. And don't tell me,' she went on furiously, 'don't *dare* tell me that Cannon is an innocent just because his wife is so clearly that. Don't make him into a hero for me. I'll never believe you. You are such a *romantic*. Don't tell me that this villainous brother put him away into prison simply to detach his wife.'

The cigarette in the other hand was finished. Pauline held the filter tip between her thumb and finger, looking at the dead end of it longingly. Sarah hesitated. An empty flat, with the promise of what it might become, seemed to make her want to slur and hurry the words. She and Pauline were sometimes awkward together in the manner of those who loved but would never understand one another.

'No. Not quite. John Smith masterminded a complex business, mainly legitimate, admirable even. Building, property development. The arrangement of explosives was a sideline. You wanted a building to come down before the bureaucrats told you to save it, they were your men. I don't know who they supplied – Cannon's too ashamed to say. There was certainly money in it. Then Cannon fell in love, married quick, became the total renegade in his brother's eyes. The illicit end of the business was discovered when Cannon wouldn't co-operate any more. He took the blame for it totally and went to prison for the best part of two years. Not before he'd pocketed a fair chunk of his brother's money. Hates explosives now, even fireworks make him crazy. He's a man of many talents.'

'Could he bomb the bishop for us, do you think?'

'No. He has a mysterious affection for clerics. One of them married him to Julie, after all. He's grateful.'

'I never know when you're exaggerating, niece, but you never fail to give me food for thought, and prayer. You're like a tabloid newspaper in that respect – I never quite know what to believe and I can never complete the crossword puzzle. Do they have anything else in common, these brothers? Any weaknesses, apart from lack of conscience?'

'Teeth.'

Pauline ignored this as facetious. 'We must go,' she announced. 'I, at least, must. You can sit here and dream if you want. I can't. I take your point. Your only real point. Only a devil would leave a flat to rot when a thousand other people *need* a room. He must be wicked. It doesn't follow he's a sadist.'

'Cannon says he is. I have to believe Cannon. No one else *knows* John Smith.'

Sarah waved from the front window to the girl in the car outside. Unsmiling, she came to the door, let them out, locked up and got back into her car again. They walked a way down the street, Sarah carrying the duvet box, crossed the road, rested against the railings and looked at the water of the canal. It looked like black jet in the lamplight.

'What a shame J. Smith owns that house,' Sarah said. 'I've always wanted to live by the water.'

'How many places like this?'

'Oh, ten, fifteen, at any given time. All of them interesting.' She lit another cigarette and did not offer the packet. 'Ironic that Cannon, after destroying his own house, hides in a property belonging to his brother. Possibly the last place for his brother to look. Can't work in the long term. Smith is looking for his brother, but not very hard. The person he's really seeking is his brother's wife. He wants to cut her into little pieces and hang her out to dry. And then he thinks Cannon will come home to him again.'

Pauline gripped the railing. '*Would* Cannon do that? Abandon *her*? Oh, for God's sake, I sound like a litany. *Why?*'

'I don't know. Cannon and John were everything to one another for most of their lives. I don't know what he'd do. But Cannon's wife is the biggest insult Johnnyboy has suffered in his whole existence. She's the one who took Cannon away. No question in *his* mind of Cannon going of his own accord. Anyway, it isn't a question of what Cannon would do – no one can predict that. It's what his brother *thinks* he would do.'

'She might die if she lost him. She couldn't stand any more violence either,' Pauline said. 'She'd crack.'

'Cannon thinks she would be destroyed if his brother found her. He's sure of it.'

'Are *you* sure?'

Sarah hesitated. A car swung into the street, catching them in the headlights. A nun and a still young woman, staring at the water, the nun crossing herself, her head bowed. A tableau for the curious: a scene of conversion on a route to Damascus, perhaps; the older woman exhorting the younger to mend her ways. It could have been an argument about the box that stood between them.

Pauline shivered.

'I have to be sure. I can't take the risk of not believing. You'll keep her, won't you? Only until Christmas. A few more weeks. That's the deadline Johnny's set.'

'Of course. Did you ever doubt it? Answer me two more questions. Now.' She counted them on her fingers. 'How do you have all this knowledge? Papers? What you lawyers call *hearsay*? Cannon? Pillow talk? And then why do you care?'

A duck swam on the dark water, a calm and lonely thing. Sarah began to explain, keeping her voice low in deference to its tranquil progress.

'I met Cannon when he turned up at the firm – he'd seen the

name on one of John's letters – and he was sent up to me as just another loser. I like him and I care because he and Julie exhibit a kind of love of which I would never be capable. I admire it beyond reason. I believe beyond reason. And what I know, yes, I've learned from pinching office files, listening to the gossips, and I've got a spy, my boss's wife, who tells me the real lowdown on clients because she gets the information he'd never share with me. Mrs Matthewson and I are friends. *And* I've listened to Cannon, and *yes*, I believe, because somebody must. And *yes*, I've got close to an estate agent or two to get the gist of this property angle, but I might well have done that anyway. I like that sort of thing. Men are such fountains of knowledge.'

Pauline picked up her box. 'Julie reads all her spare time. She tries to improve her mind.'

'Don't you *dare* to subvert her beliefs, will you?' Sarah shouted. 'Don't make her question this love of hers. You'd do it, I know you would. Look after her, but leave her mind *alone*. She has more virtues than I, Sister. At least she endeavours to save herself. I'm beyond all that.'

Pauline leaned forward and kissed her cheek, touched her face with the rough knuckle of one hand lightly. 'Hush, niece. You've the most generous heart I know. I'm not criticising. Do I ever?'

'Yes,' said Sarah. 'You do.'

'Only when I'm tired. Imelda keeps me awake.'

Sarah pecked her on the cheek. 'Take her to a dentist. I'll find you one.'

Pauline returned the kiss. 'She wouldn't go any more than I would. I'd rather face the fiery flames of hell.' It was cold. Pauline looked for something to say. 'If the interrogators of the Inquisition had hired dentists as torturers, there'd be no martyrs to the faith. They'd have killed themselves first. Why didn't they think of it?' A bus drew into sight.

'There weren't any dentists.'

'Don't be pedantic. And, if we really need one, God will provide. Yours would be far too expensive.'

Know thine enemy. Always the way – they would part on a waspish note, Sarah Fortune and her dead mother's sister, leaving each other with love and a rising tide of sheer irritation. Blood, forever coursing thicker than water; the presence of God in one life and the lack of it in the other stirring the brew. We are, Sarah Fortune told herself, the most worldly women of our acquaintance, and yet, and yet . . . she never accuses me and all the time I know she might. There was a resurgence of old longing for family love, to be accepted and *admired*. Pauline could never do either; the knowledge left Sarah bereft.

She walked down the wide street, looking into windows. I could live here, and my life would be different; I could live *there* and my life would be different again. I could have had a different husband, raised a cricket team and made them sandwiches; I could have been a nun. I have nice teeth and a body covered with scars, and I want for nothing but a new house and the fulfilment of some perverted, romantic urge. Don't tell me about hellfire, Aunt. I know. If I can't save myself, I'll save who I damn well can.

Good advice, even that held on the cusp of the tongue and only mentioned in prayers, had always been the worst as far as Sarah was concerned. Pauline always resurrected second-degree guilt. Sarah slammed the door inside her flat, changed her clothes, made her way back to the West End environs she had passed in the morning, toothbrush inside handbag. She was shyer of the bathrooms of her male acquaintance than she was of their bodies.

If in doubt, don't think, do. Look in shop windows and visit a lover. Do all of that which would make Pauline disapprove.

Wet pavements and a million cars; a loquacious taxi driver. The Bond Street lights beginning to suggest the promise of Christmas, a bedding-down into winter and serious spending. The taxi chugged in the traffic, slow enough to allow the gaze to travel across shop windows. Into St James's, with the beautifully tailored houses of dealers in art and gambling, so remote, so aloof, so arrogantly exclusive that she could see the temptation to destroy them as well as admire them. The taxi stopped. She walked through an arch into a courtyard, rang the bell on a heavy door, glanced at the window display. Inside were paintings of heroic significance. Oil-painted scenes of battles and oratory. Hunting scenes; portraits of glum dogs in packs; portraits of generals and elders of the parish; nothing suitable for a boudoir. And, beyond the paintings, a small dapper man, waiting to feel important. A nice, lonely man who liked living alone, but not all the time. Another lover and a fellow frivolous hedonist.

I like him, too, Sarah told herself, as she waited. I like all my friends and all my lovers. That's the problem. There is no rhyme or reason to my liking, no discrimination. It makes my know-ledge of the world extremely eclectic. It hides the fact that my heart is cold.

'Hallo, Mr Mole,' Sarah said, when he came to the door. 'Why do you always look so anxious?'

Drip . . . drip . . .

Late in the evening Cannon wanted to write furious letters, but he had never had much patience with words. Letters of love to Julie; begging letters to his brother, if he were not afraid of making even that contact. Johnny might regard a letter as part of the game; might use it as an excuse to renege on his promise.

There was a steady drip of water from the ceiling windows of his garret, which puzzled him since it was not raining. The roof seemed to store rainwater until long after the event, then release it into the room in minute quantities. The dripping was irregu-lar, so that while at first he had steeled himself for the next *plop!* he was now content to ignore it as he might have done an irreg-ular metronome guiding someone else's piano lesson. He put the battered armchair beneath the site of the drip, so that the sound changed from *plop* to *plip*, and was satisfied with that.

No light but inadequate electric light, and it was all his own fault. He had, after all, destroyed the house, which was theoret-ically his own but it had never been his house anyway. What Johnnyboy purchased never belonged to anyone but himself.

The destruction was a gesture of contempt that Johnny, of all people, should have understood. What was he to do? Live in it and wait for the State to take it while waiting for Johnny to cease his own, incessant calls, in case he was there? That was his last piece of destruction, his very last, and now he was hiding for fear of Johnny's presence and Johnny's voice and what it might persuade him to do.

No light meant no colour except primary colour. Poster paint, powder paint, the sort they had used as kids for lack of anything else, aerosol cans far beyond the price of what they could afford. Johnnyboy got bored with it; he never did. From graffiti to oil paint on canvas, he was never bored. This was what he had always wanted to do. From a background such as theirs it was a miracle he had ever learned.

He had meant to work on the Sarah portrait, but the quality of light forbade serious endeavour. The colours would be all wrong; the result would be garish, the paint on the palette too strong for the daytime tones he had sketched. Such lovely skin, she had. He could not resist for a minute working on the skin, including those features lodged in his memory. Little white flakes on her breasts, like tiny soapflakes . . . there! Then he put more brown in the hair. The rich auburn hair with which she played had disturbed him; a little more brown made it less luminous. Stop: he would ruin it. It was artistically dishonest of him to try to turn the portrait of one woman into that of another simply because he wished the model had been his brown-haired wife.

He had caught the facial likeness, though. They were the same height, Julie and Sarah. Perhaps it was not a cheat to change the colour of the hair, provided he did not alter the distinctive shape of it, curling down to the shoulders. He wished Julie would grow her hair into the way it had been when she visited him in prison. She had laughed at the suggestion and said she would, when they were together in a setting where vanity could be indulged.

Oh, Johnnyboy, you fool. Johnnyboy had refused outright to

meet Julie. Refused that privilege repeatedly, even turned his face away from the photographs Cannon had shoved into his hand, saying, Look, look, isn't she beautiful? They had fought when Johnnyboy had tried to tear them up, but it was useless fighting with Johnny. He won with contemptuous ease. Johnny had muscle, one of their many differences. They were no longer identical in feature and physique, not notably similar even, apart from a familial likeness only apparent when anyone saw them together. In the bed shared as children, and somehow never quite relinquished even after Johnny began to bugger him, Cannon had admired his brother's muscular development against his own skinny chest. It had not seemed an unnatural thing to do: he had massaged Johnny to order; made love to him to order; loved him, feared him, and then abandoned him. He stared at the gap on the wall where the painting of the woman had been, the one he had bought with Johnny's money. Johnny was the first lover.

Never easy to excise love, whatever kind. He knew only of this incestuous kind, and the love of Julie. One love did not replicate another: it simply predominated, so that the old one had to be hacked out of the system, the wound cauterised to prevent infection. Johnnyboy had not done that. Cannon thought he had, but at times it came back like a rogue virus, with symptoms of guilt, sentiment and a feeling of weakness so intense it immobilised him completely. *He was the first.* The love virus did this even after what Johnnyboy had done to Julie – returned, made him feel septic with it all over again. Brother; lover; twin; same flesh, same DNA. Oh, for a child. If they had a child, Johnny would know it was too late, and ever since he'd loved her he'd wanted her child. To be the father he had scarcely had. To prove himself.

Enough of that. In the absence of light sufficient to distinguish subtle colour, he would not paint, he would draw with a big fat brush dipped in vitriolic black ink. The head emerged as if it had grown from the stark white paper. Johnnyboy's smooth black hair, slicked back into control, like the rest of him; the frown-line between the bushy eyebrows he had once plucked, seeking that Valentino look in a broad face that would never allow it. One ear slightly larger than the other; the creases in the cheeks; the fold of flesh beneath the jaw that made him look as if the whole of his face was sinking; the scar to the left of the mouth.

Remembering, too, how Johnny had got that scar. So frightened of the lady dentist, they'd tried a general anaesthetic to deal with his teeth, with Cannon waiting for him in the outer room because he wouldn't have gone at all otherwise – any more than he could stay unconscious for more than a few minutes, whatever they did. But it had been long enough for the boiling-hot handpiece she had left hooked inside his lip to burn through the flesh, so that he woke screaming. Both of them staggering out of there, fighting like rats, two undersized urchins on the run. Back home to hugging in bed. She hadn't meant any harm, of course, but they blew down her door anyway. That was the day they became lovers: they owed *her* that. Even the first painful buggery had been provoked by pain.

Nobody knows you, Johnny, except me. Don't cry, please don't cry. He lit a cigarette. These were things he should tell Sarah. Make her understand that Johnny did keep his promises.

The talent of capturing likeness was a frightening gift. This was not Johnny now, but Johnny in a few years' time when the good looks would be gone, the apoplectic colour of his skin higher and the brown eyes ever more hooded. Finally the mouth, large and wide like Cannon's own, the only real point of resemblance, with fleshier lips drawn back into a rictus of a smile to show chipped, uneven teeth, stained dark. A shadowed face, hurt and lonely and cruel. Puzzled. Quickly, before any element of pity could enter the equation, Cannon inked in three of the teeth to make them blacker and added an additional crease to the forehead to indicate pain. He stood back from his handiwork. 'I must remember what an *ugly* bastard you are,' he muttered.

The *plip* of drops into the chair had ceased. Condensation, not rain, dripping from the skylight, rotting the beams. The light from the roof would be the only sign of his existence here, apart from his anonymous comings and goings in a street largely devoted to shops and offices. The end of both the dripping sound and the whisper of brushstrokes across the paper left a vacuum of silence. He stood and stretched; wished, for a fleeting moment, that he had Sarah Fortune's flexible limbs. Then froze.

There was someone downstairs.

Rotten steps led up to the attic, with a notice at the base of the steep, narrow flight informing the unwary of the fact. Sarah had secured this place, hadn't she? Made an offer subject to planning permission, written the necessary letters on headed paper to make her sex anonymous, secured a respite from further viewers; he forgot the details. She had spared him those.

But downstairs there were indeed the slight vibrations of movement. A trio of voices, climbing upwards. Cannon turned out the light and braced himself across the door. If anyone were to touch it, they would feel the warmth and know he was there. The drip from the skylight resumed with the resonance of a drumbeat.

There was no timbre of anxiety in the conversation he could hear from the room below, the words of which he could not decipher. He heard only the rhythm of it, the pauses and the hesitations. The high voice of a woman, announcing exclamations of surprise or disgust; the low voice of a man and the more youthful treble of a second male, murmuring apologies. They came out on to the landing. There was laughter, and one voice, the woman's, was incredulous. 'Someone's actually offered to *buy*? Amazing.'

'There's a large attic.' The apologetic one with the servile voice. 'Can you see? Don't . . .'

'More than I want.' The woman again, her feet on the stairs, coming on regardless with a light, swift step, until she was on the other side of the door.

'*Don't*.' The apologetic voice was becoming shrill, 'Don't go up there; the beams are rotten, it isn't safe, come *back*.'

Unlike his brother, Cannon had always admired the insatiable curiosity of women; he had always venerated women, even when he was preserved from them, but this particular example was one he automatically detested. The woman pushed at the door; he leaned the whole of his weight to the other side. 'Locked,' she said. The tread of the top stair creaked ominously.

'Come down,' the man shouted again.

She ignored him, paused, and shoved.

Cannon could imagine her, palms pressed to the door, touching his own skin through the panel, their foreheads and mouths separated by the mere thickness of wood. He imagined himself knocking a little hole through, so she might catch sight of a single eye, see him poking something through into hers. For a moment, he could understand Johnnyboy's congenital, intense *hatred* of women. Thought again of making another hole and sticking his prick through it. That way, surely, she wouldn't come back. They were both evil thoughts, which shamed him into a blush even as he contemplated them. He suppressed a desire to giggle, stuffed his fingers into his mouth. They went away, the men rebuking the woman, who was angry with them both, and they with her. Raised voices floated down the stairs. 'You will *insist* on seeing everything. When will you ever *listen*?'

'There was somebody there, I'm sure of it.'

'That isn't possible. It's dangerous.'

'I'll complain.'

'No, get *him* to complain. There's no point in us complaining; don't want it anyway.'

'*When will you evah lissen,*' Cannon mimicked, '*you silly moo?*' opening the door a crack as the voices faded away. The woman had left a faint trace of perfume: she must have reeked of it – all the better to disguise the smells of human life, turpentine, paint, the harsh soap from his hands.

For a whole minute Cannon felt instantly jolly, until the life went out of him and he dropped into the damp armchair like a doll. He lolled in it and picked at the frayed upholstery on the arm. It begged to be picked at; no wonder Sarah did it. However could he go on living like this? He was better in prison – my God, there were aspects of it he had positively enjoyed. He entered one of those temporary phases when he told himself that Johnnyboy would get bored with the game, long before his own deadline for winning or losing it, just like he did with the houses he left to rot when they ceased to be fun.

Oh, Lord, they had had fun. What else was there to do but wait for the time to pass? Sell the picture and give him back the money? *No*. The baby would need it; Julie would need it. Nor could he *bear* to hand it over to that – that – *Philistine*.

Cannon looked at the face in his drawing and saw again that they no longer remotely resembled each other, but Johnnyboy had already entered the room. Johnnyboy had the cunning he had never inherited and, in the same breath, Cannon felt the familiarity of fear.

The people had been sent to tease. Johnnyboy had always been better at games, better at everything. Probably knew where his brother was, in the way he always seemed to know.

There was not really anywhere to hide. From a ghost. A legend he no longer quite knew. From his own heart and the lure of destruction. From his own nature. From a world where he still did not understand the rules.

CHAPTER FIVE

Today I shall need an onion for the stew and another bottle of wine, William wrote on the margin of a set of notes. *Other than that, life is dandy. Why did Cannon bring me that painting to look after? Why am I so surprised that someone likes me?*

Sarah, where are you? It's too late for shopping. Perhaps you're working. He *must* stop writing in the margin of notes, as if that were the only paper he had; but he was, after all, surrounded by them. They were always to hand. William perfected the notes he had scribbled during the day in the evening, late afternoon or early morning; sometimes, such as now, at dawn, as if the very labour of it might encourage the sun to rise and the dreams to end. The notes were a record of expertise, a database for his credibility; he pored over them, wondering how he could have done things better. He did not just *need* the respect of his professional peers: he craved it. His papers in the international journals provided something of the kind. He was always looking for something fresh to write, but apart from that he yearned to describe his profession as a series of refinements and surprises; otherwise it all became pointless. Technique could always be perfected. William knew that the pursuit of excellence and knowledge (how pompous that sounded) was the only thing that could give him dignity.

In the early days of semi-idealism he had not been like this. He thought now that his was a route for a frustrated artist, or mechanic, rather than a medical man; someone who might have been equally happy tinkering round with cars, fire engines, trains, cameras and the other kind of bridges. Painting had been a passion until he recognized his own lack of vision. He could never make himself concentrate on the whole, only the part. Writing things down wasn't bad, but despite strenuous efforts he was not unduly talented at that either. Like the painting, it was the details that bogged him down in pedantry while the concepts evaded him. So he had to be an excellent dentist. That was all he could do.

And yet he wanted to write about the individuals and how temperament was such a feature in treatment; the mystery of the human response, which varied as widely as the colour of their eyes. Maybe colour and physical type were the keys to it all. Perhaps the pain threshold was dictated by the thickness of the hair, while the size of the feet governed tolerance of anaesthesia – perhaps it was as simple as that. This was too large and wide a theme: he wanted something both factual and anthropological to enhance his self-esteem. All right, then: he wanted to write about how trauma changed attitude; still too fanciful and vague. What was required in his dull circles was articles on new techniques in root-canal therapy, implantology, rather than anything with a personal touch, but in this particular dawn he wanted to write about how a terrified patient became the opposite of his former self; changed from unwilling to willing, from afraid to positively enthusiastic. He wanted to write a paper about Cannon out of sheer affection for him.

This is achieved by extreme measures, William wrote on a fresh sheet of paper while glancing at the large bundle of Cannon's notes. *First, allow the patient to develop a truly terrible set of teeth which he comes to loathe. They have made him socially anathema; disfigured him. Then get fate to make them worse. Incarcerate the patient. By this time, he will no longer care and may become very co-operative indeed . . . Encourage a suicide attempt. This often leads prison authorities to allow special treatments not normally contemplated . . .*

He sat back in his chair and tried to reconstruct Cannon's history from his very clear memory of the remainder of Cannon's front teeth. Tetracycline was a useful antibiotic for adults, no longer given to children who had yet to develop their secondary teeth because of its pernicious side-effects. Cannon had been unable to remember why he had ingested so much of the stuff: both he and his brother were sickly, he said, not subject to the best of medical or parental care from a single father with other things on his mind. At that age tetracycline made the new teeth emerge a ghastly brown shade; healthy at heart, maybe, but uneven, misshapen, with the appearance of dirty decay. The larger the teeth, the less attractive. A tetracycline smile was not a pretty sight. And there had been delayed, inadequate treatment of caries, an impatient dentist (I *bit* her, Cannon had said. I bit her so hard she refused to treat either of us again). Some phobias were more reasonable than others.

The other way of getting a patient to become co-operative is to ensure that a dental appointment is a high spot in an otherwise boring life. Ergo, it really does help if your patient is in prison at the time. His stomach rumbled. He moved into the kitchen, poured cereal, the bachelor's standby food, into a bowl and added milk. He waited for the flakes to become a soggy mess and ate absent-mindedly. The stomach continued to growl.

It also helps if the patient regards sedation by Diconal as the best time he's had for ages. It is as well to prolong such treatment if you have any curiosity about the fellow at all. He may tell you things while under the influence which he might not otherwise reveal. Nor might you wish to know.

He knew what he might write next, if this mood of frivolity prevailed: a book of Diconal poetry, a slim volume admittedly, in which he would put into rhyme all those disjointed, sometimes revelatory things that people happened to say under the magical influence of deep sedation. Like that poor boy, Andrew, with his broken front teeth, two to be extracted, two to be saved and crowned. Tetracycline would not harm him; Diconal would obliterate any memory of what William had done, as well as any memory of what he had said. Not that Andrew's lisping, fretful replies could be said to be significant. He moaned about not wanting to lose his job.

Cannon, under sedation, was rather more amusing and infinitely varied. Cannon growled. He could not keep his hands still: they conducted an orchestra with minute movements, or made tiny little motions resembling an artist with a brush, which were, in their way, endearingly vulnerable. He repeated the name of Julie in a high, sing-song voice and the name of Johnnyboy in a low hum, apparently aping the music from the radio in the surgery. On the day William had asked, Do you have any children, Mr Smith? he had moaned in his sleep about how he longed for a child and feared he could never achieve it. Then he sang that his twin brother wanted to kill his soul. When his mouth was not full, he chanted as if he was in the playground, something that sounded like a skipping rhyme. *Johnnyboy, Johnnyboy, dirty fangs, Johnnyboy, la, la, la.* He mimicked the radio.

William reminded himself to ask Cannon more about his next of kin and cursed himself for not having asked before. A *twin* brother. They might have the same teeth. There would not be too many left with the ugly distinction of brown tetracyline fangs. The very thought stunned him; he closed his eyes to savour it. He was tired; concentration, even in excitement, slipped. Sleep had been punctuated by the same old nightmares, the children, and Isabella's skull beneath her flawless skin. Isabella, rampaging through the waiting room with those two in tow, hacking to pieces the paintings on the walls. The recurrence of the image was so vivid, even now that he was awake and noisily ingesting his bowl of cereal, that William stumbled downstairs to check. He tripped on the bottom step, swore and catapulted himself into the room. All was safe, and there on the wall the picture Cannon had brought. To be exact, the third picture Cannon had brought.

There was only ever Johnny and me; everyone hated us. Afraid of our teeth.

Cannon had thought that he was paying for his extensive

treatment of beautifully crowned front teeth by bringing along, every second visit, a sketch or a small watercolour, executed with cheap materials in prison. Cannon was not paying for it at all: sleight of hand with the forms, a conspiracy with a prison doctor, Sarah, and officials frightened into fits by the prospect of another suicide attempt. They had paid for it. All the same, it had moved William that Cannon came armed with gifts; but, then, the attitude of the prison patients, the existence of whom Isabella so deplored, had always surprised him. Since his first practice, which had had a prison on the doorstep, he had always included prison patients and he had volunteered to continue at the same discounted rate long after Isabella had got him out of there. *Why?* she had shrieked. You could treat princesses and you treat *them*. *Why?* Because it was a chance to make a *difference*. And because they were churlish and pathetically grateful by turn.

Cannon had been practically dragged into the surgery, his guard agog at the poshness of it all and his charge gibbering with fear and white with pain; abscesses from broken, untreated teeth; suicide risk. William gave them both a large shot of whisky for starters. Promised Cannon he would not feel a thing and almost made him believe. Not quite. Until he became utterly passive.

The very first sketch Cannon had brought him was slightly macabre. William moved down the corridor towards the door to where it sheltered in a corner. It was a pencil sketch of his own hands, caught in the act of making busy explanations. They were sketched as if they had been held in front of Cannon's face, in front of Cannon's mesmerised, terrified eyes, watching every movement, as William, after stroking the jaw, rubbing the numbing ointment in the gum, talked incessantly while he worked, getting the needle in there while Cannon was still hypnotised by fear and the constant stream of words. Cannon, sweating with relief, when William said, We are going to do nothing today, but you see, you had an injection without realising, didn't you? Then explaining, with dramatic use of hands, pointing, illustrating, finger-wagging, cupping, expansive, what he was going to have to do after the massive dose of antibiotics had worked. You'll feel better tomorrow after they begin to take effect, and next time we'll put you to sleep, promise – the hands folded at last in an attitude of prayer alongside his face. William was accustomed to using his hands to explain; the language of gesture was less specific than words, suited him better.

And the patient had recorded exactly what he had seen in movement, and made it still. Cannon captured William's elegant hands, palms outwards, fingers fully spanned like birds in flight, anatomically correct, unmistakably his own hands down to the last crease, but looking as if they were born to bless, caress and heal. The sketch of the hands thrilled him still, made him proud. *You gotta take care of those hands*, Cannon had said. William wanted to go back to sleep. He did not want to write or to think. The light crept through his windows and revealed the clean paint, and the extra-clean mark where yesterday's boy had steadied himself against the wall. William's stomach continued to grumble. The milk had been too cold. It did not seem much to complain about.

Seven thirty and the phone buzzed. He ignored it, listened from a distance as the message recited briefly the services he could offer, implants, cosmetics, enamel facing, crowns and a whole new life, addressing the unwary in cheerful tones he scarcely recognised as his own before inviting them to leave a message saying they were going to cancel. Or whatever they were going to say at this godforsaken hour of day when the light still awaited arrival. He waited to hear if it were Sarah – she owed him explanations – but it was a man, pleading a business meeting. William did not have the faintest idea who it was. Identification of this voice required consultation of the damn notes. Maybe one of those who promised to return but never did. He moved on, tummy growling, vaguely upset, to look at the second of Cannon's drawings and the third. In his dreams, these were the first the children destroyed: his hands.

The second hung in pride of place in the bathroom, in case it should otherwise cause offence. It was of a slim, heavy-breasted girl-child perched on the end of a high bed without frills. She sat on the very edge, supported by her arms, looking at her feet, which were both just on the ground. One foot was raised from the heel, for particular inspection of the toes; she was nervous but amused, eyes fixated by the foot rather than by the audience. The room had all the appearance of an institution, a hospital ward or a lecture theatre of the old sort, bare, apart from the lights in metal shades hanging above her and the surgical green of the walls behind. Her skin was dark, the sheet, covering the bed on which she sat, white. She was an object for inspection rather than seduction. William could imagine students standing in front of her in a circle outside the picture, waiting for a description of her history, her times, her disease, while she, quite simply, waited on life to continue.

The phone burred again. By this time he was in the waiting room with the fancy sofas and the coffee machine, and the message was muted. He was looking at Cannon's glorious loan of yesterday. Then found he could not look at it. Hurried upstairs to the flatlet where he lived in his miniature space, so that Isabella could live in relative splendour with some rich paramour, whose name by choice he could not remember, for as long as she kept her nerve and her face. And her teeth. *Her teeth*.

He brushed his own. Rigorous attention to detail; like hell. Should have given her disclosing fluid, make her teeth brilliant blue to show where the plaque lingered, tell her a thing or two, get the message across. Those teeth had bitten him, more than once, in a playful bite on the shoulder which hurt like a series of minor pinpricks. Isabella nibbling and saying, *More . . . But . . . when are you going to earn more money, William? We need more*.

He left the dental floss and the whitening toothpaste, the scolding in his ears, and belted downstairs through the foyer, into the street and the cafe down the road, where he sat and consumed a cappuccino with sugar and a Danish pastry.

Sticky on his tongue, fresh as the day, souvenirs of it lodged in the precious spaces between his back teeth. Then he went back to face the morning and Cannon's loaned painting.

The sun streamed through the window, the sky was pink with promise, and William wanted to yell with delight. The painting was exquisite and he had the fascinating prospect of another paper to write. Twins and their teeth.

The flat where Sarah had stayed the night with the man she nicknamed Mr Mole, was small and potentially neat, like the dwelling of one who might have preferred to live, like his fictional counterpart, underneath the riverbank. The potential for neatness lay in Mole's insistence on the numerous fitted cupboards to maximise space, the state-of-the-art kitchen in miniature and the stark, military nature of his furniture. There were campaign chairs, which could be folded away, a chest that doubled as a table, an expandable suitcase, which could be used as either a wardrobe or a seat. He was as fully equipped to embark on a major expedition at any given time as a nineteenth-century general. The man called Mole woke from a deep and dreamless sleep to find that his place was full of foreign noises. Splashing from the bathroom, which was so close the sound could not be avoided, the flushing of the lavatory and the sound of low, musical singing. It disoriented him for a full minute until he opened his eyes.

Sarah's clothes, visible but hardly colourful, hanging not in a cupboard but on the door, the way she did. Sarah's melodious voice over the rushing of precious hot water and the indentation of her head on his pillow. A different smell to the room. They had talked too much, and he had eaten and drunk too much, was the problem. Had he or hadn't he? It would clearly be far too insulting to ask. The progress of the day would clarify memory which, so far, extended only to that of an extraordinarily pleasant, over-indulgent evening.

She had set out cups in the kitchen, pulled out two stools from under the counter, cleared space for them both adjacent to the coffee machine, which dripped, to order, sternly calling him to attention. It was still the middle of the night, as far as he was concerned: Mole's business rarely began before the end of the morning. Her preparations alarmed him, since it looked as if the scene was set for serious conversation of the life-threatening sort. Maybe she wanted to talk about *life*, their life, and how it should be further intertwined. Oh, no. He sat heavily and watched the coffee jug fill.

Supposing she wanted to discuss *them*? Supposing she wanted to move in with him? She always said how much she loved the place. They were fond of one another; comfortable together once a week or so, and she was used to the making of unilateral decisions. Perhaps this was it: the table was laid for the making of lifestyle commitments. He braced himself against the counter and counted to fifty, slowly. That was usually the length of time it took her to dress. The speed of it always amazed him, in the same way the clothes did. There would be a simple subtraction of a belt or piece of jewellery, and the more festive creature of the night before would emerge soberly clad and ready for work. The kitchen was so small she had to sidle into it and sit carefully, which she did with the maximum of grace. Hangovers appeared an unknown quantity in her life, but not, unfortunately, in his. She was picking a bad moment to tell him how much she loved him.

'Now, listen, Mole,' she said. 'Answer me this one. It's extremely important. Supposing you have a *person* . . .'

'Yes?' he said, holding his breath. 'This *person* . . .?'

She poured the coffee and he waited, tremulously.

'Supposing a *person* has a budget to buy paintings for a corporation. You know, a showy-offy collection to impress people without losing any money at the same time. Now, where would this *person* start?'

He was nonplussed, but rallied quickly. 'This *person* could have all my stock for a start. I can't wait to get rid of it.'

'Thank you for that, but no. I think the subject matter has to be . . . rather more domestic, if you see what I mean. Suitable for a very broad base of taste or non-taste. You see, the corporation doesn't know what it wants. It thinks it does, but it doesn't.'

'And what about the *person* in charge of the collecting? What does *she* want?'

Sarah sipped the coffee as if it was the only coffee she would ever drink, savouring it for a lifetime. 'The *person* wants an excuse to display the work of unknown, or virtually unknown, unfashionable artists who could do with a chance. Not money, necessarily; the encouragement of being seen. Let the rich actually feed the poor, in other words. The other instinct of this *person* is to trash the whole thing. Get them a collection which is comic, or laughable. A mimic of pretension.'

'Then it really would be state-of-the-art,' Mole said, relieved and thoroughly warmed to the topic. 'What's required is a *theme*. Then you can get away with *anything*. And you must go to the big exhibition on Saturday. A must. Has everything.'

'A theme?'

'Oh, whatever you like. Historical. Geographic. The sky, sunsets, sunrises, the sea, English landscape, Africa. Or you could make it conceptual. Poetry in motion, love and war, men at work, women at work, the movement of the seasons, friendship. Captivity . . .'

'Captivity,' Sarah echoed. '"Stone walls do not a prison make, Nor iron bars a cage".'

'Exactly,' Mole said. He was looking round himself at the smallness of his kitchen and, at one remove, the dimensions of his really rather satisfying life. Sarah was on her feet, planting a kiss on the top of his head, the whole of her a sudden flurry of movement.

'Thank you,' she was saying. 'Where's my coat?'

A green coat, to go with a sanguine temperament that did not believe in bad luck and always brought the opposite. He watched it whisk away past the paintings of battles, gathering dust on the hem as it went into the sunshine it seemed to have evoked. The careless, almost joyful slam of the door and the sight of her striding through the courtyard, fixing her in his mind. Mole was not sure if he should feel irritation or sheer relief.

Instead, on the whole, he felt absurdly disappointed.

Racing down Piccadilly for the bus that would take her back to the prison of work, Sarah remembered Sister Pauline's slower steps and all her many admonitions. My darling Pauline, she told herself, you should not worry about my morals. Men who really want *good* women will always find them; and, as for sexual licence in the current men of my acquaintance, they are almost invariably too tired.

I must account for my time, my time, my time . . . I need my job. Everyone on this bus needed their job. *I was out doing research for the art collection* . . . Oh, what an excuse Matthewson had given her. *Don't forget the exhibition. Take Cannon. Put it on the time sheet.*

Accountability simply requires inventive words on paper to explain the hours spent. The bus rolled through London, half full of people who still looked surprised by sleep. Sarah loved the winter in these early stages when the cold was a stimulant, the sunshine a catalyst and there was an explosion of seasonal hats and scarves, far more effective than the Christmas decorations. The bus was so much more convivial than the underground: chat was allowed although by no means mandatory, and there was always the view. She sat upstairs towards the front, wondered why she ever bothered with the lonely back seats of taxis. Central London: last night's playground, full of those plodding and rushing to work, drawing them in like a vacuum cleaner only to spit them out again in the evening. The bus snarled at the traffic in Holborn, where the tall buildings of the city began to close in, blocking the sun. Top-deck people were reactive to the weather, kings and queens of the road for twenty minutes at a time, able to peer into office windows with a degree of impertinence they might never have exhibited to their suburban neighbours; it gave her the urge to pull faces. There was a young man with beautiful coiffed dark hair sitting immediately in front of her, staring ahead, his shoulders hunched in misery, his newspaper ignored. Sarah wanted to touch his hair, to see if it was real and as soft as it looked, tell him how nice it was and somehow convey the fact that the day could not possibly be as bad as he seemed to anticipate. He reminded her of Malcolm Cook, the most consistent of the lovers. Today would be a good day; she had decided it. There was nothing simplistic about the Fortune philosophy, such as it was. It was the very cutting edge of pragmatism.

That was it, the right phrase: *cutting edge; state-of-the-art; interface*. She began to rehearse the outline of the initial report on her ill-chosen task of amassing paintings with the firm's money. *Consultants suggest that the cutting edge of art-investment theory indicates that the collection should have thematic unity, each work to interface with another to create organic harmony* . . . That should do it. Keep them at bay for a while. There were other things to do: look at houses; keep Cannon on cue until Christmas; keep Julie hidden; keep all the secrets and hope he was right.

I must account for my time. But there was no Matthewson lurking inside his door, waiting for her explanation. No bloodstained, weeping boy in her office either, explaining his hurt and the need for silence, because he, too, needed his job. The door was closed, the route to non-accountability clear, but she paused to listen. There was a murmuring of voices, an undertone of irritation in the blurred words, until she heard Ernest raise his. Far too early for Ernest to do this: bad for his ulcer. 'I am only a consultant,' he was saying, portentously and conveniently loud for an eavesdropper. Big talk: that should get them on the run; that was really talking dirty and laying down the law. She supposed she had better explain the nature of the *consultant* in her consultancy document on the collection; listened a while to pick up a useful phrase. And then, still at the foot of the stairs, still listening, wondering if more of the estate agents' particulars had arrived, she felt a tremor of hesitation and a desire to run away. An appalling sense of responsibility, which was tantamount to terror. She ran up the stairs and slammed the door.

Johnnyboy Smith was in that room, talking with Cannon's distinctive voice. *Don't go near him,* Cannon said. *Don't ever let him see you.*

'I don't care a shit about fucking consultants, if you'll pardon my French,' John Smith was saying to Ernest Matthewson in a pleasant brogue, which did not make him easier on the eye. All jowls and hair from four feet away. He wore a highly coloured Hermès tie, predominantly red, which looked, around that pink neck, like a cheap ribbon wound round a birthday cake, with the obvious difference that Johnnyboy would never be sweet to eat, what with that broad, short body and the way he muttered to hide his vowels, or maybe his teeth. Wait till he told Mrs Matthewson about those teeth.

'I know all about this *consultant* stuff,' Mr Smith was saying. 'You *consultants* only use broad brushstrokes, right? The . . . the minutiae are left to others. I mean, the fucking details.' Ernest could only nod.

'I hate lawyers,' Smith said, without any degree of real recrimination. 'MPs, they're all lawyers. Guy Fawkes had it right. And what's a lawyer anyway? Just a man who oils wheels so the wheels can turn round. So what's a *consultant* wheel-oiler?'

'I take an overview of what your requirements are,' Ernest said, looking earnest and bending forward to lessen the distance between him and this menace while in fact he wanted to increase it. 'In the absence of your designated lawyer, for some time, I gather, following his car accident . . .'

'His *what*? Oh, I see, yeah.'

The accent was false: Ernest knew it, but could not pinpoint it, and continued earnestly, looking at the eyes of the man rather than his teeth, '. . . then I shall isolate one or two people who can replicate what your own designated lawyer did.' There was a hollow laugh. 'I've looked at the files. My word, what a lot of them, ha ha! Property slow-moving, eh? Well, well, well, winter's here. Personally, speaking as a *consultant*, mind, I think you could maximise your investment and avoid tax rather better than you do, which means specialist skills which we can easily provide . . .'

J. Smith took advantage of Ernest's confidential stance and leaned forward himself, so their noses almost touched. Ernest remembered, just in time, not to recoil from that mouth.

And later, after he had gone, Ernest wondered what all the fuss had been about. The man was only a client; a good client admittedly, but not the best or the most powerful; there was no need for anyone to kiss his feet. God help anyone who had to kiss any other part of his anatomy, Ernest muttered fastidiously. More tales from the battle-front to tell Mrs Matthewson, though. What he could not understand was why everyone was so afraid of the man. There was nothing fearsome about him at all. Watching him making his flat-footed way out of the room was not like watching a warrior of the commercial world. It was like watching a sad clown. He wanted Sarah to see it, called for her but she did not answer the phone. He wanted to gossip, but it would have to wait until he got home. Darling, he would tell his wife, such *breath*, such *teeth*. *A peasant*. You should have seen him.

It was not the power of rendering the patient so helpless and speechless – with the rubberised insertion that isolated the tooth and covered the throat to protect them from the debris and the accidental swallowing of one of the tiny brushes he used to dig out the pulp – that made William take a secret pleasure in root-canal work. The patients hated it, and he sincerely, if sometimes irritably, regretted that, but it had the sole purpose of relieving pain, permanently, and it was the cleverness of the instruments and their current variety, the prospect of surprise and the tension it generated in himself that kept him going. Locate the canal; establish the working length. Enlarge it gently to the point where the file starts to bind. Straight files used in a large to small sequence with a reaming motion, the rotary action preparing the

canal into a round cross-section in this anterior tooth; the minimum of pressure. Watch out for danger zones, weakness in the
cavity, weakness in the instruments. Remove the pulp with infinite care, an ultra-precise form of spring-cleaning, leaving
nothing behind to infect, working slowly, mostly by hand and
wishing, for once, they were smaller. Avoid the nightmare of a
broken instrument, lodged in the dentine and impossible to
remove; the discovery of an extra canal, a canal so twisted in
shape it made the original estimate of the treatment time entirely
false and the patient would begin to fret. The omnipresence of
grave discomfort, the dentist's most euphemistic word, made
speed imperative, while the precision required dictated the exact
opposite.

There should not be such satisfaction in rendering a tooth
dead while keeping a patient sentient throughout, but there was.
William preferred them awake in the interests of greater co-
operation. And if he regarded it selfishly, the level of relief was so
much more palpable if the patient had known what was going
on. It was a horrible fact that their consciousness refined his own
concentration and improved his technique. He was actually
pleased with himself.

The perfection of the notes would have to wait. There was an
arrangement to see Sarah. He did not want to tell her about
Cannon's painting: he was shy of it and did not quite know what
to do about it apart from admire, and wonder, as he had all day,
about the motives. It was Sarah who was so clever on the human
motive; he, who was so dense, wanted to work it out for himself.

It was she who had brought Cannon into his life, but that did
not mean that she owned every aspect of the relationship that
followed, nor any more of himself than he chose to give. Where
was *she* when she did not see him once a week, more or less? He
did not ask, he guessed. He referred his own dilemmas to her
and told her stories; revelled in her intelligent interest. He wondered if he bored her, and decided he did not. It was a strange
middle ground of intimacy, which was close enough for the
exquisite comfort it provided, with no merging of identity. It

was, he realised with a shock, the only relationship he had ever had with a woman that was based on mutual respect.

Would it be different if I were more curious? he asked himself. Would it? If I *loved* her? If she really trusted me and I really trusted her? Is *love* the same thing as this big gulp of infuriating pleasure when I see her coming towards me? I must work on technique for living. There's something I'm doing wrong.

Let's walk somewhere, he had said. They met between their two places of work at Hyde Park Corner and walked the well-lit circle of the park, popular on the evening of a dry, bright day: joggers, cyclists, a floodlit football game, walkers and strolling lovers. At Speakers' Corner, a lonely figure stood on a box and shouted global warnings at passers-by, convinced of some major truth, blind to the fact that he had missed the meeting of true minds.

'A consultant,' William murmured. 'He reminds me of mine, at dental school.'

'What *is* a consultant, William?'

'Ah,' he said, tucking her arm through the crook of his own. 'I can tell you a story about that.'

'How was the darling Isabella?'

'Fine. I did *not* succumb to any temptation to torture her. In case you wondered.'

They strolled arm in arm. She adapted her pace to his long-legged stride; he slowed down. The lights of the park glowed yellow. There was frost in the air. 'I have an aunt', she said, 'who says she won't go to a dentist before hell freezes over, because she thinks dentists are torturers at heart. Perfectly placed to be sadists for hire. She has the theory that if half the martyrs to the Catholic faith had been faced with a professional dentist-torturer they would have denied God soonest. She thinks you could all have alternative careers. Hirelings to the secret services of brutal dictators. And there you were, contemplating torture, exactly proving her point.'

A jogger dressed in red huffed into view and swerved to avoid them. A puff of his breath lingered in the air.

William laughed, took her seriously. He took most things seriously. 'Does she mean someone like me would have been *useful* in the Inquisition, depending on which side you were on? What a ghoulish imagination she has. A dentist would *not* be a natural for the job of torturer. We're descended from *barbers*, for God's sake. We wouldn't be natural for it because we like to *mend* things; that's what we're here for. Second nature, professional pride, call it what you like. You *can't* destroy without wanting to mend. The dentist would be *useless*, tell her. He'd be looking at what he could *mend* after the event. He'd be putting on a show, you know, lots of blood and stuff, but everything capable of restitution. The mouth's good for that. Has this extraordinary capacity to heal.'

Another jogger, this time in sinister black, overtook them silently from behind on winged feet, padding towards nowhere.

'So exactly what would you do? Tell me and I'll tell her. She used to tell me dreadful tales of decapitated saints to make my skin crawl. I could get my own back.'

'Oh, same things I've thought of doing to Isabella and never would. Open the gums, stitch them back. Drill where it did least damage. Let the burr catch inside the cheek. It would all mend. I could drill a hole—'

'I think I'd prefer the story about the consultant. I like stories better than facts.'

He grinned, tucked her arm more closely against his own. The lights of Knightsbridge loomed ahead like a fairy palace.

'The consultant . . . Well, once upon a time there was a town where they had a problem with cats. The feline population had grown out of control, largely due to the sexual activity of one great big bold tomcat with great energy and irresistible appeal to the female of the species.'

'A serial seducer.'

'Possibly. Anyway, the parish councillors hunted down the tomcat, emasculated it rather than killing it and let it go. The cat population dropped dramatically and everyone congratulated themselves. Then, suddenly, it went up, ten times worse than before, kittens everywhere, stopping the traffic. None of the kittens looked like the old tom. The councillors met and decided, nevertheless, that they hadn't done the job properly with the old devil tomcat, so off they went to hunt it *again*.'

'And?'

'They found it, finally. In the graveyard, sitting on a tombstone, surrounded by other, younger tomcats, telling them what to do. Now that, dear Sarah, is a *consultant*.'

She laughed, and felt warm, let him carry her with the tide of people towards the other side.

I'm a consultant, she thought, the cat on a gravestone, trying to conduct the offstage orchestra, with no skills at all. Trying to give something from an old, cold heart. Trying to act on faith, without quite knowing what I should believe, with not much time before Christmas.

Trying not to fail anyone.

I think I *shall* go and try on that red dress after all.

PART TWO

CHAPTER SIX

It was always a mistake to base anything on a lie. Pauline knew this better than most. If lies were necessary, and *oh, yes, they are,* it was always better to construct the thing so that it was as close as possible to the truth, leaving the least scope for embellishment. A lie was a living thing, demanding growth: it could develop like a vine with tendrils to throttle itself; it could be a little creature growing into a monster. Like the kitten they were watching, it could trip over its own legs.

Pauline sat with Julie in the convent kitchen, a place of utilitarian warmth and ugliness. Like the rest of the building, a devotion to cleanliness outstripped aesthetic consideration without any sign of contest between the two. The radiators against the walls kept up a steady rhythm of protest: a moaning, keening sound that reminded Pauline for all the world of a high wind through an ill-fitting window and gave the impression that they were secluded on a mountain-top – which, in one fanciful sense, they were – without a view. The only thing that was beautiful as well as dangerous was the kitten that played at their feet.

Named Felicity, without anyone having the skill or inclination to ascertain its sex, the kitten gambolled on the lino tiles with no better sense than an eye for movement and a suicidal instinct towards warmth. There was an industrial-sized gas cooker, which excited curiosity and a turn of unsteady speed in the animal: it seemed to want nothing more than to get inside the lower oven designed for other things than the cooking of cats. Barred from this compulsion by an old firescreen, which Julie had found, the kitten had crawled up the inside of Pauline's leg, beginning at the ankle, mounting via cotton stocking and habit, to be rescued via a hole in the capacious pocket at the hip. Pauline had held it by the scruff of the neck, shaken it and stuffed it in the opposite pocket, which did not have a hole. 'And now', she announced, as they bared their teeth at one another, 'I'm going to sit on you.'

That, too, was a lie. In a different degree from the lie of pleading poverty, which had led to the second-rate service of the central heating, which had led to the noise. Or from the lie that had got her into the kitchen and Sister Imelda out of it, credited not only to Imelda's influenza but also to Pauline's as yet unde-tected enthusiasm for cooking. Or from the original lie that they were, all twenty-five of them, so democratic that they should all take turns at the stove, since all women can cook, a resolution which, for a while, had brought about results so unspeakable that there had been a universal weight-gain attributable to des-perate reachings for bread and chocolate. After that there was bland food, prepared with meticulous lack of imagination by five of them in turn, until the arrival of Julie and her subsequent gravitation after a fortnight from sickbed to kitchen; but then she, too, had arrived on the tide of a lie.

The radiators moaned like a theme for *Wuthering Heights*, and the kitten played with a ball of wool. There were members of this community who could knit for England. All of them were retired from active life; some of them were poorly. They liked nothing better than outings to Westminster Cathedral. It was no place for a girl who was scarcely out of her third decade.

It had been a lie to introduce Julie to the sisters as some kind of refugee, recuperating from the ailment of a violent family but bankrolled by an uncle who paid for her keep, just as it had been a lie to present her with the impeccable credentials of a believer. The poor child did not quite know how to behave at mass, although she had learned, and her earlier fumblings with genu-

flections had been put down to a certain stiffness in the limbs.
The fact that she could cook made up for many of the lies surrounding her. The sisters were incessantly curious, as inquisitive
as sparrows and readier than hawks to dissect the origins of their
guest and gossip about it to their many outside contacts, but
discretion was maintained by that strange, instinctive consensus
they were able to reach without discussion. The way to the suspicious heart was through the stomach. So much for spirituality,
Pauline thought. The kitten pounced on the wool. Julie was
scooping out the insides of baked potatoes, a staple of the convent
diet. Never before had they been served with crisp skins and a
filling flavoured with cheese and chives.

'Why on *earth*, child, do you love that man?' Pauline
demanded.

There was an eloquent shrug. 'B-b-because I *do*, I suppose.
D-d-does there have to be a reason?'

'Yes.'

'I shall have to think of one, won't I, then?' She laughed. Post-
laughter, the stutter improved.

'"How do I love thee? Let me count the ways—"' Pauline
quoted.

'Oh, the *ways*,' Julie interrupted. 'The *ways* depend upon the
means. I can love him here by praying for him. Or pretending to
pray,' she added, with an apologetic nod. 'That doesn't have
much to do with the reasons, though, does it? Here, Kitty, don't
be such a fool. Drink the milk – it's good for you.' She pushed a
saucer across the floor towards the kitten, who ignored it in
favour of the wool ball, which Pauline threw for it again and
again.

'There's a good *reason* for loving a kitten,' she said drily. 'It's
a piece of perfection. Beautiful without making any effort. No
one could say that about your husband.'

Julie seemed to consider that. The radiators whined. Never
once had Julie whined. Not a single hint of it. In fact, she seemed
in some perverse way to consider herself lucky.

'Loving the kitten has nothing to d-d-d-do with its looks,' Julie protested. 'I love that thing because it came from the gutter, like me. Rescued, wasn't it?'

Pauline was not about to dispel that myth. The kitten had been all that was left to the aged convent cat, deceased in the aftermath of a misguided pregnancy. After a dozen confinements. it should have known better. Pauline thought she would never understand the female sex.

'I can't tell you the reasons for loving Cannon,' Julie went on, 'because I don't rightly know. Because he rescued *me* from what I might have been. And because I could actually make a difference to *him*.' Her hands paused about her work for a second. Her constant industry added to her popularity. 'Can you imagine it? A man who would *let* you love him. Gives you a life, and says, "It's all yours now, tell me what to do."' She was cutting the chives, the knife slicing neatly and quietly. 'A man who'll *let* you reinvent your life and his. Wants to marry you the week after you've met, so sure is he. Abandons all his ties to be with you. Oh, no, Sister, you don't let go of a man like that.'

Pauline paused to wonder if her niece Sarah had ever found a man like that. If she had, she was perfectly capable of throwing him back into the gutter.

'My man Cannon was an unwritten page,' Julie said, 'all talent and nerves and energy and fear, and I don't know what. And if I was abused as a child, which I was, mind, I'd got nothing on him. He was his brother's creature, in every sense. Oh, he had money, if he asked, but he didn't know the value of anything. How could he? He'd been kept in darkness. A man of thirty, as ignorant as a child. You think I'm an innocent, Sister, but I'm the worldly one. The stronger one. Or at least', she added sadly, 'I was. I'm not so strong now.'

She picked up the kitten, tickled its ears and put it down. When it grew up, it was likely to be a very ugly cat indeed.

'He hardly knew the difference between right and wrong. A moral vacuum. All that misplaced talent. The oddest mix I ever saw, tearing himself to bits. I wasn't a good person, I was sliding into nothing. He *makes* me something. I made him want to live.

We'd disintegrate without each other. I *need* him, he *needs* me. Although . . .' she hesitated '. . . he needs a child as *well* as me. He needs a child because it's the only way he can really begin again.' She laughed unsteadily. Her stutter had quite gone. 'So it isn't just my life in the balance, it's his. I'm sorry, Sister. You and your niece seem to have taken responsibility for both of us. I hope you don't enjoy power.'

'No,' said Pauline insincerely. 'No, I don't think I do.'

'Nor I,' Julie said. 'But I had it and I have it still, although how it ever makes a person proud I can't imagine. It makes me weak with the thought of it, the *need* of him, the gift he gives me, the *amount* he needs me.'

'You could despise a man for need like that,' Pauline said carefully, smothering her words as she bent to pick up the kitten, which squirmed in her lap and covered the black cloth of her habit with fine white hairs. She could swear it had a squint. She stroked the cat because she wanted to hug Julie. Julie had turned her attention now to the making of pastry and, despite her general indifference to food, Pauline found herself curious about the next meal, as well as the items Julie might ask her to fetch from the shops next time. She would miss this industrious mind.

'Despise him? Oh, no. Oh, *yes*, perhaps if he was *weak* in himself, but he isn't. Oh, Lord, how c-c-c-c-can I explain it?' A level of agitation brought back the stutter. 'I know . . . I want you to know, but you can't, can you?' She paused. 'Th-th-th-think of what it would be like, Sister, if you met someone lost to the devil and they saw your *God*, saw another life, a p-p-perfectly marvellous life on the other side of the clouds, and they rushed, *rushed* to embrace it. Full of joy. And they were *determined* to embrace it, and you'd been the one who'd made them want it, and then – and then out came the claws to drag them back, beat their bones and make them bow to the devil again, all for someone else's vanity. Wouldn't *that* break your heart? Oh, tell me it would. Tell me it would matter. Tell me you wouldn't rather go to hell yourself first.'

Pauline nodded.

'A *g-g-good* man, I mean. It would have to be a good man. A good man corrupted, not a bad man or a lazy one. One with a talent to give to *your* God. Have you seen his paintings?'

'No.'

She was lifting the flour, rubbing the fat between her fingers with gentle ferocity.

'Sarah has. Perhaps that's why she never needed explanations. My husband sees things no one else can.' The bowl bounced against the surface of the table. The kitten slept. 'Am I making sense to you?' Julie demanded.

'Yes.' There was a vision, for a moment, of Sarah, her niece, embracing not her style of life, which she would not wish upon anyone, but the power of her faith. Sarah with *belief*; what a leader she could be. Julie's analogies made profound and perfect sense. They were inspired. The child had a chance. And there was she thinking that any woman who waited on a man, as well as waited for him in the face of patent unreliability, must be a fool. The bowl thumped. The whining of the radiators rose to a shriller whine. *Yeeeeeh*, followed by *uuuuuhmmm*.

'I would want to die if I lost a soul in torment,' Pauline said, inadequately. Julie kneaded the mix. The soon-to-be-ugly cat slept. The kitchen was warm. She had made Julie angry, and she felt perversely pleased about that.

'And, of course, there's another thing in this *love* business. That p-p-peculiar thing. Wanting to *fuck* him all the time. All the time. Wake up to it, go to sleep to it. *All the time*. Him, too. Like wanting to feed. *All* the time. Being hungry to get him inside me, him and his babies. All the time.'

Pauline nodded, without any meeting of the eyes. She wanted to pretend she was not shocked, but she was. It seemed slightly out of context somehow. 'Cannon's brother,' she began tentatively, willing to take advantage, test Sarah's version of things and change the subject, 'what's *wrong* with him?'

'I'm guessing,' Julie said. 'Guessing on what I'm told, but it has to be true because Cannon doesn't know how to invent things. You won't like it.'

'There's a lot about men I don't like,' Pauline said severely, 'which does not mean I have to be spared it.'

'They grew up with bombs,' Julie said, 'the pair of them. Daddy an amateur terrorist in the Belfast back-streets. An opportunist in a senseless war, making his sons the same. They grew up learning to destroy things and the dad making money out of building them again. They were children who threw stones at anything and anyone, and not a breath of religion in them; it had nothing to do with that. Escaped off over here in their teens to make good and get out of it.' She laughed nervously. 'I try to picture it. Little Cannon, throwing stones at the bomb-disposal man who might save his street from falling down. Then his dad would build it up. What chance of a moral code in that? And the trouble is, it must have been *fun*. You can see that, can't you? Running, chasing, hiding, breaking things, *blowing things up* . . . all *fun* when you're a kid. And noise, all that lovely noise.'

'But it might leave you with a great big lump of hatred,' Pauline interrupted. 'No enemies, just hate, sloshing round inside you, nowhere to go . . .' She realised she was holding the kitten down rather too hard. It squirmed.

Julie shook her head. 'Unless you have an alternating love of harmony and, by some miracle, Cannon does. Thank God for the teacher at school who made him want to paint. The only class he went to. They played truant for the rest.'

Pauline wondered briefly what it would be like to *want* to push the kitten inside the bottom oven, close the door, listen to it scrabble and scream to get out as the heat rose, confining it to hell. She shook herself. Her fingers teased the softness of the stumpy little tail protectively.

'I can't believe in a soul incapable of redemption. I *cannot* believe that.'

Silence.

'You stole from him, didn't you? It *can't* simply be pride. You must have done *something* extra. *Did* you?' More silence. '*Did you?* What did you steal?'

Julie was putting the pastry in the fridge, moving awkwardly, the answer a shake of the head. She was embarrassed, tight-lipped.

'What does he look like?'

Julie grabbed the sleeping kitten from Pauline's lap and held it against her own face. Her hair had been cropped like theirs; now it grew. Her eyes were wet. 'I don't know. How would I know? I've never seen his face. Only a glimpse of his mouth. He had the fat man put a pillow-case over my head so I could breathe but he couldn't *see* me. Then he . . . Then they hit me.' She raised a stubborn face shiny with tears. 'I don't *know* him, but I know it *was* him. No one knows him except Cannon.'

The swimming-cap made her look like a nun. A yellow rubber cap, beneath which Sarah's red curls lay squashed against her head, uncomfortable and tight, until she began to swim and forgot everything other than movement. She hated the cap because it was a rule of this club, all rules were anathema, and she did not much like swimming either but she needed her health, something to complete the vicious circle of wine and cig-arettes and all the rest, and this was one way to do it. The costume and the cap were all there was to carry; there was no timetable to maintain and the activity was mindless. Up and down, down and up, like a mechanically propelled toy, counting the lengths and often wanting it to end, enjoyable for the sensa-tion of virtue afterwards and the water itself. A slab of blue for the carving, her body making the wave, the feeling of weight-lessness, the rasp of her own breath and the sight of the far end coming closer. Turn, push off, turn; sound and reality distorted.

Hockney's blue pools; Californian blue water and a sun-filled sky; blocks of blue in those pictures that suggested languor and health. The theme for the picture collection could be the hyp-notic effect of water: no one quite immune to it; drawn like lemmings to the invitation and the threat. Sarah tried to think of the sea, floated on her back and tried to imagine the screech of gulls and the sound of waves. The water of the pool, conveniently close to the office, currently empty except for herself, lapped against the edge with the more prosaic sound of a domestic bath, and the view of the ceiling showed not sky but white plaster, peeling in places from the damp. It was a place beset by rules: caps, single-sex swimming sessions, a club run by a martinet, who ignored a falling membership in the interests of a regime. Sarah floated and wondered how long it would last. A man stood by the entrance to the changing rooms, his arms folded as he surveyed the scene. He tapped his watch and pointed at her. *Five minutes*, he mouthed. She nodded, understanding. Men only in five minutes. She lingered. wallowing in Saturday-morning privacy. On a weekday morning it was like a scene from the sinking of the *Titanic*.

As long as she was weightless in the water, the burdens of the mind became weightless, too. As if, mid-length of the blue pool, they carried themselves alongside rather than within. Threats became mere imaginings, obligations mere bagatelles, time immaterial in the face of the current challenge. *Five more lengths; just five and you're finished. Go on, you can do it.*

Another man came out of the changing area. Saw her swimming towards him, the emerald green of her swimsuit and her disfiguring cap stark against the water. He stopped, changed direction, spat on the tiles and went back in the direction he had come from. Sarah hauled herself out of the water. Ah, John Smith, oh, for a better look at you. You are shy of the public eye.

Cannon had told her that John Smith came here because of the rules. He did not like to swim in the same water as a female, in case, by chance, she touched him. As if the contact with a woman's skin would bring out a rash. What ailed the man? And what ailed her, that she should want to get closer?

Arrogance. Some dim dream that once John Smith was seen, smiled at, spoken to, he would assume some other, manageable personality, like other men, reveal his secrets, if not his desires, prove amenable to reasonable suggestions. Arrogant to assume any such thing, especially of a man who spat at the sight of a woman in *his* stretch of water. As if he owned it. She ran for the

changing room before the martinet came out to shout. A gob of
spittle lay shining on the tiles. The air outside the water was as
cold as spite. *Mens sana in corpore sano.*

Sticky damp skin refused to dry after the shower, no time left;
the cloying warmth of the changing room, the whiff of chlorine
in the hair. The pulling on of clothes that twisted and restricted
after the cool freedom of the water; the sight of dead-looking
skin on her hands. There were no easier ways of trimming
bodily excess and driving those scars back under the skin.

Dressed, warm but shivery, she went up to the gallery and
watched him swim. Two of them: the fat minder, carving
through the water with an easy breaststroke so fast and powerful the water purred in his wake; the man himself, slow and
clumsy, waddling in the water with a slow, ungainly crawl of
maximum effort and minimum result, rolling around like a loose
barrel with kicking legs; a little laughable, maybe. The man
Matthewson had described to his wife as a clown, and Mrs
Matthewson had described to her, looked clownish in the water,
with his trunks ballooning behind him. The little white whale no
one would want to preserve. Who could be afraid of a man like
that?

It was the second time she had spied on him here, the first
with an impression endorsed by her own particular spy. She
wished she had not done it. The sight, and the opinion, was
making Cannon's version of a *bête noire* difficult to believe. Sarah
counted on her fingers. Cannon, Julie, herself: they could all be
wrong. It could all be an innocent lie. Or a real lie. Maybe that
was why Cannon had said, Don't go near him.

Saturday morning and the City was deserted. Sarah hurried
in the cold, which stung the damp hair on the back of her neck,
rammed the hat down harder. She passed the policeman at his
outpost on the corner, standing in his little box and rubbing his
gloved hands. They had stood there day and night since the last
of the City bombs – the City's ring of steel against the antics of
terrorists. Cannon might have become one of these, but Cannon
was cured of his amorality. She was the one who had graced him

with total belief. She must continue in faith until the Christmas deadline. But somehow she was beginning to doubt. It was difficult to believe in a devil moulded out of hearsay. The lawyer in her rebelled at it.

Cannon woke because of the cold. Blue patch of skylight, cold feet the death of sleep. Heater, socks, stumble back to bed, looking at the light. 'That patch of blue the prisoner calls the sky,' something forming in his mind. Supposing he looked up at the skylight and saw someone trying to get in? Not trying to get *out*, as he often envisaged, engineering in his mind a series of ropes and pulleys, Heath Robinson style, but trying to get *in*. There was a construction of a canvas forming in his mind: a figure reclining across the skylight, languid and naked in the cold. If there was anyone up there, all he would do was invite them down.

It was the second week of December, light was precious; in a minute it would bloom and he could paint in it. He fell asleep instead, dreaming of the freedom of Christmas. Johnnyboy had promised.

Woke to the rattling of the door, the skylight patch now a rectangle of grey, the heater burning his feet, disoriented, but not alarmed. He was not in this camp bed, he was in prison; half alive to the sound of shouts and the pounding of feet. Lying in a bunk with his life seeping away, from four o'clock in the morning when he had first started to cut his wrist with the sharpened prong of his belt, to the sound of the man in the bunk below, snoring. Two hours, three, before anyone would notice; easier because the pain in his teeth persisted until he caused a competing pain. He remembered looking at the anatomy of his wrist with mild curiosity in the dim light. There was always light outside the cell: they were never left in the dark. Such a treasure trove of veins and sinews beneath that pallid skin. Scratching at it with the buckle sharpened against the wall, he had felt like primitive man in search of an instrument, angry with the sheer effort of it, digging into his own disobedient flesh, but at least he bled. Knew enough to clench and unclench his fists to increase the flow, the man below still snoring and enough blood to *drip, drip, drip*. Cold feet, pain and shame, and still not enough to take away the toothache. He had raved about the toothache later; long after he dozed and listened to the *drip, drip, drip,* as if the toothache had been the reason – as if it ever could be: he had lived with toothache most of his life. One pain did not take away another. All he had done was damage.

The rattle at the door was louder. Voices in memory. *Let's have you, you daft bastard. What you done?* The sound before that of the suicide squad, running towards the cell in a clatter of boots, ready to drag him back into life for trying to outwit the system. Like an army, pushing everything out of the way, tramping towards him with practised panic, fear and fury echoing in their voices. *What you done, old man, what you done?*

'My teeth hurt,' he'd said; the last thing on his mind. Bonfire Night, it had been; a few weeks after he got there. Fireworks in the sky, visible from little windows, driving him mad.

Most people talked such *shit*, Cannon concluded, relying not on contempt, which he did not feel, but on his own experience of doing exactly that under stress. He had blamed the toothache, which had nothing to do with it; it was feeling useless and desperate, and wondering what the hell his brother was doing on the outside, that had had everything to do with it . . . and wanting to make love to her and cherish her, *all* the time, and not wanting her to die, or to live without him either. If *he* himself was out of the way, *she* would be left alone.

There were qualities of sound, he had decided in prison, that presented themselves in ways that only the subconscious could judge. He was alarmed by the rattling of the door now, not frightened. The sound of the suicide squad, boots on concrete, fireworks: *they* were frightening; this was not. Prison senses had refined him, or perhaps these were senses he had already had. The instinctive knowledge of the dangerous sound; the isolation of the opposite. No one had rattled the door in quite such a fashion before, but he knew it was unthreatening. Cannon came into the full realisation of his senses with a groan. He had missed the best of the light, and that was the worst start to a day.

He knew who it was before he removed the chair; regarded her with a wariness and a feeling suspended between gratitude, mystification, irritation and a kind of awe tinged with affection. Quite simply, he wanted to be in a position to return favours he did not understand. Sarah looked like a drowned rat. He left her at the door and hurried across to the painting, standing face out against the wall, and turned it the other way round. He did not wish her to see herself naked with the scars he had given her. Or to let her know he had forgotten their appointment the way he sometimes forgot the promised daily phone call.

Sarah had none of the timidity of a trespasser: she walked round every place as if it was her own, politely enough but still as if she might have command of it, like the captain of a ship, respectful of privacy while knowing all the time she could invade any part of it. She sat. 'God help me, Cannon, you gave me a fright. Are you awake yet?'

He *knew* she would try not to end his sentences for him as he felt around for the words; she would wait, half knowing what he wanted to say before he said it, dying to articulate it clearer and quicker than he could.

'I owe a lot to the suicide squad, let me tell you,' was all he said.

'Why's that, Cannon?' She knew the answer – she had been part of the equation – but she was always trying to make him talk, about anything and everything. Practice for the outside, fear that the isolations of his life would make him even less confident, he guessed, and wondered, for the fourteenth time of asking, why she should care so much and how long she would go on believing everything he told her. It was a question he never dared ask.

'Because they stopped me. I seem to have this instinct for self-destruction, don't I? And if I hadn't been a suicide risk, I wouldn't have been allowed to get my teeth fixed. Prisoners only get stuff like that if they scare people. And if there's someone on the outside like your William. He must have fudged the books. He's nice, your William, isn't he? Why don't you love him?'

'Well, he isn't *my* William. And I do love him, for what it's worth, but he doesn't want to be loved. He wants to be approved of. Do you want to do more of the portrait? You said you did on the phone yesterday. That's why I'm here. Then we're going to the exhibition. Remember?'

He shook his head, glanced towards the covered easel. It was an old stand for an archery target, broken when he had found it. 'No, not the portrait, if you don't mind. The light's bad. Anyway, I want to think about it for a few days. Let it mellow, if you see what I mean.'

'Let *me* mellow, you mean.' She grinned at him. It was infectious: he found himself grinning back, despite his low spirits. She prowled round the room, not consciously checking for changes but noticing everything just the same. Flakes of wood had fallen from the beams and been swept to one side. It was tidier than before, as if he was packing to leave, precious few possessions since the only things Cannon seemed to cherish were his paints and his brushes even if they stopped him travelling light. Not that there were many paints: too many tubes were only confusing, he said. She stopped. 'What have you done with it, Cannon?'

'What?'

'You know what. The Bonnard sketch.'

There was a particular blank space on an otherwise blank wall, marked by a nail. The space had been wiped clear of dust, showing a cleaner surface and smear marks. Cannon shook his head slowly, like a donkey trying to distract flies around the eyes, sat down on his bed and motioned her towards the cherry armchair. 'I'm allowed to make decisions, you know,' he said resentfully.

'Of course you are. Everything is your decision. But what have you done with it?'

He stared at the ceiling, hands clasped behind his head, as if the sight of the ominous stains would give him inspiration. Sometimes it did. 'I took it somewhere safer. It isn't safe here.

People have been round. I'm sure *he* sent them. I took it to William's surgery.'

'Does William know what it is?'

'No, but he knows it's beautiful. He'll look after it.'

'Cannon, people are in and out of there all the time.'

'So? People don't go to the dentist to examine the paintings on his walls, do they? They can scarcely *think* by the time they get there. They sit, frozen, with a magazine, pretending to read it, that's what they do. And, when you come to think of it, it has to be the last place Johnnyboy would go. A dentist? Never in a million years. But he might come here. I feel it. He'll sense where I am, in time. Johnny has his own satellite.'

It was a long, infuriating speech for Cannon. 'Does it work the other way round?' she asked, trying to keep sarcasm out of her voice. 'Can you picture where *he* is? Because it would be bloody useful if you could.' He treated the question with the utmost seriousness.

'In a vague kind of way, yes. But there's nothing special about that. I know his regime and his habits, you see. I lived with him every day of my life until four years ago. He won't alter, you see. He can't. So I never know, if I close my eyes and see him in places where I expect to see him, that it's because I already know where he'll be. He was swimming this morning, wasn't he? There's nothing . . . what's the word? . . . telepathic about that. He always does on a Saturday. Same place, where he can have the pool to himself.'

'He looked ridiculous,' Sarah said shortly. 'About as frightening as a sick porpoise. Cannon, are you sure?'

'Have I ever told you a lie?'

She looked at him closely. He could look quite guilelessly stupid. The smile revealed the magnificent evenness of his crowned teeth. William's work. William had altered Cannon's life far more radically than she ever could. 'No. I'm not sure you have the knack with lies.'

'Doesn't make me honest either. Julie says I'm a moral vacuum.'

But not a liar or a thief. Sarah was prowling again. She picked up the Johnnyboy sketch, bold lines, hangdog features, black teeth. She scrutinised it. The teeth, which were like bars in the middle of the face, turned the expression into a snarl far removed from Cannon's deliberately vacuous smile, and she frowned at the depiction. 'This is what you think, you see,' she said finally. 'Your version, without him standing in front of you.' She put the sketch down. 'He *swims* like a sad bulldog. Cannon, why are we doing all this? All this running and hiding for *this*? He *looks* like a sad bulldog. He *swims* like a sad bulldog. My boss's wife says he talks rubbish.'

'That's only a photo,' Cannon said.

'What do you mean, only a photo?'

'Stupid!' he shouted, advancing like an avenging angel, taking the sketch, tearing it in pieces with his big hands. The rapid movement was so violent and sudden in itself that she might have been afraid, but she had never been afraid of Cannon. The hands were large enough to encircle her throat and throttle her; they were ludicrously large hands and, like his head, capable of independent movement, as if not connected by the same driving force of a common brain – even his fingers seemed to waggle free from each other. But nothing of his bizarre flurries of movement came to anything until he painted, leaning his whole body into it, unselfconscious, like the conductor of an orchestra, sublimely concentrated. She waved him away. Patted the air with the palm of her hand, dismissing his extremes, inviting him to sit but feeling impertinent for all that. They were both trespassers in this house.

'You don't understand. A proper portrait of a man takes time. It has time in the fabric, time in the paint. Time to watch the changes. That's a snapshot. Of one moment in time when I *thought* I could see him, did – do. I loved him, you see. I love him still. I couldn't even sketch him without *feeling* for him. What have I got, poor bastard? EVERYTHING. *Teeth.* A wife who *loves* me. A talent. And what has he got? *Nothing.*'

He sprang to his feet, lit with his own rage, precise with it, suddenly delicate in purposeful movement. He clipped a sheet of paper to the hardboard on the easel, flurried around for a pen, drew in a few strokes. Took it away and drew another on a fresh sheet, another, another. It was so frenetic she could scarcely look. Sheets of drawing paper scattered the floor with the ink drying. His brother; his brother; his brother, drawn without love in a series of cartoons that made him wink, grin all over his evil teeth, frown for a moment, distend his rubber lips, crease his brow, purse his mouth into a wavy line, look kindly, look like a savage, look like a photofit, a convict, a mad saint. It did not help. In the last he looked like a hungry ghost with nothing to feed his jowls. At the last there was love in the portrait. Her throat was sore and her mouth was dry. Cannon had begun to cough; the kind of polite cough that hurt but sounded as if it was designed to interrupt a conversation, with no other purpose, turning into a spasm of dry coughing, even as he worked. 'See?' he kept saying. 'See? See?'

She saw nothing, apart from the spaniel eyes in the sketches and Cannon's perception that no man was evil incarnate. She had never met a man who was; not even Charles Tysall, who had tortured her and given her the scars. Evil, to her mind, was a quality more shocking for rarity. She did not believe in the devil. She looked at the several depictions of the face and could only see, in her mind's eye, the clumsy body beneath it, barrelling its way across water with all that pathetic effort, afraid of witnesses. The sad clown.

'I'll paint you a proper portrait from these,' Cannon was muttering. 'I'll do it after dark. He never liked bright light much.' Suddenly he laughed, sat down abruptly. 'We used to go out after dark, you know, so no one could see our teeth and laugh at us. We never saw the light.'

'What are we going to do, Cannon?' she asked.

He liked the *we*, although he resented it. 'I don't rightly know. Wait, until the time limit. Believe him. Watch out for him. Guard everything. Until he accepts the fucking rules he set and finally *accepts*, I'm not coming back. *Can't* come back.' Then, more to himself, he added, 'Oh, *God*, give us a child.'

'Is that what he wants, the resumption of a love affair?'

Love affairs were ten a penny to her, not to him. It was his turn to prowl, picking up his coat, putting it down uncertainly, arranging the tubes of paint in neat rows. 'Yes, he wants that, and a new game. A nice fat explosion. He probably wants to blow up the Houses of Parliament with me to help. He always said Guy Fawkes was a fool for getting it wrong. Odd, isn't it? That's the only piece of history he ever remembered from school. *When* we went to school, him to history and me to the art class. I went to that. Teacher took me home and tutored me. Johnnyboy didn't like that, *nooo*, not at *all*. Beat the shit out of me for a while, then got bored with the effort. There's always hope. He always gives up in the end.'

'Perhaps if you gave him the painting?' she suggested quietly.

'No,' he said emphatically. 'No, I can't do that.'

'It's the proceeds of crime, Cannon. Money you took from him.'

'It's the proceeds of *work*,' Cannon shouted. 'My work. Johnnyboy wouldn't recognise something like that if you shoved it up his nose. Money I took to turn it into something beautiful *he* would never buy. What would he want it *for*? He'd burn it or let it rot. Like his houses.'

Nobody knows him but me.

She got up and rammed the hat back on her head. He liked the hat. It made her anonymous and less intimidating, a softer version of herself. Someone perfectly willing to play the fool.

'Right,' she said, saluting. 'I shall continue to assume your paranoia is entirely correct. You'll need a new place to stay. I'll work on it. What else does your brother do with his Saturday?'

He could not understand any more why Johnnyboy so hated women. They were the only people who ever believed a thing he said. 'He stays at home. Sport on telly, all day. Racing, football, rugger, anything. Saturday's a stay-at-home day. Too many women about. Mind, he likes the boxing best.'

'Ritualised conflict,' Sarah murmured. 'While you and I go shopping for *art*.'

'Do we?' Cannon said dubiously.

'Yes. Today you're a consultant.'

It ebbed and swayed, this almost friendship. They could be silent companions or deeply suspicious. He could move from intense curiosity about her to indifference, to introspective silence, then shout a remark apropos of nothing, without minding if she responded. She found it restful to be with someone who had no recognisable code of behaviour: it entailed a certain kind of freedom in her own. Belief in Cannon was an act of faith.

Today he had all the suppressed excitement of a child taken on an outing: talkative, with thoughts flying into questions half forgotten before they came out of his mouth, interrupted as they drove with snatches of whistled song. That was what had drawn her in the first place: the ludicrous smile, the profound capacity for happiness, however temporary; the lack of reserve when he forgot his own predicaments. The ability to lose himself in the moment. He made her fiercely protective.

'How much does lovely William know about me?' he asked suddenly, watching her manoeuvring the car, badly, into a space. Cannon could not drive: it was a mystery to him. The engine and the vehicle itself filled him with alarm.

'Nothing. Next to nothing,' said Sarah. 'The bare minimum. Unless you told him anything.'

'*Me?*' Cannon replied, watching her turn off the ignition as if it were a piece of magic. '*Me?* We don't talk about anything. Nothing personal anyway. It wouldn't be fair. *Nothing.* 'S why I like him. Accepts you without asking. We talk about everything and nothing, like we do.'

'That's all right, then,' said Sarah, and felt a stab of guilt so sharp it was like a stitch in the side. 'I've asked him to come along too, but I doubt he will. Says he's too busy.'

'Too fucking shy,' Cannon said. 'Adores you, can't admit it.'

Then, as an afterthought, as they climbed the steps, another question: 'How did you make the house fall down, Cannon? They say it was a gas explosion.'

He nodded. 'It was. But that's all right, isn't it? I paid the bill first.'

'You promised Julie you'd never do anything like that again.'

'Never. Never, ever, ever. But', he grinned, 'it was *fun*.'

'Yes,' she said, thinking of some of the ugly houses she had seen in her search for a new home. 'Yes. I can see that.'

CHAPTER SEVEN

As they mounted the steps to the exhibition centre, Sarah knew that this might have been a mistake, one of those occasions when instinct clearly foretold embarrassment and was wilfully ignored. Cannon did not like crowds: he looked at the populace pouring through the doors and surrendering bags for inspection as if they were rabid. He shuddered when anyone brushed against him, refused to part with his coat, placed the entrance ticket between his teeth while he decided what to do with it, settled finally on top pocket, right.

A vast hall was thronged with separate stands, five corporate art collections immediately opposite the entrance and, on a separate floor, sixty screened stalls run by dealers, and a balcony above with more. The big works were in the middle; the smaller round the sides. Paintings large and small, sculptures dotted like mushrooms.

'Take note,' Sarah said, *sotto voce*. 'This is where people come to *buy*. The biggest show of contemporary art. Next year you will be *exhibited*, but today *you* are a *consultant*. A *diplomat*. You tell me what's rubbish and what isn't.'

Saturday-morning hunters and spenders, full of goodwill and ready to be delighted. People with houses and eyes, eschewing the delights of do-it-yourself for the joy of looking at paintings. The presence of so many about the purpose seemed cause for celebration rather than for distress, and she tried to tell Cannon that – for the brief moment he listened. Isn't it wonderful that so many people want to *see* paintings? Not *wallpaper*. Paintings and drawings. You are my judge, she told him. Tell me what I should notice, tell me what has talent, I don't know. There was a hubbub of sound, a draught of heat, the scent of excitement finely tuned, the smell of perfume in a crowded train.

Cannon was immune, unbendable to the will of another. She had learned how a certain crispness of voice and a *rat tat tat* direction got his attention, as long as it sounded like an order, while persuasion, the method she always preferred, was more difficult to achieve. He nodded distantly, as if they were a pair sent to reconnoitre foreign territory with instructions to obey nothing but remote signals, and even then at his own discretion. He walked around with his hands clasped behind his back, the better to control the twitching of his fingers.

The corporate collections tended towards the large canvas of abstract art; paintings with titles suggesting serious concepts, such as *Life*, *Waste*, *Chaos*. Rather gloomy and colourless things, she thought; things with bubbling surfaces, cauldrons of paint, or a few spare lines occupying a vast tract of frozen wall. Cannon had to touch, jump from space to space as if he was avoiding the cracks in the pavement. He wanted to stroke the paint and work out through his fingertips how it had reached the surface; he wanted to poke at the canvas, lift the frame and stare at the back to see what had been used. Fashionably suited exhibitors hovered with unctuous politeness. In the corporate collections there was nothing for sale but reputation, while outside that the customer was God with a credit card, greeted with overpowering charm. Sarah loved a market red in tooth and claw but dressed in cultured clothes. She stared at buyers; he at the merchandise. William should have come: he liked a zoo.

It was a market ablaze with enterprise, promise and false promise. *I have been in places like this,* he whispered in her ear. *Don't condescend to me.* He had sat in places like this, he told her, and also the more permanent public places, national galleries where they let you sit and copy, see what other painters had done and struggle with the likeness until it emerged like the birth of an animal out of long, painful and envious perusal. He had lurked in these vaulted rooms, and then on building sites, watching figures at work; figures at night, hurrying past lit windows in a street, the movement of limbs he yearned to capture and never, to his own mind, did, quite. *But I know what I have to do . . . I know how each and every attempt should have the single purpose of capturing a moment of reality or perish.* He murmured into her ear, like a lover, full of indignation about the prospect of betrayal, the whispers louder and louder, the fury in him rising fit to bellow. She ran to catch him.

'Crap,' he screamed. They were facing a large canvas across which there danced something that resembled a bright blue eel. On a white background, it had a single, malevolent eye, directed towards the frame it determined to escape; its back was decorated with minuscule lettering among the blue; a splodge elongated into a creature.

'Shhh,' she said. 'Shhhhh.'

'That's what it says,' Cannon announced indignantly, touching the lettering with a grubby forefinger. She had never seen him with clean hands; imagined he had been born with hands as stained as his teeth had been, and the darkness of his skin contrasted nicely with the white background of the eel. '*Crap,*' he repeated, tracing the lettering. '*Crap, crap, CRAP!*'

'Be quiet,' she hissed, secretly enjoying the row he made.

'Pretentious *crap!*' he insisted loudly. 'Now where's the bloody truth in that? A poster not a *painting.* It says *nothing.* He's *crapped* on his own canvas. Does he know how much *paints cost?*' Spoken while he turned and hissed at the skinny girl with the suit and the bony knees and the winning smile. '*Judas!*' he yelled at her, stabbing the canvas again until the white paint bore the imprint of his stubby forefinger. '*Judas! Thirty pieces of silver for this SHIT!*' And then, suddenly, he was all charm again, hands in pockets, grinning widely, teeth first.

'These critics,' Sarah added, smiling into the eyes of the girl and taking Cannon by the arm to give an impression of safety.

'So *passionate,* you know. You'd think he was a *consultant.*' She tried to blame the increasing discomfort of the heat. They moved on, arm held inside quivering arm, hotter and hotter as they progressed. It was becoming unbearable. 'One day that person might be your dealer,' she said reasonably. But he was gone, far gone; looking at a patch of blue, twenty feet away, anger forgotten, drawn to it like hunger to food; standing there, rationing a moment of bliss, postponing the possibility of disappointment; relishing the delight; dancing, twisting his hands, the whole of him in movement.

'Oh, bless him. *Bless him,*' he was murmuring. 'Look at that fucking *blue*. He lives in there. Ohh, isn't that beautiful? Buy it, Sarah. Buy it.'

She was only conscious of the heat, rising like a tide, stultifying, claustrophobic, and the painting being a very small thing. Cliffs and an Adriatic sea, caught in some miracle of early evening, outlines blurred, the scale announced by a single, vague figure in the water, colours as intense as jewels. He bared his teeth at it, ready to consume it whole, swallow it. She watched; she was born to watch; and, all the same, they were shouting at each other.

'It's a lot of money, Cannon. I haven't got it.'

'Give it to him, Sarah. *Give it.*'

'I can't.'

It was so hot; hot and humid. The painting mesmerised. Sweat trickled down the back of her neck. The hour had passed in minutes. She glanced at his flushed face and then at the faces of others. There was something unnatural in this stultifying heat; something far more artificial than mere excitement. A girl fainted; the public address system crackled; an apologetic voice boomed over the heads. 'So sorry, ladies and gentlemen, the heating and air-conditioning have broken down. For your own comfort, would you kindly leave the building by the nearest exit while we fix it?' No urgency, but a command, nevertheless, creating an uncertain swell of movement, orderly but resentful. Accompanied children and bored companions sighed with relief; in the slow surge towards a side door, Sarah lost Cannon and did not mind. The cold outside was sweet relief.

She watched; always second nature to watch, while the tall and the small and the beautiful and the plain gathered in the side-road and waited in groups, and she thought, with a touch of resignation, that Cannon's presence always had an uncanny knack of shifting crowds. The Tannoy had announced free drinks on their return within the hour; an optimistic promise, perhaps, but the mood was resigned, although those who had surrendered coats huddled and grumbled more than the others and Sarah was glad now to have kept her own.

A favourite coat, full-frocked, voluminous and definitely green, the warmth appreciated even as the perspiration on her skin dried inside it, and she scanned the stragglers still emerging from the building. Cannon was one of the last, his face a picture of injured innocence, his arms folded crossly across his chest; a man aggrieved to have paid for a ticket only to be expelled. He shuffled towards her, her red hair drawing him like a beacon, his steps quicker and quicker until they collided and, to her amazement, he kissed her mouth, hard.

'I might have been followed,' he hissed. 'Here, take this,' removing the object inside his arms and thrusting it into the open folds of her coat. Surprise made her obey. She found herself clutching the thing, hands already familiar with the sharp corners of a frame. Cannon swung his arms in exaggerated fashion, reached into his pocket for a cigarette, which he lit flamboyantly and held triumphantly, as if for an audience. *Look, I'm clean.* Sarah's only desire was to run, far and fast, while he smiled his vacuous smile into her white face. 'You've gone pale,' he said. 'It's not so bad, is it, being kissed, is it? You could get used to it.'

She remembered to saunter rather than run. Down the road, around the corner, past the main entrance to the centre where the crowds were thickest, strolling nonchalantly, waiting for a heavy hand on her shoulder, moving on automatic pilot, and once the safety of the car was in sight, turning on him and screaming, 'You stole it . . . you *stole* that painting. Are you mad? Haven't you learned anything?'

'Be careful,' he said. 'You might scratch it.'

'*Scratch* it?' she yelled. 'You're worried about *scratching* it? What about *stealing* it?'

He hung his head without obvious repentance. 'But you liked it, Sarah. I know you did. It was the best thing I'd seen. You wanted it and I owe you, so I got it. Don't you like it?'

The grinding gears of the car signalled her reply. They shot out of the space like a bullet and, for a moment, he seemed satisfyingly frightened. She drove as if trying to forge a path through a desert in a tank; he clutched his seat-belt with white knuckles.

'Moral vacuum,' Sarah muttered. 'Moral slut. Don't you *think*? What about the artist who painted this picture? What about getting *caught*? Don't you *think*?'

'I did think,' he protested. 'I thought when the loudspeaker spoke. It inspired me.' He tapped his fingers on his knees. 'I thought, wait a minute, this is a right mess, and the dealers will be able to claim any losses from the organisers because it would be their fault, because of the air-conditioning, and there'll be insurance policies and such, and no one will really lose. Not really.' And he smiled again, smugly satisfied with his own logic.

She braked sharply; his forehead touched the windscreen with an audible tap. 'I shall have to take it back,' Sarah said. 'I'll work out a way to take it back.' And then, as the distance grew between herself and the scene of the theft, wondered whether she would. Or whether the company she kept, the life she led and the lies she told had entered her very soul.

She could not drive back. She drove on.

William supposed he had turned up to this exhibition so late because he had dithered about going at all. Sarah had asked him to go, but perhaps not quite warmly enough and she hadn't been specific about the time. He had once tried to count the hours he had devoted to indecision and found the total depressing. On the other hand, there were days when his failure to commit himself to any plan led him simply to wander about, to do things he had never intended by sheer accident and thus let his eyes light upon treasures. He had woken thinking about the paper on twins waiting to be researched, but Saturday was the wrong day for it. Instead, he had stood by his window, with his tea in hand, watching a fat man walking up and down the street, pausing and moving on, as if he was walking a dog, as indecisive as William himself felt. He drank more tea and passed the time. The seventh day of the week was a playground, a day for pleasures, a day for children, and he always felt out of sorts in it, as if he should be having fun instead of wishing there was work to fill an inconvenient gap. So finally he went to the exhibition, wishing he had not wasted the morning and the chance of company.

He hesitated on the steps, slightly disconcerted by the presence of crowds and, as he moved forward, the strange feeling of recognition he had for the fat man standing to the side of the entrance and talking into a mobile phone, looking oddly like the man he had seen in the street. But there were many fat men, and his memory for faces was poor. Fat men or thin were not excluded from looking at paintings.

There was envy as well as pleasure in seeing the work of professional painters succeeding where he had failed, but it was an old disappointment by now and it was the positive element of the envy and curiosity that had made him the haphazard collector he was. He had collected paintings and drawings ever since he had known he would never be able to make them, and he supposed, as he mounted the steps to the exhibition, that what he collected revealed what he was like, in the way books on shelves were supposed to reveal their owners. William shook his head and climbed two more steps, struck by the implications of this. By their possessions, thus shall you know them. He looked at the people, trying to guess from the colour of a coat what the preferred taste of that person would be.

He knew absolutely nothing about fashion in art. He knew, sometimes, what he liked, and on rarer times what he liked to do.

Potter. And he knew, just as he entered the heat of the hall, that he had come to look for something yellow. He also knew a minute of sheer contentment. Two hours before closing simply to *look*. It was the collector's version of complete happiness, and he could not imagine how he had ever considered resisting it.

A collector is a person who refuses to engage fully with human life. Sarah had said that, teasing him, explaining herself. William shrugged. He did not care.

Excuse me, excuse me . . .

All the way round was littered with *excuse mes*. He was aware at one point of being jostled, heard a rough voice, somehow distinct from the babble, whispering impatiently, *I just want to look, just a look*, as if something was preventing him. He did not know why all this was quite such a pleasure, apart from the general politeness of the crowd, but he loved harmony in beautiful things; the search for both dignified his life, and he supposed it did the same for others, or why were they here in pursuit of it? Oddly, his pleasure in the occasion was not diminished by all the examples of disharmony and, to his own conservative, pre-modern taste, downright ugliness: the contrast between what he had expected and what he found amused him.

Chaos, Waste, why bring them into your house when you spent your whole life keeping them out? And even here, there was no getting away from teeth. William found himself facing a six foot by six foot depiction of a gaping mouth with Andy Warhol-style Marilyn Monroe lips painted in primary colours and opened wide in a scream. The tongue lay flat and inert; the tonsils were huge. The head of a youth with a woman's lips. I'd have 'em out if I were you, he told the Mouth silently, feeling lonely in the making of this facile observation. He need not have been alone in this crowd: Sarah had said *come with us*, and he had dithered. It was the curse of inertia fed by shyness, the constant ambivalence of wanting company and yet wanting to avoid it. Sarah would have made him laugh at these obscene red lips. A child stood next to him, rapt with attention. William glanced at him. Froze.

This boy-child was so like the one of his dreams. Ash-blond hair, falling in a straight cut across his forehead; too young to be captivated by merely visual, immovable things, but significant in his fidgeting concentration, his mouth slightly open. Night after night William dreamed of a boy like this, as thin and pale and beautiful, but when William dreamed of him his dreams envisaged a sickly waif, a boy coughing his heart out from some undiagnosed blockage of the bronchial tubes. No strenuous games for this child, but quiet rooms and coughing fits and anxious parents making him petulant. The child seemed to notice he was being observed, turned on William and grinned with an unselfconscious confidence.

'Her mouth hasn't got any fillings, has it?' he remarked. 'And that can't be right, can it?'

William relaxed and actually laughed, louder than the remark demanded. Of course this was not the child of his nightmares: *that* child would be a teenager now and his sister a young adult, while this precocious boy would still have some of his deciduous teeth and pink cheeks to redeem his pallor. He was simply another blond child, out of context in his surroundings. Relief from his own ridiculous imaginings made William laugh again. 'Why should she have fillings and who says it's a she? They could be white fillings.'

The boy considered this. He had a look of intelligence, almost cunning. William found his interest fascinating. 'Well, she's quite old, isn't she? Like my mum. She should have fillings.'

'No, not necessarily so. But there's nothing realistic about her, is there?' William went on, conceding the boy's opinion as to the sex of the mouth only for the sake of conversation. 'Nothing about the mouth, anyway. Whoever painted this didn't know much about teeth. She's got too many of them, for a start. Thirty-six, not thirty-two. And look at that widgy little tongue – it isn't even alive. How many teeth have you got?'

'I *had* twenty. I lost some. I'm getting new ones.'

'Well, they started to grow as soon as you were born, so you can't stop 'em.' He judged the boy to be about ten, canines and premolars erupting gently in his mouth even as he spoke. The boy stood with his own tongue protruding, curled it over his top teeth and ran it round the edges, as if counting his incisors, a task quickly relinquished. 'My tongue usually feels too big,' he volunteered.

'Tongues do,' William said. 'And they won't do what they're told. Have you noticed? You can tell your tongue to stay still, and it might for a second, but it's got so many things to do your brain can't control it. It won't be ordered; it has to be automatic, disobedient if it wants. After all, it's got to move around about a litre of spit every day. *This* tongue looks like a piece of dry bacon. Got no life at all.'

The boy giggled. 'It doesn't look as if it would hurt if she bit it, and it does hurt when you do that, doesn't it?'

'Oh, yes, but not for very long because it gets better very quickly. Everything in your mouth does, because it has such a good blood supply. It's made to heal super quick. You could stick a pin right through your tongue and be better next day.'

'Yughh,' said the boy, his tongue unconsciously licking his pink lips, his eyes still on the painting. 'Are you a dentist, or what?'

'Yes.'

'Gross,' said the boy, and turned away, bumping into a large adult who stood close behind him, listening. William was unsure whether this remark was an indictment of the painting or of his role in life, but he hoped it was the painting. He watched the child rejoin parents, felt himself blush under their suspicious glance, and felt absurdly cheered by his small encounter. Like a child himself, he pulled a face at the painting of the Mouth and then continued to amble from stand to stand. The child seemed to have given him an excuse to behave badly. The delivering of a little lecture always relieved him and made him feel superior, as if he had done a good deed, and it was always pleasant to be critical of a ridiculously misleading representation.

But the point of a painting, he told himself, was not to be studiedly realistic. He loathed the kind that aped photography or the precision of the architect, because that was not honest: it was not what the eye saw. When you look at a face, Cannon had said, standing in front of the pictures in his waiting room – the existence of which had been the first stage in his trust of the dentist – you don't see every detail. You see the strongest lines. You record the strongest impressions first, the same way you do when you look at anything. And when you describe one person, or one scene, to another, you will be selective in what you say because you cannot hope to be complete; you can only give your own version. That's what I try to do; if I can get one off-centre moment of truth, one strong impression, that is all I can do.

Whereas I, William thought, as he wandered round, would become obsessed with the perfection of my technique: I could not allow myself spontaneity; I have had it trained out of me. I would buy the highest-quality materials, measure my brush-strokes to the millimetre, try to be comprehensive, record what I *ought* to see and miss the point entirely. I would be like the fussier patient, convinced that the world could see the black spot on a back tooth when she smiled, or the slight crookedness of her left incisor, instead of which no one would notice at all. *Stand three feet back from the mirror:* that *is what people see; rarely more than that.* No one studies your face the way you do your own. Only a lover.

'Excuse me, how much is that?' It irritated him when the prices were not clearly displayed and he had to ask, introducing a certain coyness into the whole exchange. He was aware of someone watching him from behind, probably sizing him up for financial worth, making him feel awkward. Not that he had come here intending to buy; he had come to browse because it was a Saturday – but he wanted to know, all the same. There was nothing here that had quite moved the cockles of his heart yet, but he faced a piece of prettiness, three russet apples in a bowl, looking ripe and ready to eat; a cheerful work of art for a kitchen wall.

'Eight hundred pounds.' No, he would buy a supply of apples. He moved on, warm, surrounded by enthusiasm, content to look, but dizzy with looking, then backtracked to see what he might have missed. An argument at a stall: someone returning for a painting that had been stolen; raised voices. Disharmony; ugliness. It drove him back round the hall; back to the Mouth, out of sheer curiosity to see if someone had actually purchased it, and out of perverse fascination to see if anyone would love what he had detested.

Someone did. A red sticker in the corner of its garish pink frame; a gallery girl self-importantly writing out an address on the back of a cheque; a man standing by, shuffling on a coat and ready to leave, until he turned back to survey the painting one more time, and grinned. For the second time in the afternoon, William thought his heart would stop.

The man who stood with his eyes fixed on the Teeth was very still. He seemed so rooted to the ground on large feet that he could have been one of the sculptures: no one stood so still with a smile on the face; a smile meant some sort of animation; William thought he might have touched and prodded him without any response. He was not a large man, smaller in stature than the picture, and the top of his head was only level with William's shoulder, but there was a quality of massiveness about him as if his bones were heavy. Both feet pointed forward with military precision; the features were dark and harshly handsome, marred by the smile: full lips drawn back revealing brown, uneven teeth.

The teeth marred the face worse than a scar. They marred it for a stranger – a friend would cease to comment, the brown teeth would be accepted as part of the whole – and on first sight, even to William's experienced eyes, they made the man look like an imbecile. A cretin with dirty habits, the discoloration suggesting without subtlety that the rest of him was unclean, even though the skin of his jaw hung soft and shiny from shaving, the shirt was immaculate pink and the hair shone black with health. Efforts were made to compensate for these teeth; the neatness was vulgar and aggressive. The impression of the man would be entirely different if only his mouth was shut. William closed his eyes briefly, waited for the other impression to emerge. It would not. He felt a wave of violent pity, mixed with intense excitement, like someone coming home. The face meant little to him; only a pleasurable recognition of someone sweetly familiar, confused by lack of identification and almost greeted without thinking. It was the teeth that made him want to say, *Excuse me* . . . Tetracycline-damaged teeth, the very image of Cannon's before treatment. A vision of a man out of prison, smiling at him fearfully.

They were crowded together in the small space of the exhibitor's stand; too small for a painting that belonged on larger walls. William did not pause to wonder why a man with such frightful teeth should want to buy a dreadful picture designed to shock with its totally awful and misleading delineation of perfect dentine in a ludicrously overcrowded mouth; he thought of that later, and instead, in that second, found himself looking round in expectation of the blond boy, who somehow belonged in this scene. That was his only hesitation. Apart from patting the pockets of his jacket to find where he kept his business cards. The man had turned his back again, consulted a watch, business done, anxious to be gone, unconscious of William or anyone else.

There was nothing William could say, or think to say, even though his curiosity was overpowering. He skipped to the front of the solid body to find the man still smiling and staring in a fixed basilisk stare towards the dreadfully perfect, plumped-up lips of the Marilyn Monroe tooth model. What *could* he say now? Can I look at your teeth? My word, what interesting choppers! Where did you get them? All sorts of inanities bubbled up from his throat, and instead he bowed from his great height, unable to resist a second look, and proffered his card. It was something he did when he was too shy to announce his own name.

There was no movement. William could feel his own blush rise across his face like the warm lick of heat from an oven. The eyes moved. They looked like the liquid eyes of a puppy. Cannon's eyes, but alive with surprise and a furious fear.

William was still holding out the card as the man backed away. The white rectangle looked as pathetic as a stale sandwich; he could feel the man's shock and outrage, but he could not withdraw his hand. He had to stoop to be level with the man's face. Then a blow landed on the left side of his jaw, deflected by the slight embarrassed turning of his head, but still a memorable blow. He fell to his knees, felt his hands clutch the serge of trousers, feel the twin pillars of a pair of legs. The blow paralysed; he remained in his attitude of prayer; the legs removed themselves and the mist cleared. Some semblance of dignity made him adjust to sit back on his buttocks, cross his own long legs in front and prop his elbows on his knees with his head held between his hands. This way he was abject without being servile. The voices around him seemed to come from another country; a foreign sound which, after a full and endless half minute, he recognised as whispering laughter.

He came round into fuller consciousness with a growing sensation of pain without damage. Looked up, to find someone stepping over his knees with the careful respect owed to a drunk in a place where he might be sick. There he was, with his head propped in his hands, in artistic reverence.

The man and the painting had gone. In the middle of the crowd, William was left entirely alone to his eccentric appreciation of the subtle implications of an artfully contrived blank white wall.

Sarah propped the picture against the mantelpiece. It seemed to bring light into the room, carried within itself the promise of happiness, captured the feeling of sun on the skin, the first pleasurable sip of perfect evening. She could see herself on the balcony overlooking the ocean, alone and yet complete in a minute of sensual perfection. Then, looking closer, she identified with the figure in the sea, swimming around endlessly without purpose or direction, lost in the moment. She shivered, as if some creature had walked across her grave. The bottle of wine was half empty. The wine alone could not conjure up the smells and scents of the scene in the stolen picture; only colour could do that.

Alone on Saturday night, but there was never anything maudlin about such a regular occasion, except when she sat as she sat now and contemplated the new depths of corruption that had made her collude in theft. *I didn't have any choice*. Oh, yes, heard that one before. There was always a choice in someone stealing a painting. This one already felt like a necessity of life; if she moved it, it would leave a space. But a painting was not edible: no one actually starved for lack of paper and canvas; there was *no* excuse. No, she told herself, I had no choice because if I had taken it back immediately it would be obvious that Cannon had stolen it and Cannon's low profile was a bit of a priority. She recognised, as she formulated these words to an audience, that this was specious rubbish. She was inventive enough to have taken the painting back after she had got rid of Cannon, explaining away the theft as a piece of mentally defective delinquency by a friend driven mad by the heat. They wouldn't have cared – they wouldn't care if she did it tomorrow, but she knew she wasn't going to do it tomorrow either. It was already too late.

Why was she keeping it, then? Because it had been stolen for *her*? As if Cannon were flattering her with his boldness, earning his spurs and presenting them to a favoured lady? *Crap*. Yes, there was an element of flattery in his having stolen the painting for her rather than himself, but it was also, in its way, deeply insulting. The presumption that she *would* be flattered rather than shocked to receive a stolen gift she would never be able to show; the presumption that this was commonplace and therefore perfectly fine; the presumption of corruption. *It's not so bad being kissed; you might get used to it*. She felt a prickle on her skin that she wanted to scratch. I am hardly one for such moral dilemmas, she told herself. I sleep with two or three different men in any given week; they give me things and provide me with information; I give them affection and I don't think that makes me corrupt in the way *this* does.

The mirror in the hall was dusty; it was always dusty and she never knew why. Dust comes from skin, someone had told her; whenever you move, you shed and create it, then wipe it away. She stroked words in the dust. CORRUPT. Then she wrote DUPED and ended the D with a scrawl.

Sarah Fortune regarded Saturday night as sacrosanct, by accident and by design. Saturday night alone was a sort of statement about how she lived, breathed, plotted, planned and survived with more than a modicum of laughter. Saturday night was reassessment time, Sunday committed to glorious indolence before the circus began all over again. Until, that was, this extra element intruded. *Corruption*. She wiped the mirror clean with the sleeve of her sweater.

She had believed in Cannon; she had turned her life into a series of wheels for Cannon; she had championed him, defended him and given him her faith. Why? Because there was no one else; because he had talent; because he and his wife were worth it, according to her own code. She made her own evaluations carefully and did not doubt them. Between them that pair had an enormous capacity for happiness and fulfilment. She did not care if he made fortunes for thieves and dishonest builders; she did not care what he had done in the past, which made it entirely inconsistent that she should feel such revulsion for the act of theft that had implicated her now.

'What a *selective* conscience you have,' she murmured.

She turned the painting so that it faced the wall and could no longer seduce her, but hiding such a beautiful thing felt like another sin. In her kitchen, Sarah shoved the cork back into the neck of the half-empty wine bottle with unnecessary force. The bottle slipped from her grasp and fell. No satisfying sound, merely a timid thud and the wine seeping away across the floorboards. A bloody waste, like all this bloody effort. What she saw in her mirror was a bit-player in some melodrama that no one but a dreamer would believe. She opened another bottle of wine and looked for something to do. If Cannon's imprisonment and the wife he had met on the first stop of his road to total reformation had failed to cure him of casual dishonesty, as they patently had, then why should she place any belief in him at all? Wasn't a thief also a liar?

She wanted more than anything to turn back the clock on the day that had passed to the evening that had preceded it, when she could still hold on to belief in Cannon, and all he had told her about his brother, as an obstinate act of faith, before he had shown he could not be cured of dishonesty. Before she had seen that ridiculous, harmless body barrelling through swimming-pool water. Before she had listened to the last bulletin from Ernest Matthewson's wife, relating Ernest's impression that John Smith was a *clown*. That was where the rot had set in.

She moved round her own abode, restless, the whole state of her a travesty of Saturday-night calm, peering into rooms as if she was a stranger, the pictures on the walls mocking her. There was no real reason to move house, except for the memories and the way that movement always granted the illusion of freedom, as if a fresh start wiped clean a scratched slate and got the blood and tears off the walls. She opened the balcony windows; the air bit nicely cold.

Cannon stood below, poised to throw a pebble against the glass, a method of gaining attention he seemed to prefer to ringing the bell. Perhaps another part of his fantasy life. She was coldly, furiously angry, ready to spit, but then when she opened the door, she saw him slumped and his face bloated with tears. He made no effort to cross the threshold. He had forgotten his coat and his teeth chattered with cold.

'I'm sorry,' he said. 'I'm sorry, sorry, *sorry*. It was an *awful* thing to do. Not just awful, stupid. Insulting. Sometimes I just don't know better. I can't stop. I don't *know* until afterwards. Can you see that? *Can* you? I'm so sorry.'

'Sorry for what?' she spat. 'Stealing? Or lying?'

She stared at him, the anger melting even as she struggled to retain it. She had never been able to harness anger to good effect: it always failed to have enough force and she could never make it last quite long enough to stop it feeling ridiculous, even by dwelling on it.

'I'm sorry,' he wept. 'You rescue me from prison and from fire . . . You believe me and what do I do for you? Steal. I've never stolen anything except from him, and that was *mine*. And I don't know how to lie. I just don't *think*.'

She saw him then as she had seen him first: a confused and clever child. Julie had seen the child in him. He stumbled into her perfunctory, motherly embrace and she led him inside. The phone rang. Cannon squatted in front of the fire, the reflection of the gas flames glowing against his wet face; she watched as she answered.

'Sarah?' William sounded more distant and hesitant even than usual. 'Sarah, could I see you? I could get a taxi . . .'

No. She did not want these two under her roof at the same time; it was too much. She did not want William to see the stolen painting. She did not want William receiving any explanations whatsoever: what he did not know would not harm him. She did not want him to know she had become a thief.

'Could it wait, love? Tomorrow, if you like.'

Cannon coughed; a prolonged, hacking cough, a development of the dry spasm of the morning. He needed the warmth of the fire. Her mind moved on to think about food, shelter, warmth. She had an hour to get food into him: he would never stay longer than that.

Johnny would know. He would find you.

'Oh, yes, it can wait.' There was disappointment in William's voice; it irritated her. I *suppose you had another bad dream*, was on the tip of her tongue until she remembered, with difficulty, how much she liked him. She liked them all; it was the hazard of her life to like the rejects no one else even noticed. My God, they did not know what they were missing.

'Tomorrow, then?'

'I'll see,' he said, and put the phone down sharply. Slowly, less abruptly, she did the same.

CHAPTER EIGHT

Isabella Dalrymple woke with a Sunday-morning headache and the memory of snoring during the night. She was cold because the man on the other side of the bed was warm, with the whole of the double duvet wrapped around his ample body. Not simply draped, but inextricably linked with his limbs and jammed under his chin, thoroughly, if unconsciously, appropriated. Until she recognised that fact, and the futility of any attempt to get it back without waking him, she had been unsure of where she was; there had been half a minute of disorientation and a sense of another place and more forgiving time.

In the years of her marriage William had been an agitated sleeper, who moved and muttered and sometimes spoke aloud, but he was more likely to relinquish the duvet and wake cold himself than he was to take it. Isabella thought of William with regret, tinged at the corners with a nasty little shadow of conscience that hung over her eyes, like something minute stuck to an eyelash. There was no longer any point in staying in bed.

In the scale of marital misdemeanours recounted by contemporaries, William had done nothing *wrong*; no infidelities, no serious addictions, if the dentistry itself were discounted, no unpleasant self-indulgences otherwise, no obnoxious personal habits, no outstanding social gaffes. It was just that he had done nothing right either; he had simply ceased to be an asset. All he had done for his wife was do everything she asked him to do. In retrospect, an obedient husband who pandered to the ambitions of a wife without ever sharing them was the worst kind of partner. She had moulded him and schooled him, organised him and ordered him until he was a nothing more than slightly afraid of her shadow, and all she could remember now was how he had never once stolen the duvet.

With a backward glance at the sleeping form of William's far richer, more colourful replacement, Isabella took to the bathroom. For every morning of her marriage to William, she had presented him with a flawless face over his breakfast tea, a time-consuming challenge that should have commanded appreciation and was now such an ingrained habit that she had made herself regard it as a virtue. This is the face he will remember when he goes to work. Avoid having children if at all possible: it wrecks everything.

Everything had proved capable of wrecking itself by the slow, disintegrating process of her own disappointment and contempt, and this was what she had now. A richer, shorter partner with a far finer apartment and a far more interesting clientele of friends, plus a shared interest in bigger and better. Isabella tested the water in the shower with a delicate hand. It was too hot. She felt lethargic: the prospect of the hour-long ritual of hairwash, hairdry, *maquillage*, the selection of clothes, all seemed incredibly arduous, and that was the real cause of the malaise. *If* she had still been with William, none of this would be mandatory. He wouldn't have noticed; hadn't noticed for years. She had – as she still did – bled William dry in maintenance costs to sustain a face, a style of life and a wardrobe that meant absolutely nothing to him. Which meant she had taken away *nothing*.

Life seemed suddenly to be one long series of clichés lived out against a backdrop of hope. She brushed her teeth cursorily. Life with William meant that everything about teeth bored her; her own had never been any trouble; everyone else made such a fuss. The rest of her year seemed to unfold in an endless succession of doing exactly this. She raised her upper lip in front of the mirror, the better to remove a speck, saw blood on her gums and had a sudden vision of a face without teeth. No, no, her teeth were excellent and permanent – William said so, didn't he? But if they were not, who would love her then?

He would.

The bathroom wallpaper was richly decorated with birds of paradise, which made her want to screech in tune. The world divided, he had told her once, between those who loved wallpaper and those who detested it. She was cross and tired and could remember nothing that had given her any pleasure in the last week. Except, of course, the comforting thought that, in a similar fashion to the planned stripping down of the paper in here, her own life could be altered. Nothing was permanent about the way one lived, and whenever she wanted, she could go back to the husband who did not snore.

Mrs Matthewson, loyal spouse to Ernest and equally loyal friend to the few she otherwise loved, laid the table for the ritual family lunch in a dining room of many colours: creamy yellow walls, vibrant swagged curtains festooned with brilliant blue hummingbirds, whose motif had been repeated throughout the house ever since a holiday in the West Indies. The house, which was large and solid as befitted Ernest himself, bore tribute to that vacation.

She always left the laying of the table until last, waiting until she was sure everyone was in attendance. There was nothing more insulting than a fully laid table displayed as an accusation of parental incompetence on the many occasions when her son had failed to turn up. The provision of food was one secret of marital stability – it had been sufficient to keep Ernest more or less in control – but it was not enough to ensure the consistent attendance of an emancipated son. With girlfriend, a pallid little thing with a pretty enough face mostly subsumed into over-large spectacles and an adoring smile for her affianced. Mrs Matthewson never ceased to marvel at what a good-looking, personable man her son had become. The revolutionising of his body from the grossly fat boy she had nurtured to the streamlined and athletic

male he was now had been his own work; the acquisition of
social graces and, at long last, an appreciation of his parents had
been the work of Sarah Fortune. Mrs Matthewson approved
violently of Sarah; she resisted the impulse to give the new
girlfriend the napkin with the stain, just as she would try
to avoid the temptation to pour gravy all over her skirt. Such
activities would be childish and counter-productive, and would
not achieve her heart's desire, which was to have cataclysmic
Sarah Fortune, her *friend*, back in the family fold. Forgiveness
of her son for the monumental carelessness of losing her was
beyond Mrs Matthewson, even though she privately, if not
publicly, agreed with Ernest that a marriage would have been
a disaster.

They sat. Malcolm and his father talked about the law, as
lawyers do. A careful listener, and Mrs Matthewson was certainly that, would recognise that this apparently intellectual
exchange was no more than pure gossip, not about the law itself
but the personalities in it, who was earning what with whom,
which dog was eating which, and how they were managing to
digest. Malcolm had become boringly ambitious. *Sarah would
not have let you do that,* Mrs Matthewson muttered to herself
over the grapefruit segments, turning her face and a saccharine
sweet smile to the newest replacement.

This girl was not stupid; a businessperson, with hungry eyes.
Malcolm would never go for anyone stupid, not after Sarah, but
he would, quite unconsciously, choose something more
amenable, a little less *vivid*. Mrs Matthewson watched the eyes,
enlarged behind the specs, straying away from her own. Tricky;
scenting an enemy; she was not going to engage in girl-talk with
Darling's plump, middle-aged mummy, was she? She was going
to cosy up to the men and refuse to be excluded.

'How's Sarah?' Mrs Matthewson asked Ernest pointedly,
ignoring his wince.

'Oh, very well, blooming. God alone knows what she does. As
I was saying . . .'

'When are you going to make her a partner?'

'Yes, Dad, when are you?' Malcolm, amused, was not letting him get away with it, or his mother either; Ernest was glaring, finally giving in. It was no good resisting once it was started: when they were together, the three of them, they wanted to talk about her.

'Still giving her the no-hope clients?' Malcolm asked.

'She finds them of her own accord. She seems to have an aversion to clients who either make money or have it. She *loves* awkwardness,' Ernest protested defensively.

'I wonder why.' Malcolm's eyes were on his mother, who lowered her gaze towards her food. The girlfriend ate doggedly.

'We've one awkward client she won't go near. We've tried him with everyone. No one lasts. Now, if she'd deal with John Smith and make him happy, the partnership would love her, but she won't. I don't understand her sometimes.'

All the time. Mrs Matthewson shifted uncomfortably, and began to clear the plates. The new girlfriend was supposed to say, 'Let me help.' She didn't.

Malcolm adopted his dry cross-examining voice. 'Not berthing her alongside the dangerous ones again, are you, Dad? Leaving our Sarah to handle the psychotics? You know what happens when you do that. If he's half-way mad already, she'll make him madder. Why don't you give her a decent client for a change?' His voice had risen. The girlfriend smiled into an empty face.

'She doesn't *want* decent clients,' Ernest shouted. 'She wants eccentrics. Like she wanted you.'

This time the silence was longer.

'Do you like your beef rare or medium?' Mrs Matthewson asked the girl.

'Rare, please,' the girl said.

'What a shame,' Mrs Matthewson said, carving the burnt piece off the end of the roast and putting it on a cold plate. 'Tell Malcolm about this John Smith, Ernest, do. What does he look like? So *interesting*.'

And then, much later, she would tell Sarah. All the gossipy

pickings from the rich man's table, in case, woman to woman, they were useful.

They finished the last of the overdone beef, followed it with ice-cream, and then said grace. The offer of alcohol had been made, but it was a token offer. Imelda had announced it as a challenge immediately after Sarah came into the refectory and remembered to stand for the prayer preceding food. 'Would you have some wine, Sarah? We've plenty,' she yelled, as a Christmas-present bottle was brandished like a club for the juggling. The parish priest followed its progress with a longing glance; the others with mild curiosity. Sarah could see herself sipping a single glass, for ever in debt for this special treat while they followed her consumption of it with their eyes, concerned for her soul in case she asked for a second. Only the one bottle between the thirty here present, as if a drop of the stuff would intoxicate instead of reawaken a growling need. Sarah refused politely, and prepared to drown the food in water, remembering to ask for more in order to flatter the cook. Not Julie; not today, although they wished it was. Your day of rest, dear. Let us bugger the beef.

'I wish they wouldn't,' Julie whispered to Sarah, on her left.

'Wouldn't what?'

'Buy beef at all.' She had caught from them a certain Irish intonation, a rhythm of speech alien to Pauline's crystal tones, which showed she did not spend most of her time in Pauline's company. Sarah waited for a topical reminder of beef-related disease while she and Julie ate the meat with equal feigned enthusiasm.

There was a buzz of voices in the convent dining room, none of them raised, all animated, argumentative even, discussing the day's news, the week's news, each speaker with a separate ailment that was never discussed in public except in an earnest invitation to make a joke of it. They were all slightly disabled, by age at least. They had faces without lines, bent bodies; they were old without protest; a dying breed, who knew they were unbanishable. Oh, for a life of virtue, free from acquisitive needs, never even *wanting* to house-hunt and full of appreciation for burnt beef. Sarah had learned her manners at this kind of table; she had a certain gratitude about eating, whatever it was.

'Once a month, child, you eat with us. You don't eat enough. Look at the size of you.' Not once a complaint, or a curiosity for the outside world. Plenty to talk about, especially the prospect of the Cardinal's Advent sermons in the cathedral; they all went, even most of the walking wounded. What happened here was the will of God, illness included. That, and that alone, was what Sarah abhorred rather than admired. This dependence on the will of another, either divine or sent by the National Health Service, each couched in inefficacy and mystery. She loved their capacity for acceptance, but she could not revere it. God was a perverse old man to be indulged, with a passing resemblance to Ernest Matthewson, in her view. Deities and more temporal authorities begged and deserved the challenge of sheer bloody-minded disobedience.

There was a garden of a kind, which sprouted rather than grew, the better for that on a good summer day, not now. These retired sisters had been too much in the world and moved about too much to find time to cultivate a garden. They were neat and tidy without being versed in domesticity or horticulture. The front garden doubled as a car park, the garden element revived from time to time with indoor potted plants and gifts and surviving shrubs, unlike the back area, which no one noticed until the nettles reached the height of the dustbins. The heart of the convent was the chapel, where each item was polished and revered, each statue and seat, shining with the touch of a hundred loving hands.

In the watery sunshine of the afternoon, Sarah noticed that Pauline looked frail, her skin like parchment and her movements less than brisk. It was only after dark, in electric light, that her deepset eyes looked powerful; for the moment, although she was the strongest of her contemporaries, she looked an old woman. Until she spoke, and all the authority returned.

'I'm grateful to you, Sarah,' she was saying gruffly.

'Why?' The statement was surprising. Pauline gave thanks for the existence of this niece in her own prayers, but never in public. She accepted Sarah's donations as no more than the convent's due; took it as conscience money from a heathen. She never gave thanks for charity, but if it was offered she never missed the chance.

'For your dentist friend, of course. A Christian, for sure. He phoned me to say he was willing to treat any nun virtually for free. We have to pay for materials only, now isn't that nice? He seemed to know all about Imelda, can't think how. Is he a Catholic?'

Julie was looking straight ahead, transfixed by the bare branches of a shrub, conspicuously innocent.

'Hm. I would say his religious orientation is not decided yet,' Sarah said carefully, hiding her surprise in the palm of her hand and feeling vaguely outmanoeuvred. 'He may want you entirely for research. The effect of diet on teeth, or something of the kind. After all, few people have a diet which is easier to predict. But I should take the offer. He's a very good dentist and a kind man, even though he sometimes doesn't realise it himself. Probably ripe for conversion, too.'

'Of course we take up the offer – we take up *any* offer like that. I don't care about his motives. Sister Dominic went the same day he phoned – she raves about him.'

'Everyone does, apart from his wife,' Sarah said.

'No man is a hero to his butler,' Pauline said inconsequentially, and rose from the bench where all three had sat. 'Have a word with me before you go, will you, Sarah? I'll leave you in peace with your cigarettes. I can't bear to watch.'

Julie and Sarah sat in companionable silence, Julie with a piece of mending in her lap. It was a cotton traycloth with embroidery and a frayed hem; it kept her hands busy. Sarah employed hers in the lighting of a cigarette. Each to her own. The sunlight caught Julie's growing brown hair and made it gleam against her bare face. In the warm light of a mild afternoon she looked almost saintly.

'Cooking and now mending?' Sarah enquired. 'Do you also pray? Give you a habit and a rosary and you'd become one of them. Do you think it would suit you?'

'No.' She let the mending fall, as if it embarrassed her. 'No,' she repeated. 'But it has its virtues.' Her face lit with an impish smile, dispelling the illusion of saintliness. Saints were not renowned for humour, or maybe their jokes were never recorded. 'Obedience to divine will,' she said. 'The belief that all sufferings are temporary and have a purpose. I could do with a bit of that, although I might prefer a belief that everything was *preordained*. I should love to be able to offer up pain in the belief that it altered the sentence of some soul in purgatory. Turn it into something useful. That would be nice. And I'd like to be able to pray for the baby Cannon wants so much.' The mending remained untended.

'Some of it must rub off, you know,' she continued, with the same, hesitant thoughtfulness. 'Even though I don't believe it. Because here I am, sewing and cooking, keeping myself busy to avoid going mad. I don't do it for praise or the greater glory of God, and I know that really I'm a prisoner, but I don't feel like a prisoner.'

'It's your decision. You can leave whenever you want.'

Julie shook her head vigorously. 'No, I can't. Where would I go, except to Cannon? And if I went to Cannon, John would find us. You know what I think?' The mending had fallen on the ground and Julie did not bother to retrieve it. 'I think John could find Cannon whenever he wants, whatever Cannon does. Not that he's watching him, but he follows him with his mind. He goes to the places Cannon goes to . . . He *imagines* where he is. Do you know this already? Has he told you?'

'Something similar. I don't believe in telepathy. No evidence, you see. If John Smith knows where his brother is, it's because he's sent someone to look. Or gone himself.' Sarah felt guilty. Day by day, her belief in the ultimate wickedness and the almost supernatural powers of Johnnyboy Smith had been gently eroding.

'Johnny can't imagine *my* whereabouts because he has no link into my mind the way he does to Cannon's. But he would know immediately if I went to Cannon. Then he would come and destroy me.' Julie stood, folded her arms across her chest and walked the few paces the garden allowed. She spoke with quiet certainty. 'He'd do it out of revenge for me stealing Cannon away, as he sees it, or simply out of hatred and loss. Can you imagine hating anyone so much?'

Sarah paused. 'No. Hatred is quite alien to me. So is revenge. If someone hurts me, steals from me, I keep out of their way. Take another path.'

'But you might not if the *person* who was stolen was the only person you had ever loved. The only person you were *capable* of loving. The person who made you complete, allowed you to function. You would hate the thief who blinded you, wouldn't you? The one who cut off your right arm and took it away?'

'I might,' Sarah conceded. 'I just doubt if I could sustain it – not sustain it and carry it forward into some act of malice, such as bashing them over the head with a teapot. They say anyone could kill. I don't believe I could. I might wish someone dead, but that's totally different. That's only wishing.'

She thought of her long-dead husband; the one she had loved with youthful optimism. Wanting him dead when she knew his unfaithfulness; not wanting it at all when it happened. Pauline had helped, then. Said it was God's will, not her own. In the end only God dictated birth and death. She thought of Charles Tysall's death and not being able to hasten it or even wanting it.

It was growing cold, the December sun sinking in the sky, turning Julie's soft hair into a halo, somehow ignoring her own.

'Well, the game's nearly over. Two more weeks. We've got to believe that. Don't let Cannon boss you around. Do you want a baby as much as him?'

'I want what he wants. It would be the ultimate message for Johnny, wouldn't it? And, besides, I've always been afraid that if I didn't conceive Cannon would leave me. I'm not enough all by myself. No one is. There has to be something more important than either of you.'

'Nonsense.' Sarah did not believe her. Cannon had fascinated her from the first meeting; obligation and fierce defensiveness had grown from that and, at the beginning, his wife was only his wife; a once-clever school dropout who had lost a decade to drugs, pulling herself half-way out when Cannon met her, and now the wife of dreams. Sarah had never before seen such unconditional, determined love. She did not judge or measure it, simply felt the peculiar strength of it; it infected her and almost made her ashamed. She watched him blossom in Julie's presence; shrivel in prison without her. There was a magic in her potency: she made the unlovable lovable; she was the guardian angel, who chased away the demons. She remembered Julie's instructions and her terror. *Take me away – somewhere secret. Take me away . . . don't tell him.*

Who did this to you?

His brother – take me away. Hide me – he's coming back.

She had believed then in the evil of John Smith, although she could not encompass the reasons. Looking at Julie now, diminished by the attentions of this monster but restored to health, she found the belief slipping away, like adolescent faith. She remembered the incredulity of the police. *What? She* thinks *she knows who it is? Why would this man do such a thing?* She tried to summon up the hatred she had felt then and found she could not. The monster had no shape. But Cannon lived. Cannon and the bogeyman he might have invented to scare them all.

The Christian Sabbath was a bad day for reflection.

William was not going to phone Sarah. He was not going to be dependent on anyone who was so independent of him. He was not going to become introspective either. He was going to go for a walk, like other people did, mull over the week, pretend he was purposeful. Think on his feet, in case it made it easier.

He did not love her, never pretended he did. He simply thought of her a lot. He found it difficult to make his own kind of romantic image out of someone who was, however desirable, so generous with sexual favours and yet so self-contained. He was in the street outside on a dying afternoon, making himself walk away instead of walking towards her, ringing on the door-bell and saying, Yesterday I was punched in the face and it hurts, it jolly well hurts, and you were busy, with a man who coughs.

He touched the railings outside his premises. Sharp spikes on the top, if he reached to touch them, firm iron railings beneath. He paused, grabbed two of the railings and shook them. They made the slightest movement and all he felt was the sensation of flaking paint against the palms of his hands. The railings outside his building were a series of twins, bent at differing angles, nod-ding towards one another, identical but separate.

William felt a touch lopsided, because of the bruise to his face, and a trifle brave, because he did not really care about the bruise and was faintly proud about the means by which he had acquired it. He *hit* me, he repeated to himself wonderingly. Now, why did he do that? I have never in my life done anything which would justify a gratuitous blow, so why did he hit me? Perhaps that's what's wrong with me; I've never been important enough to hit. Isabella probably wanted to hit me all the time. His shoes were heavy, striking the pavement hard, *click, clack*; he could not dawdle. That man did not like you: you made reference to his *teeth* by staring at them and you almost accused him of having a *brother*; *you* might have offended him. As someone who by dint of his trade invaded the privacy of others all the time, William was philosophical about it. Every day of his working life he com-mitted some kind of assault or was forced into statements that might cause offence. Passing the other set of railings, three doors down, he remembered the Arab princess who had arrived with her retinue and departed in disgust as soon as her translator informed her that all her teeth needed was cleaning. *Swish*. Down the stairs like a rush of curtains, flurrying with outrage.

He walked, expecting any minute that someone would come out from behind these serried sets of railings and hit him again. He felt like a bouncy rubber ball. A touch of violence had enlivened him; made him excitable. What made a man violent? William was not sure, but felt he ought to understand it; he had the feeling that Sarah would understand it completely. He had often wondered about the scars on her body; little white marks that in no way diminished her attraction, on her back, her chest, her arms. Flying glass from a car crash, she had explained, and he had not questioned: she was sensitive on the point. Scars on her *back*, from a car crash, teeny little scars rather than lacerations? He doubted it, but it was really none of his business. He would not ask a patient, How did you get that wart on your finger? and he really did not know how to ask intimate questions of a lover. He did not have a great deal of practice.

His hands were cold from his daft, unconscious touching of the railings, something he did whenever he left the building, greeting them, checking up on the continuity of his life. As long as the railings remained where they were, his life would remain as stable as it was. The railings belonged to another era; their variety amazed him. There were tall railings and short railings, railings with sharp, pointed, fleur-de-lis tops; there were sooty black railings tapering to elegant points, guarding the basements he passed, all built to repel rioters and prevent them climbing through the windows and now incorporated as part of the fabric. Dug up in the First World War to provide metal for armaments, replaced because they belonged. They comforted him, these railings. A burglar, breaking into his premises in a misguided search for drugs, had once snagged his shirt on the way out and there had been small compensation in that.

He walked briskly, making himself look at things. Perhaps he liked the railings so much because they were at eye-level, saved him looking up and noticing anything else, such as the sky and the enormity of his surroundings. Wide streets, lined with red-brick buildings, severely beautiful, designed for a stylish life. This is where Edwardian heroines might have alighted from carriages, tripped up steps to the wide front doors, rung the bell, or sent the footman to give a card, where Elizabeth Barrett was At Home to Mr Browning in a first-floor living room, the better to command a view of the street, houses fit for the distinguished to receive suitors and accommodate servants in basement and attic. He could see them now, polishing the brass bells and whitening the steps.

No shops were allowed in Wimpole Street and Harley Street, only these gracious frontages to suites of offices and medical practices. The same sort of people came to these streets now, for different purposes, deposited from chauffeur-driven cars and taxis to pay munificent bills for private health to charlatans, profiteers and a host of decent and honourable practitioners. William supposed there was not a street in central London that did not have that kind of mix, whatever the trade.

It was Sarah, really, who had made him interested in people, the view from the window rather than the view with his back to it; Sarah who had instilled this habit of walking. She was easy to please, he found on their first acquaintance – 'Come on, let's walk, discuss your case, have something to eat, oh, *look at that.*' She had never wanted courtship, only communication. She seemed so honest, so open.

He crossed the road and smiled vaguely at the cyclist he had not seen, the collision averted. A scowl was returned.

But there was, of course, this strict economy with the truth in all their dealings; a mutual, unspoken agreement not to go beyond the confines of what was volunteered. Thus he did not ask her about the scars, and she refused the details of what Cannon had done; he did not go behind the scenes of what she told him. It was similar with Cannon himself: mutual affection of a surprising kind, which did not yet permit an exchange of confidences. William was worried that he should inspire such reserve in his few friends – maybe he was not trustworthy – but he knew more about Cannon, he felt, than anyone, because Cannon had mumbled and chattered in his Diconal dreams. *Johnnyboy, Johnnyboy, dirty fangs, Johnnyboy.*

The streets were wonderfully quiet on Sundays. Cars passing *en route* to somewhere else, stopping dutifully at lights with none of the weekday impatience; empty parking bays, allowing him to see the buildings and delight in them. Turning a corner into Marylebone High Street, the wind caught his face and the bruise stung. He felt an enormous affection for his own environment and, thinking of Cannon, a surge of excitement. Ahead of him, two Arab men walked arm in arm.

He had always wanted a brother, had created, as a child, an imaginary companion to offset his own single-child status. When that companion died of natural causes, although William had created an elaborate accident on a mountainside to explain his absence, he had mourned him. Cannon had an estranged brother; that much William knew. It was not beyond the bounds of possibility that this man with the similar teeth and oh-so-similar eyes was *that* brother. Maybe, he, William, could engineer a reunion? Rubbish, but he liked the idea, and it would be a fitting addendum to his paper on the teeth of twins; a double whammy; the coup of a lifetime. A service to humanity, better than merely professional, and it would make his paper remembered. As well as make him proud. He was wistful at the mere thought.

He could go back to the exhibition and find out who had bought the Mouth. Or wait. Or tell himself, as he turned back for home, suddenly reluctant to reach it, that it was sheer imagination that had led him to yesterday's assumption that the man who had hit him was Cannon's twin. William stopped, and stared at a massive front door of mahogany, polished to such a shine that he could see in it a blurred reflection of himself. Vainly he struggled to recall the features of the man who had hit him, but the face itself blurred into a strange photofit. All he could remember was the teeth. He reached his own front door, looked at it as if it had nothing to do with him, realising at the same time how he had forgotten that part of the reason for the walk had been to buy milk and eggs. His cold, soft, well-tended hands were uncomfortably free. There were some things that were bound to be forgotten: toilet rolls, letters, the most tedious of necessities.

What was *wrong* with phoning Sarah? Why did he so often cut off his nose to spite his face? Because of the other men, who left him free of any obligation for her? He didn't care about that, most of the time. He hated admitting need, that was all; told himself, as he noticed how the door seemed oddly askew, that he was becoming old and strange.

The keypad worked, the big front door opening with surprising speed when it was usually slow, buzzing at him like an angry bee. He did not think of it at the time as he mounted the stairs to his third floor. He thought, That foyer might once have been a ballroom before they put in a lift. I wonder who danced there? And the same feeling of mild euphoria made him add, Bugger the eggs and milk, bugger everybody. I'll have beans and toast for supper and a bottle of wine.

It was deserted at the weekend. Five specialist dental suites and a penthouse suite above his own. Quiet as the proverbial grave. Thick carpets, which Isabella had chosen and the communal expense of which he heartily resented, muffling his steps to his own front door. Sarah also forgets the eggs and the milk.

The door to his suite was open, which did not particularly surprise him. William automatically assumed that any omission was due to his own negligence; he tended to apologise as soon as he opened his mouth. It was the presence of his dental records, released from their cabinet and spread, systematically, over the floor, that made him realise that this was not his fault any more than it was accidental. A large man sat on the floor by his records, leafing through them with every appearance of disinterest. He was expressionless, like a Buddha, grossly fat and unperturbed. William had a confused memory of a similar figure patrolling the street the morning before, the one who looked as if he had lost his dog.

It was so much warmer here than outside that his eyes began to water and the bruise to throb. He nodded at the man on the floor, as if to a casual acquaintance whose name he could not recall. He had the strange feeling of returning to an appointment he could not remember having made: the man looked as if he belonged, as of right. The nod was returned. William had a sudden vision of officialdom. VAT men? The Dental Practice

Board investigating a complaint? On a Sunday? It all seemed extremely silent and legitimate. He walked into his surgery, heart thudding.

There was the man with the legs like pillars and his back turned, his arms folded and his head dipped in enquiry, nodding in deference towards the drill equipment, hoisted safely out of reach on the gantry, and then, as William watched, sitting awkwardly in the dental chair, still with his arms folded, his eyes fixed on the light. Adjusting himself for comfort, finding none, slipping on the seat. The features of the man suddenly made sense. Without thinking, William approached, flicked the switch for the overhead light marked Siemens and put his foot on the pedal to recline the chair. He moved round to Tina's side and turned on the aspirator. *Slugggh*, the head of the thing sucking at nothing, *slugghh*. Where there had been silence, there was racket. The man lay, his eyes blinded by the light, his lips in a rictus smile, his limbs stiff with terror. All he did was remove his hands from his armpits and put them over his ears, as if aping the monkey who hears no evil. He made a small sound, a hiss; then the prominent red lips, which had been parted, were clamped shut, forming a wide, red line splitting the jowls of his face. William stood over him. There was no time for fear; he was simply very angry.

'What can I do for you?' he said. He moved the drill gantry so that it hung between them, in front of the man's eyes. 'If I drilled your teeth without water coolant,' he said conversationally, 'I could make them white hot. What the hell do you want?'

The man did not speak. William's anger became tremulous. 'What do you *want*?' he repeated, moving closer. And then, in a voice that sounded petulant to his own ears, 'Why did you *hit* me?'

The eyes opened wide and stared at the light, blinked and remained fixed. A large hand shot from the torso and grabbed William by the balls through his trousers. The hand gripped; William gave a sharp yelp. The grip lessened, but remained. He looked down at the brown paw clutching his groin and grabbed

at the wrist. The bone felt like the indestructible iron of the railings outside. The man blinked again and, for the first time,
diverted his glance to William's face, twisted his grip, then
relaxed it. Then he smiled. 'This is just to make sure', he said
softly, 'that we don't hurt *one another*.'

They remained like that, William and he, staring at each
other, William with watering eyes, mesmerised by brown teeth.
Then the hand dropped away. The relief was enormous. As if in
response to some command not actually made, William pressed
the foot pedal bringing the chair upright. Almost a normal chair.
The man sighed, pushed the offending hand into the pocket of
his trousers and flourished from it William's card. 'You gave me
this,' he said. The voice was extremely soft. 'You *insisted*,' he
added, as if that were more than sufficient to justify forced entry
and trespass. The argument seemed completely compelling.
William felt at a loss – again, that strange sense that the visitor
was here as of right, his presence inevitable, even familiar, and
that it was he who was owed an apology. He found it difficult to
take his eyes from the flash of the brown teeth, almost urged to
touch them. He could do so much for these teeth; he could
redeem a thousand wrongs by treating these teeth. The man got
off the chair and began to prowl, his hands locked behind his
back in a mute promise of no further intimidation. William
could do nothing but continue to stare at him, scarcely aware of
the third man, who made slight paper-shuffling noises from
behind.

'How did you get in?' William asked stupidly. It was irrelevant
how they had got in: the only fact that mattered was their presence – the *man*'s presence. The other, somehow, counted for
nothing. There was no reply. The man seemed totally absorbed in
his own curiosity. He paused in his perambulations, looked at the
battery of equipment on the dentist's side of the chair, equipment
more cumbersome than that on the nursing side. A deep shudder
shook his frame; his body trembled with profound revulsion. It
reminded William of a dog shaking water from its coat.

'So, Mr Dentist,' said the soft voice, 'you think you could do something about my fangs? I've got as far as your door how many times? Five? Six? Never made it inside until now. And I didn't need your card. Some little boy of a lawyer told me all about you. If you treat the crap inside prison, like he said, you ain't too proud to treat me.' He retracted his upper lip, let the top teeth pin down the lower lip, the better to expose them. It was an almost comical snarl, like a child competing with another in pulling faces.

That's what you might have done as a child; made people laugh at you.

There was a photocopier in the other room by the reception desk. William heard the sound of its operation and, for a moment, his sensation of panic returned with a different focus. The *records*. They were inefficiently banked on computer; he was not particularly computer-literate and it was still those pieces of paper that mattered. Without records, he would be lost. The practice would be lost. So would his academic career.

He closed his eyes to blank out the thought. Concentrated on his own voice. 'Yes. I could do something about your teeth. Veneers . . . crowns, all sort of things . . .' He faltered. '*Yes*, I could do wonders with those teeth. I've got all the relevant experience.'

'Would it hurt?'

William shook his head, without sufficient conviction. 'Totally painfree dentistry is a modern myth,' he said earnestly. 'No pain as such, or never for long. The analgesics are highly effective, although people vary in response. But it would be . . .' he struggled for the right euphemism '. . . *uncomfortable*, at times.'

'I need fillings, too. I don't want metal in my mouth. Poisonous.'

'Amalgam isn't poisonous. You don't have to have it. Resin for the cavities.'

'But you could cause *exquisite* pain,' the man stated, emphasising the word, gesturing to the drill. 'You could *disfigure* me.' The pause was poignant, as if both recognised that disfigurement of the man was already achieved.

'Your brother had no pain.'

'You're quite wrong about that. I have no brother. I don't know why you think so.'

William turned his head and, for one horrified moment, thought he saw tears in the other man's eyes. 'There's always the potential for pain,' William said. 'I've devoted my life to avoiding it.'

'Where do you keep the stuff? I'd need to know you had plenty.'

William opened a drawer. 'Plenty for daily purposes. I keep the minimum, order what I need. You could be sedated.'

'No. I need to know what's happening.'

It was a surreal conversation, he thought. He felt as if he were being interviewed, his premises viewed not from the point of examining his credentials but with some other agenda in mind. The man continued to pull faces, looking clownish, as if the working of his jaws and eyebrows were essential to the process of thought.

'Perfect,' he said. 'Let me ask you something, Mr Dentist, before I make an appointment. A test, if you don't mind. What, in your life, do you hold dearest? Or, should I say, *whom*?'

The question was oddly shocking. The photocopier made its familiar noise. William tried to remember the order in which he stored the dental records, what they said, apart from the charts of teeth. They were stored in sequence, the most recent patients to the front, the bulkier records to the back of each alphabetical index. What privacy was being invaded? No layperson could read a dental chart. He remembered how he recorded names and addresses with a note of who had referred the patient to him, so that he could remember to ask after a patient's referring friend and thus make it seem as if he remembered who they were. Part of the personal touch he had to rehearse. *What* did *he hold dearest, or whom?* At the moment, his records. The man waited for an answer. It tripped, stutteringly, off William's tongue. 'The pursuit of perfection. Professional *pride*. Technique.' He held out his hands in front of himself, making a plea for the records. His hands were shaking. 'And *these*, I suppose.'

The man nodded. 'You'll give me an afternoon this week, perhaps. Before Christmas. We'll fix it. I don't want anyone else here, do you understand? I don't want anyone watching me.'

'There are rules—' William began.

'And rules,' the man murmured.

He was moving towards the door, William following. He saw, to his relief, that the records were neatly reassembled, sitting on the reception desk. A briefcase stood by the door. What the other man had copied, he had no idea. It was what he was leaving behind that mattered. Suddenly everything was polite. Their method of entry was a mystery.

The man stopped and stared at Cannon's drawing of William's hands. He stared for a long time. Then he turned and held out his own. It seemed necessary to reciprocate, like civilised beings at the end of a normal, mutually beneficial meeting. The man wrapped William's knuckle in both of his own and crushed it. Then he lifted the hand to his own mouth and bit it. William could feel the movement of bone, jarring pain, felt as if the hand would crumble into sharp splinters. This time he screamed long and loud. The hand was released. The scream echoed into the empty hallway, continued as the door closed.

William put the hand across his mouth, moved his fingers and felt his jaw. He leaned against the door frame and looked at what he could see. Everything as normal, nothing disturbed, as if they had never been there. All the paintings still in place. The mark of an emerging bruise on his own skin.

CHAPTER NINE

The phone rang into the heavy silence and William looked at it as if it were alien. He listened to the message and heard the receiver replaced after the bleep. Slowly he flexed the fingers of his right hand, then cupped it in his left to control the tremor. Poor hand, mottled in colour, intact, the same as ever. It was a playground trick to compress the knuckle like that and make the victim scream. The body was shy of injury to the hand. A circle of purple toothmarks rose in the fleshy part between thumb and forefinger.

A series of possible and logical actions paraded themselves in the forefront of his mind without prompting him to any movement. He felt sick with a corrosive shame; paralysed by the conviction that he had invited the intrusion, played with this fire and solicited the burning. It made him responsible; he felt like a girl, guilty after the rape because she had been the first to smile and get into his car. This is your fault, William. Then, panic, mollified in part by the presence of bruises without blood; a mental check of the last tetanus jab; all immunisations in place as they always were. No bite more poisonous than a human bite.

To test the workings of his right hand, he pressed out 1471 on the phone, using three fingers and thumb. *You were called today at . . .* The number was Isabella's. She did this sometimes, never speaking or leaving a message, and he never knew if he was supposed to have known and phoned her back, whether she was lonely, whether she simply wanted a few seconds of his pre-recorded voice to prove he was still alive and earning money. He would have liked, for a moment, a touch of her unsympathetic certainty; he could ask her for help.

But he did not want *help*: he wanted redemption. He was too ashamed for help to be appropriate. Seeking help from Isabella, showing her the pathetic bruise to his face and the non-existent damage to his hand, which had made him scream like a baby, would only be tantamount to inviting contempt, while seeking help from Sarah would involve facing the briskness and wisdom of her sympathy along with an offer of strong drink. He decided on strong drink alone. *He* had got himself into this; *he* would get himself out.

William went to his kitchen and made tea with elaborate care. One Earl Grey tea-bag, indecision about whether to have lemon or milk, until he remembered there was no milk, the sharp scent of the tea a restorative. A sip of that, a slug of brandy into a glass, sipped and then gulped, which made him cough. Then he collected the bundle of notes from the desk and went backstage. He felt like a reviled actor, slinking into the wings.

The room that comforted in its mess. The reminder of the good old days of dentures and National Health practice; dangerous anaesthetics for children; no time for mere technique. Dentures and moulds on surfaces, looking as if they waited for a mouth. No one had come down here: he would have been able to tell by the disturbance of the white dust. He went back for the second glass of brandy and collected the bottle. He got ice from the fridge, noticed evidence of Tina's current passion for lemons, added a slice. The first drink had gone straight to his head. Somewhere in here was the first impression he had ever made of Cannon's teeth. He began to search feverishly, faster and faster, increasing the mess and the sense of hopelessness as he went, and all the time the bruises on the back of his hand faded indiscriminately until only the most prominent, left by the top canines, remained. He stopped the frantic searching; there would be nothing to compare but, all the same, he could swear that those teeth and the teeth that had made the impression would be almost identical.

There was no telephone here, deliberately, a decision made on grounds of economy, and a state of affairs preserved because he liked it. He wiped a surface clean with his sleeve, blew at the dust, and separated the notes into two piles. They were heavy; he found himself panting, with a vague inclination to cry, which, once recognised, made him cross. Oh, for heaven's sake, William, what happened after all? Nothing. A shock, easily treated with sugared tea, more brandy.

He made himself concentrate on the notes. They would be out of order; it might take hours to sort them and there would be patients arriving tomorrow. The thought of that made him tremble; the mere idea of ever again facing a patient without reading the notes first made him nauseous. That was what he had done with the girl-child who inhabited his dreams along with her brother; the one from whom he was sure he had removed the wrong teeth. He looked at the names on the first three folders: none of them meant anything. Without their notes they were strangers, although, if he looked at the chart, memory stirred in the way it might for a fingerprint expert recognising a familiar set of whorls. The impression left by a bite was similarly unique. He almost wanted the bruises to reappear, to evidence their own origins. It had been a nip; the man had not wanted to *eat* his hand any more than he had wanted to eat from it.

William thought of another version of the same scene: the man's teeth snapping shut on his hand, not with the nip of a puppy but the bite of a Rottweiler, jaws locked, teeth grinding on sinew, remaining like that until prised apart or the hand torn away. The notes were not hopelessly muddled, and it might have been himself who had muddled them more by carrying them downstairs and dropping a few of the folders on the way – no way to treat treasured things, how could he be so clumsy? The mere touch of the folders reassured him, but what might have been taken out? From cursory examination it seemed that nothing was missing from the first few he examined. Gradually he relaxed and slowed down. He isolated the Ms; they were all together, like a family. Ah, Mrs Macdonald, he remembered her from her chart, a lady with fine yellow teeth like a horse and a kindred liking for sugar lumps. Mr Murray, a faceless memory with a highly successful bridge between molar and premolar of which William had been proud. Miss Motcomb, a child of the fluoride age, free of dental caries. He looked for the single folder on Andrew Mitchum, Sarah's emergency treatment, and could not find it. This was faintly disturbing, but since he doubted that patient would ever return he put second thoughts into the realm of non-being, calmer now. Sister Dominic's were gone, with the notation of Cannon's introduction to the sisters. *Cannon's friends*, he had written on the front, with a reminder to keep them all together. That did not matter either: he would remember Dominic's filling. What mattered was that there would be notes for tomorrow's patients: Tina would be able to find them before anyone arrived. The relief was profound. He sorted through until he found the folder that related to Cannon, filed under that name in the Cs without fuss. The name Smith was added in brackets; there was no address other than the prison, and Cannon's prisoner number was all that appeared. William sat back, sipped the brandy and read, slowly and thoughtfully, the coded record of what he had done with Cannon and in which order over nine months. A good job, was what – but, then, the raw material had been so much better than he could have hoped. Diseased teeth, but strong and recoverable; not a suggestion of degenerating bone or receding gums; an extraordinary case of underlying health.

He remembered Cannon trembling in the chair. Remembered the man downstairs, with his shudder of revulsion, the aggression, the bravado, which were surely the symptoms of fear. He looked again at the notes and felt satisfaction. A *good job*; he was *good* at this; in fact, he was *excellent*. He drummed his fingers on the dusty surface; the pain had gone.

Now, if these two were twins, there was every chance that the mouths would be similar, but professional instinct was telling

William that *this* man would not have the same underlying
strength. There was a lividity about him that suggested otherwise; blood pressure, lines to the face that suggested familiarity
with chronic pain. And Cannon, virtually under orders and
removed from prison for the purpose of mending his teeth, had
had nothing to lose and something to gain from a glimpse of the
outside world. Cannon had been curious; Cannon had been
allowed to explore; Cannon had sat happily in *this* room. And
Cannon had a capacity to trust: he *wanted* to believe and he
wanted renewed teeth, he had said, because it would so delight
his wife. Lord, he'd forgotten that Cannon had a wife. There
was nothing about the state of his clothes to suggest it.

Would this man have the same to lose or gain, and did he
have an ounce of faith? William doubted it. Would he stand a
dozen or more long afternoons devoted to crowns and veneers?
Would he submit quietly to the needle or the offer of Diconal
oblivion? William doubted that, too. Would he be able to accept
that some of his treatment would be experimental, at least a case
of trial and error, and not everything would work first time?
Probably not. William would not be able to treat this man in the
same way as his brother, but all he knew at this point was that he
desperately wanted to try. He craved the challenge of finding the
best methods and achieving the *best* results, making a real difference to the man's appearance and attitudes, lifting a lifetime's
curse by reversing a now rare condition, the way he had with
Cannon, and against that desire the blow to the face and the
pain to the hand became, if not forgotten, at least irrelevant.

He moved, restless, slightly drunk and becoming more so; he
had consumed little food that day, and it was getting dark. He
found the darkness a relief. He picked up one of the moulds on
the table, counted the teeth. Twenty-eight in this particular
head. What if he were simply to remove the disfiguring teeth and
create a denture? The creature would endure this better, perhaps; the result would still change his appearance dramatically.
William had a fondness for dentures. His National Health practice had featured them strongly, for reasons of budget rather

than of fashion, and, ah, Isabella had been right to tread on his principles and insist he migrate to private practice, for the chance to do better, without restrictions . . . *she had been right*, without knowing why: dentures slipped, they broke; the mouth changed around them, for all that they served well. There had been dentures brought back for repair that looked as if they had been run over by a train; he remembered the dentures that had been chewed by a mimicking child, dentures chewed by a dog with similar ideas. Suddenly he began to giggle, holding his sides at the thought of a dog running away with a set of teeth, giving them to a bitch by way of courtship – *Here, have these; my master clearly thinks they're delicious.*

William told himself he was probably losing his mind and the loss would not make a difference. He laughed until tears rolled down his cheeks and he felt exhausted and sober. He rolled back towards the kitchen in search of more drink, dabbed at his face with a paper towel. It took some time to adjust to dentures: would the man be patient with something short of pain? Then he rolled into his surgery and sat on the patients' chair. Looked suspiciously to his left, expecting the man to be there, a substantial ghost, standing where he had seen him, with tears in his eyes, provoked by the denial of the existence of a brother.

Only a man then, not a savage beast. Only a man, like himself. And William wished, far and above everything else, for the chance to deal with those teeth, and then write it down for the world to know what *he* had done, and what could be learned from twins.

Write it down. Make a list of everything you want. Then look at the list and work out which of those things is less important. Specify at those things until you realise they are not very important at all and can, therefore, be removed from the list. Thus, make the list smaller. Sarah crossed out the word 'garden'.

She sat by the fire with another set of estate agents' particulars, saved as a treat, like a favourite book, to be consumed or dismissed at leisure. This is the stuff of which dreams are made.

I tell you, Sarah, you are never satisfied. If you ever get to heaven you'll say your wings are damp and the harp is out of tune. Pauline's voice, not accusing, but puzzled about the nature of restlessness.

She had to think about houses. She had to retreat into this kind of dreaming because if she did not she would think about Cannon and Julie all day and all night. And when they were safe, she would have no life left. She had to think about new homes because it was the best antidote to nagging doubt, and the vision of Julie Smith with her inscrutable face and slightly swollen belly. Concentrate.

The next flat, when she found it, would be minimalist in style, unlike this one, an overcrowded tribute to the acquisitive habits of recent years. There was this passion for mismatched chairs, which was a particular nuisance: they crept in and out of corners, always making room for another one with a kind of courtesy. There was an additional sofa, purchased purely for the colour of its sun-faded cover, sitting ill at ease with the custom-built, like a poor relation. There was a dining-room table, which dominated its own room, acquired for the splendour of its legs but redundant because she had lost the knack of entertaining. The next flat would have none of those things; these items would have to be found suitable homes, like well-behaved orphans. She was going to have bare wooden floors and walls full of paintings; only the paintings were lifelong friends.

There had been a psychiatrist lover in here once or twice, who considered that her collection of paintings showed signs of paranoid kleptomania and subversive tendency. There's no *theme* to them, he repeated; they say *nothing* about you at all; they have nothing in common with each other or with you. Definitely like friends, then. It had seemed to disturb him; it didn't disturb her. It was not a *collection*. It would seem odder by far to have things distinguished by uniformity, a series of landscapes, for instance, or a series of interiors or abstracts, instead of a jumble nudging each other for space in their diverse frames. The psychiatrist did not seem to notice that there were more portraits than anything else; he might have analysed something sinister in that. Are you lonely, Sarah? Do you have need of inanimate, undemanding company? Do you seek solace in the form of these expressive faces on the wall? Do you *talk* to them?

Only sometimes. She looked at her own list and looked at the particulars.

Was Cannon making it all up, or was he exaggerating? There was one agent, more amenable than the rest, who seemed to understand that she wanted only as much space as she could get, with the maximum of light, the greatest height of wall, to accommodate the lifelong friends and the added company they were bound to attract. If the friendly estate agent found it odd that she demanded to know, in each case, the identity and address of the vendor of the places he described, he did not say so. None of this current bundle of properties was owned by John Smith; none looked quite right, there were none of his ruined homes; but those she had seen of his were always *right*. Despite their ruinous state, she had liked them all, felt that tug of excitement which suggested, *I could live here, I could fall in love with this.* Could a man with a taste for houses really be such a horror? He, too, liked big, tall walls and ceilings half a mile off the floor. It might not be enough to make the man virtuous, but it did make him sympathetic.

Have nothing to do with him; if you see him, don't let him see you. No, I cannot ever stay in your flat; he will know where I am.

She had obeyed, with the obedience of faith, and yet what nonsense it was. John Smith swam like a porpoise and collected houses the way she collected paintings, with a purpose so random it did not bear analysis. What was wrong with communicating with him? Especially after a long conversation with Mrs Matthewson. What strange things they discussed over their Sunday lunches, to be sure. She pushed aside the particulars with their seductive photographs, drew a line through her list and began to draft a note on the same page. Stopped, fetched the fragment of the letter Cannon had given her on the way to the high court on a day that now seemed a long time ago. She would write to John Smith with a dual purpose. Purpose number one, to disobey orders and attempt to meet him on some sort of common ground. Purpose number two, the shameful one, to see from his reply if the writing was the same. She disliked this belated urge to cross-check, but she was sick of being reliant on third-party information. Maybe she wasn't such a bad lawyer after all.

'... *if you keep this up until Christmas, I'll leave her alone. Promise ... But you won't keep it up. You'll get careless. You'll realise what's good for you ...*'

A clumsy, trustworthy hand. An entirely illogical promise. He might succumb to the plea of ghastly flattery, like any other man.

Dear Mr Smith,

Please forgive me for troubling you and do not consider you are obliged to reply.

I am a respected member of staff with your legal firm of Matthewson and Co. We are seeking to create a subdivision devoted to the sale and conversion of prestigious metropolitan properties for purely domestic use by overseas clients. (We already have a commercial division, as you know.) With this in mind, I am writing to enquire if you, as a valued client, would consider reviewing the way your domestic properties are handled in the marketplace, and give me your comments as to how this might be done better. This would assist us greatly in the creation of a service-oriented, experienced team, dedicated to the service of clients in this area.

Yours, etc., S. Fortune.

If he replied, he might suggest the meeting. *If* he replied by hand and the writing wasn't the same, she was in dead trouble.

It was so difficult to believe in a mythical beast. All her own ghosts were creatures of her own creation, solidly founded on real human counterparts. She prowled round the paintings. There was nothing of her own that she regarded as an example of excellence, except the stolen one, which would never be quite hers. All the rest had been chosen because she could see they were somehow flawed. Ah, yes, they were friends all right. No one, at the end of the day, owns anything, and it was probably unwise to trust the bright ideas formed with a bottle of wine at the elbow. Ghosts, mythical monsters and enemies were all scaled down to the size of a glass.

The armchair over there was too heavy, reminiscent of the parlour of her convent school where she had sat among uncomfortable chairs, waiting for the Reverend Mother to tell her the bad news of her imminent expulsion – for precocity and subversion, for telling other girls the facts of life, for introducing Tampax and raising a petition about the food. She remembered that parlour for a burning sense of injustice and the ice of the atmosphere, marking the onset of scepticism. She got up, stretched, yawned.

The next flat was definitely going to be minimalist. Just like the next life.

They sat in the parlour, Julie and Cannon, like a pair of awkward guests, each on the edge of a hard chair, knees touching. It was at the front of the convent, adjacent to the main street door, accessed from the body of the building by a gloomy corridor and another locked door. The nuns were passionate about locks, Pauline explained; passionate without being logical, since they always seemed to assume that intruders came from the front rather than behind and they left God himself to take care of the chapel. The existence of locks was the insecurity of women dwelling alone, but still at odds with the vow of forgoing personal property. Each owned minor personal possessions in their rooms, no more, but the locked front door, the locked porch, the third lock on the door connecting corridor with residence were by now established precautions, Pauline said, because, once known, the existence of a convent drew the drunk and the lame and the abusive. Led by pragmatism, the sisters took the view that discretion was the better part of valour when it came to charity demanded after dark at an inner-city door. The truly needy would come back in the morning.

Which all contributed to Pauline's idea that the parlour should be Julie and Cannon's trysting place after conventional bedtime, provided they did not linger long or deface the carpet and Julie removed all traces of their presence afterwards. Besides, Pauline had added tartly, this is where we entertain the *priests*. The smell of a cigarette would not be amiss over the other smell of polish, surely. And the other condition was that should any sister descend upon them, armed with a weapon, they would not retaliate in unseemly fashion and Julie alone would explain, taking responsibility for either her own truths or her own lies.

Cannon was uncomfortable. The parlour was a sizeable room. He was used to small spaces; he enjoyed the sense of confinement provided by walls he could touch; he hated double-glazing and the consequent lingering of smells; he liked draughts; he was not at home in rooms big enough for the swinging of cats. The only purpose of space was to provide light; this room was large with small windows. The whole damn building was back to front, built north to south, with no regard to the direction of the sun, and even the chapel, the one room that could maximize it, ruined itself by the barrier of the sacristy and the presence of thick stained-glass windows. They seemed to try to make all their public rooms as ugly as the chapel, he complained, although that was not the real complaint. In here, even Julie was a stranger, sitting prim and proper, although their knees touched. There was greater intimacy in the chapel, disdaining God and the presence of plaster saints.

'Hallo there,' Julie said.

Ever since he had divorced himself from his brother's life and his brother's daily speech, Cannon was easily discomfited by a new environment. There were new nuances to the way he spoke now, but he did not expect his nearest and dearest to have learned a new vocabulary too. Or familiarity with new rooms and ways of being. Sitting opposite him, Julie was suddenly refined, with her skirt pulled down over her knees and a faint southern-Irish lilt somehow caught in her voice as if by accident. They could speak in normal tones and pitch in here, but he missed the urgency of their whispers.

'Lord, what a clutter,' he was saying, shivering slightly. He looked around himself. He expected the door to open at any minute and a nun to come crashing in with a trayful of tea. Not that he would have objected to such sustenance to augment the half-bottle in his pocket; nor could the nun have objected to the sublime modesty of their positions, sitting so primly and over-dressed. The chapel and the parlour were equally chilly, but it seemed intrusive to turn on the electric fire and Julie did not suggest it. The overhead lights were bare and bright, provided by a miniature chandelier with five shiny bulbs, enough to make the contours of their faces hard. She looked yellow in this light; he felt red. The mirror over the mantelpiece made him look flushed and poorly. He always smiled into mirrors, the better to see his teeth. 'It isn't so much a clutter', he said, nodding at the furniture, 'as a muddle. They've tried to cater for all occasions and ended up catering for none. They just don't know how to create comfort, do they?'

She giggled softly, but pulled the skirt further over her knees, a trifle defensive. The nuns were her saviours and her hosts: she did not like to hear criticism of them. She was coming to adopt their tastes and their economies with the same ease as her unconscious mimicry of their soft voices. 'Oh, I don't know,' she said vaguely. 'It's a room with a dozen purposes. They entertain relatives in here, for tea and coffee, then there's priests and guests, not very many, then there's meetings . . . They let people use it for meetings, so it needs to be big enough for that.'

'All these bloody *chairs*,' Cannon muttered, sinking out of his own velour moquette of drab green, so that he sat on the floor with his back against it. That was better: now he was level with Julie's knees rather than with the rest of the room. It was easier to ignore what he could never fail to notice: the garish religious pictures on the walls, the forest of armchairs, the monumental sideboard, which looked as if it should have contained a battery of wines and spirits. It had all the equipment for a riotous party, except the ambience. Perhaps if they turned out the lights and danced to the bar of the fire, but they were sombre and inhibited.

'They'll have Christmas decorations in here next week,' she said wistfully.

'Jesus,' Cannon said. 'That'll really make it perfect.'

'Oh, *stoppit*, will you? What does it matter what the room looks like? They do their best. Why should they have *style*, even if they could agree what *style* was, especially since they don't care anyway? Stop carping.'

He touched her knee. 'I'm sorry,' he said, formally and insincerely. 'It's just that when I see you in a room I keep seeing you somewhere else entirely. Somewhere where I'd like you to be. A cottage in the country, with a garden for the baby.'

'And roses round the door?' she finished for him, a note of irony in her voice, then sat back in her chair, refusing to join him on the floor. She laced her fingers together in her lap. 'Sarah said she once wanted a cottage like that. With a cat. Then she realised she would hate it. All that silence, all those dead leaves, no cars, no shops. How would you live in the country? You're a town animal, through and through. The last time you saw a cow was from the window of a train.'

'Well, we'd have to learn, wouldn't we? You can learn anything . . .'

'No, you can't. If Sarah reckoned she couldn't, nor could we. Sarah's more adaptable. Now, there's a woman with style.' There was an element of jealousy, Cannon realised with a start of surprise. He touched her again, tentatively. There was no response. 'I wonder if I'll be here for the New Year,' she went on, 'admiring the decorations. Paper chains, tinsel and a crib. Maybe it would be easier if I took to the faith. Swore myself to poverty and chastity. Learned to accept divine will . . . Gave up hoping for anything different. After all, it doesn't matter what you believe as long as you believe something.'

'Look, love, it'll soon be over. Christmas. You've forgotten. All over by Christmas.'

'Will it? Will it ever?'

He was silent, gripped with a sense of dread so acute it seemed to retard breathing. He looked up at her beseechingly, but in this light she looked distant and almost cruel. Immobile, like the statues in the chapel; a woman in the act of becoming an effigy. Angry with him, unable out of long habit to say so. Somehow on the verge of giving up. Something to do with all those books she now read. Challenging him.

'Can I smoke in here?' he asked.

She shrugged. 'Yes. Can't do it any further harm, can it?'

He lit the cigarette, watched it burn, and after three greedy inhalations tapped the ash into the palm of his hand. There were no ashtrays; it was unthinkable to put the debris in one of three wastepaper bins. They were too clean. He blamed the room for this feeling of alienation. Another fear prevailed. Perhaps Julie and he would never survive in a so-called normal world; perhaps the intensity of the love would wither if it were not clandestine, the way it had always been. Love on the run, first from Johnny's fury and refusal to meet, then the flurry of hiding from the police, love on bail, love on remand, love from the distance of prison, love like this, after he came out. Love within the framework of something forbidden, defined by Johnny's contemptuous disbelief in it. Love in a battlefield. She was sick of it; she was changing, *just like Johnny said she would*. Put her in a room with real chairs, make their contact as normal as possible, and there seemed so little to say; there was no common life between them, nothing to create intimacy, and if she was looking for *something* in which to believe it meant she no longer believed in him. Nor, perhaps, in Johnnyboy either.

'Is that what you want to do?' he said roughly. 'Stay here? Give up? Let me go? Opt for a quiet life? Oh, I'm sure Pauline would love to have you. Free labour and good food for ever. A halo at the end. Good luck to you.' He tapped the last of the ash into his hand, held the remnants of the cigarette between thumb and finger, watching it die. The room was quiet, apart from the ticking of the clock, the item he loathed most of all. It began to chime midnight, with small, undignified sounds. It looked as if it had been given as a prize for twenty-five years' faithful service and a pension. She leaned forward and touched his hair; he shook his head angrily. She rubbed her eyes, pressed them shut with her fingers, then blinked to dispel the tears. They ran through her fingers onto her wrists. He noticed the red of her hands against the white of her face.

He knelt at her feet, leaning into her knees; he reached for her face and brushed at her tears, but she still held her fists pressed into her eyes. He buried his head in her lap and, smelling the animal smell of her, slid his hands beneath the skirt and stroked her thighs. She stiffened; the tears continued; she removed her hands to press against his, stop him. 'Don't,' she said. 'Don't. Please don't.' He remained as he was, gazing at her.

What was it light did to a face? Or was it the blurring of tears, his and hers? She was no longer harsh in feature, but childish in distress, sexless, vulnerable, hurt, small, furious. 'Don't,' she repeated. 'Don't you dare.' Then softened it by adding, 'Please,' fiddling in her pocket for a handkerchief, wiping her eyes and blowing her nose. He watched all this closely. Puzzled, severely alarmed. There was something so unfamiliar about her. The stutter had gone.

'They're brave, these nuns,' she muttered. 'Some of them suffered more than you and I put together, see? Don't criticize their *style*. Or not in front of me. They're the closest thing to family I ever had. Do you wonder I should think to stay? It's so frightening outside, so n-n-n-n-nice within.' A deep breath. 'So j-j-j-just so . . . Oh, shit.'

He was ashamed of himself for welcoming the return of the stutter. Maybe he had never wanted her to be free of it, in case she should find it easy to outstrip his use of words; it was the stutter that had drawn him in the first place. Him and the builders, sitting in a caff, with them mimicking her behind her back until he intervened. Watched her smile into his eyes, look-ing only at his eyes, nothing else.

She took a deep breath. 'I'm not going to cry any more,' she stated, 'but I've come to love these nuns. We've something in common. Their life is controlled absolutely by belief in God, mine by belief in you. It's only natural that belief should suffer from doubt from time to time, isn't it? You gave up on your brother; you might give up on me. And the longer I stay here, the less use I'll be on the outside. I can't go out because you tell me I shouldn't. Soon it might be because I *can't*. And all the time Johnnyboy gets smaller and smaller in my mind. *Was* it him who hurt me? He stood in the dark and watched, and the fat man hit me. I've tried to put it right out of mind . . . I don't know who was giving the orders.'

'He wouldn't touch you. He'd always get someone else to do it.'

'Why?'

'Because he never could bear to touch a woman.'

She was suddenly completely still. 'Ah,' she said, after a long pause. 'I thought desire and hatred overcame such things.'

'Not in his case,' Cannon said, suddenly exhausted. How many times and in how many ways would he have to explain to women what Johnnyboy was like? He did not have the words or the energy and, God knows, he had tried. Yesterday, to Sarah; a dozen times to Sarah, innumerable times to Julie and they had believed him with wide eyes and open mouths at first, willing to accept what he said. Shock was the great aid to belief. Julie believed because she had suffered at Johnny's orders; how could she be incredulous now? A calm life away from him was lulling her into a sense of safety, that was all, the image of John Smith fading like the memory of a violent film developing into a series of cartoons.

'No, Cannon, you're wrong,' she said, reading the expression on his face. 'I'm not *less* afraid, I'm more afraid. It makes me weaker, not stronger, staying here. I'm preserved – like – like a jelly!' She laughed. 'They like jelly, the sisters, they like childish food.' She stroked his forehead. 'I don't have to make decisions. I grow weaker rather than stronger, and that's what makes me afraid. Not being any use to you. And if he *did* find me here, threatened me, threatened any of *them*, then I'd have to run, Cannon, I'd have to run. Far away and not come back.'

She had been so ashamed of her injuries, as if she had inflicted them herself. He had wanted her to forget them; now he wanted her to remember. The clock ticked past the quarter hour loudly. There was absolutely nothing to say and it was time to go. The rain lashed against the door as she let him out, and she made to pull him back, but he kissed her quickly and pushed her back inside. The light of the street outside made him nervous and he hurried away. Ran down the road until the convent was out of sight, then huddled in a doorway, lit another cigarette. Why should anyone believe him simply because he told the truth? Because he told it incompletely, that was why. Was selective with what he told, for fear of giving offence. Never told Julie, never told Sarah what Johnnyboy said when he went to see him, after prison, long, long before the letter. *You've got to leave her. You don't belong with her; you belong with me; we've got things to do. You wait and see; you'll come back. What? She was scarcely hurt at all. She asked for it. Let's see if she'll wait for you. I'll test her for you. The worst pain, I'll find it.*

The worst pain was loss. That was the very worst he could envisage. Loss of her; loss of hope. The worst pain for Julie would be loss of him. Johnny would know that; *he* feared the rot of his loneliness more than anything else. He knew exactly what he was doing in the waiting game: waiting for love to rot. Christmas was too far.

Cannon did not want to go home. There was no such thing. Home had always been a house owned by Johnnyboy; he had not progressed by a single step in all these years. He had regressed, because now he lived in one of Johnny's houses as a trespasser, waiting for discovery. Cold and wet as he was, he could not bear the thought of the drip through the ceiling, the damp heat, the sense of imprisonment. Where, then? Who were his friends?

Sarah, William, scarcely any other who did not belong also to Johnny, and few enough, always, of these. He would have turned back to the convent, climbed the back wall, huddled in the familiar yard, if only to be close, but he had a superstitious dread of that. The longer he stayed in the vicinity, the sooner Johnnyboy would sense where he was. And the same would apply to Sarah. He was bad news to women. He began to walk.

On the main road, he saw the lights of the night bus, X12, Charing Cross, by the long route, offering for two pounds half an hour of warmth and oblivion and, for the price of the whisky in his pocket, a borrowed blanket with the homeless. It passed down the Edgware Road and into Oxford Street, a short walk from William's. He thought of William's basement room. The messy room with the teeth where he had been allowed to go to keep him out of the way of the real clients. William would never know; it was not for William to know. He could get in easy. Lie down somewhere; that old chair, maybe. Think of his precious painting upstairs. Bonnard, sketching his wife with love for the umpteenth time. A study for a painting rather than a painting, but fresh and lovely. Yes, he could think of that. And it would be nice to sleep in the home of someone who did not even know that Johnnyboy existed. Be a guest of someone who still had faith in him.

The rain dripped through the ceiling, unnoticed. The door of the attic swung open to the push of a hand. There was no sound but that of the *plip, plip, plop* through the skylight and the sound of laboured breath. Too many stairs. Ah, a room bought with an artist in mind, for the promise of light. Steps across the floor, a body stooping to retrieve the scattered drawings. Ink depictions of a face; the hand holding them shaking. Looking at the features, the jowls, the malevolence, the age and the black teeth, snarling; the angry face; the face full of need. The lonely face; the hateful face, captured by someone who would not, could not, look at it without looking away. Finally, the face drawn with an element of affection.

He still loves me.

He tore up the black and white sketches, thoroughly and systematically, and placed them in a pile.

The steps moved, the hands took the canvas from where it
stood against the wall, placed it on the easel. Noted the abundant hair, more red than brown in this light. He could not
remember her being described as red-haired; frowned. He had
never looked at her before now. Glanced, looked away . . . hadn't
got close, couldn't bear it. Looked again. Noted the full mouth
and the long, slender legs with the prominent muscles in the
calves. Athletic legs; a figure of strength. Examined with distaste
the slightness of the breasts lying nonchalantly on the ribcage, the
hand lying across the bush protectively. He wanted to slash
the picture, pierce it at that point, extend the wide mouth, half
open to show the white teeth, but it was only with the tip of a
knife he wanted to touch; no closer. He bent, looked, memorised
each detail of the face, the colour of the eyes, the way the hair
swept back from the forehead, the small nuggets of gold in the
ears. Traced the shape of the ears and the brows; moved his
glance down, frowned at the pale flecks of paint around the neck,
on the upper arms, the shoulders. Little scars, superimposed on
the paint, added as a kind of signature, like tiny hallmarks. These
distinguished her.

The man went back to the wall and looked through the other
canvases. Scenes, interiors, playgrounds full of children. No
other women. A dozen sketches of the same woman.

This, then, was the one. The one whose face he had always
refused to see.

He took her off the easel and put her back against the wall.
Closed the door softly behind him.

CHAPTER TEN

You have to live; whatever else you have in mind, you have to live. *Always eat when you are hungry; always drink when you are dry; always scratch when you are itchy; don't stop breathing or you'll die.*

Hardly a profound philosophy, but perfectly good enough. Cannon had not phoned. The year would soon be reaching its shortest day. Another foggy, early Tuesday morning, and this was it. *Two bdrms; bath, wc, lge living room; no stairs. Convenient for transport.* Convenient for everything, as if that made all the difference. A place to put a car three streets distant, but the car didn't matter. Sarah hated her car: it distorted her view of the city; there was no one to talk to in the car. This flat was walking distance from all that mattered. A mansion block, second floor; shabby without real decay; homely. An acquired taste, she was told. Someone had died in it recently.

She knew it was home as soon as she turned the corner. A little worn; a little scarred; just like herself. Following the agent inside, Sarah saluted the late occupant with a surreptitious sign of the Cross and a hidden bow to her memory. The dead warranted respect and she needed the blessing.

The place had the stamp of an elderly occupant who had been less than mobile. There was a high armchair by a fireplace in the huge living room, next to a table, flanked by a sewing box and a footstool, facing a television, a self-contained island of furniture in an otherwise empty space. There was a radio on the table. Between this assembly, suitable for long sitting with everything to hand, there was a well-worn path across the floor to the kitchen which was small to the point of miniature, with old-fashioned appliances and open shelves within easy reach. There was a cooker of ancient but efficient vintage, an antique fridge and every indication that the occupant saw no necessity to change anything. No aspirations to anything other than adequacy and established routine; comfort without frills, nothing that required complex instructions. Someone had been here who cooked the same things, in the same way, every day; Sarah felt a profound affinity with her.

'Of course, you'd need to gut this and start again,' the agent was saying, as they peered into the bathroom. Old bath, stained and clean, disused; newish shower shoved in the corner; hardly enough space to turn round. A bedroom with a large, low bed, depressed on one side nearest the door. A lady who had learned to economise with furniture as well as with movement; she had dispensed with obstacles and would have walked through her flat in a series of the shortest routes in a rigorous but dignified routine that sustained and allowed her independence. They went back to the living room. There were two large windows, a high ceiling with a flaking cornice decorated with grapes and tastefully tinged with smoky yellow; pale, unadorned walls. The sense of empathy was as powerful as a sweet smell. The air was clean and fragrantly dry. Happiness beckoned.

'What the family should do is get some money together, do it up and *then* sell it. They'd make so much more, but they haven't time, and it's chicken and egg – they don't have money until they sell . . .'

'Who lives either side?'

'Old block for old people. They're mostly deaf. I'm not sure anyone else even knows she's died.'

I know. The light streaming through the south-facing windows turned the old carpet to full, faded gold. The empty walls were an open invitation. Shall I die here? Sarah thought. I may die friendless, but I do want to *live* here. *Now*. This minute. Perhaps I have never wanted anything quite so much in all my life. She sat in the old lady's armchair and asked again for her blessing. She looked at the wall above the fire and imagined the favourite ornament she might have seen.

An empty flat; deaf neighbours. Cannon could live here until Christmas, if she could get him in. She put to the back of her mind the fact that Cannon had not phoned.

★

'I want to buy it *now*,' she said to Matthewson, standing in his office with arms crossed, a strange attitude he thought, in someone who had come to ask for advice. She should have been humbler. 'How do I secure it? How do I make them take it off the market?' She was so fierce he almost wanted to laugh. He had rarely seen her so passionate, although when she was he scarcely listened, because it was always about some hopeless cause of a person and she had the loser's habit of defending the indefensible.

'Throw money at them. It usually helps. Most vendors find it irresistible,' he barked.

'Why can't I exchange contracts *today*?' For God's sake, she had never even mastered the finer points of conveyancing, such as delay, prudence, patience, *caveat emptor* – the essential rule of let the buyer beware.

'You *could*, if you were sillier than I thought. You can make a contract on the back of an envelope, if you want. I agree to buy 1 Acacia Avenue for *X* pounds sterling, and he, she or it agrees to sell signed by both. Perfectly valid, and perfectly senseless, of course. You could be sold a wreck with a motorway through it . . . pub next door . . . service charges. Those places have monstrous service charges. A survey, of course – got to check the roof and the drains. All that. Weeks. Get someone in the firm to do it. Usual discount, of course.'

'I don't care about the roof and the drains. I want to buy it *now*.' She sounded like a child demanding to be taken to a party.

He shrugged. She was behaving like the most intractable kind of client who would not listen. 'There's one small point,' he murmured, relishing the fact that she had asked his opinion. 'I don't like to mention it, but have you got the money?'

She glared at him.

'Have you sold *your* flat?' he persisted.

'Almost.'

'Ah.' That was news. Mrs Matthewson would want to hear about that. He sensed that Mrs Matthewson would feel a vague sense of unease if she did not know where Sarah was. So would his wretched son.

'Money?' he said again.

'Enough.'

'Well, give it to them,' he shouted. 'Give them a thousand to take it off the market and promise exchange and completion within a month. Only *don't* sign a contract. Please.'

'Not even on the back of an envelope?' She was smiling now, somehow comforted by the yelling. How is it, he would ask Mrs Matthewson, that she takes her reassurance in such strange ways? The mere fact that Ernest had failed to say *Don't do it at any price* was enough to provide some kind of moral support for impetuosity – but, then, he had liked the sound of the address. Montague Mansions, Marylebone. Faded grandeur, but still grandeur: Mrs Matthewson would approve of an easy walk to Selfridges.

'It's very convenient for my dentist,' Sarah said.

The cigarette was back in hand, sure sign of defiance, tension or relaxation, he wasn't sure, only that it was indicative of something alien. The sight of it infuriated him all over again. 'I don't *care* who it's near. Unless *it's* a client. You've *work* to do. As well as the art collection.'

'Ah, that. Don't worry about *that*.' Beaming at him, as if a hundred-thousand-pound budget was nothing. The insouciance turned charm into anger.

'But I do worry about *that*. I want a report. You're a *consultant* in this regard, don't forget. Trusted for expertise. You have to take it seriously. As long as you aren't subverting any of the damned art budget on the deposit for your own bloody house.'

The silence was palpable, thick and sticky; a boundary crossed. He had gone too far. There were innumerable times when he had accused her of white lies, evasions, abrogations of responsibility, general moral perfidy, but he had never suggested she could be tempted by theft. It was the lawyer's cardinal sin: they could lie to a client in this culture, lie to each other, but never steal. She may have once left priceless title deeds in a taxi, billed for a fraction of the proper price, given glib and erroneous versions of the law, seduced the male clients as well as their opponents, commandeered the irrational devotion of others, but stealing was another kind of sin. He was ashamed of his own tongue; kept his head bowed and wondered what to say next in the face of her righteous fury, but when the silence continued and he was brave enough to look up she was blushing. An alarming sight against the red hair; he doubted he had seen such a phenomenon before; it was almost as frightening as seeing her cry.

'There's no apartment worth that much,' she said. The door closed quietly.

Convenient for my dentist. Certainly the flat would be convenient. Half of her male acquaintances lived within striding distance. There was Mole, a short walk in the other direction; the estate agent, closer; the judge; then Master Ralph of the high court and his service apartment occupied Tuesday through Thursday; one or two more, past and semi-present, a couple of ghosts, but convenience did not dictate the choice, never had, any more than any of the nice men who wanted her near and also wanted her far. Except William. William mattered. William would like it; she and William liked the same things. She wanted to show it to him, tell him how she had fallen in love with that old lady's chair, the dimensions of the room in which she sat, the things she might have seen and the things she had left. Tell him about how she had forgotten minimalism and about that last tribute to posterity which she had found in the bathroom cupboard when no one else was looking. The old darling's dentures, looking for company.

William found that he took pleasure in the day's work, as if his fleeting acquaintance with violence the weekend before and the prospect of a stunning new client had acted as a stimulant to energise his eyes and ears, and make him notice things he otherwise ignored. It was the energy of complete distraction; the power, suddenly, to acquire extra vision; he recognised it as mild neurosis. He seemed immune even to irritation. There were dentists of another kind than himself, to whom the human contact was all and the surgery simply a means to it; perhaps he was becoming such a dentist, whose pleasure was all in the kinship with the patient. He was jovial, complimented Tina on a new shade of hair, and then said he preferred the old in case the remark smacked of sexual innuendo, but she seemed to consider any compliment at all a step in the right direction. He wanted to thank her for tidying the glory-hole, something he had noticed mid-morning when he went down there and found it cleaner than he remembered, but instead he debated with her how they should deal with the man in the waiting room who was likely to slide out of the chair at the touch of the needle. It was always the big men who fainted. There had never been a heart-attack yet; the fainters came round; the allergic survived; and this bright morning he was actually noticing the contrast of patients. Miss Mallerson, a busy barrister, flying in to discuss a variety of cosmetic treatment to augment her powerful teeth, demanding grave explanation for the sixth time of the various improving treatments she would never find time to complete. Then the dignified alcoholic restaurateur of uncertain years, as passively proofed against life first thing in the morning as he was late at night, deceptive in his calm, frenetic with misery when anaesthetic, retarded by wine, took longer to work and his raddled face, at the end, looked the same way it had at the start. *When* Mr John Smith came in for surgery, *when*, not *if*, he must ask what he did for a living because it was relevant to the drugs. Was he a boozer? Did he work with tar? Did he smoke?

He felt like the Mad Hatter in *Alice in Wonderland*. Do you know why the hatter was mad? he asked Tina. Because of the mercury he used in the making of hats, ha-ha. We don't use mercury amalgams so much in teeth any more, but they are useful. Californians want them out, you know, quite the worst thing to do, destabilises the stuff, and it wasn't the solid form of mercury but the vapour that made the hatter mad. Mid-afternoon, she gazed at him sternly.

'You'd better behave. Say your prayers. There's a nun in the waiting room. Two of them.'

The second nun had a severe face and pale blue eyes fit to scan far horizons; the first looked as if she could not speak and required guidance to cross a road. They both sat bolt upright, suspicious of the luxury. The elder admired Cannon's loaned sketch, enjoying the view of a naked woman stepping out of her bath. The other had turned her back on it.

'Ah,' said Pauline. 'Look who's here, Imelda. The inquisitor's apprentice.' She stabbed a finger in the direction of her companion. 'This one grinds her teeth. What are you going to do about it?'

Several hours later, when Sarah sat opposite him, he found himself examining her face for familial resemblance to her aunt. It was there, in the brilliant, watchful eyes and the strong chin. Hers, too, might be a gaunt face in her older years. An over-strong face, softened by the cloud of hair. Something had happened to William. Ever since Saturday he had not been able to stop looking at faces. In three days the bruise on his own had faded away to nothing. If Sarah had a child, it would look like her; she should have a child for that reason alone, even if the child looked as she did this evening. Jubilant, secretive, worried.

'I met your aunt,' he announced. 'We had an extraordinary conversation.'

'Yes,' said Sarah drily, the dryness hiding the pride, the surprise and the repeated sense of being outmanoeuvred. 'She's unique and amazing. Should my ears have been burning?'

He hesitated. 'Yes. Yes. She's enormously proud of you.'

'Well, strike me down, Lord. First I knew.'

He touched her hand, found himself looking at her as if he had never seen her before. Yes, she was definitely worried as well as happy and, in the same way he had been throughout the day, he was talkative to the point of giddiness. Various subjects would remain on the incommunicable list, Cannon's twin for a start, but how beautiful she was; what a series of colours. Pauline's eyes had faded with age; those of her niece were intensely blue, full of welcome mischief, and her mouth soft and desirable. If there had not been so much to say, he would simply have sat and stared at her.

'Your aunt refused a free check-up. She said she would save it for her martyrdom.'

'I think I told you before,' Sarah said, 'my aunt used to tell me tales of the martyrs. She considered the best way to get children interested in the faith, was blood and guts. Mention of martyrs was probably her opening gambit. She never really stops.' She sipped her wine. 'Anyway, you look remarkably cheerful on it. I was worried about you at the weekend. Cannon was shivering in front of my fire when you phoned on Saturday.'

'Oh, was he?' He had forgotten about that and it was no longer important, that brief moment of jealousy, followed now by a moment of relief. Cannon could linger in Sarah's house for as long as he liked since he was not a lover, and he did not want to discuss Cannon or have her discuss him either, not when he had such delicate plans for his long-lost brother, although, at the moment, on the third glass of wine, they seemed the stuff of sheer imagination. Cannon and Cannon's brother: that was his challenge; his only. Besides, the man had not yet made an appointment. The fingerprints on his glass seemed to prolifer-ate.

Do you like me? Your aunt liked me.

'She asked me to Sunday lunch,' he said.

For all of the familiar ease, there was something troubling about this conversation. Sarah could feel all the strings controlling her very secret life becoming entangled. There was Cannon, the loose Cannon, bringing the poisoned chalice of his friendship to William, giving him to guard a golden sketch of a painting that would not gladden William's heart if he knew either the value or the history. Cannon made people keep secrets: he was a manipulator, bringing the nuns to William's door, making all these friendships and connections into spider threads, lacing them together in a web, with a predator at the centre, waiting patiently. She felt the same chill of fear she had felt when she had known that John Smith was on the other side of Matthewson's door; an unaccountable, unquantifiable fear; a kind of toothache.

Perhaps she should explain; tell the story as she knew it right from the start; tell him how Cannon was the harbinger of bad news unless he was also an absolute liar. Tell him . . . but telling him would surely dent the shell of his innocence. She had no business sharing her responsibilities; he had not volunteered for that. So she lit the sixth cigarette and watched him watching. Regarded the frank gaze of admiration in his eyes. Almost love. She did not want to relinquish that; not yet, if ever at all. He was quite odd enough for her to love.

'Did you buy anything at the exhibition?' he asked, jumping topics with accustomed ease.

'No.' Another stab of conscience; a vision of that stolen canvas; a reminder that she could lose that look of liking so easily.

'Nor I,' William said cheerfully. 'I didn't join you, but at least I went. Thought it was a load of rubbish, mainly.' They were both being evasive and finding it all too easy.

'Any more bad dreams?'

'I think they're being temporarily displaced by new challenges. Shall we eat? I've been talking too much. I don't listen to *you*.'

The bubble of her news had been blown away and no longer

seemed as important. 'I've fallen in love,' she said, watching his face fall, enjoying the expression. 'With an apartment. The person who lived in it left her dentures behind. Do you think I'll need them?'

She looked at him smiling at her, and felt unaccountably lonely. Felt, in the pit of her stomach, the same airtight bubble of despair. Ah, William, I cannot trust you to *like* me. Nor anyone else either. I must put my trust into bricks and mortar. There was nothing else to trust. And, as if he knew about the slippage of faith, Cannon had not phoned again today.

Cannon had no illusions about the durability of bricks and cement. A home was not a castle. No Belfast boy growing up in the seventies could ever think that. Stones and wood became fragments, like bones; a home was a flimsy thing, flung down on to the ground out of spite, out of a liking for the insurance money, or for an unscrupulous builder like Daddy to have the chance to put it up again. The bomb was simply another form of blackmail, like a threatening letter, easily deployed.

Cannon wanted his wife and child to have a home with thick walls and a serious front door to foster the sensation of safety, but he himself had no such illusions of permanence. He knew how soon a building could be destroyed if no one watched. That rumble of destruction, that cycle of wanton damage and noisy renewal was the music of his childhood. All he really cared about in a room was the quality of light. Or its absence. Whether it had pictures on the walls. Otherwise it would all come to dust. The interior was not important unless it surprised him somehow into noticing, and it had to be beautiful or outstandingly ugly to do that – like the convent or the prison at one extreme, but all the same he liked it here. William's ambience; the smell of him, per-haps. It was a very strange sensation for Cannon to have friends. He wondered if he would ever quite get used to it. Being around William's things gave him a quiet, intense pleasure, which was nevertheless tinged with the guilt of trespass. He tried to tell himself that if he had asked William for a billet for this second night, William would have said yes, but he knew that this avoided the issue because he had not asked for fear of a no, and a no would have prejudiced something as precious as it was fragile. Cannon had scant talent for friendship. Johnnyboy had seen to that. *When me and Julie have a house, William, will you come and see us? Julie would like you. I like you. Be god-daddy to a baby, will you?*

Besides, he had always liked mess, the stage in the construction of a thing, painting, building, when it was a mess. That was when it was full of promise, long before the disappointment was clear in the vast difference between what was envisaged and what finally emerged. Mess was the thing he liked in here, even though he had tidied a little. William would not notice, surely: the room seemed so little used. William told him so, all that long time ago when he had let Cannon explore. A glory-hole. Dentists are hoarders: they throw away nothing except ideas.

He felt guiltier, too, watching William go out in the evening dark before he himself got in. Guilty about relying on the fact that, although William had a nice eye for a painting, he was not really an observant man, let alone streetwise. He simply did not *expect* violation, as Cannon did, all the time. He didn't see life as a series of booby-traps. There were sets of teeth, mounted on a card, like buttons. He found those in a cupboard, grey with dust. There were the dental moulds on the table, looking as if they kept one another company. Yes, he liked it here. He could sleep in this battered chair, eat his sandwich in peace, drink water from the tap, look around and feel peculiarly safe, and if his hands itched with the idleness he would sit on them. Enforced contemplation. Use the nail-file left by Tina to file his nails. Nothing wrong with doing nothing until the early hours of the morning, although it seemed a long time in prospect. After an hour, the guilt got to him again: he had only wanted a sympathetic, private place to do nothing but *think*, but his dedication to furious thought about what he should do next, other than play out the waiting game, was simply creating confusion. Feeling guiltier still, he began to wander.

That William was out for the evening and the night was something of which he was fairly certain. He had not looked like a man popping out on an errand: he had looked like someone washed and dressed, carrying a bag, locking up with care. Dear William. Cannon found there was no toothbrush in the bathroom, the old rogue, out for the duration. His kitchen was empty of food; if he had to eat, he would not be eating here. Cannon's deductions made him feel cunning and, at the same time, treacherous. Privacy was not something he had ever been able to value much, but he knew that other people did.

A small, neat bedsitting room William had, featureless in style. A functional kitchen, again with no other mark of individuality apart from the colour of it, as if he saved his efforts for the bits of his domain other people saw. Or as if he was on the brink of moving on and did not care. All that mattered here were the waiting room, the entrance hall, which was the first thing they saw, and the surgery, where they would recline in various states of anxiety until they got up, looking at nothing except the light. He remembered looking at the light until his eyes closed; remembered William's kindly face even better and his hands most of all. You could judge a man by his hands. He drifted into the waiting room, noticing how the blinds were drawn, another sign of William's absence for the evening, a fact to be celebrated and also deplored. Cannon half wished he would come back through the door, whistling. He decided he could risk raising the blind.

The glow from outside lit the picture in the centre of the wall – as if it needed light, containing so much of its own. The painting he had loaned was its own complete world. There was Bonnard, not quite at his best, sketching his wife as she got out of the bath, the way he had sketched her a hundred times, beautifully fleshed but delicate. Fastidious in her toilet, pink and gold in skin, captured in the glow of his constant fascination, the little brown dog in the corner. A deliciously clean, gorgeously familiar body, totally unselfconscious either of the gaze or the desire of a husband, the gloss of familiarity suggesting *husband*, rather than mere lover, content to be exactly as she was. To Cannon, it told the whole story of a life he himself wanted to live. Painting his wife, again and again and again, making love in the bright light of the day with every brushstroke. Feeling the weight of her arm round his neck, the touch of her breast on his bare arm. Julie in sunlight for ever.

They had seen it together. *Could you ever love me like that?* she had asked. As if she could not know that he already did.

He lowered his gaze, and wanted to weep. Johnnyboy could never even look at a picture like this; it had been bought with Johnnyboy's money and it could never, ever be returned. Johnnyboy would slice it into ribbons rather than own it. It represented connubial happiness; a vignette of fulfilment. Johnny would not want to know about Bonnard's life.

He moved to the other side of the room, viewing from a distance, aching with longing, suddenly tired. He did not want the chair in the basement room; he wanted a bed and the luxury of dreaming his way into oblivion. A state of nothing in which he would wake in a sun-filled room with her by his side; watch her go to her bath and know she would come back. Let him know before she left the house.

A bed. A bath. But he could not sleep on William's bed or use William's bath, not without asking. He could use the basement room, because it seemed to him that such a room belonged to nobody and everybody. The sight of the clean coverlet on William's modest bed made him feel ever more the intruder; he stared at it, saying to himself, *I am sick of always being in a place where I must not leave traces. Sick of it. Sick of reliance on kindness.*

Madame Bonnard might not have been kind for all he knew, but she was *there*. Go, get out, *go*. Out through the basement window. No. He felt safe here. He had felt peculiarly safe here from the very first visit. Dear William had no idea what he had done, overturning the fears of a lifetime. Dear William had no idea of what he was like. He did make a person feel safe. Although not safe enough to take the liberty of sleeping in his

bed without prior permission. Not when he was contaminating
his life enough already.

William would not miss a piece of stale cheese from the
kitchen fridge. No one downstairs would miss one of those six
lemons past their sell-by date. And he *would*, one day, share a
little of Bonnard's experience. He *would* leave his mark on the
world without his mark being some destroyed building in a
street, looking like a gap in a row of front teeth and an invitation
to misery first, and the profit of a stranger second. There was a
taste of salt on his tongue from the cheese, which stuck to his
teeth. Leave no traces, sit on the stairs. He had washed in the
junk room in cold water, still felt dirty. Finished chewing.
Stopped with a terrible, weary sense of fear, mouth open.

Nobody hears what goes on in your mouth except you,
William said. What is loud to you and visible to you is inaudible
and invisible to anyone else, unless you happen to grind your
teeth, a sound with a certain resonance. He loved to lecture, did
William. Cannon was on the last set of the stairs, which turned
a corner into the waiting room, part of which he could see. He
was absolutely sure he had never turned on a light – who needed
a light to look at the Bonnard painting? There was one now.
Cannon detested any kind of God, but he thought of the nuns
and prayed. You bastard, God, will you ever give me a night's
sleep? Will you ever give me a moment's grace of feeling safe? I
sold explosives to thieves; I was never big-time enough for terrorists; please, God, don't stop my heart, not yet, please. I am
safe here. We only have to get to Christmas. Johnny would never
ever be here. He could never even look at my wife's face. He
would never come inside the premises of a fucking dentist. Tell
me I'm wrong.

And yet there he was, crossing Cannon's line of vision, in front
of the painting, which he ignored, confident here as if he had
been invited, so oddly at home that the first thing Cannon felt was
a spurt of jealousy. This is *my* place, *mine*. *I* found it, and there
was a sense of *déjà vu* in that. How many dens, how many hiding-
places had Johnny uncovered when they were kids? How many

caches of paint and paper had he ruined before he gave up? Beyond count, and here he was again, doing the same. Johnny was talking to himself, suited and spurred with shiny shoes, as if for an appointment, convincingly debonair, fooling himself. Oh, how the devil did anyone with Cannon's use of words ever begin to explain the chameleon existence of Johnnyboy, when nobody else in the world had ever known him, ever been *close* to knowing him? Hirelings, paid and fired. These days, he was like a potentate with a series of speechless eunuchs who never lasted long. He looked so lonely down there that Cannon wanted to leap off the step and touch him, hug him, but he was paralysed. The first touch would never be the last; touch him, and his own soul and his own hope were as dead in the water as floating fish. No one would ever know. If he killed him now . . . if he killed him now . . . if he killed him now. He sat instead, the salt on his tongue, his mouth slack, watching, listening.

Johnnyboy, in his suit, was trying to read, trying to check from the notes in his hand. There was another presence, out of sight, calling back, a fucking eunuch fatty – they were always like that, big, sexless, brain-dead.

'Look . . . there's another one . . . "C's friends," it says. He doesn't have any friends. She must be with his friends. There's no one else. Why couldn't that little bastard Andrew have got this far? Pay people, they focking let you down. Do it yourself. Only way. Christ, will you look at that rubbish on the wall? Sort of shit *he'd* want to paint . . .'

Cannon smiled. He did not know why he smiled. Once, they had only smiled for each other. Now the very intonation of that hectoring voice made him smile out of sheer recognition, bite back the desire to answer. He bit his knuckle instead. The figure moved out of sight; not far, three steps at most, the voice fading.

'Writes messages to himself, this fella, only in pencil, on his focking notes. Tells you who knows who and where they live . . .'

A distant voice, murmuring, indecipherable, discontented. Johnnyboy had filled his small horizon with similarly servile voices, muttering now, 'Nuns, focking Sisters of Mercy.'

The door clicked shut. He was not the only one who knew his way out as well as his way in. They were gone and he was here. Shivering.

Wanting to blow up this place now Johnny had been in it. Make it disappear.

'Can I ask you something, Sarah?'

'Anything. Shhhh, you're shivering. Here . . .' She held his arm across her body, his hand to her breast, her body nestled into him. She had pulled her hair beneath her head, so that his chin could rest on her shoulder in the crook of her neck, and that, to William, was the sweetest piece of generosity. She made room for him; accommodated her small self against his length, made herself fit. Made herself belong, without making any demands. Was this a kind of kindness, he wondered, technique, or the sensitivity engendered by serious affection? Was it simply a question of practice?

'Have you ever posed for Cannon?' He moved his hand and stroked the curve of her hip. Soft, the bone firm beneath.

She moved, closer into him, covered his hand with her own. 'Yes. It was rather uncomfortable.' She shook slightly with remembered laughter. 'Cannon doesn't go in for creature comforts. And it wasn't me he wanted to paint, it was his wife.'

'Tell me about his wife . . . his brother.' The body, relaxed after love, tensed. William regretted that. He adored her like this, as floppy as a soft toy, sleepy, close.

'No, my love, I won't. Let him tell you himself if he wants. It's a long story, which he can tell but I can't tell for him.'

'All right.' The warmth he had lost padding to and from the bathroom was fully restored. He remembered the curve of her back as he had got back into her bed; the way she moved her hair to make a resting-place for his chin.

'Besides,' she said sleepily, 'that wasn't what you wanted to ask, was it?'

'No. Not quite. Am I a *good* lover, Sarah?'

She could have laughed at such a question at this stage in

their knowledge of one another. How long was it? Two years, on his reckoning, since his first sight of her in that small office of hers, less than that since they had become lovers, almost imperceptibly. A drink at her place, several; a casual invitation, why don't you stay? A scene repeated more times than he could count. Understated passion, remarkably satisfying, marked by a gratitude on his part that denied the asking of any upsetting questions. What a fool he was to ask such a question now, but it was suddenly important to know that he did, actually, please her. He rewarded her; he paid any debt he might have by fixing things; he took on her acquaintances as patients; he tried to keep things equal; but did he delight her, as she delighted him?

She stirred in his arms, raised his hand to her lips, brushed his fingers against them. His right hand, the one John Smith had bitten. Suddenly he wanted to pull it away, retreat to his native state where all questions were superfluous except those justifying purely factual answers without opinions attached. Back to his own world, where the biggest mystery of the day was why, without scientific explanation, a solution of hydrogen peroxide could stop bleeding. It took an effort to repeat his question.

'Am I?'

'As a matter of fact, you are. Do you think I *pretend*?'

'Well, *no*. Perhaps I just needed to know in words.'

She was wider awake now, turning with a *phumph* in the bed so that she faced him and held him by the hair. He thought for a minute she was going to grab him by the ears and beat his head against the pillow. The curtains were never closed in Sarah's room; she said she was afraid of the dark. Ambient London light through the window showed only the hollows of her face. She kissed his nose, then his mouth. He wanted her to say something more.

'William, I'd like to kill that wife of yours for what she did to you. You're a marvellous lover. You've got the heart for it. Makes you good at whatever you do . . . let it take you over. Makes you a good dentist and, yes, a good and generous lover. Will that do?'

Not entirely, but he nodded. There was something else he wanted to know and wanted to hear, but for the moment, in a state of contentment, he could not remember what it was.

Do you love me? Do I love you?

CHAPTER ELEVEN

No. He had not seen Johnny, or heard his voice. There was nothing to indicate the presence of anyone else. The two men he had heard, the one he had seen, were figments of his imagination. They were nothing of substance; Sarah was right to suspect the soundness of his mind. Cannon blinked. He was stiff, as if he had sat still for a long time, fallen asleep without knowing and woken cramped and uncomfortable. He was not entirely sure of where he was, leaned forward and put his head in his hands.

There was no way Johnnyboy would ever come to a dentist. No way. Nothing in their subliminal understanding of one another would make him cross that barrier. The sheer smell of the place would make him sick, the way he had been sick the first time they put him in the chair and held him in it. Projectile vomit as soon as the probe hit his teeth. A grunt of disgust; the lady dentist wanting to hit him, except she didn't want to get so close. The twin, Cannon, watching from a corner. Johnnyboy refused to cross the portals without him. Johnny would never, ever go to a dentist, not if the pain killed him first. He'd had two of his teeth pulled by a barber later, and that was all. So it was a dream, then.

Cannon could still feel the taste of salt in his mouth; looked through his hands into the waiting room, comforting himself. Better to be losing his mind.

Then he noticed how the light was on down there. He had

not put on the light. He could see what he wanted to see without that; he had merely pulled up the blind. And then he heard the voice, echoing through his head with its resonance of disgust. *That's the kind of shit my brother would paint.*

If only he could paint with Bonnard's joy. *If only* . . . How fucking ironic that Johnnyboy, who could not recognise talent, could not recognise what his brother had done with his stolen money. The desire to scream with outrage roused Cannon into the present. Of course it was Johnny, standing there, defacing the painting by the mere looking at it; there was something unique and corrosive about Johnny's capacity for disgust. The repercussions of what he had seen and heard intruded like a bad headache. This was what he, Cannon, had done, in return for William's great contribution to his life and William's tentative friendship. He had brought Johnny inside the door in his wake, like a wave of disease. A confident Johnny, too, who did not give a damn about who saw him.

Jesus, God, do something.

He ran down the last of the stairs, snapped off the light, stumbled further down into the safety of the basement, pulled the door, as if it was a shield. It was stiff and warped; it would not shut. It seemed so typical of William that the door would not shut – there was no need to *close* it because William had nothing to hide. And not a single clue how to protect himself either. Such a calm, skilled man; professional in his own field, devoid of any of the black arts he would need against Johnny if Johnny had singled him out for attention. *Why?* William didn't have so much as a stick, let alone a knife or a gun, in the same way that he had nothing to bar his doors. William could not hurt a fly, and now here he was, caught by a spider. *Why*, and what *did* he have to keep Johnny out?

You could only threaten Johnnyboy, not persuade him. What did William possess for that? A useless, gentle temperament was what. Cannon prowled in an agony of self-recrimination so intense it burned. He was disastrous to the people who liked him; he should not be alive; he was a walking piece of damage.

His eye lit on the detritus in the room. Bottles, jars, old packets spilling out of shelves with an air of abandonment. Cannon
stopped and stared. Ah, Christ. Save me from my promises.
Jesus save me, even though I don't believe. Hydrogen peroxide,
somewhere; he'd seen it. What did William say it was used for?
William and his lectures. Stopped bleeding; no one quite knew
why. And over there, that old-fashioned disinfectant, in packets.
Mix crystals with water, clean the lav. And over there, more of
this redundant stuff. And, over here, potassium permanganate
in disguised form, crystals again, the sort of thing he had found
in his gran's cupboard before she, too, died; he remembered her
creating out of it a dark purply-greenish mouthgargle – *This'll set
you right*.

He groaned, and he wept a little and brushed away the tears.
There was the makings of destruction in here and the same old
urge to use them. Some of the things he had played with as a
child, bless him. Making big *bangs* out of household stuff, the
way they made them now out of fertiliser and shit and subversive
handbooks, and he had made them out of nothing without even
knowing the names; just knowing what worked. High explosive,
bigger, faster bangs and greater risk to health; low explosive, less
dramatic and in the end more fun for a kid. He allowed himself
a moment of moral superiority: it was so easy to make a bomb
now – all you had to do was steal the stuff, no art to it, no art at
all; no guesswork. Probably no fear either of the kind that now
drove him mad even at the sound of fireworks. Never, ever again
would he do such a thing. Johnny had made him go on doing it:
it was him who had the knack, not Johnny; him who had the
knack with everything except the orders.

Never again. I shall never again destroy anything, or make
anything that can destroy, he had promised his wife, who had
made him repeat it – as a Catholic repeats *Kyrie eleison, Lord
have mercy* – until the promise was etched into his brain, made
him forget that it had been *fun*. Wicked fun, she said, and all the
more wicked because you never saw the result. You ran away
before you saw the cost of it or you sold it to someone else and

didn't see. We didn't *kill* anyone, he'd protested. How did you
know? How many lives did you ruin? All promises were made to
be amended, because Johnnyboy was on the threshold;
Johnnyboy knew nothing of reason or art or anything, any more
than dear William knew how to stop him coming back.

*Listen, William. You've got to be on the right side of the door
yelling to him that if he comes any further forward you'll blow the
door into his head; he understands that. Tell him you've got a nice
piece of high explosive.*

He began to assemble things, like a cook in readiness for a
feast. He poured the disinfectant crystals onto a cleanish part of
the stone floor, ground them beneath the heel of his boot. He
took the torch out of his pocket, flicked it on and off. There were
batteries around here somewhere, bound to be, or he'd bring
one. Johnny won't be back tonight; doesn't need to be; something planned. OK. Squeeze the juice from the lemon left in the
fridge; improvise; put the mix of the crystal powder and the peroxide solution and the lemon juice into this bowl, cool to near
freezing, maybe outside the window – God, it was cold out
there. Leave it a few hours. Use the torch: break the glass on the
bulb, give it that little bit of intense heat from the naked fila-
ment – better still, cross the wires from the flex of that old
Hoover . . . Take it away, Joe. Tell *him* what you've got in
here . . . Tell him to take his gorilla home, or else.

Cannon stopped and looked at the muddy mix in the shallow
plastic bowl. Yes, Sarah was right. He had lost command of his
brain. *Next task, tell the darling fool how to detonate the thing, point
it, keep his distance.* Poke it towards the door like some fucking
lion-tamer in a fucking circus. Oh, yeah. Easy-peasy.

The light that filtered through into the basement was changing slowly but perceptibly. Winter dawn, heralding itself two
hours before the real event; a witching hour, and if he were
Dracula he would begin to think of going home. Oh, yeah. Dear
William would blow himself into smithereens before he could
detonate or control a homemade bomb, although he might be
fascinated by what was in it. He might be able to do amazing

things to teeth with all his know-how, but he would be just as likely to drink this mix as use it. He'd be the same if you gave him a gun: he'd only want to take it apart. Give the bugger a knife, he'd cut bread with it and give you a slice. Cannon was monstrously tired and appallingly sad. He stared at the contents of the bowl as if it were urine in a potty. What a waste of effort, born of a fevered mind. What was he to do? Surreptitiously explain to William, say, Here's a bit of useful knowledge for you, just in case of – *what*?

He moved towards the ancient fridge with the tread of the defeated on a long march to nowhere, holding the bowl, not sure what to do. It was all absolutely useless. After all, he was not good at anything, directionless without Johnny.

Finally, he flushed it down the sink. He picked up the lemon he had squeezed, bit into it and chewed. There was still salt in his mouth.

Then he tidied all trace of his presence from the basement room. Stuffed his possessions into his pockets and squeezed himself out of the window. The cold of the railings bit into his hands. The daylight held no promise. There was nothing to do but wait. As the light reached the room outside the surgery, the answer-machine clicked and whirred. *Please speak after the tone.* A quiet, apologetic voice hesitated before speech.

Julie preferred the convent chapel when it was lit by the moon and a couple of candles, or when it was illuminated by electric light in the evening, not the way it was now, merely dim, the windows aching to admit the purer light that the heavy coloured glass denied. None of the sisters could bring themselves to use electricity for a task, when daylight would suffice, even if the light was scarcely as adequate as it was in here. Their sense of economy often outweighed convenience, but it was invariable. A room so dim mid-morning oppressed her. After dark, it mattered less. She was grateful for the winter and the dearth of daylight glimpsed through windows, because it was the light that reminded her she was in prison.

'Help me,' she murmured.

A place of enlightenment, in one sense, but still a prison for over three months now, although she had hardly noticed the first weeks. An existence so artificial it was ludicrous. She was trying, before God, to continue to see the sense of it, not that she believed in God. Life was far too random a matter and people far too various to have either one Creator or one Controller, surely, but she did believe in saints, and that was a kind of concession. If Cannon had opened her eyes to visual beauty in his critical fashion, making her notice and admire, then this place made her at least acknowledge the existence of the kind of soul that needed no such stimulus.

They needed symbols, these women, ritual and statues to give form to belief and turn the ephemeral into the real. My, she was learning such long words from Pauline and her books. Three hours' reading a day and it had become curiously addictive. You'll go back into the world a heathen, Pauline had said cheerfully, but a bit more literate than many. She would certainly not go back the same, but then she had not been quite the person they thought when she first came in. She was already altered.

Julie had brought the kitten into the chapel with her for the daily cleaning, not an invitation of which Imelda would approve but a venial sin rather than a mortal one. The kitten was company; it skidded on the high polish of the floor and attempted to suffocate itself inside a duster, but she could scold it in her normal voice. 'You stupid little beast, you! Behave or I'll strangle you with a sodding rosary and then which direction would you go? Heaven or hell?' The kitten was also something to hold; light, warm, soft and resentful, a poor substitute for human skin. 'You gorgeous little sod,' she said admiringly.

Imelda was suffering from the aftermath of dental treatment and was behaving like a tragedy queen, resting. She kept going on about the marvels of the dentist's waiting room; beautiful curtains seemed to be the stuff of her day-dreams. Julie tried not to envy her the joys of her excursion, only because although there were moments when she herself would have risked fire and injury simply to be *out* of here, if only for an hour, there were others when she was peculiarly reluctant to go. She smothered the jealousy with the realisation that she could not possibly envy anyone a visit to the dentist, because such a thing terrified her, even the smell made her tremble. Cannon had been stoic in the face of it; she admired that, especially since she had not actually noticed his appalling teeth when they met, only ever his eyes. At the moment, she envied his comparative freedom.

The kitten made play with her ankle; its claws were sharper as it matured. 'Sod off!'

She was dusting the statue of St George, flicking at it with absentminded violence. The tip of the spear poised to enter the dragon's mouth snapped off and fell to the floor with a *clunk*. The kitten pounced on it. 'Hell and fucking damnation . . .' Julie suffered a moment of panic, feeling shifty and sacrilegious. Then, in a gesture that surprised her with its swift spontaneity, she found she had made the sign of the Cross over her own body, touched first her forehead, then her breast, then each shoulder, left to right, just as *they* did two dozen times a day, not only in prayer, with grace before and after meals, in here, anywhere, but at moments of stress and impatience, a calming gesture, but also one of warning, an admonition. She was horrified to catch herself in such an act: she had already assumed the seductive rhythm of their quiet speech; now she was assuming the movements of their hands. Next she would be wearing their talismans and soon there would be nothing left of her original self.

'I'd rather go to hell,' she said out loud. Jumped as a hand fell on her shoulder.

'Would you really? I'm sure not – whatever the alternative you were hoping to avoid. Hell's for eternity, a difficult concept I find.'

'An eternity of having your teeth filled,' Julie said lightly, thinking of Imelda, who had been the sole topic of conversation last evening, and hoping that Pauline had not heard her swearing,

mild though it had been. Or seen her making the sign of the
Cross; she was even more afraid of that. A vain hope for this
gaunt gentlewoman of silent footsteps: Pauline missed nothing.
Julie adored her, but the intense affection was tinged with a fear
that went slightly beyond profound respect. Pauline had more
than a touch of ruthlessness.

'And, yes, I did see you making the sign of the Cross, child.
What a curious thing to do when all you had done to precede it
was snap St George's perfectly dreadful spear. Don't worry, my
dearest, don't worry. It really doesn't mean that God has *got* you,
like St George supposedly *got* the dragon. Not that George was
really after the dragon. He was only after the maiden, after all.
Most men's ambitions centre on the carnal, in the end.' She
tapped the dragon's nose. 'They have to be the way they are for
the furtherance of the species. It afflicts them all the time, even
when they do it with each other into old, old age without any
discernible result. And they know, of course, by another version
of the same instinct, that the women will look after the progeny
long after they've gone on to plant some more. So don't trouble
your head about St George's spear. He only wanted to get the
dragon out of the way. A rolling-pin would have done.' She
touched the broken spearpoint with her foot. The kitten skit-
tered away.

'Why did I make the sign of the Cross?' Julie asked, ashamed
of the aggression in her voice.

'Oh, Lord, for the same reason you wave *thank you* at someone on a zebra crossing for failing to run you over. An automatic
reaction against a repetition of danger or embarrassment. Really,
it doesn't matter.'

The St George of the statue had rosy cupid-bow lips, pursed
in concentration. No primal scream forming through open jaws.
The dragon looked like a larger version of the kitten, rolling on
its back; not much of a contest, for all of its feigned agony,
pathetic beast.

'But what if God had got me?'

Pauline sat in a flurry of sudden consternation, settled herself.

'What if? I'd be delighted if He answered my prayers, but the occurrence of that isn't frequent so I'd also be surprised. *What if?* would be entirely for you to discover. It wouldn't prevent you from loving your husband, if that's what frightens you about it. Indeed, if you saw him as an instrument of God as well as a mere man, it would make you love him more. Is that what you mean?'

Julie shook her head.

Pauline went on, 'If this casual invocation of the Holy Trinity meant a realisation that no human love is complete, totally fulfilling and providing all the answers, you'll merely have taken a step forward. Several steps. It may make you judge him differently. Sceptically. Want something more reliable to love. Not *instead of*, as well as. You wouldn't believe the flexibility of religious belief. If it does damn-all else, it puts things into perspective . . .'

'*Stoppit!*' Julie yelled, holding her hands over her ears. And then, more quietly, 'Stoppit. Stop *it. Stop doubt.* Stoppit.' She hesitated; she hurt. Old bruises came to life. She wanted to shout, 'I'm *pregnant.*' 'Why is it that I could live by myself for two whole years when Cannon was in prison and never waver in the way I felt about him? Never waver in my complete conviction about whatever he said, never *doubt*? What are you doing to me?'

'I? Nothing. God might be working on you. There might always have been the need for another kind of faith. You've never been among religious people before, have you?'

'*Contented* people,' Julie murmured. 'Contented with a fraction of what I hope for. No, I've never dwelt with people who are content.'

'Well, don't let the appearances fool you. Why do you think Imelda grinds her teeth? We can't all be free of doubt.'

'What? Not even you?'

'Especially not me. But this has nothing at all to do with me. And it wasn't the same, being utterly faithful to Cannon when he was in prison and you weren't. Now the position's reversed and it surely gives rise to resentment, doesn't it? After all, it might be all his fault. Or his *fantasy*. But your injuries were real, child. Entirely real.'

Julie turned on her with quiet fury. 'Yes, they were, weren't they? Only I'm no longer sure who it was inflicted them. A man who refused point-blank to look at me, couldn't bear to see me. Put a pillowcase over my head so he didn't have to. Got someone else to hit me. It *must* be his brother – oh, God, I *hope* it was his brother. There was nothing I would not do to keep Cannon. *Nothing.*' She smiled uncertainly. 'Maybe it was all simply an act of God, bringing me here.'

Pauline laughed shortly, the sound of it loud in the chapel. Her reverence for the place was casual. 'God moves in mysterious ways, but they aren't usually quite so convoluted.' She touched Julie lightly on the shoulder, brushed her hair back behind one ear. It was as if she knew how much Julie longed to be touched, even as innocently as this. 'Would you like to *try* to pray?' Pauline asked. 'It's easy, really. All you have to do is just imagine God the Father does exist and chat to him. That's all there is to it, really. You don't have to praise him, you can complain to him if you like. I would, if I were you.' She bent down and picked the tip of St George's spear off the floor. 'A bit of Elastoplast, I think,' she said.

'I'm hungry,' Julie said. 'Ravenous for food. Help me.'

Sarah sat and looked at the mess on top of the desk. She had put all the estate agents' bumph into the bin, thought of the new flat and quietly applauded. Yes! Thought of William and smiled. Thought of Cannon and frowned. Enough was enough. In between everything else she had found a new place for him to squat: *her* new flat with the deaf neighbours. Throw money at the problem, Ernest had said, and she had. An immediate rental agreement, pending exchange of contracts, expensive but worth it. Cannon and Julie were going to bankrupt her, but that did not come into the equation.

There were more art catalogues and a letter.

Dear Mr Fortune,

*I have got your letter of today about 'domestic properties',
'specialised services' and all that stuff. I don't find much
wrong with estate agents, personally. At least they tell you
what's going on. This is just another way for you lot to
squeeze more money, right? On account of foreigners who
want flats having more dosh.*

So, I'll think about answering your questions, shall I?

*Mind, I don't see why I should advise you lot anything. I
pay you lot plenty enough already and I don't go much on
lawyers. I think you're a load of tosspots, reely.*

John Smith

She agreed with the last sentiment, albeit with reservations. She
could quite understand why any member of the paying public
might consider a lawyer no more than a highly trained thief
extracting money from grief and necessity, a servant with an
exaggerated sense of self-importance, not in the other guise, as
protector, which was the way she saw it. Someone who led
others through the minefield of highly regulated contemporary
life, stuck with them and brought them through to the other
side. That was what she did, when allowed.

So, Mr Smith, I may have you on a hook. I may get to have a
proper look at you at last. What will you think of me? Shall I be
able to make human contact with you or will you spit? The writing was similar to what she had seen; similar, but not identical.
The spelling was different and the result inconclusive.

The mirror faced her on one turn of her restless pacing.
Window open for forbidden cigarette smoke. No, there was no
way she could make herself look like a boy, but she could probably make herself look less like a woman. Scrape back the hair,
omit the makeup, try to look pale and uninteresting; add specs.
She rather liked the idea of disguise. It was only an extension of
daily life to assume the colours of her surrounding company, not
for camouflage but to make them feel at ease. An actress, playing a number of parts.

Cannon. Who still had not phoned. If Cannon was telling the truth when he said there was no answer to the terrible threat of Johnnyboy until Johnnyboy was tired of the game, then she would have to find the solution for him. Blackmail of the kind Cannon had forbidden. After all, at one remove she knew quite a lot about John Smith's business. The countdown to Christmas was short, but it was still too long, even if John Smith *had* promised. She had the sense of time running out, even before Pauline phoned. The office this morning was hot and stuffy.

'Where have you been?' The mere sound of that authoritarian voice sparked the guilt that had lain pretending to be dormant. Pauline reminded her how little of her own life she seemed to possess, but it seemed wrong to complain about that. She shut her eyes and tried to recall the moment when she had seen the new flat; a moment of unalloyed, undistracted happiness. As if it was ever going to be hers.

'I've been nowhere, Auntie.' Pauline hated being called Auntie. 'I've been busy doing nothing. As always. You know how it is.'

There was the sound of heavy breathing. Sarah doubted she was using the convent phone, sited in the hall next to the dining room – not for confidential conversations and sparingly used as necessity demanded. Sarah had offered to buy them a fax and met a barrage of puzzled faces. Why would we need it?

'How soon can you come and see Julie? How *soon*?' She was whispering urgently, sounding childish, as if enjoying the conspiracy, relishing the keeping of secrets. No wonder it had been easy to persuade her into such discretion: she was a closet spy.

Sarah glanced at the letter from John Smith, ending with his illiterate signature. *Ridiculous* secrecy: the man could not even spell. He was a clown who swam like a piece of cork on legs, and she herself was delaying because she was no longer able to believe that any of this had been necessary.

'Why should I?' A weary question, sounding grudging. Julie was her responsibility was why, just as Cannon was. She had made them thus. Was it laziness and wanting her own life back that made her resentful? But she loved them both, Pauline and William, too. It was just that none of them seemed to be aware of it. 'Oh, I don't mean *why*, I mean why now? It's only a few days since . . .' She was sounding apologetic, and cross for feeling it. Why could she never do *enough*?

'Well, if you came today, most of them are out. The sermon in the Cathedral . . .'

'*Why*?'

'Look, things move fast with the human soul,' Pauline hissed. 'It doesn't stay consistent. I'm worried about her. Cannon's missing two nights. They argued. She's getting frightened. She's also getting addicted to this way of life. Thinks it's easier than coming out. She's starting to *pray*.'

'That's your fault,' Sarah said, icily calm in her anger. '*Your* fault. You can't leave well alone.'

The breathing became heavier, indignant. 'Do you think I want a *convert* at any price? Well, I don't. I don't want someone I can mould into belief simply because they're weakened, impressionable and fearful. Especially someone who feels they're being abandoned. Not much of a gift to God, is it?'

'I can't make her happier. Cannon's the only one who can do that.'

There was a snort of derision, an unspoken curse. *Men*. 'I wasn't suggesting you could, but you could alleviate this sense of abandonment. Come and talk to her. Make plans for her. Cannon's not communicating. Tell her there's an end to this charade. Give her *some* version of what might happen. Tell her he'll do anything for her. As she would for him. *Anything*.'

Sarah was silent. Pauline had always asked the impossible.

'She's afraid of the frailty of love.' And Pauline added, saving the best until last, 'I've a feeling she might be pregnant.'

Perhaps it was something he had done or said; perhaps it was the imminence of Christmas, and a time when his clients consulted their budgets and decided their teeth could wait in the interests of other, less important and purely seasonal spending, but business was not brisk, William decided. This did not worry him unduly: money had never worried him much, apart from a vague discomfort about the fact that perhaps it should – in the way that a new suit or a different piece of wallpaper should excite him and didn't quite. In fact, anything that had to be *shopped* for, money included, was always a trifle disappointing. He surprised himself by thinking that what he really appreciated in life were the surprises: the events, the gifts, the people wished upon him unexpectedly before he had a chance to head them off. Sarah; Cannon; a truly unusual set of teeth presenting themselves for his inspection; the challenge of John Smith. The surprise to the eye or the emotions of something exquisite or hideous. He was not sure whether John Smith was a real person or an event. Whatever he was, there was something stupendous about his arrival. He was a gift without wrapping.

Early in the morning William was home, Sarah and he embarking in their always separate directions. Wouldn't have to be so early if she moved into that flat she'd described. He liked the idea of her living nearer; definitely liked it, a lot, so much so that he wished he could remember the address she'd told him before he'd been distracted, wished he had told her about John Smith, but on the whole was pleased he had not. She was so damned helpful. He wanted to deal with John Smith by himself; create an achievement all by himself, alone and unaided. I'm not such a klutz, am I? I can make a real difference to two lives. And I'm a good lover; *me*. She had said so.

What he liked about John Smith's teeth, and by the same token what he had liked about Cannon's, was the fact that they were so much *worse* than what he normally saw and they belonged to rather unreasonable people. The rest of his patients were *so* reasonable, so prosperous, so educated about the state of their fangs that they arrived at the first sign of trouble and did what they were told, boringly, so predictably co-operative they scarcely needed him at all.

By eight o'clock the wintry sun began to creep into the

corners of the room. There had been a touch of frost as he had walked down the road and the railings flanking the door felt frozen to the touch. Shop windows, black, and what would he buy her for Christmas? A rubbish van was collecting black sacks left on the pavement; there was something positive about the place looking cleaner even as he watched.

One of the blinds was up. William frowned. He could not remember leaving it like that and he was precise about such things. He pulled up the blind that was down, releasing a shaft of sunlight. It fell on Cannon's painting, and he stood before it, lost. A woman in her bathroom, drying herself. Ready for her *toilette*, a dress strewn over a chair, the only furniture in a simple room with painted stone walls, a rough-tiled floor against which the nude had guarded her feet with bright-coloured slippers. A small selection of glass jars on a shelf, backdrop to her ease; she would not hurry for anyone; there was no preening in the pose, no apparent knowledge of the observer. Had he, William, ever regarded Isabella with such frank admiration, been allowed to gaze at her in this way? No; he could not remember it; nor, he imagined, could she. He could only recall the degree of lust, which did not comprehend details, and could not have stood back to observe her. Did not look, only wanted to grasp. He could also recall that the details of her *toilette* were always secret: he would glimpse her going into the bathroom, glance at her during her cursory scrubbing of teeth, but by and large Isabella never stayed *au naturel*. She emerged from behind closed doors fully armoured for the day. It was the finished product she presented for admiration, never the body, as if she had hated it.

William felt a great stab of pity for her, and shame for himself. How little they had known each other. How intimately, by comparison, he knew Sarah, who would sit joyfully naked for all the world to see and not care what it thought. She was the one happier without the clothes and the accoutrements, a creature requiring no second skin. He must ask Cannon about the painting. Why did he never *ask* things? In his heart of hearts, he did not want to know it was stolen.

Into the surgery, and yes, on this blithe, refreshed morning,
holding on to his high spirits of the day before, he was proud of
the place, too. *Clever* design, William. *No* immediate view of the
chair, another little space to sit and talk about it, a corner to turn
and a feeling of space. He had hated tiny surgeries. They got in
everyone's face. There was no painting or piece of distraction
facing the chair. How long since he had decided on that? When
Tina had said there was no need, or because he had realised
that, whatever he put there, it would have to be something *he*
liked and it followed from that that someone else might dislike it.
The wall in here looked bare. Fussily, busily, getting himself in
motion for the day, William proceeded into the hallway and
removed Cannon's drawing of his hands, placed it on the empty
hook opposite the chair. Surely no one could take exception to
that. Then he washed his hands carefully, reminding himself of
how precious they were. Humming, he admired the order of all
he surveyed and pressed the answer-machine button for messages. A sibilant voice, oddly without resonance, hesitant,
instantly familiar.

*Tomorrow afternoon, Mr Dentist. The whole afternoon. And no
one else there, you get me? No one but you, or I'll go as soon as I
arrive, and you'll miss out on all that cash. But I can't have anyone
watching, can I? Smith.*

The words themselves were hectoring, but the tone ingratiat-
ing, almost pleading, as if attempting an apology.

Click. Beeeeeep. The sunshine seemed to depart from the
room. William slumped. Examined his hand for the disappeared
mark of a bite. Didn't the man realise it would all take so much
longer without a nurse to record and assist? But then again, how
would he know? Sarah would say, Do not do this. You have an
awkward patient with high expectations; you *never* see such a
patient alone, especially females. What defence could you offer
if he sued? What protection would you have?

I don't care. I want to.

He looked in the appointments book. It was so much easier
than the screen. Five for tomorrow afternoon, the names as

meaningless as usual without the notes, all short appointments, no one booked for more than half an hour. No sedation, no anaesthetist to inconvenience, all capable of cancellation; nothing major. How *dare* the man give such short notice? Why the hell should he cancel? He hated to cancel, it was unfair and irresponsible, but he knew as he reached for the phone, formulating excuses and unaccustomed lies, that that was exactly what he was going to do. Tell them to come back next week or the one after; they were a biddable lot; so *good*; so respectful. Tina would be delighted with an afternoon off. Everybody would be happy.

And yet, when he looked at his hands, they were shaking. Long, elegant fingers, shaking like twigs in a breeze. Not nearly as confident as the hands Cannon drew. He was not used to telling lies. His fingertips tingled and grew pink. Sometimes he thought his whole life was his hands.

Cannon had not phoned, had not phoned . . . had not phoned. The realisation repeated itself like a litany. He had rejected the idea of a mobile phone – typical Cannon, rejecting anything that made life simpler. Addicted to complications. And fantasies. He must be sulking in response to the increased scepticism that had come to surround him. Cultivating other credulous friends. Doing something to upset his wife. Making a mess as usual. The bright daylight outside made her angry. She had promised to find him the new place to live; she had fulfilled the promise; and still no phone call. What the hell did he think he was doing?

The small space of her office had the effect of multiplying the anxiety she had tidied away; she felt she wanted to push the walls aside. Maybe the daft bastard had gone on a bender, that was all. Not an entirely unknown phenomenon in Cannon's unpredictable life.

Lunch-time, at last an excuse to exit. Running downstairs, carefully past Matthewson's door, avoiding him, too, in case of question – *I must account for my time* – the green wool coat flowing out behind, such was the speed of her. A pause in the vast reception area with all its empty walls; a nod and a grin to the woman behind the desk. Out into the sunny street with an arm already raised for the taxi. Yes, Cannon was going to bankrupt her. Traffic made her snarl. The taxi-driver wanted to discuss it, as if it was news, but found her aloof and discouraging.

She had never come to the attic in the middle of the day. More often, it had been in the earlier hours of morning, or long after the afternoon dark had taken command. The street was busier than she remembered: she felt conspicuous and told herself she was not. She was an office worker, like all of these coming out into the cold to find sandwiches and dream of going home soon. No one would notice her entering the only domestic residence in the street, that empty place no one cared for. It was not her, it was Cannon who would look out of place here, but no more so than the man on the corner selling the *Big Issue*. If anything, he was smarter than Cannon. She unlocked the door and went in.

The chill was ominous; she could sense from the first floor that he was not there. 'Cannon?' The sound of her voice was muffled by dust and the creak of the floorboards. Polish these, mend that, it could be a lovely house, she told herself, as she forced herself onwards and upwards. It was only an empty house with a harmless squatter; the worst that could happen was discovery. I am John Smith's lawyer, she would say haughtily. He gave me the key. Take me to your master.

'Cannon?'

The door to the attic at the last set of creaking steps gave easily as she pushed. The emptiness inside was a relief. Half-way up, the vision that had haunted her all morning since Pauline phoned had increased in intensity, become sharper, so that she almost expected to see it. Cannon, dead or dying in here, giving up on his allies because he could sense they were giving up on him. Cannon, lying on the cherry-red sofa, beginning to stink, victim to his despair; the artist artistically disposed in death in his garret, an image he might like. Another image had clashed with the first: she had seen herself coming up here to find there was no roof, that he had blown it all away, leaving nothing but sky and dust. The last thought occurred too late for her to guard against it as she closed the door behind her. He may have booby-trapped the place. Even if he had sworn on his solemn oath never to play with fire, he might have done that. He was mad enough. He kept his cash between the first beam and the roof. The beam sagged dangerously.

There was nothing. A stale smell of nothing, not the sharp smell of turpentine she associated with this place. He had not been messing about with paint in the last day or more. There was none of his leftover heat; no sign of activity. As tidy, in preparation for imminent movement, as she remembered it from last time.

There was the single difference that all the sketches of Johnnyboy's face had been torn. Ripped across and thrown in a heap, showing signs of systematic, rather than furious, destruction. That was Cannon all over, destroying what he had done, always at war between the making of something and its breaking down. So he had at least been back, then. There was a half-eaten sandwich on a chair. Cannon lived on sandwiches and yet he loved good food.

It struck her with a terrible conviction that no one with Cannon's love of light would ever consent to live like this unless they believed it was entirely necessary. Whatever the real nature of the threat posed by his brother, it was certainly real to him. Utterly real, for him to confine his free spirit into this and insist on separation from his wife. She had not done him justice. But he had done some sort of justice to her. Her portrait rested against the easel, turned towards the light from the window in the roof. He had done further work on it, lovingly, it seemed. Toned down the colour of the hair, and then added more of the red. He had caught the likeness in the body and the face; captured something essential in the attitude of careless abandon. It was a sensual portrait, which was not, at the same time, sexual. Not like the Bonnard, which was both. She wondered if he was pleased with it. Moved closer, admiring her mirror image rather than herself.

We form our impression of a face from a distance of three feet, at least, William said. It was only a painting that allowed the impertinence of closer scrutiny, touching, squinting, looking for flaws in the skin. He had found hers, the tiny scars on the breasts, slightly whiter marks against sallow skin, not disfiguring but oddly enhancing, like freckles on a sunny face. And she had thought he would not notice.

'Cannon, where are you?'

A pigeon cooed and tapped on the fanlight, startling her, making her want to run. But she did not run. She found a pencil and wrote a message, 'Darling, where are you? Phone me,' and then ran downstairs and into the street, locking the door behind her as if it were her own house.

CHAPTER TWELVE

I must account for my time; I must account for my time.

She sat at her desk, facing the screen, typing with disinterested fury. The law required such a vast number of words. There is *real* life, Cannon, real work: look at it. If I keep on skiving like this, they'll all lose patience. I won't be able to help anyone else because I won't have a job and I won't have money and I shall never be able to pay for the flat. There are other clients, Cannon, you aren't the only one.

Where did a man go all day? Where did he disappear?

The afternoon seemed endless, anxiety, as well as anger, extending each minute into an hour. Where would he go with his depressive nature, his capacity for intense joys and miseries? She remembered him running towards that fire, saw it mirrored in the screen; remembered that he had a valuable life but a frail one, and why, oh, why, had she ever taken on the burden of it to neglect it now?

Thinking: trying to remember anything relevant about him, affection sneaking back and catching her unawares. Cannon was at his most unpredictable when he had done something of which he was ashamed; what *might* he have done this time? Unless that fanciful ogre, his brother, had found him and spirited him away. What *did* Cannon do with his day?

You can sit as long as you like in the galleries. They're half full of weirdos like me. Some of them with sketch-pads, some of them just sitting. It's the best thing about London. That's where you learn.

And which one do you like best, Cannon?

Oh, I circle around. I always come back to portraits. I like the living dead.

This time, leaving the office, she remembered not to run, to look calm and casual as if slipping out to a meeting, even remembered to invent one and write it into the open diary on her desk. Matthewson sometimes snuck up here to see who was hiding. *Research into art collection; portraits.* He might not believe it, but it was a record all the same and almost true.

Believe in your instincts. The brightness of the day had faded mid-afternoon, and the city began to prepare itself for dark. A pavement artist outside the National Portrait Gallery began to clear away his chalks, regarding his depiction on the stones without sentiment, indifferent to its imminent destruction, counting the takings.

She moved through the vaulted rooms of the gallery quietly, feeling foolish and conspicuous. The few guards were yawning towards the end of the working day. What a job; what sublime boredom. The thought of that made her quicken her step, moving from one incurious gaze to the next, wondering what they would do if she was a thief strong enough to snatch one of these heavy frames and run with it. Surely portraits were too personal for thieves. As if anything were too personal for thieves. She found him finally, sitting, head propped on his hands, staring at a portrait of a bearded Victorian premier surrounded by his family, and the relief at the sight of him cancelled out the irritation. She sat. If Cannon was remotely surprised to find her there, there was no indication: it was as if they had met an hour before and met again by prearrangement. She thought, wryly, that his erratic faith in telepathy must have extended itself beyond its application to his brother, making him assume the same quality in her.

'Sometimes', he said, by way of introduction, waving at the noble lord, 'it does one good to look at a thoroughly second-rate piece of work. Which this is. This painter was doing what he was told, as if someone had said to him you can paint it any colour you like as long as it's blue. It makes me feel better. If I spent all my time looking at artists with vision who paint like I want to paint, like Bonnard, it would make me feel hopeless. I'd want to go back and white out everything I'd done.'

'Or tear up your drawings,' she suggested.

He shook his head in unfeigned surprise, shocked at the suggestion. 'Oh, no, I never do that. I'm never angry enough to do that. Put them out of the way for a while. Then use the other side of the paper. Paper costs money. Where have you been?'

'Come on out, Cannon. We can't talk in here. They'll think we're plotting a robbery.'

He followed her, shuffled level with her down the road, into Trafalgar Square. There was the dull roar of traffic, muffled into background noise by the well of the square itself and the sound of the fountains. Nelson, on his column, towered above them. There was a dilatory shifting of people, meeting, greeting, crossing; movement towards buses, trains, entertainment, home. He seemed unnaturally calm for a man who hated crowds, but the space was large enough to absorb them, no one came close enough to push or to touch.

'Never mind where I've been,' Sarah said, pulling her coat around her against the cold of the bench, trying to avoid pigeonshit. There was an enormous Christmas tree in the centre of the square. Another year gone. 'You didn't phone. I'm sick of you. We're all sick of you.'

He nodded in agreement, dull in response. 'I'm not surprised. *I'm* sick of me. I just don't know what to do. So I don't do anything really.' He took a deep, shuddering breath.

If he chose this moment to cry, Sarah thought she might hit him. He did not cry; she waited.

'I go and look at paintings of patriarchs and father figures. Wishing I'd ever had one. Wishing I could be one. A man who was able to look after his own.' He shoved his hands into his pockets. Even in the cold open air, the coat still smelled. 'I thought I might just disappear. It would be better for everyone. Better for Julie in the long run. None of this had any point. Johnnyboy's always known where I was. He's been up to the attic. He's been to William's place. I saw him. He'll get to you next.'

Oh, nonsense. She did not say it, thought it. What had William to do with anything? William had been protected from knowledge. She didn't believe in unconscious communication. Nobody would have been to Cannon's dwelling-place: it was an almost perfect hiding-place. She was sick of pandering to fantasy. Then she thought of the torn-up drawings in the garret. *Oh no, I'm never angry enough to do that. Paper costs money.* The cold from the bench struck through into her back, chilling her spine.

'I suppose the *other* thing I could do', Cannon was saying, 'is simply go back there and wait. He'll be along, sooner or later.' His hopelessness had a quiet intensity she had never seen before. She did not know quite how to rouse him. It grew colder with the darkness; the lights of the grand buildings surrounding the square began to glow. She did not know if she wanted to humour him or believe him.

'Pauline thinks Julie may be pregnant,' she said. No forethought to the statement. It simply emerged as the only positive thing she could think of to say.

'What?'

'Your wife. Having a baby. *Maybe.* I don't suppose you take condoms on your nocturnal visits, do you?'

She looked straight ahead, not quite wanting to see the effect of her statement, guilty for making it on such shaky information. Pauline might have said it for effect; it might not be the truth. They were none of them masters of truth: they all made guesses and stuck to them. She could sense him uncurling beside her. Moving from his slump with head in hands. Standing with his hands in his pockets. Then, with his arms above his head, locked into a stretch. Then one hand on hip, the other raised as he performed a jig, like a drunken Scottish dancer ignorant of the steps but feeling the tune, hopping from one foot to the other, singing tunelessly, louder and louder as he moved until he stopped, breathless, punched the air and yelled, 'Yeah!' in a voice loud enough to slice across the sound of the traffic and the water. The pigeons, which had begun to approach their feet with the constant optimism of pigeons, flew upwards in an untidy arc. Cannon was transformed.

'Oh, yodleodle*deeeeeee*,' he sang, pirouetting with his hands on his head, changing the steps into a kind of hopscotch over the paving-stones, not touching the cracks, as far as the brink of the fountain. She thought he might climb into it, but he put his hands into the cold water, splashed it into his face, hopscotched back, jumped up and down. YES! YES! YES! Sarah leaned forward on the bench and laughed long and loud because he was comical, and out of sheer relief to see him thus: the other Cannon, reminding her of why she had fallen into devotion to him, for all his intensity, his absurdities, his intolerance, his moods, his talent for outlandish joy, latent in his paintings, patent now. She would always love creatures of extremes; the ones impossible for cohabitation; those who saw what she never could. He would weep for a fallen leaf and shout for joy at the colours of a tree. He could make a bomb or paint the soul in a face. She grabbed him and pulled him down.

'Cannon, I said *might* be . . . And it hardly improves the situation, does it?'

She hated to rain on his parade; he had the knack of making her feel cruel for the slightest attempt to restrain him – and how would this man ever stay alive without Julie to direct the dreams?

He sat so abruptly that the solid bench creaked. He was suddenly sober, but his face was still split by his widest grin, which made his mouth look like a cave. A passer-by glanced at him curiously; he glanced back, then pulled his hand down from forehead to chin, as if wiping off the smile with a cloth, pretending to be solemn. It reappeared immediately. Sarah adopted her dictatorial voice, uncomfortably aware that she could sound a younger facsimile of her aunt. Bossyboots.

'Look, Cannon, whether she is or she isn't, this whole charade is at crisis point. We don't just *wait* any more. I'm going to see Julie *now*. You're going to come with me. You're going to march in there without thinking of who might be watching. The hell with it. Why should anyone be watching? Then we sit down and talk about plans, four of us, like civilised human beings capable of making them. Then we either take Julie home or arrange to take her another time.'

'Home?' he echoed. '*Home?*'

She shook him impatiently. 'Another apartment. I've got one lined up. My home if you want. Anywhere'll do.'

'No,' he said. 'Johnny'll find us.'

'If I hear that *one more time* . . . So you say. So you've always said. And what if he does? You barricade the doors. You call the police—'

'Who won't believe a single thing I say. I'm a con, a liar, a thief who cheated my own brother . . . The police were never an option.'

'Of course they are. For Christ's sake, if they didn't weigh in for liars and thieves, they'd be out of a job.' She paused. 'Are you a liar, Cannon?'

'No.' Without hesitation. He was sober without being depressed, sitting still and thinking, a rare state of stability for him.

'Good, just checking.' *You lied at your trial; I helped you.* 'Shall we go, then?'

'Wait a minute, let me think . . .'

'Don't think, Cannon. You either don't think at all or too much, without any good results either way. Come *on*, Cannon.'

'I'm not sure . . .'

'Well, I am.'

The crowds *en route* to somewhere else had gathered momentum; the traffic growl increased; they were leaning close together, heads almost touching to hear themselves speak.

'This flat . . . How will Julie manage?'

'A bit of rudimentary furniture, enough. More than you're used to.'

'Only I don't want her lifting things.'

Cannon stood decisively, brushing himself down as if what he did would make any difference to the state of his dreadful coat. 'I'll have to go back to the attic. Get some money. Come with me?'

She hesitated, furious at his assumption that she should. She did not want to go back there; shuddered at the thought of the place; wanting to keep a strong hand on his arm, but gripped with repugnance for that grim place and the torn drawings. She wanted to say, 'Never mind about the money,' but she had little enough to give him, twenty maybe, sufficient for the taxis, not more than that from a bank account looking a little leery at the minute. Surely he could go alone; no sense in duplicating tasks. And what was it he'd said about William? No time to ask. She fished in her bag for cash. 'No, thanks. You go, quick. I half promised Pauline I'd be there at half five. The nuns are out, more space. Meet you there, OK?'

He nodded. She watched him lope across the square, scattering more of the pigeons. He gave a hop, skip and a jump, twice, took chocolate from that everlasting pocket, threw it. Optimism rewarded.

Perhaps her own would be rewarded, too. Sarah did not want to move; she stretched inside her coat and closed her eyes. There was nothing but the roar of the traffic and the insistent splashing of the water. She calculated the differing time it would take at this crowded hour to reach the convent. Taxi or tube? She thought of economy as much as speed, rose stiffly, listened to the raucous music of a cacophony of horns and descended, like a thousand others, down to the trains.

He was absurdly happy and he was not going to be afraid ever again. He opened the window of the taxi and let in the cold air and the noise. He wasn't going to be afraid any longer because *this* settled it. New life settled it, redefined everything, because there was going to be a child with *his* blood and his bones, and that made all the difference. Because a man could love his wife with his body and his mind, which he did, and more, but his soul would enter his child. The child would be the ally to make him strong. A male, surely; a little man. He would hold the child like a shield against Johnnyboy; the child would be the final *proof* that he was gone from Johnny for ever. Gone from being buggered, gone from the intimacy, living on a different planet from the one they had shared. The child would be proof that he had become not merely a defector but a different species, a new kind of animal altogether; no longer, in Johnny's eyes, simply an experimental lover, indulging himself in an affair that Johnny would find unspeakably repellent and thought he could squash to death like a bug; Johnny would see what he was. *Look what I've made, Johnny. Look what I've made. Now do you see I can't come back?*

There was a pause for self-recrimination in the back of the cab. Was he so little and so cowardly in himself that he had needed this promise of new, innocent life to confirm his own certain footsteps? Was he as feeble as that? Was his passion for his wife not sufficient all on its own? He chewed his nail and watched the blurred passage of the world outside; someone ran across the front of the taxi as it slowed for lights; the driver swore. Oh, yes, love for Julie was enough; it was everything, but perhaps not quite enough to quell that greatest fear of all. The fear that, one day, Johnnyboy would be diabolically clever and try the simple expedient of seeking a reconciliation through charm and guile without any threat of force. He hadn't learned a thing, Johnnyboy: his cruelty was powerful, his need insatiable, his kidney punch the worst on earth, but the power of his affection and his tears and his longing, if ever he admitted it, well, that put any kind of threat into the shade.

The taxi lurched round a corner. He was thrown back against the seat. Remembered Johnny with a hand pressed over his mouth, both of them hiding; the fear all the time that Johnny would *beg* him back, plead with him. That he would forget to hunt and bully, that he would crook his little finger in some awful act of kindness and tap into the common sap that made them. That was the real fear.

But not now, not any more: now this had happened, and Johnny had left the ultimate threat of sweet persuasion too late. He would never win now, because there was so much more to lose. *Yes!* He bounded up the steps and into the shabby house, which hid its dereliction rather well, careless for all his thinking. The office workers of the street were in full, colourful exodus, hats and scarves donned, the girls with silly shoes incapable of keeping out cold or wet; he had a fleeting memory of kissing Julie's feet in her practical slippers, feeling the thin skin of an ankle. He ignored the faint scent of Johnny inside this house, because it was impossible to explain and he wanted to concentrate on things he could explain, but it was there all the same. Definable only to someone who had slept with the brute for all those many years, knowing every smell of his body from the peculiar stench of his sweat to the gentle aroma of a freshly soaped chest. No, he had not been forced to love Johnny; not at first. It had been as natural as breathing . . .

He could hear Johnny breathing in here, the pulse of the house; ignored that, too. Crashed through the door to the attic, wishing he had asked the taxi to wait. More haste, less speed, Cannon, my lad.

His stash of cash was under the beam, above the portrait of Sarah without her clothes. Sarah, another convenience, how generous she was; wouldn't he love to do without her, like *they* wanted to do, shedding Granny when she tried, in vain, to keep them in order? And, Christ, how was he going to earn enough to keep a wife and a child? Haste made him clumsy; the boards creaked. He glanced at the painting of Sarah: it was good, very good, provided he did not compare it to Bonnard, and that way lay the death of all endeavour. He had talent; he had to believe it; there was a child to consider and the child had talent to be nurtured, too. He yanked at the beam, fingers exploring impatiently for the plastic bag secreted up there with the survival money inside. Didn't trust banks: you couldn't when the State said you owed it money. He fetched a chair to stand and reach better.

There was only the one wooden chair, a spindly thing suitable for a bedroom. He stood on it regardless, reached again, heard the leg of it snap, clutched at the beam and hung there for a moment, thinking, This is funny. Then the beam cracked, broke, fell, hit him a sneaking, soundless blow on the back of the head as he landed; sent him crashing forward, colliding with the make-shift easel, both of them spinning down noisily. Then he was lying on the floor with a dead weight across his shoulders, plaster and dust cascading into his hair like hailstones. He tried to lift himself up; could not; tried to breathe; could; lay where he was with the cold imagination of having been hit by an explosion. Stay still, think about it; no pain yet; blurred vision, his heart pounding. Remembered, quite inconsequentially, a remark Sarah had made about this room. It's rotten, she had said, but not that bad. And there's not a single beam high enough for a man to hang himself. Such faith she had in him. He felt delirious, ridiculous, with some half-remembered sense of happiness and optimism. He closed his eyes against the grit, reached forward, exploring with his fingers, finding, to one side, particles of plaster and dust, pieces of torn paper, which were oddly unexpected, and then straight ahead, the canvas of the portrait.

The last thing he remembered for a while was that the surface of it was still slightly soft and sticky. Oil paint took a long time to dry.

Sarah rang the bell at the door of the convent and wondered idly how many times she had done this – dutiful visits to her aunt, when she was a child and Pauline in some other institution, nearer what was then home and a long way from London, a place with a similar door, but attached to a school. The convents she had known, her own school included, melded into one another in a single sensation of smells, lack of comfort and a deceptive façade of gloom to hide what was behind: laughter and warmth often enough, charity, devotion, talents and tensions, a code of conduct that kept everything in place.

She noticed the dearth of lights in windows; two, far left, for the two sisters currently bedridden, the rest in darkness, sure sign that most of them were out. Off to the Cathedral, Pauline said, to hear the Cardinal in the afternoon, busloads of them from all over the place, but I've heard enough from priests so I'll keep the home fires burning. In virtual darkness, it seemed. No one here would ever leave a room empty with a light burning: they had a second sense for a switch. They closed doors quietly and turned off the light behind them, like polite guests in some-one else's house, ever aware of cost. Sarah had lost almost every aspect of her convent training; all she could remember was the habit of quiet movement, so ingrained that it was natural unless she made herself stop, or some mood of hilarity prevailed with the housework, some excitement overcame the well-absorbed reserve. It was not much to have taken from a moral education; a small souvenir out of otherwise comprehensive rejection. She had not lost it all. There was still that belief in redemption . . . for others.

She remembered, also, the slight and controllable sense of claustrophobia that preceded her like a high-noon shadow as soon as she came here, some memory of small rooms and scold-ings, *Sarah Fortune, you are beyond hope . . .* a feeling of inadequacy because she could never, ever get it quite right. Could manage the decorum, but not the obedience; found the rude books about sex and made sure the other girls read them. *Stop sniggering, will you?* She rang the bell again, turned to survey the off-road parking space and the road beyond while she waited for someone to come from the back of the house to the front. A car moved slowly down the quiet road, pausing, as if looking through the trees for a number on one of the great big houses that flanked either side. The door opened. Pauline made a mock bow and ushered her in with a flourish.

'Cannon shouldn't be long,' Sarah said.

'Ah, a double pleasure.'

To Sarah's relief she detoured away from the parlour. It was a room that echoed; it was more suitable for a summit confer-ence than a cosy chat; she could see visiting dignitaries snoring in there on the pristine moquette, sleeping out of self-defence against the dizzying patterns of carpet and curtain. She followed to the kitchen, where the warmth hit like a soft blow. Julie was by the industrial oven, her face flushed. There were trays of cling-film-wrapped food on the table, cold meats and bread and butter, a pan of soup to one side of the hob. 'They'll be hungry as horses when they get back,' Pauline said cheerfully. 'A good sermon from a high-ranking cleric always does that for them. Say hallo, Julie.'

She isn't a child, Sarah wanted to shout. Let her speak for herself.

Julie smiled a greeting, which lit her face, turning it from interesting to beautiful, despite the fatigue. Sarah turned to Pauline. 'You're a tyrant. Julie's a paying guest, remember?' She did not add, *paid for by me*. 'You make her work too hard.'

'I do *not*. *You* try and prevent her. I can't.'

'Stops me thinking,' Julie said. 'I'd rather not think.' She tucked her hair behind her ears; it was damp. 'Can we go some-where else for a minute? It's so hot in here.' It was warm, certainly, without being uncomfortable, but then Sarah had not been labouring over a hot stove. Hers was the easy life: she could see it in Pauline's eyes.

'We'll say a prayer in the chapel, shall we?' Pauline suggested brightly. Julie nodded and moved ahead of them. Pauline and Sarah followed. 'She *likes* the chapel,' Pauline whispered to Sarah, irritating her with the assumption that Julie might not mind being talked about within earshot, like a deaf old relative. 'She feels at home in it, these days.' Was this new, or a piece of invention? 'Cannon likes the chapel, too,' Pauline added.

It was chill enough in here to reduce a fever. Sarah had left her coat and regretted it; the other two, a unit, did not seem to notice. It struck her for the first time that there was a purpose to Pauline's voluminous clothing: it was the equivalent of wearing an adaptable blanket at any time. She herself was dressed for an overheated office, skirt and blouse inadequate for these more Spartan conditions, and there were further advantages in being a holy nun like Pauline, such as never having to worry about co-ordination, whether the shoes would go with the skirt, the skirt with the blouse: she could simply stick to the shroud and put the equivalent of the handbag in the pockets, without vanity as if she had none of that commodity. Which she did have, the darling, in plenty, but vanity of a heavily disguised kind properly belonging to a producer of a play who might dress with deliberate insignificance in the knowledge that it was he who was pulling the strings and creating the scenes. Sarah tried to suppress the suspicion with which she regarded both Pauline's inscrutable face with the marble skin and Julie's guileless exhaustion. How melodramatic to insist on the chapel, as if it were a lay-by on the road to Damascus and Pauline, if not the embodiment of Paul's vision, at least the official breakdown van who collected him for the next leg of the journey.

'There, now,' Pauline said, making sure they were all uncomfortable. 'Julie and I have had such a lovely quiet day together, haven't we?'

Why this dreadful condescension? Was it saint to sinner? Or was it Pauline, mother appointee, becoming overprotective on the discovery that her darling little flower was in a delicate condition? Sarah looked at the statue of St George around which they seemed to be marshalled, wondered what the pursed-lip princeling thought he was doing waving that stick.

'I told you Cannon'll be here any minute,' she said. 'Can you hear the doorbell from here?'

'Oh, yes. There's a pager on the wall, a quiet one . . .' That was Julie, confident in these surroundings. A waitress with slightly buck teeth, marvellous eyes and enormous dignity. Sarah felt foolish. There was no disingenuity in either of them; there was only her intense irritation at feeling so much at a loss, that convent feeling of guilt and powerlessness. She had her arms crossed over her chest, defensively, less against the cold than the sensation of their innate superiority, married woman and professional celibate. Maybe all *tarts* felt like this in such a place. Maybe it was Pauline being so condescendingly motherly to her

new charge. *You always were an attention-seeking child, Sarah.*
Still jealous at thirty-five, are we?

'Look,' Pauline said, 'you've got us wrong.' The *us* hurt. 'We
like the chapel because we like the chapel, right? And it's perfectly fair to sit here if we're waiting for Cannon to join the
discussion, isn't it? He's far more likely to come in the back way
than he is the front, if he follows established custom. Never quite
took to the parlour, did he, Julie? Prefers the clandestine.' Julie
nodded. 'If he can't get in the front, he'll get in the back. So
don't worry about Cannon. You didn't say you were bringing
him anyway; the later he is the better. Gives us more time to sort
things out.'

'Are you pregnant for sure?' Sarah asked, avoiding Pauline's
eyes and staring straight into Julie's tired face, fascinated by the
changing expressions that altered it so much it could have been
a different face; she would be similarly and dramatically altered
by different clothes, another chameleon. They had something in
common then. It was difficult to describe the change of mood:
a sad face in repose; utterly attractive in laughter; the huge eyes
of a madonna, mirroring the amazement of discovery. She
would be divinely patient with child and husband, given her
chance. How they would all grow together, like a twisted and
fruitful apple tree.

'Pretty sure. Sure as I can be, short of an announcement from
the Archangel Gabriel. And Cannon won't have any reason to
think the thing a supernatural object rather than his own, his
very own.'

There was a note of irony, foreign to her, a new tough self-
assertiveness. Perhaps the result of a day with Pauline, to whom
ironic understatement was second nature. Sarah could not see
Julie being ironic with Cannon: he would not comprehend it.
With Cannon she was sweetness and light, not sickly sweet, but
firmly indulgent of his primary status and her integral part of his
life as the decoder of his language and his needs; his passport to
reality. There was pride in the symbiosis, the being the other
half; she made it admirable. Feminist claptrap about finding

oneself would find as much house room in Julie's repertoire as it would in that of any of the sisters here. Her kind of love made its own ultimate demands and she would obey them completely. Seen in the context of Julie's generously self-sacrificing soul, perhaps a temptation to include love of God into the equation was not so surprising. Pauline had said it once: if you love completely, the heart expands, and calcifies. She always made it sound like a disease.

They may have been right, Julie and Pauline. The coolness and sense of space in the chapel refined thought, gave an instant access to perception in a place where the distraction of movement was minimal and concentration on the non-peripheral was ordered. Personally, Sarah thought being locked in a cold cellar with a few crates of wine might have the same effect. Why had she never noticed before the strength in Julie's arms? Born to hug a man and cradle a baby, quite clear about it. She felt a moment of envy so intense it was painful, followed by a wave of protective feeling that was equally intense. Nothing should harm her; nothing. Beneath that currently calm, strong face, she had all of Cannon's fragility. It was only the combination that gave them the strength. Didn't matter if they bankrupted her. Someone would. Perhaps she could be godmother to the child.

'Some women put on weight very quickly, don't they?' Pauline murmured. 'Not that Julie is yet.' Still talking about her in the third person, as if impending motherhood made her a subject for discussion rather than a presence. 'Can't be more than a few weeks, can it? But all the same, if she stays here it's going to be a little difficult to explain. Nothing insurmountable, provided I don't have to confess to carnal goings-on in the sacristy, but tricky.'

'She isn't staying. Are you, Julie? We can go straight away.'

Julie gazed up at St George, then at Sarah, then down at the floor, frowning. '*He*'s still there, Sarah. Still there. Cannon would never leave me now, not if he knew. But he's still there.' Sarah thought for a minute that this was an oblique reference to a saint. There were a lot of them around.

'Who?'

'Johnny. And, child or no child, I'll come apart at the seams if he ever comes near me again. Especially now.' Her voice rose. Pauline patted her hand. The wedding ring gleamed a dull gold, insignificant in all the protection it promised. Pauline's rosary beads were more effective, weightier and at least potentially useful for something. They looked ten times more likely to ward off the evil eye. They clicked with the smooth *click* of polished bone as Pauline moved.

'But *why*, Julie? He's only a man. A bad man, but only a man.'

'He's much more than a man. He's the dragon in the story,' Julie said. She was attempting to smile, but it did not mask the weakness of the fear.

'And a man is nothing compared to God the Father who created him,' Pauline interrupted, impatient with it. 'What a shame none of you ever once thought of asking *Him* to intervene. Still, better late than not. And you've had the benefit of *my* intercession for months now. Go with God, child, and if you don't believe in your own prayers, believe in mine.'

She rose with a shushing of robes, ever the leader. 'Come, it's cold in here. Where the devil is that husband of yours? You'd best have something to eat before you leave. The gannets aren't due home for an hour or more yet.'

They moved in a slow trio towards the door, Pauline standing back for the youngsters to go through first in case either of them should forget the golden rule to turn off the light. How strange this place was, Sarah thought, that it should exert such an effect, creating as it did an aversion to going inside, followed by a reluctance to leave. Bye-bye, chapel. You can't get at me, God, but sometimes I wish you could. She stroked the gnarled foot of St George's dragon as she moved round it. There was, predictably, no response, but her hand felt warmer for the contact. Poor old dragon. Then Julie clutched her arm, her mouth forming into a scream.

The swing door was shoved by a heavy hand and hit Pauline

squarely in the face – contrast to the way in which it was used for sidling through. She fell backwards against the final pew, scrabbling for balance, and hung on, uttering a sharp scream, which sounded oddly girlish. Then she moaned. In the ensuing split second of silence, blood began to pour from her nose. In the same tiny interval of time, Sarah had the absurd notion of a divine punishment, about to be inflicted upon them all for the temerity of leaving the chapel without a genuflection. Pauline's hands moved, clumsily, as if searching for something lost; and Sarah realised, with an unbearable stab of pathos, that she was trying to make the sign of the Cross. A gesture of futile courage.

Oh, Lord, that fool Cannon, coming to find them with all the speed and tact of a raging bull.

'Cannon?' she mouthed, starting forward. 'Cannon?'

The door swung on its hinge, a door bidden to silence. All three backed away from it, Sarah and Julie clutching Pauline, dragging her back with them towards the altar. She seemed reluctant to relinquish the knob of the pew, clawing at it with bony fingers white in the light, the other hand splashed with red.

It was not Cannon; there was no apologetic voice. Only a cough, like someone preparing for an entrance while adjusting a costume. Then the door opened and two men came inside. One was grossly stout, a caricature of a man built out of rubber tyres arranged in sequence from his neck to his knees and a rolling step to accommodate the thickness of his thighs, the other slight by comparison. A thickset man all the same, with a breadth of shoulder and enough height to tower over them. A whimper came from Julie's throat, muted by the knuckle she placed in her mouth. The larger man held the kitten by the scruff of the neck; it seemed smaller than a piece of fluff and made no protest. He placed it gently on a pew, where it sat and began to lick itself. Sarah felt a moment of pure terror for the kitten. Wanted to tell it to run and hide.

She knew exactly who it was. He did not look quite so foolish now, Johnnyboy. He looked like Cannon on a good day, with his grey jacket and brilliant white shirt and hooded eyes, which darted glances round the room, uneasily guarded against coming to rest. He looked a useful kind of man in here, where he was not swimming like a porpoise and his strange proportions were hidden by his suit. She knew who he was, and she knew in the same instant of sadness that Cannon had been right. The chapel did not affect him; the presence of a nun of senior years with blood gushing out of her nose did not affect him. There was no conscience of any kind to influence. None.

He paused in his progress towards them, shielded his eyes with a cap, as if their presence blinded him. Julie began a slow keening.

'Stop that,' he said mildly. 'Whoever you are.' Then louder, a trace of nervousness in the voice. '*Stoppit.*'

She stopped, dropped her head and let her hair fall across her face. It had grown long. Pauline came to life. Her voice shook, still held an unmistakable note of authority. 'Get out of here. How *dare* you?'

He seemed to consider this clichéd rebuke faintly amusing, came two steps closer. In unison, they took two steps back, like a single animal with six legs. Sarah could smell Julie's fear: it rose with the power of perfume, bringing with it the smell of the kitchen, talcum powder, acrid sweat. Now that he was closer, shortening the distance between them, gaining confidence, she could smell him, too. He extended a hand towards Pauline, let it drop, shook his head.

'My brother's *friends* . . . His powerful *friends* . . . a bunch of *women*. Oh, come now, Sister. Don't worry. What on earth would I want with a woman like you? It's *Julie* I want. My brother's *wife*. She owes me something.' Julie began to whimper again. Sarah felt for her hand across Pauline's shoulder, grabbed it. The grasp in return was soft, as if she were already giving up, had known this was going to happen all along and was unable to fight it.

'Look at me,' he commanded.

Slowly, all three raised their eyes and stared at him. The larger man was motionless, simply a fat man, standing still, waiting for his cue. Johnnyboy held their gaze until his own faltered and fell away, talked over his shoulder to the companion. Any hint of nervousness had gone. He seemed almost relieved.

'Well, that's easy,' he said. '*He's* made it easy. He's a good artist with a likeness, you have to grant him that. We'll just make sure since there's two to choose from.' He turned back to them. Crooked his finger at Sarah.

'Come here.'

Pauline was grabbing her, putting the crucifix of the rosary into Sarah's hand, begging her to hold it, go no further than that short lead. She detached it gently, squeezed the cold silver into Pauline's palm and moved forward. There was a sweet sense of freedom in moving at all.

'*Mrs* Julie Smith, as I live and breathe,' he murmured. 'Well, he certainly captured the likeness, didn't he? I could almost be proud of him for that.' He was close enough for the spittle to reach her face; it seemed to require an extra act of courage for him to speak with such venom. She remembered the way he spat. A small gob landed on the floor. Imelda would clean it up in the morning, she thought, along with Pauline's blood, her own, too, perhaps. Julie's whimpering intruded. There was a sniffy sound and a *yeugggh* noise of anguish from Pauline. Sarah sensed she could scarcely stand or speak. The thought of her helpless like that was shocking. She wanted the power to usher the two men out ahead of her like a flock of sheep, letting the door close on safety.

'My, my. I can see his point, I suppose. Pretty enough and Irish enough looking for an older hen, though I did think you were younger. He never described the hair. Magnificent, isn't it?' Again, the over-the-shoulder remark to the silent companion, met by an indifferent nod. 'Couldn't bear to look at you, could I? Covered your face and only saw you in the dark that time. No, *he*,' jerking his thumb backwards towards the fat shadow, 'was *him* covered your face, right from the start. Hurt you. I didn't want to touch you, you disgusting piece of . . . but I did, didn't I? Not much. Women *like* to be touched. *You* did.'

Another gob of spittle on the polished floor. She wondered where the kitten was, diverting her eyes and her mind from the spotlight of his hatred. The man behind was wearing big boots – surprising they had not heard him: rubber-soled perhaps; black and dirty, making marks on polished floors.

'You *are* Julie Smith?' Johnny asked, suddenly doubtful all over again.

She said nothing and, out of a perverse instinct, smiled at him. In a reflex action he smiled back, revealing a set of brown, uneven teeth. They looked almost artificial; joke teeth worn by a child to give offence on Hallowe'en; they made him look dead, tingeing his skin with their own appearance of rottenness and giving him the look of a sarcophagus. Lips like Cannon's, but pale and greedy. As soon as he was aware of the smile, he stopped and spoke through the pursed pocket of his mouth. 'See if it's her. Make sure. Bound to be her.'

There was a muffled sob from behind. The fat man came forward with his waddle of a walk and with one easy motion, ripped Sarah's blouse from the neck. The buttons held. He yanked again, exposing a lacy bra and a collarbone. It had been a good blouse; she mourned it. There was a strangled gasp of outrage from Pauline; Sarah closed her eyes. Don't, Pauline, don't speak. There is more nudity on a beach, and I have been here before. I've done this kind of thing before. The big man was prodding her, as he would a piece of meat for tenderness, fat fingers tapping her breastbone with a hollow sound, reminiscent of a doctor tapping a bronchitic chest, touching with the same degree of indifference. He was feeling the tiny raised ridges of the white scars. Nodded. His hands rested on her neck; she knew he could have snapped it. There was a minor sense of relief in the understanding that this was not his purpose; it brought her to her senses. The man stepped back, waiting orders.

She remembered the oil painting of herself in Cannon's attic and suddenly understood the nature of the mistaken identity. The fat hands were confirming it.

'Of course I'm Julie Smith,' she said. 'Who else would I be?'

Part of her wanted to hear an emphatic denial from the two shivering women behind. Longed for the sound of words, saying, '*no*, she isn't, I am; *she* is,' in a convincing chorus, but there were no such words. The other part was relieved that they kept their silence. That was what she wanted them to do, however intense the feeling of treachery.

'What do you want?' Pauline's voice was old and querulous.

'Only her. Nothing else.'

The foolish kitten went to play around the fat man's boots. He scooped it up and held it aloft. They could all see him, dashing it against the knob of a pew. Or putting it on the ground, under the boot.

'Give me the kitten,' Pauline said faintly. He swung his arm, and threw it gently enough in her direction. Sarah could hear the swish of robe and click of beads as she picked it up. The beads were no guard against the devil. She kept her gaze on Johnnyboy, but he could not return it. He clicked his fingers, like a man calling an animal to heel, and moved towards the door. The fat man came back towards Sarah and, with one enormous hand on the back of her neck, propelled her forward. She resisted, but his fingers spanned her scapula; her head was level with his shoulder; there was no choice. Still she waited for the words of denial, which did not come. The fat man seemed to relent slightly at the sight of Pauline's bloodied face as she sprang towards him and he shoved her back with ridiculous ease. Johnny was beyond the door, holding it open.

'We'll bring her back,' the fat man whispered. He seemed, temporarily, in awe of the place. 'She's only going for . . .' he hesitated '. . . for *treatment*. We'll bring her back. Honest.'

The last hint of conscience and then they were gone, the steps they had not heard in advance only audible in retreat. By the time Pauline had stumbled down the corridor after them and looked wildly into the road, the car was long gone.

CHAPTER THIRTEEN

No real pain yet. Only a dull pain like a stiff neck after a night spent in a draught. A pain in the neck; laugh about it. That was what Cannon had been doing when he came up the stairs, laughing, and that was what he remembered when he opened his eyes. There was a trick they had practised as children suffering minor wounds, such as grazed knees or cut fingers. They would concentrate not on something better but something worse. Stare at each other with their almost identical eyes, Johnny and Cannon, saying over and over again, This does *not* hurt, not *really* hurt, does it? Think of something that *really* hurts . . . something *really* scary, like the dentist, and this one will go away.

Cannon tried it now; thought of real pain to put this dull ache into perspective. His fingers touched the stickiness of the canvas; he imagined himself touching the heat of Sarah's neck, feeling for a pulse, finding it. Those little scars of hers must have involved real pain, like the cigarette burn Johnny had once inflicted for fun, sneaking up behind him, stubbing it out on his bare back. That was real pain, like the dentist Johnny so feared and he no longer did. Johnny always lied about what pain was. The worst pain was loss and the worst result he could envisage was remaining as he was, beaten into accidental submission by one of Johnny's dilapidated houses. *Laugh* about it, go on. *Man who plays with fire since age of four dies under falling beam.* Johnny never used to let houses rot. It was loneliness and despair made him do that. Three years of wilful neglect could bring down the beams of a house. Cannon thought of the house he had destroyed on Bonfire Night and what a pointless piece of destruction that had been. As if Johnny would care. All this time he had thought he knew what made Johnny tick, but no knowledge was complete.

The joists in an attic floor, he remembered, often marked the point in the building process when the contractor ran out of the best wood. Rot might have made the broken beam lighter. He could not *stay* like this; it was *ridiculous*. He heaved and, like Prometheus unbound, he was, if not free, free enough to raise his torso and shuffle the weight of the broken rafter down his body and onto his buttocks. Then he lay, twisted to one side, grabbing the portrait with its wooden stretcher to use as a lever, shoved under the beam, raising it a fraction before the fragile frame of the stretcher snapped and he slithered his legs free, like someone curling away from a snake, leaving the skin of his coat. The portion of beam rolled to the floor with a dull thump like a sledge-hammer, bounced and landed on Sarah's portrait. He stood uncertainly and gazed at it briefly, looked at the hole in the roof and then back to her. There were notes from the money stash scattered over the floor, one or two directly across her face. Sarah with ten pounds sterling over her lips, more on her bosom.

No real pain yet, but he hurt. His shoulders were stiff, his left arm curiously reluctant to move as he tried to use it to hail the cab. He wanted a drink. The darkness had come down like a curtain at the end of Act Two. Not final, but determined. A taxi stopped; he flung himself inside.

'Aren't you a bit cold, mate?'

Cannon looked at his torn sweater and dusty trousers. The temperature was irrelevant, the question perfectly stupid. 'What time is it?'

'Seven o'clock, near enough. Where to?'

It felt like the middle of the night; still early and the roads full. He felt he had escaped lightly from a stupid accident and the omens were therefore good; he was smugly pleased with himself, bordering on the euphoric, apart from a monstrous headache, into which there nudged that memory of happiness. Julie and a baby; the end of rotten houses and the old identity. Singing to himself softly and tunelessly as the cab rolled along. '"Rock-a-bye, baby boy, Go to sleep, son."'

The door to the convent was open. The ground floor blazed with light so that he was almost shy to go in, used as he was to its cautious darkness and the single light from Julie beckoning him inside. He should have been here at least an hour ago and he waited, humbly, for the chastisement of women, only mildly suspicious of the frenzied activity inside. Into that suspicion there crept the other fear about Julie and how she had come to belong where she did not belong; a little nag of doubt about her. Sarah would dictate and they would obey. Sarah with the ten-pound note stuck over her mouth and all the good ideas.

There were flitting figures, like a nest of moths disturbed. He pushed past a sister who seemed so pleased to see him she must have mistaken him for someone else, apologised automatically and crossed into the parlour. There, more of them were huddled in a posse, clucking like quiet hens, Pauline resisting the attempts of Imelda to hold her hand; Julie curled in a tight, cold ball into one of the chairs, uncurling and racing towards him with a cry, flinging her arms around him, grabbing at him and holding on like a limpet. For a full moment, he enjoyed the sensation of public embrace. It seemed years since they had ever hugged openly with other people watching, but the pleasure and the pride were fleeting. Pauline's voice cut through like a whip. Her face showed the presence of tears, as did the face of his wife, but in Pauline's case, the weeping and the shock were under control. Her face was altered and aged, the sight of her iron grey crop as startling as if he had seen her naked, the voice unmistakable.

'Your brother and his minder took Sarah away. Because they thought she was Julie. There's no comparison, is there? Why would he do that?' The voice rose in anxiety. The crucifix on her rosary beads was curled inside her palm as she shook her head. 'And . . . *we* . . . *we* let him do it. God help us.'

Her head was bowed. Imelda murmured to her. She sat back obediently, neck stretched, contemplating the ceiling. There was a red handkerchief in her lap. He was slow to smell the blood. 'I am so sick of kindness,' she said.

'He's going to come back, the man said they were going to come back. Cannon, we've got to go before they come back. Before he realises – oh, Cannon, we've got to go – now.' Julie's voice was high with hysteria, shrill, demanding, insistent. 'NOW.'

'Shut up,' Imelda said.

To think, all this time, he had been waiting for this. Waiting to find that Johnny had taken his Julie away; waiting and hoping not, while those who had once believed him had ceased to believe him, so that he himself had grown careless and hopeless, and all he could feel now was relief, because *something* had happened to show he was right and because Johnny had kidnapped the wrong one. He wanted to snigger at the mistake because it was all Johnny's fault for refusing to look at Julie's picture in the first place, refusing ever to meet her, couldn't look at her face even when he had had her beaten, serve him right. But after the relief, there was speechless rage, and outside that he was only aware of Julie's hand clawing at his arm, pulling him towards the door and the outside world.

'The police are coming,' Imelda ventured comfortingly, as if that would be the answer to everything. 'I don't know why you didn't call them at once.'

'Because we were waiting for this gentleman,' Pauline murmured. 'Well, Cannon? Are you going to go and leave us to explain to them? What shall we say to the officers? We don't even know where he lives.'

'He wouldn't take her there,' Cannon said quickly. He shuffled his feet. He never did want the police near Johnnyboy; always tried to save him from that. Besides, he would never take her home; never. 'I don't suppose they said where they were taking her? Or why?' A foolish question. He wanted to be gone,

out there, anywhere with Julie, even if it was nowhere, running
in the dark, and he was finding it difficult to consider anything
else while she still pulled at him in panic, even though he knew
there was something wrong with his reaction; something abom-
inably selfish.

'She'll be *all right*,' Julie was screaming. 'They said they'd
bring her back. He *promised*. Sarah's always *all right* – she's a
survivor. Don't think about Sarah, think about *me*. Get me away
before he comes back for *me*. She did it for us.'

There was a moment's silence and her hand dropped from
his arm. 'They're only taking her for *treatment*,' she gabbled. 'He
won't hurt her as soon as he knows she isn't *yours*, why should
he? And that's why she let it happen. To give us time to get
away, don't you see? Come on, Cannon. *Come on*.'

There were echoes of similar, brisker orders from Sarah.
'Come *on*, Cannon.' Julie was in a rage of cowardice and he
could not blame her for it. *Treatment; taken away for treatment.*
Giving us time to escape. He tried to justify it. They won't hurt
her, not *really* hurt. And if Johnny were to wreak his revenge on
Sarah, surely that would spend his forces and be the end of it.
There was always a limit to his energies. He wouldn't do it twice;
it was over; the loss of face, the wasted malice would exhaust
him; they were free; he knew it; they should go, now, anywhere,
and never hear of him again. He thought of his own cowardice
and what it had created: Sarah's portrait, prominently displayed,
part of him wanting to say, I told you so, don't say I didn't warn
you. I *told* you and you stopped believing me. Let her take the
brunt. She would outwit Johnnyboy, with her hands tied behind
her back, a woman like that; she was clever with men, a *tart*. She
knew loads of men.

Not men like Johnny. She couldn't imagine a soul like that any
more than sweet, gentle-fingered William could. No one could.
He could feel Pauline's eyes, gazing at him; her pale face glowing with pain, the voluminous handkerchief red with blood; the
fine nose, bloated. What was the worst pain Johnnyboy could
envisage to inflict on the woman he perceived as enemy and

thief and rival? Going for *treatment*. He knew where they had taken her and knew in the same breath that no policeman would believe it or act on it soon enough. Julie was clutching him again. Freedom had a price. Somebody else was paying. He kissed her and ran from the room, followed by the sound of her screams. 'I've done everything for you. *Everything.*'

It was not a special kind of car, Sarah noticed, as they drove away through the dark streets. Nothing about it designed for the conveyance of prisoners, no extra locks on the doors of a middle-range saloon. She could never remember the makes of cars – disinterest foxed the memory – but she tried to remember details in case she was asked and because it helped her to avoid the present. Blue: the inside of it was blue and the back of Johnnyboy's head was blackish grey as he drove with quiet precision. Perhaps she could get out if they slowed for a light; he was a careful driver, never exceeding the speed limit. Perhaps she should open her mouth and speak, but all she could have uttered was an instruction to go back and collect the right woman because that was all there was in her mind to say and she did not want to say it, not yet. Not until the convent was full and Julie was protected. Give them an hour. She felt for the handle of the door.

No need for locks. Only the big man, holding her hand like a father in the back seat of the limo taking the bride to church, proud and protective and possessive, his hand large enough to crush the bones of her wrist, the way he could have crushed the kitten. He had spared the kitten; she took some comfort from that and hung on to his final, hurried, whispered words and their suggestion of conscience. Don't worry, we'll bring her back, he'd said. She felt the loneliness of the condemned, the fear of the sacrificial victim led towards some altar in the presence of a crowd who applauded the ritual and would not let anyone spoil it. She had never quite understood the existence of evil. The blue upholstery stank of newness.

She could see where she was going: there was no subterfuge

about it, no blindfold; no twists and turns. They were soon in
the familiar territory of the West End with shoppers still streaming home, and hope rose like a bubble. It was all so ordinary;
in a moment, she could step out and join the throng, run
across this road and down the next and slip into the side-door
of Selfridges to meet Mrs Matthewson, or plunge into the
stuffiness of the tube. They had cruised beyond Piccadilly,
across Bond Street, pausing at the corner where the Mole lived.
Past the house of another lover; there would never be any
rescue provided by lovers; there never had been. Lovers were
solace, not power; the strongest of emotions, the weakest links.
Then they were in William's territory, the district of doctors:
civilised, handsome, full of the promise of a cure. If they passed
his house, she could wave at him, scream for help if she had
such a thing as a voice left. An hour, and the convent would be
safe. Cannon would have got there. Useless in a crisis; better
than nothing. Take Julie away, you fool. Take her away. From
inside the self-contained vacuum of her life she thought of the
people she loved and doubted if any of them would try to help
her even if they knew the danger. She doubted it without bitterness. Each to his own life. She had never expected much and
she was not sure of what the danger was. Only that it was
immense. She made herself small and silent and unobjection-
able.

Not only William's territory but William's street. She recalled
his kindly face with a desperate surge of affection, wanted to see
him running along beside the car, tapping on the window,
saying, 'Stop, stop, stop. You've made a mistake.'

They stopped.

Early evening, and the city, as far as he could sense, was lingering at the breakpoint between day and night. William would
have liked a town crier to patrol this street, telling the hour, every
hour, and confirming that all was well. Not that he doubted it as
he surveyed the surgery with no more than the usual anxiety,
checking the cleanliness, the detail, taking it in with a pride that

no one else shared. He had dusted the reception area as if it had not been done early in the day and would not be done again, first thing in the morning, by the cleaner. He liked the way he had designed it, so that when one moved from the reception to the surgery there was only another pleasant vista towards the window when the door was open. William mourned the necessity for closed doors. He crossed and looked out. Traffic subdued by double glazing into no more than a distant buzz; lights catching empty windows. In the waiting room, the paintings glowed with their own life.

He always liked the building best when it was empty. Felt like a king in a castle, forgetting he was the mere tenant of a few rooms with his throne undermined by debt.

It was perverse of him to want the place to look comforting for tomorrow's patient, especially since the patient was not due to arrive until the afternoon, and heaven knows what disturbance there might be in the morning. Nothing arduous; he had checked. This evening would be alone with the journals, thinking time. The elaboration of his preparations for John Smith could mean nothing more than the fact that he was afraid of the man, and he decided that that was not the prime motivation for all this fussiness. The fear was of failure. Not being good enough even to inspire faith.

This is silly talk, William, and you were never any good at communication, he told himself, as he went down to the basement, finding no comfort in the chaos the way he usually did. There was an atmosphere here that he did not trust; the cold from the window, which since last week would not shut, warped by the wet. The place did not feel as if it belonged to him any more, but then, looking at his life, he did not think anything belonged to him. Back upstairs, checking again, suddenly a little bit lonely and wanting to talk, having a chat with the paintings, the way he did sometimes, although he was not usually quite so sober when he resorted to such inanimate company. Wanting Sarah, because Sarah would understand this, but pushing the thought from his mind. Good athletes and, possibly, good dentists should put such feeble need for womankind from mind on the eve of combat. But it wasn't combat: it was nothing more or less than *treatment*. They might do *nothing* tomorrow. No one was going to give him a medal for this. He wasn't even sure he was going to get any money.

The phone rang at the desk as he tidied things round it. He interrupted it, reluctant to hear the sound of his pre-recorded voice. 'Yes?' he barked.

There was the sound of shuffling and adjustment, a gasp, as if the person phoning expected the anonymity of his recorded voice rather than this distinctly personal, impatient reply. Followed by a sniffing sound, a hawking into a handkerchief, a tremulous sigh and a sob. A patient with a post-operative problem – bound to be one of those. He softened his voice. 'Yes,' he murmured, 'how can I help?' professional solicitude creeping into his tone like a wheeze.

'William? Is that you?' Isabella's sobbing grew earnest. He could feel himself melting, slightly. Who was it said, 'Let me not go to death surrounded by wailing women'? Some king who was spoiled for choice. It didn't strike William as a bad way to go if one had to shuffle off the mortal coil in any kind of company at all; women rather than men, any time. A wailing woman was one in need and William liked to be needed.

'Isabella? What's the matter?' *There, there, there,* he wanted to say, but it might sound condescending. He took refuge in a cough, the way he sometimes did when searching for a patient's name, hoping the spasm would jerk it into memory.

'Nothing,' she said. 'Nothing, nothing, nothing.' The voice trailed away, leaving behind it William's unsteady breathing. He flattered himself that her occasional calls to the answer-machine might have been something to do with concern for his health, but this was the first time she had taken the risk of communicating unhappiness. The sound of her distress provoked a series of responses: irritation, grief, concern, foolishness, guilt, and that shameful pitter-patter of the heart which had become his neurotic condition as soon as he heard her voice. Nightmares about Isabella and the children; daydreams that she would come back through the door and beg his forgiveness.

'I made a mistake, Will, a bad mistake. I misjudged you.'

He had once longed to hear such sentiments, but now they left him disconsolate and strangely annoyed. Why was she the only one who ever diminished him by calling him *Will*, and why say this *now*, when he had other things to think about, choosing a time when there was no possibility of his indulging the slightest sense of triumph?

'Do you think we could try again? I miss you so much.'

Missed him? Such as, shacking up with someone richer while receiving maintenance without gratitude? That was *missing* someone? All the same, he felt a flush creep up from his neck and over his face and, if it wasn't quite pleasure he felt, it was a close relation, which he managed to control, as well as the silly smile on his face that made him vaguely embarrassed as if she was there, watching. The pause stretched into half a minute.

'Will ... there's no one else, is there? No one special, I mean ...'

No one. Just Sarah. Mysterious, adorable, dependable Sarah. A tart with heart and morals.

'Perhaps we should meet and talk about it.'

'Can we do that soon?'

'Well, yes. Soon.'

He was staring at the door, not even half listening to her. A crucial conversation in the history of his life, and he could not pay attention, because there was someone outside, knocking against the door so hard it vibrated. He had the ridiculous thought that it was her on the other side, only pretending to talk from a distance.

'Like now?' Isabella was saying plaintively. 'Oh, darling, I'm so unhappy ...'

'Soon.'

He was slamming down the receiver, not quite believing that he had actually done that and choked her off. He watched, with his fingers still touching the lifeline of the phone, as the door opened abruptly.

John Smith first, smart and unsmiling, Sarah next, and the fat man who had gone through the records bringing up the rear. John took the key from behind the desk, locked the door behind himself and gave the key to the fat man. It was a heavy door, like the separate door to the surgery, guarding against crazies in a misguided search for drugs even in these respectable quarters. The presence of all three in the small area by the desk was at first astounding then immediately claustrophobic. John's aftershave was oppressive and the silence was overwhelming. William gave his indecisive, nervous cough before he spoke, sounding officious. 'Mr Smith, you've got the time wrong. You're due here tomorrow. Not today. Tomorrow.'

John Smith sighed, spoke softly, shaking his head at the error of such blithe assumptions. 'Oh, no, it was always going to be today. Tomorrow's too close to Christmas.' He ushered Sarah forward, without touching her. She was held by the fat man's meaty paw on her neck, making her stoop under his weight, preventing her eyes from meeting his. 'And *this*', he was still murmuring, 'is the patient. Bring her in.'

'Sarah . . . what are you doing?'

'Julie,' she said. 'My name is Julie Smith.'

She was propelled past William's stupefied face into the surgery. The fat man hesitated on the threshold for a second, disoriented by the absence of the chair in his immediate line of vision, then saw it round the corner. It was low to the ground in this resting state, easy to shove her into it. Following, watching with increasing agitation, making small, inarticulate squawks of protest, what puzzled William most was her calm lack of resistance, as if she had already learned the futility of it. She was not easily coerced – that much he knew; she was as stubborn as a mule, and it followed that there was some form of conspiracy between them. A joke, a trick, a mystery designed to make him look a fool, like a strippergram victim at a party, all of them knowing about it except himself. Then the fat man, with the efficiency of a policeman in a second-rate film, produced a piece of tape and attached her wrists to the supports at the side of the chair, so unlikely and deft a set of movements that William could not believe it, even though he was beginning to perceive the sickness of the joke. The fat man found a scalpel out of a drawer to cut the tape. They had been here before. She lay as still and uncomfortably posed as a plastic mannequin in a shop window. Only the abundance of curling red hair, spilling over the back of the chair, showed her to be real.

'A woman's crowning glory,' John Smith was saying dreamily. 'Her hair. They can seduce a man with hair like that. The smile's more important, don't you think?' He was locking the surgery door, putting the key in his top pocket. 'Cannon was always a sucker for a smile,' he went on, 'because of the reaction to his own. Must have dreamed of a smile like hers.' He paused, remembering something, his face sad. The figure in the chair remained immobile; William could see that only her fingers moved restlessly, as if trying to signal, looking for something to clasp. John Smith seemed to remember where he was and his purpose, looked at William directly and spoke with the author-itative patience of a teacher to a recalcitrant child.

'And it was that smile which hooked him,' he went on, '*stole* him from me. *My* lover, *my* heart, *my* flesh and blood, *my* soul, *my* reason for anything. And then *you*, Mr Dentist, *you* did the rest. You gave him his film-star teeth, so that when he looked in the mirror he didn't see *me* any more. Made him think he was different from *me*. Kid himself he was no longer part of *us*. And how can I live without him? Answer me that, will you? I rot inside, is what happens. I rot away, like my houses.' He was shouting by now, wagging his finger, coming closer, so the spit-tle landed on William's face. Then he controlled himself, became calmer. 'No, I can't blame you for *that*. Such a conscientious fellow you are. But it does seem fair you should share the punishment. Don't get me wrong . . . I'm not asking much . . .'

He perched on the ledge to the far left of the chair, still not looking at her, legs crossed, relatively relaxed, the sweet soul of reason. 'I don't want you to *kill* her,' he added conversationally, as if they were simply man to man in a bar, discussing a friendly proposition of mutual interest. 'It would be *dreadful* if you did. What *you* have to do is wreck that smile, tooth by tooth. I mean, there must be a way of poisoning them at the root, just like someone did with mine. Murder them and that fucking smile. No anaesthetics, of course.' He looked at his watch, businesslike. 'How long do you think it will take?'

'I thought it was *you* who wanted treatment,' William said. 'I want to treat *you*.'

'No. How long will this take?'

The obscenity and seriousness of the revolting suggestions finally penetrated William's shocked and sluggish mind. He punched John Smith on the jaw. The blow jarred his wrist, seemed to recoil like a heavy gun, thumping into his shoulder as if he had missed contact with flesh and hit the wall instead. He was as fragile as paper, all height, no density, no skill for a fight. John Smith returned with a punch to the abdomen and a series of kicks to the legs. The room swam; he was on his back with John and the fat man leaning over him solicitously, so easy they were scarcely short of breath.

'You forgot to tell him something, Mr Smith, sir,' the fat man whispered. Their expressionless faces mesmerised him, and out of the corner of his eye he could see the fat man's enormous boot, pinning his forearm to the ground with enough pressure to hurt extremely.

'Oh, that,' John Smith said carelessly. 'I forgot to mention that. Silly me. If you don't do what I say, my friend here is going to stamp on your hands. *Pulp* them. Your precious hands . . . and you do *love* your hands, don't you? You even have fucking *drawings* of your own hands about the place, like other stupid idiots have portraits. *Pulp*. Not a whole bone left, even the little ones. I hold, he *stamps*.' William swallowed the scream. The foot pressed against his arm relentlessly; the pain increased. Then the fat man held his right hand lovingly, tut-tutting under his breath, bent the fingers back until William gasped. He could picture his hand dismembered, all those complex bones rearranged in a pattern of red on the clean white floor.

Sarah's voice, sounding resigned: 'Better do as you're told, William. You need your hands.'

'Why?' William screamed. '*Why?*'

'Because she's a thief,' John roared. 'A fucking *thief*.'

'You aren't a thief, are you, Sarah?' The body on the chair seemed to wilt and remained utterly silent. It perturbed him almost more than anything else. Smith's smell was a disgusting mixture of adrenalin and scent. William hated him.

'And it's not called Sarah, it's called Julie,' the fat man stated, then clamped his mouth shut, aware of speaking out of turn. William looked at him. Of the two, he might be the one with conscience.

'She's—'

'Shut up, William. If you don't do what they want, they'll do it themselves.'

Yes, they would.

They seemed impervious to the sound of her voice, both of them jittery now, anxious for something to begin, as volatile as crazed insects, mad with captivity. William was on his feet, hoisted without effort in arms that felt like girders, standing upright, clasping his hands and gnawing on a knuckle as if he were a baby instead of the puppet he felt. The fat man was handing him the white coat. The door was locked, the building was empty, and that mystery person in the chair, his lover, his best friend, seemed to encourage them by her very compliance. And his hands, his trembling hands. He could not live without his dextrous, sensitive hands. His mind went back to the bonfire, the last time he had worried about his hands, wondering then if he would risk them, for love, for rescue, for his living, for his pride, for anything. The fat man was holding out his white coat. It reminded him now of the uniform of a butcher: high-necked, double-breasted stiff white cotton, the better to absorb the stains. *If I don't do it they will; better me than them; what will they do if I renege?* He imagined an amateur let loose with a high-speed drill. Mind in overdrive, brain going tick, tick, tick, like a bomb, making his voice sound as clear as a voice that belonged to some other person entirely, another kind of man. The Inquisition's torturer, paid by the hour, with an agenda all of his own.

His hands were stinging as he pulled on the gloves that would make the allergies worse; his hands remembered pain in the way he hoped the mouth did not; hands were impossible to mend. Why did Sarah fail to deny she was a thief, and a thief of what? Affection? Lust and trust? For the slow passage of time expended on putting on the gloves, he hated her, too. For all the trouble and the disquiet she brought along with her reassurance; for never letting him know her. Never letting him be needed or letting him near. The resentment was temporary, gave him that distance he needed to *think*.

'There's one thing I need to establish,' he found himself saying. 'I mean about your priorities, Mr Smith. I presume you aren't coming in for treatment tomorrow, even though I have blocked out the time, so I'd like to be paid, please. And for this. Two thousand, minimum. Be fair. I can't keep myself on less.' He needed them to believe he was a torturer paid by the hour; he needed, in one way, to think that himself. There was a nod in response, a glint in the eye suggesting admiration, a hint of true minds meeting. The hatred burned like a furnace beneath his skin. 'And there's another thing,' he continued, 'which I need to know before I start. Priorities. I can't do two things at once. Sure, I can disfigure her, but simply pulling teeth will take two minutes. What is it you want? A wrecked mouth and pain? Or do you just want me to take out her teeth?'

'Pain,' said John Smith. 'Pain and all the rest. But pain.'

'I can, as you suggest, poison at the root, so they drop out later. Very painful too. Will that do?'

'Yes. That's what I told you. Drill in the poison. *Do it.*'

He prevaricated. He tried to say that the injection he proposed was disinfectant saline – they didn't want her dead, did they? No syringes, John Smith said, not unless I say so. Only needles for stitching. They would ration what he could use: scalpels and drills, the elevator for extraction, the clamp he used to keep the mouth open. It seemed that John Smith had made an inventory of the equipment and was not going to let him use a syringe. John Smith wanted him to use the drill without the water coolant. He liked the idea of a tooth glowing hot. Impossible, William said. This one works with the water or not at all.

One lie, another lie. They let him give her an antibiotic; dries the saliva, he said. They all seemed to be getting along fine, even cheerfully. William popped the pill into her mouth, watched her swallow obediently while he tried to communicate with her eyes, pretending he was talking to them, but talking to her.

'Reminds me of the Inquisition,' he remarked. 'Or any era when the professional torturer was employed. They were never paid enough. Needed a union.'

The fat man laughed uncomfortably; John Smith didn't. *Remember what we talked about, Sarah? Remember walking in the park? Remember what I said a good dentist would do? Put on a show . . . a performance. Avoid destruction. Trust me.*

'Stop talking.'

By now the identity of the patient was totally irrelevant. She was just a thing. John Smith could look at her now, arranged himself to watch. Fascinated and disgusted and determined. The aspirator in her mouth made its liquid slushing sound and, unable to delay further, William found his scalpel.

They wanted blood; they should have blood. Apicectomy of the lower central and lateral incisors. He found himself lecturing under his breath: this is the second line of treatment after root-canal surgery has failed. And why does it fail? Because it is impossible to prepare and fill the apical third of the root, for whatever reason: because it is persistently infected; because there's a broken instrument blocking the canal, so you can't reach it from the occlusal surface, so you have to get in there, through the gum. As if poisoning the roots.

He would concentrate on the lower front teeth. They were so much less visible; it was the upper buccal surfaces that were the aesthetic hallmark of the mouth, but John Smith would not think of that once distracted by blood. William pulled down the lower lip, held it with a lightly weighted clamp. A clamp holding the mouth open and an uncontrolled, hanging lip made a person look subnormally stupid; Smith would like that. He fussed with the equipment as long as he dared, mincing round it, delaying until he could not delay. Apicectomy was safest on the incisors and canines. He cut an incision across the gum level with the emerging teeth. Perfect gingiva; perfect teeth; he winced as he did it. Then he began to cut down behind his incision in a chiselling motion, keeping his hand steady and his eyes focused on the task. He released the gum and the periodontal ligaments, revealing the root of the tooth and the alveolar bone. He could never do this without being reminded of a precise butcher, shaving meat from the spine of a carcass. Such central teeth; such a lot of blood. Maybe the blood alone would satisfy. He had the horrible thought that he had overdone it and maybe it would have sufficed to cut a single flap for a single tooth rather than four. He peeled back the section of gum and ligament neatly. The gum flapped over the lower lip; the effect was garishly hideous. *Stay still, Sarah; stay as still as you can so I don't make mistakes.*

The movement of her head was limited by the chair; she was rigid with pain but braced against it. The aspirator slushed at blood; he kept on adjusting it. Keep still: this is difficult enough without an assistant, especially under such watchful eyes. Her head seemed fixed to the back of the chair, heavy and immovable; there was, so far, an appalling control in her, co-operating with him, understanding, he hoped – oh, God, he hoped she understood. She was staring, fixedly, at the light, as if it could save her. Staring, but she could not keep her tongue still: it moved incessantly, poking over her lower teeth in her open mouth, interfering and insulting.

'Make her stop that,' John said, his only words in minutes. 'Make her bloody stop.'

'She can't stop it. No one can.'

'Cut it, then.'

'No, there's a better way.'

William had never done this before, but he had seen it done. He took a long, curved needle with silken suturing thread, stuck it straight though the forward flesh of the tip of the tongue, doubled it back and tied it round the prominent third molar to the left. The wisdom tooth was gone: he could secure the thread without much difficulty. There – did that look savage enough? The gurgling, gagging sound in the back of her throat had all the makings of a scream. He adjusted the aspirator again. That was what it meant to be tongue-tied.

He continued to chisel, revealing more bone. More blood. John was restless, waiting for the drill, shouting for it. William could no longer avoid the drill. Bloodlust was not enough.

The appalling thing was that he was proud of his technique. He could not do this without being absorbed.

Cannon crawled through the basement window and crept up the stairs. There was something wrong with his left arm: it functioned, but badly – no force in the grip. Outside the surgery door he listened and heard, briefly, the high-pitched whine of the drill. There was a strange, distorted, semi-human sound in the wake of it; a pause for either discussion or argument; the unmistakable sound of Johnny's guttural laughter; the sucking noise of the aspirator, louder than anything else, and, again, that deep-throated moaning like someone mimicking an animal. Would they kill her? Would Johnnyboy watch as William's hands were smashed to pieces? It would hardly bother what passed for his conscience to do that to a dentist. Was it Johnny himself who wielded the tools of torture? No, he would always delegate under threat; no one understood that about him. And what, from the other side of a heavy locked door, could he do about it? They would hear if he called the police. There was no time to call the police – it was too late for that and this was his task, not theirs. It had nothing to do with anyone else. It had to do with Johnny

suborning everything Cannon had and everything he was,
maiming and corrupting his friends in the process. If only he
could make the anger so cold. Then there was the drill again,
followed by that same unbearable, inhuman sound.

Cannon was back in the basement. Almost a second home, he
knew it so well, knew what an arsenal it was. He was calmer now,
cool even, aware of the left arm throbbing. Let's play a game,
Johnny, the way we used to, remember? One of those boyhood
games. We did it before; I can do it again, even though I promised I wouldn't. He would have to remember his instinct to get
the mixture right. Potassium permanganate crystals; throatwash. The sugar, in a well-handled, sticky packet left ready
for someone's tea. The malfunctioning sterilising kettle for
dental instruments, which would contain it. Fate provided the
tools. William never threw anything away. It was insane. He
could destroy them all, but anything seemed preferable to the
sounds Sarah made.

*The purpose of the apicectomy is to sustain an apical seal at the end
of the root, to prevent the invasion of bacteria . . .* Once the apex of
the tooth is exposed, excise. They would have the smell of burning, which was not burning but dentine dust. The apex of the
first incisor was easy to find, marked by a bulge. 'I've isolated the
roots,' William said. 'Now I'll poison them.' The bleeding was
still copious. He thought only of the technique; ignored the
tongue that strained against the knot; the hands in the shackles
turning bruised and blue, the wrists raw with burns. It was a
final cruelty that she could neither clench her fists nor scream.
Her eyes had the vacancy of a dying dog he had once moved to
the side of the road, careful of the bite. Tears flowed quietly
from her eyes into her hair. The lead X-ray apron he had laid
across her chest as extra ballast to steady her was littered with
debris. He pushed away the high-speed drill.

'Why are you doing that?'

'Slower drill. Hurts more.' Slower drill because the high-speed
would lock itself in the bone. The slower drill did less damage:

John Smith would be more familiar with its vibrating sound. Choosing the site carefully, he began to drill not the root but the bone. Denser, harder; marginally less painful. Look out for the mental nerve; damage that and . . . The drill had a different, vibrating, droning, louder but less sibilant sound. It echoed in his ears; he could feel it in his own bones.

They needed more blood and he needed an excuse to stop. He let the burr of the drill catch the inside of her cheek, watched as all that copious blood supply responded to the wound. It would take him a while to mop up. Perhaps, by then, John would have tired of this, but he looked on with the rapt attention of a keen student. The fat man huddled in a corner with a handkerchief held against his mouth, but still warily observant of what William did rather than what the patient suffered. The flaps of the gum still hung over her lower lip. Unless John tired, he would have to move on. Drill further holes in the bone, big enough to see through. Windows into the mouth; the drill again; the fine spray of healthy bone.

'There,' he said. 'That's enough for now.'

'No,' said John, standing over him. 'It isn't enough.'

William took the elevator he used to raise a tooth for extraction, deftly punched a hole in the atrium of her mouth. Blood poured out of her nose.

There was a bucket for the mix, crystals and sugar, treated with respect, but hurriedly. Three parts to one, and he was filling up the spare space with lumps of plaster. No detonator; this little mix required none. Cannon was hurrying up the steps, like an anxious cook with a meal for the master, the steriliser kettle upturned, his finger blocking the aperture in the lid. A fire – he could simply start a fire with this. Why not? But he had to get through the door and get *her* out. William, too. And he would have the advantage, because no one but he would be expecting the bang, if it worked. They would be dazed. He was visualising the layout of the surgery; he had been in that chair often enough to know it by heart, always conscious of his surroundings, always trying to catch sight of something new to avoid the Siemens letters on the overhead light. You should decorate this ceiling with wild colours, he had suggested; make a distraction. Or I could paint my face, William had said. But there was nothing wrong with William's face. It was a kind and gentle face, worried and infinitely reassuring. Sarah's, too, if it was still recognisable by now.

Cannon remembered the layout: the chair round the corner not in line with the door; the little seating area; the window further beyond. He let a little of the mixture trickle out of the steriliser as he walked backwards, slowly, leaving a snail-like trail to the basement steps, then skirted round it and placed the upturned container close to the surgery door. It sat unsteadily on a small heap of mix, looking untidy and harmless. Cannon hesitated. A piece of homemade explosive like this was not entirely predictable: it might simply burn; it might do so much more than he intended. All he could think of was the fact that the fragments had no choice but to travel in straight lines and not round corners. Still he hesitated. *Cannon, you always overreact, you stupid creature – you do too much or too little, nothing by halves . . . No judgement of your own responses, indolent or frenetic.* Sarah's voice from the back of his head, scolding with affection. And then, as he hesitated still, that terrible, gurgling sound of agony. He ran to the shelter of the basement stairs and flattened himself against the wall. Hesitated again, watching the flame of his lighter.

The thudding whine of the drill . . . the third hole in the bone. She would not, could not faint away, and all William could wish for her was the mercy of oblivion. He was pausing too much, going too slow, his lack of dedication becoming obvious. John Smith was impatient, beginning to move about, and it occurred to William how pointless was all this deployment of skill. They were still going to tread on his hands, and he had the added, tired fear that at any moment now John would seize the drill himself, that all the careful watching was only for the purpose of establishing how it worked. He would push the dentist out of the way, activate the machine in the way he had learned through his close observation, drill through the incisors, shatter the exposed roots . . . or he would grab the scalpel and lace her face with wounds. That would be true disfigurement; this, so far, was not. John began to prowl, stood behind William, breathing down his neck. William's coat was soaked with perspiration, his hair wet, his hands slippery. From the fat man, now standing at Sarah's feet, there rose a stench of vomit.

'I think we could do with a drink,' John Smith said, and moved towards the door. 'You're playing games with me, Mr Dentist. You know that?'

'Games?' William screamed. '*Games?*' He pointed at the hideous mouth. 'Look at what you've made me do.'

John Smith shook his head, reached towards his top pocket for the key. 'You wait until I start. Then *no one* will want her back.'

Cannon lit the fuse.

CHAPTER FOURTEEN

The sound of an explosion always brought tears to his eyes: jubilation, of a kind, to a toddling boy; later, in his early teens, they were the tears that mourned anticlimax, a touch of regret, until finally they became tears of horror that it was now too late to stop it. Cannon's forefingers were firmly wedged in his ears, but the blast still shook his feet, his knees, his skinny ribcage, and the tears followed through eyes squeezed shut against the flash. There was always the desire, again as a child on a piece of wasteland, to run towards the sound immediately, until he learned better the wisdom of waiting to see what the first flash did. The flash and the flame were worse on his side of the door, the sound of splintering wood lost in the settling of the debris and that sudden, wonderful silence. There would be fires; he remembered the surgery and its mostly metallic contents and tiled floor. Then he remembered wooden-framed pictures on the reception walls: he had forgotten the vulnerability of those.

The dense smoke was grey white in colour; thicker than the mist of dawn, but penetrable. There was a crackle of flame, the tinkle of glass from a window he could not see. The light-bulb central to the reception area remained intact and burning. Something else was burning, with a sickly, oily smell. Cannon stumbled towards the surgery door.

A huge, squat figure emerged, screaming, tripping into the crater left by the bomb, stumbling ankle deep into the hole, the body falling forward, saved by the hands. Then he was crawling until he was upright, arms thrashing a passage through the smoke so that Cannon could feel the draught of his progress across the room to the outer door, howling as he went, like a drunk baying for the moon. He could hear him shaking the door, the howling turning to sobbing, the door released and the flat footsteps running away. A survivor, then. A ludicrous, unbidden thought crept into Cannon's mind about how Johnnyboy never could keep the hired help. How he might have enjoyed this.

Then he was shouting himself, standing on the threshold, avoiding the hole and the shattered door, screaming, '*William! Sarah! William!*' The far window had gone: there was splintered wood, the lights in here still burning; the intense heat of an oven and the spotlight over the dental chair shining down the blessing of Siemens. The aspirator still gurgled.

Cannon's brother lay at the furthest end of the room, in a straight line from the door, tidily out of the way. Cannon noted the figure on the floor, familiar even in the smoke; familiar from any angle. He looked for William, who stood like a long thin rag doll, hands loose against his side, back against the wall around the corner, his whole body numb. Cannon shook him, the response was nil, shook him again, harder, and then slapped him across the face. William prised himself away from the wall, his eyes beginning to focus on Cannon's face, then on the rest of the room, then on Sarah. Cannon followed his roving glance. Bile rose in his throat. Both of them were covered in blood, Sarah's mouth a wound clamped open, her lap a repository for blood. The bomb – no, the blast did not go round corners. The bomb had not done this. *William* had done this.

'Christ, Jesus . . .' He moved, in some instinctive attempt to block Sarah from William's sight. William came back to life, snarling, screaming at him, 'Get out of the way, get out of here,' pushing Cannon away, pummelling at his chest even before he recognised him.

Cannon retreated, suddenly shivery; watched. He could not

go to Johnnyboy, not yet. It was not Johnnyboy he had been trying to save.

'Get me an icepack, you cretin – *now*.'

'Where?'

'Fridge, behind me – are you blind?'

William was hovering over that dreadful mouth. There was no sound from her, the lip hanging like a foreign object belonging to no known creature. The eyes were closed. He wanted to remove the weighted clamp and the clamp that held the mouth open, close the mouth and let everything rest. No. Scissors; remove suture to free the tongue, no, leave that till last. Bring the flap back up, stitch, and, Christ, in this smoke, the place was rife with infection. Work. Don't go too fast.

Cannon found the icepack and put it down on her lap. He moved towards the figure on the floor. The smoke was clearing efficiently through the broken window; it blurred rather than ruined his sight, and his eyes still stung. There was a distant sound of sirens. Cannon dreaded going closer. Perhaps only part of Johnny had been in line with the door, not all of him.

'See what you've done, Johnny? See what you've done?' Cannon said, kneeling next to him. The eyes were open, the chest heaving for breath, the clothes torn, a gash in the forehead. The tip of a key was sticking out of his bosom below the left nipple, giving the faint illusion that if it were pulled and turned, he would spring to his feet like a mechanical toy. Such a little key would not kill him. 'Didn't mean it, Johnny. Didn't quite get the mix right, did I?'

The hand, which had been clawing at the groin, reached out, feeling for his own. There was a huge splinter of wood sticking out of the palm. He did not seem to see it. The sirens had grown closer, deafening in a static whine outside. 'At least somebody noticed, didn't they, Johnnyboy?' Cannon said. There was the flicker of a smile.

'We never did get round to the Houses of Parliament, did we, Johnny?' He patted the hand ineffectually. 'Now, don't die on me, Johnny. Don't do that. See, no one else knows me like you. See, we didn't care about fuck all, did we, Johnny? I'll be lonely without you. There'll never be another bastard like you . . .'

There was a whispered sound from the pursed mouth. Johnnyboy was still hiding his teeth.

'You won't want her now, will you?'

'No, Johnny. No. No. No. I want you.'

Two mattress sutures. Enough to hold it. Stuff the mouth with xylocaine gel . . . No, benzedrine hydrochloride, good, topical anaesthetic and anti-inflammatory. Release the tongue; unclamp the jaw. Let the lip hold everything in place. Hope the bleeding'll stop now. Icepack. Trust the mouth to heal. The ambulanceman coming up the stairs would treat for shock. Do everything in the right order, you fool, don't *rush*. He slit the ropes with the scalpel, reset the chair to bring her upright, chafed her hands. And all to the sound of Cannon's keening. There were shouts from the other room.

He took off his filthied jacket, folded her hands, tucked the jacket under her chin for warmth. The heat had faded fast: a damp chill filled the room, smoke drifting from behind him. He stared at her vacant face, wanting to wipe away the blood. No, not yet; too tender to touch.

Cannon's keening was down to a steady sound, a slow howling of grief.

What to say? He did not know what to say; he never knew what to say. *I have disgraced everything I ever stood for.* Lies would be best for now. William moved to the shattered door and looked beyond. Three masked men in the room, looking like aliens. He noticed how two of them were stamping out small fires. He looked, as he always automatically looked, for Cannon's picture on the wall, looked again. That was the one smouldering on the floor. He knew it by the remnants of the frame.

He carried her through the clearing smoke. It was dark outside: they would mistake him for a rescuer. No one was going to admire his technique. *She was in the middle of treatment when the bomb went off,* that's what he would say. He set her down on the old dental chair by the basement stairs. He kept his hand over her mouth to make sure the lip stayed closed. She breathed raggedly though her bloodfilled nose. It looked, even to his own eyes, as if he was deliberately trying to stop her from speaking.

She was never going to love him now.

CHAPTER FIFTEEN

On the feast of the conversion of St Paul, three weeks into the New Year, Pauline sat and bowed her head in prayer. The chapel was warm. No one should be asked to conduct intimate conversations with God in the cold: life was too short for that.

The ability to pray was slow to arrive. It was no use talking to the Creator and expecting Him to direct what she wanted to say into the consciousness of others when more direct communication was required. She could not hold the necessary conversation with God. All she could do was hold imaginary conversations with the human beings she most needed to see and pray for the intervention of the saints to send those people to her door. Her conscience was far from happy. She seemed to have alienated her acquaintance. Sarah, beloved Sarah, who never seemed to know how much she was loved; Julie, who was maintaining the silence peculiar to those who had revealed a little too much of themselves and were ashamed of it. Julie, with her bitter words between the time Cannon had left and the others had arrived, none of them to be believed, because fear and fury made liars of them all. Pauline apologised for her lack of concentration and told the Lord it was just as well He had made her a nun and not a priest. She would never have been able to obey the ultimate strictures of the confessional.

They had been given copious quantities of wine over Christmas. Pauline seemed to have consumed the lion's share and felt relieved that the supply was not endless. So easy to take to that kind of thing, especially if one had an obsessive disposition. In a minute, she was going to sit in the parlour and smoke a cigarette since in the hierarchy of sins it seemed entirely unimportant. She felt the bridge of her nose, still tender to the touch, the black-eyed bruises no longer more than permanent shadows. Her fine proboscis would remain tender for months. As an excuse for bad habits, it was adequate.

Forgive me, Lord, I betrayed my niece into the hands of sinners. I did it for the best of reasons, namely that she was *stronger* than the victim they intended to wound. She knew more about life; she was *less* vulnerable; she was the cleverer. Had there been a chance that they might have taken me instead, I would have gone. You know that, Lord, don't you? But I told a silent lie, and let my own flesh and blood suffer, and I cannot see any justification for that. Or, more to the point, I do not for the life of me see how *she* will ever see the justification for that. I have tried to see her, Lord, and she has evaded me. Can I blame her? But I *need* her, Lord. I cannot carry this burden.

And give me the right words to say to this man. He has even more on his conscience than I.

William sat in the parlour, indifferent to his surroundings. He flexed his hands, extended his arms and held them rigid to see if his fingers still trembled. The tremor was improving, so that he was only noticing what was not visible to anyone else. He doubted it would ever quite go, which would not matter one way or another if the General Medical Council, at the end of their deliberations, should decide he was still fit to practise. Early indications showed a tendency to leniency; there was a shortage of dentists. Sexual misbehaviour alarmed them most, and this particular patient had lived to tell no such tale. Had not only lived but had exonerated him. It was the dentist who had lost his innocence.

Pauline glided into the room at the same time as William began to nudge himself out of his reverie and notice where he was. There were three statues of saints. Perhaps in another life he would collect icons, the better to bless his existence. He thought of the destroyed paintings, drawings and sketches that had occupied the reception-room walls and reflected without regret that the patients had noticed them as little as he had noticed these. Pauline came towards him, looking relieved to see him. Two people, sent to limbo.

'Don't call me the inquisitor's apprentice, will you?' he said. 'It's the kind of description which tends to stick.'

She shook her head. 'I wouldn't dream of it.' She inspected him closely, eyes examining for the details of thinning hair, requiring a comb. Longer hair than she remembered, thinner limbs, too, the face gaunt and the hands restless – a man fighting the demons of his own wretchedness. The mere presence of them made her feel stronger. God put her on this earth to *do* things, not to loll around in a self-indulgent mess of recriminations, and nor should he. She was not going to have it.

'Do you smoke, William? No? Well, don't mind if I do. Imelda will bring us some coffee in a minute. Do you know, she doesn't grind her teeth any more? We're all very pleased, I can tell you. You did a good job there.'

'I doubt the connection, but thank you. I'm glad someone's better for seeing me.'

He was not going to say, Smoking is bad for your teeth. Life was bad for the teeth. The people who smoked managed to stay alive. Cannon's brother had scarcely smoked, William had been told, and he was the one who was dead. William was suddenly unsure of why he was here but, then, there did not need to be a particular purpose, apart from the critical need of each of them to talk to the other.

'Are you *sure* she'll make a full recovery? *They* say she has. They tell me things, you see. I'm her only relative so they have to, even though she doesn't want to see me . . . but are you *sure*?'

'Everything I did was deliberately done to cause minimum long-term damage. The capacity of the mouth for recovery is miraculous. You see, what I did was—'

'Yes, yes,' Pauline interrupted. 'Quite.' She had considered the detail and did not want it rehearsed.

Silence fell for a minute, until they both began talking at once, both wanting to avoid contemplating the pain. Pauline had knelt in prayer, trying to assume that pain to herself, offering her own injury as inadequate compensation. The problem with prayer was the rarity of seeing the result.

'Cannon? What about Cannon?' Her voice prevailed over his, but he had the better information.

'In his brother's house, with Julie, for lack of anywhere else. Unhappy – how could he be otherwise? – even though there are compensations. The child – he thinks of the child. He's on police bail for the explosion, doesn't know what will happen any more than they do themselves until they've done with enquiring. But they found the fat man, you know. Not *found*, as such. He found them.'

'Don't tell me what he said.'

She drew on the cigarette, looked round for the priest's ashtray. Why them and not her? Imelda whisked into the room with a tray of coffee. Weak and milky, the way William hated it. She dumped it down with a crash, smiled at him warmly, scowled at Pauline and left.

'We're a little bored, that's the truth of it,' Pauline said. 'After all the excitement. And Cannon, now. He'll be relatively rich, I suppose. The brother's will . . .'

'There wasn't one. He inherits anyway. There's no one else. He offered to pay for the surgery. I said no.'

She clicked her tongue, stifling the unworthy thought, *And perhaps he'd like to make a contribution here, too*, a thought that had no place in this conversation but was second nature to anyone like herself, whatever the situation. She had spent her religious life begging shamelessly for things. What she wanted to ask was, Do you think she will *ever* forgive us? and what she asked was, 'And your surgery? Is that coming along?'

'Yes. It's workable. Not beautiful, but workable. Buildings can mend very fast. Like the mouth, given money. I don't want to work. I desperately don't want to work. But I have to. I've got faithful patients. I don't want to send them to anyone else and they don't want to go.'

'That's entirely right, William. Couldn't be more right. That's exactly what you have to do. Work. And the damage . . . what about the damage?'

'Not as bad as it seemed. As Cannon said, he's good with a bomb.'

'Not *so* good. The effect was the last he intended.'

'*Was* it?'

There was another lengthy pause, devoted to the sipping of boiling coffee that tasted of nothing, offset, in William's case, by a sweet digestive biscuit that stuck to his teeth. They were failing to comfort one another; a little awkward.

'I wonder if *she* knows how much we love her,' Pauline said. 'She never felt able to believe that anyone would or could love her, which is probably why she believes in the safety of numbers and being needed. And fun, of course. Never could believe in being loved after that unfaithful husband of hers . . . and that sadist and . . . Never mind. She'll come round and bounce back. She always does. She's got a long memory but a great talent for forgiveness.' She seemed to find that reflection infinitely reassuring.

'I didn't know anything much about her history,' William said wonderingly. 'I didn't know much about her at all.'

Pauline glared at him, suddenly changing from the concerned confidante with an equally troubled confessor into a matriarch approached disrespectfully by an unsuitable suitor for the favours of a daughter. 'Well, you'd better find out, hadn't you? Go and find her.'

Cannon had thrown everything out of the living room into the back garden. Everything. Julie had not tried to stop him. They would not be here if it were not for her condition: he would have stayed anywhere rather than here, but this last of Johnnyboy's houses, the one currently occupied, would be free of rot and awash with creature comforts. He had always done that: gutted the bathroom and installed something new, new kitchen, new carpets, for the pleasure of becoming bored with them and moving on to install the same kind of thing all over again. Cannon hated the stultifying warmth of it: he could feel the smell of Johnny in his nostrils, oozing from the pores of his skin; he did not know if he wanted to eradicate it or preserve it. Windows open, both of them used to the cold. Not a stick of furniture left in the room and not a picture either. Julie remained quiet throughout this exercise, helping as help was requested whenever he forgot his constant instructions to her not to exert herself. He would regret this later. Perhaps.

She had the strange recurring desire to *pray*. Found that she crossed herself when he wept, warding off the devil. Saying thank you for salvation. Wanting to *pray* when she crossed the road.

He had whooped with glee as he levered the desk over the window-ledge and watched it fall, crashing through the branches of the tree. He had screamed with delight as he tossed out the ghastly painted-to-order battle scene with its garish reds and postured figures. He had yelled with rage as he slung the huge silver bird of prey to follow the painting. Then he had sat and wept. He wept often, at the slightest stimulus. Wept in her arms and huddled in corners; wept in the lavatory beyond what he thought was her hearing, when he thought he had wept too much. Now he laughed. He did both in turns.

She was trying to be patient with him. Filled with lassitude, a strange reaction to promised safety, she was passive rather than patient. The realisation that Cannon was the inheritor of a dozen decaying houses was slow to arrive. They had never occupied more than a corner of anyone else's abode. This felt dispiriting, palatial in a way she disliked – another reason why she was not going to stop him turning it into a barn. The thought of sleeping in sheets Johnnyboy might have used gave her nightmares. She chose the ones still wrapped in their brand new packets; there were many of these from which to choose, as well as brand new towels, bath mats, napkins, cutlery. He had been a man fastidious to the point of mania; there were goods newly wrapped beyond the point of contamination, but when she imagined his fingers touching them, if only in the process of purchase, she shuddered.

'It's stuck,' Cannon was muttering. 'The fucking thing's stuck. Think I'll go downstairs and shake that tree.'

'And then it'll fall on top of you.'

'No, it won't.'

'Leave it. It'll fall one of these days.'

Such a robust tree, with big careful branches that looked, in their winter state, like a series of frosted feathers fit to make a nest. They did not sleep in Johnny's bed. That was gone on Christmas Eve. There was another bathroom, too, unused like the room beside it, virtually shrink-wrapped, waiting for the visitor who had never arrived.

'Both of them stuck.'

'Let me look . . .'

'That silver eagle. And that painting of the mouth. How could he buy that?'

The silver eagle swayed in the branches like an anxious predator devoted less to hunting than fear of flying. She could almost feel sorry for it. Almost. The torn-up carpet revealed a fine wooden floor. She was hungry; always hungry. Today's rage of destruction was almost spent. Julie wondered, with a brief moment of dread, swallowed by inertia, how often this might happen, and what, if anything, might provoke it. The question seemed best answered as the occasion arose. She did not want him to cry. She wanted him to look at her without his glance ever sliding away. She wanted him to adopt this glorious south-facing room as his studio and paint her again and again, like Bonnard with his wife. She mourned the Bonnard sketch.

He sat back in one of the two remaining innocuous armchairs. They had muted rose-coloured fabric, which did not seem to offend him.

'Houses. I might have to go back to being a builder. When they've decided if they're going to charge me.'

'No,' she said. 'No, no and no. You're a painter. An artist.'

'A good builder's an artist, too.'

'We'll just wait a while, shall we? We've g-g-g-g-g-got to this by a series of miracles, lovely. You can wait for another.'

He had found Johnny's stash of booze and cigarettes – odd that he should keep it. He had never had much time for either, so Cannon said. Unlike his brother, who was not an alcoholic in the making but not a temperate being either, prone to binges. She had lived with those; she could handle them; she loved him; it was simple, if not for the fact that this house had been waiting for him, not for her, stuffed to the gunwales with things they did not need. Fully equipped for the advent of a baby. She was used to her tiny room in a silent place. When her energy returned they would not live here. Let him wreck it.

'I'm doing all this,' Cannon said, 'and then I suppose I'll wish I had something of him left. Something to remember him by.'

She was very quiet. It was a knack to know when he wanted her to be quiet and when he wanted the intervention of speech. She was grateful for the lassitude. It made her slow and diplomatic. If in doubt say nothing, or go to sleep.

'I should go and see Sarah.'

'Not yet, lovely. You saved her, you know. You don't *have* to go. Not yet. Besides, I went. I told you I went. I went for both of us. She's fine, she's moving house. You went to see William, I went to see Sarah. I told you she sent her love.'

'Love? Are you sure?'

'Sure I'm sure.'

'We'll get her and William to visit when we settle,' he announced.

'Yes, yes. Of course we shall.'

Crossing her fingers and saying to herself, *Of course we shan't. We begin* here. *We begin as if we really began* here, *at this point in our lives.* Our friendships are going to depend on exactly what we create from *now* onwards. Our lives are going to exclude *anyone* and *everyone* who knew us before now. *Every single one.* Clean slate, fresh set of canvases. She wanted the stink of white spirit, ink and oil, and the smell of his righteous rage when the work was not going right. She would sneak inside his studio and preserve what he did. Someone must. She loved him. If he went back to prison, it would surely not be for long and the child would tie him to her. She had earned her spurs. Who would believe the fat man?

He crossed to the window, looked down, cigarette burning with its comforting drift of smoke. She would always see him thus, free of grief for a moment, letting the laughter light his face, smiling into the dark as she heard the warmth surge into the radiators with a teeny *click, whoomph*. He began to close the enormous sash window and shut out the dark, looking down as he did so at that stupid silver eagle caught in the tree, clutching at the branches like a last survivor against the stiffening wind.

'The lawyers want me to help organise their art collection, did I tell you? Strange people, they are. At least half human.'

'Come inside,' she said, 'you'll get cold. And don't worry about the charges. It'll come to nothing. You've the best legal help. Andrew Whatsit and Matthewsomething. The best.'

'I'd rather Sarah.'

'She's a witness, lovey. She can't do both. And . . . well, she wasn't the best lawyer, was she? An amateur compared to these. They're the *real* experts.'

The wind shook the branches and the silver eagle crashed to earth with all the aplomb of a sparrow. They watched it land on the barren January grass, alongside the painting of the mouth.

'Got a message from William. He says come and see him. You've got to take special care of your teeth when you're having a baby. So I said you'd go, all right?'

No. No one who knew us in another life is going to know us now. He would not believe it, but that was exactly what was going to happen. She had absolutely no doubt about it. There were other dentists.

But there was only one husband, who would never know how

much he was loved, and only one baby. She would do anything to preserve them from the past. There was only the future.

'Perhaps I wouldn't mind so much if I hadn't just painted it,' William quipped to the patient, a man who expressed only the mildest curiosity concerning the changed décor of the premises of his dental surgeon. The patient accepted without demur the explanation of a minor gas explosion of a purely domestic nature, ignoring any coincidence between this and a story he might have read in a newspaper, because it suited him to do so. The dentist's problems were peripheral to his own toothache and quiet dread of the drill. Conversation was not what he wanted. William could answer questions about the changed state of his rooms quite casually once he had decided that a minor gas explosion was really what everyone wanted it to be, marvelling at the speed of the repairs and blessing his insurance company. There was only the memory of blood on the floor, and the consequent need for the place to be reconsecrated, as if it were a church.

Cannon's bomb had avoided the essentials, a straight line of damage removing the window, making the hole in the floor, then leaving the souvenir fires, which did the greatest harm. A decorative disaster. William was surprised to find that he did not mourn the destruction of the pictures in the way he had always imagined he might when he visualised theft or vandalism. Perhaps possessions really did not matter; perhaps the life in the lost paintings, even Cannon's piece of beauty, were pieces of borrowed life and never owned by anyone at all. The bareness of the walls was an excuse to start again, take a different direction; think anew. The drawing of his hands still occupied the prime position opposite the chair. He hated it there: it was a reminder of what he had done, and that was why it would remain.

Nightmares jumbled into long, weird narratives and recriminations. What *else* could he have done? The girl-child with the missing teeth, the boy with the amalgam stuck in his lungs frolicked into his dreams along with John Smith, smiling with an empty mouth, and Sarah, who had never told him anything. If *only* she had told him about Cannon's twin none of this would have happened. But, then, why should she infect him with dangerous knowledge? Guilt was so much worse when there was no one to blame.

'Right, all finished. Don't eat anything hot or solid for the rest of the day.' The patient scuttled away; a face forgotten.

He was trying to remember if he had actually received a message from Sarah not to contact her, or whether it had simply been a friendly directive from a police officer that it was better they should not for fear of each contaminating the story of the other, he supposed. No collusion. The yearning to see her, numbed in the beginning by the appalling knowledge of the exquisite pain he had caused, however careful he had been in its infliction, grew in intensity, not only every day but every minute of every day. Seeing Pauline had been a pale substitute.

There was so *much* requiring explanation, irking him, the relevant nudging at the irrelevant, elusive memory getting in the way. Such as Cannon's Diconal murmurs. Remembering the day he had asked conversationally in a line of chat during that one-minute interval between the needle in the arm and the onset of oblivion, not really expecting a reply, *Do you have any children, Mr Smith?*

The ramblings that had followed in his sleep. *No kids, not yet. Tried for a year. Think I'm firing blanks.* William thought of Cannon with intense affection and not a little envy, tinged with regret for a bizarre friendship suspended into a dim, fading promise.

He sat in the reception room on one of two borrowed chairs, looking at the fresh plaster of the walls waiting for paint. God was good all the same, Pauline had said. If Cannon had not known there was a beloved child on the way, he might have died of grief for Johnnyboy. He quite understood that Cannon would not come back.

A patient had cancelled. The afternoon was young, the decorators due tomorrow, and he was profoundly tired. He was never going to bother locking his doors again; there was no point. He would open his practice to the street.

Isabella crossed the room, heels loud on the paper temporarily covering the floor, sat next to him, waiting with the impatience of one arriving for an appointment promised twice, postponed and now arrived. She had been sympathetic to an annotated version of his disasters learned from a headline, which had been swallowed the next day by a greater headline about a different kind of bomb in the City and a suspected resurgence of Islamic terrorism, William's face and his name easily forgotten. He had refused offers of solace and help, but now, finally, here she was, looking at the bare walls like a person hungry to weave a spell on it with wallpaper and swagged curtains to cover the cracks, beautifully, informally dressed, not quite in command of her agitation, but trying. They did not even greet one another.

She came straight to the point. 'William, you look awful. You need someone to take care of you. I told you I was wrong about everything. Can I come back? *Please.*'

Visions of a comfortable nest, food on the table, sofas long enough for lounging. A flat somewhere replete with tasteful design. Wonderful coffee in the morning, beef cooked to perfection, Sunday lunches with friends. Clean sheets, no domestic decisions; the hum of an efficient washing-machine, fine china and fragrant flowers. A dozen irritating tasks per day, supermarket included, abdicated to her efficiency. An organised life. Always a sufficiency of bread, eggs, milk; the daily newspaper of choice.

A brittle body to hold in bed. Magazines, not books. No pictures; no nakedness as they grow older. Conversation of *absolutely mind-numbing banality.*

'Have your gums been bleeding?'

She gasped, looked on the verge of outrage, then lowered her fine eyes to the hands clasped in her lap. 'Yes. Nothing odd about that, is there? I mean, what has it got to do with—?'

'Everything,' he said. 'You must go to a dentist as soon as you can.'

'*William!* Did you hear me? I want to come back. I've been so unhappy . . . I know I could make you happy. I did before, didn't I?'

There was no answer to that. Except to say, *yes*, you did, and *no*, you didn't. She would cling to the power he had given her. Given her willingly, foolishly, completely, so that he could not even blame her for wielding it. Or failing to believe it had ended. It was never a question of her releasing him from the spell; it was he who had to dispel his own illusions.

'You can't come back,' he said loudly. 'Because I love someone else. I've loved her for a long time.'

There was a new kind of silence after Isabella had left and he remained where he was, sitting in the chair and looking at the empty wall. Not crossing to the window to watch her go across the street. A free, uncluttered silence, as if there was one less thing buzzing round in his head and the traffic outside had ceased out of sheer respect for his sudden clarity of mind. All he could feel was relief. At least now he knew, and even if the knowledge came too late, it was still of a joyful kind. He closed his eyes, and thought briefly of what colour he should have for the walls. Remembered he had chosen the total anonymity of white and thought, I can do better than that. The outer door creaked again. Someone stood by the desk, just out of sight. He thought, with mild frustration, She's come back . . . I'll have to say it all again. Leave me alone. He squeezed his eyes shut, clenched his fists, felt tired.

'Mr Dalrymple? You haven't changed. Remember us?'

He opened his eyes. A trio. One large mother and two golden teenagers, all smiling as if posed for a camera.

'Mr Dalrymple . . . we've been looking for you for years. Moved away, you know how it is? Couldn't find you, lost your card. Then I saw your name in the paper, and thought, *There* he is. So I brought them back to re-enlist. You remember my children, don't you? Are you all right, Mr Dalrymple?'

The girl, flashing fine symmetrical teeth, no gaps, her face as pretty as her early promise had suggested; the boy, bored, tall, healthy, with the build of an athlete and cheeks like rosy apples, looking like a youth who might have accidents, but never illnesses.

'Never had a single problem since you sorted them out,' the mother said proudly, as if this was solely his achievement and nothing to do with their inheritance. 'So we came back.'

I took out the *right* teeth for that pretty little girl. If that boy Adrian had ever swallowed amalgam, it did not hurt him.

He recognised a moment of profound happiness, which was similar to standing under a hot shower and sluicing off the stickiness of the day. He struggled to his feet, hand outstretched with not a tremor in it. 'I'm very pleased to see you. Of course I remember you. Very well indeed. Shall we make an appointment?'

The second dentist, a professor organised by the investigators, had told her that there would be no long-term damage. He must be a man with steady hands, he told her, able to think as he worked; an excellent and creative surgeon. Sarah tried to distract herself with the reflection that this was the only time she would be examined by a professor without paying for it. Holes in bones are nothing more than holes in bones; they heal, he said. Everything in the mouth heals, even with infection, and you have none of that. Tell me, what did he use? How long did this *procedure* take? Purely scientific interest, you understand. What happened to you is of far less importance than *how* it was done.

That was the way it was: they all had the mindset of engineers exploring either a problem or the history of it. She found it difficult to be pleased that someone so admired dear William's skill. Then, with the looming of the terrible empty week between Christmas and New Year, a time when in previous years she would have lain deliciously low with a crate of wine, she hated his skill; forgot she had encouraged him to use it; forgot she had, in one sense, volunteered, and that *yes*, she had understood what he was doing and why, forgot everything but dull, residual pain, a sense of violation, night sweats and nightmares. The knowledge of being nothing but an *it*. A piece of flesh vandalised for a purpose. She had hated him then.

When the second dentist asked her to open her mouth, she could not do it at first. Whimpered and refused, her tongue pushing at clenched teeth. The touch of his instruments and the closeness of his scrutiny were little kisses of horror. Even his hand, powerful, broad and dry, shaking her own on leaving, had felt like a claw. Better the devil you know, with hands like a pianist.

On the fifth or sixth of January, she could not recall which, since the days were blurred, punctuated by nothing more than darkness and light and the obliteration of messages on the answer-machine, she walked down the road in the early morning dark and put the remainder of the Valium prescription into a rubbish bin. Shoved some noxious household rubbish on top, so that she would not be tempted to return and fish through it later, wiped her hands on her trousers and went home and washed her hair. Took every single picture off the walls, dusted them and propped them in layers in doorways, according to size. It took brute strength and hammer blows to dislodge the nails supporting the lifelong friends. Then she sorted out the contents of her wardrobe, preserving only what she loved best and putting the rest into sacks. Her labelling of these was precise, laborious and clear. There were good clothes, not so good clothes, and clothes so mistaken, so shrunken, so far too well worn no one would benefit from their existence, kept out of sentiment or laziness. She piled the last category on the kitchen floor and systematically cut them into very small pieces with a pair of sharp scissors. Then she threw the kitchen plates she had always disliked out of the window at the back, listened to them break in the back garden. *Good.*

Tomorrow she would go and see if she could find that red dress in the sale. She knew it would be there. Opened the wine; wrote notes in a small, crabbed hand.

William is one of the nicest men you could ever meet. You can't

*stand the fact that he hurt you, even though it was a situation where
you knew, and he knew, that there was no choice.*

*He couldn't love me and do what he did. Yes, he could. He saved
you from worse. What do you think you've done to him? What does
it feel like to be a torturer? Is it worse than being tortured?*

It achieved something . . . didn't it? YES. The survival of a partnership; the possible survival of a child.

No matter which child.

Earlier in the afternoon she had taken the painting Cannon
had lifted from the exhibition to the post office. Sent it, carefully
overwrapped, to the dealers described on the label on the back.

That was the day before Julie came round, cool on the heels of
the policeman who wanted to check with her what the fat man
had said and then retracted. Spoke a whole lot of rubbish and
then took it back, troubled first by conscience, then by fear of
the consequences. Julie, sitting in the corner of the barren living
room, looking at the ragged holes in the walls where the pictures
had been. Julie, hell-bent on the survival of what was hers and
knowing beyond doubt that the pursuit of love justified everything and anything, wanting co-operation, looking at Sarah as if
she was an *it*. Thanking her as if she was a stranger, relieved to
see she looked *normal*. Asking odd, airy questions about inheritance between brothers, DNA between twins and a mixed bag
of queries that showed an overburdened mind in an anxiously
pregnant body and making her final announcement on leaving.
They were the same height when they stood up to say goodbye,
like actresses paired for a part. Julie made the final announcement.

Cannon says William loves you. He'll never stop, Cannon
says. You mustn't let Johnnyboy win with him too, you know.

In the silence, Sarah lit another of the cigarettes which were
bad for her teeth, blew a defiant smoke ring into an empty room.

If William thought he loved her, he had better fight for it. She
could not quite stop crying and she was not going to try any
more. If he could not recognise her from closer than three paces,

no one could. And in the absence of that close scrutiny of love, liking would suffice. It was recognition that mattered.

Yes, it was worth it. Even with the lies.

They were all safe. If there were any thanks, she had not asked for them anyway. She would keep the secrets. Begin all over again, with an empty slate.

Julie found a church on the way home. A silent place, empty of people. She needed to pray.

Listen, Lord, forget it. He raped me, right? Got that? He came round with his fat mate and his pillow-case, put that over my head, no lie about *that*, told me to get lost and I told him to get lost too. Stood three yards away and told me Cannon would never be able to get a kid, said he tried hard enough with all those other girls when he was younger, never stopped trying, if you get my meaning. Obsessed with babies. Nothing happened. That's what Johnny said. You want one, better be mine, be mine, be mine . . . that's what he would want . . . you aren't enough to keep him. Who do you think you are?

And I believed him, Lord, for a minute. Let him take me from behind so he didn't have to look. Then he went mad with disgust and I went mad too, because I must have been insane to think Cannon would never stay with me without a baby. Or think there had been other girls. Anyone with Cannon for a second would know there were never any other girls. I dived over the stairs; I threw myself against walls; I clawed at my skin, long after they hit me. I screamed at him and he laughed. I *know* whose baby this is. Does it matter, Lord? Blood tests wouldn't tell, because the blood will be the same, and even You don't know, do you? Fine God you are. Cannon wanted something to remember him by. Now he has it. And I love him.

Is that all right, Lord?

The bubble of happiness blew as large as a balloon and drifted away. She does not want to see me, or maybe she does. She forgives me, or maybe she doesn't. The decorators come tomorrow and I shall *not* have the walls painted white. I am still wearing my gloves.

William reached the green across the road from her flat, sprinted across, rang the bell. No preliminary phone call, like other men, he was simply *here*. Muttering under his breath the opening line, 'Anything you want fixing, lady?'

Empty. SOLD written on the board outside. He was always slow.

She had said she was moving. She had said she had fallen in love with that new place, lovingly described. Street name? He could not recall. Description, rough location . . . YES. He had nodded when she told him about it, got the idea. There were highly distinctive railings outside; he had a rough idea where he had seen them.

He hailed a taxi to take him back to his own front door. After that, he had to stroll in a way which was precise and casual, because if he was to see her in the headlights of a car, she might be running. He began to walk in slow concentric circles.

Looking for the other sign that said, SOLD.